The X-or Story
By Dr Joe Ireland

Publisher details: Dr Joe

© Dr Joseph Ireland, "Dr Joe", 1983
Edition 1.2 © 2018 ISBN-13: 978-1502731210 (CreateSpace-Assigned)
Current edition ISBN 9780992329464
Printed by Lightning Spark

National Library of Australia Cataloguing-in-Publication entry

Author:	Ireland, Joe.
Title:	The X-OR Story
Edition:	2nd, with pictures
Target Audience:	Young Adult
BISAC:	Fiction / Science Fiction / General
Pages:	584

This is a work of fiction. All the names, characters, organisations, spell descriptions, and events portrayed in this book are products of the author's imagination. Any resemblance to any organisation, event or actual person (living or dead) is unintentional.

A world hidden deep in humanity's future.
A planetoid devouring entire civilizations.

Paradise, or prison? Oppression, or Resistance? Freedom, or subjection...

... and is there really any choice?

The enigma, the telepath, the prodigy;
each grow through friendship and trial.
Is freedom a right, or a choice?

More wonderful titles by Dr Joe & Creating Science:

Delightful high fantasy for the thoughtful young reader
Choice, set free
1: The Quest of the Tae'anaryn
2: The Tae'anaryn and the Wizard's Apprentice
3: The Tae'anaryn and the Paladin's Squire
4: The Tae'anaryn and the Enchantress's Chrysalis
5: The Tae'anaryn and the Spear of the Troll Prince

An engaging science fiction adventure that introduces real science concepts to readers.
Space Chase 1: Arrendrallendriania
Space Chase 2: Elizabeth
Space Chase 3: Daniel
Space Chase 4: The Mechanizer

Thrilling young adult science fantasy adventure.
The Dragon Riders of Pearl
The Dragon Riders of Pearl 2: Seven Worlds
The Dragon Riders of Pearl 3: Return of the Plague
The Dragon Riders of Pearl 4: Rage of the Dragonmen
The Dragon Riders of Pearl 5: Twilight of the Giants

And for the budding scientist:
Creating Science – Dr Joe's book of science
experiments and activities

The X-or Story

To my wife, my kids, my parents, my muses, nature itself and God.

Based on a dream I had when I was 8, around 1982.
Started seriously writing when I went off from work due to stress, 2001.
1st published draft 2014. This is a long project…

Enjoy your journey, and feel free to send me your thoughts and
experiences: xor@drjoe.id.au

The X-or Story

Contents

Book 1
X-or

7 years ago

Hello??

HELLO!!! Her screams echoed, unheard in the thick blackness. The world was dark.

Daemon! she cried in the silence of her mind. *Daemon!!*

Water trickled down from somewhere. The noise from the highways above; the low dry groaning of an ever-dying beast. There would be tanks up there by now, "no passing parade" her brother had called it. How she wished she could have never gotten into this mess in the first place.

Somebody was near her now. She could feel the heat of their thoughts, shielded by copper banding. She fell silent, throwing up false indications on her own mind. If it was her brother Daemon he would recognise the signals. If not... well, she was sick of the underside and what life here meant anyway.

She hid behind a collapsed concrete pillar, forcing her thin adolescent figure into the black crevice. She felt the coldness, shielded now and cloaked in blackness. No psychic or ordinary soldier would find her. Darkness, dampness. She touched her medallions, the one her brother held, before they left on this mission. But there was silence... and she didn't dare breath.

Another mind passed her shielding; a weaker mind, with familiar markings. For a moment she paused, shielding tremors. She recognised its similarity, brought with her his smell. Trembling, she let down her mental casing.

Daemon, she dared to whisper, *is that –*

Immediately she perceived the first mind still there, now only meters in front of her. An animal mind, dangerous and hungry. Lowering her shields may have just saved her, for though she could not see in the dark, it obviously could. Silently it had stalked her and now she was trapped between concrete and death. Forgetting all caution and succumbing to irrational fear she screamed out in voice. 'DAEMON!!'

A sudden burst of light energy in the visual field filled the immediate environment: The Emmissionaries were alerted to the two fugitive spies' presence. The being was silhouetted in the growing light. It was a ground dragon, rearing on its hind legs and bearing its razor teeth.

Again she screamed, unarmed and too frightened to think.

1

Suddenly two plasma blasts from behind exploded into the hunter. It fell, dead, across her terrified, but living form. A humanoid stepped out from behind the dead beast.

It was Daemon.

---++---++---++---

Daemon saw that her mind was a temporary shambles. Shaken by fear, his sister had quite lost it. It reminded him of the time he left the turquoise beetles on her bed when they were six. *Sheelaakah,* he consoled. *I'm here.*

Spoken in the silence of their minds her shaken state still refused to hear his words.

Whoa sis, you are off line! Well, round two over, we'd better get out of here.

Her state disappointed him. She was by far the most advanced of them. Why would she lose it now? War wasn't easy on anybody, by no means, but her? He knew that there would be time to think later, right now it was time to go.

He heard the sounds of the Emmissionaries moving closer. The Emmissionaries; hunters, ruthless enemies. And he, the outlaw. What excitement this had all been... initially. Pity he and his sister Sheelaakah had been spotted, but not recognised, where they shouldn't have been; in the reaction chambers. Pity they'd been fiddling with things they shouldn't have been fiddling with; like the governance cells. Oh well! Win some, lose some. Usually they lost, but not always. And not this time.

The sounds were closing fast. Daemon threw his flare into some sort of lead iron pipe. They would miss the light but not the heat, especially with aerial help, if they had any. His sister now clung desperately around his neck. He tried to calm her but it was useless.

'Daemon! They'll find us now!' She wept silently, verbally now.

'No.'

A low drowning noise came from above. Wasps. Aerial help. Anti-gravity surface attack craft.

Oh no.

He touched his communicator, amplifying his mind, sending a direct message. *Guys, we need out.*

Teleport impossible, was the reply, *they've got a trace on it.*

He dragged his terrified sister behind some rubble, forged in photon blasts centuries ago. They stumbled into an old sewer canal, long abandoned but still reeking. He couldn't help but smile, perhaps the stench would help

Shee straighten out a bit. Down a long corridor, into the growing blackness, rancid water splashing in their footsteps. Down a narrow branch-off. Down another larger tunnel. Voices, though they'd be safe from Wasps now.

This way, he instructed his sister. Her glassy, listless expression struck real fear into his heart. She should have been afraid, but now appeared dispassionately numb. Down a dark corridor lit only by the phosphorous algae. They were leaving a trail, he knew, stirring up the water and extinguishing the algae as they passed through it. Daemon spotted an iron platform, noisy but algae free. They crossed it.

Lights. Soldiers.

They pressed themselves into the crevice of an old, rotted pipeline, smelling worse than the rest. They'd need bio-medical remediation after this little flight, if they ever succeeded. Daemon pushed that thought out of his mind. Concentrate…

The darkness shielded them, and the soldiers ran by them to the tunnel they had just exited. Sheelaakah sighed a silent sigh of relief, her flowing blond- brown hair caked in mud and other foulsome stuff making her look quite bedraggled. With fear still lingering in her eyes, grey in the darkness, he could see his twin wanted only peace.

Well, we'd had her chance at peace. They all had, but that was long ago. She knew the risks before taking the mission. Risk was something they lived with, living as prisoners on a world that had annexed their own small moon five years ago. Help was so very far away: fifty million light years from a galactic senate that still denied their plight and every plea for help. Peace was even further, living in oppression in the city or fear in the wilderness beyond. A thousand years away from their peaceful ancestors on Earth when humanity had first begun to colonise the worlds, reaching out into the stars only to find a galaxy filled with life of all kinds – including their own…

Metallic sounds abruptly adulterated his revere into history. Biomechanic whining. Daemon saw the fear in his sister well up, a scream stilled only by the aid of his own mind.

An Emmissionary was stalking them.

---++---++---++---

Freya watched the children playing happily with their new toys. Freedom day was such a happy time. Her husband was helping their oldest son Robert unwrap his new Seren Defender doll, while their youngest child,

Little Gem, jumped excitedly over having received a brand new 'passage of lore rights – part two' game.

'Why yes,' she agreed. 'Isn't it wonderful what the peacemakers have brought you this year!'

She missed joining in her children's festivities on the floor between the pillars of the Arch, but she was going nowhere. Eight Earth months pregnant with only sixteen days, seven hours to go, and she wasn't shifting from her comfort lounge. The world she lived in could be seen from the terminal on any of the four million different channels. Not many, but they weren't the most needful of families. She and Dave had opted for this life and though it did mean heavy concessions, it was far more rewarding.

New giggles burst from her children punctuated by her husband's hefty, powerful laugh. Everything tended to be powerful with his strong masculine figure. You had to be in his line of expertise - artisans such as he were few, but some still survived, though his blacksmith trade at the foundries was more for tourists and history students than much else. He did have a talent with the men and iron he worked with. He could have even been a soldier but he was never the rough sort. He was her soldier. And she his beloved wife.

---++---++---++---

The Emmissionary passed their tunnel, its powerful lights turning sable blackness into day. The pipe they were sheltered in covered the heat of their bodies, and Daemon covered their minds with his sister's help. Her fear concerned him; as long as they had no means of tracing that...

He knew their next step was to reach the surface. Now that the hunters knew where they were, it wouldn't be long. They'd have most exits sealed already. Daemon looked at his watch, only seven minutes until the Resistance's transport would pass over, right as their enemies rocket launch would disrupt their own traces. They had to be up to the surface by then.

Quickly they moved down the tunnel again. If he was right, there would be another exit ninety or so meters from their original entrance. Maybe...

As they half ran, half crawled through the narrow silence, bestilled of thought, Daemon carefully studied his sister. He relied only on visual stimulus, which was what he was best at. She was exhausted and terrified. This mission had drained her. It was a routine sabotage mission, a diversion for higher motives, something to give the suburb leaders something to think about while Resistance made some major vehicle moving, and one or two other things. He didn't know what. It was better not to, with the enemy's mind probes. All had gone well until he had made a mistake, just a minor one, and given away their identi and sicuracode numbers. Well, they were off the system for good now, but in a few hours the Resistance would get them back. No worries. New names, new roles, new thought patterns. How tedious.

Shee tripped in the blackness, crying out as she fell. Daemon tried to pull her up but he couldn't.

'Daemon, I'm cramping!' She cried. He felt the pain shooting up her leg. Quickly he straightened her offending limb and applied mental amnesia as best he could. She bit her lip to stop from crying out again. Daemon realised how badly affected his twin was. She couldn't even use her mind to stop a cramping leg. Her fear of being captured kept her going, but when they got home she would probably concede. He could not let that happen! Again he tried to pull her up, but again she refused to come. Risking being traced he probed her mind. She was slipping, and already had partly conceded. Traumatised by exhaustion and fear, she was thin and the cold dampness was sapping her strength.

Tenderly, he picked her up in his arms and began to move on. She was lighter than he remembered. Briefly he recalled how just six years ago on their tenth birthday he had picked her up like this and thrown her, gown and all, into their city lake on a world they'd been forced to leave behind. She was so mad at him that time. He pushed the thoughts behind him. He had to concentrate now, to shield them both. His humour had left him. It was time to focus.

Strange, he thought, *how when she is weaker I feel stronger.*

Stumbling up a steep embankment the noise from the highways was heard again, even though they were in the underground. His sister lay limp in his arms, and his breath was visible in the damp air. *Concentrate!* He had carried her before. Then Talmagion fever had left her paralysed. He'd never told her how afraid he was for her then. He drew his mind in and tried to concentrate to make sure their mission wasn't a failure or that they were captured. Concentrate,… concen –

Voices from behind cut off his thoughts. *A patrol!* They couldn't see him, yet they soon would. Their goal was death, or worse, capture.

---++---++---++---

'Captain, the transport is ready for take-off.'

They were in the command section of the Resistance transport. Once it had served farming communities of Ptrus Prime. Now it was outfitted in military strength. Inside it carried a precious cargo of secrets the Galaxy longed to forget, but now would be forced to acknowledge. When they succeeded, the fight would soon be over.

The officer that spoke addressed his leader, seated at the controls behind him. The older man stroked his neat chestnut beard thoughtfully as he eyed the scene before him. He looked at the sergeant's face, honest and trustworthy. He looked at the control panel. All systems checked out. Shields were up and the diversions had worked perfectly. Timing was crucial. The waiting was over. In two and a half minutes they would finally be free.

'Initiate launch and prepare to jump to Hyperspace.'

---++---++---++---

Daemon ran as fast as he could now, noise mattering little. He knew that the transport was launching and that he had just over two minutes to get where it could get to them. He carried his sister on his shoulders, and though she was thin she had become dead weight. Her unconscious mind was cold to him now.

The cold air stung his face, hurting his lungs and draining his strength even more. Desperately he stumbled up the slope, his legs were weak, and his arms complained over their impossible weight. On he ran. Stumbling. Scraping. Clawing.

He reached the ladder. It was their last hope. Resting Shee at the base he slapped her face gently, using what energy he could of his own mind to awaken hers. *Sheelaakah… Sheelaakah!*

'Let me die...' she pleaded, mind so numb she could no longer reason.

---++---++---++---

A bright flash lit the morning sky.

'Oh daddy!' cried his daughter Little Gem. 'Is that a Wasp?'

The children ran to the window. A noise approached from the distance. It was no Wasp, the man knew. The smile quickly left his face, and he felt his fists clench in tension. More like some kind of transport. The kind of transport he may have guarded twenty or so years ago, before crashlanding on this place, before finding Freya, and falling in love. But that was the past, his wild adventurous past, never to be repeated and never to be revisited. He'd made it this far and now he was comfortable. There was no turning back. There was no point. Things were peaceful now. There were no crazy missions to fly, no senseless heroic cause to uphold, and no fighting an impossible enemy that could just crush you anyway. And he'd been crushed. But that was the past. Things were peaceful in his life. Now things were OK.

'Honey?' His wife's voice interrupted his thoughts.

Freya was concerned. She knew so little of his past – didn't need to, didn't know if she even wanted to. She'd grown up here on Seren, knew little of the outside galaxy, except for what she'd learnt from the terminal or at schools.

He looked up and smiled his warm smile at her. But she knew how it troubled him every time a flock of Wasps passed by. Well, that was his choice living on the outer suburbs. Not the greatest social advantages perhaps, but the Emmissionaries were so helpful in keeping everything organised and running as it should. Who would want to live on a planet or system with a less centralised and protective government anyway? The worst place inside Seren Citadel was a thousand times better than the best anywhere else in the galaxy. It was safer here, and she liked it that way. Nothing like voting or riots, not like in other, undesirable places away from where they happily lived. No, this was the best place in the whole universe, a peaceful place. Yes, the scans were... uncomfortable. But no place more peaceful, safer, or like a dream unawakening! There was challenge and opportunity, with comfort and the latest technology available. A great wall protected their giant citadel, and the most impenetrable force shield in the known Universe protected the entire planetoid! Who would want to live anywhere else? Yet sometimes others did, but rather than turn them loose on the galaxy the rebellious lived out their lives in the wilderness beyond. All were free to choose between the two, but she would never choose to live anywhere other than Seren city!

And that was the truth of it.

---++---++---++---

Daemon was not about to let his sister choose to concede.

Death won't stop them from getting what they want; besides, you're getting a proper hero's burial. What am I talking about! Were both getting out of here! Sheelaakah! Live!

Then he dared to send the full strength of his will into her fevered mind he discovered the cause of her unconsciousness. Another mind had taken residence, probably at her fear over the animal's attack. *Forges!* She recognised it too, so holding hands he placed his right palm with the copper band on her forehead. The other mind was strong, very strong. But it was Shee's body it had tried to own. Their two minds fed on each other's indomitable love, the bond the twins had shared from conception. Sheelaakah had forced these parasites out before, so the mind slowly slipped and lost its control, sneaking away silently without leaving any trace of its sinister identity, and Daemon could get no reading.

Sheelaakah now stood fiercely. Daemon looked at her in the darkness. *Cute,* he mused. Her eyes shone out from behind her tangled hair, staring in affection at her twin brother Daemon's taller, darker features.

She knew she could trust him. As a matter of fact she knew him better than anybody. He had just saved her life, again, but there would be time for thanks later. She knew that they had to get out, so turning she started up the ladder.

Two bursts of fire! She looked down to see Daemon fallen away from the ladder. They'd been found.

Daemon skilfully and quickly returned the blasts, and Shee, though shielding her own mind, could feel the agony of three soldiers wounded in the return fire. She mourned for these souls. Trapped by ignorance they didn't know they were fighting against those who were only trying to free them. But the ignorant in Seren city were so many and those who knew the truth, so few.

Shee was hidden by the small opening that led into the large tunnel below, but Daemon was in the open. Five other minds took shelter in the cavern, so she would have to dispatch them with Daemon's help one at a time. Quickly they took the first, willing him to sleep. Then the next, but something was wrong. He became confident, as did the others. She felt them retreating, gloatingly.

Then they heard a metallic sound, and biomechanic whines.

'Daemon, get up here!' She screamed.

She saw her brother leap up on the ladder's edge. He hadn't begun to climb when a flash of light from the Emmissionaries laser tore the phaser from his grip. Sheelaakah knew what to do. Biomechanic technology made these machines particularly susceptible to pyrokinesis. She began to burn out the circuitry.

The soldiers were moving in on her brother, so she hoped he could deal with them while she took out the machine.

One mind closed, three still to go. The machine moved closer to the ladder, the soldiers hidden behind moving with it. Her brother was unarmed except for his mind. She was grateful it had chosen to anaesthetise him personally instead of shooting him down. Classical capture manoeuvres.

Two other minds fell numb and the last, realising what was happening and struck with fear they suddenly retreated. The mechanic beast entered Shee's view down from the ladder. Daemon was pinned between it and the wall. Gold plated prongs issued from one of the lifeless beings many arms. Daemon worked frantically to fry some circuitry, but it was of no use. The neural network and backup systems evaded his every fevered attempt.

While barely a dozen meters away, two arms suddenly slashed from the iron denizen's form and cruelly pinned her brother to the wall. Desperately, she destroyed circuit after circuit but it still advanced. The gold prongs flashed the sparks which would still her dear brother's consciousness where he could be made to serve the enemy.

Shee, he called to his sister through his mind, *unplug it!*

Quickly their minds struck at the cold fusion reactor. Primitive. Thoughts like flames created power surges which flooded the nano-sized networks. With a gurgling sigh the iron dragon shuddered to an ignominious death, golden prongs centimetres from Daemon's heart.

For a moment he paused, refusing to believe their success, then hurriedly pushed the hulk of dead machine away from him. He stood on the base plate to get a higher grip on the ladder. They had won.

Suddenly Sheelaakah's mind was violently darkened. The psychic attack from somewhere else catching her unprepared. She fought the darkness to see the thought-slain Emmissionary spring miraculously to life. Sparks flew as it spun around, knocking her brother away from his ascent, out of her vision.

Flee, were his last words. *You've got but a moment!*

---++---++---++---

The roaring grew louder now, and his children jumped excitedly at the approaching craft. The foundry man turned to face the window so that his wife couldn't see his expression. Low drone, high pitches. A roar as octane fuel burned bringing the craft to the speed of sound and on to twelve hundred kilometres per hour where it would jump to hyperspace – if it was a transport. The ship passed high overhead, leaving a white trail in the planetoids trapped atmosphere.

It wasn't a government ship. He could tell by the sound of the engines, which he could also tell weren't in the best condition.

He listened for several more moments, and then his brow furrowed. It should have gone into hyperspace by now. But instead it was gone, suddenly, completely. He was startled.

It worried him, because he knew what it meant.

Freya read her husband's body language as the ship left for hyperspace. Though her children cheered she felt she heard him holding his breath, and saw his hands clench. She knew that something troubled him about the Wasps, because he would get all tense occasionally. She never asked him much about this. He seemed unwilling to discuss it, and she was glad just to have him.

He turned again and smiled warmly at her, and she smiled in return. Everything would be OK.

'OK,' he thought, 'nothing to get worried about, it's not my business anymore.'

But he couldn't help worrying when an unscheduled transport passed over. And what about the power fluctuation earlier this morning? Perhaps it was the Resistance again. Some 'super shield' protecting us. Yes, he knew it would hold them nice and safe. No one would leave Seren while the skyshield was in place.

Freya called him over and kissed him warmly, drawing his attention to his children playing happily beneath the family's annual peace arch. Soft, relaxing music played over the channels, and she rested her hand on his arm. He tried to get into the spirit of things, but it had left him now, though he tried not to show it to his privately concerned mate. He secretly knew what that ship was, and what its fate would most likely be.

The same fate as any who resisted…

---++---++---++---

Twenty or so minds flooded the corridors from both directions, pinning the Resistance warriors in a trap. Sheelaakah climbed the ladder and pushed on the opening. It didn't budge. Her mind felt numb as her invisible assailant attempted to knock her unconscious. Her shielding began to fail as it struck at her repeatedly.

She looked down. Sounds of fighting, men wrestling. Her brother would hold them off for those few moments she needed.

The power unseen attempted to flood depression into her mind. Her limbs went weak, but she fought it off. Then there was just plain darkness. It was more sinister, yet she knew the tactic well. She slung a mental attack of her own, offsetting her assailant. But it laughed, toying with her. It still had not unleashed its full venom.

She took out her hand-held configuration computer she'd used to mess up the governance cells in the reaction chambers causing the power fluctuation all over this planetoid they were imprisoned on. She slammed it into the opening, wedging it ajar. Shoving it aside she pulled herself half up.

Then Daemon fell unconscious. She screamed and began sliding back in. The enemy took full advantage and tore open her mental shielding, leaving her open to its bidding. Suddenly strong hands wrapped around her arms and pulled her up. Silence filled her anesthetised mind and she was quiet. She stared into the face of her deliverer and screamed internally. A black clad soldier, with a whip of long hair trailing down past his waist.

Out of the breach, into the core my dear. A voice spoke both to her ears and to her mind. Sheelaakah turned unwillingly to face the man who spoke, seeing only his eyes, the lightest shade of grey. He held her transfixed in his power and stare, and studied her soul.

'Oh, you need not worry about your twin Daemon, he will be treated as a … guest. Or rather, perhaps I should say; a host.'

Her fear took control of her body, as she began trembling uncontrollably.

'Oh, poor Sheelaakah.' Her enemy crooned. 'Cold and lost are we? Well not lost as your little transport with its pathetic bearded leader now is…'

His voice cut off as blue light suddenly flowed all around her. She heard her enemy scream and saw the black guards leap at her, passing through her as she slipped away. Her enemy's mind lost its grip on her, allowing her to begin control of her own feelings and thoughts as she was taken by site to site teleport far away. She was free, and the light intensity gathered into the familiar marking of the arrival dock.

Sheelaakah collapsed into a semi-conscious heap, allowing the altruistic hands and minds come to her aid. She felt their warmth.

Sleep Sheelaakah, an important sounding voice like a mother's said. But she could not sleep.

'Daemon, my twin,' she murmured, clawing to sit up and pushing the aid away from her. 'Daemon?' she begged, too weak to see properly. 'Daemon, did you get him?'

Her mind summoned the last motes of energy she had left, and she probed nearby for her Daemon.

Another mind softly touched hers. It knew truth was the only reality she needed, and that she must face it.

I'm sorry, it said compassionately, feeling her pain. *He didn't make it.*

Sheelaakah collapsed to the floor, and wept bitterly.

Interrogation

Commander Sheelaakah glanced at the room into which the prisoner was unceremoniously thrust. It was small, and apart from the dim light in the ceiling nothing shone at all. Windowless permicrete walls surrounded a single dull red circle where the prisoner stood, or occasionally, be allowed to sit. The entire area thrummed constantly with a powerful force field and myriad of other energy patterns useful in 'persuasion', even now the unshielded mind would be brought to great grief within its crimson circumference. It was not meant to be a friendly room, and it looked as if nobody had bothered to clean it in the past two centuries.

A single guard stood at the opposite wall, armed and alert. He wore the formal colours of the Resistance: deep green chameleon trousers and dark jacket, with a neuro-transceiver around his headband. His short boots were polished well, a tradition dating back to pre-galactic senate times. He held at the ready an aqueous rifle. A somewhat antiquated weapon, but at least the ammunition was plentiful.

Still, it was the single prisoner who stood in the centre of the circle, arms cuffed behind him, that earned the greater portion of her attention. He was only a little taller than average, which made him taller than her. He looked unafraid, and his stance was that of a soldier on trial – proud but not presumptuous. Perhaps that was just the way he always stood? He wore a tattered shirt, not too heavy, so she could see his muscled form underneath. He might have been about her age. She noticed the scars along his chest and one across his cheek, old but still visible. Obviously neither had received correct treatment. Amazingly, he had no shoes.

The guard approached her. 'He had these on him when he was found. The power cell is aged and little use for more than basic heat or maybe some light. He appears to have made the knife himself. He claims there are no others with him and offered no resistance.'

1 A remarkably clear conscience

She pushed a lock of chestnut hair from her forehead, scanning him lightly with her mind. For a trespasser he seemed to have a remarkably clean conscious. She decided that for this procedure the more physical means of interrogation at her disposal would not be necessary. The guard handed her the power cell and a rudimentary knife, which she examined curtly, then moved to stand directly before the captive, outside of the circle. He looked across at her, his admiration all too obvious. She had met too many overconfident spies sent from the Oppression to infiltrate the Resistance to be beguiled by this one.

She had already lost much to them. This one would learn to fear her.

'Begin,' she stated forcefully.

The guard hesitated over the inactive protection wards, but decided to not question his superior. She read in his mind the thought that added vigilance would compensate.

She examined the enigmatic prisoner.

'These restraints are not necessary,' he complained in a confident voice, yet not arrogant.

'We shall see,' she countered. 'Remove his copper banding.'

All humans were psychic, they always had been, but few could match her talent and abilities. The rest wore copper bands around their heads to amplify, or more often than not, render useful their natural talent. They also felt the bands gave them protection, and they did, to a small degree. But a determined individual could usually penetrate their defences with strength and skill. And she herself, Commander Sheelaakah, honoured as one of the foremost up and rising among the chief gifted of the Resistance, was generally regarded as an unusually determined individual.

The guard removed the band from around the prisoner's head. He offered no resistance. She noted the simple band, sufficiently effective, yet well-worn and untempered in several years. She wanted to find out how long he had been hiding in the deep underground, and where his journeys had taken him.

'Prisoner,' the guard began, 'by authority of mandate seven sub mandate twenty-three, you are found guilty of using stealth and failing to report to camp authorities upon entering into base section level two. You are therefore accused of being a spy for the Oppression and will submit wilfully and co-operatively to this interrogation. You have no rights...'

Sheelaakah waved the guard to silence.

'You understand the necessity of this procedure,' she explained simply. 'We cannot trust any at their word alone. You say you entered the area by accident, and had no knowledge of our presence? We do not know that you are not a willing or unwilling spy for the Oppression. You will submit to this mind search without hesitation or reservation.' And as a quiet after thought she added, 'not that it would matter.'

He nodded. Eyes an almost too bright a shade of green glowed at her from behind raven locks of his straight dark hair. *You examine me,* she thought to herself, *and like so many others, you underestimate me.*

'This will not be pleasant,' she warned him, and began.

Immediately his mind opened up to her. His audible gasp filled the small room. A kaleidoscope of thoughts and feelings barraged upon her. She chastened herself for her momentary loss of control. He was too keen to be known by her. *How annoying.* Quickly she restricted the flow of knowledge, speaking to his soul.

You are called Matrix. Why have you come here?

'I was rejected.' Pain-filled images flashed past her consciousness: His violent ejection from the citadel; being torn from his parents, disowned by his father; asking the wrong questions and getting in trouble; lost in the wilderness and travelling through the underground; deep underground; surviving alone; surviving for a long time. Alone.

She was as used to reading minds as others were of speaking, and the manner in which experience was exchanged. Whole images and their emotions changed as quickly as words, and time was of little consequence to all but a few individuals. Experiences were usually shared from the most powerful to the least intense. Also, memory faded and changed over time, as did recollection. People rarely recorded facts as much as their reaction to them. True recall was possible, though much deeper and harder to seek. She recalled how all individuals she'd examined showed some reluctance to being read. All except this one. His experiences cascaded upon her like water on desert sand. He could be a danger if he learnt anything important, such as anything about their Resistance.

Still, she was suspicious. Few survived the underground, and none alone. His openness made her cautious. And how could he deal so openly with such intense experience?

She questioned him on how he survived deep below the surface where powerful forces and unknown inhabitants dwelt. Immediately what he showed her made her nauseous; the uncooked rodents and fungi, learning by experience what things were poisonous. Then there was the occasional friend, the alliances with unlikely beings. He had learned to find happiness in the simplest things in his sunless world, like a gratitude for glowing bacteria. The memories were a curious story she found she wanted to read.

But then she was angered again at her lapse in focus, so she drove deeper into his awareness. *How did you find the Resistance, and enter past the second gate without detection?*

He claimed he merely wandered, attracted by human presence, but as cautious of their motives as they of his. If she hadn't sensed him he would have continued watching for days until he discovered if they could be trusted.

Still, he was too anxious to be known to her.

Lies! She said to his mind. *You are a spy and a thief. I will have the truth from you.*

'But I speak the...' he tried to say, but she drove her awareness into his being like a knife. Conscious, yet still open to her thoughts, he fell to his knees in pain while she stood unmoved. He was showing remarkable sensitivity to the force field, and it was a wonder that he wasn't already overcome – forced and over willing to re-live traumatic events without compassion or censure.

What happened next surprised her. *I speak the truth.* He spoke telepathically to her mind. Never had a non-native telepath managed to communicate in such a manner during an interrogation. He was using the very link she had established to communicate with her. With a moment of metal chagrin she threw up her mental shield and drove the mind probe deeper.

Memories of such pain flittered past his mind, awakening the defence mechanisms he had learned. Yet he strove not to use them. She grew annoyed. *He must be hiding the truth very deeply,* she assumed. Stealing herself, she knew she must look deeper, though the flood of recall from his wounded past might drown him forever.

Deep sweat broke out on the man as he fell to the floor. His breathing became constricted, and blood fell from his nose. Again his memories opened up to her; a brush with another gifted, who had tortured him similarly, stung her mind. She steadied her control and observed him. He was in extreme pain yet tried to remain open to her. Despite his best efforts semi- conscious defences broke through, quickly crushed by her experienced mind. His wrists began to bleed against the cuffs.

Whoever he was, he had a remarkable pain threshold.

Again, his memories colluded with his claim of telling the truth. She felt his terrible loneliness and sense of betrayal. Yet also observed his desire to live. She saw his deepest aspects of self, buried deep within his unconscious. She learned the violent acts he had not wanted to witness, the violence which had become his unwilling means of survival, his dread of surrendering to despair and loathing for those who did; including those he loved. His hidden fantasies and things he had never wanted anyone to know. He begged her to stop.

Perhaps I should? She mused, but she did not. She was a step away from the essence of his being. Yet for some unknown reason he fought to not resist. His claims were substantiated with his thoughts - even psychics could not hide the truth this deeply.

Finally, despite her better judgment, she drove her mind into his one last time, and would forever wish she hadn't. For as she tore away all his mental defences, broke open his memories to touch the very edge of his soul... and in the moment beheld him in a way that would bind them forever. They were kindred souls, much like...

'Innocent...' she was forced to admit, then the link broke violently off, leaving him convulsing uncontrollably on the floor. She almost collapsed against the wall and stared in fear at the man whose soul she could never touch again. The guard offered his assistance but she pushed him angrily aside.

She turned to leave, yet took one last glance at the man Matrix, whom she had left unconscious on the floor and so mentally unshielded that even the non-gifted could pick up the incoherent scattering of his thoughts, which would remain confused for several weeks until he healed, if he did not die...

She had been deeper into his mind than any other; not even her twin brother Daemon. But she knew it was only because Matrix had allowed her, despite the risk it posed to him. She was shaken, and as Sheelaakah slammed the door shut on the interrogation room and walked briskly along the corridor she was deeply disturbed. It wasn't until sometime later that she realised something she could never explain;

Her wrists hurt...

The Healing of Matrix

The first thing Matrix realised after regaining consciousness was the terrible, unremitting pain. Nothing else made sense. Thoughts mingled in confused conversation like an angry crowd, and he had no memory of where he was or even that he was. For a long while he stared at the ceiling.

Eventually he noticed another dull pain and was drawn to it. He stared at it for a long time, but it would be several days before he recognised his hands again, let alone the medical implement that they had attached to the back of it.

The quiet yet incessant babble of his thoughts were broken by the waking memory of a cruel voice: *I will have the truth from you!* – punctuated with dark and contorted images. He tried to flee, to get away. The images crashed down on him, and he tried to hide from them like a child from a thunderstorm. But they thundered on. He saw a young girl hiding in a stone crevice, a woman standing strong interrogating a man, saw someone very dear captured by laughing men in dark clothing.

He then heard voices, from outside his mind. They sounded urgent, yet competent; though they made no sense to him.

'He's going into autonomic shock. Four cc's Postmodulum. Try to stop the convul – hold his arms!'

And then a different, higher voice. 'Four cc's administered. Psychotoxin levels still increasing. Raising administration.'

He looked to see arms tied with silver bands, while he was trapped in a lightless cave. He heard another voice within jeer: *Let's see how well you do blindfolded!* Immediately he was blind. Black masked assailants kicked and punched him, breaking his ribs. They were going to make him leave the citadel like this? Was this … his memory?

He tried to flee the pain and suddenly there was a rush of motion as though an elevator had just come to a stop. He looked down and saw a stranger; a man with black hair twisting violently on a bed. He looked somehow familiar, and longed to help him. All around him was the most profound silence, almost peace. Two figures rushed about the convulsing man, his arms tied with silver bands. He felt himself drawn to a small female. He felt himself seeing the man through her eyes and felt a stab of fear that he might not be able to save this man who had been unfairly treated. He was angry at the person who had done this to this man. How could she leave him like this without properly closing his mind! Wait, his soul is moving again. He must return to his own!

With a gut wrenching pull the elevator moved again and he was surrounded with distress, and sound, and intense pain.

'Psychotoxins critical! Pulmonary distress, collapse imminent!'

'Ten cc… forty cc Noradrenalin! Hold his arms!!'

'It's having no effect. What do we do now?'

'...We pray.'

He felt dark hands close over his neck, squeezing the life from him. The blows intensified, but slowly weakened. He struggled against the strangler, to no avail. As the strength left him he heard the words; *You will submit to this interrogation...*

---+++---+++---

'Matrix? Awaken. It is morning again.'

He felt like he'd heard those words recently, but could not recall at all when. A name... his name? He fought consciousness as a sound sleeper avoids waking, knowing the dreamer escapes the pressures of the waking world in the pleasant land of sleep. But he did stir.

'My dark-haired charge,' the familiar voice continued, 'it's a fine day and I'm in a good mood. Perhaps we'll give you a bath again... oh! You're awake!'

A blurred figure moved into his line of vision. He tried to focus. He felt something touch his forehead.

'This will help.'

Immediately his vision began to clear. Then he realised that it was another mind that touched his, and the sensation invoked a primal fear. He pulled away, but was still too unaware of his body to move much. The figure above him broke the link and grabbed him arm.

'It's, ok. You'll be ok. Hush Matrix.' Her voice was calm and reassuring. She gently stroked his hand and face. 'I'm sorry. I should have realised. Hush, you are safe. Safe here. Hush.'

She began to sing softly, enveloping him in her song. Her voice was high and gentle. Matrix sensed her pure intent. She wore some kind of single colour uniform. In the peace of her song his thoughts were silent and his head hurt less. He let it carry him to sleep.

---+++---+++---

Matrix heard voices in a room nearby, and realised the light was too bright, which was what woke him. He tried to sit up and realised his head hurt too much. His mouth was dry. He wanted to know where he was, then he realised he had no idea when he was either, or of the passage of time in the outside world. He tried to relax and remember something, but his thoughts were disjointed and fleeting.

'Good morning Matrix. I sensed you were awake again.'

'Wh... who are you?' His tongue felt like a baked brick.

A figure moved into his line of vision. At first it was hard to focus, but eventually he made out a short female of the human Irid sub-species, known for their mathematic and telepathic tendances. She had the wide cheekbones and large eyes, typical of her race, with a small nose that quite suited her. Her hair was red, and sparse by human standards. She wore the uniform of an Irid aid, or nurse. It reminded him of a visit to the hospital as a young man. Her presence felt... comforting.

'I am your aide, Matrix, your nurse. Your progress is quite remarkable. I brought you some orange juice Matrix, just like you ordered.'

'Ordered?'

'Yesterday, we talked for nearly half an hour. Don't you remember?'

He tried to, but felt like he could only remember his name on account she kept on using it.

'No,' he confessed, but was glad to hear he'd apparently asked.

His bed swiftly rose till he was almost in a sitting position. She manoeuvred a straw into his mouth.

'No matter. Drink in small doses.'

He had trouble swallowing, so she helped him by putting her hand behind his neck. He didn't know what she did, but it helped. He figured it must be some form of telepathy, and for some reason that made him nervous, but he was too thirsty to care. He soon finished.

'There. Did you like that? Can I get you anything else?'

'No. Just something... for the migraine.'

'Sorry, nothing can be done about that little piece of pie. Don't look so disappointed! You've suffered *severe* psychotrauma. We nearly lost you.'

Matrix sensed the sincere concern she had for him. He supposed that by her vocation she also remained day and night to care for her patients. It brought back a vague memory of someone convulsing on a bed.

'How long have I been here?'

'Two weeks now.'

'Two weeks!' It had passed as a dream. 'What 'app, wha, 'appened?' The H sound suddenly seemed to be too much to manage for the time being.

She smiled, then allowed a strange understanding expression to cross her face.

You're not ready to know that, she spoke telepathically. Matrix suddenly broke out into a cold sweat and instinctively began to tremble, and his nurse again began to stroke his hand and face. She started to hum a familiar tune. Before she'd gone too far Matrix hummed along with her and his fear echoed into silence with the final notes.

'You've been here too long!' she stated.

He laughed, but it hurt.

'You will recover soon.'

'Where am I?' he asked.

'I cannot tell you that.'

Suddenly another voice spoke from the door.

'Our patient had awoken! Good morning Matrix.' A tall human female walked in, and she seemed as though she had a talent for looking important.

'Good morning sir,' he said.

'I am your chief healer.' She looked at the aide, and Matrix sensed a brief conversation occurred to which he was not privy. The chief healer nodded and began checking instruments and dials.

'How do you feel?' the chief healer asked.

'I have an 'eadache.'

'You will, for some time, but it will subside. I hope to have you out of bed in a week. Your progress is quite remarkable.' The chief healer bent over to check his forehead, and Matrix realised he was wearing a headband of some sort. As soon as he noticed this he realised he could focus his mind more.

'I complement you on your work, Pip,' the chief healer said to the aid. 'No doubt his recovery cannot be ascribed to his abilities alone.'

'Thank you.'

'Second year out. She's the best,' the doctor indicated to the Iridian with admiration.

'Oh shucks,' the nurse replied. 'You lie!'

At those words Matrix's headache grew suddenly worse. He was quickly retired to bed, and left alone to sleep. He began to wonder if he would ever leave that bed and return to the world outside.

---+++---+++---

He stared blankly at the cards. It had been four weeks now. He was grateful for the constant company, but his Irid aid Pip was a hard taskmaster.

'It's the second,' he said, 'it has this shape to the left of the circle.'

'Good, your spatial ability is improving. But no, it's the other one.'

Matrix groaned in exasperation. 'I've had enough tests for one day. Why do we do so many?'

The nurse looked at him with her large eyes. 'You want to know? For me, I do it to discover what occupies your mind most. Plus its part of this hospital's requirements.' She paused to arrange the cards. 'You are quite lonely.'

Matrix stared at the sheets, trying to ignore wondering how she could have known this after a spatial acuities test. So he changed the topic. 'For a Resistance, you're much better equipped and organised than I think people realise.'

She looked intently at him, ignoring his attempt to evade the question.

'Oh all right... They threw me out of the citadel when I was sixteen, seven years ago. Since then I've been surviving on my own. Guess I had some help. But it's a long story. I don't really want to go into it.'

He looked at her and she at him. He hoped she would ask no further questions.

'You've an interesting story Matrix, and one day I hope you will trust me with it.'

She seemed sincere, but who could he trust? She seemed to sense his fear.

'That's alright. It's not like this is a Confronting or anything. You only need tell me what you want to tell me. But,' she said sincerely, 'as I've said, I will insist you be honest with yourself. No hiding truth from me when you decide it is time to talk. You can cry or yell or anything you want here, and I won't let you hurt anybody. There is nothing to be ashamed of. Remember,' she added cheekily, 'I've seen you naked.'

Her mischievous twinkle lit up the room. He didn't want to admit it, but right now, he couldn't live without her. Just her presence was enough, even the sound of her breathing helped him to sleep deeper at night.

'Will you be staying in tonight?' he asked, embarrassed that he suddenly sounded so forlorn.

'No, my charge must learn independence. Besides, I want to get home to my children.'

'They're lovely,' he mused forlornly at the memory of most mornings here. 'I'll miss you, y'know.'

'Don't worry, you'll be in here for a couple of months yet.'

They chattered meaninglessly until it was time for her to go. She touched his forehead with hers in that odd farewell and was gone again for the night.

Matrix curled up in the sheets, best bed in almost seven years. How odd life could be; one moment chasing pig rats and the next personal care at someone else's expense. Voices were out in the hall. He knew he could stop that with the push of a button, or turn off the light. But he kept them on. He even kept the 'do not disturb' sigil switched off in the hope that, perhaps, someone else might come in and disturb him yet again, and he would not need to feel alone.

He wondered why he hadn't cried yet. It felt strange. He was twenty-three and still a child. Most of his friends, those who had been too wise to question, would be finishing academics this year. Yet here he was without them in a hospital bed of the Resistance of all things. Still alive too! Now that was more than a miracle.

Yet he was sad. He'd missed out on a lot. Seven peacemakers and six birthdays spent alone– except for the year with the mutants and the one spent strapped to a Dymoc sacrificial altar. He had to laugh; there certainly was a story to how he got out of that one! He smiled. Guess it hadn't been all bad, and he was still alive. And now, here he was. Perhaps, somehow, he was meant to be here.

Then his thoughts soured as he remembered the Citadel with its two trillion inhabitants who had, by their silence, condoned his and countless thousands of others to being banished out here into the wildness beyond, being left to die or rot to death, living in chaos on whatever constituted survival.

He wondered if he would ever go back, or was there no going back? What would he do now? Join the Resistance? Or maybe recant and get back into the city and civil life? No, these people had stayed out in the wilderness beyond to build an organised group. But they were the enemies of civilisation, "refusing to live under law, becoming a law unto themselves: Reaping the harvest of their actions in the lawless wilderness." But then, perhaps that had all been a lie as well? Matrix still didn't know for certain. All he had done was question, and continue to question until it was too late. And yet... he still had questions...

But to join the Resistance? It was a challenging move, but perhaps better for his personal survival; or for regular meals at least.

The sounds from the corridor kept him distracted from answerless questions. He found himself recalling his mother's seventh-day roast.

Ample, with lots of gravy. He missed her. Most sensible Seren youth didn't leave home until they were thirty: he at sixteen, and that by force. He tried not to think of her crying as they took him away. He tried not to think of his father's righteous denial of his son, comforting his spouse as their second son was taken to the courts. He tried not to think of the trial, the false accusations and image footage, and his so-called friends' testimonies. He tried not to think, and then finally he succeeded. Biting the cushion he thought of that song Pip sang often.

He did not believe in luck. Whatever destiny had kept him alive in a dead world for seven years and had brought him here would have to guide him further. He would find his way, eventually.

Choices

'You are currently at location seventeen, in a Resistance stronghold south of Border Mountains within the Wilderness Beyond leading to Moonscape. All this, of course, is south of Seren City proper, about twelve thousand kilometres from the Citadel's wall. We are at an underground facility because, as you know, our location and activities must remain clandestine. You are welcome to stay, but if you choose to leave you will do so without anything you came in with or anything you gained here. You will be left at no pre-specified co-ordinates and will be required to fend for yourself. This is your choice.'

The Resistance official spoke directly and sincerely to Matrix. They sat with Pip at the patient's lounge, on Matrix's first day outside the hospital rooms where he'd spent the last three months. They'd decided he had to know sooner, rather than later, so that he could begin to make his decisions. Things were starting to happen, and he had to make a choice. It was a harsh line he thought, but adequately fair given the circumstance.

Matrix turned to his Irid aid. 'How long 'til I am discharged do you think?' Although she'd saved his life, countless hours with this person was getting at times, well, tedious. He'd spotted a nice couple of girls he wanted to meet, but they seemed shy with his nurse always at his side.

Pip replied, 'Well, you're up and about now. To be safe and assure complete recovery you'll have to wait almost another month.'

That made him instinctively impatient. Turning to the official he asked impetuously, 'I've heard about this Resistance, but I never knew it was so well organised. You people really want to take down the system?'

The official looked gravely at Matrix. 'Don't be flippant, young man. You know very well what is going on around here. We would be happy just to leave this planet, but we can't. They threw you out, but you can't leave can you? Nobody can.' The strain on this man was obvious.

'Come on Terric, you'll stress him out too,' Pip argued. She was so protective it was annoying. More often than not though, she was right, and usually knew what was wrong before Matrix even noticed symptoms. She'd taught him how to swallow and walk again, he owed her that.

The official stood to leave. 'Just remember those facts young man. You have 'til you recover to decide.' He turned and walked quickly away.

Matrix turned to his aide. He examined his Irid nurse, and knew her well enough to know that she was troubled about Terric. Did she worry about everyone's state of health?

'He'll be alright,' he counselled.

Pip feigned surprise. 'Really, becoming bit of an aide yourself? Doesn't surprise me; you've the planetoids best tutor!'

They laughed and the tension left. They chatted on less grave topics for a while, but eventually Matrix had some things he wanted to know.

'Pip, what happened to me?'

'What do you remember?'

'Not much. I was hiding outside the walls when the guards spotted me. I ran for a while, but they caught me and brought me in. Things get pretty hazy around then. Pain… struggling… and this meaningless image of a … brown haired woman. Can you help me?'

Pip was silent for a moment, as though driven with thoughts she did not want to express. Instead, the admitted, 'I remember sensing your arrival before you came into my care at this hospital – on the third day of the week, about the ninth hour. They'd brought you in from the other place having administered only bare psych first aid. The careless fools had put you in stasis, and you were busy degrading anyway. We took you out and began operating. You see, you were caught sneaking outside one of the outer bases and taken to interrogation. For reasons I cannot share the interrogation went badly. Unfortunately your interrogator couldn't accept that you might have been telling them the truth, so they took 'extra measures', which were utterly unwarranted. They nearly killed you. Anyhow, they got you in to us just in time and by grace, you live. And that woman, she is not a fleeting image. It is Shee that did this to you.'

Matrix sat lost in thought for a moment, and she left him privately there. Eventually the aide continued; 'One thing we still don't know, my patient, is what you were doing outside the walls in the first place.'

'I told you, I was just looking. This is the most people I've met since... years. Seven years below ground. I'm still not exactly on top, but at least I know where I am. I wanted to see what you were up to; I had no idea who you were.'

Pip looked at him, but she didn't have to be a telepath to tell he wasn't telling her the whole truth. He sat back then, and she watched him get lost again in his thoughts; what kind of lives did they live in the citadel nowadays? Did they still live double lives – making all the right appearances during the day, and indulging in all kinds of lust and dishonour during the night? Did they still condemn the children who questioned?

Angel

Arriving at the club on 15th she drowned her thoughts in reckless hedonism.

Her real name was Alasia: but she was becoming known as the Princess of Pleasure. She'd chosen her company this night for his stunning beauty and wealth, and she deserved only the best. Heir to a throne of the beauty queen and accustomed to getting what she desired.

The club, hidden deep within the citadel, was full of aspiring, status-minded, fashion-sensitive, wealthy party-goers – her type of people. She knew them, their secrets, their hidden desires and their fears. She was one of them and one of their best, and they respected and feared her. Anybody who was anybody in this Circle knew her. She was Alasia, popular, well liked, naturally beautiful.

The floor shook with hypercharged music and multi-coloured lights froze the silhouettes of dancers drugged to euphoria with excitement, and the drinks, which were available both over, and under, the bar. Entering the Club took special permission, which Alasia had held for longer as long as her career had lasted. She did not need it now. She knew the Doorkeeper well, so very well. This was her type of party.

2 Alasia, Princess of Pleasure

But it wasn't in music that her passion lay, but in the illegal source of income that she so lucratively plundered from the public coffers. Her true source of wealth lay in trading secrets – a dangerous, exciting, and lucrative ... hobby.

So as she descended the stairs she waved charismatically to those who knew her, and those who pretended to. Her face was unforgettable, and was becoming known to other circles quickly as well. Her notoriety was on the rise, and her presence requested at more and more events. People would be honoured to meet her, and she could have her pick of men for the evening.

Her companion helped her remove her coat and sat her at their reserved seats. What she had on underneath was illegal on the streets, and she'd designed it herself to be provocative and sensual. As the band would not start playing for several minutes she allowed him to take her to the dance floor full of enviously attired people. The dance was a tuneless rhythm of repetitive sounds, perhaps new, unrecognisable - though nobody cared.

Although it wearied her, she did her best to ignore his bodyguard nearby. He seemed accustomed to it, a statesman such as he. Should they ever decide on permanency in their relationship she would be assured of the continued lifestyle; that pleased her. He pleased her. He was handsome, and attractive - though spoilt, and she didn't like that. She was used to getting what she wanted, and did not like the thought of having to live with someone so accustomed to a similar existence. No perfect match ever existed nor ever would, so few permanent relationships existed. Besides, they would live a normal permanency for those of their clique, open to the occasional relationship other than between themselves.

He lifted her off her feet, and he laughed. They were making quite a scene on the floor. He was quite a dancer and tonight, he was hers.

The song ended and people clapped, some resting between songs while the relentless beat still continued unbaited. Alasia noticed her ears ringing, but knew they'd grow numb soon. She looked into her companion's eyes and kissed him. He kissed her too, and the warmth of his kiss surprised her, though she tried to hide it. She would go home with him later, unless she was more impressed by another. He had no claim on her, and he knew it. It kept the spark alive in their own union, and kept him hers when she wanted him.

She was Alasia, Princess of Pleasure. This whole party could have been for her. She was noticed by everyone, and wanted by all. She could have any man, or anything she wanted. She was hot property.

And she knew it.

Premonition

Commander Sheelaakah was in a forest, like the gardens back on the colony she grew up in. She immediately knew it was a dream, at least it felt like a dream. She was on the outskirts of a forest when suddenly she was afraid, and began to remove herself back into the forest. There, blocking her way, was a huge dog arrayed for war, collar spikes glistening in the moonlight. On its haunch was written in a paint so red it could have been blood, the number five. It walked calmly past her, glancing over at her as it passed. With its company she took courage, and began to approach that part of the forest where the source of her unnamed fear awaited. Then there was a familiar presence, her spirit guide.

'Sheelaakah,' a voice whispered. A quiet voice, yet one laced with such power and understanding she could not help but be a little nervous. It spoke in wisdom and agelessness. Sheelaakah breathed a sigh of relief. In all the universe there were so few beings that could enter ones dreams from a universe away. It was a Seraph, the one called Whisperer, and her visits were rare.

'Whisperer,' Shee answered. 'I have been shown a dream, but I don't know what it means.'

The voice didn't answer, but spoke a message. 'You must join with the Dogs of War of the fifth regiment. You are needed.'

Shimmering light coalesced into feint lines, the silhouette of a bear forming in the light. Shee trembled and stepped back. This rarely happened.

'You are troubled,' Shee dared to whisper.

The being repeated its message, seeming to strain just a little as though it took great effort to come to where Sheelaakah was. 'Join with the Dogs of war of the fifth regiment. The war continues unabated. You are needed.'

Sheelaakah was uncertain, her mind filled with a thousand questions. When Whisperer finally spoke once more, she looked directly at her, eyes filled with sympathy and wisdom. 'I see you have many questions, and that is natural. Your heart is greatly burdened. Are you so unsure of what you have to contribute, or why these things *must* be? Perhaps that is necessary. If you lack direction, go first to a Confronting; clear you heart of burdens. Then will your feet be lightened to walk the path that was chosen.'

Sheelaakah grew nervous at that suggestion. Always; she had been the one others relied on, or the one others answered to. When one attended a Confronting they faced their weakness, their failures, their questions. Confrontings had a tendency to force one to be honest with themselves, and in all honesty, she was not keen on attending one.

A soft breeze blew. The spirit continued, touching her face in kindness with shimmering glimmers of light and fire, meeting her gaze with eyes that seemed older than eternity, and deeper than forever. 'Join with the Dogs of war of the fifth regiment. The time of the First Great war is upon us. I am sent to prepare you. You *need* this service. Let it change you forever.'

Swirling lights grew together suddenly, and vanished. Sheelaakah woke suddenly, the kind of unusual awaking that throws the sleeper into full consciousness. She'd had a dream – very lucid and terribly clear.

She sighed, and sat up.

Whisperer had never seemed so troubled, nor so close. Non corporeal entities were common enough on Seren, bound for the most part by the same laws of society and physics that governed corporeals. But entities like those of the Seraph, such as the one she called Whisperer, came and went as they pleased. They seemed to be unbound by time in knowing all the affairs of temporals, such as herself. Whole religions had begun when their presence had first become detectable, even when it was usually only a few who could detect them, or believed in their existence. All this didn't help Shee understand what was going on.

Commander
Sheelaakah
The X-or Story
(c) Dr Joseph
Ireland 2016

3 Commander Sheelaakah, rising promise of the Psychic division

She lay back down, exhausted. Higher entities had a way of exacting it out of you. Shee pondered the message so important it was repeated three times, engraved powerfully on her mind. It had left more questions. What great war was this spirit planning, and what was she needed for? At least one thing was clear. She was moving camp to one of the hundreds of war units. Why this particular one? And why was it so important that a Seraph herself would send a message personally to tell her?

The diplomat

Alasia had kept the cat waiting for over half an hour, but it had made no difference.

'You called?' She asked, annoyed. It was a very good party till he'd called.

The cat licked its paw. Empathically, with thoughts beyond words, it informed her that it was time for her to work again. It also told her that it knew she would be late, and that was why it had called early.

'You *forge fired...!*' she was lost for words in her anger, and hidden admiration. 'Oh, I hate my day job!' she complained, slapping the crystal book down on the banister, hoping it would break but knowing it couldn't.

The cat looked up at the approaching craft.

'I know,' she answered his unspoken thoughts. 'I'll do all the talking and just leave all the work to you. Run my 'little speech'. You know, it was really a very *good* party that I was at, are you sure we couldn't have left this to someone else? Karen loves her job, why not... yeah, yeah, I know.'

She hadn't been at work for over two weeks. Everyone worked on Seren, it was law, but few people had a life. And few people knew about Alasia's secret life.

'I hate being sober,' she complained. 'Besides, civics bore me. I can't see what you find so interesting in all this. Hey, since it's my *moral duty* to accompany you today, surely I can have a little fun?'

One look from the cat silenced that thought completely. She knew it would, she was just teasing, and it knew it. Reaching out she picked it up and helped it down to the floor.

'You'd better make this worth my while, Firo,' she said to it. 'I've some real work to do.'

---++---++---

'Thi delta, you are cleared to land. Proceed to docking port ninety three. Seren government welcomes Diplomat Gral to your three day tour. Your guides are waiting.'

The diplomat shifted his coffee from where he was trying to read. Usually half prepared, he often found he had little time between his wife and girlfriend for a professional job. Sighing, he looked up at the Senetcraft's wide-angle view screen to the vortex that was forming in the protective shielding. A strange mega metropolis shone underneath. Their destination: The Seren Citadel. His inforvisor beeped to indicate it had information to share, but he set his computer for direct synaptic download, he could study it all later.

World shields such as this had been his speciality and passion at the academy. Despite missing half his lectures he'd managed dux for his project on the Pllallath-seven archshield, managing a decent social life as well. It was soon after that he was approached by a lower senate official and offered a post in the government research labs. The monotony drove him insane within two months, and he was almost glad when a freak accident created no small stir within the settlement. He'd found himself swept along in a tirade of media and government investigations that would drown most. But not himself. He surfed the tide of opportunity and soon landed a job in civic representation. He had learned then that one of his greatest talents was in lying to people, and the natural conclusion was to move into politics.

The small craft trembled as it rode through the narrow end of the vortex, which closed immediately behind them. Many such shields were employed around planetoids such as this one, usually just to hold in the air or keep away excessive sunlight, though it was an established fact that none were quite so detailed or as large.

But enough of hobbies, he was here on official business. The 'Seren City' as it was called had recently entered the Utopian system where he and one hundred and seventy million others resided. So the research colony at Breakers Point had, like so many of the other civics, decided it proper protocol to send official delegates to discuss rights and trade issues. Who better than himself to represent his new home? Besides, it would make an interesting assignment before he returned to Terran 4 to see family.

The diplomat remembered, because the knowledge had just been put there during the synaptic download, that the Seren City was first settled 930U (3280 AD), just prior to the great war which symbolised an end to the tyranny of the Galactic Overlords. Originally it was a large asteroid circling the Terra Solistus blue supergiant in the Menonian cluster, millions of light years away from Earth. It may have been inhabited previously, but no records were kept. As the colony grew, mostly due to refugees from the warzones, it acquired an internal power source. After the truce of 1214U it gained independence, and in 1220U it gained Tesser capacity and moved to the outer reaches of the galaxy. It continued to grow in size and capacity as people fled to one of the few colonies that was not and had not been involved in any wars. Internal strife was rare due to the highly centralised and efficient government. In line with the discovery in 2128 AD of non-corporeal life, and the following repercussions, a non- corporeal entity of reputed extraordinary leadership capabilities was elected leader in 1272U, whom the people had honoured with the title 'True One', and has served successfully in that capacity ever since. In spite of being seven hundred percent larger than most non- planet colonies the Seren people refuse to divide their mega metropolis into smaller parts, claiming more effective management as is. Current population – roughly two trillion sentients.

Diplomat Gral marvelled. A lifeless rock turned into a living stone. It had the appearance of an oval shaped megalith almost the length of earth's moon, a little, perhaps like an egg. One end was entirely aglow, the top fifth a super city to rival some of those found on the inner colonies. Most of the population lived, and died, here. None left apparently. Surrounding this city was a relatively uncharted wilderness, though why that was so, he could not tell. It encircled the entire planetoid in a forest that gradually thinned with the artificial atmosphere towards the opposing end. There lay the propulsion and refining section; an airless wilderness thousands of kilometres wide. There five gigantic metal pillars stood, each two thousand kilometres at the base, which joined at their ends and stretched down to the planetoids surface like a cage. It was a stark difference to the tower of light that was the centre of the megacity, residence of the True One, and part of the shield generator.

The Senetcraft flew over the city that just seemed to grow ever larger. The city itself was mostly green, a little strange for a planetoid, but as he looked closer it was dotted with white towers and deep crevices for housing.

He found himself pondering this 'city paradise of peace': did it have a dark side?

He searched his memory for some clue. To his surprise he recalled a discussion with his boss he'd never had. He only ever heard rumours that the technology existed for a synaptic download to do that. His employer, Diplomat Plause, was standing by his desk like someone had visualscoped him.

Darn you Gral! I knew you'd settle for a download before you put in some real effort. It's that girl of yours. I still can't believe your wife lets you! Anyhow. This Seren system that comes out of nowhere... Look, there's a concern in the senate...

His recall was cut short by the outer seal on the door breaking open. He hadn't even realised that they'd landed. The diplomat sighed and picked up his jacket. The trifling concerns of ignorable city officials would have to wait. His assistant entered the senetcraft's main room from the chamber and smiled, placid limbs of steel and plastic holding out his briefcase.

'Time to work, sir,' it said with its ambrosial voice.

'Yes,' mumbled the diplomat. The inner door opened and he strode confidently to the exit. As he entered the doorway he paused to examine the surroundings and allow the surroundings to examine him. *What secrets do you hold Seren?* He thought. Then he realised that his welcoming party consisted of only two: a cat, and of the best looking human women he'd honestly ever laid eyes on. She looked at him with a cold politician's smile, as though hiding something... mischievous. And he found that immediately interesting.

Oh, he thought wickedly, *I know how you got your promotion.*

--- +++ --- +++ ---

She smiled, and took on her professional persona. 'Welcome to Seren City, Diplomat Gral. I am your tour guide Alasia.'

He nodded at her silently. He was much more handsome in real life.

Alasia watched as he raised his hand in an age-old greeting. 'Diplomat Gral welcomes the Seren Planetoid to the Utopian system on behalf of the research colonies at Breakers Point. I know we will both benefit from our transactions.'

Although a formal greeting, she could tell he meant it personally. Behind him, his assistant, a biological android, carried a single briefcase. She knew he would be recording every word they said, and she knew better than to underestimate the silent machine who was instructed to never address her directly or speak unless spoken to. She assessed the diplomat as a typically arrogant and self-obsessed lower Senate representative.

What fun...

'Our tour will consist of a brief overview of the facilities and capacities citizens share in living on, "the safest rock in the Galaxy". We will proceed first to the briefing room, then on to the refineries and lower civics, stopping at various places of interest such as the Mezzanine, Seren Library and the People's Palace. Our tour concludes tonight at a tavern known as the 23rd and fourth. Feel free to ask questions at any time, understood?'

'Understood.'

'Good. Please come this way.'

--- +++ --- +++ ---

He had to admit, she had great legs. Gral determined she was what would make this visit memorable. He only hoped they could lose their assistants this evening when he and this Lady Alasia went out for some drinks at 23rd and fourth. Nice name for a place to meet. He listened to her speech, delivered with sincere professionalism while she took one too many glances at his chest.

'Seren was officially founded in nine sixty U, thirty years after first settlement. What began as a refuge to lone wanderers soon became a haven to those seeking peace from the warzones. As a result, ingrained in our education and daily life is the symbol of the peace arch, given to us by the peacemakers to remind us of our duty to our future and past and the need for constant vigilance in maintaining peace and order. The peacemakers, on the first of the first, enacted the four hundred and twenty three codes of conduct that are the basis of our city's law, beginning with the right of each individual to choose their own life journey.'

Her speech continued, 'Seren itself is a circular city covering the entire northern hemisphere of the Planetoid, covering a total surface area of the Atlantic ocean on Sol third. While we see only the surface from here, it extends almost a thousand kilometres underground. The surface and the tower of light are kept white due to the artificial lighting, as Seren often enters regions of space where no adequate natural sources are available. As you can imagine, a system of this magnitude requires a massive amount of power; twenty Terahertz per nano second, which is generated in part by the gravitic field its counter clockwise spin generates, and by electrical potential between the surface and the atmosphere. Industry is assisted by Cleon and or EGF generators deep under the city at the refineries. Some out-dated fission generators are occasionally used if necessary.'

The tour continued, most of it an official spiel obviously held on file back at the colony, but still a decent amount for someone to memorise. They paused as he took in the view from their window. His attention had begun to wane when his guide suddenly pointed skyward.

'Our city is protected by the most powerful artificial energy field in the known universe. In spite of occasional hostiles from without the system, Seren has managed to defend herself and her people for over a thousand years 'til the present day being third of the second, two thousand, six hundred and twenty U... You do use standard galactic time units at Breakers Point, I hope?'

He smiled at the comment as though she'd meant it as a joke. 'So what brings you to Utopia?' he asked, hoping to disarm her.

She paused as though wondering why he'd ignored her question, but deciding proper protocol was to answer his. 'Obviously, Seren has a lot to offer and gain in the way of trade. Seren requires energy in any form, and raw materials of almost any sort. Mining ceased back in twelve twenty four U. We also offer technology and armaments to any just cause.'

She stopped suddenly and turned to Gral. 'However, Seren's most pressing need is citizens. There is no greater resource. We are a growing mega metropolis with all you could ask. People are power, and power to unite a warring galaxy in peace. You do want peace, don't you Mr Gral?'

Her unexpected leap in intensity surprised and offset the otherwise polished diplomat. 'Ah... Yes! Of course. That's what brings you to Utopia, no?' Nice save.

She didn't seem convinced, 'Two trillion inhabitants and no major civil unrest in history? Nobody has achieved that before. We've found a way, diplomat. We have more to offer than you could pay for.'

Whoa, he found himself thinking, *a fanatic!*

The diplomat glanced at his guide and realised she was maintaining eye contact longer than was conformable. Eventually she looked away and continued in a business-like fashion.

'Our second stop is the industrial heart of Seren; the refineries. In case you were wondering, although most work is automated we do sport some handcrafts and even the occasional smith or other arcane forms of material management. Artisans, potters, etc. Power wastage is kept to a minimum, and all forms of terrestrial matter are recycled at one hundred per cent.'

They exited the corridor and got on a travelator. Slow, but scenic. Within minutes the Tower of Light could be clearly seen in all its glowing glory. Diplomat Gral could not help but stare.

She must have noticed this, and continued. 'Seren tower holds most of the rulers of the system, who live in accommodation no more nor less luxurious than anywhere else on Seren. The force field is broadcast from here, which protects the city.'

'So why the wall then?' The conversation decelerated instantaneously to an unexpected halt. The question had come without warning, not from the diplomat himself, but his assistant. The diplomat and his guide turned to look at the lanky machine.

Gral scowled at his assistant, why on earth had it spoken?

--- +++ --- +++ ---

If it had've been the Diplomat, she might have managed better, but Alasia was put off by the unexpected 'outburst' from the silent assistant. Such a delicate issue as well, perhaps it knew something? The cat hissed in displeasure, almost tripping over himself in indignation at the breach in protocol. Clearly, Firo had been caught off guard as well.

The diplomat began apologising for his assistant's unprofessional behaviour. She waved him aside. It was time for the line again. 'Not all of Seren is hospitable. There are always those who cannot live within the bounds of civilisation, nor do they receive its benefits and protection. Since it would not be of good conscience to release them on anyone else, they are allowed to live under their own rule in the wilderness beyond the wall. Their civilisation is, well, uncivil and often violent, though they are kept in check by our security forces and have never succeeded in disrupting the public peace. Unless they are guilty of serious crime they are free to return to the embrace of the citadel any time they choose.' She turned to the diplomat. 'Most of them choose the citadel, or live the remainder of their lives in the wilderness.'

'Interesting way to deal with criminals,' he admitted.

'Effective,' she replied, and glowered at the assistant in an attempt to dissuade it from asking any more questions.

For dinner

Alasia grinned.

'That's one thing I don't get,' Gral complained as they finished their second drink, 'is why downloads aren't more common?'

'Really?' She asked disbelieving, but allowing him to sit very close to her now. This was all too much fun. They watched the dancers swim about in the music, relaxing now that the real work for the day was done. Maybe it was good luck that she'd been called into work today after all? He had such handsome eyes. 'It's probably the amount of effort it takes to make sense of them. Most people are too lazy.'

He plucked the stone from his brow, and Alasia raised an eyebrow. Removing mental protections such as this was unheard of in Seren. 'This little crystal can download into my mind almost anything I need to know – languages, routines, protocols. Yes, it takes time to assimilate it all, but it makes learning so much quicker. Really, what did they do before crystology!'

Alasia felt the enthusiasm rise unbidden within her, ancient history was one of her pet topics, and he'd surely mistake her enthusiasm for interest in him. 'They'd been developing computer systems for hundreds of years on Terran third... '

'You mean Earth?' He interrupted.

'If you must. And they'd been developing faster and faster systems. Well, imagine their surprise when they found out the best and most stable devices for carrying and calculating information were already naturally formed? Now imagine their further surprise when Kringal and Trellwaki in 1958 AD found out that crystals not only can hold almost unlimited information, but that they were all, already, full of it! Can you imagine that? So many questions about the formation of the worlds, the movements of the stars, snippets of conversations and powerful emotions ... all already faithfully recorded by the stones under their feet. It revolutionized everything,' she adjusted her seating.

'Of course, the repercussions of these results were ignored for hundreds of years, tragically. But when they got into it finally they discovered the crystals in each world form a kind of symbiotic bond among each other, much like a computer based system they called the 'internet'. Given the right technology, which took several dozen years to develop once they got around to it, they found they could store and trade all sorts of information, memories of ancestors, thoughts, hold conversations across vast distances like they were sitting in the same room-'

'You're joking right? Didn't they know about soul prints?'

'Oh not at all, they had an inkling with echoes and soul parts and such. There were a thousand different philosophies. They did not know that all matter generates a soul print, and that at conception a new soul print begins to form organised by matter into a sentient being, though we believe this theory had occurred to some.'

'So what did they think about death? Did they not know that sentience ends at death and the soul print is recycled into the Universe?'

'At first, then they almost all tried to erase it from their civilisations memory!' Alasia mused, literally fascinated by the misconceptions of past civilisations. She was about to launch into comparative philosophy between Terran and Mythonian home worlds.

'Where did they think humanity sprang from?' Gral asked, moderately curious.

'They didn't even know about the Seraph,' she mused romantically. 'They had all sorts of ideas, including evolution.'

'Evolution!' He scoffed.

'Indeed. Purposeful creation was one of the least popular 'myths.' '

'No way!'

'Yes. Dissemination theorem was still four hundred years away from crystology.'

'Unbelievable,' he stated.

'Indeed,' she replied. 'Humanity has changed a lot since that time-'

'Well, this is all very interesting...' He lied in interruption, 'but tell me, do they dance on your world?'

It was a redundant question; dozens were dancing about them already. But before she had a chance to display one of her favourite talents... someone expectantly invited themselves into the conversation.

It was Karen, her best friend.

And she was holding the cat.

'Alasia!' Karen charmed, 'so good to see you here! Warm the people,' she said in an old gesture of fellowship dating back to Seren's pre-Tesser days, giving her a hug. Then she turned to look at the diplomat, 'oooh,' she said covetously, 'and who's the meat you brought to dinner today!'

'That's...' Alasia began, moving to push Karen gently aside before she stole her date away. But then Firo, the cat, leapt up onto the bench. He had a dangerous look in his eye, and he stared hard at Alasia.

'… diplomat Gral,' Alasia finished, the fun flowing out of her.

'Diplomat, no way! You're off world? Wow, I *like* that,' Karen gushed, and started chatting the diplomat up.

Alasia just stared at Firo. *This is just business,* he threatened her, and Alasia knew immediately that her services were no longer welcome here.

She looked over at Karen. Something was so very wrong about what she was trying to do. She was flirting, but her voice… something wasn't right. Alasia knew her friend well enough to tell it was just a put on. She was forcing it. And she was trying to get Alasia out of the picture as soon as possible.

'Karen?' She asked.

Firo growled.

One hidden glance from Karen silenced her, and took the party right out of her. In a single look Karen communicated that everything would be all right, that Alasia needed to leave, that this was all just work.

But her voice said, 'Oh, your boyfriend called. He's having a party up on fifteenth this evening. He's asking for you!' She gleamed.

And the cat stared.

'Oh!' Alasia smiled, joining whatever game Karen was playing, 'I forgot! Do tell him to save a place for me. I don't suppose you feel like taking care of Gral for me? He's not from around here.'

Karen's eyes hid a silent panic, yet her thoughts begged Alasia to leave.

'I'll see you 'round,' Alasia said to Gral.

'I dunno, it's a big galaxy!' He smiled.

She smiled back and didn't care for all that galaxy if she ever saw him again. It was offensive to be pushed off a date like that, even for work. Why was she being kept out the loop? She hated the government, but she'd never dare think that in public. So they wanted her out then? So be it then. There was a place she knew, a place where people went to break the rules of a government that hated them: It was time to drown her thoughts in some reckless hedonism once more.

Three heroes

Matrix lay on his back, arms behind his head, lost in thought. He had been discharged from the hospital that morning, and was glad to be out of there! Pip had seen him off tearfully and with one of the longest hugs he could ever recall receiving in his life. After that last month spent in rehab he now felt better than he had in his life.

He had seen his interrogator once – she came by on some official business. She looked smaller than he remembered. Their eyes had met, but not even a glimmer of acknowledgment let alone recognition. She probably tortured people daily, or at the very least, had a chip on her shoulder the size of a construction beam.

He sighed. It had been two months now since he vowed to forget the brunette, a vow he found himself breaking daily. She was annoying him and she wasn't even here. How good it would be to just forget.

--- +++ --- +++ ---

'How good it would be to just forget,' thought Angel as she turned away from the man she had just been with. He was handsome, and a patient lover, but he looked terrible without make-up. They'd met at the nightclub and he'd recognised her from a virtual magazine. She realised quickly that he would pay generously to live out his fantasies, and had let him spoil her for the prize he sought. Now he had it, and she had what she wanted. So everyone had every reason to be happy.

Without warning her partner started the rare and infuriating habit of snoring. *Restructure your subconscious resonances!* she demanded in silence. Now thoroughly disgusted, it was all the impetus she needed to slip quietly from between the silk sheets and tip toe into the bathroom. The last thing she wanted to do was wake the bore, though the way he was sleeping even that seemed impossible. She realised she should probably be sleeping too after nine days, but the drugs hadn't worn off yet. Besides, it'd been a wild week and they'd helped make the recent events… bearable.

She switched the screen to mirror and examined herself. Tall, attractive, full figure. Yes, she had that, and that is what others saw. Perhaps all they saw.

Almost without thinking, and in need of distraction, she set the screen to text, fast display. It served well its purpose, and soon she was immersed in her reading. When it came to distractions, and other people's secrets, having a near flawless memory did have its benefits. She kept up with the news, and had actually invested most of her small fortune. This meant forging a few different names of course, which took some clever programming and one or two favours for the boys down at Civic info. Her stocks were doing well. She set some to sell from one that she had put a small amount into as an experiment. Eventually she tired of this and activating a low level security code 'borrowed' from someone else with a need she checked some of the latest research into inter species trading forum while wrapping herself in a bathrobe. Boring even of this, she moved on to theoretical maths – her most secret indulgence.

Well, at least it's a hobby. Kept her alive between parties. She'd left her regular partner tonight; made him cry, but she needed some space. Something had changed in her, though she didn't know what, and being thrown out of a date seemed to drag it all out. She needed some time, and was spending it wildly. She caught herself yawning, and realised she probably only had a few hours before she would sleep for the next two days straight.

The man shifted, spoke the name of some woman she didn't know. He lay half uncovered under the sheets, and suddenly Alasia was so nauseous she felt sick. She dressed quickly, gathered her belongings and scribbled some pretentious love note on the screen using something she found in one of the draws, and went to leave. She took one last look realising she was probably letting go several hundred credits worth of thank you presents but really couldn't keep up the act any longer. He had what he needed and she'd got what she wanted, but it made her smile.

She thought cynically as she left, *I do to life what life did to me.*

I do to life, what life did to me. Shee thought bitterly as she bowed her head. She was in the Confronting, where one's hidden truths are made evident and dealt with, least they become the enemy. What she loved had been taken away from her, and now in fear of love she tried to hurt what loved her. Alone between her and her healer she faced now what she could not otherwise admit.

You fear to love. This issue has always been with you, but more so than when your brother was taken. Now it has come again?

Sheelaakah wept silently. To cry was to be strong at the Confronting. *Yes. The pain makes me strong, yet at times this hurt influences my actions in ways that I wish it wouldn't. I am driven to express this pain in ways that afflict others.* 'I wish I could tear out this burden!' She screamed, 'but I cannot!'

The room was dim and silent, with none but the two women and the scent of healing herbs.

And this pain, you want to tear it out?

'Yes!' She hissed. 'I am unkind to my attendants and others. I am harsh in judgement and motivated by hate. It is a burden too great, I…'

'Shee,' spoke the healer, 'you are avoiding the issue again. We seek to cure the cause, not the symptoms.'

Sheelaakah looked up at her doctor, a tall blond woman who had a talent for looking important. Though her psychic inferior she was much more complete as a soul, as a pure instrument in the healing of minds.

I fear to love, spoke Sheelaakah, somewhat factually.

The aide waved her hand in the air before Sheelaakah's heart. Shee almost instinctively drew back, but submitted. Again the flood of tears flowed as the automatic defence was lifted away. That was why the healer was here, to help Sheelaakah confront herself; to stop her from hurting herself any longer.

For a while Shee just wept. Then she began again, 'I just wish I could stop fearing to love.'

'Do you wish to tear out this fear?'

'Yes.'

'You cannot.'

That surprised the young Commander, though she might have advised another of the same thing under different circumstance.

The aide continued. 'You must confront it, not deny or repress it. You have these many years and now you see it is still there and just as potent as ever. It has always affected your actions, only now you notice it. Anger is not your enemy, it but hides a repression of a part of yourself crying to be heard. You cannot destroy it. As a part of you, its strength is drawn from you. Look within. Confront and know the pain, see it for the hidden strength it really is. You will see it as never so frightening as you told yourself it was.'

The penny dropped. Sheelaakah saw herself too proud to admit she was deeply wounded by loss. She saw how she had never allowed others to be close to her for fear of first loving, then losing them too. She had decided that she was unworthy of love and would keep pushing, never accepting love even of herself. The healer spoke again, 'Shee, this all began again when you interrogated that young man. Why?'

'I do not know.'

'Do you love him?'

At first startled, Shee knew better than to hide the truth from herself or the doctor now. She looked within. 'No, no more than I love all life. It was his eyes, his confidence… He reminded me… reminded me of my brother.'

'Is that why you hurt him, because he had hurt you?'

Her lips trembled, and again she cried.

'I think so...' Sheelaakah trembled... 'Yes,' she whispered.

--- +++ --- +++ ---

'Yes,' he whispered to himself. 'I can't believe I said "Yes".'

Matrix couldn't help but chuckle to himself. He rolled on his bunk as another soldier entered the barracks. Beneath him lay another man he'd met earlier that day, an old hand, one of the lieutenants. Matrix smiled. "Dogman" he called him, he had a nose a little like a dog. And he wasn't just saying that. He actually had canine genetic inheritance implanted long ago within his ancestors.

Matrix found that being in the Resistance was like paradise, so far, to a young man who had slept the past seven years on little more than stone or moss. He was determined to make the most of it, and learn what was really going on. He realised that the hospital had given his soul time to recover over much more than the botched interrogation. Fear and loneliness had been his constant companions for some time. Now he held them like medals of honour. He had been to the underworld, for seven years no less, and survived! None few were impressed. He achieved few moments of happiness, and focused on them. Still, it was good to be out.

On the other hand, Matrix wasn't sure how he'd cope with not being allowed to make up his own rules now. Suddenly someone called out from the other end of the barracks. 'Well, it's a new boy! They say you're in from the underground!'

Several voices laughed unkindly. Matrix sat up to see a tall arrogant humanoid standing in the hallway not too far off. It had his shirt off, so that Matrix could see the enhanced masculine build of muscles. He was barrel-chested – almost inhuman. Indeed he was, for as a bio-mech almost half its body was concealed machinery. His skin was dark, and oddly tattooed in symbols meaning something to him in whatever years he had served in war. His hair was short, thickly curled, and dark, and deep set eyes shone momentarily crimson with the tattoos across his skull. An almost imperceptible vibration in the floor marked the artificial increase in combat readiness in this half man, half machine.

'Skion, unit leader. Just agree and he'll leave you alone,' recommended the dog man in a whispered voice from the lower bunk.

Matrix was incensed. The first time in years he associates freely with human company and already he was beginning to resent it.

He glared at his accuser.

'Well, someone with a little feist. Welcome to the Scorpions. You ready for the initiation?'

He stood with half a dozen others and looked, thought Matrix, disappointing in that he needed their support. The cyborg pulled out some brass knuckles, and smiled. His actions sent a vivid image to Matrix of just what he planned to do with them. Painful, but not injurious. He stepped towards the new recruit. 'You ready worm boy?'

The air grew tense. Matrix alighted from the bed and stood facing the unit leader in the corridor between the beds.

'No,' Matrix said.

--- +++ --- +++ ---

'No,' she said to herself. 'No walking, I'll take a taxi.'

Angel had no trouble hailing one, having arranged it while leaving the building. She got in and instructed it to take her back home.

Staring blankly at the ever-lit streets, now dimmed for the night time, she fondled the necklace he had given her earlier that day. Something like a family heirloom, but he didn't seem to miss it much. She'd talked him out of it, and so what if he was almost thrice her age? It was no more than those who came to that place intended to do.

The street became a tunnel which would take them speedily and directly to their destination. It was a part of town she hadn't been in before, but much the same as anywhere else on Seren. They passed over one of the reserves too quickly for her to appreciate it even if she'd wanted to – apartments as tall as mountains, capped in evergreen forests so all appeared natural to the untrained eye. Eventually they came to her residence and she alighted.

Yawning she approached the front door that opened automatically at her presence, recognising her individual energy signature. She stumbled in and was disappointed to see she'd forgotten to instruct a bed setting before she'd left nine days ago. She padded to the cabinet and took some more drugs, grabbing a lepidolite orb to make the sleep mean something. Without any conscious effort she cancelled all appointments for the next two days, including the photo shoot.

Settling under the covers she suddenly found herself wishing she had company. Chastising her childishness and grabbing the blankets she covered her face.

--- +++ --- +++ ---

Shee covered her face, and sat in the recovery room drying her tears. It had been a long afternoon, but well worth it. She planned to spend a pleasant evening with the office lynx before retiring – it had such a nice personality, and its relaxed thought patterns would do her good, and allow her to focus on someone else. Her journey in was over, and she hoped to be calmer and fairer now.

But she missed having a true friend. Life at times could be lonely.

A messenger came to the door and was held up by the healer. She heard her say the commander was to recover and not be disturbed.

Shee, however, couldn't help herself and wanted redemption. 'Tell the general I will avail myself eight hundred tomorrow. And no, I wouldn't like a peppermint tea.'

The messenger looked startled for a moment, never intending to ask either question out loud, and left rapidly. The chief healer turned and gave her a stern "Don't do that, dear," look.

Sheelaakah enjoyed her talent even if it was employed at times in the soul draining business of covert warfare. At times it was all too much for a twenty three year old who'd grown up much too fast. Eventually she left for her own quarters with the feline in tow. She reached her room and fell straight on the bed. The lynx soon made itself comfortable as Shee lay on her back, trying not to think.

--- +++ --- +++ ---

Matrix lay on his back, lost in thought. The prison beds were a lot less comfortable than at the barracks, but still better than some alternatives. It had been a good fight, his first in some time where the purpose wasn't kill or be killed. It was invigorating, but sobering. He had won a battle, but may have started a war. In retrospect, the combat might not have gone his way had he not managed to 'plug' the unit leader's mechanical arm into a power conduit. It delit the entire barracks for several minutes, but there were some spectacular fireworks from this Skion's arm in the meantime. He only hoped that in his victory he might have won greater respect of the others.

Almost on queue the prison door opened. They brought the half machine in with medical implements on his right arm and leg, and the gash on his head healed but still apparent. Minimum aid was delivered to

47

prisoners. The force field went up between them. Two days to sort out their differences, then court. Since it had gone public it could mean demotion for Skion and expulsion for himself. Odd how life worked out, same day as joining the Resistance.

He secretly wondered if today he hadn't done the right thing.

They helped Skion onto the other bed somewhat roughly. He didn't say a word. Matrix nursed his badly bruised cheek and aching torso. He sighed and lay back down.

--- +++ --- +++ ---

She sighed and lay back down. As she drifted off a fleeting thought escaped of the generous man who had made this night profitable. And she slept, alone.

--- +++ --- +++ ---

She slept alone with only the company of the lynx, still feeling very much without a true friend. It had been a long two days.

--- +++ --- +++ ---

A long two days of imprisonment, and despite his company, he felt very much alone. Matrix lay on his back, arms behind his head, lost in thought…

Dogs of War

The two men did not speak the first day, and it wasn't until almost midnight that someone entered the prison.

It was Dogman, with two others from their unit. 'Well guys. I've brought the good news!' He said proudly as he moved into view. 'Someone here got a promotion!' He continued, gloating.

Skion barely sat up, while Matrix was straight at the bars – he knew better than to touch them though. 'What are you talking about Dogman?'

He scowled back at Matrix. 'Fighting in the barracks, disruption of property, unscheduled scrimmage leading to bodily harm. Skion, you're back as foot soldier. As for you recruit, you got pack duty for the next month. No mech assistance. This has left some positioning for someone.'

'Oh no,' groaned Skion, sitting up slowly. 'Demotion I can live with. But I'm afraid I'm going to have to kill myself if you are made unit leader.'

The three outside the bars saluted smartly. 'Dogs of War!' shouted Dogman, followed by a sharp bark like salute from the others. In spite of better protocol, Matrix and Skion looked at each other and exploded in laughter.

'You'll learn that salute soldiers, or face correction,' Dogman said jabbing his finger out at them. It only made them laugh harder.

'You gonna beat us wid a stick?' teased Skion, laughing loudly.

'Sit us in a corner, Dogman?' joked Matrix.

Their unit leader stared at them. Matrix knew he could tell that they were only joking. Even if they were both better warriors than he, no-one else was better qualified in the unit for leadership. Had Skion been killed, Dogman was the next most likely for the leadership, though he clearly enjoyed as little association with the egotistical warrior as possible. He waited until the laughter had died a little.

It took a while.

'My name is Glenn,' he said quietly.

Then the laughter died.

Again for a moment they stared out of the prison at him, and relinquished to the situation with their silence.

'I'll see you both in two days for unit parade. Anyone's guess why you're both still in my unit.' He gave his salute, which Matrix tried to imitate, but collapsed in a fit of laughter again the moment he left.

As the soldiers left, one of the escorts remarked acidy to the other: 'Those two hold no protocol! One wonders what their place in an army is!'

'They're the best,' whispered Unit leader Glenn Bakerson. 'They can afford to laugh.'

---++---++---

The visit from their unit leader was all it took to get them talking. Within minutes they were swapping stories like brothers. The mood went from silent hate to open contest. It was a marked improvement.

Matrix learnt the taller man was eight years his senior, fighting with the Resistance for almost sixteen years. He'd been working as a mercenary with a security forces division for a galactic trading federation. Then he'd been inadvertently annexed with his crew and the supply vessel they were defending ran too close to Seren. They'd hardly noticed they'd entered the energy field, but whenever anyone tried to leave, they died.

'How'd you get involved in the Resistance?' Matrix ventured to ask.

Skion remained silent for a moment. Matrix found it a little strange to talk to him as he had two voices, the mechanised one answered all the logical questions, the other swore and insulted openly and on a regular basis. It was this voice that answered. 'Once we'd fought off the Kinerigan, the Resistance gave us peace, Wormboy. Pretty soon we figured out that we weren't just leavin', then all bets were off and it was all for themselves. Forge! Lucky I swore to serve the Resistance and took the warriors along with me, or they'd all have burned each other ash in a day!'

Matrix lay back in thought. It was probably true, but he could tell this guy liked the sound of his own voice, or voices. 'What's it like, in there now.'

'Inside the city?' Skion lay back soberly. 'Nothin's changed. Guys at the top still pushin' people and they thankin' them for it.' Then his mechanised voice spoke, 'Nobody leaves this planet. We have yet to succeed. But we will.'

He spoke as if his presence alone would bring this about. His human voice continued. 'Media puppets still dancin'. You wouldn't believe the stuff they come out with. Make it out like they got angels for politicians. Still. People go missin'. And though they deny it,' he leant forward, whispering in emphasis, and Matrix found himself leaning forward in interest, 'the annexing. It's still happening.'

It was dramatic. It was the Resistance's line. It was one of the lines which had got Matrix asking so many of the wrong questions years ago. He hadn't meant to get mixed up in all this. But since he was here, he would make the most of it.

'Hey,' Skion asked. 'How 'bout you. What are you doing diggin' yourself up from underneath, Wormboy? What you doin' underground anyway?'

'I guess I got lost.'

Skion scoffed rudely.

'It's true! Seven or eight years ago, when I was sixteen, a few of my college friends and I formed a fraternity. Part of our mid school finals. Well, I started challenging the lines. You know those things are all about the fors and none of the againsts of the system. Well, one foolish day I stood up in finals and questioned whether a government from above, like the citadels, is more than government from within. You know, that the first is impossible without the second. That sort of stuff.'

Skion looked confused.

'Anyway, the school council asked me to recant, I didn't; it was valid opinion. Well, I got hauled up before a court. Something went wrong, I was set up. They got my journal and put things in there. I was made an example.'

Skion husked, 'They only put people out here they never want to see again.'

Matrix laughed. 'I know! Anyway, a group of mutants attacked shortly after I got out. I escaped down a tunnel. I got lost. Took my sweet time to find the surface again. I just went down. Don't know why.'

Skion sat silently.

Matrix knew he didn't believe him.

'Where'd you learn moves like that?' Skion asked. 'You fight like it's all you done.'

Matrix felt proud. 'It is. Oh, I had some help. Won junior open martial arts on the Tsalmak province three years running. Still didn't prepare me for the underground. I spent most of the time squashing bugs. You learn to think fast, not use your eyes... though I've seen a lot.'

He tried not to sound too proud. In all, he'd been rather busy the first quarter century of his life. Like so many others, learning like any kid at home for the first few years. Next day fighting for his life. It had been hard, but his stay at the hospital had been a good way to start again with people. He'd sorted some of it out then, at least he felt like he could face people again. Yet, it still felt that there was some barrier he put between himself and anyone else. He felt... out of sync with the reality everyone else created.

' 'sides,' Skion asked, 'whads wid that knife?'

'This?' Matrix asked. It was ironic, he hadn't used it in the fight, so they'd let him keep it. Perhaps they felt he'd recover better with his only personal belonging on his person, or perhaps they felt it fair since he was in prison with a mech warrior – a permanently armed individual. He toyed with the short knife in his hands. Then, running it along the round let out a shower of blue and green sparks.

Skion raised an eyebrow.

Then, using the same edge and only the mildest of pressure, Matrix gently slit the edge his blanket like a hot knife through congealed fat.

Skion raised the other eyebrow. 'Self-sharpening?' His mechanised voice purchased.

Matrix smiled. 'I can't believe the telepath didn't figure it out! I made this blade myself, but I had good help, from a copper shard I found just after leaving the city. Point is, about four years back I won about one fiftieth of a gram of *motile* bronze! It lives inside the copper now, keeping it sharp. Wouldn't trade it for the planetoid. Oh, maybe the planetoid. I live with this blade more than any weapon you could offer me. It has saved my life more times than a phaser, than a whole ballista could you believe!'

He laughed, but Skion only huffed.

'What about you?' Matrix asked. 'I've never actually fought a fully armed and trained mechman before.'

Skion smiled. With his good arm, he formed a cannon. He suddenly twisted around and pointed it at Matrix, who did not flinch. The protections in the prison were surely good enough, and if they weren't, they would have disarmed him first. Still, it was an impressive sight.

'Is it all so biological?' Matrix asked, eyeing the mucus that leaked from the cannons end.

Skion laughed. 'Not all, but the enhancements are help'n.' Then his mechanised voice continued. 'Transformative implants are placed prior to adolescence. These can be reconfigured at any time using xenotropic retrovirus DNA reprogramming. I can form weapons, tools, even certain animals given the correct configuration, however,' and here his human voice took over. '... I feels like *reduce* for two weeks every time I do!' Skion laughed like it was the funniest thing.

Matrix smiled, but didn't see the joke. Skion seemed far more biological than machine, but looks could be deceiving. He wondered if Skion could form an extra limb or something?

He toyed with his permanently resharpening blade. It was a curious thing - with all the wards and defences that were common nowadays it was almost impossible to shoot a person, even with something as indiscriminate as a cannon. Animals and objects, yes, but even house pets enjoyed their owners luck and other protections. It had reduced a large portion of ultra-modern warfare to hand to hand combat, which was what *he* had always excelled at. Few had the level of ability to synchronise with objects that made them great marksmen, and that was another thing he used to be good at, when he was back inside, seven years ago.

Suddenly shouts came from along the corridor. Prison guards rushed past signalling. The prison door flung open. At first, neither of them knew what do.

'What's the scrimmage?!' Skion demanded.

Suddenly an alarm sounded. 'We're under attack. To your posts!' and the gate guards crashed open.

'Not a day to rest,' complained Skion, smirking.

'C'mon!' called Matrix, sheathing his blade and running ahead. 'Time to redeem ourselves!'

Skion strode quickly after him, downloading his orders and transforming his body into battle and not repair mode.

'What's the problem?' Matrix asked the guard struggling past him.

'Bugs.'

The colour Black

Later that evening, black booted footfalls echoed out across the giant cavern, crisp heals against crumbled stone. The remnants of the gun towers lay like crumpled spider legs on the ground, and the bodies of the slain Resistance soldiers a fair and even sprinkling. The other guards worked quickly and professionally to secure the area, even though they knew the Resistance would no longer be a threat from this outpost.

Although trained almost exclusively in the mental arts, he knew enough of war to see there were nowhere near enough bodies to count the three Resistance units they had expected to find here. Either they had fled or were routed.

But as he entered it was the single prisoner who lay before his new master, arms cuffed behind him that attracted his attention. He pushed aside his own hair, as long as a whip, and of which he was justifiably proud. He watched as his superior officer and mentor lifted the unconscious prisoner by the collar. The band around the prisoners neck had been intended to end his life before interrogation could be possible, but now it was too late for that.

'You are accustomed to the manner of psychotraumatic interrogation, my apprentice? Watch.' His master said, then he spoke to the prisoner, firm, yet patient 'Where are the others? Show me in your mind. Remember…'

--- ++ --- ++ ---

He had lost consciousness sometime during the second battle. First the bugs, then... yes. Black guards. He'd been shot. He couldn't feel his legs. Nor indeed his whole body. He felt a peculiar floating sensation and wondered if this was what it was like to be dead. He saw nothing but a grey cloud. There were sounds. Was he still alive?

'Where are the others?' A voice asked. It was firm, yet patient. It must have been somebody, important. 'Show me in your mind. Remember...'

'I don't understand.'

'You are... Yarnk Degling. Soldier of the Dogs of War. You were defending this outpost. But there were others. Where are they now?'

Without quite knowing why he answered. 'Yarnk Degling. Soldier of the fifth – Dogs of war. Stationed to defend Resistance outpost fourteen North. Joined two days ago by the seventh and eleventh. At 9:15 morning time we were defending against a Bug hoard.' He struggled in his recall. 'At the suspicion .... government involvement. The unit leader of the fifth, the others called him Dogman, he smelled the wounds. She, she sent the others away.'

--- ++ --- ++ ---

His master paused. He sensed his master knew more than he was ever going to share.

'Token, you are a clever boy. Join us in this one.'

'Yes Sir.'

His mentor, an incredibly patient man, allowed his younger mind to enter this prisoner's soul. He sensed the pain held in check by his master, and was chastised by him for entering at the wrong point. Gently, he guided him.

--- +++ --- +++ ---

Yarnk seemed to be floating again. The mist was very opaque, yet so light. Where was he? He wasn't alone, how did he get here? He had the feeling he had been having some kind of discussion with a superior officer.

'Show me,' a voice said. 'Show me what happened here.'

'Wh... who are you?'

'I simply am. Now show me.'

'Show you what?'

A scene flashed before his mind. He was back there, only, now others were watching too. They were very interested. They seemed dark and powerful, but interested. Were they the true leaders the guided the Resistance?

He was standing on the outposts outer wall. He was firing. Bugs. Countless. Meter high omnivores with pincers large enough to cut a human right in half. The clattering of their black and red exoskeletons accompanied by their screeching filled the cavern to almost deafening.

'Pull back!' His commander shouted. Firing they retreated to the inner wall just in time. The bugs had already stormed the outer wall and were prevented from taking the courtyard only by the lightning field on top of the inner sanctum. Two gun towers sat atop the outer wall, and soldiers worked feverishly to prevent the monsters from engulfing them and the men that manned them. Several bugs had broken into the inner courtyard before the field had been activated, and were wreaking havoc.

He kept firing. Screams as one of the gun towers was eventually overrun. One less turret gave the bugs greater chance. They began to climb the walls over the field. Unless something happened it wouldn't matter soon.

Suddenly the second tower began to tilt. The bugs were dragging at its base. It started to fall. Towards them.

'Look out!' cried somebody. He leapt out of the way as the entire gun tower smashed onto the inner wall cutting across the field, snuffing it out like a candle. The ants began to climb the walls.

Somebody pushed past him, towards the wall. A voice from behind called the man to stop, but he turned and yelled something to them all; 'We're doing it all wrong!' The running soldier shouted.

Interesting. One of the watching voices said.

Don't trust the interpretations of your host Token. You must make them yourself, it is why we are here. The other dark observer stated.

Yes master. The first voice replied.

He wondered who was speaking, for they were not part of this memory. But suddenly the dark haired man from his memory leapt from the wall into the writhing mass of insatiable insects. He stared in horror as the man landed in the middle of them, back against the outer wall, and the time and the battle literally paused in disbelief. Without a breath this man bellowed a war cry and started attacking the bugs with what must have been ... a knife.

He lowered his aqueous rifle, and he and several others tried to keep the creatures off the knife man, but it was a doomed task. Whirling and slashing, he leapt into the hoard like a madman and should have been killed a thousand times.

Whatever it was, it was working. The bugs on the wall had turned back down to the fray. Despite the efforts they were closing in. Then suddenly the man slipped and went down into the mass. His heart sank.

Suddenly another soldier slid down the wall, a sound like the crack of thunder ricocheted through the cavern. It was Glenn Bakerson, newly appointed leader of the fifth. In his hand he held a weapon the soldier barely recognised. A gun. A primitive pulse gun. Invented over millennia ago, used to propel small mass projectiles using chemically based explosives. Ancient, and noisy.

The bugs paused. He fired again, making everybody's ears ring. The bugs began to lose morale.

Primitive indeed. Is the Resistance so poorly armed? The dark observer questioned. He wondered what they were, was this real?

What else did you learn? It was a correction and a question.

They're... innovative? The first dark voice replied, heedless of his own questions.

'Push them down the pass!' cried a unit leader a voice from the wall. Beside the outpost ran a river. They had planned long ago to force enemies into this narrow pass where they would either be gunned down or crushed to death in the press.

The bugs pulled back from the inner wall. They looked to attack again, but a shot from the pulse gun sent them careering along the wall into the pass. Guns and lasers blazed as thousands were cut down in minutes. Few survived.

The dark observer mused: *So, they were not defeated by the bugs. Look at the memories, it still doesn't explain why there were so few of them when we our forces arrived later.*

Watch. The other replied.

A cheer went up from the walls. Soldiers scaled the walls to hoist the heroes onto their shoulders for a victory lap. He found himself tending to others when his unit leader motioned him to follow.

'Footman Yarnk Degling, we have a special visitor from command today. You and two others are to complete a bodyguard. She will address the men who...'

His voice trailed in memory loss. As he spoke a young woman moved into view. It was Commander Sheelaakah, a bright promise of the psychic wing. No *wonder* they'd won today!

--- +++ --- +++ ---

Token felt a bolt of electricity pass through him. It was her. *At last.* After so long!

Do not lose concentration for infatuation pupil! His master commanded powerfully. He winced, and felt his mind focus again. He'd ached to savour the image, but stifled his resentment.

--- +++ --- +++ ---

They approached the celebrating heroes, and unit leader spoke. 'War was upon you today men. News of your actions will reach headquarters, we can guarantee. There is someone here who would also like to thank you. May I introduce Commander Sheelaakah.'

He only saw her from behind, but he could see the reaction on the others' faces. Dogman, the unit leader, straightened to attention, and the tall one with medi bandages did too. The one with dark hair who had first jumped off the wall turned pale, and refused to look her in the eye.

She was saying something he couldn't hear.

'Our duty,' responded the unit leader.

Then the one with black hair spoke. 'Our duty, Commander, but...' he spoke openly to the woman. It was bold of him, and rebellious. 'There's something I don't understand. I've met bugs many times before. Killed scores of them. But I've never seen any so dedicated. They were almost... they were driven.'

Mark him, commanded the more mature dark observer to his underling.

'Private Matrix!' commanded his unit leader, Dogman, obviously wishing to smooth things over.

Commander Sheelaakah waved him aside.

Impetuously this Matrix continued, 'Bugs fear courage. Oh believe me, the nastier they get the deeper you go. You've just got to know them. They're smart. If you're too much of a threat they'll leave you alone. Our tactics, we virtually invited them to attack us hiding behind walls. When we came out fighting they judged us too confident to fight. And that weapon thing helped too. Still, they should have run off earlier.'

He'd probably face military correction for improper use of protocol. The commanders conferred in glances.

'Just what are you saying, Wormboy?' One of them asked.

It seemed a pretty harsh name to call him.

--- +++ --- +++ ---

Suddenly the cloud cleared, but was filled with a haze of pain.
What happened then? The voices asked him.
'Who are you?'
I like to watch.
The vision seemed so unfamiliar. What was he doing here? He'd been here before. It was a memory. Was this death? No he shouldn't be here.
Continue soldier. The powerful voice inside him mind commanded.
I'm detecting psychotoxic shock Commander. Perhaps...
No, it won't matter soon. Continue!
'But I don't want to.' He felt something like pain. It was his. It drew closer, he was somewhere.
You will continue.
'I don't...'

--- +++ --- +++ ---

Again he was back in his memory. He was watching the officer discuss something.
The man Matrix paused before replying. 'I think it was a set-up. They had no reason to just attack like that. We were just in the way. Perhaps they were fleeing something?'
The Dogman, a Unit leader, was sniffing the strange wound on the back legs on one of the insects. Rumour had it that it gave him hypersensitive smell, could tell what had caused wounds. The Commander had sent the others away, leaving the Unit leaders, herself and the two heroes, but he watched from a distance. They conferred. Suddenly the Dogman said something, and the entire entourage started for the inner wall. Yellow alert was sounded.
It had all been a set up. The ants... the Oppression was onto them! They would be coming next! The black guard...

--- +++ --- +++ ---

The prisoner started convulsing. He was nearly dead. He fought the reality. He fought for consciousness.

'No!' He cried. 'You won't have this from me! I won't te...'

'This outpost can no longer serve the Resistance. It will be struck from official records and become a haven for refugees. It will no longer be a danger to official Resistance activities. If the Oppression know we are here we are all in danger. You are to divide into the three unit groups and head back to the surface; from there you hopefully will be able to re- establish contact with headquarters.' The psychically gifted Commander instructed the soldiers.

They mumbled among themselves.

'We will require volunteers to man the outpost after we have left,' she continued. 'They will prepare to receive and assist any refugees that enter. They will need to wear E-G collars to prevent capture. We must prepare to leave within two hours, preferably sooner. Who will volunteer?'

Yarnk remembered his hand went up.

'Commander,' said one of the other unit leaders. 'Why do you think this happened?'

'I don't know,' she replied. 'This has been an unexpected turn of events, but perhaps fortuitous. I have a task that will require a small group. We need answers. The only reason the Oppression can have for wanting to flush us out of the area is that they are planning another Annexation.'

'But,' spoke the other, 'we are at least four thousand kilometres from the Maws. I wouldn't expect they'd need-'

'It's because they are planning a very large one this time,' she said factually, and walked on.

'How large,' asked the man Matrix, an innocence about him.

'I don't know.' Unit leader Bakerson replied softly, 'four thousand Kilometres? Could be millions...'

The young man watched as his superior officer and mentor held the prisoner by the collar, the E-G band around the prisoner's neck inactive.

'Where are the others?' Taalk demanded.

The prisoner, now delusional, answered. 'At the suspicion of government involvement. The Dogman, he sensed the wounds. Shee, Shee sent the others away.'

His mentor, an incredibly patient man, was growing tired of dealing with this pathetic non psychic. 'The others?'

'Three groups, split up. We stayed behind to help the refug...'

'But there are none. The government takes care of all who will, does it not?'

'No!' he resisted.

From where he was standing, the apprentice could see his master's features. The familiar yet unremarkable change of countenance, which meant his mind was taking control of another's. It was a skill he aimed to master soon. 'Does it not?'

'Yes,' the weak minded prisoner quickly conceded. 'We are safe.'

Apprentice, the master spoke telepathically to him, *inform command that we have several prisoners. Also, the wilderness is now cleared up to the specified four thousand kilometres, and they are free to proceed.*

Done, he responded.

The master turned his mind to the prisoner again. 'Yes, and soon you shall experience profound peace. You do want peace.'

'Yes,' he answered weakly.

'Good. Your leaders. Where did they go?'

'I don't...' he winced in agony of soul.

'They... Shee... she took a small group... The others, all headed off to the surface. I don't know. We are fighting the Oppression. Must fight!'

The man struggled against the mental control. The apprentice stood unmoved, awaiting his master's signal. It did not come. With extreme effort of soul the prisoner broke free of the mind control, awakening to full consciousness. He looked about in panic, finding himself surrounded by fully armed black guards, his outpost destroyed. He reached for his weapons, but found his unrestrained arms would not move.

'Don't resist.' The master counselled. 'You will have a better future now. You will serve the people as an ageless minion in the underfoundaries. You will never be tired-'

'No!' the pathetic rebel screamed. 'You will not take me! You will not turn me into one of your zombie...'

He would never finish the sentence, and his last conscious thought was staring at two eyes, the lightest shade of grey.

Questions

Matrix looked about him. The mood in the shuttle craft was different. Even though these were some of the most elite soldiers of the Resistance, they were silent as if preparing for a war.

Which, he had to admit, begged the question of why *he* was going along today.

There was Dogman, his unit Commander. He had his head bent as though praying, fingering pieces of metal that held memories from home, trophies of war, and his personal identification should his death be so violent as to leave nothing more. He had broad shoulders and a broad nose, large hands and a solid brow. He was a career soldier, who in another time, or another world, might have just as happily been every bit as much a baker as his surname indicated. He was in charge here, now Skion had lost rank.

The mechanised soldier took point, gazing out into the sky as they tore past the rapidly thickening tree line. He was a head taller than any natural man and broad enough to fit another two men inside him – as part of his natural bulk or mechanised enhancements it was impossible to tell. He looked out with intensity as though he was the kind of cyborg that never looked back, never held on to the present, never did anything he chose to regret.

Among them three regular soldiers waited. Himself, and two others. They looked concerned, like they knew they were walking into death, and they knew it was *she* that was taking them.

She just stood there, next to the mech man. But Matrix knew better than to think in her direction. It was she who had insisted on this mission almost as soon as they'd realised the ants had been driven towards the defence outpost in the first place.

'We need answers,' she had told them. 'We need to know why the Oppression is pushing our forces back from the maws. We need to know what it is they want, and how it is we can take it from them before they use it without remorse to do evil. And,' she added as almost an afterthought, 'we need to know why it is so easy for them to displace us…'

The soldiers had looked at her with uncertainty, some dug their heals in the dirt or cleaned their weapons in order to avoid her gaze.

'And the only place to get answers is back in the citadel.'

They mocked openly, an impossible breach in protocol. But she'd suffered it. When she spoke it was in a voice soft. 'I will ask only for volunteers; only those without the fear of what we have to do. There is a place to go, and we need only the fearless to get there. I believe, no, I know we can do this. It must be done.'

And so the six of them waited inside a shuttle craft as it tore through the sky, well beyond the safety of the Resistance lines. They took a circuitous route around a large, forested area – too dangerous with the other races around, like the Kinerigan. Then they flew below the tree line to approach the wall, hoping not to incite any mutants.

'Approaching the outer veil,' the pilot stated.

The Commander winced visibly at the effort of concealing their combined psychic wakelines from the eyes of the enemy, and the mechman's crimson eye took on a darker tone as he reprogramed their energy signatures to be virtually undetectable.

But most of all, unseen to any eyes, were the prayers and will of the Resistance citizenry, combined with the strength of the Evernet programmers that would shield them and that would continue to shield them wherever they went. They would detect as a random assortment of souls, constantly changing so the enemy would not find them. To the eyes of their enemy they would look like citizens, faces and soul prints taken from colluders within the wall, or phantoms made up by the Resistance itself.

It was a desperate measure, a vain hope made up of four trillion prayers. But it would have to do.

That was when Matrix got his first real sight of the great wall that divided civilisation from the wilderness beyond. It seemed black in the fading light, stretching up several kilometres in dark hexagonal patterns. He knew of many, many exits along that wall: no citizen was forcibly kept inside… but he knew of no way back inside.

As if reading his thoughts the Commander spoke up. 'We have an arrangement with one of the gate keepers I hope to be able to use,' she whispered. 'Let us hope his honour yet holds out.'

They set down in the underbrush a stone's throw from the wall. From its crescent bright lights pierced the darkness and searched the wilderness beyond. They stood in a small group, yet no one bothered to tell Matrix what to do.

'Just keep up,' Bakerson told him in a professional tone.

She forged a golden rope of light, and tied one end around her wrist. Then she took the other end and walked around the group, tying it onto her other wrist. They were completely encircled around, and he held the rope in his hands.

Matrix was ecstatic. He'd heard of this happening, but never lived to see it before.

They walked up an enormous ramp to the terrifying metallic gate that kept chaos out. It was riddled with sigils of unwelcoming and fear, clearly not intended to encourage those of this world from returning to Seren's light.

When they reached the top, she knocked on the door three times. A cloaked man materialised in front of her.

'Do you wish to return...' He started, then looked beyond her to the group she allowed him alone to see. '... return to the city, woman?'

'I can,' she replied.

A light from the wall turned about to face them, but with a wave of his hand it passed thankfully away. The cloaked man opened a door within the gate and allowed her to walk through. As their small group crowded into the booth within he spoke quickly and quietly while inscribing a small sigil on her hand.

'You are maid Torlight,' he intoned. 'You are hereby assigned to the forth and Dzenon washing and abasement division. You are to report there within three hours or they will come looking for you. I assume your penance is complete, or I will have to incinerate you if you attempt to return to the wilderness beyond, which I am sure will take place the day after tomorrow. Never let me see you again.'

He said the last phrase with particular sincerity, then pushed open the inside door.

It was a factory, or a museum. Few worked there. Someone approached her, looking to assist a 'returnee'. She would not even see those behind the golden rope, consciously, but would assist them anyway. New clothes were hastily found, but she didn't even notice that it was not the robes of the penitent she gathered, but the cloaks of the working class.

It would not protect them as their warrior robes did, but it would have to do.

They proceeded to leave, and Matrix took a quick look over at the man who'd let them in. He was watching them, closely, as they filed out now without the rope, disguised as employees of the city.

He's marking our faces, Matrix whispered to his Commander.

I know, she replied. *A double agent was the only way we could get help. However, please don't talk to me.*

The man stumbled then, as though he'd forgotten for just a moment to stay awake. When he did regain his composure he looked around and smiled to himself, seeming to think *whatever was I doing out here again?*

We have less than three hour to be away from here, at best, the Commander informed the group.

---+---++---++---++---

'I need questions,' the master whispered to his whip haired apprentice. 'For answers are easy, but only in asking the right question do we find truth. This Sheelaakah you covert is a threat, a danger to us all that must be dealt with. And this 'Matrix', he was not foreseen. There is a ripple in his destiny that concerns me, one that I know we must study further. I determine the Seraphination of them both. And there is one that will give me those questions.'

Token, the apprentice, said nothing; he was too wise to question his master now. They stood in the silent graveyard that was the defeated Resistance outpost. The black guards had piled the bodies up high, setting them out in a mockery of symbolistic good. It would do them no good now, it was their end.

The ritual was long, and complex, but still the student said nothing. Knowing the danger of disrupting his master's concentration was too great. So he stood instead, brushing his hair as dayness turned to darkness on the surface, and the noise of plundering soldiers into silence sometimes towards midnight. They had hurried in their theft, feeling too the severity of the hour, and the need to be far, far away as the master Lord Admiral Taalk brought a demon into this world.

The apprentice sensed it before he saw it, and a moment later the bodies desiccated as their vital fluids were drawn of to give life to a new body: The Hunter. It was old science, hidden away in every almost every world in the galaxy. Every world except this one, and those few chosen to keep this knowledge sacred from the ignorant masses.

The guards cowered or fled, but the apprentice stood. His role was to ensure the wards held, and that the veil that concealed their arrogant rebellion against all things natural would go unheard on this world until it was too late.

The demon rose, a humanoid form holding a wicked bow of suffering and loss, made from the bones of its victims. The being itself was composed mostly of bitter mist and memories, almost invisible to weak minded mortals. To his eyes it appeared to be wearing a cloak this time, though he'd seen its menacing features and eyes of abyssal darkness in many pictures and diagrams.

The master trembled, but breathed in deeply. The demon did not move, or attempt to test it bounds.

What impressed the apprentice the most was not the power of the incorporeal creature, or the legends surrounding its unbroken record at successfully returning its quarry dead or alive to the summoner. No, that which impressed him most was the apparent ease with which his master had summoned it.

'Commander Sheelaakah,' Taalk ordered it.

The being nodded, and seemed to stare out at the cavern with unparalleled malevolence. Even the elite soldiers had fled now, fearing in their ignorance for their eternal souls in the presence of such a creature.

But the apprentice smiled. He had lost his soul a long time ago, no demon could frighten any more.

'Silence her in this world,' Taalk instructed.

The demon nodded, and when it spoke its voice was a terrifying whisper of unmitigated vengeance. 'She will die.' It looked up in the air, as though sniffing. 'She walked here, just this last day.'

'Here, demon,' the apprentice boldly interjected.

His master tensed, but said nothing, as the apprentice knew he wouldn't.

He held the now dead Resistance soldier by his useless collar, 'This man was the last to see her.'

The demon said nothing, but glared at the apprentice as though deeply offended by him impudence. In almost an instant the demon was standing in front of him, and he could not stifle a gasp of fear at its speed.

'Ignorant fool,' it muttered with spite. 'This bereft body has no further use. No, what I seek is near, but not this desiccated husk.'

The demon smelt the air again, and at it summoner's leave, walked past the wards and off towards the fallen tower. There, a moment only later, it split open the rock to reveal the corpse of a fallen Resistance soldier, one who in death and desperation had hidden himself within the foundation of the tower in the hope of never facing the world beyond death that Seren offered all who disobeyed her.

'Impressive,' the apprentice muttered.

His master stayed him from speaking further with a single thought.

The demon knelt down to examine the fallen man, and breathed in the lingering essence of his soul print deeply.

'This one touched her, she brushed past him before the final conflict. There is the touch of her spirit, the remains of several of her skin cells. This is all I need.'

The apprentice stifled a smile – it was never all a demon needed.

'Oh, that, and perhaps a drop of blood from you, my master?' It said to the Admiral.

'Take a drop from my apprentice,' he ordered, 'he would do well to lose it with his pride.'

He wanted to protest, but knew he had nothing to bargain with.

The demon was on him in a thought, gripping him by the wrist. He tried not to struggle or cry out, but his breath was fevered and ravaged as the demon dug his nails into his arm, drawing not one, but three.

The crimson orbs levitated over to the corpse.

'You may want to look away,' the master teased him.

But Token, the apprentice, would not. He knew what the demon was about to do, and how illegal this was on any thinking world. Yet he also knew how all this would be blamed on the Resistance, causing them to sink further and further into confusion and despair, and the right thinking citizens of the city to hate them all the more. It was the perfect punishment for those who chose to live outside her laws, but Token was here only for himself. He wanted to know how to send demons after his enemies one day soon too.

But he did not let his master know these thoughts.

The blood drained into the dead soldiers forehead, and for a moment there was silence. Then the corpse began to bloat, swell and deform. Sand began to rush towards him. There was the baleful cracking of the bones splitting and reforming, the unholy rending of once mortal flesh. Within a heartbeat, a new creature stood, made of sand, his own blood, and the corpse of a fallen enemy. It was an abomination, a nightmare...

'A Golem,' the master smiled.

The creature breathed out a blast of fiery sand, and turned into living dust that swirled on its own breeze.

The Hunter looked at his creation, and smiled, 'By the gift of your apprentice I, myself, have given it life, and the fallen solider has given it flesh. Now it knows her touch,' the demon explained, 'and it's knows only the need to destroy her.'

Then the sand formed a whirlwind, a vortex in the air.

'And I will follow it,' the demon said, 'and we shall wonder... what is the hour in which Commander Sheelaakah will die?' It smiled knowing malevolence, and in the next second the demon vanished, somehow following the vortex as it floated down the corridors and towards the sky above.

The master nodded, 'A powerful question, indeed...'

The apprentice wisely began tracing sigils of light and health on his wounded arm, pushing the darkness and warding the sin out. To have been touched by such a creature could turn a normal human to madness, or uninhibited wickedness.

The master laughed. 'Come, we have more important things to attend to.'

The golem

They took the long way around. As Bakerson had told him: it was the only safe way to travel.

Matrix felt uncomfortable, but he couldn't tell why. In the end he convinced himself it was just the fear of being in the citadel once more, where everyone was watched. But he had a gnawing feeling in his gut that wouldn't go away, that didn't go away just like the time he'd done something he'd have to live with for the next seven years. But it was worth it then. Perhaps it would be worth it now.

They were taking a transport, late during the night cycle, across the ambrosial fields – immense farming lands the city used to support its massive inhabitantry.

'I suppose ...' he begun, but his unit leader shook his head. It was hard enough to hide their mental signatures without great effort, saying his thoughts out loud might be a disaster. All it would take is a local citizen to carry a warning thought to the black guard and they'd be arrested in seconds, or at least have a fight on their hands.

Suddenly the feeling returned, even more tangible than before. Without knowing why Matrix stood up, looking out towards the back of the transport. There were about twenty people with them, and they all looked at him.

Officer Glenn spoke up, 'Friend, the journey is far from over, sit down.' He said in a friendly manner, as if to an old acquaintance.

Matrix knew he was making people nervous, but there was something... Even so, the Commander was sitting still, looking out the window, so he returned to his seat. Nothing was bothering her, well, nothing except his breach in the unspoken etiquette civilians shared in public transport inside the –

The transport gave a sudden jolt, accompanied by the screech of metal and stone being torn apart. With a grinding wrench the entire rear end of the cabin was torn off, taking a few late night citizens screaming with it as it crashed to the ground at several hundred kilometres an hour. And there, from the outside of the craft, a hideous beast of sand and bone was clawing its way desperately into the craft. Citizens panicked and began to work their way along the walls from the enraged monster. The transport began plummeting out of control.

'A golem!' Skion shouted. A moment later his arm collapsed and reformed into its biological cannon.

'Officer, d–' Bakerson began, but Skion either didn't hear him or didn't care. He blasted the golem full in the face as it tried to scramble into the transport.

'Enough!' The Commander shouted, and with a mental command all the remaining citizens collapsed into unconsciousness.

The golem slung two fierce javelins of stone at Skion, but he deflected one and caught the other.

'Return fire!' The Commander shouted, and the two guards as well as Skion lit up the air with blazer and microline fire. Matrix had nothing.

Bakerson was nowhere to be seen.

Screeching defiance the creature crawled out and fell below the craft. The transport was just beginning to level out, and they were left standing in silence for a moment.

'You don't suppose you know where that came from?' One of the guards asked.

'It's after us,' the Commander replied. 'Someone knows we're in the city, but not where exactly. So they sent it – '

Matrix almost saw it before it happened, the tentacle clutching through the windows and grabbing the Commander. So before he could think he yelled out, 'Get down!'

She ducked only just in time.

The guards returned fire, but not soon enough. In a breath the unhallowed being had grappled the Commander's arm. Without thinking

Matrix spun around and kicked out at the stone tentacle with all his spirit. It snapped like a twig.

The Commander stood up then, and thrust her palm out against the creature. It looked like classic telekinetic manoeuvre, but instead of the usual wave of force Matrix experienced a strange sensation, like pins and needles. In its wake the being disintegrated into dust and sand.

'What was that?' Matrix asked her, looking at her hand in curiosity.

'I should ask you the same thing. That was *stone*.'

'Of course,' he replied. 'Break the spirit and the flesh is dust,' he explained from teachings he'd received even here in the city, many years ago.

'Indeed,' she replied, then answered him loud enough for everyone to hear, as though he was only one ear that needed her council. 'Once the golem got a hold on me I was able to determine who its driver was. I cast him out, and the golem lost all cohesion.'

'Does that mean they know where we are?' A guard asked her, twitching with nervousness.

'Indeed, and their Wasps will be here in moments. But we have tactics and technology of our own. Matrix, men, take a personal object from every passenger here. That will buy us some time as they try to sort out our personas from the others here. Plenty of time to disappear once more.'

'How much time,' he asked her.

She walked off.

'About an hour, if we're lucky,' a career soldier told him.

'Are we lucky?' Matrix asked. He didn't believe in luck.

---++---++---

The Hunter raised his eyebrows in surprise. This was an unexpected turn of events.

He'd heard her voice, that was good, and the voice of one or two soldiers.

But one of them had sensed him, even before he'd manifested the golem. The man had looked right at him. Then, thankfully, he'd doubted his wisdom and sat back down.

He would be a dangerous adversary if he ever learnt to use that ability properly...

Scanned

Something was wrong.

Everything meant she should still be unconscious, and had been for at least a day. But now she was wide awake. Perhaps there was some negative attachment from her lover? Or sent as punishment by her ex? Perhaps her metabolism has subtly altered recently? It was impossible to tell! But one thing was for certain; she could not sleep.

She went to a party, but the noise still didn't save her. Sleep hadn't erased her offence: being hauled off a date was the last thing Alasia expected, and she took it out on her fans. They knew she was there, but she refused to sing. Some of them took it badly. Some of them might have even been in pain, but she refused to listen to their psychological angst. She was annoyed, and she wanted them to feel it too.

Try as she might there was no way of spying on Karen and her diplomat. She was just too good, and had all the scrying devices covered. But she didn't need to see inside to know what was going on, or what was going to go on.

Or how badly things were about to go for Karen if she did what Alasia expected her to do.

It was a good enough reason to stay awake…

---++---+++---++---

The Commander is being boring, Matrix thought to himself as quietly as he could.

Of all the soldiers there Matrix had to assume he was the most recent to have actually ever seen the city. The others were only barely holding their anxiety in check.

They were in a crowded mezzanine, with short yet colourful market stalls along the edges. Citizens came from all over to spend the handful of credits they'd earned this week, since none would run over to next week: it was one way all things were keep equal. Children chased each other in circles or flew bright kites in the gentle breezes. It was a happy place.

The soldiers stood all around the mezzanine, always in sight of each other. One was looking at ribbons a stall, another chatting to a young couple not far from where the Commander was sitting. She was feeding birds. Matrix could only assume she was either looking for signs in the patterns the birds lay out or conversing with someone over the Evernet somewhere. But he could confirm neither, and so was left to conclude she was deliberately being boring.

He sighed.

Resisting the urge to follow protocol he sidled up to his unit leader, Bakerson, who scowled at him internally as he approached. The camera's would know they'd spoken.

'Good Morning, citizen,' he said.

'Morning,' Bakerson replied from unconsciously clenched teeth.

'Fair day the breeze,' Matrix replied in an old phrase. It meant, "so what's happening."

'Yes, nice breeze,' Bakerson replied inappropriately, jaw tight.

Matrix decided not to test this soldier's further ignorance of Seren idioms at this point. He looked so tense he might just shoot him in the head right now.

But Matrix smiled. 'So, Good'man, have you tried the roasted chestnuts? They are quite good, I've done so myself.'

'Not as yet,' he replied, sinking into a minor comfort. 'I am waiting for a friend, and I think he might not be coming. I expect I'll be leaving soon.'

'Really?' Matrix asked, quite surprised at the little innuendo, which meant he'd suggested they'd be leaving soon. Then he realised his reply was probably making that very obvious to any who listened. 'Well, then leave you must! I may tarry, or not. I've an afternoon solicitous to enjoy and this place is well coloured. I...'

He stopped short.

There was a familiar tingle along the back of his neck.

It was a feeling he'd not known in seven years, and he knew what it meant. One look at Bakerson told him, however, that his unit leader did not know what it meant, though his eyes were wide with fear.

'Best to lie down then!' Matrix said with a familiar joking smile, Bakerson took his lead, as was everyone in the plaza. Even children.

What happened next was not what he'd expected, though a moment thought revealed that since he was no longer a legal resident he had nothing to fear. But the others, the real residents, either lying on the ground or resting securely in a chair, did.

The scans were never painful, at least they'd always told him that. But he'd never seen one from outside. A whole plaza of inert, softly twitching people. It was a form of seizure. Blank stares in their eyes as the Government read their thoughts and histories, and, if the Resistance was to be believed, changed their minds.

A moment later it was all over and people begun to stand up and resume conversation as if nothing had happened. A baby cried, they sometimes did, since the scans usually didn't start till they were two and it probably was a bit of a surprise.

Matrix looked over at Bakerson, his face dark with chagrin. Matrix didn't need to ask to know what he was thinking: *and this happens twice a week?*

The seduction

Seducing him has been all too easy, thought Karen as she submitted to another barrage of kisses. It had taken a day to work him off Alasia and into her care, but they were in her apartment now, past the stage of pleasant conversation or even seductive touch. She pulled him towards the couch. 'Gra!' She breathed another uncounted time. 'Take me.'

She felt his hesitation, but they were too far gone to turn back, unless she did something stupid. He paused unnecessarily, but her kisses convinced him. Perhaps she had been too easy? Perhaps he was suspicious? It made her nervous, but there was no turning back now. If he caught on to something before it was time, well, it wouldn't have been worth it. She was scared.

She thought of Alasia, and was grateful that her actions had spared her dark haired friend. She would never have done what was required now, required for the safety and benefit of trillions of people.

At least, that's what she told herself.

For a fleeting moment she thought of the ramifications of her actions and found herself wondering if it was such a good choice. She knew it wasn't, but that it would be worth it to her. Besides, it wasn't like she was going to ruin his entire life, just his reputation. But she crushed the thought again as she had a thousand times that day. She knew how to play the game. In order to survive others had to fail, besides what was the worst thing that could happen to him?

The cat sat unnoticed in the far corner of the room, his near perfect visual memory recording everything. A perfect memory that could be accessed like a movie even weeks later. She waited until he was pressed against her and she laid his hand playfully across her mouth. He smiled hesitantly, but went along with her fantasy.

Then she screamed.

--- +++ --- +++ ---

They were in the middle of some very passionate and mildly kinky foreplay when her eyes dilated and she'd suddenly screamed. Her touch became violent claws, and he found he had to grab her wrists to stop her from scratching him. At first he couldn't tell if this was part of the game. Then she screamed, 'Enforced!'

Diplomat Gral tried to jump away, but found their legs entangled. She held him there, terror in her eyes. What on earth was she doing!?

'Please don't do this,' she begged.

He looked at her in disgust. It was all happening too fast, whatever it was that was going on.

Suddenly he heard a familiar sound and saw the room alighted with the blue glow of a site to site teleport. He looked around him just in time to see a black clad guard high tackle him off her and onto the floor.

He'd been set up.

'Wait, no!' he protested.

They dragged him to his feet.

'You've got some explaining to do criminal!' said the guard. They swiftly anaesthetised his arms behind his back.

She sat crying in the other guards arms.

'No, you don't understand. She invited me in, she started it!'

'How could you take advantage of me!' she screamed.

'You asked for it!' he roared back, and then realised what he had just said. 'She did, she said she wanted... wait!'

Lower Foundries

'Why are we here?' Matrix asked. He'd only been here once before, on a school excursion. He'd hated it then. He hated it now.

Thousands of kilometres of nothing but factories that rimmed the outer city right alongside the wall, all hidden underground. Everyone who worked here ended up looking course and weathered, even if they took inventory in the offices. But there was a lot to be made for two trillion inhabitants, counting the humans.

'There is a contact I'd like to meet,' the Commander replied. 'A disaffected government official that was easy to bribe. I just need to get access to a terminal inside the walls, I should manage from there.'

'Why didn't we do it as soon as we got in?'

'Every alarm in the city is expecting just an act. Besides, there was another contact I was hoping to meet. One more malleable and willing. But that chance is lost to us now. I propose we back track, confuse our pursuer, or confront him.'

'You're the boss,' Matrix saluted weakly.

She gave him a strange look, like a smile hidden against a condescending scowl, but said nothing more of it.

They were moving as a group once more, pretending to be employees heading to their government assigned duties. They were a motley lot, different sizes and genders, so it would not have been too suspicious. They had taken an underground skip through the glass cylinders. They entered a large transport cavern. Literally thousands of vessels, transports and skips loaded and unloaded citizens. They purchased their tickets and Matrix was pleased to see the Resistance programmers were doing a fine job – they even managed to get them new names and identities, synch codes and programs, all in the hour or so since the last attack.

They also managed to get them a ride on a skip together, though not in the same carriage. The ride was swift and uneventful, and for a moment Matrix lost himself in revere, able to pretend he really was once again a person of the citadel with a normal life, and silent goals. He pondered, even for a moment, just staying on that skip, letting the other soldiers get off on their stop.

But there would be questions, and in the end, he realised, he believed in their cause.

They got off at the Commander's telepathic signal and followed. Within twenty minutes they found themselves as a lose group outside a small office, attached to a few thousand apartments. There, the Commander spoke to the bell hop.

They stood scattered around the street, allowing others to pass by. They hid themselves in the crowd, looking like men delaying a trip to work, or chatting to a friend, or stopping to read a sign.

They did not look like a handful of dangerous Resistance soldiers keeping a hawk eye on a single female who was speaking to a bell hop.

Matrix alone had the audacity to stand close enough to her them speak.

'Good lights to you, my lady. How may I serve my city tonight?' The thin faced, aged man smiled.

'Kappa Serenade,' The Commander said, getting right to business.

The man visibly tensed, but his aura was well hidden.

'Not happy to have you people visiting me right now,' he said. 'How many you got with you?'

She didn't answer his question, 'I need a terminal.'

He looked about, and noticed Matrix, 'Beside that green eyed lackey, I mean.'

She was silent. Even Matrix knew it was dangerous to challenge her, yet the old man didn't flinch under her stare.

'You might find one down the lower foundries that might work,' he said in a helpful manner. 'As for my people's, they are all spoken for. There are none I can help you with.' He said, a note of finality clear in his voice.

It was looking like the Commander would have to force one out of him. Matrix knew that would not be pleasant.

'However...' the old man began with his helpful smile, 'I'm surprised you aren't a bit more curious about ... recent events.'

He saw a puzzled look cross her face.

'Here, look here,' the old man said.

Matrix's cover was broken, so he stepped up to look at the screen anyway. It was a lesser story, something you'd have to dig around to find. It held information about some kind of off world diplomat who'd be leaving tomorrow morning.'

'You people are usually more careful about this kind of thing. I'm surprised you aren't all over him.'

One look at the Commander told Matrix she had no idea, but that didn't mean the Resistance wasn't trying to contact him anyway.

Her voice was stiff, and her breathing carefully measured. 'Bell hop, I thank you for this news. There's not much I can do about it. But, please, my terminal is playing up and I need to contact my *brother* for his evening council, he has not been well of late.'

The Bell hop didn't smile for a moment. 'Imbalance and illness are rare and troubled events...' He agreed, sharing in whatever innuendo she was playing with. Her 'brother' was no doubt some kind of agent, or Resistance informer.

'Please,' she begged. 'It's just... there's been some big changes recently, a little more than we can handle, or explain. I really, really need to see my bother.'

Matrix noticed it, the subtle telepathic signal, the gentle alterations of his thoughts. And the bell hop, perhaps because he had a conscience, was going to agree. It was on the tip of his mind to help her and she hadn't forced anything from him.

But the explosion of darkness in the centre of the street swept those thoughts away.

Matrix armed himself with his knife in moments. It was probably what set off the alarms, but the seething darkness would have done that as well. It was a non-corporeal. A demon. In less than a heartbeat it drew back an enormous bow of ebon and blood.

The incorporeal. Matrix recognised it immediately as the pilot of the gnolem.

It loosed the ammunition.

Matrix could have handled one arrow, but the demon shot off two. Commander Sheelaakah was quick, and had warded herself, but it was clear in the moments before the arrow struck that this was no mortal projectile. Matrix narrowly managed to parry one away from her with his motile bronze knife, green sparks heralding its change of course.

But his breath caught in pity as he saw the second speed towards her shoulder – and miss completely.

Matrix faced the demon who'd spun around to deal with the other soldiers when he heard the Commander gasp. He turned to see the arrow was not aimed at her at all, but had pieced the chest of the bell hop.

'Please, don't concede!' She begged with genuine sorrow in her voice, reaching out to hold him.

He said nothing, but before he died, he pushed the news article about the off world diplomat towards her once more.

Then, instead of fighting, she reached forward and wrenched out the broken arrow.

Another two arrows of darkness and flame sped towards them, but Matrix deflected them both.

'How do we deal with-' he began, but was cut short as the demonic being shot out the stone pillars above where Bakerson and two other guards were trying to sneak up on it. With a pang of fear and sorrow, he saw them covered by several tonnes of stone.

In the next instant the creature was shot in the back by the other guards, but instead of dying it vanished in tendrils of black smoke. For an instant there was silence, the scattered citizenry peeking out to explore the ruins. Then the creature reappeared behind the two soldiers and slashed out at them and the two citizens they were hiding with, without mercy or distinction. The screaming started again.

'Now what?' Matrix asked.

Skion was there in a moment. For a second the Commander just stood there, then she began to walk off down an alley.

'Hey aren't we?' Matrix began, but the Skion held a finger up to his lips.

'This is not how we deal with this kind of adversity,' his mechanical voice replied.

Matrix hurried, confused. Demons were plentiful in literature and lore, and they all had a weakness, let alone a name by which they could be controlled. They only had to identify it, but instead they were walking off on it and the soldiers it was slaying.

But Matrix knew he could not face it alone, so he followed.

'I don't understand…' he said, voice caught with sorrow.

'Follow Skion,' the Commander ordered him. He knew her voice well enough to know she was hiding powerful emotions. 'And don't look back.'

Matrix knew better than to look back. He *knew*. But he also had a deeper knowledge, and that was that he'd eventually do whatever anyone told him was the one thing he could not do.

So he looked.

The demon materialised through the ground before Commander Sheelaakah, but she stood tall and unafraid. Even as it menaced up to her she knelt down and wrote a simple symbol at its feet.

Then she smiled victoriously, and turned her back on it.

It did not cross that symbol. It could not. A demonic scream of frustration and defeat tore from the abyss that was its mouth, but it did not follow them.

The three of them had escaped.

The stories

We've had a change of plans, she told them telepathically. *We need to get to the city of light at the centre of Seren. There's an off world diplomat staying there.*

Why do we need to see him? Matrix asked without permission.

She scowled internally at his breach in protocol, Skion frowned openly. But she answered him anyway. *For centuries the Resistance has been gathering witnesses, stories. Evidence of the Oppression's deeds. Evidence they desperately do not want to fall into the hands of the galactic senate. If that were to happen there would be a public outcry. Seren would be held responsible for her crimes, and we, all without the wall, would eventually be allowed to go free.*

You truly believe that is so? he asked.

She nodded telepathically. *It's not much, and it might be years before we see anything come of it. But it's something in a world oppressed. We can't even get one of our own people off world, and that would be the ideal situation. This is the next best thing, our next best hope.*

So they were off to see the diplomat, and now there was only himself, Skion and the Commander. It did not look good, but perhaps they'd do better as only three. Still, it left not even an hour to mourn.

Matrix gathered his courage. *Then where do we start looking?* he asked them.

We need to find out where he is staying and then hope by some miracle we are able to get to him. We need terminal somewhere out of the way, any will do. You actually know the city best of any of us, I was here ... a long time ago, but I remember it poorly. Find us a terminal, the Commander instructed him.

Matrix hated the foundries; they were dark places where uncreative people tended to dwell. But this was important. *I recall, from a school visit we made here seven or eight years ago. They tend to keep tertiary adjunct terminals down at the eateries. If we find one, a little out of the way, it should be able to keep us up with the major news stories, even if it's empty of any other real information.*

The Commander nodded. 'It'll do,' she said with a gentle smile.

'This way,' Matrix replied. They moved down, deeper into the residential area's that surrounded the foundries. It was progressing towards night time in this area, so the curfew was soon to take effect. He deliberately headed towards the lighter industries, hoping any curious guards would take their circuitous course as nothing more than an innocent deviation from their assigned night duties. Employment was effectively decided by the state, in spite of what they said, but some lenience as given in how one got to work.

Eventually they found an old terminal by a disused factory, waiting beside a quiet street of what must have been empty houses.

More evidence of a planned annexation? Skion suggested.

The Commander ignored him, and turned to a stone statue that was the terminal.

This one see's little use, she thought.

Matrix turned towards it as well. A terminal, a direct line to the interconnection of all the data, information, and minds that were on Seren – and more especially those within the walls. Each and every individual wore a stone on the band around their heads that allowed even the least psychic of individuals to enjoy the benefits of the Evernet. It was much more than data storage or even reminders for meetings. It was a meeting of all sentience, a place where all knowledge could be shared.

And this one was broken.

Matrix punched the stone computer right in its face. It wouldn't feel it, of course, but it still make him feel better. The frustration had boiled up inside him, till he realised why; he liked that puppy soldier. He'd miss him.

But there was something that Matrix knew he'd miss even more if it was taken away – the chance to live for freedom. At its heart this very issue was what had got him thrown out of the citadel seven years ago, and it was what drove him now. Yet they'd come all this way, sneaking past guards, hiding their auras from a malevolent oppression, fleeing from an otherworld demon that was not supposed to even exist on this world... and the stupid terminal was broken.

'Stand down, soldier,' Skion's mechanical voice demanded, even as his human hand shushed him and his human eye looked at him with pity.

'I just wish,' Matrix said the obvious, 'that at least this terminal was working.'

'I never held out much hope for it,' the Commander whispered, standing unusually close to him. To them both. After all, it was night, and they were being hunted by a demon. 'Come, we need to keep moving. We need to find where that diplomat is staying.'

Matrix knew it was true, but he hit the terminal one more time for good measure. To his eternal surprise it flashed momentarily to life. In that moment his unconscious mind found a scattered memory in its vast database; *News report. Diplomat Gral Bakerson, Utopian research colonies at*

Breakers point. Arrested for attempted enforcing of a local tourist guide. Taken to capital prisons... and its voice faded.

Matrix stared at it in wonder. Yet it wasn't the fact that it had worked that surprised him the most. He'd never been a part of the Resistance when a telepathic news report like that came on. Everyone knew about the subconscious messaging that went along with reports like this one, but he'd never felt them wash by him like this. He felt the rage, the indignity that one within the walls had been so abused. Then he felt nothing, his new allegiance stripping away the brainwashing almost instantly. It felt strange.

The change of heart

Alasia knew all the gossip even before it had reached the public, one of the many enhanced social networking virus's she's released years ago to keep track of the people she cared about. So it was no wonder that she was there when the black guards left Karen's apartment.

She'd watched them as they'd performed the healing rituals, given comfort to a woman assaulted. And Alasia had almost laughed at the futility of it all. Karen wept, she swore vengeance, she poured out tears of gratitude; all like an actress in an old romantic film.

It was all so *fake*.

And *that* was not like Karen at all.

So Alasia waited until the last of the healers had left, two assigned black guards standing outside as "comfort".

'What was all that about?' she demanded to know, emerging from the shadows.

Others would have been startled at her presence; she was moderately good at sneaking up on them. But not Karen. Alasia knew Karen was every bit as clever as she was, and so she knew Karen would know she was there.

The flow of meek sobbing gently subsided, and in a moment Karen's normal confident demeanour had returned, though she still sat.

'I see you waited till the cat had left,' Karen accused her.

Alasia scoffed, 'That individual annoys me.'

There was a moment of silence.

Karen shifted, clearly displaying her annoyance that Alasia was so able to piece the shroud of dishonesty that surrounded her. But she did not ask her to leave.

'What was all that about?' Alasia repeated, a twist of anger delivered with her shaken words.

Karen glanced at her, and Alasia read that look. She was looking for a place to hide from Alasia's accusations. That, or she was looking for forgiveness.

But she said nothing, so Alasia filled the silence for her. 'I read the news reports,' she explained, 'and the black guard's file. But I know you better Karen. Why did you set that man up?'

Karen didn't even bother feigning a gasp. 'You think you know what's going on "Angel"? You think yourself wise because you are very good at finding out other people's secrets? But you are *innocent*, like a *child*. And children need protection.'

The accusation hurt, for in all their years Karen had never told her she thought this way of her. But Alasia hid per pain behind her smile. She could tell she was getting very close to another secret, and that was moderately exciting.

'That hurt,' Alasia accused her, 'and I forgive you. But whatever duress the Government has you under tonight –'

Karen cut her off, 'Duress? *Ignorant* child. *Foolish* whelpling. Have you walked where I did tonight? Have you seen what my eyes have seen? You think you are wise, but you are a child. In knowing false pretences can you handle the truth? Have you beheld all I have seen and not turned away? Go play with your toys; go back to the presents men give you. Leave the real work to the women.'

Her smile died. A sudden rage sparked up inside Alasia, more than she had ever known at Karen's insults. She sure knew how to strike her, 'How dare you!'

Karen continued, 'You children stay outside in the garden, lolling with the pretty flowers. I'll get to work inside the kitchen, where sometimes the *meat* gets *burnt*. I did what was necessary.'

Alasia felt the tears in her eyes, and an almost insane desire to flail this woman's ego with bighting words of her own. But at that last statement Alasia heard a tremulous falter in Karen's voice, an almost imperceptible flutter of the left eyelid.

Karen was hurting.

Alasia looked at her, 'I've known you better than a sister. Why? Why do you do this?'

Karen backed up, the defence of anger crumbling in Alasia's soft words. 'I...' she faltered to say.

It was her plan all along, Alasia realised, to drive her away... like a conscience.

'I know you better than this,' Alasia repeated, soft kindness falling from her lips.

Karen looked at her angrily. Sighed, and buried her face in her hands. 'They never asked. Just hinted. They wanted the diplomat dishonoured so that they'd have something to hold against the Utopia system, get them apologising. Get them feeling ... unworthy before the light and order on Seren. So I played their game for you. Because I knew you wouldn't. You're too ... kind.'

Alasia was stunned. What Karen had done... what she'd just confessed to... she should be in prison for the rest of her life.

But Alasia knew that would never happen now. She was at *their* party. And what she'd said was always so true; Alasia had never played their games, though she knew she'd been invited. She only hurt those that hurt her, played games for business. But this, this was criminal. It dishonoured a world – hers and theirs.

She didn't know whether to slap her, or hold her in her arms and help her weep.

Their conversation ended with the most acrid insult Alasia knew she had, 'Who are you? And what *do* you want!'

Hunters end

It all seemed simple enough, Sheelaakah hissed to herself. Unless there had been some momentous alteration in protocol they would take the diplomat to the capital prison. They had made their way to the city now, co-opted the identities of prison officials and simply walked in. Now she sat working one of their terminals.

It was a simple prison break, but the entire facility was much larger than she'd been told.

She sighed, and closed her eyes. To seek deeply like this was sometimes dangerous, and she had to be shielded. But the two soldiers left her were guarding her, and she felt she could trust them.

Sheelaakah allowed her mind to wander, emerging deep within the subconscious link between all minds and souls in reality. To seek intuition was one thing, but she was looking for someone. 'Guide me, Whisperer...'

Her eyes flew open, and her gaze fell on a certain cell block and number. She smiled. It was quiet, out of the way. It would be a fairly simple matter to redirect resources and leave the place entirely vacant for a break out within only a matter of hours, trusting to her talents and the determination of the Resistance.

Then the air grew cold.

Contacting Seraph would sometimes accidentally accomplish this, though no one knew why. Was it some treaty the demons had with the Seraph? Or a natural result of reaching into the distance between realities to speak with the Seraph that somehow also alerted the demons? Either way, it had to be done.

But the Hunter had found them, once again.

She barely had a moment to reinforce her wards before it was upon them, the violence of its claws barely deflected by her will. But even as she saved their lives she knew she had been cornered into making a mistake. The alarms were almost instantaneous. They had only seconds to escape before the black guards would arrive.

Its violence threw her to the ground, so she was only able to imagine how Matrix was able to keep its claws busy. Skion was in there too, fast enough to wound it. But before she even had a moment to lift her head she felt it somehow manage to cut Matrix with an arrow, stabbing just below the deltoid muscle and right into the vein that ran there. Matrix didn't even cry out.

Sheelaakah did all she knew she could do, filling her two soldiers with clarity and resolve. It was what she was best at. There were few runes she knew that could keep it away from them now they had returned the violence.

She began to draw the heat away from it. Cryogenics she hated more than anything, but it would weaken a beast that drew strength from the living. But the battle looked grim and she was barely able to roll herself away from the frantic melee.

Suddenly, with a terrifying crack, Matrix somehow managed to sunder its bow with his heel.

The demon let out a pitiful wail of frustration and pain. The horrific noise would have started citizens from their sleep for many suburbs, chilling dreams all over the city. The two soldiers moved to press the attack, but Sheelaakah could sense it was all a ruse.

Pull back, she whispered to their minds, and they chose to obey.

The beast stopped roaring, and smiled at her wickedly. She had seen through its bluff.

They stood close while trying to put some distance between it and them. She erected a common warding field around them, glistening blue in the nightlight. As the distance improved so would their chances. And if the Black guard found a demon they would concentrate on it, naturally. But that thought brought little comfort, for if she or her soldiers were ever captured it would be all over for them, and notwithstanding any of their words or memories the entire event would be blamed forever on the Resistance. It was a bitter thought, but they *had* to survive, even if only so that they Resistance could not be directly blamed this time.

Then the demon stopped.

What is it doing…? Matrix asked, his voice clear in spite of his wounds, and once more Sheelaakah was surprised at his ability to work within pain and fear.

The demon rose up, and Sheelaakah felt the fear in the buildings nearby. But no one was going to come to their aid. It took a handful of its arrows, tipped with human bones, and with baleful intent fused them into one. It became a javelin.

Matrix moved to the front. He was going to attempt to push the javelin aside, and she knew he stood the best chance of it of the three of them.

But Sheelaakah also knew, with perfect precognition, that he was too damaged. That if he did this, he was going to give his life so that they could get away.

In the very instant the demon drew back its deadly weapon a blue light flooded the area from the left. Skion moved, his arm becoming a cannon, to deal with the black guard.

But instead a bright light, like daytime, filled the area. Skion held his arm down only just in time. A moment later a service trolley arrived… driven by officer Bakerson. There was no black guard at all.

Get on! he ordered.

No one waited to be told twice. They flung themselves on the trolley and it began to speed away. Matrix managed a cheery, 'Hey!' in greeting to his fellow soldier as it did.

And in that moment the javelin struck.

But friendship is a powerful thing. Together Matrix and officer Bakerson grabbed the projectile in mid-flight and captured the demon's weapon.

They heard it scream in frustration, screams that would soon die in silence. She took the weapon from their hands; it was all that she needed. She found the runes in its aura; spoke the words of banishment taught most children from their youth.

A moment later the demon was gone, forever.

The escape

Several kilometres under Seren tower was the capital prison. Enforcing, Gral had been informed, if proven was punishable by death, or worst, eviction into the wilderness beyond. His career now lay in ruins. He'd been set up. One sly manoeuvre he hadn't seen coming and now he sat on death row. He knew he was never going to leave Seren now. They had shamed him, his family, and the colonies he represented. Even if he did get out, home would never accept him back, and if a miracle occurred and he did escape, he would be a wanted criminal most likely worthy of death.

He spat the bitter taste from his mouth. His assistant would most likely be required to leave immediately, with more than actual evidence of his 'crime'. All of Utopia would know soon, and diplomatic relations strained. But why? Why had he been used as a pawn in this charade? What could they gain by disgracing him? Hadn't they come to seek assistance of Utopia? What is it that they wanted!?

What was it that she'd wanted?

He'd strangle her if he ever got the chance. Then he'd really get capital. The time alone had given him time to "recall" the warning he'd ignored in his rush to get business done. He was embarrassed.

... Gral, the council of Utopia is suspicious. This planetoid has been loosely linked to several mysterious occurrences in the outer arm. We're concerned. We don't think it is all it claims to be. Gather what intelligence you can without getting them suspicious. We're counting on you. Be extra cautious...

He jumped as the hum of the outer prison door opened. Blazer blasts ricocheted from the hall outside, then silence. Footsteps approached his cell and some form of key hit the lock. Perhaps death was early for its appointment?

Suddenly into the light stepped Karen, her shirt torn and lip bleeding, with nothing but jail keys in one hand, and a weapon in the other. She took a faltering step inside.

'You little bi...' the diplomat began. He would have added violence to offence if he wasn't afraid someone would be guarding her. But she stood unmoved, eyes brimming with tears, her phaser unraised. She stared at him for a moment, then collapsed, and in spite of himself, he lunged to catch her.

'Gral, I'm sorry,' she began.

'Well somehow "sorry" just doesn't cut it baby,' he said woundedly, but softened when he saw her look. He could tell she was no longer playing games.

'The guard. I think I killed him. You have to get out. I found out something I shouldn't have known. They're not going to kill you at all Gral. They're going to...' her voice died.

The diplomat held her. He wasn't sure whether to trust her or try and hold her hostage. But the prison door remained open.

He held her up to his face. 'Listen Karen. I don't fall for your games twice, what is going on here?'

She choked back a cry. 'You've got to get out. I have a cargo booked. Use this to impersonate me. You have to get to your Senetcraft and get out of this system immediately. Your assistant is booked to leave in less than an hour. He can't stall for long. He knows too much too. You've got to get out of here. Other lives depend on it!'

The diplomat's head was spinning. Again, it was all happening too fast. 'How do I know this isn't another trap?'

She stared at him. 'You don't, but you're dead already.'

That much was definitely true.

'What about you?' he asked.

She fumbled in her hands and brought out an identicard. 'We have to trade places. I can only fool the system so long. They'll find out soon. If we both left the alarm would be immediate, so I've switched our identities so that you scan as me and I as you. By the time they discover I got on the ship, which is really you, you'll already be gone. This identicard has details; they're planning some sort of invasion. Please. You've got to tell the United Council what happened to you in Seren!'

She began pushing him towards the door even as her tears cascaded anew. What did she know? For a moment he felt to be a gentleman and refuse to escape at her expense. As if reading his mind she continued.

'No-one will believe me. I have already lied, and betrayed my people tonight. But it doesn't matter. The less you know the safer we are. You have to tell others you were set up.'

'The Senate will never believe me. They think Seren is a floating isle of paradise!'

'Then why can no- one leave?'

His blood ran cold. So there was more she wasn't telling him. He had never heard any suggestion of this. He turned to leave, half expecting to be cut in half with a blazer. He turned back to her.

'Remember, a prison cargo,' she insisted. 'Get to the Senetcraft and leave right away. Use plasma burn off to hide your body signature and hope no one recognises you. You were on the public terminal earlier today.'

She came to the door and blinked through a smile. 'I'm sorry for what happened. I used you for personal gain without realising I was the one being used. I suppose it's only fair that I receive what I gave to others, and am only made free by accepting their punishment.'

He stared incredulously at her, not at all understanding her sudden... religiosity.

'I promise I'll get out,' and he smiled in return, 'and I won't forget you.'

But he knew she didn't need that promise. He had met death with fear and scheming. For her, the impending death or worse seemed to be the only way to make her whole. She must be crazy. She smiled as he touched her cheek, but not in that he should remember her; that in now that he should live.

He ran out leaving her standing in the open prison cell. Within the hour alarms would sound as the guard was found mortally wounded and a prisoner escaped. Perhaps she would fear then?

Death at the Prison

Something was wrong. Matrix could tell by the way Commander Sheelaakah tensed up. They had made it all the way down towards the capital prison now, and were preparing to enter in as disguised officials. Then the Commander turned, and conferred with Skion for a moment.

What just happened? Matrix asked.

Just wait, Bakerson told him.

Finally she turned. 'We're too late,' she said, her eyes overflowing with sorrow. 'The programmers in the wilderness beyond just intercepted an Oppression report, and sent it to Skion. There's been a jail break. The diplomat has escaped. We're too late.'

'Too late?' Matrix asked.

'Yes, too late!' She insisted with apparent indignity. 'They'll have his ship locked down immediately. They'll find him soon, and he doesn't have the kind of help we have.'

Bakerson sighed, but Matrix couldn't. Somewhere deep inside he just *knew* it was not too late. Fate was always trying to help out; they just had to… insist.

'No, it's not too late. Scramble their communications. We need to give him more time. We can still save the diplomat.'

She nodded, 'That I can. And the Hope?'

'What of it?' Matrix asked.

'How will we get the Hope to him if he flees?'

'That's a chance we have to take.'

'Perhaps, if I may speak freely,' Skion's mechanical voice suggested, 'if we do get into the cell you can telepathically scent him out, locate him that way. We *may* be able to use the prison site to site teleporter to get you to him.'

'Perhaps there is still hope,' Bakerson smiled.

'Even so, it will take a miracle,' the Commander agreed. 'Against the combined will of the entire citadel looking for his death? I don't know how he will manage to escape.'

Matrix answered, 'Because the will of those within the walls are not the only factor in play here. Those outside number those here two to one. We have to trust to those prayers as well.'

The Commander paused, thinking deeply. 'Then, perhaps… let us hope your "faith" is well placed, officer Matrix. We may be going to our death, finding a memory of a prisoner in the fortress of our enemy. But we have bested a demon tonight. It can't get much worse than that.'

'It can,' Matrix said, 'if one ever gives up the fight; the fight to be as free as they can be. That, I think at least for me, is much worse than dying for a good cause.'

She smiled at him then, a disarming smile of gratitude. In a flickering moment he saw the human within her, the woman who was battling impossible odds, who had lost more than perhaps even he could imagine.

For just a moment it struck him how beautiful she was, but the thought did not last.

'Then let us pay this prison a little visit after all,' she said.

---++---++---

The prison was not what they expected. For one thing, it was deserted.

They walked on in silence. This place felt very wrong, even to Matrix.

It could be a trap? He suggested.

No one replied; they were just as much on edge as he.

They followed the path the Commander took as she traced out his psychic imprint. They found his cell in moments. The door was open. With Skion on guard the other three went in.

'A woman lay here.' The Commander said, but the comment made no sense in the vacant cell of a lone diplomat.

'Can you find his scent?' Matrix asked.

'Yes... but... it is masked somehow. There's another entity here that's blocking me.'

Suddenly the floor bulged underneath their feet. Matrix leapt back, but Bakerson was paralysed. Skion turned to blast the encroaching incorporeal but it seemed to know his strengths, and limits. It thrust out its clawed hand and threw him into the far wall with a deft telekinetic manoeuvre.

The Commander was muttering some kind of power, the room filling with heat as it drained from the monster. But it was too skilled, and almost seemed to expect it. It had brought heat to spare and in a moment swept her from her feet. She lay silent on the floor.

Matrix stood alone to face the beast.

It turned to look at him, and Matrix could see it was exactly the same creature who had attacked them by the broken terminal. Somehow, it had survived.

Or been brought back.

'How?' he wondered.

The creature paused, and it spoke, its voice the rattling whispers of vengeance and death, 'Mortal, I will have great pleasure in your death. But first, we have questions. What are you? What are you capable of? I will pull your existence apart one fingernail at a time.'

Matrix knew he had very little time to act. 'You know so little? And yet you knew we'd be here? How is that?'

It hummed, and Matrix could feel its invisible tendrils of hopelessness and fear weaving themselves around him. 'You are born of this world, yet not. You are different. How is that? My caller will want to examine your DNA, take the measure of your soul print. Matrix, come with me.'

'Never.'

It laughed, the bitter solitude of hell. 'Like you have a choice.'

'I will always have a choice, even if all this is left is the right to deny my enemy the power to choose how I *feel*. You are darkness, and the darkness always contains... hidden options. And if you ask me, I would say that I don't have to come with you at all today. You can only convince me that I have no other choice.'

The demon sneered, 'If you're so confident you still have choice then you can claim the price of your companion's souls here. Come with me and I will let them live. Perhaps they will yet fight their way out of this place? That soldier outside, I see you respect him even as you revile his confidence and strength. And this genetically altered one here, you care for him as a brother every bit as much as he cares for you. As for this woman, the bond between you is already very strong, I think you would not risk any harm to her if you could.'

'That's your price?' Matrix gawked, in hindsight a very arrogant gesture, 'am I worth all three of them?'

The demon sneered again, realising it had only fuelled his determination. 'Then will take your consciousness. All it would take is a single touch. I am darkness to you, and death, and fear. With a single touch I can drag you screaming down to my abyss. There you can witness your friend's fate, fates you could have avoided if you'd chosen to.'

'Sorry, that would be your choice, not mine. I am not guilty if you choose to slay or torture them. No. You are not pinning that on me.'

The creature drew back, almost surprised. But the moment didn't last. 'I am going to kill you now, Matrix.'

That was when Matrix suddenly began to wonder if he had another option. So the being could kill him with a touch? The creature of darkness could extinguish the light of his soul, just like that? All his life he'd known about the human soul, the light that gave one light. What if that light touched, instead, the darkness? What if all the hope for life, freedom, and compassion reached out and touched the darkness?

What if he touched the demon with all that?

Suddenly his hands burst into white flame, and the demon flinched involuntary. It was aura, and he wasn't sure how he was able to see it. But he knew right away he had a weapon against fear and darkness: understanding, hope and light.

The demon swung out at him, and with reflexes born of seven years of survival he caught it effortlessly. Matrix was dimly amused that this was happening, wondering all the time how it was even possible. He wasn't a gifted, or priest. Yet he had something the darkness feared. The creature cried out, and swung wildly with its other claw. This time he swung the blow on, lifting the massive being out of the ground and crashing it onto the floor. It split the stones as it fell, and before he'd even thought about it, he'd grabbed it by the throat.

It struggled, twisting will all the rage of hell. But he held on, held on with every determination of life in a world this entity did not belong.

For a moment their eyes locked, and the demon seemed confused, then lost. There was nowhere it could flee from the blinding light of his touch. It could either struggle forever, or surrender to the light and release its existence of pain and death.

It chose the latter.

---++---+++---++---

Commander Sheelaakah woke up moments later, Bakerson and Skion stirring almost immediately after her as she sent out the message to them. They rose from the floor.

'What happened?' She asked, standing.

'What is that fire on your hands, Matrix?' Bakerson asked.

Matrix shrugged, letting the light die from his hands. They felt like they were burning now, but he sent that light up towards the stars, and his hands felt cool once more.

'Deemon!' Skion's human voice muttered, 'Where? Waa?'

'No time.' Matrix ordered. They needed organising. 'Commander, can you find the scent? Skion, can you access the teleporter from here? Bakerson, are we safe?'

They all responded well to orders.

Commander Sheelaakah spoke first, ignoring his breach in protocol completely. 'Got it. He's just outside the shipping platform right now… Bakerson, you and Skion take the inner halls to deal with any intrusions. Matrix, you are with me. Skion, can you get us there? Skion?'

'One moment please,' his mechanical voice insisted.

The Hope

Gral's heart raced as he stormed across the mezzanine. To his left two black guards stood, armed, yet unalert. If they'd known who he was, or even asked the question to themselves, it'd all be over in a second. Yet somehow the thunder of his heartbeat did not give him away.

Then he saw it; the Senetcraft. It was only four hundred or so meters away, resting on the platform. It was still here. Somehow the gods had allowed his assistant to stall successfully for time.

He paused a moment, gathering his thoughts. If he showed any fear...

... he walked calmly towards the mezzanine doors.

Then froze.

Between him and his exit stood his tour guide, the dark haired 'angel'.

---++---++---

Alasia knew he'd be here.

She smiled. She knew what was happening now, and what was even more entertaining was that she finally knew *why*. She knew he'd escape the prison. He was too clever and Karen, too kind. She'd look her up again one day, find out how she'd managed to arrange a jail break. Clever Karen.

She was leaning up against his exit door like she was waiting for a date, and as soon as their eyes met she simmered at him with her gaze. He was in her power now – and whatever she wanted, he would have to do. Two lazy guards at her right, seven more in the corridor below. She could call them all in an instant, and he'd be taken.

He didn't even pause. She saw the fear in his eyes, watched the fevered heartbeat along his neck, observed the way his shoulder muscles tensed. He was terrified. But he barely paused. He was too professional to give himself away just yet.

It was cute.

Or was he simply confident because she was alone? There was no cat, no trace signatures of noncorporeals of any kind. It was just her, and his destiny.

She smiled at him, enjoying every moment of the game.

She stood in the doorway, and he walked right up to her, almost pressing every inch of his manly frame against her. She found herself caught up in his moment, influenced by his desperation, trembling in his desperate will to live.

Yet she held all the power. All of it.

'Angel...' he whispered.

She only had to give the signal and they would all be here. He would be taken to prison, and she might be a hero.

Yet even as she though this, looking over at the black guard, she found herself waiting. What? What was it for? Did she need him to beg? Did she want him to threaten her and give her an excuse? Why did she wait?

Gently he put his hand on her chin, and invited her to look in his eyes. They were dark as mahogany, tremulous ripples of fate reflected in his cornea. He was not pleading, he simply asked.

She had nothing to lose by letting him go. They were as blind to her presence here as they were to his.

He had insulted her. She had so much to gain by turning him in, except... some part of her just didn't want to.

It was not something she could explain. She was one of the most "liberated" of Seren's citizens, knowing the law so well as to get most of what she wanted. Did she just want to see how much she could get away with?

Or was it pity for him, or her friend? Was there some kind of rebellion inside her, knowing that in letting him go free she would strike a subtle blow against all that was inside this world, all that held them prisoner here?

Without word or explanation, she slid aside. Not so much as a pace away, but far enough so that he could pass.

He looked surprised, then grateful. He looked, and she knew he was trying to read if she was telling him the truth. But there was no time to find out. He had to leave. She turned away from him, and allowed his breath to wash over her as he gasped out a sigh of disbelieving gratitude.

And he was gone.

---++---++---

Gral left the door, waiting while it slid shut, then held his breath. He knew the moment she left, his guide, and assumed that for now he was safe. She'd let him go, for reasons he could only imagine.

Two hundred meters.

Immediately he perceived another problem. There were four black guards, one a lion, standing about at the entrance of his ship, and they were alert. Beyond them, still as stone yet as alert as sentinels, two of their autonomous metal and stone guardians waited. The Emmissionaries, twice the height of a normal man and a hundred times more dangerous. He knew at once they would be trouble. And he knew at once they would die before they let him or anyone get on his ship.

He did not know what he was to do, but he knew he had to keep walking. If they saw him turn around he would be arrested for sure. So he walked confidently, walking towards his death. Praying some god might save him. Suddenly the last words his "date" ran through his panicked mind, lost words spoken in a prison cell;

'In freeing you I am made free. They might take all I am and know, or all I care about and even my life. But they cannot control me. They used to, because I let them. Now I choose, because I'm not afraid even to die. In that, I am free.'

Yet he was not prepared to die. He felt his footsteps falter, the fear bead out on his forehead. He saw a guard turn in his direction.

Suddenly a man and a woman arrived, a site to site teleport, interposing themselves between him and the guards. With casual indifference the woman wandered towards the guards, but the man turned to speak to him. He had riveting green eyes.

The man whispered, 'Diplomat, I'd like a word with you, if I could?'

Matrix breathed a mental sigh of relief as, thankfully, the diplomat stopped. He was a professional, that was sure. His bearing strong, his chin confident. But Matrix could also tell that he was afraid. *Terrified*. He was stopping only so that it gave him time to consider his options against the four guards that stood between him and what must have been his goal – a small intrasystem spaceship, large enough for only two.

'What is it?' The diplomat said, blinking unconsciously as he spoke, a sure sign that he was supressing powerful emotions, mostly fear.

Matrix deliberately paused to make sure he had the diplomat's full attention. 'Where you go now is up to you. But I beg you, take this stone with you. It is a parting gift, from *all* Seren.'

The diplomat looked at the little diamond in Matrix's palm, then back at his ship, 'What is it?' He asked.

'Oh,' Matrix explained, 'you needn't worry about the path to your vessel there; my friend will be taking care of that for you. But I have a favour to beg of you. I understand that you have had some trouble here of late? That does not surprise me. This world has a way of creating trouble for all those that do not bow to the higher power. You are not the first to suffer this kind of indignity, not in the least. This is our story.'

There was a pause, a moment of eternity, then a scintillation of glee as an unconscious agreement took place between the two men. The diplomat walked on, but he reached out and allowed the simple diamond shard to be placed in his outstretched hand.

He took the stone, and left.

Epilogue

The most important factor in this battle was that it be invisible. There could be no alarms. There could be no bodies, not so much as a scratch on the floor.

She smiled as she approached. Two men, one woman, and a lion. Beyond them, the Emmissionaries. Naturally, the female had to be dealt with first. The high order command to find sleep was focused entirely on her. She fell without a sound.

The others reacted immediately, and with precision training. Sheelaakah didn't have time to think, only to be. Telekinetically she removed the communication device from one man's hand, he was intuitive enough to have not even bothered to attempt a subtelepathic call for help, unconsciously aware that she'd already placed them inside the interdiction wards so subtly not even the lion had noticed.

The second man had raised his hand, a gem of ruby glistening inside a bronze hand guard, clearly a pyrotechnic enhancement for his palm light. The pillar of flame that tore from it in the next second was expertly deflected by her with practiced skill, but she didn't have further time to act while he adjusted as the lion had pounded.

She ducked under as it flew right over her. It roared, but she almost unconsciously manipulated its rage to sound like hunger to any who heard it. The first man already had a short sword out and attempted to stab her, but she twisted away from the blow and carried it on, catching his ankle in hers she pulled him to the ground. A simple curse was all it took for him to miss his footing and land chin first on the floor, knocked out cold.

The lion had turned, but it too fell unconscious a moment later; the great strength and power of a lion a disadvantage when they forgot to breathe.

Then the second man grabbed her from behind, pinning her arms.

With a single whispered curse she pierced his brow light with her will. He froze, and a second later succumbed to her deadly intent. He was overcome with fear, trembling, clutching at his heart he fell to the floor. While she touched him he would not move, but soon he, too, would succumb to welcome unconsciousness.

And that was when the Emmissionaries arrived.

She dodged the first ones swinging blow, pausing nanometres before striking the stone where she'd stood only an instant before. As she ducked under its chest, she withdrew her already raised hand, a symbolic gesture as she telekinetically tore its entire power circuitry to dust. It fell dead at her feet.

Before it had even hit the floor the other machine, with dispassionate rage, leapt towards her, threatening to crush her even if she managed to unplug it. Arms became scythes, and its shadow darkened her world. For one instant, for one breath of a moment, Sheelaakah recalled that terrible day seven years ago when one of these machines had pinned her to a wall. That day, when they had taken her brother.

With a violence born of rage and perfected through years of training, she poured all her strength of retribution into her psychokinetic manipulation, rending the machine to shreds from the inside in less than a second. It left her exhausted – but she stood, unharmed. Unhindered.

A moment later she felt the diplomat walk by. For an instant they shared a glance, which might have lasted for eternity. She saw in his eyes the familiar fear of what she had just done, all with apparent ease. She saw him wonder if he had any choice about whether he took the diamond or not. She saw him dying inside as the world he knew, the illusions with which he had built his reality, was stripped away from him in a day.

And she hoped, hoped with all her heart, that he would pity their plight, perceive the will with which they fought for his and their freedom, and not deny them this simple request... though it was clearly no longer in his best interests to do so...

... only time would tell.

Book 2
Rescue

Prologue - Book 2

(Today)

Water trickled down from the concrete pylons above. They were huddled together, shielded from minds, fearful of detection. The refugees hushed the children. She dared to light a candle made from some sort of wax. It was late, and the rendezvous team was even later. They should have been here by now, yet they weren't.

A sudden noise from far off caused the people to cringe, and children wiser than their years to shiver. They listened in silence, but nothing else happened.

How long have we been here now? She wondered. If the others didn't come soon they would have to move back into the caves. No- one wanted to be in there but, ironically, it was safer. She wiped the sweat from her brow and administered another dose of the medicine. It made breathing possible in the rarefied atmosphere, even if at times she swore she could feel the worms swimming about in her lungs.

There was the noise again. Like a short sharp earth shake, or thunder, so deep and resonating. She had never imagined this world, now their prison, as somehow alive. But now it seemed full of hellish machinery on an unstoppable flight through the galaxy.

A child approached her. She motioned quickly for her to stay low.

'Montsi,' the child whispered, 'why did this happen?'

She pulled the child's dark robe around her, and held her close.

'I don't know Cherrin, I don't know why any of this has happened,' silence passed by them on another journey through eternity.

Soon another child, the one who always dressed in green, who had been waiting by her side the whole time in silence, whispered; 'They are here soon, Montsi,' she spoke prophetically, as though knowing her thoughts.

Time lapsed, and then the child, her eyes black in the darkness, spoke to her again, 'Don't be afraid.' The child waited patiently, so unlike the others – a child imparting comfort to the woman. Jacinth was special.

Montsi crawled over to the rest of the group. She held Petrie, the autistic. He had been good so far, in spite of his fear. She went to comfort him as much as to be comforted. The score of children looked up at her, and

Montsi exchanged glances with the other three tired and worn adult workers. Last night, they were all tucked into soft, warm beds.

Marcuus, a co-worker, crawled over to her.

'Piniti needs to go to the toilet,' he whispered, not daring to use any other form of communication.

'Can she hold it?'

'I don't think so.'

'Go back a little way into the cavern. Use this vessel.'

He nodded, and left.

She was proud of herself. She could not hide her fear from the others, but she could show them how she dealt with it. She did not like being in charge under the circumstance, but it would have to do.

Suddenly there was a loud crack, followed by the earth shifting violently beneath them. The children screamed.

'Right!' she ordered, 'Everyone back into the cavern!'

She stood up and began pushing the children toward the tunnel. She turned in time to see the metal arm of one of their robots sweep her from her feet, dashing her head onto the hard earth. She fought to stay conscious.

The robot advanced on its decapods like a prehistoric spider. The children ran screaming in all directions, but she knew they would not get far. All except one. From the corner of her eye she caught the glimpse of a little girl in green moving *towards* the machine. It saw the child coming, and paused momentarily to consider this behaviour. It did not pause long, and raised a deadly limb.

And kept it raised. For all its violence it did not strike, but waited as though it was expecting something to happen.

'They're not allowed to harm us,' Jacinth explained calmly, calm as the depths of space - though unparalleled fear drove Montsi almost to insanity. Without waiting to comprehend the impossibility of this situation she grabbed the child by the shoulders and tried to drag her from the machines reach, though it scurried to keep up with them.

Then Jacinth suddenly stood her ground. 'They're here,' she quietly announced.

Suddenly a massive bio-electrical blast hit the decapod right on the side of its head, toppling it instantly.

Montsi stared in disbelief at its sudden and complete downfall. Then she remembered the children. Jacinth was already beginning to walk away, and she moved to stop her, but then noticed the dark figures approaching over the crest of the crater. Every instinct made Montsi want to run after the child, but experience told her to trust someone whose gift of prophecy was so much more powerful than her own. She and the other children followed, but at a distance.

The first figure, a man, approached Jacinth and swept her up into his arms kindly. They stepped into the candlelight. They were an unlikely crew, two females, one brunette, one night black. Two males, and while it may have been a trick of the light the second might have looked a bit like a dog. There was a third male, extremely tall and muscular, but outside the ring of light, standing watch.

The young man who held Jacinth was the first to speak. He came right up to her, so that she could clearly see his eyes, almost too bright a shade of green from locks of raven hair. 'Welcome to Seren. I hope you can like it, you'll probably never leave.'

23rd and fourth

(7 days ago)

I-olo Tilk, Understudy to the Supply and Reconnaissance Admiral for the Resistance munitions wing eyed the report with grave concern. The Oppression had made an unexpected move. Within a week all Resistance outposts up to four thousand kilometres from the dark side of Seren had been either cleared or decimated. They'd had no warning, no time to prepare. Almost a full tenth of their operations were compromised or destroyed. Once again, he had the nagging feeling that the Resistance only existed because the Oppression let them. He sighed. It was time for another internal spy purge.

He stroked his ebon chin, an old habit, picked up from time immemorial, and contemplated. The government was a slippery adversary. Such a large offensive on their part would mean they were planning something big. He sighed deeply, then looked up at the assistant who was still waiting at desk's edge.

'There are reports of no survives from outposts Gamma twelve and North fifth. Several incidents involved indirect government involvement, but there is more disturbing news,' the nervous secretary said.

The Understudy looked at him over his report.

'Commander Sheelaakah made an un-notified transfer to North fifth a day before it was destroyed. We have not heard from her.'

'Are you suggesting!?' demanded the Understudy.

'No! N... Not likely sir. We've scanned all available Oppression intelligence. There is no indication that she has been captured.'

'But not impossible,' the Understudy finished. A stifling moment of silence filled the room like a listless breeze on a humid, windless day.

'There is indication, sir, that North fifth may have managed to detect the government plot and evacuate only hours before. The Oppression documents indicate a much smaller battle than would be expected from three full units. We've sent out intelligence supplies; apparently they may have divided into three units and heading back to centre via the surface.'

The Understudy stood, 'Treble the search parties: she is one that is far too valuable to lose! And remember, others will be looking for home as well.'

'Sir!' the experienced secretary questioned, 'that is a significant commitment, are you sure?'

The Understudy's look silenced him. 'Also, prepare to inform our units within the wall, as well as the underground Resistance inside Seren to go to level Delta propaganda.'

'Sir?'

'That's right. I have to bring this to the Circle for confirmation. We may no longer be safe...'

-- + -- + -- + --

The phone rang again. He ignored it obstinately. It was rude, and he wished it could hold conversations until he wanted them.

He looked up. 'You'll have to leave now.'

She nodded, gathered up her clothes and hurriedly left. He activated the panel, but not before wrapping himself in a loose robe.

He recognised the shrewd conspect of the general representative of Government works sneering back at him. 'Senator Breen; leader of Government foundry works. Night robes at midday? You're feeling relaxed today.'

'No, no,' the older man stumbled. 'Just... taking it a little easier today. You know how it is.' He winced, knowing how much a fool he sounded.

'No, I do not,' the younger man tersely replied. 'Have I caught you at a bad time?'

'Not at all, go on Representative.'

'Three days ago, a small group of Resistance operatives were able to enter the citadel, and have been causing no end of trouble, at one point even involving a *demon*, no less! They went silent for two days and we thought they had left. Then central informs me of a most embarrassing breach of security today. They were recently seen attempting to gain access to several terminals within *your* factories! This sort of incident will not be tolerated again! If you need help in securing your jurisdiction-'

'No! Not at all Representative, I mean no disrespect but-'

'Understand this Senator. Your position is at an impasse. One more breach and you will be serving, not leading, the factories.'

The Senator had no reply.

A tense moment filled the room then the Representative relaxed visibly. 'But don't worry; I know you will keep your area secure. And as for the fugitives, Central command informs me that Lord Admiral Taalk himself has been monitoring their movements. He is taking care of the matter, something about sending in an apprentice. He has requested that you approve the movement of a unit of black guards to these co- ordinates. We don't need to worry, not for us to meddle in the affairs of Government.'

And the screen went blank.

Senator Breen sunk into a chair, stroked his greying beard and rested a tired hand on his stomach. He was getting too old for this. Only six months until retirement, and now some more of those forge-fired Resistance people stirring up trouble for the rest of them! Thankfully, most citizens never found out about this kind of trouble – only those directly involved or serving the people in government positions, like he was. Life was much simpler fifty years ago. He'd make *these* Resistance fools pay like he always had for causing this latest trouble.

They would all pay.

--- + --- + --- + ---

Hours later, Alasia sat alone in her apartment, wiping the tears from her face. *How sad. How noble.* How he'd sacrificed their love to serve the government. And to think a mere two months later he would die trying to rescue a transport full of children from the gravitational collapse of Omega four. But that wasn't until next episode. Participating in these old classics was still a favourite indulgence of hers, one that few of her friends knew about.

She checked the time. It had moved faster than she'd expected, and now it was nearing departure time for the next series of social engagements. Hurriedly she gave the tissues to the automaton and headed for the bathroom, finishing the lines from the movie as she went.

It squeaked its protest, something along the lines of "You're running yourself to the grave with this lifestyle" or something equivalently ignorable. She faced her bathroom mirror and deactivated the business pages she was browsing earlier.

'Party set zero one,' she ordered, and investments turned to reflection. Immediately any evidence of tears was gone, as well as any evidence that she'd slept for the past two days – apart from this morning's festivities. As a finishing touch, the mirror added a soft glow to her cheeks.

'Set hair to… forty centimetres.'

Obediently it grew to the desired length.

'Set fringe straight,' and it obeyed.

She looked herself up and down. The slim leather outfit with gaping cleavage that she was already wearing would more than do for the occasion. But something was missing. She examined her profile.

'And cup size C.'

She commanded – they obeyed, and she left.

Her guard was already waiting for her outside, and silently lead the way down to the platform. A handful of hopefuls were gathered outside, but the warding sigils kept them from getting too close. Her friends weren't there yet but were set to arrive right on time, which kept the wait blissfully short and the need to smile and wave to a minimum. Someone had told them about the party tonight.

And as she waited, she noticed someone had brought a young girl with them, or perhaps the child had brought herself. She looked no more than twelve, with straight, dark hair just like Alasia. For a moment their eyes met, and it brought Alasia disturbingly back to a time when she was that age – when things were simpler, at the end of her age of innocence. It was about the time her career had begun, and what it took to make it happen. She wondered what her life would have been like if she'd never met the promoters – never been through the rites. She wondered if that young girl held ambitions to become the next 'Angel'.

For a moment she wanted to run up to her and scream, "DON'T!" Then she wondered what on earth she was thinking. Around then the limousine arrived, and the train of thought was buried under the traffic jam of the present again.

It was time to think about the party.

--- + --- + --- + ---

Matrix entered the 23rd and fourth and looked around. Palm trees adorned a roughly circular room with several alcoves large enough to fit some tables in relative privacy, all within adequate view of the stage at one end. The floor sloped gently down towards the centre, where a circular bar floated like an oasis. It was designed in colonial wood, the oldest surviving interior design he could imagine - apart from stone arches and columns. The sea of people within moved slowly about, the calm before the storm. Although still early, the bar was filling quickly. It looked as though they might be expecting some choice people. Perhaps they had picked a bad night?

He waded through the crowd and was rescued by the bar. Mists filled the air, creating the atmosphere people liked. He sat quietly. Commander Sheelaakah was already off towards the far end of the room. It had been many long years since he'd been inside the walls, and they had just walked in like residents. The new identity they had given him was working well. Seven years ago he had been tossed out with the garbage, beaten severely for his questions. Now he sat like any other resident at a bar. The streets remained the same, the unending sea of faceless humanity a drone. Like a fledgling eagle unable to fly - still a victim of circumstance, still not free. Still not neutral in the place that sent him away long ago, now its enemy, and its victim.

Matrix waited until a tall and keen eyed bartender, who looked like he had been marooned there for some time, approached him. Matrix ordered the only drink he knew the name of, and wondered if he'd made the right choice by the brief unquestioned pause of the tender. But Matrix had learned to look all his decisions in the eye, and the tender quickly provided the drink and wisely left him alone.

He wondered when the others would arrive. It had been three days now since the battle with the bugs at the outpost, and the victory he had helped secure there. In reward for his knowledge of the denizens indigenous to Seren the Commander had required he accompany them on this fate daring risk back into the citadel for answers. He was wondering if that was such a good idea, or if the whole idea of joining the Resistance was. But in a way he felt he owed them something, after all, they had healed him. And the Commander was... sorry, perhaps. They hadn't discussed it yet, let alone made eye contact – except that professionally. Yet he was here, her only defence for now. It was inexplicable, was this her way of apologising, by trusting him? Or did she still threaten him? She'd only spoken to him in short exchanges of direct instruction...

Still, at least he'd found good company in the man he insisted on calling Dogman, even though he knew the other hated it. Matrix suspected a good personality such as this Glenn had was a comfortable consolation for many people, and he noted that he took all his responsibilities very personally and sincerely. He was a man men would trust instinctively, a man of little words but much action, a man who always played for the home team. Even if he lacked spontaneity, he was a supportive friend. He found it hard to remember to call him "Unit leader" on most occasions, as it brought back the humour of a situation in a prison cell barely a week ago.

There were others, however, called on this journey he found far less sufferable. His wounds from the battle were much improved, but he still could not bear the audacity of the man Skion, who wore his arrogance like a medal. To be fair, he was a skilled warrior and technical expert. He had brought down a dozen black guards single handed three days ago, and had broken into a foundry door with his bare, biomechanically enhanced, fist. They fought well together, back to back – having become well acquainted with each other's combat strengths in the barracks not a week before. It's just he found the mechanised man... unbearably arrogant. He was condescending, self-motivated, ridged. He only knew utter obedience or complete self-service. Something was very wrong with that.

Matrix looked at the brew and noted with some consternation that no one else was drinking anything similar. He considered that a swift conclusion to his chocolate milk might arouse the least suspicion, as was his strict orders from the Commander. She was as warm as ice, and as sociable as a pit viper. He wondered how someone with so much inward facing energies could survive in such a self-sacrificing cause... or perhaps it was the very reason.

She did have an engaging smile, when he'd seen it once, and at that thought found the memory of her working its way into mind once more, and far more often than he wished. She was mildly attractive to him, he had to admit, though he could not fathom why. She had been from the first time he'd heard her voice... at any rate, he'd decided that she was no longer on his list of interesting females. Now that list was empty.

Matrix found himself again pondering if he was the right choice for this cause, or just lucky to have been in the right place at the right time. Still, running from the law was better than running from wild Rynahs.

Another couple entered the bar, and he wished sincerely they'd had the sense not to. Danger seemed to follow them. Who else would be coming to the 23rd and fourth tonight?

--- + --- + --- + ---

The limousine was full of attractive women, their bodyguards in the cars in front and behind. One of Alasia's friends had proposed a night out to celebrate a new employ, and they were out to party. They were talking about the usual things, and what some of their other less well-known friends were up to.

The conversation was turning to fashion when Alasia found herself staring out the window. People passed by on the street. Some turned to look at the limo, and she wondered what they were thinking. She wondered if they ever felt lonely. Lonely was the code name for one of her investments. She began toying creatively with some possible options. And when that got a little boring, she began absent-mindedly generating new fractal sets. She was on a real spin when someone shoved the dosage into her hand. It brought her quickly back to reality. She thanked them and smiled.

'Angel, are you all right?' Crystal asked. She was one of Alasia's oldest acquaintances, and perhaps her closest friend. They met at a publicity fund for one or another of the government projects, and became friends straight away. She was always trying to get Alasia to try blond like herself, but so many did nowadays, and blond just did not suit Alasia's taste. Alasia recalled how they'd been through quite a bit of life together. She had helped Crystal to recover after a painful breakup, or the disappointment when her sponsor had taken another job without her consent. They had had some excellent times together too, but had never been truly close. Alasia knew there was much she did not know about Crystal, and many things she would never willingly reveal about herself either.

'Yeah sure!' Alasia forced a smile, and took a dose quickly. Soon, the feelings would go away anyway. 'What were you saying?'

'The 23rd and fourth! It's a classic night bar, real atmosphere, great for parties. Heard of it?'

Groan, not there again! Alasia thought. 'Yes, tends to be... crowded.'

'Oh, c'mon!' another from the other side of the limo called. 'It'll be fun!'

'Maybe we'll get you up to sing!'

The others laughed.

'Besides, you might meet somebody...' Crystal teased.

--- + --- + --- + ---

Sheelaakah glanced about her before activating the terminal: a sign of her apprehension. The bar was quite full, which could work either way for them. It irked her tangibly to have had to come up here. The plan was to lay low for a couple of days at a Resistance safe house, to rest and heal, and it had done them good. Even so, she hadn't dared contact central, at least not yet. She hopped they'd be able to intuit that she and the others were safe, for now. They would have surely felt the drain on their resources, the echo's in their group psyche. The Hope had been planted, but it might still be years before it germinated.

This morning she'd brought her group back up to use a terminal at the lower foundries, but her security code had already been compromised. They'd only barely managed to fight their way out once the Oppression had discovered where they were. Some poor foundry representative would get a severe reprimand for that. Her tactic of heading deeper into the Citadel appeared to have helped throw off any pursuit. It had been a long three days since the incident at the outpost. She hopped to finally get some answers here.

This terminal was a translucent sphere about thirty centimetres in diameter, glowing softly in the nightclub atmosphere. It could be accessed by others, but she found one that was alone. She considered waiting for unit leaders Bakerson and Skion to arrive, but decided against caution in favour of action. Most people seemed intent on the dance floor or the attractions on stage.

She looked at the globe, standing out against the darkness. If that was her choice it would be expedient to activate it soon. She reached her hand out. The noise and crowd of the bar accelerated to a great distance away, and she stood alone in a room inside her mind.

The Terminal spoke, *Please state your identification.*

Omega Serenade, one nine three Alpha Kro forty two. Morning song.

Welcome Ms Serenade. The walls vanished, filled instead with a surreal mezzanine. Shee faced a library, and instantaneously arrived at her destination. There a guide met her, looking out from within a hooded cloak.

What wisdom ye seek?

Take me to the gardens.

He responded to the secret code, and escorted her inside to a private room. Living art lined the walls, including a virtual window that looked out onto the 23rd and fourth, where her body waited for her consciousness's return. Ironically, it did not seem quite so crowded from where the security probe was positioned. At least she could check on herself from here.

Terminal. Access secure file. Pre-set Alpha Alpha. Lock current files into doc series B. Continue analysis.

Several of the pictures froze. *Success.* Now provided the others in the outside world did their job, she should get her job efficiently done.

--- + --- + --- + ---

Matrix stared into his drink, a millennia-old practice. He found himself wondering what Pip was doing, then wondered if he would try and contact his parents and see how they were doing. Then wondered why he would even want to - they had held his funeral almost a decade ago.

He scanned the area. Dogman and Skion hadn't arrived yet. Perhaps they were in some trouble? The bar was full of shadows, and it was impossible to see from one horizon to the next. Then the far smoke cleared for an instant, and he held his breath. A tall man stood alone in the corner, dressed entirely in black. He couldn't make out if there was the insignia of the black guard on his uniform. Though they had once been his allies, now, they could mean trouble.

He ordered another drink.

--- +++ --- +++ ---

The Carer watched over the children as they played. She enjoyed her job on the little research colony at Breakers Point, far away from any of the conflict that seemed to afflict the rest of the Galaxy this past decade.

'This is your new student, Signor Montsi,' the superintendent said. 'Her name is Jacinth, and she will be yours for several weeks while she is assessed. Here is her daily routine.'

Montsi read the report briefly, then her brow furrowed.

'But there's nothing here. No autism, no Obsessive Compulsive. Why has she been brought here?' She questioned.

'Yes, so unlike the others; but they are all so unique. That's why they send them to us, out here in the Utopian research colonies. She won't be here long. I know you will help her fit in,' he replied, not answering at all.

The carer Montsi turned back to her children. The games they played were strange and disjointed, not at all like "normal" children. One did nothing but spin the disk on a toy survey satellite again and again, but could recite any conversation he had ever heard. Another child could not read, yet would add any length of numbers faster than he could recite them. To another, a toy floated unaided to her grasp; the rare and untempered gift of telekinesis. And others with stranger habits and talents still; Petrie, who sometimes would bang his head against walls, or pick at his fingernails until they bled. Yet his contact with extra dimensional beings was undeniable. Verbally and mentally, Petrie was speechless, but had developed more subtle ways to communicate. He was so helpless, and perhaps for this reason, perhaps her favourite.

But being special wasn't the only reason they had been brought to the research centre. They were all special, capable of so much. And they'd all came unannounced: just the information briefs and they were hers to care for. None were aged before two and beyond eight – they were the charge of other faculties. Yet while all the children were incredibly gifted in some way, most also bore intractable disabilities, both emotionally and mentally. She and the other carers were to make them feel at home, and to educate them while the resident experts deliberated on what was to be done for them. Most children in the major colonies were detected much earlier on. These children often came from the war zones, or were never treated in time for curable diseases. It was sad, and ironic that they were sent for help to an isolated colony such as this one.

However, isolation was one of the reasons the research colony existed here at all. Isolation, and also the rare minerals and spatial anomalies, that were the main reasons the colonies had sprung up at Breakers Point near the Utopian System over the last three centuries anyway, a hundred million kilometres from the centre of the galaxy.

Jacinth stood where she had been placed, quietly watching without speaking. She seemed about almost six years old, and was completely absorbed in what the other children were doing, but at the same time daunted by the unfamiliarity of it all.

'Her parents?' Montsi asked.

Yet as the words left her mouth Jacinth answered. 'They are in my office.'

'They are in my office,' the Superintendent reiterated, a bit surprised. Then confided quietly. 'She has advanced temporal perception.'

'A prophetess?' Montsi ventured.

The superintendent nodded soberly. 'They're apparently sending a Senate research elite, scheduled for next month,' he whispered.

That raised eyebrows.

'Please make sure she stays well and happy,' he announced, making sure everyone would hear. 'She should only be here for a short stay.'

She nodded, and he turned to leave. 'She'll feel right at h – '

'Montsi!' one of the children, Cherrin, suddenly called, 'Tuktuk is touching the plants again!'

Montsi left Jacinth to be introduced to some activities by another carer while she scurried across the floor to halt the child. As he touched another leaf, it turned brown and fell to the floor.

'Tuktuk, you know not to do that!' and she helped him put his mitts back on and return to his building blocks. One day he'd get the hang of it. Maybe.

Jacinth would fit right in here, she thought.

And so the Carer watched over the children as they played.

Paradise end

(6 days ago)

The lights were beginning to pulse by the time they arrived at the 23rd and fourth, a sure sign to Alasia that she had taken enough medicine. They exited the limousine with a flourish, a path already cleared by their entourage and security long before, holding back curious onlookers. They headed inside quickly to avoid distraction.

Alasia smiled as curious onlookers waved. 'What a gorgeous little hovel!' she gleamed with pleasure. Indeed, the outside of the bar was welcoming, with tight-shirted bouncers and wide open doors.

'Told you this would be a night to remember!' Crystal replied, laughing.

'Indeed,' Alasia replied, grabbing her hand and heading in with the others.

--- + --- + --- + ---

Unit leader Glenn Bakerson watched as the Skion gave the taxi a frustrated kick. They were having trouble at the taxi rank, and he was losing his temper.

'Attempt this! My tag was fully operative at seven hundred owwerrs. Maybe your out-serviced scannin' equipment is bruisin' the difficulties!'

Bakerson could tell the mech soldier was getting nervous. Never mind that the data key embedded in his hand was a fake anyway, he still used force of personality to confront difficult situations.

'Look bud!' said the robotic driver, mechanical eyes swivelling out of the dashboard. 'I've given the system its third, and unnecessary, over check. Naught is wrong with it! Presume something be wrong with your hand-'

'Nothin' be wrong with my hand, service; fully dated.'

He swiped his hand over the scanning plate again. Nothing. Time was getting late and they still had a few blocks to walk before they reached the 23rd and fourth. They could not afford a data key problem; by law they had to report it to the authorities immediately, and that was not an option.

The mechanical eyes drew closer out of the cab. 'Look chum, I'm afraid you'll just have to report it. I won't debit you for this ride, I'll even drive you to the nearest outpost and we can charge it to them. Unless you've got something to h-'

Skion grabbed the appendage and curled it violently out over the bonnet. Glenn tried to stop him, though he was sure that even despite its make Skion could probably tear it out of the dash.

'Process this, screwbolt. I am fully serviced! Something is faulty with your scanner *and* your maintenance routines. Something is always the-'

The eye turned to look Skion boldly in the face, 'By law I am required to-'

Suddenly Skion lifted the entire car off its gravity pad. Several citizens stepped back, and others turned from across the way. At this point Glenn knew he had to do something. On pure intuition he grabbed Skion's hand and hoping against hope slid it across the scanning plate. A small beep, and the computer responded 'Kro Therrum. You have been debited fourteen units for this journey. Have a good night.'

'Can I go now?' asked the cab boldly. Even as a machine, Glenn thought, it sounded choked up.

Skion laid it down heavily.

'Non-sentient,' he mumbled in one of humanities unkindest insults to sentient machines over the past century.

They headed quickly for the bar.

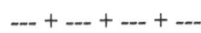

Sheelaakah was just about done. From the terminal she'd been able to gain some vital information and patch a small line that she hoped the Resistance would pick up and acknowledge.

All at the same time she'd been scanning the entire area. Most conversation starters where stopped before they'd even began to approach her. There were so many minds and all in a self-induced state of reception. That's what they came here for; to disengage their issues with the thoughts provided by this location. They called it a good night out, or some anarchic term, like 'getting drank' or something.

In that way the soldier Matrix stood out like a sore thumb. She was a little disappointed that a man of his survival instincts couldn't subvert his nervousness and newness better. What was it about this place that made him so anxious? He probably didn't even know, and she could see no reason to find out. It briefly crossed her mind to ask herself why she'd brought him on this journey anyway. Auspiciously it was because she had a personal policy of seeking out talent, even unusual talent, whenever it was found, and testing it for the service of the Resistance.

That was what she told herself, though no logical reason could really be brought to bear as to why this untested warrior was in her entourage this evening...

Pressing unanswered thoughts away she accessed screens quickly.

--- + --- + --- + ---

Despite the din, his drink made a cheerful plink as Matrix laid it on the bar top. Its taste had been adequate, but he was beginning to feel truly edgy – beyond uncomfortable. The 23rd and fourth was a classy joint, but experiencing one of her busy nights. The major focus on one end was the stage, now flickering with some exotic dancers like the sun reflecting off the ocean on a hot day.

The ice swam in his drink. Dancers moved across a crowded dance floor like bracken on a pond to the tuneless, noisy sounds, blown on the winds of a driving rhythm. He tried to look up at the Commander without looking like it, but instead his eyes met another woman's, a very attractive one. He glanced away for a moment, but she did not. She reminded him of a black cat, though he did not want to be noticed. When he had first entered, he'd sworn to himself to stay out of trouble, presumably from the black guards.

Matrix didn't know now which was worse.

--- + --- + --- + ---

Alasia had headed straight for the bar and drank a Topi full and straight and much too quick. As her drink hit the bar top, she noticed a dark haired man sitting alone. He looked a little as though he wanted to keep it that way, and a lot like he didn't belong here. She stared at him for a moment, and was certain he had beautiful eyes; a fact she shared with her entourage. He turned to look up, and then twice as quickly to look away again.

She concluded she deserved to move to where she could get a better look in his eyes. Her friends dared her to.

So she did.

It only took a few seconds to organise with the synthetic musicians. Lights turned to centre stage, bathing her in sheer white. It was the moment, and she felt the rush that came with it. She started to sing; voice free and resonate like butterflies landing in proximity. She brought the room swiftly to a standstill, admiration in their silence. It was why they called her Angel. As she started her song, improvised and unprepared, she looked at her audience. She smiled at her entourage and their encouragement was not needed, but very welcome. She moved seductively across the stage, wholly living in the moment.

The 23rd and fourth was busy, its residents rough and weathered. She pondered if it might be better to stay on the stage tonight. She reached down in time with her song, new each time it was sung. They approved. She could feel their response, though she was not more psychic than most. It was something she couldn't explain, nor felt the need to. Just a gift. The music she spontaneously composed over eighteen lines rose again. And he was there, still looking like he didn't belong. He continued to stare into his drink, and did not look up.

She held their attention, and it brought her a satisfaction that nothing else could. Yet still the dark-haired man did not look up, and it annoyed her. She felt the frustration express itself in her voice. She let the music change, as it would with her mood. She started down the steps and onto a table, much to the delight of its occupants. She sung about rejection, of betrayal and threats. Her song was from the heart, of unpaid sin. Onto another table. The song now was heavy and intense, and the crowd moved and passionate. She picked up some man's glass and sipped it luxuriously between measures, rewarding him with a stiletto-healed shove to the floor. It brought great satisfaction to herself and the crowd.

But the dark haired man did not look up.

She allowed herself to be lifted up onto a levitating table, and carried herself over the audience. She caught a glimpse of her bodyguard who looked like he was having a time of it trying to do his job. She carried herself to the far side of the room and right on beat and the end of a line she smashed the glass right on the edge of the table. It made her smile;

management would not like that one. The tinkling was carried across the room, echoing in the silence.

She sung now of reconciliation, of letting go and resignation. Slowly she brought herself towards the man who did not look up. She stood up, the full length of her thigh bathed in the light. Low tones and long notes rested across the room as did she, kneeling down to invite his chin with a single finger. She let her note travel to an eventual conclusion, and the people gave a rapturous applause.

Then as she finished, he looked up. Soft eyes, a beautiful emerald colour. She realised that it was what she had wanted; to see his hidden eyes. And suddenly, and the thought surprised her, she was struck with shame at having uncovered his hiding when all he wanted was to be hid. He looked... almost hurt.

Her guard helped her from her podium and she was welcomed and whisked away by an adoring entourage.

But she knew she had to see him again, if only to apologise.

--- + --- + --- + ---

Matrix looked up to find the gorgeous woman thankfully gone. To be of a truth, he was partly disappointed, mostly relieved. The sweat was almost unbearable. What had made him so conspicuous? The crowd seemed to go about their business again, and he breathed a sigh of relief. Someone nodded approvingly from across the bar at him. He smiled and nodded uncertainly in return.

Matrix thought about how he had been cornered once by a ground dragon. Tall as a bear with talons like knives, glistening in the light. It was terrifying and glorious all at once. It reminded him of that. A woman so influential and entirely... unafraid.

But again she reminded him again of a black cat. And she had crossed his path.

The colour black. He was edgy now, but something deeper was making him nervous. One could perhaps expect nervousness after something like that. But... no. It was something more. A sense of destiny or fate. He looked up to find the black guard unmoving by the door. He recalled then that they never travelled alone.

'Excuse me, Master,' the bartender said charismatically. 'From the gentlemen over on table seven.'

'Err... thank you,' Matrix said, accepting the drink that was ushered into his hand. He looked to where the tender had indicated. Three characters raised a glass in his direction, and he raised his in return, not knowing what else to do. He was at a loss now. The Commander would torture him again for certain, he was sure of that. He wasn't even allowed into these sorts of places when he lived inside the walls and he'd had no idea of what to expect. Perhaps he should try to sit somewhere along the walls, but the Commander was expecting him to be here. He did not have time to ponder his options as someone approached the bar from the left.

'You seem alone,' a woman's voice said.

His breath caught, and he did not answer.

--- + --- + --- + ---

He did not answer, but she wasn't surprised. She only half noticed her guard taking a seat not too far away. Her friends looked encouragingly on from their vantage point across the bar.

'Come here often?' She attempted to continue a conversation he wasn't having.

'No,' he softly replied.

Alasia was getting a little frustrated at the way he played the game. She would not admit it, but she was beginning to feel uncomfortable. But she decided his silence would only make her more determined.

She continued nonchalantly, 'Well, aren't you a talkative one! You are new here.'

Again, no answer. This was not going well.

'Let me see,' she teased, 'you are hiding. Yes, and you are not from around here? This place, these people. They make you nervous.'

He looked up again. His eyes were a riveting emerald green. She could become so lost in those eyes.

'I need... to be alone,' was all he said.

But she would not accept that. She felt it was a challenge, and as she realised he would talk, even to dissuade her, it raised her confidence. She allowed him a moment to sip his drink, which he seemed to find distasteful.

She pondered; though he claimed he needed to be alone, he did not leave. 'We all value our privacy, in it we hold our secrets. Sometimes privacy will find you, sometimes you just have to acquire it. At times, I've known men who claim to want privacy but desperately seek company. Men like that tend to seek solitude in crowds.' She paused to see if he would speak. 'If I embarrassed you back there I'm sorry… but I don't promise I won't do it again sometime.'

He did not say, but she could tell he was listening. Perhaps he was one of those men. Those had made some of the more interesting men she had met.

'But if you want to,' she teased nonchalantly, 'I can leave you… alone.'

He turned to look at her, though she did not know what he was about to do. Then his gaze slowly and deliberately shifted to the door. Alasia turned, and what she saw made her feel tense, though at other times it was not an uncommon sight. A pair of black guards was entering the 23rd and fourth.

'I am not the only one here tonight with secrets to keep,' he whispered.

--- + --- + --- + ---

Sheelaakah continued to scan for information.

Commissioner Vox. Orders twenty thousand kilo tri-lithium to inner maw. Dated… one week ago. The Government council covertly orders suppression of all Resistance activity up to four thousand K of the dark side. Just this week. Makes sense, what could it mean?

She sensed she was getting close. On habit she glanced at the outside world. Officer Bakerson and Skion were about to arrive, and Matrix looked like he was talking to someone. A woman. This was not tactical. Could he not help himself?

A tremor crossed her sixth sense. She realised another high level psychic was somewhere near. She had to hurry.

--- + --- + --- + ---

Glenn followed Skion as they hurried into the bar. Immediately he was beset by the fragrances and scents around him, the drinks at the bar, the things being consumed and the things that shouldn't be. So this was the sort of area they were entering? Without looking he knew a clean-shaven middle aged ranking black guard was waiting by the door. Another plain-clothed guard was mingling several meters away.

'A patrol with four guards just pulled up outside the building,' Skion mechanically informed him. 'Two of them are wolves… can you locate the Commander?'

Glenn looked about, and spotted a quiet corner far off. Someone was accessing a terminal from there. Simultaneously he and Skion noticed Matrix. Glenn could tell Skion was angry by the way he immediately straightened and tensed. Matrix was talking closely to a woman. Or more so listening, by the looks of things.

The warriors moved to improve their situation. Matrix was still sitting near the middle of the room, which had the potential for disaster. He'd always wondered if this young enthusiast from the tunnels really knew how to serve the Resistance.

Skion suddenly motioned to Glenn as they pushed through the throng. One of the black guards was pointing an orb stone at Matrix, and now at Matrix's woman. Matrix saw it too. And without making a fuss or a hurry, the black guard began to move in.

--- + --- + --- + ---

The man she was talking to, or rather, not talking to, faced his drink. Alasia touched the back of his hand.

'You're in trouble, aren't you?'

'No,' he said. 'We both are.'

--- + --- + --- + ---

'Success!' whispered the Commander as the data screen she'd been searching for finally revealed itself. Without adieu she exited the terminal, carrying the information she had accessed in the stone at her copper banding. She turned to find Matrix.

Then she saw them.

Two black guards had worked their way behind him while another made a conspicuous entrance through the front of the crowd. Suddenly Matrix threw his glass to the floor and quickly stood up. He was unarmed, but the guards had tried to take him by force. Holding the woman's hand he managed to turn in time to strike one unconscious with unbridled ferocity as he leapt across the bar. Twisting, he swept the feet out from the other guard, who was polished off surprisingly by another beer mug to the back of the head from the woman.

'Why'd you drag me into this!?' She screamed at him.

Black guards began pouring through the entrance.

Skion, what now? Sheelaakah asked.

Head for the back exit! he replied, as the mayhem quickly degenerated into an all-out bar fight in paradise.

Clear a path to the back exit, cover the front doors, Commander Sheelaakah ordered.

Although Matrix was surrounded, the others were actually well positioned. Sheelaakah was monitoring the black guard's conversations. The deluge of light she unleashed on the black guards caught them completely by surprise. Bakerson threw out his stunning rune and many guards fell unmoving to the floor, blocking the entrance. They were pinned down and unable to get more of them in. Skion drew his quarterstaff and Glenn, blade and shield, managed to keep the ones already around the bar down as people everywhere headed for cover. What was meant to be a precision assault was quickly looking like some unfortunate black guard Commander was going to lose a promotion. They must have underestimated their numbers. Even so, it was unfortunate that they had found them here. She would have to learn what had given away their position.

The Commander turned again and headed quickly for the back exit. The bartender was easily controlled and she kept him from blasting a new exit in his bar. With screams and constant blazer fire Matrix grabbed the strange woman by the hand and they all headed for the exit of the 23rd and fourth.

The whip-haired apprentice waited as the screams and light blasts echoed from inside the pitiful bar. He felt they would have their work cut out covering up this one. Then he sensed her nearness, and revelled in her unique talent. She broke around the corner with the man Matrix and the singer. They halted quickly at the wall of his thirty fully armed black guards, shrouded by his gift until this very moment. Seconds later two other men turned the corner and they, too, froze. He smiled at them and stepped forward while caressing a thin braid of his long hair that went down below his knees. He was not armed. He did not need to be.

At his telepathic signal all the fighting stopped. He looked at her. Sheelaakah: the highest promise of the psychically gifted wing of the Resistance. The richness of her soul and rebellious beauty excited him. He smiled at her obvious disdain as he approached. 'Out of the core, into–'

'I know you,' she hissed in full consuming spite. 'You were the black guard that pulled me from the underground sewer the day my brother was taken. You were with Lord Admiral Taalk.'

Without looking, he sensed the feeling of the others. They'd been surprised at the passion in their Commander's voice. They would be much more surprised by the time he'd finished with her.

'I am Officer Token, apprentice prime to Admiral Taalk,' he started calmly with a tone he'd learnt from his master, and then added with a commanding spite all his own 'You are dissidents and spies! But the Government will see you are returned to your place. Just look at the disorder you have caused tonight,' he said persuasively. They did not answer.

'I owe you one,' the woman Sheelaakah said calmly.

Her assault surprised him. He had expected it, but not this way. It was sly. She'd offset him with sensuous thoughts and plunged her mind into his being as he inadvertently left himself open. His shielding went up. She battered against it, but his headache grew worse. To his surprise he found her working her way through his pain while allowing him to believe he was defending himself against her.

He clutched his temples and fell to his knees. His nose began to bleed. The guards behind looked around without knowing what to do: They'd never seen him on the receiving end of psychotelepathic torture before.

She stepped closer and intensified her attack.

Weapons were lowered in confusion as the psychic duel continued. Her allies looked around, not knowing what to do. Two more men may have exited the bar, but he was unsure of that in the unabated assault that afflicted him. His guards' confidence failed, held in check only by their commanding officer, but the ranks of the dissidents grew in confidence, apparently believing themselves a match for the wall of low ranking soldiers he'd brought with him. Another wave of telepathic energy surged into him. He tried to channel it into his copper banding, but to little avail. He attempted to overcome with pressure several blood vessels in her mind, but she stood against him. He felt his breath leave him.

He steeled against her assault and slung his unkindest at her. They stung her, but she wounded him. In the gathering blackness he tried to show her what they had done to her brother. The assault bounced off her unassailable will.

--- + --- + --- + ---

Sheelaakah heard shouts and new light blasts. The long-haired man fell to the floor in front of her. Matrix might have said something. They began pulling her away. She resisted, but was too overwhelmed to assess what kind of danger they were in. He had been a desperate and skilled adversary, and might have done better if he hadn't have been so gullible. She regained her presence enough to realise she had to move her feet and legs. They pulled her away with a forlorn cry of realisation that she would not have the pleasure of destroying him today. She started to collapse into someone's arms, and the world went very dark.

It felt like hours later when something cold touched her desiccated lips and a deep cough tore itself from between her ribs.

'Shhh,' she heard Matrix say. 'It's OK Commander, we are safe here.'

'Where are we?' she coughed.

'Seven levels below the 23rd and fourth. You scattered the black guards. We're waiting on Skion.'

She tried to sit up. Matrix helped her. They were in what should've been an alley, only there was no sky above. It was damp. Feint light struggled from the entrance some distance away. Unit man Matrix was here, a silhouette against the faded glow. She looked out, and caught a glimpse of Unit leader Bakerson somewhere near taking the look out. The image then tilted on its side and she found herself caught in Matrix's arms again.

She paused a moment to gather her thoughts, chasing them like scattered deer. She looked up again, and then she saw the woman with hair the decisive tint of ebony. At first she did not recognise a face. Then she was intrinsically afraid of the stranger. At a moment of thought she recalled the face she'd seen so briefly before, and she stared into the other's black eyes.

By force of habit Shee reached out with her mind, but only weakly, and the other was a bastion of secrecy. Had she had her full faculty she might have been willing to try harder.

Instead she just smiled weakly, and passed out again.

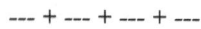

Matrix waited as the footfalls turned into Skion's approaching hulk. Three minutes. 'You are late.'

The taller man just glared. 'Time. We must leave,' he stated.

The group stood – four warriors, a gifted, and a singer.

'What about her?' questioned Skion gravely, motioning a mechanised limb towards Matrix's new friend.

Her dress trailed about her like a waterfall as the singer stood, and she answered for herself with impetuous confidence: 'Just get me to a transport site. I'll be fine once I leave this suburb.'

Matrix and Skion shared a glance.

Skion motioned the way for her as a butler opening a door, but she did not leave immediately. Instead, she walked over and looked down at the Commander. 'Is she someone important?'

Nobody answered her.

She went with them into a dark corridor, across a narrow street and down some mechanical steps, after Skion had deactivated the scanner reader. Dogman approached the others and the guards carried Commander Sheelaakah.

'The Commander did not manage to contact Headquarters. We will have to try again, outside the city walls,' he informed them.

'How do you propose we get there?' Matrix asked.

Skion answered, 'I believe I know of a location. There is a breach at the ninth section of the wall. Plans for the extension were changed. It is not fully sealed, but is reinforced by many enemy units. It is a strategically operative action as the Oppression will not expect it.'

'I don't like it,' replied Matrix. 'There are less places to run, and the surface is easily searched. We should take the sewer tunnels under-'

'Your experience in subvert tactical operations is questionable,' Skion's mechanised voice stated tersely.

'I've been places you have yet to imagine,' Matrix retorted.

It may have escalated, as it often did, but the discussion concluded with an order from the Dogman: 'We take the tunnels.'

Alasia looked down at the brown haired psychic. Her pulse was too fast, and her breathing shallow. It had been almost an hour since the excitement at the 23rd and fourth, and their going had been greatly slowed by the unconscious brown haired woman. Now she was beginning to come to once more, and Alasia had an opportunity to practice some aide she'd learnt time ago.

'Can you stand?' Alasia asked.

'Yes, I think so.'

She looked into her eyes. Too dilated. And they showed signs of respiratory and psychotoxin shock. 'You probably should let them carry you.'

'No,' the other woman insisted, and stared back at her with those firm hazel eyes. She was a woman, if not a fool.

The one they called Commander struggled to her feet. Two of the men tried to help, but she was unwilling. 'I'll be all right!' She insisted.

She stood, but only by force of will. And she rewarded Alasia with a look that could freeze a star.

'Well then,' she countered, 'you walk. But don't say I didn't warn you.' Being upset would probably help her focus. Besides, this one *really* had some issues.

The "Commander" took a faltering step, and finally consented to one of their arms. In retribution, Alasia took another's, the dark haired man who had dragged her into this in the first place.

This was the most fun she'd had all year.

He walked in silence. She could tell he was still uncomfortable, more accustomed to war than women. She enjoyed his boyish discomfort.

'You know,' she began softly, 'Thank you for saving me in there. You are ... very brave.'

He did not answer.

'You must be very strong.'

He might have mumbled something. Eventually he spoke. 'I am Matrix.'

'And I am Alasia. Angel to my friends, so you can call me Angel. You are an honour to know, Sir.' It was very formal to call him that. Perhaps it even surprised her. He seemed so tense, and she was making the most of this, after all, it might mean a suspended sentence or some other form of recompense for all the fun that they'd had.

'I didn't mean to drag you into this,' he said gallantly. 'They were coming for you too, they'd seen you talking to me, and I needed to drag you out of-'

'Only I "drag" myself, Sir. You are quite the one to think to make my choices.'

He was uncomfortable. He really had no idea what she was, but he was different. Too hard, and too sincere, to have lived any life she knew. 'What brings you into this area of the City, Sir?'

Suddenly he stopped walking and looked straight at her. He held her by the shoulders. For a moment she thought he might try for a kiss, but he answered with surprising severity. 'We're with the Resistance, Alasia.'

124

As though she'd never met anyone from the Resistance before. She had. Turned one or two over as well, if they'd upset her enough.

'You are?' She feigned in wide-eyed innocence.

He nodded gravely. Now he was too much. 'We're trying to... well... we need to get out of the city. Alasia... Angel, I don't want to bring anyone into this who doesn't want to be. It is, as you say, your choice. We can attempt it on our own but I fear they may think you are with us, and I don't-'

'Don't worry about me,' she argued instinctively. He was so ... genuine. She had never met a man like him before, and underneath, it made her a little nervous. She found herself leaning backward, and he gently let her go.

Someone called out from the back of the group. 'She's fainted again.'

Without notice or adieu Matrix was by the psychic's side. Despite herself she looked at them, and wondered what might have been between them. The woman's face looked so much older than it should be. This Matrix looked like a hero from the Terran wars.

'We have to get her to a hospital,' he was saying.

'As soon as we're outside the walls,' the puppy soldier said.

What! Were they going to just walk out? Oh, there *must* be secret passages then! They had formed a circle around her then, trying to help. They were quick to forget she was there listening.

'Is there someone we can trust here?' Asked one of the other men.

'I know someone, that is, I can refer you to someone who owes me a favour. But you'll have to visit him alone, I'm already late.' Alasia interjected uninvited.

They all turned and looked at her.

--+--+--+--

The children played happily as Montsi watched. All seemed pretty quiet. Joel looked like the sedation was taking effect and that he would not bother them for a while now. Tuktuk's mitts were still firmly affixed, and the twins happily engaged in Boolean algebra. She sighed. It had been a big day. Things had been inexplicably tense; no one could tell why. At least it wasn't the solar activity, passing comets or errant ley lines. Apparently one of the patients in the adult ward had even taken an almost unheard of epileptic seizure, but now things seemed calmer.

She heard movement outside in the hall and decided she could afford a peek. Surprisingly, it was the manager talking to some other staff. They were expecting some visitors soon. Knowing it was better to know from the source first, and not to let the children tell her, she poked her head outside. 'Expecting some visitors, are we?'

The superintendent turned mid-sentence and spoke enthusiastically. 'The Research Governor himself might be paying a visit to the facilities here at Breakers point within the week! I was going to tell everyone at morning council but the word is already old, so it's not a secret.'

'Not much is within these walls,' the other staff member mentioned humorously.

'True. But why would he be coming here?'

'There are some unofficial test flights he has asked to be present at. We've planned to invite him to this ward for inspection. I can't guarantee he will ask to see your work, but there's always that chance!'

'Well, he's welcome any time he likes, within the regular hours. I'm sure the children will be at their usual, and that ought to liven up his visits!'

They smiled at the thought, but the superintendent quickly spoke. 'Well, yes they do. But keep that in mind. He is due in six days from today.'

'We will. Anything else?'

The superintendent looked around in thought. 'The Seren Planetoid just entered Tesser, and has left the Utopian system.'

'I trust trade went well.'

'More or less,' she replied.

Montsi knew the "less" he spoke of was that rather embarrassing incident with one of the diplomats they had sent. You'd think he would have had more decency that that. Apparently he was still at large, hiding somewhere. Best to put that behind them now, fate would catch up with him on day, and punish him then.

'Well, let's hope for some more 'more' then, shall we?' she said.

'Good idea. Well, back to work!'

Montsi turned and almost walked over little Jacinth. She bent down with habit to straighten her emerald green headband.

The child spoke. 'The Governor isn't going to come to class,' she said matter-of-factly. 'In fact, he isn't even going to set foot on Breakers point.'

'What makes you so-' but child was gone, and didn't miss a beat at her turn of Mah-jong. Montsi knew better than to pursue it, but there was a foreboding finality in what the child had said. She was using her 'prophet of doom voice'. Montsi had quickly come to know that voice from the time one of the children had burnt himself, or when Chanah had taken a turn. Jacinth had seen them all long before they happened, and timed them each to the moment. Now she'd told her something else, and said so much with so little.

Montsi wondered what it could mean, other than not needing to straighten up the bookshelves... she did not know.

Time fast spent

(Morning, 5 days ago.)

He struggled through the darkness about him. Events from the past and creations of a future fused incoherently in a downpour of images. They were all too loud, too sharp, and too painful. Token struggled to regain his lost mastery. His body was probably writhing in fits of agony again. He felt detached from reality, and covered in pain.

For a moment the restless images began to clear and a familiar mind entered his, mocking him with truth, *You are wounded.*

Master, please, please, help me! He begged piteously.

No. You will learn strength from your weakness. You were a fool to underestimate her, as I knew you would. Now I shall have to take matters into my own hands. Don't worry. Leave the work to me now. Important things are taking place, we cannot risk having them interfering. Rest Token. Your adversity will make you stronger. Rest.

The voice and mind began to recede and the agony beset him once more.

No Master Taalk, Please! He begged, but the voice was gone.

Alasia had returned home to find others had already let themselves in.

She looked into the face of a man she did not know. He was aged, sporting short hair of grey wintry strands. Although he looked old, he spoke and acted with vigour, implying a passion he found in his career. His voice was calm and authoritative, and his eyes were the lightest shade of grey. He wore the same black uniform, but without the broadened shoulders or even a cape. He was unarmed, and curiously didn't even wear a copper band on his brow, or any sort of banding for that matter. No one she knew lived nowadays without a headband of some kind. Alasia might have felt better inclined to speak with him, apart from the dozen fully armed black guards he'd apparently felt the need to bring with him.

By the time she'd entered her bodyguard was already on the floor with a weapon at his face. Her very first fickle thought was that now somebody would have to clean up the blood... but then she'd noticed the guards. They were a more elite group than most. Their faces were concealed behind black metallic masks, and they'd taken up position all over the room. Into her choicest recliner sat the old man whom she now studied. Admittedly, the unexpected scene had actually caused her a moment of contemplation before she'd decided to act.

'How dare you!' Words flung like stalactite daggers from her icy lips. 'If you have any inclination-'

'Alasia, calm down,' he said soothingly, as though all this had been an unfortunate misunderstanding between children. 'You surprise me. Usually you treat your guests to a better reception.'

She stood up very close to one guard and stared right into his black masked faced. If he noticed her, he made no sign. They were trained well. 'Usually,' she retorted, 'they don't bring so many of their friends.'

The old man laughed. 'You will excuse the guards; we thought you might be bringing some of your new associates over.'

She turned to look at him. 'My friends are out at the moment.'

He waved her casually aside, 'Oh, I wasn't referring to *those* friends. I meant the new ones. The ones you met tonight.'

Alasia swallowed her apprehension. He was too calm. So she was in trouble. The Government wasn't usually this sudden, or severe. Maybe she really was in as much trouble as that man with the emerald eyes had hoped to avoid for her? Yet who really was he and those he travelled with? And who was this ranking official before her? Perhaps he too would succumb to... persuasion.

A mind touched hers. It was the old man's, *I know your thoughts, child. They are an open book to me.*

Alasia stepped suddenly back. She quickly recalled all the schemas and incantations she'd learnt and practiced to avoid mind reading. The guard on her left moved unexpectedly in an attempt to remove the banding from her head, but an icy glance from the old man stopped him in mid-motion, and he returned to his vigilance.

'Who are you?' Alasia demanded, suddenly aware that the tension was more than evident in her voice.

The old man laughed. He seemed to find this entertaining. 'Lord Admiral Taalk, High Commander; Supply Admiral and psychic division of the government. And you,' he spake, looking into her, 'are suspected of Resistance activities.'

Alasia gasped a half-practised, half-genuine gasp of disbelief. She felt a little dizzy, and steadied herself on the nearest soldier, whose arm was like iron – very good for leaning on. This old man was very high-ranking indeed.

'So, talk,' she demanded - no sense in burying suspicion with thin lies.

At his signal the entire group of soldiers moved swiftly to leave. Her bodyguard was hauled swiftly to his feet and out the door. The Admiral motioned for Alasia to sit, and offered her one of her drinks he'd helped himself to.

She continued to stand.

He looked up at her and smiled, and relaxed back into the chair. 'Four days ago we monitored a transaction of illegal investments from an apartment in the southern blocks. Our tracers returned the information back to you, though I admit, we had to convince the owner of the apartment that talking to us was the best thing for the People.' He sat forward in the chair. 'We know you were there 'Angel', and how you profited by this man. Your actions were illegal, and shunned by all right-thinking citizens of the State!'

His words smashed into her in sound and thought, rendered potent in his practiced telepathy.

He sat back in his chair. 'Nevertheless, we might be able to forget this little incident, even let you manage those accounts, once you change the names and return them fully to the rightful property of the People. And assuming you stick to the lawful employ provided you by the State.'

Alasia slumped into a chair. 'You don't understand, he was alone and I...'

Oh, I understand child. You are young and fresh. And he offered you... incentives. It is a mistake too often made by the youth. Don't worry, he has been reprimanded for taking advantage of you. Now, we need to assure the People that you have their interests first at heart.

'In voice, please,' requested Alasia. He was a very powerful psychic not to require a banding or some form of link to communicate directly with her. She knew what was to be required of her. Something like this had happened to one of her more ambitious friends in the government tourist agency just recently. Come to think of it, she hadn't heard from Karen in too long a time.

'It is an assignment that I think will suit your particular talents well, and, oh don't worry Angel, I wasn't referring to *that*,' he said, leering at her.

He tried his drink again. 'It has to do with that small group of dissidents that are within the walls.'

'Really,' she replied sarcastically.

'It would be advisable to listen child. The dark-haired man you met tonight is an enemy to the people, a corrupter of minds. He is travelling in the company of a high ranking Resistance leader and her other bodyguards.'

'What is it you expect me to do?' she demanded.

'Child, ask not what you must do for the People! I cannot force your will. All we ask is that you help us capture and liberate these dissidents for the sake of Seren. You do want peace, don't you?'

She glared at him in obstinate silence, oozing disdain at the rehtoricity of the question. *Of course.*

'Good, then it is settled. You place this message stone on any one of their persons, preferably their leader. We will come. I know that you will find the peace of conscience your heart needs for your services. After all, we wouldn't want your actions to cause you to a restriction of your options in life, would we?' His voice was soft but authoritative, as though he'd had this conversation a thousand times before.

Alasia sat in silence, looking at her nails. One was looking a little out of shape, and she would have to attend to it sometime. But she had heard the message, and permitted the small black orb to fall into her palm.

He hadn't asked. Just hinted...

... so they'd finally found her anyway? So what, she could still find a way to make this fun.

The old man sat forward and looked at her seriously. 'These rebels are dangerous people, Alasia. Take care. That woman leader is responsible for countless acts of terrorism, sabotage and murder. I'm not pretending that this isn't dangerous. Take care, young one.'

His palm brushed her forehead in blessing as he stood to leave. Her body guard, little more wounded than in pride, took post near the portal and shut it respectfully as the grey-eyed man softly left.

She continued studying her hands.

Alasia began to think. He was far too high ranking for this to be a minor assignment. It meant something to them. And why they should send her? Perhaps she really had come to their attention much sooner than he let on? Her mind raced over options and issues for what was not said, as much as what was. Why had they not sent a denizen, or a spy after them? Didn't they already have someone in there? Perhaps they weren't as efficient as they liked people to believe? Was that why the Admiral did not deal with this himself? Perhaps there was some way that she could profit from all this yet...

She stood, and went to access her terminal. It was surprisingly willing to share government information previously more difficult to obtain, the first of many 'gifts' for her new assignment, no doubt. Texts on espionage, Resistance activities, and detailed personal profiles on all individuals involved in the assignment were all set to direct synaptic download. After some digging, information on some low-level covert government operation protocol was also available to her. What was most interesting of all, however, was that the new books open for perusal also included alpha level codes and operating instructions for tutor level government spies.

Perhaps life was about to become more interesting from here on after all.

--- + --- + --- + ---

The door rang again. He ignored it obstinately. It was rude, and he wished it could hold conversations until he wanted them.

He activated the panel, but not before wrapping himself in a loose robe. He did not recognise the two men who stood before him, nor did they give any indication of why they were out at this hour.

'Senator Breen, leader of Government foundry works?'

'Yes, it is I. Who are you, and what are you doing out at this forge fired hour?' He asked in a gruff, aged voice.

'It's my friend here. She has been hurt. We were told you might be able to help. Could you, please?'

'And just who is it that might have told you?'

'Someone you might know by the name of Angel?'

Her! What would she be doing collecting this kind of favour?! He looked out at the two men again and the unconscious woman he could now see that they held. She was a reasonably pretty woman with chestnut hair. He pitied her, but considered for a moment following protocol and turning them away. They could be trouble, or mean harm, but the men looked sincere, particularly the broad shouldered one that spoke. Besides, if Angel had sent them, he knew it would not be prudent ignoring her collecting on the favour he owed.

He scanned their identi-chips before deciding, then as they checked out, he opened the door and invited them in.

'Ursha!' he called to his assistant and aide. 'We need your help here.'

The golem aide walked unquestioningly in and began investigating the woman they laid on the broadchair. Administrator Breen watched the young men. It looked as though they had been in some sort of trouble. The black haired one bent over the woman, while the broad one spoke. He had genuine, almost puppy dog type features.

'We appreciate you doing this for us. We owe you the greatest favour.'

'Who are you, man, and what brings you to the foundry council offices?'

'We're inspectors from KiKaan province,' he answered, looking down at the female. 'Assistor Michelle experienced some kind of psyonic episode near a gravinodic field several hours ago. We tried to look for help but facilities are somewhat wanting in the foundries themselves.'

'Oh really, I inspected them myself only two weeks ago and I found them to be quite adequate.' Replied the senator boldly, but without conviction.

His aide spoke up, 'she is suffering acute, but minor, psychotoxin shock. I don't know how this could have been caused by anything other than a trained telepath.'

'Can you treat her?' the dark haired man blurted, almost fiercely.

'Of course she can,' replied the senator. 'I'll have security increase the scans. I'm glad you came to me with this, boys. I'm sure you'll understand the need to keep this incident... quiet.'

'If you're suggesting we keep this out of our reports!' The black haired one said indignantly.

He was waved aside by the broad one. 'Provided she is cared for.'

His aide initialised treatment, and was explaining something to the dark haired man as the senator went to get drinks. He occurred to him how this could turn out to be the opportunity he needed to restore his standing with his superiors. If there was trouble – was there ever not trouble – and he resolved it, well, then that could be very good for his career.

On getting the drinks, he checked his terminal for reports, and scanned them for the visitors from KiKaan province. To his surprise, none were listed as government surveyors, only assistance and utilities. How had these strayed so far from assignment? The woman in the next room began to speak deliriously, a good sign, just as he was entering the room, questions poised on his lips.

'You young men-' he began, and the ill woman interrupted.

'Officer Glenn... the long haired... Did you-' she sat bolt upright. 'We've got to get this secret information to Resistance headquarters immediately!'

The room went deathly silent.

'You're not from KiKaan province, are you?' The senator stated.

--- +++ --- +++ ---

He sat alone in the shattered remains of his once proud office. He waited, for he knew they would come for him soon. To have let the Resistance people into his own apartment, to have helped them! It would be the final act.

They'd managed to blast a new exit into his wall. A giant mech soldier with a gun for an arm had made it the instant after she'd finished speaking. Their escape was impressively well planned. By the time security was around they were already half a block away, and then into a skipper and straight up to the upper city. They had disabled the defences and timed it beautifully. There was little anyone could do to stop them.

There was an explosion down the hall. Probably the door he'd locked in a last moment act of defiance at their coming. It wasn't fair. After all he'd done for the people! And now they were coming for him. And he'd never gotten to finish that book he was writing – a third-person autobiography of a mistreated youth who rose to become the Senator of the foundries of the greatest city in the known galaxy. It would have been an influential book, he was sure.

There were footsteps now. His aide and servants were long gone. He was alone now, for none stood by him. He recalled his son, and was proud of him in spite of his self-servitude. He would serve the people well. He recalled a woman, who once thanked him tearfully for restoring her employment after she had been brought in from outside the wall. He wondered why he had never collected on the favour she owed him, but then realised, it did not matter.

Shadows crossed his doorway. They were here.

He stood then to face them, and for the first time in his life seriously wondered if perhaps there was a God, and if now was a good time to find out. Because if there was, it would only be a moment before he knew.

Request for sanctum

(Evening, 5 days ago)

Alasia watched as the Resistance operatives crossed the crowded mezzanine, bouncing on her heals nervously. They had moved quickly in only one day since they had left the foundries. Their leader was up again, undoubtedly after being treated by that fool factory senator. At least he'd had the decency to answer the favour he owed her. She walked briskly beside the large man who wore a cape over one arm. The others were there, forming a rough circle around her of several dozen meters. Impressive! You could not tell they were a group unless you knew what to look for.

The man she had been searching for was on the right flank now, dark hair shining in the light of a forgotten sun. Watching him, she found herself thinking how easy this was going to be. Betrayal was not her specialty, but self-servitude certainly was. All she had to do was to make them trust her.

She alighted from the carriage, her veil waving in the wind. She was accustomed to being outside, but not to being alone. If she wanted to succeed, this was something she was going to have to get used to.

Their group was turning towards her and the carriages, as she had anticipated. She waited till it was time, then moved to intercept the man Matrix. Perhaps it was the oldest ploy in the book, but it would work for her today. No sooner had he crossed her path than she all but stepped right into him, dropping her entire bundle. Without thinking, he bent down to help pick things up.

'Oh, I'm sorry, I wasn't watching where I was going,' she apologised.

'That's OK,' he said quickly, keeping an eye on his friends.

'No, really, I shouldn't have,' she moved into his field of vision.

'No, it's OK,' he reiterated impatiently, and stood to leave.

'Perhaps I can buy you a drink?' She said.

'No,' he replied sternly. 'It's-'

He paused to look beyond the veil, then turned abruptly to leave.

'No, wait!' she begged, surprising herself at the sincerity in her voice. 'I need you, your help. They found out. I had to get away. I have nowhere to go...'

He turned to face her. 'You'll be no safer with us.'

'I don't think so,' she said.

He looked her over. 'And you'll need to be serious; once we leave, you cannot return.'

She did not believe him.

'I can look after myself, and you,' she informed him impetuously, yet almost promising herself.

He looked impatient. With a swift gesture he motioned her to follow, and then as an afterthought he turned and carried the bundle for her.

By the time they reached the carriage the others were not impressed. They stood looking down at the two. The brunette flanked by the strange, stout man and the large one with the cape. They were hidden from the daylight by the carriage roof.

'She will mean bad luck to you if you take her on Matrix,' the stout one was saying. 'You should think with your... heart.'

'Hearts can change.'

'It is unlikely that she would provide a tactical advantage,' the taller one spoke deeply in what might have been... tact.

'Perhaps, but I have right to sponsor whom I will. Besides, she has requested my help.'

'You cannot help everyone, you know,' the tall one responded. He was gruff and masculine in a way Alasia found attractive. Probably half machine. Even better...

'I answer to no man,' she said, glaring defiantly at the three. 'Besides, you may find my talents... useful. As you have once before.'

They conferred in silence.

'She has helped me once, and you Commander,' the man they called Matrix stated. 'Now I intend to help her.'

There was real intent in his voice. It saddened her. Was he so untouched by the world? How did a man like this ever come to be? The others looked uncomfortable. The brunette stepped forward and finally spoke.

'You would leave all you have here to assist us? Why?'

'There is nothing for me here now.'

The other woman looked at her, and soon Alasia felt another mind reaching out. A powerful mind, it reminded her of the Admiral. It softly caressed her thoughts, studied her motives. But not too deeply. It was not intrusive, just curious. She felt as if the other woman greatly wanted the truth, but would not take it, at least not yet.

'You renounce your pledge to the Government?'

'Yes.'

A moment passed as the psychic considered, then she asked another simple question, 'Are you telling us the truth?'

The others looked surprised at the question, as if she should know or didn't usually ask. And if it wasn't evident until now, it certainly was in the way she looked at her: the psychic did not trust Alasia.

She glared back at the woman on the carriage, 'I am willing to start a new life. I don't expect your trust; I would not give it easily if I were in your place. But you'll find I have more to offer than you are willing to admit.'

She stared confidently at them, and it seemed to convince the others. That, or the doors were signalling the need to close. They hurriedly stepped on. They had managed to draw a little attention to themselves, but it looked as though that would pass on. Alasia and the brunette exchanged cold stares, until Matrix deliberately or accidentally positioned himself between them, looking at neither. The others relaxed.

Their leader whispered something to Matrix, who then began explaining basic protocol to her. The basic message was stay low and out of trouble until "We can get you to safety".

'Why are we using voice?' She whispered closely to his ear.

'Because the government may be expecting telepathic signals,' he whispered so close that she could feel his breath along the back of her neck. It felt good. Perhaps he was beginning to relax?

'What about the sensors?'

'That is what he is for,' Matrix replied, pointing to the cloaked man. 'He is a mech man. His fittings give him some unique abilities.'

'Oh,' said Alasia, though it was something she already knew. 'And who is she? Some kind of telepath?'

'I'm not going into details, but yes, and she is very important.'

Yeah, to you, thought Alasia. He was playing right into her hands, but she knew she could not use the stone, not here, not while the psychic was undistracted. It would take time, perhaps days.

Then the large man shifted in his stance. Matrix ended mid-sentence and began talking about the weather. The psychic took a seat and stared out, looking in every way as common as any of the occupants of the scenic carriage.

'It's the sun I think,' Matrix was saying. 'It's the green hue that really brings out the gardens. I think we should stay here for a few more weeks after trading. Surely the Government can afford the time?'

'It's the copper ions in the nebula that bring out the hue, not the sun, remnants of a battle over a thousand years ago.' Corrected Alasia, though Matrix looked like he didn't really know what she was talking about. Their discussion continued for much the same, he commenting and she correcting. It was a game she played sometimes for men who thought they knew too much, though he just needed some livening up. She could see it was beginning to annoy him, and that gave her some sadistic delight. He was rescued only when the caped man moved position again, and the psychic stood to talk to her.

'Perhaps you can help, Alasia. We need to get to a terminal. One that is a little out of the way.'

'Certainly, there is one at Tigre Park.'

'No good,' claimed Matrix. 'Last time I was there it was in an open park. Not very defensible.'

'Well,' said Alasia. 'How about Rikka? The terminal there is right inside the wall. Near the nineteenth pylon. You should be right to access it there, though it'll take half a day to arrive in this carriage.'

'Perfect. Can we use your codes?'

'Yes, but you'll only have fifteen minutes at best. Less to be safe. Even less if they expect us to be together, we have been seen in company, you know.'

'Convenient, isn't it?' The psychic stated with surprising accusation. What was she playing at, and if she was a telepath?

'Yes, quite,' Alasia shot back.

The cloaked man moved again and the argument was brought to a sudden halt. They waited out the rest of their journey in silence until it was time to disembark. Alasia wondered what she might have done to warrant such ire from their leader, though she had been unkind when she was wounded before, and psychics were such strange people. It was probably her clearly repressed desire for this man Matrix, though what the connection between them was, she could only guess.

Alasia shook her head. They didn't look all that dangerous. Disliking this woman was only going to make her task easier. She knew also, that when she succeeded, there would be other "favours" to be asked of her in her new relationship with the Government. She wondered if, perhaps after all, there was such a thing as fate, and if it had always designed for her to end up in this placement.

---++---++---++---

I-olo Tilk, Understudy to the Supply and Reconnaissance Admiral for the Resistance munitions wing sat in grave concern. His reception at the Circle had not been what he'd expected. They had been cold, cut his report short, and dismissed him early. As always, he'd not seen their faces, and as always, he was left assuming they knew many things he didn't.

He passed down the corridor and looked at some art that had been placed there by one of his assistants. He realised there might have been a window there, but they were almost a kilometre under the surface, almost an hour from under the wall. It saddened him.

He puzzled once again over the information as he had this past half week. All organised Resistance four thousand kilometres from the maws were destroyed or forcibly abandoned. The enemy was going to attempt something on a larger scale, he was sure. But what was the Resistance going to do about it? The Circle had been silent. Perhaps they, too, were afraid.

As if on cue his chief assistant spoke.

Message for you sir, Beta Priority. Unknown caller and origin.

He hurriedly activated his armband and the blue light filled his vision. When it cleared he was standing in a room with no doors, his private office.

He activated the terminal. A soldier he did not recognise was on it. 'Your name and rank.'

'Glenn Baker. Unit leader - Dogs of war. I speak on behalf of Commander Sheelaakah, leader-'

'It relieves me greatly that you are safe. We have not heard anything. How is the Commander?'

'Occupied in surveillance, but safe. Understudy, we have urgent information.'

'Speak.'

'I am downloading to your location details of government activities accessed by the Commander inside Seren. Our recent visit to Utopia is no accident: The government is planning another annexation.'

'We feared as much, but the details you provide us with will be invaluable. The Circle expresses its profound gratitude for your efforts.'

'Sir, my men?'

'Two thirds of the troops that abandoned the outposts have returned. Many of your troops are among them. Now, tell me more of the Commander?'

'She suffered low level psychotoxin shock in an encounter with an unknown government telepath, but she has recovered.'

'She will need further medical attention.'

'She insists she is all right, sir. What are our orders?'

Before answering, as he was inclined to order the Commander to report to the hospital, the understudy looked briefly over the data. He had to look twice before he understood what he was seeing. This annexation was more than double the total of the entire previous decade. It would mean the annexation of the entire Utopian system! The blood drained from his face and his fingers paled.

'*Get* to the Maws immediately. We have to get a message to the Utopian system. Monitor activities and await further instructions.'

'Yes si-'

He was cut short as the link abruptly broke. In the moments remaining before I-olo Tilk thought he saw light blasts and smelt the char of burnt flesh. He remained there stunned for a moment, and then broke off the link.

His mind was racing, until he reined it in. They had to assume the Commander was now dead. An incalculable loss - but her sacrifice would live on. This information would assist the Resistance adequately prepare for the newest annexation. Their sacrifice would be remembered.

For always.

Very annoying

(4 days ago)

Admiral Taalk gazed into his crystal sphere. The ambush at Rikka had been a complete failure. These rebels were proving remarkably resilient, a factor, perhaps, of their self-sacrificing devotion to their cause. The woman he had sent was in their midst, but as yet had not fulfilled her assignment. It was indeed a concern. Perhaps she was growing attached to one of them? Or to their cause? It was a possibility.

They were talking now. Their leader, the chestnut-haired female Token had underestimated, was certainly the most interesting. Now he watched her: So focused, so intense. But he could see inside her. It was her pain that drove her on. Images of her life flashed briefly before him. So, he mused, was he also a memory of her soul?

They were separating into three groups now. His new spy had again lost her opportunity. Perhaps the battle had not been a complete loss. Even if the spy failed she was still fulfilling her role. She worked well with the others – they were a skilled group. And while she held the message stone he was free to monitor those she travelled with.

He looked to see which path the leader took. She travelled now with only the Cybot. Tactically very impressive. The admiral watched her move on, without wasting any time on unnecessary thought, gracefully and deceptively gentle. No wonder many had underestimated her gift. Her face was still young, in spite of the war she insisted on maintaining.

Suddenly she stopped. For a moment she paused, and then she spun around to look directly at him. She'd found his scrying sensor. Suddenly the image quickly twisted and blurred, and he found himself staring at an opaque, lifeless stone.

Impressive.

She was good.

…very, very good…

--- + --- + --- + ---

Sheelaakah looked out on the endless forests of the wilderness beyond. She'd only ever been here twice before, and each time the trees impressed her with their sheer height. A hundred men around could not circumscribed the smallest ones, and no direct sunlight would ever reach the ground. But they were alive, and deep. The sheer weight of their combined age inspired her, reminding her of the insignificance of her own life against them.

'Come,' Bakerson offered.

She'd felt his rising nervousness, but been lost in the space of the giant trees to notice.

'Yes,' she agreed, forgetting rank for a moment in the depths of her meditation, deeply grateful to be away from the deadened sway of the endless minds of the city within. The wildness was like a breath of fresh air in many ways.

A flash of light stove past her consciousness: Bakerson was in danger. Telekinetically she removed the spears from the air before he'd even noticed they were there.

'Mutants,' he roared, filling the near bushes with the fire of his weapon. Their enemies fell back, wounded.

'I count almost a score of them,' Sheelaakah informed him. That was not too many, if they could intimate enough of them. She reached out, finding their group mind. It was strange, dissonate. Violent… yet afraid. It would not be hard… it should not be hard…

But it was.

She looked up to find Bakerson standing over her. What was happening?

Sheelaakah's last conscious thought was to notice the poison tipped blowdart thorn protruding from the back of her right hand.

---++---++---++---

By now Alasia was beginning to get on Matrix's nerves. She would not stop talking, as though something was gnawing at her conscience.

He was back in the sewers again, after seven years. The fighting at Rikka had broken out in the tunnel while Dogman was talking to someone in Resistance and then the Commander had required they divide into three groups, each with the intent of passing the kilometre thick wall that surrounded Seren city. The masked black guards had brought flight suits this time, making them harder to evade. Having Commander Sheelaakah and her intense psychic abilities had helped immensely, and improved moral. But they were separated now and in three groups making their way over, under and through the wall. It was no great surprise, but the Commander had ordered Matrix and the singer – Angel as she wanted to be called – to form one group and to take the under wall tunnels. The singer insisted then and now that it was all a plot to have them killed, but Matrix saw it as a test of his navigation and knowledge of the underparts of Seren.

She was complaining about the moss now, complaining that the Government allowed these tunnels to exist which apparently she, and no-one else, knew about. Complaining about a stylist and a magazine. Complaining, complaining. Perhaps it was how she dealt with her nervousness?

'Look,' he finally said in exasperation, 'here, have this.'

'What is it?' she asked, taking the coloured cube from his hand.

'A multifaceted Hexagonal Polygon, just something I picked up inside the citadel. Each of the six sides can be arranged to make patterns or to be of one colour, and it rotates around its three primary axis. It is an ancient mind puzzle, by the people of Terran Third I believe. Got it a while back. It should keep you busy.'

Matrix smiled and turned to the tunnels again. It had taken him six months to master it after acquiring it one day long ago.

The tunnels. Again they branched. He took the one leading up because, from experience, those were the ones that were safer. Still, they were tramping through dampness, Alasia somewhat unsteady. And though she seemed distracted by her task, it didn't stop from talking one bit. 'I once had this opportunity to speak at a convention for family and affiliated businesses. It was quite an experience you know. They were talking about resourcing for advertising, you know, how hard they try and publicise it. So few choose it nowadays. Anyhow, I met this guy, professor of theoretical maths at the eighth university. He told me about this fifth dimensional polygon. It reminds me of this one.' Pause for breath. 'They try and sell love you know, with their value-laden advertising. But I think you can't buy love. You can't even control it, just float down the torrent of its motion. Beginning and ending all the time. Frankly I don't know how some couples keep together for a lifetime.'

'It's a commitment, I think,' Matrix tried to input.

'Oh, I know how they say that it gets deeper with time, like some sort of spiral with change and continuity. I just think you'd get giddy doing that all the time and... There, finished.'

Matrix turned to stare at the cube, all six faces aligned in a single colour each. He looked up at the woman.

'Elementary. See, if you assign an alphanumeric to the central square, then a number to each of the remaining 8 faces per side moving from left to right...'

The rest was lost to him.

'...and it's all quite simple really. So is this the way were going?' She asked and walked on.

Matrix hurried to catch up. The puzzle had afforded him no respite. Perhaps the Commander really had sent him to be slain by her incessant chatter? It was becoming a distinct possibility, and Matrix was beginning to wonder if there wasn't an element of truth in what Dogman had said about her being "bad luck". Still, she'd solved the puzzle easily, and in under two minutes. What else was she capable of?

He had to find the Commander again. He was wondering how she was doing. Either that, or he would be driven mad by the singers incessant nervous chatter. Surely the Commander and Skion had found their way outside the wall by now?

But the tunnel, and the singer, went on, and on, and on...

--- + --- + --- + ---

By the time Sheelaakah came to the blood was beginning to rush to her head and pulsate painfully against her temples. Her banding was off. They had used some form of poisoning to anaesthetise her, then taken them to their village outside the citadel walls. It was ironic; a tragic, careless exit from the citadel after their heroic flight from the ambush during Commander Bakerson's communiqué with Resistance headquarters. She was beginning to think that dividing their groups was not a particularly sound idea after all, though it was obvious that some long-range psychic had knowledge of their location and they needed to divert the prying eye. Otherwise, they would again have been easily found out back in the citadel eventually. At least she had dealt with that threat. Intuition told her that it had something to do with Alasia, though she had no proof. Now, however, their fate was no better.

From where she was hanging, upside down, Sheelaakah could make out the humanoids amidst the forest and trash yards. They were tormenting a male - Officer Bakerson tied half naked to a pole next to the campfire. They were poking him with red embers. He stood unmoving, in obvious pain, yet refusing to retaliate.

Shee peered to her left. They had torn Skion's arm off and rigged him to some sort of generator. They were using him to power the dim lighting from the macabre scene.

'Careful,' a profoundly deep voice spoke from outside her line of vision. The harassment ceased. 'Their Priestess awakens. If she tries anything, knock her out. We'll eat her tomorrow.'

Sheelaakah did not have to move to recognise the clear signature of a fellow psychic that spoke. He was a tall male, with an unusual mental signature. She took a good look at the figures around Bakerson, crouched and deformed. They appeared female, like unfortunate witches, vexed with warts, unkempt hair and rags for clothing, their skin a pallor of mottled blue. They stared in a mixture of awe and fear at her helpless state, then returned cackling to their debauched entertainment.

A sudden movement caught her eye. Now off to the left she saw a humanoid armed with a huge club watching over her, and she knew that at the signal that club would send her to silence again, or worse. She stared at the man, and at first wasn't sure of what she was looking at. He was deformed and twisted in the lamplight, bald all over and covered in impossible muscle. A mutant.

So they had fallen capture to the hated mutants, barely making their exit from a disused refuse channel from the city. It was then she realised who must have spoken. So, she would finally have the opportunity to meet Karl Brek'anarl, the mighty leader of the mutants. Rejected by most citizens of the galactic empire as genetic impurities, Seren was no exception. Yet still the mutants managed to survive in the wilderness beyond, affiliated with neither the Resistance nor the Government. They lived off the trash that filtered through the gates of the city, and other more unfortunate travellers. Their cities stretched for miles and were violent, unspoken places everyone chose to forget.

Officer Bakerson roared in pain. They were attempting to push something into his eye.

'No!' she shouted, and struggled against her bonds.

The females cackled a wicked glee.

A strange sound like a bark issued from the deep voiced male, and the crones stepped away from the bleeding soldier. She saw her mutant guard move, but he did not strike. She watched Glenn straighten, and then his eyes widened in awe at the figure which began to appear from Sheelaakah's right. A mammoth of a man, twice the height of any she had beheld previously. His skin was scaled, a mottled blue, with huge caresses of muscle underneath. His teeth jutted from his jaw like tusks. He wore no clothes except the barest fur loincloth, and his copper banding looked like it had been welded into his very scalp. He crouched down, and tilted his head to look at her. He reached out and held her by the throat with two callused inhuman fingers.

'I give the orders here,' he said in a voice so deep it was difficult to hear. Shee was repulsed by the gore on his hands, and the acrid venom in his breath. She strived to gain control of her mind, and would fight before he gained any victory in her suffering. She looked at the monster, and decided not to grant them an offer to join the Resistance. If they chose to live like beasts they were welcome to die like them.

'Who are you?' he quietly said, and as she looked into his eyes, was surprised to see the spark of humanity within.

She spoke. 'Commander Sheelaakah, of the Resistance-'

'A valuable prize, should we need to bargain with the unevolved within the walls!' He shouted to the others, who cheered in praise. So she had misjudged his potential for rationale after all. If she struck hard enough and forcefully enough she might be able to render him unconscious before he could do anything.

Slowly he turned and grinned a wicked smile. 'All I need do,' he said, and with his two fingers painfully jerked her head back and towards the earth. There was incomprehensible strength in those fingers. She felt Officer Bakerson's empathy at her plight.

A voice from behind suddenly called. 'Nimka! Brek'anarl, go shum Te tak-ri!' The titanium grip loosened and suddenly let go. A figure step boldly and swiftly into the light.

It was Matrix.

--- + --- + --- + ---

His life was beginning to flash before him, when his colleague Matrix had intervened. They had the Commander by then too.

Next thing he knew, his tormentors were lifting him down from the pole and untying his hands. He fell face first into the dirt, but was lifted kindly by the very females who had been harming him. They looked truly sorry for what they had been doing.

Unit leader Glenn now lifted his head to see them taking the Commander from the tree where they had suspended her feet first. She looked very angry. He heard Matrix's voice off somewhere close, and he tried to look. But all he could see was the huge mutant who had single handedly subdued both he and Skion after they had poisoned the Commander just moments before.

Skion. Glenn looked around to see him. He was tied up to some sort of mechanic device. Glenn limped his way towards him, while the female mutants tried to support him. He approached the machine, but did not have to touch to know: his soul print was not there.

He turned desperately, looking for aide. Incredibly, the singer with black hair was also there. She was trying to put something over his eye, but Glenn pushed her aside.

'Skion!' He cried to the others, 'he's in trouble!'

Matrix came quickly, as did the Commander. One of the females started shaking some beads over the silent soldier's head, while another salivated heedlessly over his human muscles.

Despite his weakened condition Glenn pushed them disgustedly away. Skion was wired to some sort of generator, his entire mechanic arm missing. He heard shouting. Others were crowding in.

'It's OK,' the Commander consoled him. 'There is nothing we can-'

'No, it's not,' he desperately replied. He looked into the face of the soldier he respected. 'He must not die today.' Something about it was all wrong. He tried pulling the false wiring from his body. The lights died.

'It is not his time!' He repeated.

Matrix put a hand on his shoulder, which he shrugged off.

He did not know what else to do. He knelt. The singer leapt back in surprise – he'd heard such evidence of faith was illegal on in the City, and was not always tolerated by the Resistance. The female who had shaken the beads tried to stop him, but was stopped by a single bark from their leader. Glenn only prayed for a moment, in silence, as the camp watched. His worry stilled like a lake, and he felt a calm fill him from his inner soul. Somehow he knew, it would be all right.

He stood, and looked at Skion's sunken form.

'Live!' he shouted, and with nothing more to go on struck Skion full force in the chest with his open palm. Nothing.

'LIVE!' he cried, and hit him much harder. Suddenly the wires began to come to life. Light flooded the area from the remainder of the contraption that held him.

Skion drew a deep breath and opened his eyes.

The Commander went to him and held his eyes open, 'Skion. Are you on line.'

'Functions at ... eight per cent. But I am op.. operative.'

There was an audible sigh of relief from the allies. The mutants hid now in shadows from the light, all except their leader who stood, still sceptical, by the fire. Glenn knew to the mutants that bringing someone back to life usually took dozens of shamans and surgeons wielding the best medicines available, often nanoprobes and crystals of very fine vibrations. He'd done it with nothing more than faith.

It was some time before any of the other mutants would help the Resistance people remove Skion from his generator, or even touch him. They had probably never seen anything like it.

To be honest, neither had he.

--- + --- + --- + ---

'We were ambushed shortly after we exited the sewer. I was anaesthetised by darts, Skion by the militia. We weren't expecting mutant activity in this area. What of your story?' Sheelaakah asked the others.

'Well,' spoke Alasia on behalf of Matrix, 'he half expected it, and we had a choice of three exits. Lucky he chose the one he did, or we might not have found you in time.'

Shee nursed her aching arms. Indeed it was true. His knowledge of this place had saved them all again.

'Now we wait until morning to move on?' suggested Bakerson.

'Indeed,' Sheelaakah commanded. 'We have time, and cannot arouse suspicion. Let us hide in the crowd tonight.'

'Are you sure about that?' inquired the singer.

'What? Don't like your taste of life outside your walls?' A resonating, deep voice asked again. It was Karl Brek'anarl, the mutant leader. Sheelaakah felt the circle of allies tensed.

Matrix invited Karl to sit with them, to the veiled displeasure of the others.

He moved to crouch on the ground, not exactly in the circle around the fire, but within arm's reach of most of them. Skion sat welding his gun arm back on, and did not flinch or acknowledge the mutant leaders presence in any way.

Matrix seemed to feel the need to apologise on their hosts behalf, 'You must forgive the mutants; their ways are not our ways.'

'I know!' Alasia gasped, 'not too friendly to guests, are you. What were you doing that to Puppyman anyway?'

'Softening him up for eating,' Karl said unapologetically.

There passed a moment of silent horror.

'Now what!' Asked Alasia, her voice belaying a hysterical tone. 'Do you eat us too?'

'No,' replied the mutant patiently, 'we do not eat "Je tak-ri".' He said, turning to Matrix, 'our "Friends".'

'Friends?' inquired Sheelaakah in disbelief. Had they not been tortured only a few hours ago?

'Yes!' replied the giant tersely, as if impatient that they should require an explanation. 'Your Tak-ri here saved you from being tonight's dinner. Tak-ri is "friend" in our language, and friend is sacred in our belief. You are welcome to all we have, which is more than we need to survive.'

The others turned to look at Matrix. Sheelaakah knew they had many questions, but they would have to wait for that story later.

The giant stood. 'We are "GoKu nu-kia",' he spoke loudly with a broad sweep of his mutant hands, ' "People of the Evolution", born to greatness, living in sin. The confrontation of all that the unevolved do not understand, and so they fear. We have walked the valley of death, and it has returned us changed! We are the living future, and we will prevail! And though the unevolved now reject us their children will one day join us in our enlightenment!'

His sermon predicably gained the admiration of the mutants present, and while inspiring to them, made the allies feel unbearably uncomfortable.

But the giant seemed to enjoy their discomfort. He turned to face his people. 'Tonight!' he cried, 'we have gained new Tak-Ri!'

The mutants roared. There must have been dozens of them out in the shadows. Some music started up, played on skin drums and lengths of pipe. A monotone with some sort of flute sounds high above. It was driving, primitive music, far more alive than what the mutant's coarse appearance might have otherwise dictated. Some of them began a form of leaping, circular dance in the dusty circle by the fire.

It was catchy music. Even Sheelaakah had to admit to feeling its beat. Officer Matrix was almost straight to his feet, and leapt in uninhibited joy around the fire. His eyes gleamed of primal intensity. It wasn't long before he pulled the singer protesting to her feet, but she was such a natural, and quickly impressed the mutants. Officer Bakerson permitted himself to be involved, after checking first with her, though there was still much hesitation on the part of the soldier and the others.

Shee looked at Skion. He sat unheeding the music. He would not get up this night, and emanated that attitude in his posture and bearing. He appeared focused with the delicate circuitry in his arm.

Shee found herself staring into the distraction of the flames. It was burning brightly, and seemed to grant her privacy in an overcrowded place. It was noisy now, and so strange that they had gone from enemies to friends in a single moment. Shee was still wary, and was not going to let herself go this evening. She never had. Unit man Matrix was having enough fun for all of them, and seemed to have previously established good rapport with their new associates. But they were not to be trusted as allies, not yet.

The singer was making a stir, now; dancing with the giant Karl. She slid provocatively about him, looking into his eyes, although not half his size. She seemed to be enjoying the challenge. The others stopped to watch. She was very good, Sheelaakah had to admit.

She thought of herself dancing, and the thought made her uncomfortable. She realised she had only ever danced once with a man, at least that she wasn't directly related to. Daemon, how she missed him still! He had always been the social one, and allowed her to be shy. Once, when they were still home, they had been at a graduation dance, and someone had asked her for a dance. It wasn't until later that she learnt it was her brother who had arranged it all.

People seemed to keep away from the Commander. She was different: conserved, shielded, and too powerful. In some way Shee preferred it to be like that, always. There was too much lost in the past.

Sheelaakah allowed herself to return to a memory. She was only eleven at the time, but old enough to know what was going on. She was at the education facility, when suddenly all their communications had died.

'What's happening?' Her friend asked.

'I don't know,' their teacher replied calmly. But something was very wrong. They all felt it. They waited for a few moments before another teacher suddenly entered the class.

'I think we'd better get the children home.'

They started nervously for their possessions. Minutes later at their lockers her brother joined them.

'Cool! No School! Isn't this convenient!' he bragged.

'Daemon,' Sheelaakah said, 'something is wrong.'

He did not reply, but she could tell he felt it too. Things were too quiet.

Then the sirens started. And then the screaming.

They were home within minutes, it being a very small colony, towards the outer rim of the galaxy. They were preparing to terraform a fertile world, a dream that never would be. Sheelaakah was running towards their home. The ground was starting to shake; the entire defence fleet was launching. People were evacuating.

Mom! What's happening! A young Sheelaakah cried.

They colony is under attack. We have to leave.

No! Why! Who would do this?!

'I don't know,' her mother replied.

They were inside, grabbing what was most important. In that moment Sheelaakah and her brother were thrust into adulthood, and learnt what it meant to be afraid. She was just grabbing her computer stone when she first saw it – a giant tusk of metal and stone that was reaching across the stars. It would eventually fill the sky and turn it dark forever. Their world had been invited to join the great Seren Dream. They had been annexed.

Suddenly Shee was brought back to the present as the music stopped and people cheered. She stared into the fire again. Alasia had done well; the giant stood with a curious smile on his countenance. Then the music started, wild and free. It was a furious beat, and a simple repetitive dance. Shee almost wished she could forget her pain and be in there dancing.

Suddenly a hand was in front of her. It was Matrix, sweating and smiling down at her, offering a dance.

--- + --- + --- + ---

Matrix decided that Commander Sheelaakah would not benefit from more time alone, and she looked as though she was waiting to be asked to dance. So without a moment to reflect he approached her, and she did not notice until his hand was extended directly to her.

She looked up startled, she had not expected this. At least, conjectured the man, she was relaxed enough to let her mind journey.

She stared straight back at him. She did not move, but neither did he. Her surprise quickly changed to a curious expression, one of begging, or of threat. He felt she was saying; *Do not invite me in, I will only hurt you again...*

He stood unmoved, and smiling, for she also looked like a woman, and a lonely one at that. In the wild foreign he hoped she could forget rank and enjoy the moment with him, for he wanted to know her, and wanted to forgive and understand her. Besides, it had never been his policy to let a girl pass a night without a dance, and he wasn't to change that now - and she needed it even more than she knew.

She sat unmoved, his hand towards her. The soldier to her left, Skion, stopped his work momentarily and looked at the ground in front of her. If they spoke, he did not know. But when she looked at the same patch of soil the mech man resumed his labours.

The Commander looked up at Matrix, and for a moment he thought he saw the woman beneath the warring fugitive. She might have even desperately wanted to let her hair down, but feared, lest it could never be gathered up again. She looked passed him, to the swirling dancers. He motioned again for her to take his offered hand.

Suddenly, her look brightened and she grabbed him, smiled something he had never seen in a smile before, and almost dragged him to the circle.

Alasia was pleased. So the icy telepath had finally decided to melt just a little? She wasn't much of a dancer, few others were. Except that little mutant with all the fur. He was a natural at this genre, and he had such class. She danced with him now, a truly ferocious and energetic style. He moved with grace for his structure and had adapted well to work his nature and body in with his form of dance. Not at all like that brute they accepted as leader. Now she had finally met someone who she could say honestly had too much muscle. At least he was still male, and was still affected by her. She could tell. Her head was at just the right height...

It was a strange thing, but Alasia had to admit she was enjoying herself. These people were primitive, yet resourceful, and they had a native tempo that she could be well with. Her first day ever outside the city walls and things weren't so bad. So, she didn't ask what they ate for dinner, and she was planning to stay awake all night so that she wouldn't have to sleep on those pathetic covered hammocks.

It wasn't at all like she imagined it would be. When Matrix first led them out of the sewer, and pressed on without pausing to at least clean themselves up a bit, she was furious. Then he ploughed into the clearing after dragging her by the hand into the "village". Well, it wasn't a village; more like a forest with garbage hovels for houses. The smell was only barely better than the sewer, but by then she was acclimatised. Anyhow, he dragged her into a clearing without telling her what to expect, and there were the others being tortured by these monsters! It was all she could do to prevent going into hysterics. She held herself together by pretending it wasn't happening. That all this was part of an interesting discussion topic she would one day bring up.

But Matrix walked in yelling in some language she'd never heard, and right up to this giant mutant. Next thing they're all good friends and rushing to help each other out. Just like that. "Oops, small misunderstanding there. Sorry about almost eating your friend, eh, no hard feelings then?"

What were they expected to do?

Then she tried to forget, because she could not explain, the strange and sacred moment when puppy soldier brought the robot guy back to life by hitting him... it didn't matter anyway.

She had managed to make a few friends of her own tonight, though Matrix was yet to pay her the courtesy of a second dance. Little wonder, men like him seldom wrought up the courage to ask, preferring the dance daisies like the psychic, which was probably why they danced together now. They, like most, formed a kind of circle around the fire, but there were couples who still took their own feelings to dance as they wanted to in the fast, free music. She would have to ask him herself later.

They cheered as another dance closed. She stole a glance again at the psychic and the soldier. She was smiling what looked like the first real smile in decades. Her face had a healthy colour, and she was sweating in the humid night. She stumbled backwards, and found herself supported in the arms of the man with whom she had danced. And there she stayed, for far more than a moment, until another dance started.

Then, without word or explanation, she left to return to her seat by the caped manbot. Matrix watched her, without speaking, as she walked away, without looking back.

Suddenly Officer Glenn, the one who looked like a dog, grabbed Alasia by the arm. 'Danger!' he breathed quickly to her. 'Get ready to leave.'

The drums started up again. People began to dance. But the music drummed quickly to a stop as their leader slowly stood up. He looked out into the night, and hushed the others. The other camps hidden amidst the trees fell quickly silent as well.

Alasia was standing by the others. The caped robot man began preparing, affixing his arm fittings quickly, the stone in his forehead turning ugly red.

'Bikes,' whispered Bakerson.

In the next moment Alasia heard them too – what must have been an army approaching. Their leader let out a roar to rival the great waves of Seren Lake. It filled the sky and startled her. Immediately the place became a flurry of activity. Weapons were drawn, fires doused and people ran screaming.

They were there in seconds, coming quickly through the trees. There were hundreds of humanoids on bikes and plasma boards, roaring like dragons. All wore black and silver studded armour, their banners a dark shade of rebellious blue. They fired indiscriminately at anything that moved. Skion launched a volley as a mob of bikers rode towards them. Most fell, but their armour was strong. They kept coming, and quickly.

Suddenly a huge shadow crossed their view. It was the mutant Karl. With one hand he tore off the head of the nearest biker. Another sped towards him with a lance. He picked up what looked like a tank turret and easily parried the blow. In the same motion he lifted a huge battle axe, as large as a normal man, and brought it down upon his foe with such force it split helmet, driver, and the bike in two.

'Griisha! Tok to nak deninsom! Bi Su, Tak-ri!' he bellowed to them.

'Hurry!' Matrix called. 'We need to take this tunnel. It will take us to a… um.. transport.'

Screams and light fire were all around them now. Matrix led them towards a nearby tent, led to a cavern and greater safety. As she ran, Alasia stumbled to the ground on something. Mistakenly conceding to curiosity, she turned to see what it was.

She started screaming as the full meaning of war finally introduced itself to her. The disembodied head of the furry mutant she admired dancing with that night lay owner-less on the ground.

--- ++ -- + -- ++ ---

Matrix couldn't stop her from screaming. She was still screaming hysterically as he pulled her into the tunnel. She swatted defencelessly at him, trying to push him away from her. Matrix then wrapped his arms about her and dragged her further into the darkness. Several light blasts lit the cavern and Alasia began shrieking again.

They came to a cross section. The others were there; Commander Sheelaakah and unit leader Glenn Bakerson. Skion took up the rear. He pulled Alasia up to his Commander, begging her with his eyes to do something.

'She must face it alone!' The Commander callously instructed.

Matrix was struck. The humanity of the dance had obviously already worn off her; perhaps she was made of stone.

'Which way!' Dogman Glenn Bakerson shouted over the din of the nearby battle.

'Down! And to the left!' Matrix replied.

They ran down the corridor. He shouted at Alasia, commanding her to run. It seemed to help; she started taking responsibility for some of her own steps. They fled into an open storage area. Mutants were running everywhere, and did not have time to bother the allies. Deeper and deeper they went. Matrix recognised this tunnel. He'd been here before. A long, long time before.

They passed by the aquariums and past a small settlement. It became quieter as they descended. It was about this point that Alasia finally had the decency to faint, which in some ways made carrying her a lot easier. The air became moist.

'We have to take this elevator now.' He informed the others. They had reached a metal platform, and below them stretched what seemed a bottomless shaft. The lift was a dysfunctional gravity port, lowered by pullies on the deck. Without speaking Skion took the giant lever and began their slow descent in the open carriage. Soon, the only noise was their own breathing and the slow grinding of the gears. They would be safer if they could reach the transport, the battle would not touch them here.

Alasia looked deceptively calm now, her dark hair ungathered across her face. She was quite light, he thought. He looked at her thin and almost perfect features, now limp in his arms, and wondered why she had come with them, and why she had sought him in the first place. She was quite beautiful.

He looked up to see the Commander watching him unemotionally with large, dark eyes. In the next moment whatever impasse was between them was broken suddenly as Skion spoke.

'We are here.'

Matrix turned to see their transportation waiting for them. Karl had done them a great favour. He knew about the Resistance, and hated them less than the Oppression. Now they could reach into the deep underground within a day, and perhaps meet up with the Resistance there.

'Come,' Matrix said, 'they're ready to go.'

'Go?' Asked the Commander. 'How?'

'In that,' he replied, pointing to the wall.

The others looked at it. It was a strange pulsating form that swept gently away as it reached the roof. It was partitioned in sections, a dark shade of mottled purple. Each section was almost ten meters wide and reached out to the ceiling thirty meters up. They seemed to grasp it all at once: it was something alive.

'What's wrong,' teased Matrix, 'never travelled in a gargantuan rockworm before?'

'There were good reasons Resistance people avoided the deep underground.' Bakerson confessed on their behalf. 'Rockworms are just one of them.

--- ++ -- + -- ++ ---

Many hours later, Sheelaakah looked out over her unlikely crew. Alasia started weeping again, her face buried deeply in her hands. They still hadn't stopped shaking, she noticed from her vantage-point along the wall. It was cold, and they held on to their seats as they were accustomed to when their section of the worm gave another heave. They were travelling in a living cave, a giant worm over two hundred meters long, burrowing its way through the fractured rock. The mutant people had fitted it with a carriage inside sections of its interior. It was impressive, and a little claustrophobic, with a constantly shifting roof and moist, warm air. They were accompanied by the unrepentant sound of exoskeleton scraping along barren stone.

Soldier Bakerson was still seated by the weeping woman in silent empathy. His large hand resting close, but not touching. His presence would be comforting. The rest of them weren't listening any more to the woman who sat crying. She was traumatised, even a non-psychic could easily identify that. *But,* Sheelaakah thought, *in the greater scheme dealing with it fairly well.* It was, to her, a confronting. She was leaving her world and learning what life meant to "resist". Perhaps because of this she would become stronger. Or break. She was an unknown woman, with an unfamiliar mind that made her difficult to read.

Their passage gave a sudden jolt. Matrix, their guide, spoke without looking up. 'Change in rock structure. The worm will make the minor adjustment.'

Alasia stopped crying and let her hands fall from her face and onto her knees. She spoke flatly. 'What kind of adjustment?'

Matrix continued to eat, striving to spear whatever it was with his cutlery.

'A minor one,' he replied, without caring to look.

Alasia's knuckles whitened with anger.

Sheelaakah wondered, he seemed to have become uncharacteristically brief since they'd entered this giant worm.

'A minor one! What can be so 'minor' about all this!' She screamed rhetorically, her voice rising. Bakerson visibly tensed, while Matrix ignored her and officer Skion continued his regeneration undisturbed.

'I don't want to be here,' said the singer.

'There is no better way to travel through the underground of Seren,' replied Matrix.

'I wasn't referring to the mode of transport!' She shouted. 'It's this place, with you! Oh, what am I doing here!' She moaned and began crying again. Then she kicked a nearby chair fiercely away from her.

Perhaps she wasn't doing so well.

--- + --- + --- + ---

Hours later, the tears were long dried now. Alasia wiped her clammy face with weak hands. It was humid inside this horrid worm. And cold. She was feeling numb now. Having relived the horror of the battle so many times inside her mind it had finally lost all meaning. But seeing that head, fallen at her feet, the look of death in his face – that she could not forget it.

She never would.

She cried softly again. The others did nothing. No one to comfort her. It was strange. Were they frightened too? Or had they seen so much of this that they could not face someone who was pained by it?

But there was that soldier who looked like a puppy. He sat, head bowed, close by. He had not moved since she found herself in here. Had she fainted? Now that wasn't usual, for her, but nothing about this was. She regretted ever coming. She wanted out, very badly. She thought of her bed, the one that shaped itself, and its cushions, always so soft. It was so good that she sometimes didn't need to dose herself to fall asleep.

That would explain some things. Her last dose... two days ago. At least that explained why she couldn't stop crying. Or why... or something. She started sobbing, but there really wasn't anything left in it now.

The soldier puppy moved. She looked at him, and for a moment thought his lips moved. Perhaps he was praying? But then she dismissed the idea. She looked behind him, to the Robot man. He was so big and gruff, so mechanical, so unmoved and unfriendly.

She missed her friends. Would they ever sing together again? She turned to look at the psychic. Now she was taking the soup and reading something. She looked unperturbed by anything, and that just made Alasia even more angry.

Then she remembered the stone. She would get out and never play part again... Maybe she should just offer the message stone to the woman? No, she was clever, they were all wary of her. But it left Alasia wondering if this service to the People would free her, or would it only mean more "opportunities" to serve the People, like her friend and the others they'd heard of? Once you were in, you were in, and she was in deeply now.

So it was gone, all gone. The past would never return. She could not go back. As soon as she realised that it took a weight off her chest, and she stopped crying. She hated the Government, even for no reason, but loved these Resistance people no more. So all there is, she thought, was to look out for herself. She just had to pass on this message and be rid of a few insignificant Resistance fools.

--- ++ -- + -- ++ ---

Sheelaakah sighed as another hour passed.

'Where are we going?' Alasia eventually asked.

She was beginning to regain her composure, Sheelaakah realised. Perhaps there was something else to occupy her mind now?

'We're travelling towards a transport terminal where we can get a ride to a Resistance base. We will await the Commander's orders there.' Matrix gestured symbolically towards her.

Sheelaakah watched as Alasia looked at him closely.

'It has been an interesting day,' Alasia said, almost all of the tension leaving her voice. She took the hem of her dress and wiped her tear stained face. 'So tell me Matrix, tell us all. Why do you do it? Why are you here, fighting for the Resistance?' She spoke with almost natural clarity.

Sheelaakah felt the tension rise slightly in her body. Her turn was coming, and she did not want to answer that question. This was not the time to play skeletons in the closet. But she had to admit that she was curious to hear the others' answers, at least in voice.

Matrix did not look up. 'What is this place?' he asked calmly.

'You mean here, in this worm?'

'No. I mean this world.'

It was a loaded question, but Alasia handled it well. 'It is to many, many things. To most of its two trillion inhabitants, it is known as the Seren planetoid.'

'Closer to six trillion, those outside the wall aren't counted in the censuses,' Sheelaakah interjected one of her favourite facts.

Alasia flashed an angry, tear streaked glance towards her and continued '... and to most of those two or so trillion, it is heaven, a place to practice peace and discipline, family and community. To most it is home.' She proclaimed with superfluous grace.

'Yet to me, it is prison,' Matrix replied unequivocally to the woman by the wall. 'We both have lived the majority of our lives inside the walls. I left seven years ago because I was asking too many questions. I had the gall to ask why freedom requires the wall. Then my father betrayed me into the hands of the Government and they sent me outside that wall, after a few "parting reminders" of what happens to those who disturb the peace. I wasn't supposed to survive that.'

He looked across at the singer and became animated with long kept anger. 'The Government seeks to make your choices for you, it wants to control you. With knowledge and experience, it has almost become the perfect organisation to do that. But they cannot command the human soul. I was forced to leave because I could not remain silent. Because I could not stop asking questions.'

He glared in passion, and then sat back into his chair like it all meant nothing to him. After a moment he looked to officer Bakerson. 'And you, Dogman?'

Bakerson shifted uncomfortably, and replied. 'Actually, my grandfather's world was annexed over eighty years ago. He and my father both fought in the Resistance. They just wanted to return to their farming communities on the far rim, but the Oppression wouldn't allow it. After fifteen years of unheard petitions they turned to the Resistance for help. We've been fighting ever since.'

'I believe I knew your father,' Sheelaakah found herself speaking in unprecedented familiarity. 'He was Bakerson of the twelfth cannonry. I met him once as a young officer. He took his work very seriously.'

Officer Bakerson took obvious pride in the compliment, 'He was a fine man and a great example.'

'How about you, Mech man?' Alasia asked after a pause.

Skion looked up from his regeneration. He paused a moment, as if he might have considered the question beneath him. His mechanised voice informed: 'Sixteen point nine years ago I was a paid mercenary of the Congo Englomerate. The cargo I was defending fell into the energy field and we were trapped. Now I am a warrior of vengeance to this cause. In time, the Oppression will fall.'

It was a heavy comment, laden with years of hate for his enemy. But he continued in his deep, human voice. 'Now you tell us, princess: Why have you come to leev outside the walls that raised you?'

Once more, Sheelaakah got the impression that Skion did not trust Alasia either.

She attempted to deflect the question with grace. 'I am a refugee of difference. My life, different from what most are accustomed within the walls. I cannot be proud of everything I have done in life. But I live for the minute, and this minute finds me outside the wall.'

'You chirp like as if you can go back,' he replied.

She, however, did not reply. 'We have not heard from the Commander,' she evaded instead.

It was the moment Shee had dreaded, but silently prepared for.

'Yes, let us hear,' Matrix put in.

Shee felt a curious peer pressure, not eased by Unit leader Glenn's obvious discomfort at their teasing their superior officer. But Sheelaakah felt to speak anyway. 'I too, am from an annexed world. We chose to resist those that annexed our world while claiming to have "saved" us. We joined the

Resistance immediately, and I have served them ever since with all I have and am. I "do it", because one day, I will be free. Once day, I and all who choose to leave will do so, and find a new world of real peace.'

Alasia looked at her. Shee had not told the full story, and sensed that Alasia knew there was more to be told.

So Sheelaakah continued, speaking to her. 'You've said yourself that this world is many things to many people. And that it is. Why do we resist, when there is a life of 'infinite peace' offered within the walls? For it is not freedom. In there, we must surrender our wills to the Oppression, and serve them. I will not. Yet elsewise the government will not let us go, not to protect the galaxy from our rebellion, but because it doesn't want others to know what happens here. Seren and its people placate themselves by labelling us as criminals and then locking us out of the wall. It claims to prevent we "dissidents" from spreading lies and evil to other worlds because we are in a prison here. But this world is a prison to all, within and without the wall. Whether you believe their lies or not, you are not welcome to leave. You who have grown up inside the wall, have you ever seen a night without the energy field which surrounds this Seren Planetoid?'

Alasia did not reply. She just sat back in her chair, clearly thinking. She had a strange mind, this black haired woman, and it was impossible for Sheelaakah to read what she was thinking, without force. Some people were a little like that.

'You know, it has another name,' Alasia stated flatly, as if changing the conversation or boasting a little known fact might improve her confidence that night.

'What?' Matrix asked.

'The X-or System.'

It was a name Matrix had obviously never heard of, but Sheelaakah had, on occasion within the higher circles of the Resistance. It was very interesting to hear it fall from the lips of a simple singer.

'What does that mean?' He asked, always willing to be drawn inadvertently into her mind games.

'I have no idea,' the singer replied in obvious sincerity.

Montsi was stuck explaining things to her superior officer again. '... the medicine has not been working,' she was trying to justify. 'Tuktuk has been rebellious all day, and the synchronisation has fallen right out from underneath Petrie. I'm beginning to think the Governor picked the worst time possible for this visit!'

He sighed. 'Yes, the adult wards have been having no luck either... How is our new student doing, Jacinth?'

'Oh... just fine. Not much happening there. She's quite normal functioning really. Can get a bit... spooky.'

The officer laughed at that.

'She is talented... still, nothing I know can explain the behaviour of some of the other students.'

Marcuus was walking past, and invited himself to the conversation 'And have you seen the space borne Mill? They're all heading out to the asteroid circuit... they say they only do that when trouble is brewing... Wooooo!'

'Oh please!' The superior said.

'Shut up!' Montsi chorused, and hit him playfully on the arm.

They smiled at the joke... but no one had anything else to say.

The sea of sparks

(2 days ago)

Alasia alighted the giant rockworm's carriage, placing her hand in Matrix's outstretched palm. *He is a kind man,* she thought. She looked about, and found that they were in some kind of giant cavern, so high the roof disappeared in the blackness. How long, she wondered, would it take to reach the roof here? At least she was no longer upset.

She started momentarily as she noticed the caverns hundreds of occupants. About them stretched a throng of short, stocky humanoids, going about their business. It was some kind of transport hub, the likes of which she had never imagined before. There was a kind of covered shed made from metal sheets and hewn rock. The metal work was exquisite, and far beyond the workmanship usually afforded a common wall. It was ornate with some form of story, hieroglyphs, as were most other walls they encountered. Their group was quite tall compared to the stocky humans about them. Few, if any of the natives turned to look at the tall strangers in their midst, as though they were used to this kind of visitor. Alasia found herself staring in wonder.

They were extremely broad and muscular, twice that of any man she knew, excepting perhaps that manbot. Twisted ropes of muscles ended at shoulders as wide as the limbs themselves. Yet they were also very short, a head shorter than she on average. Most of them wore earth and stone coloured vests, which displayed their immensely wonderful muscular arms. At first it was difficult for her to discriminate gender amongst them, till she realised that the females wore slightly shorter beards, and tended to braid them differently to the males. Their skin was earth brown or a ruddy deep red, and their eyes almost invariably brown or black. They were, Alasia observed, a very busy people.

They left the ornate stone and metal shelter where they had alighted and headed for what might have been some form of taxi rank. The hewn stone pavement spread before a well-kept street, lit by what appeared to be primitive incandescent lights.

They pressed through the throng. The others in their group were standing closely in the crowd. The mech soldier was almost twice the height of the short, busy humanoids about them. The soldier puppy looked a little nervous in the crowd as he stood vigilantly by the ice princess. Their Commander looked entirely unperturbed by anything, but Alasia had had enough experiences with psychics to know that she was on high alert. It was unfamiliar territory to all of them – all but Matrix, who the mech soldier called Wormboy. Rank was not strong among this group of 'elite terrorists'.

The "taxis" where more like sleds, pulled along by giant armadillo-type creatures. Matrix was arguing, or talking, with one of the drivers. He apparently did not speak the language as well he had with the mutants.

Alasia wasn't trying very hard to hide her surprise.

'Who *are* they?' she asked Matrix in reference to the short humanoids when he abruptly finished his animated conversation with one of the beast drivers.

'Hmm? Oh, Derringer. Commander-'

'Derringer!' Alasia blurted out in surprise as her eyes swept the throng with a new mixture of awe and surprise. 'I thought they were extinct.'

'No,' the icy Commander replied with exacted patience. 'They were assimilated along with the rest of their world over three hundred years ago. They all decided en mass not to join the Oppression and have lived here ever since.'

Matrix replied in a softer tone. 'Their isolationist lifestyle suits them well here; they actually refuse to believe they've really been 'assimilated'. Just moved address. They prefer the dark understone anyway.

'However,' replied the Commander as though she was letting out a company secret. 'They do pose a threat to the Oppression. They are a significant, unified force *outside* the Seren walls. As such, they do not want the citizenry to know they are down here.'

'Why not?' asked Alasia genuinely. She was intrigued at the success of such a cover up. There must be hundreds of thousands down here. Possibly millions.

'Because,' replied Matrix before anyone else could, and in an almost playful whisper, 'they don't want us to know that they are happy.'

Alasia looked about her with newly opened eyes. They were busy. If they didn't all *look* that happy, at least, they did not seem miserable. They had been annexed apparently. That meant that three hundred years ago their home world was destroyed and they were forced to live on this world instead. Sometimes it happened. People, even large groups, turning up from other worlds. Usually they were genuine refugees seeking asylum from the war zones. But that was not how the others made it sound this time. Was it possible that the others were forced to leave their worlds? Abducted perhaps? Just like these others had claimed... more fuel to the old rumours...

Yet it was as she looked about the throng that she remembered her task and felt the stone warmed against her skin. She looked about, and found that the others were distracted enough observing another animated conversation between the driver and her dark-haired Matrix. She thought she might be able to place it now, and be rid of the terror it meant to follow this group, but the ever-vigilant manbot stood between her and her prey. It would make it difficult. This was the sort of objective that permitted no second chances, so she had to be sure.

Matrix turned and spoke. 'It's taken some doing, but I've found a driver that will take us to a Resistance outpost, where we can take a real transport. It's only a few hours, umm, drive, on the sleds. There is a catch though. Alasia, he wants you to ride up the front with him.'

She was startled. 'What!' she insisted indignantly, but before she could protest further, the others were already getting on the unsteady, but solidly built sled. The driver patted the cushion next to him with a toothless, wry grin.

'Interesting talent,' Remarked Skion from beneath his cape, from where she could see his amused, unhidden smile. The driver offered his hand. Perhaps it was pure shock, but before she knew what she was doing she was sitting uncomfortably next to the grinning, broad-shouldered driver who gave a quick click of his tongue. His armadillo padded off at an impressive pace.

--- ++ -- + -- ++ ---

'Oh no,' Alasia was saying excitedly to the short, stocky driver beside her. 'It's much faster than I expected. Much faster than most of the others too, I expect.'

She'd made her driver, Punnib, smile again at the compliment. 'Yes, indeed. I raised him from a hatchling, you know.'

'All by yourself?' Alasia asked with unbridled curiosity. She knew it got the short Derringer talking, and how he loved to talk!

'Of course!' He replied proudly. 'All Derringer children are instructed in the work of their fathers. I am the fifty fourth in a long line of 'Ro Rocan' – drivers you might say. The records don't go back much further than that. I trace my father's right back to the 'manu manucan': the birth of our race long ago back on Sol four.'

'Oh yes,' replied Alasia, who liked to know everything. 'During the, oh my, um...'

'Genetic experiments for perfect miners? Is that what you're not planning to say?' He said with a wry grin. Alasia had to admit she was caught out, but he saved her further embarrassment with his own continued speech.

'We call it the 'Manu Manucan': birth of the first man. Our type of man that is. People of that time had no idea what they were doing. It was a gift of the Gods to create us out of the clay the scientists "thought" they were manipulating. You know, though I don't think many people of your kind will tell you, that it was a batch that the scientists were going to reject that was the birth of our kind. That was an act of the eternal Hand of Rock to give us the miracle of life. And we have flourished wherever we exist, thanks to His ever benevolence.'

He spoke about his religious convictions with such ease, and not at all a hint of apology or holding back in knowing she did not share or begin to understand his beliefs.

'But I see,' he continued after a brief pause, 'you are somewhat uncomfortable of our speech?'

'Yes,' she had to confess. 'I've never met someone so, you know, who believed in a god before.'

'You are from within the wall then, aren't you?'

She was surprised to realise he knew that, and wondered what else was obvious to his unique point of view that may be obscured to hers after what was beginning to look more and more like a very sheltered upbringing.

The driver laughed. 'Don't look so surprised,' he chuckled warmly. 'We Derringer aren't as unaware as some might like to think. We watch, we observe, and usually, we keep well out of the way. And on the topic of "ways", look where we are!'

Alasia was a little surprised at how quickly the journey had taken them. Also surprised, because it looked like they were stopping nowhere. The cavern continued forward, yet it was no longer lit by the floor lights that had accompanied them for the past hour as they travelled through progressively smaller villages of the Derringer. Yet other than that, there seemed no cause to stop here. There were no transport hubs, no other transports, and certainly nothing that might have resembled a Resistance outpost.

'Why are we stopping here?' Asked Matrix suspiciously.

The driver shot back an uncharacteristically brief and forceful response in some language she did not understand. Matrix spoke a broken word or two in what may have been supplication, but the driver did not respond. Eyes straight ahead, he spoke.

'Surface travellers, the line ends here.'

'You'd never get involved, would you?' Matrix said quietly, as though it were an accusation. He then spoke to the rest of them. 'We go on foot from here. It should only take half a day. Besides, there is something interesting I think you all should see.'

'Little of your sites could interest us, Wormboy,' Skion demanded, his voice sceptic, perhaps frustrated at the turn of events.

Matrix did not respond, and Alasia thought him very brave. It was obvious that those two had some sort of rivalry going.

Matrix paid the driver, and with apology gruffly led the expedition further into the twilight of a dimly lit tunnel. They did not travel long before Alasia felt the air, usually quite warm this far underground, begin to cool. She did not know what to make of it. There was a sound, at first too feint to notice, and if the others did, she could not tell. It was like distant thunder, a constant rumbling which could have been, well, anything. So when they rounded a bend and entered the great cavern, her anxiety coalesced into speechless awe.

Before them was a cavern, impossibly large, that stretched all the way to the horizon and even further. Far away in the distance lightning flashed constantly on jagged islands between the cavern roof and what was the largest body of water Alasia had ever imagined could exist. It filled out in all directions with no indication of there being any other shore other than that one they stood on. Bare rock gave way to black sand that washed as regular, dark waves washed quietly along its length. It was a sea, an ocean, hidden hundreds of kilometres from the surface of the Seren planetoid. She was amazed.

As if to read her thoughts Matrix spoke. 'It goes all the way to the centre, you know. Two thousand kilometres deep. It's used to create the electric potential to partly power this huge planetoid, and without it, we could not go into Tesser. But they don't want people to know that, because, if they did, they'd realise we didn't need to trade in energy after all.'

'I never imagined...' began the Commander in awe. She walked past Alasia – brushed past her in true distraction. Had Alasia not also been filled with amazement she might have remembered her mission, but not until the opportunity had passed.

Yet in a swift step the manbot moved to prevent the Commander approaching the shore any further.

'Stay back,' he ordered. 'The water is electrically active. If you get to close, it may kill you.'

'It's true,' claimed Matrix, displaying almost proudly some form of scaring on his forearm. 'Besides, it's highly saline. Not at all good for drinking. You can float really well in it though... but I think you'd have to be dead first.'

'I never knew...' confessed Alasia. It was even less than a rumour, scoffed at by all right thinking citizens of the Government. Or Oppression, depending on who you served. 'Are there, I mean... are there living things down there?'

'Definitely, though I hope you never meet them. Squid the size of a transport, and sabre toothed fish the size of a dwelling. They're the ones you'll meet at the surface, anyway. Scores of Kerrin too. And the deeper you go... Leviathan, whales. The Derringer have found the remains of dark sharks, too. And the whole ocean is attracted to the centre of the planetoid. It doesn't look it, but it goes right around. You'd end right back where you started if you felt like walking along this beach for, oh, a year or so.'

'That's very large,' said the puppy soldier in awe, but it was so obvious it sounded almost ridiculous to hear.

'Well,' continued the Commander, nodding in gratitude to the manbot by her side. 'Fascinating. Thank you, Matrix. Now we know.'

'You mean...' he began, talking only to the brunette now but loud enough for all to hear 'that the Resistance didn't know... you... never asked the Derringer?'

She did not answer, just looked the dark-haired man in his emerald eyes and said nothing. Perhaps she spoke telepathically, but Alasia presumed that she did not. Her silence was a confession.

'We'd better keep going,' Matrix said. 'We need to get to a Resistance base, and the way is quite dangerous. It might take us a little longer than I'd hoped.'

--- +++ --- +++ ---

The child sat in the middle of the floor, crying defiantly. It was the kind of ear-wrenching wail a child gives when they *want* to be heard and *don't* want to be comforted.

Notwithstanding, Montsi tried again to console him. 'Petrie, you don't need to cry so-'

Suddenly there was a loud thud as one of the other children knocked the fishbowl to the floor. Fortunately for the fish, it was sealed and flexible, so it bounced a little before coming unceremoniously to rest at the child's feet.

'Lap'ta!' the teacher cried. 'You know we don't touch that!' She patted the wailing child on his head while another worker picked him up. Montsi rushed over to right up the fish before they became too much of a curiosity.

It was an exhausting day. The children were very distressed. What could it be? Certainly not the weather, there wasn't any on this isolated rock. Montsi found herself wishing in a moment for the tranquillity of Earth, her mother's home. There she could rest by the Mediterranean lake and take in the fresh breezes. Zapthaniel, her younger brother, used to bring her orange juice each morning.

Suddenly a new eruption of fighting brought Montsi back to reality. Two of the children were tugging and wailing defensively over an ignominious toy of which there were dozens. Montsi moved to placate them, and had barely begun before another child caught her attention.

'Montsi!' Piniti wailed out in her nasal, anxious voice. 'Tuktuk's touching the plants again!'

She turned and there he stood, the plant they'd nurtured all year, entirely wilted, leaves of autumn scattered around the young boy's feet. He held one up and, through a hole, peered uncomprehendingly at one very frustrated, very frazzled teacher having one very bad day.

A New Response

(Yesterday)

Commander Sheelaakah breathed a welcome sigh of relief. It had almost been another day before they arrived at their destination. They had been fortunate enough to catch a ride with a military transport out on long range patrol, and that quickened their travel immensely. Now they arrived rested and well fed at a Resistance outpost well away from the battle with the mutants that had occurred only a few days before. Commander Sheelaakah looked about thankfully at the familiar sights and senses of a Resistance outpost, busied with civilian and military personnel. They were at Alpha Numerous, one of the more solid and less secret underground Resistance bases. It was more a refugee camp that anything, filled with citizens from all aspects of life. The base was primarily agricultural, with a fortified tower at its centre to protect its residents.

She noted Skion dismounting the carriage, and wasting no time approaching a military terminal for tactical downloads and updates. His dedication was an asset. Matrix and Bakerson talked excitedly, and Sheelaakah basked in their optimism and the familiarity of the scene. The singer, who had proved so useful in making friends and talking her way out of the strangest of situations, looked as though she might approach her, but then decided against it for some reason. Shee realised that she knew as much about Alasia as the wind knows of an iceberg. Much she hid beneath the surface, and though it was a fact that she could force the truth from this woman, she knew it was far more prudent to wait. It was a long-held belief she took of telepathic mind reading, that those who communicated of their own volition would reveal more of who they were, and how they would react, than under duress. *A conviction recently strengthened,* she thought. Yet like a fleeting insect, a thought buzzed passed her consciousness that Alpha Numerous might be the perfect opportunity to finally relieve themselves of the singer. Here she could readjust to her new life beyond the confines of the great wall. Sheelaakah was certain that this facility was a place where, no doubt, her unique talents could be put to good use.

Yet with that thought came a second intuition which gnawed at her brainstem. The five of them had the potential to work together despite fundamental, indeed extremes, in character. Officers Matrix and Bakerson seemed to approve of her company. Skion was always hunting for tactical advantage and saw her, and indeed, Matrix, as a debilitation to their unit. But the Commander knew that their situations far often called for cunning and delicacy, which was far from his area of expertise. He would obey all orders, for it was in his nature and programming to do just so. Alasia, whose presence was disturbing to herself, did have some fascinating abilities; yet far too many secrets. Perhaps it would be prudent to keep her under closer observation for the present.

Then a disturbance caught Sheelaakah's senses. Amidst the throng it appeared that someone important was coming. She didn't wait long to find out. Surrounded by his retinue of bodyguards was none less that I-olo Tilk, Understudy to the Supply and Recognisance General to the Resistance. She had only seen him once before. He was a tall, ebon skinned man with broad shoulders and rich chocolate eyes. His dress was immaculate and his pace impatient. He wore the deep earth shades of the Resistance High Command, with high collar and tall, dark boots that struck the earth purposefully as he walked. Sheelaakah had received orders from him at times; always concise, compassionate, and direct. It was known that he carried on this work as a matter of principal, not promotion. Those who knew him spoke of him respectfully - but not many people knew him for it was far safer that way. However, even as an enigma, his reputation had risen to fame, so as he came through the crowd it made no small stir. Without a pause he walked directly up to her, halting all conversation in his wake. He spoke broadly, precisely, and deliberately very loudly.

Like a prince, she thought.

'Commander Sheelaakah,' he commenced, dispensing a swift formal salute in her direction. 'We are immeasurably grateful for the information you have given us, and to see that you and those that travel with you have escaped death at least three times!' He paused, and took a commanding sweep to view those she travelled with. Then he continued specifically and loudly enough for the entire crowd to hear. 'The circle has indicated that it is time for the New Response. Commander Sheelaakah, is your strike team ready to depart?'

She paused momentarily, not understanding what he was referring to. A New Response? That was only a pen and paper contingency. Nobody ever really expected it to happen. Now the man, second only to the circle itself, was calling for it, for her to accomplish it, in the middle of a mezzanine! Was there some report that she had missed? She sought for something meaningful to say, not wanting to confess her uncertainty to this ranking official. Then she saw his eyes spoke an urgency she could not ignore.

'Of course we are,' Matrix replied impetuously for her, as he far too often did. He turned and called the others over. They gathered quickly.

'Good!' I-olo Tilk said brusquely, seemingly unconcerned for the complete breach of formality. He reached for her temple and placed a small stone aside her banding.

'Here are your orders,' he instructed.

The download only took a second.

'Right!' said Commander Sheelaakah promptly. 'We're off!' The crowd let out a cheer as, without any further explanation, they remounted their transport and headed straight out again into the unknown.

--- ++ -- + -- ++ ---

The two women sat in silence. It was difficult to talk to Alasia, noticed Sheelaakah. When she would answer it was with innuendo or hidden with intellectualisations. It was frustrating. Even simple topics became secrets with Alasia. But talk was something they had time for, now that I-olo was sending the five of them out to moonscape for a secret assignment. Sheelaakah tried to continue the conversation politely.

'So you graduated Prime, and that four years early then?' she tried to ask the singer with all the genuine politeness she had.

'Indeed,' replied Alasia. 'But not as quickly as I ought. See, I had trouble catching on to sub-telepathic synching.'

'I see, but you have it now?'

Sheelaakah gave a start as suddenly they rounded another canyon bend twice as fast as they ought. She felt her nervousness rise sharply. 'What are you doing?' she asked anxiously, voice choked in tension.

'Oh c'mon, you're not a little worried about canyon passing are you?' Alasia teased. 'Besides, you told us we had to hurry.'

'I did not mean this sort of hurry!' Their transport gave a lurch as Alasia piloted it violently across a turn at just the last minute. 'I'm afraid you're going to kill us,' in spite of herself, she jammed her eyes shut in denial of the situation.

The craft slowed slightly.

'Not used to flying something so small and manoeuvrable, eh,' asked the Raven-haired pilot. 'It's really quite fun. It's been a bit of a while since I got out and about.'

She stared at her, and thought that just maybe she would keep an eye on her from one of the back quarters. But the men were there now, resting before battle. She would need some time herself to go over I-olo's orders, and it was beginning to look more and more like such a time was *now*.

A silence passed the cockpit accompanied by the two women. They were speeding along a desolate canyon, trying to stay below scanner range, though at this speed they were pretty safe anyway. It must have been somehow cathartic for this dark haired woman to race along at near death speeds. She had first confronted death in a particularly voracious form only a few days ago, and still had not entirely adjusted. She kept very busy, very distracted.

They rounded a corner sharply.

Alasia lubriously mused: 'Only two more hours of this and we'll be out of the wilderness beyond and into moonscape. Remind me to take a nap then, it's been a while and I need my beauty sleep.'

Shee pondered the audacity of that statement.

'We're at war,' she commented, unsure of whether that held any meaning to Alasia or was she as forgetful as a snail.

'Oh,' replied Alasia, as though it was the first time she had heard. 'In that case, just get me up five minutes earlier so I can straighten my hair as well.'

It fascinated Shee how this woman had the ability to truly frustrate her with so little effort. She paused a moment to sublimate the impulse to anger, and tried to relax a little. Trite as she was, she surely meant no harm. She'd been through a lot recently. Neither spoke for a long minute, except the magnetic field generators and the harsh, enthusiastic manner in which Alasia piloted seventeen tonnes of reinforced aluminium oxide at almost fifteen hundred kilometres an hour.

'I'm sorry,' said Shee to continue their discussion. 'But we don't have a terminal on board.'

'I *know*,' the singer commented rubbing her chest without inhibition, discomfort visible on her face. She rounded a thirty degree curve at twelve hundred kilometres an hour by flying downwards to give herself extra space. Even further alarming was the fact that she did it one handed. 'It's been a little while since I had a maintenance, I'm half a cup larger than I'm used to. And this morning, I had to brush my hair! I don't mind living outside the walls but do they have to be so *primitive!* I mean, I've got to get to a terminal soon, I've been in cheek rouge for three days!'

Sheelaakah did not respond. She could not. Shee had shaved her hair bald once when it got in the way, and her hands now were long scarred and harsh. Her skin was naturally aged. Why had she allowed it? Because it was not important! In that moment she succumbed to blind rage at her pilot's extreme fickleness. She was tempted, sorely tempted, to order the ship to stop and then she would *show* this pompous singer what it meant to bleed for freedom. And not another, her own blood which had spilt a dozen times since her war had begun. How important was hair when your twin brother was dead?

'I suppose I shall get used to it,' sighed the singer after a long moment of silence between them. 'Besides, I'll get a maintenance as soon as this little tiff is over.'

That did it. Sheelaakah stood, trembling in an effort to maintain control. She placed her face right up to the dark-haired woman and whispered, full of acid and spite: 'It never ends, you irresponsible, shallow wench. You care more for your presentation before men to fathom the death we all will soon face! I have been through hell and back, and then returned again and again. You nails will crack, you skin will spoil, your hair fall out. But, if you never give in, never yield, then maybe one day you will know what it means to be free. And until you relinquish your desperate clinging to false gods of vanity and appearance; until you are prepared to lose *everything* and keep vigilant as the eternal price, *you will never be free.'*

They stared into each other's eyes. Alasia looked calm, but Sheelaakah knew her words had told her something she was refusing to admit. Shee turned slowly, surprising herself at her passion and composure. Quietly she left the cockpit and headed for some privacy in the transport to prepare for the upcoming war.

It was a remarkably smooth ride from then on.

--- +++ --- +++ ---

"Wench?"

Now, that stone was going on *her*.

She would pay ... with her freedom...

--- +++ --- +++ ---

Commander Sheelaakah. This is I-olo Tilk. You are hereby ordered to proceed to section nine of the outer maw and observe an unprecedented Class five annexation by the Oppression. You are to assemble a strike team and assist in gathering information on types and suitability of refugees. It is your responsibility...

But it wasn't the usual commands in the synaptic download which disturbed Sheelaakah. There was something about the message, something subtle. She left the rest area of the transport for more private quarters near the rear. There she sat in the white noise of the engine and imagined silence. She listened closely.

There, a voice. Male, concerned, authoritative. I-olo? Yes, the voice intensified. But still she could not make out any words. Why would he hide a subliminal message in fairly routine orders? And why had he made New Response so public, or did they now know? Those that were with her did not. The message was being annoying, it was very well hidden.

She circled out her rune, and slowly the message became clear.

Sheelaakah, began I-olo, his voice passive and sincere. *Something is wrong. What I have to say must be sublimated once it is heard. My reception at the Circle, our governing head, had been cold to say the least recently. I fear they are hiding something from me that we have a right to know. It is becoming apparent to me that they don't seem to care about the next annexation, only that we assist those that that do not submit to entrance into the citadel. We cannot afford to fight the government in these terms! Hopefully these things will be resolved shortly; I am speaking with another understudy soon. Yet there is a more pressing matter.*

I've considered what the government stands to gain from annexing a minor research colony. There are over forty thousand people there, of high calibre, as well as some sensitive Senate research and quite an amount of material. It is their boldest move yet. Too bold. I hold my suspicions that they may be after a more auspicious prize. A small colony at Breakers Point plays host to a research centre for gifted children. Why they would want these children, I do not know. But intuition informs me that we must acquire them first, and at every cost.

What we have here, in essence, is a New, New Response. I don't care about the other refugees. Whatever you do, find those children! They must not be allowed to fall into the hands of the Oppression! In children...' His voice trailed in conclusion *'...there is hope.'*

The battle

(Earlier on today)

Inside the Seren citadel, without warning, the transmission suddenly went dead. Freya, proud mother of four, took the interruption to stretch out and find a more comfortable position on her couch. It was mildly annoying, but they'd soon have some reason for this rare occurrence. It was her afternoon off, her children out at training and her seven-year-old at the occasional carer. So in short, there was nothing important to do this afternoon anyway.

She looked out at the mantle at her joining photo, when she first took her dear husband. Across it lay her favourite momento of him, an ornate little hammer, a scale replica of the one he would use each day in his craft; wielding it expertly in his large, sweaty hands in the tourist forge. She laughed as she remembered him bringing it home one day, the real one that was, for the children to examine. None could lift it, not even herself.

The terminal relit. There it was; a minor readjustment in the shield matrix. Perhaps they were entering an asteroid belt, or some hopeless space pirate making a futile attempt to disrupt peace on their world? It wouldn't matter anyway.

The student watched as the scanner suddenly went dead. At first he thought it might have been another power surge, but looked up to notice that the range visuals were black as well. He wondered if he should be getting nervous, but brushed the notion quickly aside. He checked the other instruments. NavCom, subspace, dissolution, TK3. Even radio transmissions were all silent outside a half a million kilometre radius or so.

Now he was getting nervous. He called out to his superior across the room. 'Sir, we are having some sort of problem here.'

'What sort?' The superior asked, moving to check in on things.

'The instruments, they're all silent.'

'Have you checked the power?'

'Yes sir. Power is all functional. It seems to be a problem with the scanners themselves. They seem...

A shadow began to cross the room. From outside the window they could look out at the stars and the sun. Now, something gigantic was beginning to move unexpectedly across Utopia's only sun and cast a shadow on the research colony.

Then, he felt fear.

--- ++ -- + -- ++ ---

Charles hadn't stopped crying in half an hour, and Pietre was refusing to communicate entirely. If yesterday was bad, today was tragic. They had doubled the staff then and still no success. Something was very, very wrong.

Montsi looked up to try again for something to explain all this. The children were distracted, and not at all themselves. Then she saw little Jacinth, packing her bag.

Montsi came over. 'Child,' she said in worn kindness, 'it isn't time to leave just yet.'

The child didn't look up. 'It will be soon,' she confidently replied.

Montsi watched as the hat, then coat and then ribbon all went in. She was wandering what to say next when the child spoke.

'C'mon Terric, and you twins. It's nearly time to leave.'

'Jacinth!' Cried Montsi in exasperation. Sure enough, the three boys stolidly stood and headed for their bags. She was hard pressed to get them to stand up for her, and now they were taking orders from a peer? On the best of days the children constantly surprised her, now the surprise might just be enough to kill her!

Suddenly there were shouts from outside. The door burst open.

It was Marcuus, his face pale with adrenalin. He did not pause to draw a breath before he shouted: "The colony is under attack! We've got to get the children to safety! Now!'

It took a moment for Montsi to comprehend the incomprehensible. How could this be happening? Who would do such a thing? What were they going to do? The children? Marcuus began pushing them hurriedly out, but little Jacinth was already leaving, and as she crossed her carer's path she put a glance to her transfixed teacher, restoring a moment of clarity.

Again, pondered Montsi, *she is right, and I am wrong.*

--- +++ --- +++ ---

Alasia expertly piloted the craft into the Resistance hanger, her bout with the psychic scarcely forgotten. Moonscape was far more desolate than she had realised. There was almost no air here, as far away from the City as one could be on the opposite end of the Seren planetoid. The transport had brought them to some kind of hastily constructed military base; very small. Half a dozen long blue fighter craft lay on a recently flattened landing pad. Pressure tents and sealed transports dotted the near field and beyond that, nothing but grey stone. The warding stones their only defence against detection. Occasionally the land was pitted with small craters or broken with fault lines. Dust kicked up under the feet of soldiers and returned slowly to the ground as they hurried in their preparations for war. The stars, ever visible, twinkled behind the energy field that surrounded their world. She stood up, and pressed herself to the window. It was bleak.

Then she saw it. A mountain; sheer and ridged, that ascended straight up and grew dark into the heavens. The maw. One of five actually. She had never seen one. They weren't in many pictures of the planetoid. Actually, they weren't in any, she realised. She strained to see the end, but it was out of sight. Somewhere it ended, and somewhere tracing the maw to its end, solid metals replaced the stone. She assumed they had something to do with the transport of the planet, but was no fool to have also heard otherwise. She imagined that the maws would look like a kind of cage from far away, if Seren was viewed from this side on. But who would want to look at it from this end...

They hurriedly left the transport to make their way down a narrow, billowing plastic corridor for one of the larger bio-dome tents. Commander Sheelaakah was already helping out, talking to an assembled war council. She was a strange woman, this Sheelaakah. Not so easy to betray. Since their little speech, when Alasia was flaunting her piloting skills just to provoke her, she'd given her too much to think about. The provocation had worked all too well, she'd been so caught up in the moment of a burning ice queen she'd forgotten her task. She tried to ignore Sheelaakah's words, but found them pressing against her underconsciousness far too often.

Then Skion joined her.

She looked about at the disorganised and divergent group of volunteers who would try to fight a government a thousand times their strength in size and number, and wondered why.

'The attack has already begun,' the Commander was saying. 'The giant energy field which traps us in this world is now being broadcast over the entire Utopian system. The Utopian defence forces have begun to prepare a counter offensive. Our mission is simple: rendezvous with a small group of refugees from an outer research colony, children mostly, and bring them safely back to this base. The majority of the Oppression forces will shortly by engaged with the Utopian defence fleet. Our task will be accomplished by surprise assault on the third flank. We are to break through enemy lines and guard their transports to this base.'

Six blue-suited pilots, as well as ranking ground officials and gunners, were seated in a forum around a circular stone table. Projected to their minds from its nondescript surface lived a scale envisagement of the upcoming battle. Alasia could clearly make out the planets, and the highlighted lines of Utopian defence fleets quickly forming to deflect the upcoming assault. The Seren government craft were by far superior in might and numbers. It appeared the Utopians battle plan was to hold off their enemies long enough for the civilians to escape. Very valiant of them, she thought.

'Now remember,' the brunette continued, turning to face the assembled pilots, 'we are outnumbered twenty to one, so ensure you engage minimum offensive. Remember that, soldiers: there are no targets of opportunity tonight. The majority of the Oppression forces will be engaged in de-align with the colonies defence systems, but they won't be busy for long. We are to break through, get the refugees out, and rendezvous back at base immediately.'

'What of the other civilians?' asked Matrix.

Sheelaakah suffered his interruption. 'They are to be assisted as per usual protocol. After the Oppression has finished destroying their world they will be rounded up to the detention zones. Most of them will probably choose a life within the walls. Those that don't will eventually join the Resistance. It's one or the other-'

'Or you can be eaten by the mutants,' Alasia muttered.

From the safety of glowing holograms and calm speeches, war seemed so... pretend. Despite herself, Alasia was fascinated. So this was what it was like; to see a world annexed. Now that she thought about it, it was no real surprise to her that such things took place. It was the greatest non secret amongst those in the know at the citadel. Officially, the line was that they were rescuing war torn civilians from insecurity and embracing them in the arm of peace in Seren Citadel. But she knew now that not all people new to Seren were refugees *before* they came to live inside the wall.

'What makes these children so different?' A unit leader questioned.

'Owing to the recent attacks on our forces, the Resistance does not have the resources to mount a proper counter offensive. This is already more than we could commit too.'

The room waited. Alasia knew she had not answered the question.

The Commander sighed, and continued. 'We don't know. Pilots, your stoneships are waiting. Are we as one?'

The assembly nodded or clicked their approval.

'Dismissed,' she commanded, and the room broke into organised dispersal.

Matrix arrived at Alasia's side to stare out the window. She thought he looked almost disappointed.

'What is the matter?' she asked, though she knew.

He sighed deeply. 'It happens... it really happens. All those years, all those rumours. And now, still, there seems to be nothing I can do about it.'

They waited in thoughtful silence, and stared out the window into the starlit blackness where a battle had already begun.

--- +++ --- +++ ---

Lord Admiral Taalk waited on the bridge of the giant battle fortress, the largest of three. His antipasto of war had already been served: their communications were shut down, and the first squadron had laid a strafe across their exposed flank. Their shuttles and escape pods were already launching, but that would only make them easier to herd in. There was no escape, and it wasn't the thirty thousand fighters at his command, nor the two million ground troops waiting for his signal that would stop their prey from ever getting away, from ever telling anyone about what had happened here. It was the energy barrier, thrown around an entire system. Nothing would be left, just cosmic dust and planetary flotsam, as the gigatons of raw materials were consumed by Seren and made to be a part of herself in the endless kilometres of the underfoundries. And again, the galactic senate would be unable to respond. For all they knew Seren was a billion kilometres from here, while a little research colony and its inhabitants would vanish mysteriously. The conquest of another world was... intoxicating.

But that conquest hid a secret. He had been forced to use all his influence, all his powers, to convince the council that this was the next, *necessary* step. But the Utopian System itself was just a trinket compared to the *real* prize he coveted.

'Lord Admiral, the second squadron is in position. Shall I give the signal?'

'Tell me, general, is the Resistance responding?'

'Yes sir.'

'Good...' but he paused as a tremor crossed his sixth sense. He looked at the Resistance detail. Typical. Considering what they must have known they were facing it was surprising that the stubborn organisation hadn't been able to mass a more substantial counter attack. They had a large battle cruiser, hidden out in moonscape, which often caused them trouble during annexations. But it was nowhere to be seen today. Was this small fleet the best they brought? ... Or was there more ...

He brought out the scrying stones, mapped the terrain with his old scry stone. Yes, there was more. They were hiding a small force at the edge of one of the pillars. He smiled, his grey eyes narrowing in spite.

'There,' he told the general.

The man hid his humiliation well. 'Thank you, Lord admiral. We had not noticed anything until we shone the beacon directly at them.'

'What of their forces?'

'We estimate two hundred troops, nine tanks, and they are preparing to launch six stone ships.'

'Stoneships!' mused the Lord Admiral. 'Primitive, wieldy, staminous stoneships? Why would *that* be?' He was almost incensed.

He thought for a moment, then he replied to the unasked question of the general, for he knew what he was thinking. 'No, let them come. It will make things more... entertaining. But, send in a small strafing run for now, let them know we know they are there.'

--- +++ --- +++ ---

The children were scrambling onto the carrier. People were running all over the bio-dome. It had been twenty minutes since the first shots were fired, though it felt like only seconds. Montsi's heart was racing.

'They're jamming all signals, we can't get a distress out,' cried Marcuus.

'Even if we could, we are too far out to be helped,' she replied. 'What of the fighters?'

'The firsts, three thousand attack quads, are going to escort us and three other transports to section beta Karie. We're leaving in four min-'

'Jacinth, WHERE'S JACINTH!' Montsi screamed. Without waiting to count the other children she raced back against the tide of fleeing civilians

179

towards the nursery. Running frantically between doors, screaming her name. She was so young. After what felt like an eternity she found her, calmly talking to a message stone, then popped it into a drink bottle.

'Jacinth!' she wailed, grabbing the girl viciously by the hand. 'We have got to go!' she cried, the child's life far more important than the message she cared for.

She looked up at her, angry that her project was disturbed, then, deciding perhaps their situation might actually have some gravity she picked up her little letter and a bottle, and ran with her. Their going was slow, helped no less by the little girl who insisted on cramming the lid onto a hopeless glass container as they ran through the abandoned space station Montsi had lived in for most of her life, and would most probably never see again.

Matrix's sullen vigil turned to sudden horror as the enemy flew a strafing run over their heads. The pilots were barely halfway to their stone ships at the time, too far back to head for cover, and too far forward to head to the safety of the bunker. They stood little chance, and had no warning. Three wasps cut the night sky with searing flame powerful enough to melt boronium, so it was no wonder that it vaporised the pilots unlucky enough to be caught in the way when they passed.

Matrix and the others watched in stunned silence, then pandemonium broke out. The tanks opened fire, but it was too late. They had been found.

He heard the Commander's voice over the dim. 'Tell those remaining pilots to get to their craft! Launch immediately!'

The message got through pretty quick. Skion and Glenn were up and running in the rarefied atmosphere. Alasia stood nearby. People ran in all directions. They would have to abandon base now, and they were three pilots down even before the launch. Things did not look good.

Then, unexpectedly, Commander Sheelaakah was by his side. 'Am I to understand Matrix that you have experience in this form of craft?'

'I was level five in neural interfacing, if that's what you mean.'

'Good enough,' she said swiftly, turning to some others. 'Corporal! Get this man suited up for piloting a stone ship!'

There was a brief pause while they summed Matrix up. Deciding on action over thought, and quickly brought him a space suit.

'Level five?' said Alasia, sounding impressed.

The ground crew gave Matrix no time to reply while they helped him into the suit. It was light, not much more than a good jacket. It fit tightly, and would protect him from the airless wilderness, even the near freezing temperatures or radiation extremes of space for days, until he starved, at least. People in the early colonies had worn these as fashion accessories. The helmet needed some extra adjusting, but would allow a full range of view, and not obstruct the bio neural signals he would send to pilot his ship. He tried not to worry – it had been over seven years.

As if sensing his concern, Sheelaakah halted the dressing just before the helmet went on.

'Just in case, you might need this,' she said.

She stood before him, and reached up to touch the copper band that embraced his head. Pushing back any mistrust, he relaxed as he felt her enter his mind, and for a moment things became blurry. Then suddenly they snapped back into perfect clarity. He felt very focused.

Probably to not be outdone, Alasia planted a kiss on his cheek.

On went his helmet and out he went into the air lock.

The first thing Matrix recognised was the substantially lower gravity field. This far away from the city all that was left was the natural pull of the planetoid, which was not actually very much. It took a step or two before he began running after the others. The turrets had taken out the three wasps that had done so much damage, but that didn't mean there might not be others coming, maybe hundreds.

He arrived at his ship in record time. The others were already in and ready to launch, their sync field causing the nine tonne stone ships to hover above the ground. There were no thrusters on this craft – they flew in their own inertial field. Matrix pondered his craft. The stone ships were several times longer than either wide or high, breaking into a two opposable clubs at the far end. The entire craft had the appearance of being made of carved blue lapis lazuli, and their wieldy yet tough appearance was descriptive of how they fought. What they lacked in manoeuvrability they made up for in strength and bold firepower, and they could absorb in their stone layers blazers that would melt most alloys in a nano second.

Matrix pondered their battle plan as he lay between the stone headpiece; they had intended to use these ships as a diversion; fast, powerful, able to take the heat. They were going to punch a hole through the lines and draw the fire from off the transports. But this advantage was lost now. They would have to improvise.

As soon as he was linked to his ship's systems he lost all sense of his body. It brought back his experience years ago, though it was in a different kind of ship, and it was all training then. For a brief moment he questioned what he was getting himself into. The others were far more experienced. Perhaps he was trying to get himself killed? He did not know.

Or was it to save someone else?

His arms became the stone clubs, and the sensations of his legs powered the propulsion field. His eyes blurred, and took on the entire vision provided by the spaceship's sensors - a three hundred and sixty degree view. It focussed quicker than he had expected, and he wasn't at all as nervous as he had anticipated. Perhaps it was something the Commander had done?

It was an interesting sensation to take flight again, and Matrix had to admit he was doing better than he expected. He hoped Sheelaakah hadn't noticed his initial confusion between 'up' and 'down'. So it was that the handful of freedom fighters lifted off with the messy personalisation of individuals, forming quickly as they invited him into their military formation.

Matrix sensed through his ships sensors his enemies long before they were in view. He could have begun firing from that distance, but they were conserving the energy for their defence. Over sixty attack planes waited in formation, and while they watched, twenty pulled away and circled towards them.

'Remain in formation,' their flight commander instructed. 'When they complete their first fly past open rosette and we'll catch them in our cross fire. They should break up their ranks. Are we as one?' their flight leader proposed.

Instinctively Matrix knew something was wrong, but continued the count off with the others, preferring the unity of compliance than the disharmony of dissent. The tactic was sound, but he feared it lacked spontaneity. Even so, he kept his peace, not willing to challenge the more experienced officer.

As it would turn out however, he was right. The fighter planes doused them in a shower of blazers which their heavily armoured craft absorbed well, but by the time their bulkier craft had circled around all but none of the attack planes in the cross fire remained. Formation broke down as each stone ship was pursued by two planes, which, like piranhas, took turns taking bites out of the craft. Glenn alone managed to disable a fighter off Matrix's ship. Within a minute anguish cracked over the intercom as their flight leader required a pull out. Obligingly their enemy regrouped as well.

'They're enjoying this, aren't they?' A pilot observed.

'We're out-classed in these redundant vehicles!' Skion growled angrily.

'Calm down soldiers, we're not finished yet,' their leader paused to think. 'We have to try to draw them out, keep on each other's tails. Prepare for a wide arc open loop formation. Are we as one?' their leader began.

'No!' Matrix injected.

Muffled over the intercom he heard Skion's mumbled objection to Matrix's open one.

'You have a better plan?' their lead pilot began.

'As a matter of fact, I do,' Matrix began, realising how forward he must have sounded. 'We're fighting like fighter to fighter, not like stone ships to fighter. We need to make better use of our unique situation. I recommend we try a close formation, and punch straight along their front line. We might not be able to catch them in our crossfire, but we certainly will catch them in theirs.'

'The tactic is unsafe,' protested Skion. 'We would be placing ourselves in the middle of their attack wing, and would likely suffer several collisions.'

'But it does have merit,' their leader put in. 'Stone ships can take a lot of heat, but their fighters cannot. At such close proximity their manoeuvrability and over confidence may work against them.'

'Plus we can clear the path directly ahead of us with no difficulty at all,' Matrix explained, a little cheekily.

'We'll give it a try, but we begin with a wide angle to twelve degrees east. Let them think we are trying a berthing run. That should help pack them in a bit tighter. Are we as one?'

Skion did not sound convinced, but they all agreed to attempt the procedure to the best of their ability. Swinging out wide they headed towards their enemy, making the appearance of cutting across their enemy's front. This was a logical tactic, for while they would sustain heavy fire they would also be in a far better position to target the enemy. At the appointed signal, however, the stone ships suddenly collapsed their formation until they were touching each other. Instead of a moving ring, they were now a compact bullet. Instead of heading in front of the enemy, they were crashing right through the centre.

The pay-off was spectacular. Most pilots, salivating at the prospect of their prize, were unaware of the trap they had sprung on themselves. They kept firing, even as the six ships passed rapidly through their midst. Several collisions resulted, and a few fighters were destroyed by their own over-enthusiastic comrades. The resulting chaos was fuelled by an obscuring cloud of debris and radiation that temporarily blinded most of the fighters. The following rosette from the stone ships devastated their ranks.

'You new guns, get to the transport! We'll finish them off,' their leader instructed.

'Affirmative,' replied Dogman, now in command.

The three antique fighters turned and headed quickly out into the star-filled sky.

--- +++ --- +++ ---

Alasia watched out of a star-filled window. It had been three anxious minutes since the stone ships had left. She was finding it hard to stand still.

'They have engaged the enemy,' a cool voice declared softly.

She turned and was somewhat surprised to find it was Commander Sheelaakah, talking to her. Wasn't she supposed to be running the show?

'Fifteen, no twenty fighters. Hmmm, they have their work cut out,' she mused smugly.

'You sound very confident,' Alasia commented. She was not at all bothered at how this woman knew about a battle occurring several hundred kilometres away in unmarked space, but she had seen far stranger things.

The brunette did not move. Just stared out of the same window, concentrating. Alasia thought how she might have been made of wax, she seemed so artificial. Maybe she was an android? They hadn't done a very good job on the lips, or the nose for that matter.

The noxious brunette continued to speak. 'Their first attack … is unsuccessful. Nine to one hit ratio. They'll have to do better than that,' she added under her breath.

'You seem very curious to know what is going on,' Alasia commented. It was a subtle accusation, designed to aggravate her into an actual conversation. They had said nothing for hours, and now she was trying to pull her into talking about a war she could not see.

'They are trying, no, Matrix had another idea.'

Alasia noted a small smile play on the lips of the Commander. Perhaps... 'Missing someone?' Teased Alasia unkindly.

The Commander just turned slowly, looked at her from head to toe, and walked away.

How aggravating, thought Alasia.

--- +++ --- +++ ---

Montsi was pushing the children frantically inside the shuttle. A man came to the door, looking momentarily to assess the situation but not its needs.

'Get the children inside!' He yelled white faced, still not in control real of his emotions.

'We're trying!' Montsi screamed in reply, loud enough to pierce his fractured nerves. The launch bay was on fire now, something the final attack run had left them with. They were the final transport to leave. Montsi looked up at their old city, and as she did, she saw someone in the control booth.

'Marcuus! Marcuus! There's someone in the Tower!'

Marcuus came to the door. If she'd had time she might have wondered how he could have heard her in all the panic, but as it was, she did not.

'It's OK,' he said, racing to her side. 'He's staying to make sure we all get away safely.'

'But he'll...'

'I know,' came Marcuus's subdued reply.

Suddenly there was a lurch as the transport prepared to leave. Montsi looked down at the ramp and was horrified to see Jacinth gently placing her bottle just outside the gang plank, patting it kindly.

Montsi ran screaming down the ramp and grabbed her, in the process knocking over her little bottle. With surprising strength Jacinth jerked her hand away and in one deft manoeuvre righted the rocket. The child slammed her fist on the launch pad, and the little rocket, made of nothing more than a small bottle attached to a child's propulsion cylinder – a toy, shot up into the airless wilderness of the research colony and away among the blackened stars. Montsi was then unsure what frightened her more; that this little girl had nearly been left behind, or her smug, satisfied grin as she walked calmly into the waiting transport.

Marcuus helped pull her in as the doors sealed behind them. The children were in hysterics, except for the autistics who showed no visible signs of knowing what was going on. But Montsi could sense they knew of the fear everyone was feeling. The ship launched with a more violent jolt than she had ever experienced, and sped towards the bio-sphere's bay doors, held open to the last possible second by the sacrifice of a lone, unknown person.

--- +++ --- +++ ---

Sheelaakah waited in the silence, though her thoughts were filled with noise. Through her telepathic link with Matrix, of which he seemed unaware, she was able to monitor the battle with greater accuracy and speed than the instruments in the control tower. She could, equally as well, relay and receive information with the command centre. She saw the three stone ships rapidly approaching the base. Several transports were already in orbit and preparing to leave. The stone ships moved with several other small fighters to defend the transports as they begun to flee.

The rendezvous had been a success, thus far. She listened as Officer Glenn briefly discussed arrangements with the leader of the three transports. The pilots had received their communiqué and were expecting the stone ships to rendezvous with them.

Sheelaakah wondered if Matrix was losing concentration, for his gaze had turned and shifted towards the planet. A single transport was breaking free of the launch pad as it succumbed to flame. She reached out through him with her mind to sense what the transport carried.

It was the children.

'The children,' he whispered, for no known reason. Then roared over the com system 'Stoneship six to transports! There's another ship down there!' He said urgently.

'We've just located enemy fighters approaching from behind the station,' the transport Commander replied. 'We have to begin the jump into hyperspace. Sorry pilots, that transport is on its own.'

Without thinking Matrix suddenly broke formation and dove towards the small research colony. He drove towards them with their combined passion. The others stoneship pilots were amiss; What was he doing? He should be protecting the other three transports? The lone transport was barely a hundred kilometres from the base when it was attacked. Two fighters had broken away from the main group in an attempt to damage or disable this craft. Matrix dove towards them at breakneck speed.

Within seconds he arrived, engaging the enemy fighters. He did not stand much of a chance. He fired continuously at the craft that deftly dodged his attack. Flying on impulse, Matrix drove his craft directly into the path of one of the fighters. Unprepared for the tactic it did not move away in time, and shattered as the two ships collided. Matrix was thrown forward for a moment, and his weapon systems immediately shut down. His craft lay motionless for a second, before he could regain his composure and reassess the situation.

The transport they were fighting to defend had already lost its hyper drive, but was safely retreating towards the vast emptiness of the Wilderness beyond, while the remaining wasp turned and concentrated its efforts on him. Matrix tried to evade, but its vastly superior manoeuvrability gave it a decisive advantage. His ship was taking heavy fire. Suddenly the assault ended in a fireball of metal and gas.

'Enemy fighter has been destroyed,' Skion stated calmly over the intercom.

Sheelaakah relaxed. Quickly she sent him a message for the transport to meet them at a specific rendezvous. They had to save the children.

She turned to gather her surroundings again. She was still in the makeshift defence shelter, but people were preparing to retreat. The first three transports would have to be redirected before they tried to escape, but that was in the capable hands of the military now. She was needed to assist those that were in the lone transport that Matrix had just saved. They would need to rendezvous with them as soon as possible.

'Alasia,' she said, turning back to approach the contemptible woman who stood isolated by the window. 'Would you care to accompany us to rendezvous with these children?'

'Why me?' she asked, not turning to look at her.

'We need to abandon the stone ships and recover the pilots. After that, we can meet the new refugees. Aside from your talents with people, and I suspect, of all ages, you are a far better pilot than I. The others here have more than enough to do. We can use the transport we came in.'

'You sure you trust me?' Alasia said.

'I choose to,' she said with unfaltering brown eyes.

The two looked at each other for a brief moment.

'Good!' said the taller woman. 'Let's go pick up the boys then!'

Epilogue – Book 2

(Now)

Water trickled down from the concrete pylons above. They were huddled together, shielded from minds in fear of detection. The refugees hushed the children. Marcuus watched as his co-worker and manager Montsi dared to light a candle, made from some sort of wax. It was late, and the rendezvous were even later. They should have been here by now, yet they weren't.

Marcuus tried not to think about the fate of the other transports. Those that had managed to reach hyperspace hadn't been heard from since. They were destroyed, he was sure. They <u>all</u> should be. It was the brave actions of the three pilots in the antique ships of stone that had spared him and the others in his transport from either death or capture: so far. The fact that they were the last to leave had perhaps saved them, and they were able to avoid the worst of the battle; not that Utopia stood any part of a chance. He did not know who to trust, but the leader of the stone ships had arranged a meeting place and time. They had used escape pods and set down somewhere at the rendezvous point, sending the ship on autopilot far away. It should buy them a few hours from the scouts of their enemy.

Deep in the distance a sound like thunder or an earthquake kept the children silent and afraid. He looked down to find a child tugging at this coat.

'Marcuus,' the child whimpered. 'I need to leak.'

'What! Now?' He whispered harshly. Her bottom lip quivered in the darkness. 'Oh,' he consented. 'OK, wait here Piniti.'

Marcuus began crawling towards his manager. He looked over the tired group of around twenty children and three other adults. Last night, they could have never foreseen this event tucked into soft, warm beds.

'Piniti needs to go to the toilet,' he whispered to her, not daring to use any other form of communication.

'Can she hold it?'

'I don't think so.'

'Go back a little way into the cavern. Use this vessel,' she instructed confidently.

Marcuus was impressed; she was holding herself and the rest of them together remarkably well. Yet he had barely gone a pace when suddenly there was a loud crack, followed by the earth shifting entirely beneath them. Everybody screamed.

'Right!' he heard Montsi order. 'Everyone back into the cavern!'

The ground behind them heaved upwards. A giant, spider like machine tore itself from the earth and swept Montsi and several others to the ground. It was huge, and looked impossibly heavy. In the twilight its dark multipodal form approached with alarming swiftness. Marcuus was transfixed in panic. It raised up a powerful limb to strike. In a moment Marcuus saw his life flash before him. He was going to die, and he hadn't even graduated yet.

He waited, but the machine stayed motionless in the air. Suddenly he turned and ran feverishly into the caverns, forever regretting that he had forgotten entirely about the children. Soon he realised that no one was following, and he made his way cautiously back outside.

The machine toppled over, its head still steaming from some energetic or plasmic weapon – most likely.

Over the crest of the crater dark figures had approached. Some of the children were reciprocating the advancement. The first figure, a man, approached a child and kindly swept her up. They stepped into the candle light. They were an unexpected group: two females, one brunette, one night black. There was the dark-clad soldier who held the child and a muscular one that reminded Marcuus of a Doberman pincer. There was a fifth male, cloaked and tall, but further out in shadow.

The young man who held the child was talking to Montsi, but Marcuus was quickly busied in organising the children. So these were the pilots who had saved them? Their transport had set down nearby, probably what had attracted the machine. As quickly as they could they got everyone onto it, and left for who knew where.

--- +++ --- +++ ---

Commander Sheelaakah lay, arms behind her head, lost in thought. It was another message from I-olo Tilk, using some form of thought projection device as he was no telepath, to communicate with her.

...We will take the children back to Kappa Roe. There, they can be assessed and kept safe. It was a successful counter strike. I'm sure I can convince the Circle to be pleased.

Thank you, she replied telepathically, *but again, most of the credit goes out to the efforts of those that serve with me. It is their actions which have brought us this small victory today.*

Indeed, I'm beginning to think you work well together, he observed.

Indeed I think we do, all of us, mused the Commander.

--- + --- + --- + ---

Aged grey knuckles turned white against the command chairs arms. He did not need to listen to the full report.

'Eighty two per cent success rate. Over two million civilians rescued from the Utopian system. Most losses include military and-'

'What about the research colony at Beakers point?' he asked, his voice harsh, rigid.

The soldier paused, no doubt fearing at first that he might have done something wrong. Quickly he scanned the report. The solder felt relief. 'Yes. Three transports, oh dear. We were unable to prevent them going into hyperspace and they have been destroyed. A fourth was disabled as it tried to leave. It has been found abandoned on the surface of Moonscape.'

'Abandoned?' The aged grey voice questioned threateningly. 'Then there were no children?'

'No, Sir,' but he did not understand. He thought the conquest of two million citizens as well as the natural resources of their colonies was enough. He did not understand that in losing the talents those children possessed to the Resistance, they jeopardised the True One's plans for decades.

What had gone wrong? The sages were all aligned, the voices had spoken. Somewhere, somehow, a rogue element had entered the master plan and foiled them. They had destroyed all Resistance activities for over four thousand kilometres, and yet somehow they had managed to rescue the exact object of his obsession as it lay in his grasp.

The soldier trembled at his unhidden rage.

'Find them. There are twenty children being sequestered by the Resistance somewhere near the Annexation. Find them at any expense and bring them all to me!'

NOW!!

Book 3

Abduction

Prologue

The grey eyed man watched as the speaker addressed the prisoners, or as they were called, the refugees.

'People of Utopia. I am the one you may address as "The Speaker". Your world has been destroyed by an attack of Kinerigan pirates, which caused your main Cleon reserve reactor to reach critical. We, the people of Seren, were able to detect the catastrophe as we had only recently entered Tesser from your location. Wasting no time we returned to our place of departure, and have scattered your foe. We cannot think of any reason why these enemies of the people would strive to endanger your world and your peace, which you have earned through diligence in your time. We have evidence suggesting that the Galactic Senate itself has attempted to disservice one of its own senators, by having him seraphinated at the expense of your lives and freedom. Unfortunately, the entire system has been irradiated and is devoid of any hospitable worlds now, as it begins a slow but inevitable implosion towards the gravity well at the centre of the sun. You cannot return.'

The Admiral, along with the others sent to oversee this annexation, looked out over his balcony where the most recent batch of a few thousand fugitives stood, frightened, confused, and so mentally exhausted as to accept as true any coherent thought they were presented with. It was the usual mechanism for dealing with new citizens who had been annexed from other worlds. Their initial futile escape attempts from the attack would usually land them somewhere here on moonscape, where they would be swiftly 'rescued' by the black guard. Provided they survived the denizens the government employed there to help remind them to be humble.

In gratitude they were hurried to this compound; told very little, and fed even less. In fright and exhaustion, not to mention the susceptibility hormones that were added to the atmosphere in this compound, they were introduced to their new life. Here, they would be told what to believe had happened to their home and how Seren had, again, saved them. Here they would be offered the chance that they had rejected while they had the choice to join the great Seren dream. Here, they could become government citizens entitled to all the privilege that living inside the Citadel meant to them.

But it was more than that. There were innumerable papers to fill out and examinations to pass. And a million more if the government decided to make it so. Only the worthy ever saw the light inside the city. It was a test. Who would comply; who would submit to their new government.

And then, if they were chosen, there would be housing to arrange, new state employment to deliver, new genetic pairings to arrange. Soon, those who chose to live inside the walls would assimilate into Seren culture and the unconscious participation in their own imprisonment. Those that did not were free to live outside the walls, and the living hell that that meant.

Those that chose to believe the lies that he, and so few others knew about, were welcome to the freedom and peace, of self-improvement and knowledge that it meant to be a welcome citizen of Seren.

Those that did not would live out a conflict-filled life until either they submitted to the government that made them 'free', or died a brief, ignominious death in the wilderness beyond the walls.

Either way, they would never leave Seren again.

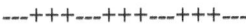

The refugee looked up as "The Speaker" finished. He was very handsome, he thought, with flawless features and convincing eyes. There was such sincerity in his voice, and unyielding conviction came with each annunciation. His face filled a wall the size of a building. About him, brief scenes flashed of the destruction of their little home colony: Utopia. Hordes of strange pirate ships had attacked the planet, disabling all communications in their wake. The destruction was immense, until the massive Seren Planetoid had re-entered space and fought for them.

He had been on a large military vessel which was almost destroyed, until it had crashed entirely onto the surface of Seren. They had spent the next day fighting off strange, horrible beasts which had attempted to feed off them and their craft, until a contingent of Seren black guards fought their way through and rescued them all. They were starving and half dead anyway, and they were taken to this strange "refugee" compound and given some thin soup. He had not slept in days.

The Speaker continued. 'Life as a new citizen of Seren has immeasurable benefits. No longer will you fear attacks from within or without the system. All citizens are issued with this individual identification sigil which fits within the skin on your right palm and forehead. With this individual sigil you will be able to access information from the government terminal each of you will have in your very own home. Housing is allocated according to need, and you will find that they will exceed all requirements. All material needs such as food and clothing are provided to you by the state. As you may know, there is no need for currency on Seren. All who contribute will find their needs met by the government, which makes the identity sigil necessary. All, from the waitress, the seamstress, to the Presiding council, are allocated the same basic resources for their needs. Inequality simply does not exist on this world...'

It made the refugee wonder. He was so tired, so hungry. He was young, had not even gained rank in the Utopian defence fleet yet. Just a dylusian system trainee for the gamma assault fleet. It would be many years before he gained rank, and would be able to afford to eat at the restaurants or permitted to attend the parties the ranking officers would always brag about. Yet here he was promised equality. It seemed so nice... but something about it seemed so wrong. Perhaps it was a forced equality? Perhaps it was just another party line – that equality was the illusion while the truly privileged lived in extravagant opulence.

He reflected on the strange battle that had brought him here. Those pirates fought so well, too well in all his experience. Even the gunner main had noticed it.

He did not feel comfortable here. It was not his place.

'Seren has no internal conflict, and all citizens have equal opportunity for enrichment and advancement. You need not worry about being tired, or hungry, or unfairly treated, for as a civilian of the Seren planetoid the Government will be your constant watch, your perpetual provider. All you need do is accept the oath of unity and receive your individual identification sigil and your future of peace is assured with us.'

The Speaker was so convinced. The young refugee looked about him. Some people were beginning to file towards the reception booths. He moved to talk to one of the black guards that were protecting him and the others. A tall man, with short blond hair and rich blue eyes staring meaningfully from underneath a strong brow. He turned to look at the refugee before he had even begun to speak.

'Sir, I was wondering, I have family on Terran fourth. Will there be a transport departing-?'

'I'm sorry,' he was cut short. 'The recent battle has damaged our shield. We will need to be entering Tesser soon and-'

'But sir!' the young man protested, 'all I need is a transport, or even an escape pod. I just need to wait around in Utopia for a few hours until the Galactic Senate fleet arrives.'

'I'm sorry,' the tall, blond soldier consoled placing a strong, large hand on the refugee's shoulder, 'we need to re-enter Tesser-'

'No!' the refugee shouted. Others stopped, and turned to look at the commotion. Another black guard stopped what he was doing to walk up beside the first one.

The refugee continued, his belligerence simmering. 'Listen. Your Speaker claims that the pirates are scattered, right? That gives us plenty of time to just wait around.' He was too tired and anxious to be polite any more.

'But the system,' began the second guard closely, 'has been irradiated. You'd barely survive a few minutes-'

'What are you talking about?!' The tired, frustrated refugee cried. Many others were listening now. 'If the system was irradiated by Cleon meltdown then that means it's primarily Gamma and Throxta particles. Base shielding one would be able to counter that indefinitely! And don't bother saying it. The gravity collapse is going to take decades! Anyone with basic essential physics knows that!'

Another guard approached, they were paying this a lot of attention.

The blond one continued, the anger growing on his countenance. 'You wouldn't last an hour with all that flotsam out there. The colony was destroyed, and you'd need-'

'Escape pods have thrusters, Duuur, or have you forgotten that!' The angry young man said sarcastically.

The black guard straightened and looked him right in the eyes. 'Your world was never worth saving anyway. Look at you, full or anger and losing control. You don't know what purpose really is! You think your world was good, it was full of conflict and injustice. Just think about it! This is your chance to join us in the great Seren dream!'

Something about it was wrong, and that last phrase was all it took for the refugee to realise that nothing, in space or hell, could ever convince him to live on any part of this planetoid.

---+++---+++---+++---

Admiral Taalk was watching the refugees from a balcony high above. He waded gently in the tide of emotions the refugees were feeling. There was one. A disturbance. He opened his light grey eyes. Some refugee was talking to the black guards. They were getting angry. Good. He reached out his mind, but was frustrated to be blocked by the refugee's copper banding, and he had a mental signature that was somewhat unique. The Admiral was too far away to do much but observe, but that did not bother him. It had been a very long time since he had been able to watch an annexing. This would provide an entertaining diversion to an otherwise dull portion on the whole as people surrendered to their ultimatum.

---+++---+++---+++---

He looked in the tall soldier's eyes. Why wouldn't they just let him go? Someone touched his arm.

It was an old man. 'If we took one of their fighters, we could defend ourselves if we had too. I have residents in Phoebus. They would be more than adequate to compensate the Seren System for any loss relating to this matter.'

'No,' the blond soldier said emphatically. 'You are all war refugees and need looking after. You don't know what you're saying. Let the Seren government-'

'I'd rather take my chances with the flotsam,' the refugee said calmly and then turning to the others, 'who is with me!'

'Grab him!' The blond guard ordered.

---+++---+++---+++---

The discussion had become a brawl, much to the admiral's fascination. So, someone had decided to do it the hard way again. The guards made their way quickly towards the young man, and would have subdued him in seconds, but an old man, one he had not noticed, swung a walking stick at the nearest guard. A brief bolt of lightning leapt from the innocuous rod and thoroughly paralysed the tall, blond guard. Within moments the young refugee was sprinting across the grounds, and would never turn to see the example the remaining black guards quickly made of the old man who had tried to get in the way of law and order on Seren.

---+++---+++---+++---

As the refugee ran he heard shouts, saw people running. He knew he only had a few seconds. If another guard didn't catch him soon those giant robots they called Emmissionaries might. He saw some fighter planes, wasps they called them, far out along a launch pad. Closer was some kind of transport. He ducked behind a transport crate and pondered. Quickly he activated the control mechanism and sent the crate along its gravity pod towards the transport, while he calmly stood and began walking quickly, but not too quickly, towards the Wasps. The ruse worked, the guards begun blasting the innocent crate to shreds while others worked their way around to the other side. Several refugees were caught in the cross fire, and he hoped they were using some kind of stun or disable setting. But then, the create was on fire...

He walked up to the three wasps. Their pilots were out on the ground talking. They were initially distracted by all the action on the crate, so by the time they noticed him he was barely twenty meters from them. As soon as they saw him he started firing at them with the gun he'd managed to grab from the blond guard just as the old guy had zapped him. He was horrified as they were struck dead from the volley. Why, why did they not set their guns on stun?

Reality came quickly back to him as a pillar of fire erupted just by his left. They had found him again. He raced onto the Wasp and threw on the mental sync shield. It activated quickly, which was also odd. Perhaps the pilot hadn't set any security as he'd left, or were all their ships designed to operate for just any pilot? It was unusual. But he wasted no time to take off and head straight into open space.

For a moment he was alone, then more than a dozen, no, three dozen craft appeared on his scanners. They were after him and in for the kill. How would he escape?

The Radiation! If he could get into the old colony he could mask his signature in the radiation field. Perhaps he wouldn't be such an important target if they were in such a rush to leave...

He took a direct course. Before him lay open space, which was divided from the refuse and radiation of a destroyed colony by a powerful energy barrier. Surely these craft had some way of negotiating this field. Yes, some codes. A sequence. A vortex begun to form in the field. Opening out into open space. He would be free.

---+++---+++---+++---

The admiral watched as the stolen wasp collided unceremoniously into the invisible barrier just within the vortex it had created.

That was the fate of those that chose to resist.

It is pointless to resist the power that is the great Seren dream, he whispered to the unconscious minds of all who cowered here.

Part 1

Friends

Sheelaakah was laughing. She couldn't help herself. It was the way he had with the children; you wouldn't think they were refugees by the giggled delight they were expressing. Matrix had some kind of footwear on his hand and was personifying it to the delight of his audience. The story that went along with it was unapologetically ridiculous.

They were in a refugee tent now, their transport already taking off to assist others. She had contacted headquarters with news of their success, and I-olo had assured her that the circle would be pleased. The tent they were in now was large, like an airport lounge, with makeshift benches and seating. In spite of this most of the children forsook the seating arrangements for a large circle in front of their entertainer. Their carers, four in all, ever vigilant, smiled in the circle of laughter. They sat outside on the edge of the small group and kept a close watch. Most of the children acted like children, but they were all in some way strange, unique. They all had rare talents. It was why they had been brought to the research colony that the Oppression had recently annexed. And while it was a remote possibility, it was not at all impossible that it was the **only** reason their system had been attacked at all. There were far more psychically gifted amongst them than statistically expected of a group of twenty children all under the age of ten.

She scanned their minds. All shielded as was the custom, but there was a lot she could tell from years of experience. Their minds young, but so few were truly whole. One of them was powerfully telekinetic. Another wore strange mittens of which he was perennially conscious, though he never looked at them. He wanted so badly to take them off, but feared retribution if he did. He could not follow the story that was being told, but laughed because the others did. His mind was severely impaired.

There were autistics there. And one, definitely a telepath, but his autism prevented him from communicating in any way. He stared out at the world from the lap of one of his carers as she unconsciously dabbed the drool from the corner of his mouth again; the one in charge called Montsi. Yet as Sheelaakah reached out his mind was far from blank. His unresponsiveness was compensated by heightened awareness of his environment that reached very, very deeply. It seemed to her that he was, as much as the woman whose unwavering vigilance kept the children, busy watching, and acutely aware. Even if he was physically incapable of communicating what he knew with the others.

One child sat near the front. A pretty little girl in a one piece deep emerald dress, her hair a single tail tied in the same colour of ribbon. She looked about five. She was totally engaged in the story, and laughed out loud at the antics. She had delicate Terran features, with natural lighter streaks of blond among the long brown strands of hair that were her own. Her eyes were evenly spaced jewels of agate; a deep, almost black iris's circled by untainted obsidian. Her head band was equally delicate, the copper tastefully etched with dark green runes. Sheelaakah knew she was aware of being watched, as most children are. They did not seem to mind her being nearby, and studying them from the moment they first met. She had felt the need to say little directly to them. But this emerald girl, she had no obvious talent, nor apparent flaw. It made the Commander curious, why had she been brought to the research colony?

Standing across the grounds was Officer Skion, a bulk of a being and a perfect soldier. He stood so coldly and aloof that none of the children dared approach him, or any of the busy army personnel. It was what made this scene so unique – a handful of giggling children among a semi-permanent army base. Skion was holding position at the door. Keeping watch. She reached out with her mind. He was very occupied, and unusually serious. Perhaps he was concerned, as she, for the children's safety, and this gave him extra reason to express his militant demure. She decided against any communications to disturb the low-level telepath, who might otherwise not be telepathic at all without his enhanced bio neural circuitry.

Another eruption of laughter from the children. Unit Leader Bakerson entered the tent, and nodded in her direction. Permitting her to probe his thoughts she learnt that an armoured transport would be passing by within an hour to take them to outpost Kappa Serenade: A far more hospitable place. The officer then turned and invited Skion to join in the storytelling, but he only glared a response.

It only then occurred to Sheelaakah that apparently Bakerson was Skion's inferior in the Resistance until an infraction involving Matrix had caused him to lose rank. Incredible! That explained the veiled tension between the three. At times the male pride would express itself as great competitiveness, particularly between officers Matrix and Skion. It had assisted them to peak performance on more than one occasion. Their rivalry was driven also by mutual admiration, but such would never be confessed. It gave Skion added impetus to not participate in the Matrix driven revelry.

Men are so... layered, mused the Commander. She could read their thoughts, and had looked into a few of their souls. And for all that, she would often wonder if she ever truly understood what drove them, or what caused them to make the decisions they did at times, or how they could be so unaware of their feelings and yet so unequivocally driven by them. Men were, as yet, a mystery to her.

Sheelaakah searched about for Alasia. She was next door helping some wounded in both body and spirit. It amused the Commander to see the nurturing side of the self-absorbed singer. Shee indulged the thought that it might be on account of something that she had said recently. It was ironic; she'd brought Alasia along to help the children, but she was far more adept at assisting the adults. Sheelaakah turned her mind quickly away, because she did not want Alasia to think she was spying on her.

Matrix was telling an interesting tale. He was making use of one hand, wrapped in a black joining band and the other was wearing a shoe.

'Oh no!' The shoe was saying in a high falsetto voice. 'Not by the hair of my chinny, chin, chin!'

And then in a deep voice; 'Then I'll huff, and I'll puff, and...'

'I'll blow your house in!' the children chorused.

The black wrapping began huffing and puffing to the delight of the children. Within a few seconds it had blown itself entirely out of huff and puff. Matrix continued. 'But it couldn't break into the third little emmanent's home because....' He paused, and began to look worried. Shee almost forgot herself, it was a story she had never heard before. But there was something about the ending that was making him uncomfortable...

...he was thinking *because the peacemakers had provided the third little eminent with a powerful energy field to protect him.* So that was how the story ended. That was what they taught the children who grew up within the walls.

'Because,' said Matrix. 'Because the third little eminent never gave up. No matter how big and scary the big bad space wolf was, he could never scare him. He was just too brave. Like you. Are you brave little eminents?'

The children cheered their agreements. One of the little boys flexed his muscles. The carers were a mix of fear, judgement and condoning.

The little jade girl stood up. 'Yes we are like the third little eminent. But Sir Matrix. We won't be staying. One day, we will be going home.'

'Oh Jacinth!' Said the carer Montsi suddenly brought near tears, 'be brave! We will be home one day, won't we?'

'Yes,' whispered the little girl Jacinth, placing a gentle hand on the carer's cheek. 'But you cannot come. You have to stay here and take care of people. It's all right. You won't be sad.'

What an odd thing for a five-year-old to say, thought Commander Sheelaakah.

--- +++ --- +++ ---

Then there were those who did not conform, but their bodies would be of use anyway. The man with grey eyes watched in glee as another Resistance soldier succumbed to the drugs. His body wrenched in pain as the soul print finally left it. The pale luminescent green tubules began to detach themselves from his veins and arteries one at a time. The mind control devices firmly lodged between his cranium and neck vertebrae relayed that vital systems were beginning to return to their anticipated parameters. His brain waves resembled those of a living human during deep, dreaming sleep. His breathing was slow and deep, and his galvanic skin response equivalent to a deeply relaxed man. He would never again need rest, never be confused about who to obey or what he had to do. He would serve as a mindless minion in the lower factories well below Seren where nobody would see him. Where no one knew where the forgotten were sent.

The man lay unblinking on the surgery bench, when a red hot iron descended from the Emmissionary above him and branded his new name into the flesh above his brow.

'931372458,' addressed Admiral Taalk, indulging one of his oldest past times. The man sat slowly up.

'Welcome to the dream unwaking! You don't need to fight any more.'

The man turned to look at the Admiral, the stare of meaningless death in his eyes.

'Now,' began the Admiral, 'it would have been far more pleasant for you if you'd told us before all this. But we will get the information we need from you anyway, and then you will be sent to serve in the refineries. Commander Sheelaakah, where is she?'

'I do not know,' the dead man responded.

'I *told* you so,' his apprentice tersely responded from behind him, coughing in the process.

The admiral slowly turned to face the impetuous apprentice he had allowed to come with him on this interrogation. He pressed his mind against Token's fragile spirit, which had no defences. He winced, and returned to his brooding in the medical chair.

'After all this time,' the Admiral mused exasperatedly to his long haired apprentice, 'it's only the psychochemates that are even keeping you conscious at this time, and my help. You'll not learn unless you listen!'

'He'll answer every question, but he does not know what we need. I could see that even during the torture.'

He stared at his apprentice's bravado, and it made him smile. Token was so *irrepressible*, Taalk mused. If he didn't get himself killed he might actually be a good choice for a replacement when he retired in a little over a decade. Provided he could keep the people's good above his own, most of the time anyway. He smiled as Token took another dose of the medicine. All this talking was making him vulnerable.

'You must listen for what we are looking for. Observe. 931372458, you were one of the pilots of the stone ships, correct?'

'Yes,' he replied in a monotone. 'Till I was liberated by the Government.'

'Tell us what happened.'

'After we engaged the Government fighters, six stone ships were ordered to leave and defend the transports. Three transports escaped into hyperspace, and the fourth was disabled. We managed to save the fourth transport, and abandoned the stone ships in moonscape. I was captured and liberated by the government fighters. The refugees were stolen by the Resistance, but I don't know where we took them.'

Lord Admiral Taalk mused. If only they'd captured him a few minutes later, they might have a better idea where the Resistance people were, and where they could find the children. None of the key personnel had revealed any truly useful information today. 'What were your rendezvous co-ordinates with the refugees?'

'Omega Nova. Until we realised that we had been discovered. I was not informed of the new location. That information was passed on to Unit Leader Skion-'

'There!' said the Admiral. 'You see! Now we know this man does not have the information we need!'

The long-haired adept stared in bored amazement and the old man, silent in vindication. Lord Admiral Taalk gritted his aged teeth silently admitting his apprentice had been right all the time. It was incredibly frustrating. Since the forge fired Resistance group had left the citadel and the telepath had detected his link he had been unable to use the message stone to spy on them. It was extremely frustrating. Perhaps if they could be lured back into the city he could get a better reading on their situation? No, that would not be a quick enough solution. He needed another, and a cruel suggestion began to form itself within his mind. Maybe...

The situation

The crowd was cheering wildly as they set down at Kappa Serenade. It was a welcome respite for the refugee's, Matrix could tell. But it was time to let someone else do the job. He had thoroughly enjoyed the afternoon entertaining a transport- load full of children. Most of them anyway, those that could listen at least. They were quite attached to him now and crowded about him. The carers were having a time of keeping their enthusiasm in check.

The transports wide doors opened and gave the children a start. They were greeted by the wave of celebration that awaited them. Slowly they, and the other refugee's with them, made their way down the gangway and into the waiting aid. Blankets, supplies, offers of help. It was the custom of the Resistance to welcome new refugees like this, though Matrix had never witnessed it before. They had so little but gave so much, and divided extra attention to the contingent of children that came this time. Armed Resistance soldiers assisted moving injured people and equipment, while dozens, almost hundreds of aid workers swarmed over the group eager to help. It was a fascinating site.

Matrix heard someone calling his name, and turned to see Alasia waving him over to one side where an unusually brightly coloured building lay. It must have been adapted to welcome the children, he assumed, and began leading the throng through the crowd towards it. Then some army men behind him gave an amused laugh. Alasia's waving had caught their attention, and they took the liberty of waving in return. Matrix turned to look, and for a moment she just looked surprised, frail hand resting against her breath. Then she returned a full smile and enchanting wave that started from her hips and would have stopped an entire unit.

There she goes again! thought Matrix.

Suddenly Commander Sheelaakah was by his side. It made him wonder how she always knew how to find him, even telepaths usually had to 'look'.

'Officer Matrix...' she said something more, but it was lost in the din of excited citizens and children. He tapped his banding in an ageless gesture.

Officer Matrix, began the Commander, her voice now as clear inside his mind as an echo in a vacant room. *Please take the children to the shelter.*

In the communication of their minds there was no doubt as to which shelter she meant, the coloured one Angel had indicated. *There they can receive medical and recreational support. It will be their permanent shelter until they can either be adopted out or placed in professional facilities. There is, of course, the chance that some of their parents will be located. The facility here will be grateful for the new assistance.*

What do you mean?

Oh, the new carers. You were right, they probably will never leave. I'm led to believe this facility was somewhat under-staffed, and this new development may benefit them.

Matrix realised how different she sounded when communicating with him this way. She had lost some of her cold informality that he was accustomed to, and she had told him more than he needed to know as though she had succumbed momentarily to the primal human drive to share important information. It made her seem... nice.

She was pushed back out of his field of view by the crowd. They were nearing the edge now. The children had stayed fairly well organised, because they were all looking towards him. Shee, ahem, Commander Sheelaakah hustled to catch his eye again. *I need to report to Resistance headquarters.*

You'll tell them we got the children?

Of course. It's why we came, she replied.

That's good then. I'd like to know what they will ask of us next.

Who can say? Will you take care of the children until I return? I'm asking a favour of you Matrix.

It made him pause. It sounded like a personal request. In that moment it almost made him, uncomfortable. But he brushed that aside. The Commander was a clever judge, and would know what she was doing.

Yes, now take care of yourself, he replied as she left, trying to sound professional but realising it probably came across as quite person. He turned, and she smiled the same smile that she had given him when they'd danced. He recalled how she'd fallen into his arms, her lovely womanly form pressed unmistakably up against him. He'd been too afraid to touch her, but felt wild enough to carry her away that night. He remembered her scent, the caress of her hair. How he wished he'd had the courage to hold her then! But she had escaped without a word. It would have been his first time since, well, ever really to have held a woman.

But this woman. No. It could have ruined everything. What did he know about relationships? He'd never had any, not really. How glad he was that he hadn't held her that night, when she had escaped out of his reach. She could be so cold and unforgiving. So capable of giving... pain. One could never maintain a relationship with one so unreachable.

He tried to give himself a dose of reality. She was his Commander, and relied on him to act professionally. It was only one dance. It didn't mean anything.

--- +++ --- +++ ---

I-olo Tilk! The voice boomed. He fell to his knees in appellation and covered his ears in pain. *Do not presume to know the mind of your council!*

I'm sorry, Majesty. I thought this news would please you. I did as I thought best, as I thought you would have done-

Fool! The voice roared. It was Majesty, one of the circle and leading powers of the Resistance. He did not know, nor ever would, who this person really was. All he knew is that it was the first and foremost authority on Resistance military activities. Its knowledge was almost... deific.

Peace, a soft feminine voice chided the Majesty. It was Tact, his superior in information and spying. She always seemed a step ahead, *I-olo is but a child. His folly a factor of our own-*

Folly? What folly, wondered I-olo in desperation. What had he done to upset them? The voices conferred in discussion as though he were absent for a time.

Eventually Tact answered his unspoken questions. *You used Resistance faculties to save a transport full of children, which might have saved four times that in capable, able adults. I thought this lesson would have been obvious to you by now: the greatest tactical advantage is always gained with the least comparative loss.*

You are replaceable, you know, spoke Dale, the physical aspect of what the Resistance would create and manufacture; and always aware of what functioned, and what did not. *Each link must be strengthened, or replaced.*

Dale, spoke a commanding, deep masculine voice. Voice, that was his name. The others all stopped to listen; his was the only undisputed opinion at the Circle, though it was not given often. His was the only voice that had never presented a physical form to the Understudy. No features, no form, no apparent age. He was treated as some kind of leader by the others. *Do not count this to his fault, he is, after all, our pupil.*

What must I do? pled the Understudy.

Imagine all those poor children, crying and afraid right now in that brute army facility, Tact said and then paused to allow I-olo sense his regret.

That was an error in judgement officer Matrix did in turning from his course after seeing that lone transport, and a greater error in the others moving to protect him as well, remarked Majesty in his most unkind voice.

I-olo, began Tact, a disembodied hand resting gently on his anxious cheek. *Here is what we must do. Send Commander Sheelaakah back into the Citadel, and make sure the same bodyguard she has previously been seen with does not accompany her, reassign all the officers. Have her place Alasia in a propaganda Resistance cell near the lower towers. Then return and inform us as to her success.*

I-olo trembled. He thought about her words. *But Circle, this group has shown remarkable abilities in spite of flagrant differences, I do not believe-*

GO! Roared Majesty, and the sub telepathic link was broken off so violently that it threw I-olo to the floor, and he was unable to move for several hours.

New mission

Taalk slashed through another pile of papers. They flew like butterflies in a curtain around him and landed helplessly on the floor. He crashed into another pile, his usual icy façade cascading before his continued defeat, their destruction as the only satisfaction in his aching frustration. They had to find those Resistance people! They had to complete their project. He was failing in his mission and this would mean the others would not be pleased. All their searches were turning up nothing, the Resistance hiding the children ever so well. Something had to be done.

He paused before taking the inevitable step, but knew his options were down to one now.

He walked inside the symbol etched into the floor and performed the archaic ritual. There was One he knew he could rely on when mortal wisdom failed. The being had not failed him, not since their first agreement many years ago. This again would cost him, but success was worth the price.

Light was replaced by darkness as the candles were extinguished in a windless breeze. Swirling black fog coalesced into a human form he knew better than to look up to. The air about him was unbreathably dark.

'What is it you want?' It asked in a powerful voice, no louder than a whisper.

He tried to speak, but his frame shock. The power held his tongue. Though it asked, it already knew.

The form breathed out a deep sigh. 'Yes. You have failed again. The war... you did not pay the full price for success to me this time, and this is the lesson you needed to be taught. Do not fear. I will bring her to you. The Jade child: Jacinth.'

He gagged under the effort to maintain the visage. Slowly the form faded and the room began to return to normal. Its spectral voice trailed off into a small eternity. 'I will bring you the Jade child....'

Taalk fell to the floor gasping for breath. Almost half an hour had been exacted of him during this one brief visitation. He sensed that something was afoot. There was a war going on. To what did he refer? He chastened himself. There was always a war, but a particular battle was about to take place. And he knew which side he served, and which served him.

So. The Jade child would be brought to him. Fascinating. Then he would wait, and see how this would be brought about.

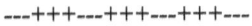

Matrix found himself sitting by Sheelaakah, laughing happily as they drank their chocolate milk. They had gone totally silly now, and were comparing moustaches. Alasia was entertaining the soldiers in a rowdy dance, which they didn't care to listen to anymore. The Commander had finally informed him what drinks were appropriate to their age, but then had carelessly left the ordering up to him now that he had complained that alcohol had given him a headache. It was what had broken the ice for them, she having erupted in unbridled laughter as he almost choked on the burning ale. He could feel himself losing control, though Shee had assured him that the enzymes prevented intoxication. It was just as well. He wasn't sure what was happening, but Sheelaakah was spending a lot of time with him since the remaining children were safely tucked into their beds after his custom-made bed time story.

'You're a bad influence on me,' she complained. 'Look at me! What am I doing *indulging* in pure entertainment with, all these _men_.' She looked about the room, almost uncomfortable that she had reminded herself. He didn't want to see her frown, and battered her arm with his glass.

'Don't worry, we both need to get out a bit. Besides, it's her fault,' he argued, pointing towards the black clad woman on the stage. 'She brings it out of people.'

Shee looked at Angel for a moment, and then stared dejectedly into her glass. 'She's beautiful, isn't she,' she questioned rhetorically.

'Ohhh,' said Matrix, trying unsuccessfully to disagree.

'Go on, admit it. Stunning. And she loves the attention.'

'You handle the attention alright.'

'Yeah, but they don't *know* me,' frowned the Commander, 'and it's all orders; do this, do that. None of them know me. And I don't want them too.' She looked out on the crowd of cheering soldiers.

Matrix thought she looked almost in disdain, or distrust at them. Had she forgotten that he was one too? He moved into her field of view a little so that she could disarm her with his smile.

She made a double take and hit him on the arm, but it broke the mood.

'You're beautiful too, you know,' he said, before he'd realised how much he meant it.

Sheelaakah looked stunned. She almost turned away, as though she could not believe him. Then they both broke into laughter again.

He'd meant it though. He thought she was beautiful. Her brown hair, which under any other circumstance might appear nondescript, cascaded beautifully around her face, with that lock on the fringe that would get in the way at times like this, and she would be constantly brushing it aside. Her eyes were quick and attentive, framed under two curves of brow. Her figure, which she so often might have claimed to not care about, was unmistakably feminine, and her posture and baring noble under the least of circumstance.

She gazed shyly out from behind her fringe and for a long moment they just stared at each other.

Matrix felt suddenly very in control of the situation. He thought it might be nice to hold her hand.

Unexpectedly he found Alasia making her way across the bar top towards them, dragging the crowd along with her, breaking the mood. They jeered and smiled at her as she went singing by. Matrix and Sheelaakah relaxed back into their stools and exchanged coy smiles.

'It is good to get out a bit,' commented Sheelaakah, probably pretending she didn't just read his thoughts. 'I never do. I had a brother once, and he used to have enough fun for both of us.'

'What happened?' asked Matrix before he could think to stop himself.

She shrugged. 'The Oppression got him. He's gone now.'

'Ohh,' said Matrix, unsure of what to say.

'It's all right. He was a good man. Boy really, it happened over seven years ago. But I can't forget. He was my twin, you know.'

A silence passed between them.

'Was he a psychic as well?'

'Yes,' said Shee. 'The bond was very strong, we would often...' and her voice trailed off in the din. Quickly she spun on the stool and looked at him. 'Anyway,' she said briskly, 'it makes me uncomfortable and I don't want to talk about it right now. Some things are better unremembered.'

'I concur,' he said wholeheartedly, and she smiled a sweet, affectionate smile that made Matrix want to ask her to dance. She looked as though she expected it, but she waited until he spoke anyway.

'May I have the pleasure of this dance?' He asked.

'You may,' she replied.

It was a simple moment, but genuine fun. He was surprised at how unshy he felt, how much he was permitting himself to be himself in the company of this female. The dance was energetic and liberating, and it ended faster than he had expected when she threw her arms around his neck and gave him an entirely unexpected hug. He was struck with nervousness and only managed a symbolic pat on the back before she let go – but he'd managed to hold her! She was smiling his smile, and looked quite happy.

He'd... held her.

Just them the soldier Bakerson came to the door of the barracks. Matrix looked up and saw him, and Sheelaakah turned to see what caught his attention. With a falling depression in his stomach Matrix watched as the

Unit leader saw them and walked quickly over to the Commander. He whispered something in her ear, as she glanced up at him.

He knew this dance was over.

'I must be excused,' was all she said, and her face took on the countenance she bore when she was at work. The ice shield had gone up. With a brief bow she turned to exit, and Matrix put a withering glare at his comrade Bakerson.

'What?!' Questioned the Unit leader, completely unaware of the unforgivable crime he had just committed.

---+++---+++---+++---

Many hours later he sat in confusion on the side of his bunk, very annoyed. Something was wrong. Unit leader Glenn Bakerson lay on the bunk across from him. Matrix sat on the edge of his bed, fidgeting. Dogman must have eventually had enough of it, for he spoke exasperatedly.

'What's the matter?' It was the opening Matrix had been asking for.

'It just doesn't make sense!' he complained. It was a frustration gnawing deeply at him. 'Why would they command her to leave so soon?'

Glenn continued cleaning his knife. 'She's a Commander. They're very busy,' he said matter-of-factly.

Matrix fidgeted some more.

'But that isn't what's really bothering you, is it?' he asked.

Matrix looked up in irritation. 'Oh, and I suppose *you* would like to tell me just what *is* bothering me?'

'If you want. You don't like the transfer because you don't want to be separated from Commander Sheelaakah. You see, you're in Initas: the first of the seven stages of love.'

'What!' he cried out incredulously. If it weren't such a noisy place his shout might have attracted more attention. 'You don't know what you are-'

'Oh yes I do!' challenged dogman, laughing good humorously. He pointed to his upturned snout. 'I've got the *nose* remember. I can tell things that you aren't even aware of. You and her, phew! The pheromones! Let me tell you, that is why I never go into those places. The *hormones*! So when I say there is chemistry there, like you don't already *know* there is chemistry there, I know what I am talking about.'

Bakerson seemed out of place getting all animated with his speech, But Matrix could tell he experienced a private world of scents that was impossible for him to share. Matrix smiled a wry smile, and looked at his friend as he lay back down on his bunk and continued his toil. OK, so he was growing attached, but he didn't want to admit it. He'd never found himself affectionate to a woman before. It was like a drug. It made him do things. Maybe that explained why he felt the way he did.

Otherwise, he might not have minded that their little group was being reassigned all over the Planetoid. Sheelaakah and Alasia were to travel back into the walls to help place Alasia in a spy cell. Skion was back in rank, and was being assigned to lead a new ground unit 'Scorpions'. Matrix had been left with Bakerson's 'Dogs of war' unit, the fifth. They didn't seem to mind where he ended up.

It didn't make sense; they worked so well together.

Or maybe it was, what did he call it, just Initas. Seven stages. He made it sound as if he had taken a course towards an inevitable seventh conclusion, and it had all happened so suddenly, so unexpected. He didn't know what to think. It wasn't right, breaking their group up like this, but what could he do? It was time to move on, let fate decide what was important.

He needed some distraction. 'C'mon then,' he said, and dragged Bakerson up and into the mess hall.

Some men were playing some kind of board and dice game. Dogman protested, but Matrix insisted. They walked up the board, and for a moment he couldn't decipher what was going on, then it hit him; they were gambling.

Matrix watched in fascination. That was illegal, all over Seren! This *was* a strange Resistance. Very... open minded.

He turned to Glenn and whispered. 'Do you know what they are doing!'

The unit leader looked sad and shrugged. 'Don't get attached. C'mon, Matrix, let's go get a drink.'

'No, wait, I want to watch a moment.'

'It'll do you no good friend, it is psychologically addictive. C'mon, I'll get you a chocolate milk-'

Matrix watched. There were many squares with numbers on a green table. Small round counters, which appeared to represent some form of token currency - also illegal, or simply not practiced, in most parts of the galaxy. Someone rolled two hexagonal cubes, pitted with uneven numbers of dots. The soldiers cheered and booed, and a rapid exchange of tokens took place that Matrix could not follow. It was a strange game.

'Eh new man, you wanna play?' said a rough looking guy that looked like he was running the game.

'Oh, I dunno...' said Matrix.

'C'mon' the others cheered. He looked at the table. The guy in charge held up two red tokens.

'Here, I'll lone you your first shot. Just put these on any square, and if your number comes up, you're a winner!'

The group cheered as others put their tokens down. Matrix stared and the table and at the circular tokens in his hand. He took a sigh and wondered where to put them. He looked over to Bakerson, who stood by the exit and clearly wanted no part in this.

As Matrix looked about he noticed, down on the floor under a nearby table, one of the refugee children. An odd little girl in a deep green dress. She was playing a one sided game with another little boy, who stared blankly out into space. A little ball bounced on the ground, and as it did she reached to pick up some curiously shaped objects before it landed again. She was singing a little song. 'When you play a game, play it fair. On thirty six, place it there.'

'Hey new man, you ready?' The rough looking guy said.

Matrix looked at the board. Sure enough, there was a thirty six, and no one had placed any tokens there. Well, he figured, what the heck. The dice rolled down the table, and most people groaned in disappointment. Suddenly a fair number of tokens were being pushed his way.

'Well! The new guys a winner!'

People clapped.

The game runner spoke: 'Try your luck again...'

Matrix shrugged. The little girl was singing again. He had to listen very closely to hear her.

'When you play, play again. Twenty eight is more the same.'

'Twenty eight,' said Matrix. One or two other token joined him in the hope of rubbing off some beginner's luck.

'All of them?' Asked the game runner.

'Yes,' said Matrix, though he noted that most people divided their tokens around.

Again the dice flew. Again mostly disappointment.

'Hey! Someone shouted. 'He's won again!'

The crowd cheered as now a considerable number of tokens were pushed his way again.

'Let's see you do that again,' challenged the game runner, looking just a little threatening.

'When you play, here's one more run. Pick the number thirty one.'

By now the entire crowd was watching. Several other tokens joined his on the appointed square. The game runner kept his eyes suspiciously on Matrix, and looked decisively disappointed when the predictable happened. His face grew dark, and the game runner stood.

The cheering stilled.

'Let's see him do it again,' the man said dangerously.

The little girl sang. 'Every game must have an end. Time for us to leave my friend.' The she held up her ball in the palm of her hand and stared over it to Matrix. She smiled knowingly, then gathered her toys and took the autistic boy by the hand. 'C'mon Petrie. It's time to leave,' and they headed towards the door.

'Sorry,' said Matrix. 'But I'm just not feeling inspired anymore.'

'Please, I insist,' said the game runner dangerously.

Bakerson stuck his head into the emerging conflict, and stared the other man down.

'Well, a very lucky day for the new man!' Said the game runner, and the people relaxed into their game once more.

'Well, what are you going to do with all your credits? They are only valid in this camp, and only at half of the vendors,' Bakerson whispered.

'I have no idea,' confessed Matrix. 'Drinks for everyone!' He shouted, and was everybody's best friend for the next half hour – including the game runner who seemed to have a hand in the drinks department.

After a while Glenn's discomfort began to reach a new peek.

Matrix began to feel sorry for his good friend. 'Let's leave,' he said to him.

Bakerson agreed with such a large sigh it was as if he'd been holding in his breath.

They headed for the exit. As soon as they left they turned to the barracks on the right, but Matrix arrested his momentum seeing the jade clad child waiting alone in the centre of the path.

Glenn stopped, turning around to watch.

Matrix looked at the little girl who always wore dark green. The one who'd helped him make so many 'new friends' tonight. She looked past Bakerson and directly at Matrix. He nodded, ready to hear her message, and she flew at him, grabbing at his arms.

'You *have* to go to her!' She spoke with anxious conviction. 'If you don't, they will take her away and we'll never see her again!'

'Good heavens!' said Bakerson, kneeling down to try and disentangle the girl, 'whatever are you talking about child?'

Matrix knelt down and held the little girl by the shoulders, sensing an urgency beyond understanding in her eyes, and they gave penance to an unconscious anxiety he had been repressing for hours. 'Commander Sheelaakah, my friend. She is in danger, great danger isn't she!'

Now one of the carers walked up the girl. He seemed embarrassed that she had escaped his vigilance and was now talking with these professional soldiers.

'A temporal perceptive?' Matrix asked the carer.

'Yes, but she's never been properly assessed,' he said, smiling in a weak apology.

'But has she ever been wrong?' Matrix persisted.

'Marcuus?' Another carer called.

'I'm sorry,' the carer apologised as the child tried to struggle in his hand, 'we need to be going, sorry to have disturbed you officer.' He took the child firmly by the hand and began to take her away, while she seemed lost to forge her thoughts into words.

'She is in great danger!' The child said with passion, 'The pretty one with wavy brown hair. It's a trap!' she fairly screamed.

The carer dragged her struggling against him. As they rounded the corner the child called out again, 'You have to go to her!'

Suddenly Matrix felt very calm. He knew what he had to do. Without waiting he ran to the barracks to pack his belonging. He was just finishing the last when someone entered, and the barracks grew quiet.

'What do you think you are doing, soldier?' Asked a commanding voice behind him. He turned, it was Bakerson already flanked by two other soldiers.

'You don't have to come,' said Matrix quickly.

'Soldier, I order you to cease this activity quickly!' Matrix's senior officer continued.

For a moment Matrix paused. Then he turned and looked at his unit leader, placing a hand on each shoulder and staring resolve into his eyes. 'Look. The Commander is in trouble. Or if she isn't yet she will be soon. I can feel it, can't you feel it?'

Bakerson struggled in a conflict between his heart and head. 'Look, I'm sure the Resistance sages would have noticed...' but his voice trailed off.

Even Matrix knew there was no certainty in temporal perceptions.

'You'll lose rank if you leave on your own this time. You'll never be welcome in the Resistance again.'

Matrix turned and continued to pack. 'That's fine, I'll survive. I make no sense of these large scale conflicts anyway.'

'You're prepared to risk everything on the... prophetic comments of a strange child!?' He growled.

'You probably would – for *her*,' Matrix replied. He did not mean the Commander, he meant... he didn't know what he meant.

Dogman may have flinched in the anguish of conscience. 'All right!' he said, 'the Commander is due to pass through Dengii province soon, and that is on our scouting run anyway. Well meet up with her then. And we leave immediately. Dogs of war!' he called, and all the men, including Matrix, barked their salute. They were all gone in less than an hour.

Betrayal

The timing was perfect, thought Alasia. How broadening an experience it had been to be with the Resistance for this short time. Most of it she was willing to forget – some of it memorable. Least of all the horrible green eyed man that she had gotten into all this for, then left her for this brunette that would never melt for him. Perhaps she would exact some revenge on him one day, or worse, just forget about him and he would forever suffer never knowing what he might have had.

Being angry had made her into a consummate professional. She knew her job, and what she had to do. The stone was already placed, and it was only a matter of time before they came for her. There would be much to profit from all this.

Their conversation was light, and deceptive. The ice princess had melted, and lost some of her edge since letting that man in. Now she was unaware of the small onyx stone that rested in her cuff. She might have noticed it, even been unable to ignore it, had it been pointed out to her. But not knowing had made it invisible to her. The two women chatted peacefully.

'So when I get in the walls,' Alasia was saying with deceptive calmness, 'were going to meet up with Sharon Corps. A Resistance cell. There we will go our separate ways and probably never see each other again. How sad, I'll miss you.'

And she thought how final that last statement probably would be.

The Commander smiled. 'I doubt it, you surround yourself with friends. Life at times, can be lonely.'

'I know what you mean,' confided Alasia. 'You'd be surprised how lonely my life can be.'

The Commander did look surprised. Alasia noted how vulnerable she had become in the last day, since she linked up with Matrix just before that battle at the maws.

'It's true,' Alasia said. 'You can have a thousand associates and a million false friends. But tell me, who can you really confide in this existence? No one really. Not even our lovers.'

The Commander looked sad.

Alasia smiled. She had changed the conversation topic without really altering the topic of conversation. 'I'm sure you'll see Matrix again,' she consoled, though she did not see how that would be possible.

The Commander drew a breath and quickly replied, 'Oh, that's all right. He's just a soldier, like all the rest. I'll probably see him around.' She sighed, but Alasia was not content to leave it at that.

'He's more than that to you, isn't he?'

The telepath turned to look out the window so that Alasia couldn't see her blush. It made her laugh. My, how unschooled this Resistance expert was in the fundamental art of love! A fatal flaw in the statue of an ice princess.

She stumbled a bit for words, but was still being honest. 'Well, I suppose... he is a friend then. Very sincere, you would have to admit. Not many men like him. Not many people really. Yes, that would... a friend. I haven't had one of them for a long time,' mused the Commander.

It almost made Alasia sad to see this spark of humanity in this woman's eyes. But it was her fault, making herself vulnerable. 'Remember you can't trust people, Sheelaakah, not even your lovers.'

'Oh it's not like that!' argued the Commander, but Alasia knew enough about love to see that that was exactly what it was.

The transport suddenly slowed. The Commander stood to see what was happening, while Alasia concealed a dark smile and sat back. Freedom at last, and a decent terminal before her aching breasts drove her insane.

'Unexpected EM turbulence Commander,' the pilot was saying. 'It's disrupting our propulsion drive. We should be through it in a -'

His voice was cut short as an explosion ripped through the cockpit, vaporising the driver instantly and throwing the Commander against the bulkhead, rendering her immediately unconscious. Alasia checked her briefly to make sure she was alive and then headed toward the cockpit. Most of it was gone, and the craft was barely managing a controlled descent on impulse. Two Wasps cut the evening sky. They were circling around for another pass. Quickly Alasia set the shields to a signal frequency that the Oppression, sorry, the Government used to signal friendlies. A moment later a signal beamed directly to the cockpit, establishing a subtelepathic link between her and one of the pilots.

Designation, he ordered.

Bri-Gran Rho, Alasia replied, hoping that they responded to the coded signal for government operatives.

Signal received. Please set down at these co- ordinates.

Alasia looked at the non-existent cockpit, her hair flying wildly in the open breeze. *Are you crazy?! I'll be lucky to land this tub alive after your uncivilised lout! Bri-Gran Rho out,* she shouted angrily and broke off the link.

They were going down fast, and she needed to do some very primitive steering to keep from dying this early in her career. Then she threw herself into a chair and flashed up the restraining mechanism. The trees from the jungle smashed into the undercarriage of the craft, spinning it wildly but slowing it sufficiently that when they finally hit the ground it was little more than a violent jolt. As soon as she was certain she was all right, Alasia opened her eyes. Somehow they had hit upside down, and she had to crawl from the wreckage.

Then she remembered the Commander, she had to find her to get credit for this effort! Carefully she crept back into the ship. She was nowhere to be found. After a few anxious moments Alasia found the Commander with the help of a locater from the craft. She lay motionless on the ground where she had been dashed against a tree when thrown clear during their dizzying decent. The two wasps flew overhead again, and then circled back to base. They would send more appropriate aid shortly, before midday most probably, as long as the mutants didn't find them. Alasia bent down to check the Commander.

She was still breathing, at least. She had broken both legs and several ribs in the fall, and was covered in multiple bruises and scars. Alasia crawled back into the craft and grabbed a portable medical kit. Then, to keep herself occupied, she tended to the Commander's wounds. The medical stones were to keep the Commander alive, and the pseudo plasma would compensate adequately for the blood loss till her body recovered. Most wounds and deep cuts were tended with the balm. The broken bones were trickier. Alasia set them in the fluid belts, but had to cut a branch to fix a splint for the second one. The re-fusing of the bones only took a few minutes, but would require a few days to properly heal. Her basic medical training had paid off again, and oddly enough, she was almost enjoying herself, in a clinical kind of way.

Yet the Commander was still unconscious nearly three hours later when Alasia pronounced the job done. *Now, where was the blasted rescue teams?*

---+++---+++---+++---

'There! You see that!' Matrix was pointed to an energy signature on the mid-range scanners.

'Yes?' the pilot spoke, clearly aggravated that he had insisted on peering over his shoulder the entire journey. 'But that's almost forty minutes outside of our territory. It would take a significant detour to investigate.'

'It's the Commander,' Matrix argued towards his Unit leader. 'She's in some kind of trouble. It looks like a weapon signature to me.'

'Soldier...' Bakerson asked the pilot. 'Can you identify the energy signature.'

'Yes sir...it was a wasp forward turret, striking tritium alloy.'

'Could be a Resistance craft. Was there an emergency beacon deployed.'

'Only the automaton. Wait. There appears to be a sub telepathic link in progress. I had to shine my scanners directly onto the area to detect it.'

'That's good enough for me.' Bakerson confided. 'We're going to take a look. Don't worry, we'll make the rendezvous tonight.' The unit leader informed them.

---++---++----

'Matrix, we have to send the men back.'

It was almost three hours later, and the men were getting ornery. They had been searching on foot, but still had yet to locate any sign of the craft. Commander Sheelaakah was probably using some form of shield to avoid being found. Or, perhaps they were too late.

'Fine,' Matrix told him. 'Call off the search if you want. I'm not coming.'

'Neither am I.'

'What?' questioned Matrix, not believing what he was hearing.

Bakerson simply turned towards the others. 'Men, I want you to head back to the rendezvous. Officer Matrix and I will remain behind to search for survivors. If not, we will meet you back at base in two days. Are we as one?'

The men whole-heartedly gave their approval and filed back onto the ship.

After they had left, Matrix spoke. 'What's going on?' he asked.

'You were right again. That craft was the Commanders. I can, almost smell it. The breeze in this forest is most unusual, it's as if... anyway. Let's put these things down and travel up wind.'

'OK,' said Matrix, though he wondered why his unit leader did not think to use this tactic while the others were around. Perhaps there was some reason.

---+++---+++---+++---

Alasia tore another scratch on her arm as she pushed between branches. She swore to herself. Hours had passed and there was no sign of a rescue mission. She was beginning to get suspicious. She had left the Commander under a sanctuary field and gone in search of the portable communication transponder. The forest was thick, with spiked lianas that grew high and thick from the ground only to disappear in the near total cover of the canopy high above. The trees were large and old, and the forest floor undisturbed in centuries. It might have been quite beautiful, but this was the third leech she had removed in under an hour.

The tracking signal was growing stronger now. Finally! She found it, hidden in a sharp, prickly bush. It took a full ten minutes before she succumbed the inevitable and, ignoring the pricks of a thousand needles pushed her arm in and retrieved the transponder from a wickedly spiked bush where it had landed several dozen meters from the craft.

'Bran Gro Rio,' she said desperately. 'Please respond, we are in need of assistance...'

Nothing. Nothing at all. Finally in exasperation she returned to the craft and to guard her prey.

The Commander awoke at her footsteps, and gave a start, then a winced. She touched her delicate ribs, and did not look well.

'Take it easy. We took a blow there. They haven't found us yet. You broke your ribs and your legs. You're going to have to stay off them for a couple of days.'

'Wha... what happened...?' the Commander asked weakly.

'We took a blow. You've broken your legs. We have to wait,' Alasia spoke clearly. Better not to let the Commander know the truth, at least not yet, in case things didn't work out the way she planned. But the Commander did not hear. She looked at Alasia with unthinking eyes.

'Here, take this sedative. Now go to sleep.'

The Commander nodded and then passed out. She seemed to do that a lot.

Whether it was the sedative or the wounds, Alasia did not care. She didn't really like to watch people suffer, and didn't want to watch the Commander right now. Pain was best kept at a distance; it meddled with her inner harmony. The sun was sinking behind the trees, and soon it would be night. It would probably become quite cold in this dank forest, so she went to get some blankets. Sleeping under the stars was a romantic concept that she promised she'd try one day, and today looked as good a day as any. She checked the energy levels on the phaser and went to get the blankets.

She was lost in thought on her way back, but it only took a second to register. Off in the distance a twig snapped. She immediately was afraid, and dropped the blankets to grab the locater. Humanoid. She hid herself inside the sanctuary field and prayed they were the right people. She could hear voices now. They weren't trying to be quiet. Something was wrong.

'Noc! Too. Splithith!' The Commander spoke suddenly, delirious.

'Shhh!' whispered Alasia fiercely. 'They'll find us!'

The Commander continued to mutter under her hand. After a moment she fell silent again.

The voices were quiet now, but the footsteps became louder. They were heading right towards her. There was no escape now. Alasia clutched her weapon and pointed it in their direction. They'd better be the right people or they would be dead. She forced her trembling hands to stop. How she could have used a dosage now! Some shadows flicked through the forest undergrowth across the other side of the clearing their craft had torn, and Alasia waited until she had a clean line of sight.

He was looking up at the giant craft which was lying on its roof, its cockpit entirely blown out, and wondering how anyone could have survived this incident. Then a blazer carved a neat hole in the tree next to him. He had his knife out in microseconds when he suddenly heard a woman call out:

'Matrix! Thank the peacemakers I missed! What are you doing here?!'

He turned around to see Alasia running towards him. Bakerson hid still concealed in the forest.

Alasia ran and threw her arms around his neck. 'I'm so glad it is you. How did you find us? It doesn't matter. The Commander was hurt. You'd better take a look,' she said.

'How badly?' He asked the singer.

'Oh, pretty badly. Say, are you alone or did you bring anyone else with you,' she asked as they hurried over to the sanctuary field.

'No, Bakerson is in the forest, I took point. Oh dear.' He bent down to look at the Commander. She was badly bruised, and her ribs and legs were bandaged. Alasia seemed to know quite a bit about field medics. He gently touched the Commander's cheeks. She awoke.

'Oh, Matrix,' she said, sounding pleased to see him. 'My friend, I knew you'd come for me. I just knew you'd come,' then she went back to sleep.

---+++---+++---+++---

She went back to sleep. How <u>infuriating</u>. Alasia bent down to check the Commander's pupils and to gently yet furtively slip the small black stone from the woman's cuff. Now the government had missed their chance! Matrix. If he were alone... but there was that sharp-eyed puppy soldier as well, hiding somewhere out there. Now she didn't know what to do.

It wasn't that she wasn't afraid to let Matrix die or anything. She just didn't want him to suffer. They wanted the Commander. And it was her job to deliver her. They wouldn't get the others as well. At least while there was this chance that they might discover what she was really up to and escape to tell the Resistance. In the past she had never let them tell the others, and these would be no different. In her business, it was important that you knew when to keep a secret.

'What do we do now?' Matrix asked.

'We'd better make a stretcher,' Puppy soldier said emerging from the forest, looking handsome in the bedraggled muck of the jungle which accompanied any who travelled through her. 'There is a unit stationed three kilometres of here. We might be able to make it before night if we all hustle.'

'What!' protested Alasia. 'There is no way you are dragging me through this jungle. I nearly died in that crash, and I'm staying right here.'

He paused for a moment, then continued fixing a stretcher up out of parts from the ship.

'Suit yourself,' he said casually, 'but the Oppression will be out here soon to check things out. I'm surprised they aren't already; they are usually more prompt than this. And after night the Bark pythons come out to drink the night air. You'd be a lot safer with us, but it is your choice really.'

He sounded uncharacteristically blunt and brief. She twisted her heals as she pondered her options, and then decided it was probably best that she stay with the Commander till this project was seen through.

'All right, lead on,' she murmured.

Matrix ducked as a bolt of lightning cut the tree in half just behind his head. They were getting closer now. Blasted black guards. They had found the wreckage and managed to track the fugitives to this location. Matrix, Bakerson, the Commander and the Singer. The latter had even suggested that they try negotiating with the guards, but he had decided to open negotiations with a wide field spread of Bakerson's stunning rune. It didn't appear to take many of them out, and they were slowly being surrounded even though they were trying to remain unseen. If the Commander were available then maybe she could have helped, but she was unconscious, and night had all but fallen. If they'd tried for hand to hand combat it might have swung their way, but clumsy as it was they had pinned them down with random wildfire.

'What do we do now!' He whispered to his unit leader even as another tree erupted in flame. They were pinned down hiding in a large hollowed out tree trunk that had fallen a century ago, which had found a resting place in some kind of gully. It offered minimum protection from the frantic arrows and blasts of the black guards who had been pursuing them for over fifteen minutes.

'Your form of negotiating is going to cost us our lives Matrix!' The singer hissed. An explosion rocked the forest.

'You know,' answered Matrix, 'call me the eternal optimist, but I believe that something good will come of this one day.'

Alasia stared at him in disbelief, and was quite speechless for perhaps the first time in her life. It gave him an immense sense of satisfaction.

The firing rate doubled.

'Oh yeah, really great. Now they're going to kill us for sure!' Alasia screamed.

'Shhh,' Dogman hissed. He was listening intently to the sounds of gunfire.

Then Matrix noticed that they sounded different too. 'You hear that?' He asked.

'What?' questioned Alasia.

'The gunfire. It's not directed at us anymore.'

'What are you talking about?' demanded the singer.

But Matrix heard it too. Shouts now, though he could not make them out. There was a battle going on. Someone else was out there too!

Almost suddenly the battle stopped and the forest was reverently silent. They heard footsteps, and it only took a moment before they found out who it was. Around the corner of the trunk came a mech soldier, a tall and muscular man.

'Skion?' he asked unbelievingly.

'Weel, weel, look what we have here – a worm in a log,' he sneered, and helped them all to their feet.

It took quite a bit of convincing that it wasn't some sort of plan to ostracise him. It wasn't until he saw the report of the Commander's ship going down three kilometres outside his patrol base that he finally believed their story. His troop had been out on patrol when they had registered the gunfire and made haste to their location. The Commander would now have better aid from Skion's medic unit.

It was all rather fortuitous really; somehow they had found themselves together again.

Together again

The next day she was up again, limping softly around. She was not nearly as insistent on refusing Matrix's aid or his arm as she had been under a week ago at the 23rd and fourth. They were making their way towards the portable subtelepathic link Skion's unit had. They were resting after their hasty departure the night before, into some forgotten paths through the forest the Resistance had built long ago. They would not be found here.

The Commander limped up to the unit, and eased herself carefully into a chair. She smiled up at Matrix. 'This may take a few moments. Will you wait?'

She knew did not need to ask him, but he nodded just the same.

The link only took a moment for her to establish. His presence was a comfort now, and it helped her ignore the pains in her legs and side. She was nervous, keenly aware of how vulnerable it made her now that she had let him in, just a little. And that was above and beyond her physical injuries, perhaps this was a wound that would never heal. But all at the same time it seemed the only sane thing she had done in forever.

The answering call reawakened her concentration. *I-olo here. Commander Sheelaakah: You do not die easily,* he remarked jokingly. *It seems the Oppression is on your case.*

It might seem so, but no more than any of the others. I am replaceable. Tell me, do we have any information on the attack? And what are your orders now?

No information I'm sorry, which is unusual. Some things are at the moment...

She wondered what that meant, and as if he knew her thoughts, he answered.

Well, well, the five of you are together again. I must say I approve, even though the Circle does not.

And at this Sheelaakah was definitely worried. It was not like an Understudy to betray the confidence of the Circle like this.

Unless... he continued, *they either wanted you dead or captured.*

Sheelaakah was stunned. She did not know what to think. What was he talking about?

Commander, I want you to rest up with this current unit for a few days before continuing. Have them move towards Beta Numerous. I doubt the Oppression will be expecting you to remain near your current location.

Understood, she replied, and allowed the link to fade.

She opened her eyes, and Matrix was still standing there.

'Is everything all right?' he asked.

'Yes, well enough for now,' she said, somewhat deceptively.

He looked surprised, but did not ask any more. Slowly they shuffled off to lunch.

She listened to Alasia complaining; field rations were not her fare. They had been on the slow march for two days now and were nearing the Beta Numerous Station, another of the less secret Resistance cities. She still stood only for a few minutes a day, and took comfortably to riding in the litter they had made up for her. She would find herself sitting, or lying, and staring blankly at the canopy as it passed high above. This was one of the few beautiful parts of their planet prison, though she had never really noticed it before. Now there was not much else to do but think, or talk to someone until she grew tired again. There were plenty of people to talk to, but for now, she felt like silence, and gazed up at the passing trees and branches.

Matrix was by her side again. 'I see you are awake now.'

'Awake? Was I asleep? Oh, I must have dozed off back there,' she said.

'You've been asleep for almost two hours,' he commented.

'Really? I never noticed,' and she wondered how it was possible that she would sleep and not remember it.

The soldier in front put her hand up for the unit to halt. They waited tensely, listening to the calls of the far away birds and the hustle of the wind making its way around the foliage above them.

'This area is sufficient to rest. We hold up here for now,' Skion said after a few moments, and they relaxed.

'What happens now?' Matrix asked.

'I really don't know,' Shee answered. 'Perhaps you would care for some field rations?'

'No, thank you,' he said in thinly veiled disgust. 'I've... eaten all of mine.'

'Oh, but they are so good for you!' she insisted with a rare hint of sarcasm. 'Pure energy and all essential additives blah, blah, blah.'

They laughed. Some of the soldiers, apparently, developed a taste for the dry, crusty biscuits, but not them. Alasia soon walked up to them.

'You'd think they could have built a chair for me too, don't you?' she asked Sheelaakah in half hidden good humour. 'You get carried about the *whole time.*'

'Speaking of which, it's time for some exercise. Matrix, will you help me to my feet?'

'Certainly,' he replied.

They wobbled unsteadily as she took to her feet. She stretched and took a good look around. 'It's such a nice day and a beautiful sky. Anyone know where we are?'

'Backwarn. Apparently,' Bakerson replied. He was always within a pace or two of the litter.

'Ahh yes, our favourite watering hole,' Sheelaakah commented, half to herself.

'What do you mean?' Alasia asked her.

'The Seren Planetoid comes to this system often. There is nothing else out here, and it's very far out along the northern rim. The Oppression seems to feel safe here... gives them time to digest their latest meal. Not many stars during the night cycle admittedly,' she mused, but her voice trailed off as a hush suddenly fell amidst the soldiers. There was no sound except for the avian species in the trees and the wind that passed between them. Matrix looked out quietly.

'Skion is scanning the area. Something is passing – '

Suddenly the serenity was torn asunder as the sound of gunfire and shouting split the day air. Sheelaakah could make no sense in the whirling rush that followed. She found herself thrown onto the stretcher and raced back off into the forest. She had to do her best just to keep from falling off, which would have been extremely painful. There were shouts and sounds of combat all around. Eventually the men carrying her stopped and took up a defensive position. The forest became deathly silent.

What happened? she asked.

Shhh, he signalled, and she waited in silence for another hour, not daring to move.

---+++---+++---+++---

The forest was deathly silent. He was kneeling on the ground now, fondling his spear quietly, sniffing the air. She was watching him from inside a hollow tree trunk where he had thrown her only moments before. It had caused a bump on her head, but she had refused to cry out this time. It had gotten her such a severe scolding the last time. And he would be mad this time too: her constant chatter to cover up nervousness had been forcibly ceased over an hour ago, and she would give him no cause to blame her again. He was awfully fierce underneath, for a puppy soldier, Alasia thought.

Their unit had been attacked just as things were beginning to relax. In the resulting confusion they had managed to get separated from all the others. She had run screaming through the forest and would have run straight into a carnivorous plant if he hadn't have grabbed her. Their journey from then on had been everything but pleasant. The first day she had tried to stop the thorns grabbing at her dress, and tried to avoid stepping on anything unpleasant. Now she was beyond caring, her clothes in tatters and her life in perpetual risk. They had spent the night pretending to sleep in the trees and batting the small bighting insects from their bodies. And since a thorn had penetrated her delicate footwear designed for city travel he had tied some thick, and rudely uncomfortable, bark to the souls of her shoes.

The stone she had collected off Commander Sheelaakah rested in her breast pocket where it had remained since the government had failed miserably in responding to her success in finally placing it. She had not yet fully swallowed her ire at their incompetence, and had determined that someone was going to answer to her wrath at their folly one day. Yet she had not forgotten her mission. There would be another time. Though she could not understand why they had failed her, someone would pay.

Without warning Officer Glenn suddenly shot up from his vigilance and leapt with his spear violently into the forest. To where, she could not see - she'd shut her eyes and tried to pretend she wasn't there. He roared, or rather barked a battle cry and crashed through the brush for a few seconds. There was the sound of a violent scuffle and the lone cry of a blazer blast.

She waited for a moment of eternity, listening to the sound of her constricted breathing. It seemed too loud, and echoed in her ears against the tree trunk. It added to her fear, and her fear added to her need to breathe more. It was very frustrating.

A twig snapped. Someone was coming. She strained against the fear and innate desire welling up inside her to get out and run. Eventually curiosity overwhelmed her and she slowly peered around the edge of her tree anyway. The puppy soldier squatted on the ground, studying some instrument he had picked off the corpse of one of the black guards he'd just slain. It was some kind of grey rectangle stone with what looked like a small, round opal on the opening face. The entire unit fit neatly into his hand. She resisted the urge to chide him, and instead crept towards him and whispered. 'What is it?'

He took his time in answering. 'It's a transmonitor responder, we can use it to track enemy movement. This is good.'

She winced involuntarily at the volume of his voice, although he was talking at a normal volume, it had been days since she had dared anything but a whisper. They had said exceeding little, except what communication was vital, since he had pointed the sharp on his spear millimetres from face and commanded her to keep silent "lest they be discovered". For a man who looked like you just wanted to pat him, Angel had learnt the hard way not to play games with him.

'You're speaking out loud?' she whispered.

He held the responder so that she could see the opal. Its colours were shifting, and it looked quite pleasing really, but she could make no sense of what it meant.

'This responder,' he was saying, 'indicates that there is no enemy presence or scrying sensors in several dozen kilometres. We should be safe for some time now.'

Alasia felt a wave of relief wash over her. A lump formed in her throat, but she fought back any tears. She had not realised how afraid she had been.

'Well, I'm glad that little stint is over. When do you think we will arrive at Beta Numerous now, Dog Soldier.'

He took no offence at her disrespect, as he was probably used to it by now. Surely he knew she used insults to deal with her tension.

'Now that we don't have to creep? Less than a day – provided it is still there of course.'

'What do you mean? Where will the others be?'

'Oh, they'll be there, I know it. The Oppression unit we ran into was probably sent to raise Beta Numerous, we were just too close. I doubt they would have captured the Commander, she is very resourceful despite her condition. The others will have continued to head to that outpost precisely because the enemy would not have anticipated it. We should be safe there, for a time. And you can get some hormone supplements...'

'What is that supposed to mean!?' Alasia demanded, delighted at the first opportunity to raise her voice and get angry in what seemed like years.

'The period of women is upon you,' he stated, studying the little device in his hand.

Alasia was stunned, it was so arrogant of him to assume... besides, it was impossible. She talked angrily, as at an impudent youth, 'Excuse me, learned sage, but for your information I have been... altered and I have never had one of these... period of women!'

The soldier refused to look up from his task, but snorted in disbelief. 'Say as you will, your hormone levels have altered a lot these past two days. The cycle is an integral part of your body even if you lack... the equipment. I'm sure you know that.'

Now it was Alasia's turn to scoff in disbelief. 'And just how are you supposed to know about *my* hormone levels.'

He put down his device and looked at her. He tapped his largish and slightly up turned nose.

'And just what is that supposed to mean?' she demanded.

'Humans can smell far more that they are aware off. My genetic heritage allows me to be aware of what I smell. I can actually only detect a few thousand more scents than the average healthy male. But considering they can respond to several hundred thousand it's surprising they don't notice more. I am simply more aware of what most people already know on an unconscious level, but rarely take the time to notice, or they brush it and most of their intuition away. That's why.'

She was not sure how to respond to the reply or if she fully understood it, so she said nothing. He led the way into the bush, but they had not gone far till she began to feel hungry again.

'Do you think, Dog soldier, that we can stop for a rest?'

'As you wish. Care for an apple?'

'A what?' she asked.

'An apple. Have you never seen one before?'

She had not. 'Isn't that some kind of flavouring additive?' she asked.

He laughed, and reached up to a twisted tree that seemed to be struggling for light for a small, roughly spherical reddish object. He yanked it off the tree and offered it to her. She took no effort to hide her disdain.

'I can't believe you would eat that without *any* kind of processing,' she began, but knew what the answer was.

'Oh, I'm sorry,' he falsely apologised. Quickly he rubbed the apple against a somewhat cleaner part of his shirt and offered it to her again.

'You've *got* to be kidding.'

'No, I'm not,' and with that he took a ravenous bite out of the side. It nearly made her retch to see a man eating unrefined food.

'Mmm, juicy!' He said happily.

'Hand me a ration,' she said unhappily.

'You don't know what you're missing!' he happily with a satisfied grin.

'Oh yes, I do,' she said and snatched the packet from his hand. She tore it open and began devouring the cracker, which sapped up all the moisture from her mouth in seconds and left her clamming on the dry paste. He must have noticed, for he took pity on her.

'Look, Alasia, sit here. I'll get you lunch.'

She sat unhappily down on the log he offered her and watched him while she nibbled the tasteless biscuit. Openly he cleaned his spear with a wash stone, and then he cut a large apple from the tree with surgical precision. Out of his pack he produced a reflection disk which was quickly turned and polished into a rudimentary plate. A knife served to take the red outer layer from the apple to reveal a soft white flesh underneath. He then cut that into several small wedges and doused it all with the clean water they carried. A quick pass under the sterilizer and he pronounced her feast ready.

'Surely you don't want me to eat that?' she asked, hungry enough to eat anything.

'Look, it's processed and everything. Here, I'll eat one first.'

He popped a wedge into his mouth and chewed deliciously. 'Mmm. Here, try one.'

'No.'

'Try one or I will tie you up and feed them to you.'

'What?! You wouldn't...!'

He looked at her, saying nothing.

'Very well then, just one,' she consented

'That's all I ask,' he replied.

She picked up a soft piece. It was moist to the touch. It looked like nothing she had ever tried before, and its colour was so pale. But she was starving. She took a sniff, and it reminded her of an intoxicating drink she had tried once. Good. Carefully she put it into her mouth and tried chewing. Its texture was soft and gritty. It might not have lasted if the puppy soldier wasn't monitoring her every move. Then she tasted it, a rich, full sweet taste.

It was *delicious*.

Cautiously she attempted another piece, and then another.

Two hours and twenty-seven apples later she decided that she was ready to move on.

'C'mon slowpoke,' she said. 'We're going to have to hustle if we want to make that base by nightfall.

The soldier stood from the pile of apple peelings around him. He had accidentally broken a branch when she sent him high into the tree to get an extra big one, and been required to 'process' them all. He rolled his eyes.

'You'll smell like apples for days,' he said.

'Too bad,' she curtly replied.

And on they marched.

---+++---+++---+++---

It was not till late afternoon before Sheelaakah was able to contact Resistance headquarters.

Beta Numerous has been attacked, I-olo was saying. *Worse still, they have the children.*

What! How is that possible? Sheelaakah asked.

Well, the Circle ordered a furtive transfer of several of the children just after you left the refugee camp. I did not want you to know for security reasons. I told nobody, not even those assigned to perform my requests. I do not know how the Oppression came by such information, and we're left to hope they just snatched them out of opportunity or spite – but I can convince myself of neither.

Commander Sheelaakah was communicating with her superior on the sub telepathic link that what was left of Skion's now decimated unit still had.

They had been scattered, but a small group had managed to stick more or less together. Unit leader Bakerson was absent, as was the singer Alasia.

Then the Oppression has demonstrated remarkable information gathering capabilities recently, she commented.

Agreed. Too remarkable. We must take great care in these things. Commander, I fear I may need to make a personal request of you this time.

The Commander was silent. This was not within the realm of her professional experience.

But before I do, I have a direct order. Go on to Beta Numerous and rest until the first day of the next week. That will give you time to adjust and heal, to help them rebuild, and to await to gather any other survivors of your recent assault. I will contact you at sunrise, day one. Understood?

Yes, she replied.

Sunrise - Day 1

Day one came all too quickly, and it found Sheelaakah pacing slowly in the growing daylight. The five days had given her ample time to complete stage one recovery, and the splints no longer cumbered her legs. They were still tender, and she was exhausted well before the end of each day.

In that time, Officer Bakerson and the singer had successfully negotiated their way to Beta Numerous with several other wounded soldiers. The equipment at the faculty was already stretched to their limits with the unprovoked attack. It was there that Sheelaakah had discovered that six of the children, aside from army personnel and equipment, had been sequestered from the faculty before they'd even had a chance to dent their pillows. The Oppression tried to make it look like a strike to obtain lithium deposits held at the outpost, but the absence of the children made herself, and many of the others, very wary of what their enemy considered a military target nowadays.

Matrix had spent his time profitably practicing range accurate weaponry, which required an extraordinary sync capability, and one which he had extraordinary aptitude. They had not spoken much since their arrival, and the Commander was apt to admit that was her fault. She was beginning to feel vulnerable, and had pushed him away. It was apparent that others were aware of their mutual attachment, and she'd noticed others discussing this matter amidst themselves, though it was all but any of their business.

She realised it placed him in danger too, and compromised their work, somewhat.

So now she waited, nervously, wondering what would be asked of her this time.

Commander, a voice in her mind begun.

She activated the link. *I-olo. How bears tidings?* she asked. He was one never to exchange protocol, just swiftly to business.

Not well, he replied. *In the time you have been recovering, we have located the children. They are being held in the upper factory facilities...*

But that's... she interrupted. *Oh, I'm sorry, Understudy.*

He mused, *I know what you are thinking. They are being held there like raw material resources, are they not? We have no idea what that facility is like, and no way to get in there. We cannot reach these children. We had expected them to take them to a research facility, but this is far better guarded. We will not get in without a fight.*

I have no idea how we will do that, Understudy. That facility is in a constant state of flux. We cannot enter and leave by the same route, and we have no way of telling in this labyrinth how we will ever find the children. It will take months of preparation.

And as you can appreciate, we do not have the time. You and I share the same goal, but the Circle does not. I know that you will find a way to reach those children, if you really want to... he paused, leaving her to think. He was being very subtle, and she wondered what he might be hinting at.

Anyway, he continued quickly. *The Circle requires me to order you to resume your previous mission and head out towards the citadel with Alasia.*

He spoke so abruptly, he almost sounded unconvinced. Sheelaakah was at a loss. What did he want her to do? How did they share the same goals? And how were they to find the children? Why would he tell her where the children were and then order her to an entirely different mission?

Understudy... she began.

You have your orders, his curt reply.

Then it slowly began to dawn on her. *Yes, I do,* she replied.

Matrix covered his ears in mock pain.

'You want us to WHAT?!' questioned Alasia incredulously.

He listened as the Commander repeated herself. 'I want all of you to come with me to save the children. We have to go back to the citadel-'

'To do that would be in direct violation of all our orders. I would have to let go the name, as would you,' Skion reminded her.

'I know this mission requires unprecedented sacrifice. We would be enemies to the Oppression and only weakly linked to the Resistance. But the Understudy has made it clear to me that unless we do something for these children the Circle will not. I'm counting on you all and the unique abilities you carry.'

'But,' Matrix found himself asking her. 'Why would you be going against the Circle to do this?'

'You do not have to, but I intend to try without you.'

'So why are you dragging me along?' demanded Alasia, arms folded in protest.

'You know more about tact and subtlety that any of us. Your programming ability with computers is almost innate, I am told. This mission is going to require a great deal of that. And... you are a formidable pilot,' she humbly admitted.

'What is this factory like that they are being held in?' Matrix asked.

'It is surrounded by a constantly altering megalith. A 'maze' if you will. To get in we need to decipher the key that they apply each day: it is some form of multi-functional equation. I believe that we can do it.'

The group looked about uncertainly.

'We'll I'm certainly in!' cried Matrix.

The Commander and Dogman exchanged glances.

'Very well, I'm in too,' Bakerson conceded.

Skion nodded in agreement.

'Well,' said Alasia, 'I guess that leaves me.' She looked uncomfortable for a moment, then for reasons of her own, agreed to go.

'Just one question, what happens to us if we succeed?' asked Dogman.

'That remains to be seen,' replied the Commander, breathing out a sigh. 'The Circle will probably censure us, but we will have saved those children from a fate worse than death.'

'What happens to us if we fail?' Alasia asked.

No one answered.

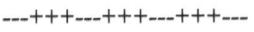

---+++---+++---+++---

It took Alasia another day to prepare. But that evening at their final briefing, indeed, their last formal acceptance in a Resistance stronghold, Matrix had brought a surprise for them all.

He stood behind the little girl, facing them. 'She can help us, I know it.'

They studied the little child, dressed in dark green and looking placidly out at them all. By the look of her, Alasia judged her to be only five and a half.

'What can she do for us?' She asked the question they were all thinking.

'She has a talent,' he argued, 'one I've never seen before. She can predict things.'

Puppy soldier bent down to study the child while talking to the others. 'How did she escape the attack?'

'I avoided the black men by hiding behind the cooling system. Petrie and I were quite safe, and he knows when to keep silent.'

Then it was Commander Sheelaakah that bent down to look closely at the child. 'Her mind is unimpressive in every way. And she is still a child.'

'I'm standing right here,' the child protested.

'I'm sorry,' the Commander replied. 'Tell me child, is what officer Matrix says true, can you see the future?'

The child stared at her for a moment, her feet shuffling uncomfortably. She looked out at the other adults, in what was either nervousness or that porcelain expression of uncertainty that children have when they honestly don't know the answer. When she spoke, it was with a shy childlike resignation accepting the will of adults over her own. 'I will help you rescue the other children from the big factory that always changes.'

'Oh, did Matrix describe their location to you?'

She did not answer.

Instead, Matrix spoke, 'No, I told her nothing. She came up to me as if expecting something, so I decided to ask her if she would help us, and she said yes. And if you've downloaded my report, it was her insight that saved you.'

The Commander looked at him in an unreadable expression, but said nothing, instead asked, 'How did she know we were going to the factories?'

No one answered.

'If she possesses this remarkable talent of foresight, then perhaps it would be wise to have her with us?' remarked Puppy-boy.

'I'll take care of her,' Matrix promised them.

'Oh no you won't!' It was one of the children's carers, a tallish female with dark hair. 'Jacinth, I wondered where you had gotten to! Come with me now!'

'They need me to find the other children,' she stated quietly.

'I was going as her guardian,' Matrix tried to say.

'That child goes nowhere without me. You are skilled warriors, but only I know how to care for the needs of a child. I am Montsi, the carer. Where she goes, I go.'

Skion growled his discontent, his biomechanics turning a deep crimson to match his fervour. 'Are you all burned in the head?!' He huffed in exasperation - clearly, he was beginning to accept that they had all lost rank already. 'It is enough you even <u>think</u> of bringing along a <u>child</u>. Now you want her nurse as well?'

Matrix sprang to her defence, if only perhaps to contradict the older man, 'but she does have a point. Where the child must go there must be one to care for her. We all have our roles in this group. I can protect this child –'

'And entertainer her,' Alasia interrupted, momentarily stalling the argument.

'- but who will care for her?'

'You cannot seriously expect us to bring along a civilian?' Skion complained.

The carer spoke up for herself, 'I have had first year military training, it was compulsory at Utopia, plus I have run the three minute mile in higher school. I can take orders and know what to do to survive.'

'Commander Sheelaakah,' Skion turned to his now equal, 'we cannot be expected to bring a civilian on this mission unless we expect her to die.'

'It does seem to be the unwise decision,' Glenn said, sounding uncertain.

'Well, I suppose we could use a carer once we've rescued the other children...' Alasia mused out loud, while Skion glowered helplessly at the sky.

He fell to debating the issue with Sheelaakah, based on logic as he saw it.

Quietly the child whispered in Montsi's ear so that only he and Alasia could hear. 'Don't worry, you will come. You are the only one that can come. You have to ... or I will not come home again.'

'Do you know what we're going to face? Do you have any idea what you're getting in to?'

'Yes,' she replied in a resigned maturity that vastly exceeded her age.

'Look,' Matrix suddenly challenged the arguing soldiers; 'go to the camp, speak to the soldiers. See if you can find *anyone* with first grade caring who is willing to join us. Then they can come instead. You will find no one and discover this carer is the only one who can come, let alone who should.'

'Now hang on,' Montsi began to protest.

Sheelaakah shook her aside with a hand. 'Fair enough, I agree. If you can find any please bring them here and we will discuss this till we are all in agreement.'

Skion, however, took the opportunity to face his visage to a smiling Matrix. 'These are some of the most broadly skilled and dedicated soldiers of the Resistance *worm boy*. YOU will be eating your words this day.'

He and Bakerson were gone for almost an hour, and Matrix spent the time demonstrating his seer's ability with a game of dice. Within a minute, everyone was rigorously impressed. To her credit, Alasia came up with the most inventive tests of the child's skill, but shortly declared the child dressed in jade either had a skill she could not explain or otherwise truly was a prophetess. Toward the end of the hour the child announced the others were returning, and they all stood for the news.

Skion circuits glowed a dim scarlet, so it was the Bakerson who spoke. 'There are none.'

'Well, well, well,' Matrix chimed, but then waited.

'Four hundred beams!' Skion bemoaned, 'n the only reference was to some carer who had apparently run the three minute mile back in higher school.' He scowled. He threw his fist down and walked off. 'I'm going to burn the recharge,' he called over his shoulder, leaving Matrix grinning broadly.

Another point to me! He thought out loud.

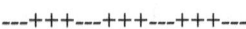

'Now, it's almost too late,' Sheelaakah said to him. 'We're all packed, how can you have second thoughts at this late minute?'

Officer Glenn paced nervously back and forth before her as she continued packing. He was dreadfully nervous; she could tell that by the look of consummate worry on his face. He had never done anything against principal, or the Resistance. Neither had his fathers; it was very difficult for him.

'It's just... I just...' he stammered. He was at a loss now without protocol. And she knew that he could not bring himself to call her by name;

Sheelaakah. They were "equals" now, neither holding any official position in the Resistance any more. Yet he could not bring himself to call her by name.

'It's all right, Glenn. You'll get used to it in time.'

He half-huffed, half snorted from his gently enlarged nostrils. He was a man of structure and order, and when that was taken away, his world lost a great deal of security. She knew he would have to re-establish some form of order, at least in his own mind, before becoming comfortable again.

'The new system is this, as I see it,' she said, 'is that we operate as a group of like-minded individuals who share the same goals. Things may not always work out, but we can rely on each other.'

'And what is to become of us *after* the mission Commander?'

'Stop calling me that,' she chided. 'Besides, I don't rightly know. The Seraphs will guide us.'

'Are you sure of this course of action then?' he asked.

A day ago she might have disdained him asking such a question of her. She looked at him, and he looked as lost as a little boy. 'Of course I am. How do you feel about it?'

'I am... honoured at being chosen for this mission. I...' He looked about, grinding his boot into the dirt.

Sheelaakah just watched him and waited for him to continue.

In a moment his fleeting glance met her waiting gaze and he continued apprehensively. 'Actually, I am afraid. I feel compelled to join you, as though we were on the edge of a very powerful storm, which we are to be drawn right into the centre of, and yet our very survival seems dependant on our ability to consciously enter and ride out the storm.'

Sheelaakah was surprised. She had never heard Officer Bakerson communicate in such poetic terms. Her incredulity must have been apparent in her face, but he continued.

'I am determined to join you in spite of the danger and the dreadful war going on inside me between compliance with the Circle or obeying your request. I have never truly fought this kind of battle before.'

She looked at him. So he was still 'obeying' somebody. His refusal to act independently could be a downfall in the situation they were about to create.

'So why all the pacing?' she asked him directly.

He sighed, a deep, heavy sigh like the waves at dusk rolling in their contemplation of eternity upon the sands.

'It is too much. It all seems... beyond us.'

'You are used enough to war Bakerson. Could it be that you fear losing the structure you and your fathers have followed? The Resistance. You crave the power of an individual hidden in a crowd of millions of Resistance soldiers, and now you are alone.'

'Never alone,' he said, not seeing the reverse psychology she had enacted in him. 'In the Resistance I had structure. I knew what rank I was aiming for. I had comrades, family perhaps; wherever I went here in the wilderness beyond. Now I am leaving the family, that structure, behind. It is not easy.'

His face quickly brightened and his back straightened as he came preconsciously to attention. 'Thank you, Mistress Sheelaakah for your insight and council. Forgive my trepidation, it will not happen again. I live to serve the Greater Good.'

He executed half a salute, then nervously sat upon his backpack, cleaning a spear.

Poor soldier, Shee thought. He was intent on serving someone, honour if not structure, that much was certain.

A swift hand fell sharply across her back, and she turned around, brow furrowed in protest. It was the man Matrix, smiling disarmingly as he twisted his overlong fringe from over his brow. Behind him was Alasia, who had saved her from the crash, looking a little bothered with her arms crossed against her chest. It appeared Matrix had dragged her here.

'We ready to go?' he asked happily, heaving a backpack up.

'Yes we go.'

They turned to see Skion returning, loaded with more weaponry than had ever been standard in the Resistance. In his right hand, he carried a massive long staff inlaid with crystal. It was used to send a high intensity shock to bring down wasps, or break through stone walls. She had no doubt he was capable of using it in as a hand to hand combat tool as well.

'I am prepared,' his mechanical voice declared, robotic eye sparkling a dangerous red.

'Then don't forget us,' the carer Montsi sounded. She had with her the young child, and both were dressed in travel clothes and sported a rugged backpack for the journey. Sheelaakah could sense she was trying to hide her fear over taking herself and a child into a war zone, but was even more determined to have a part in rescuing the other six children under her charge that had been abducted for the second time in a week. She also hid a complete faith in Jacinth's gift, which far surpassed any tenuous confidence she may have had in her own abilities.

The seven companions took one last look at the Resistance stronghold. It was time to move on.

On how to rescue children

What do you mean? No one should be separated after such success! Usually it takes days to get an operative inside the walls. Yet this group has been in and out again in less than that time, the Understudy to the machinations protested.

Indeed, I-olo mentioned. *Things have been cold at reception recently. I cannot guess their intent.*

None can, and you are the brightest of us, Understudy. I still don't understand the purpose of this call?

I needed to check up on some details without anyone knowing. It took quite a bit of work really. I want the information on the cell the Circle instructed Alasia to be put into. Furthermore, I am certain you will explore all possible leads to how the Oppression knew about the children. I want you to follow them up and let me know prior to your official report. Will you do that for me?

Of course, Understudy. But won't that report arrive at you personally anyway, after it is reviewed by the Circle? Hmm, I sense a need of discretion in such things. Very well then, I will talk to you as I sit down to draft said document. Give me half a day to obtain the necessary supplies. Thank you for this chat.

Very good, I-olo replied confidently, then found himself thinking, *At least this man could be trusted.*

--- ++ --- ++ ---

Sheelaakah winced. The battle continued unabated, and the child squealed despite her usual calm under similar circumstance. Three more black guards fell as they rounded a corner, just out of reach of the handful that followed swiftly behind them. She clung to Matrix's back, which was as best as they could do under the circumstances.

Sheelaakah stopped as they passed a side passage. It wound its way undividingly deeper into the complex, but it would do. She paused and gathered her energies, sending a telepathic signal down the tunnel, then raced to join the others.

Three seconds later, as the contingent of guards ran up to the branch, their leader signalled a halt. Without questioning the illogic of it, he ordered his men to continue the pursuit down the long, unbranching tunnel. She could feel his thoughts. He was sure they had headed in this direction. He could almost feel their retreating footsteps. They were just out of sight. Any second now and they would surely come into view ...

The fugitives now relaxed, and breathed heavily. Matrix put his charge down, and she refused to appear ruffled as she corrected her green dress and braids about her. They all puffed heavily, except Skion who merely exhibited a deeper crimson from beneath his breast plate. Montsi breathed heaviest after the chase, and was soon beside the child as she was ever want to be. She bore the trail without complaint, but was not used to the constant vigilance of covert warfare.

Bakerson was the first to speak. 'They're not pursuing.'

'Options?' Sheelaakah asked. Though no longer the official leader, they all obliged her the unofficial role. She assumed it was due to custom, and her having asked them to join this crusade anyway.

'We could try this door,' suggested Alasia. 'Looks like a simple system. Give me five minutes.

The others waited with a mixture of patience and nervousness as she attempted to alter the colours of the stone in the pedestal with that at her temple. Seconds dragged into minutes and the others couldn't hide their nervousness.

Finally she spoke. 'Skion, we seem to be dealing with a biologic system, you'll have better luck talking to it than I.'

For all her intellectual talent, Alasia had her limits. Skion moved his muscular form in front of the dais and attempted to surgically meld with the security system. His first attempt failed, and he reformed for another attempt. That too was thwarted with a small shower of sparks.

'Careful!' Matrix hissed. 'We don't really want to set off another alarm.'

Skion turned his dark features and glared at Matrix. Both stood their ground in their old rivalry. Suddenly the taller warrior's arm shifted rapidly into a large axe. In less than a second he had spun around and split the entire dais. He stepped quickly forward and hauled the doors open even as his arm resumed its regular form.

'Weeel now,' he jeered, 'What'd ya know? No alarms!'

'Even so, they'll register the shock wave in under a minute, we have to go,' Alasia replied with a scowl.

Skion pretended to look disappointed at her criticism.

Everyone followed into the darkness. Soon light began to fill the area, courtesy of Skion's staff. It was one of its many useful abilities.

They were in a small exit faculty, right underneath a subjunct service utility. It looked like a forgotten basement of an industrial facility. Pipes and tubing ran riot, clashing into dark utility hoods and rusty cupboards. Debris was strewn disorderly around the room, which apart from the platform they stood on, had a rough, unhewn appearance.

They spread out to quickly examine the area.

Glenn called out, 'looks like an old system port!'

Alasia quickly approached the port. She looked unimpressed, but necessity prevailed and she quickly accessed. Her body took on a slightly rigid stance as most did when their minds were travelling the Evernet.

'Yes,' she confirmed, slightly dreamily. 'It's an old quaternary adjunct. Must have forgot it was here.' She paused before continuing, 'we are in luck. There is a corridor right beside the left wall. It leads to an under-access of the North Gate. We'll be at the facility in under five minutes.'

'Good,' said Matrix with an air of frustration. 'Those guards won't follow us in there. Not into the Labyrinth anyway. Will they?'

The question was directed at her. Sheelaakah answered, 'not likely, not with the abolyths in there. Skion?' she asked, indicating the wall.

He replied that he understood her request, forming his thoughts into the clear open page that Sheelaakah found easy to read. *I will open an exit for us.* Though to the others, he made no visible reply. Just walked towards the wall that was indicated. Suddenly a young voice called out.

'Wait!'

He stopped and turned towards the little child who had called out. He stared angrily down at her: she was wont to stop his projects too often, though not even one tenth his bulk. Montsi stood protectively and unflinching behind the young girl, matching the mechman's glare.

'Sensor sweep,' Glenn commented, holding up a small grey block with an opal in it. Skion looked even more incensed, but they all knew that had he initiated any sort of energy discharge at that moment, as tearing a hole in the iron wall required, they would have been rediscovered quickly, and perhaps been unable to escape. He waited until Glenn gave the all clear and then proceeded to demolish the wall.

The passage beyond was long and dark, and insisted on carrying ridged, rusted piping that echoed the unknown distances from whence they came. After a few minutes, the travellers stopped.

'This should be about it,' Alasia commented.

For a moment they scanned and surveyed the area above. There were no conscious entities up there, Sheelaakah could tell.

'Mechanist movement negligible,' Skion reported, and at her silent signal begun cutting a large hole in the roof. It took only moments.

First he helped Glenn heave up, then when all was clear, he lifted Alasia who glided confidently to the new level. Matrix refused Skion's aid, and taking a running leap off the near wall caught hold of the exit and pulled himself quick up. Then he turned, placed a huge hand on the floor. She stood on it with practiced confidence and he lifted her up. With a hop, she stood on the next level.

And as she came up she caught her first living sight of the lower foundries north gate. It was immense. Tall pillars of stone stretched upwards to the invisible cavern roof several kilometres above them. They appeared ancient, and looked like they might have once had writing on them. They were of a dark, marbled stone, yet the undecipherable words were large enough to provide hand holding, should one feel inclined to scale them. Montsi stood beside her.

'Immense,' was all she could say.

They approached the entrance. Beneath the massive doors was a wide, semicircular platform. On it was a small, silver dais that led directly to the labyrinth beyond. It was unlocked, and tessered them quickly inside. There were no guards, as Sheelaakah had anticipated. It was apparent that they thought no one foolish enough to enter, and as it was the night cycle on Seren, there would be no transports to the north gate for several hours. They stood now on a similar stone platform, but before them stretched several tunnel openings and within, the sounds of shifting stone. It appeared the whole labyrinth was the insane idea of a not-so-slightly megalomaniacal manager several centuries ago, but since it was reliable, no one had thought to remove it in all that time. From deeper within, the calls of strange beasts could be heard.

'Who *makes* stuff like this up?' Matrix asked.

'Oh, you know; infinite resources for self-improvement – the great Seren dream promises to stretch all limits of personal talent, and to show it all off too,' Alasia explained.

'Over here!' Glenn called. He had located another system interface, though this one for the factory itself.

Alasia pushed him aside and linked in.

'Multi layered encryptions. Oh, a dipolic fractal. This should be fun, might take some time. You guys take it easy.'

She continued muttering to herself as she tried to break into the computer system. The others rested, partaking of their rations or engaging in their private thoughts. The child and her carer both got comfortable on the hard stone paving. The others stood guard and waited, and it was only moments before the child was asleep. In the time they only once caught a small herd of abolyths eyeing them, but Matrix threw a dagger at the biggest one, which caught it on the rump. They ran off bleating. The child barely stirred.

Almost three hours later Alasia finally spoke. 'Forge fired interface!' She swore in wrath. She hit the glowing stone with her fist, and then in excess rage removed one of her shoes and struck it several more times. She returned to the others muttering. They waited for her to speak.

'It's too hard,' she complained. 'Maybe if I had a week, certainly, but this is too complicated. I even tried deciphering this labyrinth to see if we could navigate it, but the algorithm is too complex in this short space of time. I don't know what we are going to do.'

The group waited in silence.

Eventually Matrix spoke. 'Well, we've brought her all this way. Perhaps our little green gem should wake up and show us what else she can do?'

No one spoke. Their options were limited. The gate where they resided was one of the few static areas of the entire labyrinth. If they left it, even for a moment, they might never be able to return. And under constant threat of the abolyths, they would soon be worn down and destroyed. It was an untested, crazy idea.

Matrix shook the child in Montsi's lap gently. She woke and stretched happily. Staring placidly before allowing her eyes to meet his. Neither spoke, till after a moment Jacinth stood.

'It's time, isn't it?' she asked no one in particular. She stretched again as she looked out over the changing landscape, then spoke commandingly, beyond her years. 'Very well. All of you listen. I'm only going to say this once. Follow me and stay no more than ten steps away. If I stop, you stop. Don't ever anyone step in front of me, no matter what. Stay close, understand? We go.'

She gave them no time to consider, but with a polite smile began walking placidly towards the nearest entrance. Montsi had to hurry, and was a little stiff rising as she had been holding the child for over three hours. Glenn helped her to her feet.

As soon as the child reached the beginning of the maze the child stopped. Waiting only a few seconds, she began walking towards a solid wall. Almost as she was to touch it, it shifted before her as if to let her through. Beyond it was a corridor. Sheelaakah barely had time to reach the others before the new entrance was sealed shut behind them.

For a long time the child led the group in this fashion. It appeared that they were heading roughly towards the main facility. Without warning their guide veered to the left, and as she did a new entrance appeared as the wall slid below the ground. The corridor that seemed so straight was suddenly blocked, and they hurried to catch up.

She was standing, waiting. Then she spoke. 'Whatever happens next, don't attack them. Follow.'

The wall ahead slid open as the child neared it. Skion roared in alarm. Beyond them was a large cavern filled with nesting abolyths. Their huge heads lifted from the earth their giant tusks as their domain was trespassed. Several bulls shuffled to face the intruders.

'Wait!' cautioned Glenn as Skion aimed his gun at the nearest one. They scanned the area quickly. The monsters were not attacking. Not yet.

The child had paused as the door opened. Sheelaakah sensed that though she was calm, and had anticipated their presence, even the young prophetess was impressed by the size and appearance of these monsters up close. But she did not take long to draw in the image, and was soon off walking amidst the beasts.

Sheelaakah noticed that the young girl chose a path well out of tusk reach of the abolyths, but which none the less a path that lead straight through the centre of them. The other hardened soldiers took up a cautious watch in the rear, but held their fire. They knew that if anyone startled the beasts they would soon be in the centre of a rampage.

Then they stopped in horror, as the young girl walked right up to a milking mother and placed a hand on the horny tusk of the beast. 'You see.' she said, stroking the ivory and patting the coarse hairs on the monster's head. 'You judge them.' She smiled at the beast, and then walked on, leaving the speechless adults a little more than ten paces behind.

Their strange journey continued in much the same way for over three hours. The child would walk, turn suddenly, and then stop unexpectedly. Once she chose a strange path over a wide-open area, till Matrix strayed and was almost taken to premature death by a flurry of dark, black tentacles. Another time the child waited for nearly ten minutes before a shifting opening, then she suddenly and unexpectedly walked forwards as it changed yet another time. Alasia was almost left behind then. Eventually they came to a platform similar to the one they had started on almost four hours previously.

'We're here,' the child stated, and her shoulders slumped. Looking at her, it appeared as if she had been awake for days.

Matrix rushed forward and picked her up. She rested in his arms for a moment, limp as a blanket.

'I think she's a bit worn out now,' he said, stating the obvious.

'Then we rest here,' Skion commented, and no one argued.

---+++---+++---+++---

'So how is it you know so much, Skion?' Alasia was asking him. 'I mean, you have only been in the Resistance for a few years.'

'Yes, this is true,' his mechanised voice replied, unusually serene as he cleaned out a weapon that they'd brought. 'But remember, I have certain, definite, advantages. These additions are a part of me that extend right to the centre of my mind. I can become any number of things, such as living cannon to a hover bike, with the right additions of course. We did not bring them today. We should not be needing them, once we free the children.'

Alasia pondered his reply. It sounded a little practised, but with men who were part machine, you never could tell. She wondered what motivated him.

'Tell me, if you would, what brought you on this mission. You used to have a command all of your own?'

'That command,' he replied emphatically 'is unimportant. To serve the Resistance is.' She was taken aback, and he noticed he had been abrupt. 'There is a certain... sense of satisfaction that I derive from key missions such as this one, where the risk is greater and the talent, diverse. I may yet lead many more missions, should this one prove successful.'

'You know, you're not so gruff when you get you on your own,' she whispered. He stared at her with dark eyes, and she noticed for the first time the crimson and azure circuits that hid within his iris'.

He was pondering her as well, and his human voice teased again, 'And you, singer. What deemon possesses you ta follow the Commander?'

She dismissed the question with pre-prepared grace. 'Oh, it's not the Commander. It is the children, and, now I think about it, I suppose it is the chance to test my skills, measure my limits, that sort of thing.'

He laughed a brief, derisive laugh. 'If there is one thing oppos' the Oppression will teach you,' he lectured as a hardened battler, 'it is new definitions of your leemits.' His mechanised self-continued. 'I once hunted an entire black patrol for three weeks without stopping. In the end, there was only myself and my unit leader alive; but we prevailed. My colleagues thought us dead after one week.'

He laughed at the apparent irony. 'We'd taught them; new limits.'

His eyes drifted into fond memory of the time he had been a hero, possibly to the look of speechless admiration in the eyes of those who had succumbed to lesser limits. It was impressive, thought Alasia.

'You must be proud,' she said.

He lay back, arms behind his head. 'Perhaps I should be,' he agreed, and commenced resting while Alasia looked about the tired people she was with. Suddenly they looked just like any other people she'd known. Except maybe Dogman with his funny nose. Montsi lay humming to herself like a mother with the child literally curled into her lap. Sheelaakah was resting, staring at the ceiling too far to be seen above, lying on the rug that Matrix had in a timeless display of chivalry laid out for her. He was not resting, but keeping watch, or at least, stabbing his knife dejectedly into the stones beneath his feet. Glenn Bakerson was on the other side of their group, napping, or resting his head against his spear, but his head would lift up every five minutes or so just to scan the area. It was very quiet now.

---+++---+++---+++---

He allowed a smile purse his thin grey lips. They had come, just like it had said that they would. And she was with them. It was impressive, he thought, how such a little child as she had managed to navigate without fault the entire labyrinth. If only she could have known: it had been in more than record time as well.

Taalk folded his arms against his chest, and thought. His bargain had paid off again. He was where his Master had told him to go, and now, in time, her talents would be his. How high the price had been, but a price he was willing and able to pay.

They were coming!

On how to enter the upper factory facility

Matrix was frustrated. Skion had disagreed with him for ten minutes over the best way to assault the tower, until all the others had given up and left the two to sort things out. They opted for a compromise, with Skion placing tactical charges around the structure, and Alasia opening a disused loading port for them. It was two hours before the workers arrived, which would hopefully add to the chaos that would allow them to escape. All things prepared, they were ready to being their secret assault on the tower.

However, they had barely moved twenty meters into the upper factory facility before an alarm sounded. Plan B was put immediately into action as Skion's charges left a pair of gaping holes around an old generator. It would greatly hamper capture efforts with automated repair crews taking up most of the corridor space, racing around haphazardly to extinguish flames and re-enforce struts. It would make their going slower, but much better concealed.

The troop managed to hitch a ride on one such transport, cutting the travel time between sections. They were alarmed when it unexpectedly veered off course.

'I've got a trace!' Skion explained, and everyone jumped free just as soon as Sheelaakah had jammed the power circuits.

'This does not look good,' Matrix commented. They were on a transport bridge crossing a massive tunnel. It was nearly forty meters to the ground below.

'Get down!' Jacinth screamed. Moments later a shower of lightning arrows began to put holes in the bridge work where they were standing. They jumped into the back of the transport, which seemed impervious to the energy blasts.

'Great!' Alasia commented sarcastically, 'now what do we –'

There was a deep rumbling sound from in front of the transport, where none of them could see, followed by a louder rumble as the bridge behind them tumbled into the cavern below.

'Great!' Alasia now screamed. 'Now we're trapped!'

The soldiers worked to return fire from the safety of the transport at the automated guns which sighted them, but it was little use as they targeted anything that moved and could fire almost continuously. Soon, there was a soft buzzing sound over the incessant fire.

'What's that?' Montsi asked.

'Wasps,' Sheelaakah said.

'No,' Skion replied. 'Wikons. Androids on jet packs.'

They were there in seconds. The battle was brief as they were protected by energy fields, which deflected the allies' assaults, but allowed them to disarm the humans without trouble. Of the three, two Wikon survived the counter attack, and ordered the Resistance to surrender.

'Stand behind me,' ordered Sheelaakah. While the others had been using force, she must have managed to infiltrate the machine's system. Without warning, they both suddenly shut down.

'Adequate,' remarked Skion, and began interfacing with the first Wikon's system, while the other had fallen just outside the truck. There was a moment of riot as the automated cannons began to fire again, and then they fell silent. The second Wikon twitched, and then begun to move, having repaired it's system. It stood up and began to point its weapon at the group. Then it disintegrated.

The blast had come from the first Wikon on the floor, still interfaced with Skion.

'It's quite simple really,' he said. 'Once you know what frequency their shields use. This one will serve us now.'

It was less than a minute when the newly converted Wikon ferried them all across the broken bridge, in spite of the barrage of arrows, which were harmlessly absorbed by its shield. Within minutes they had located an Evernet access port.

'Well,' commented Sheelaakah to Alasia. 'I suppose now that they know we are here, we might as well not keep it a secret from them. Let's create a little diversion...'

It took them less than two minutes to reprogram the system with literally thousands of phantom copies of themselves, running around and causing all sorts of mischief electronically. Alasia had even prepared several mutating viruses to entertain the system while the real them sought their goals. The phantoms headed for virtually every conceivable Resistance target, while their real target, the children, were quickly located.

---+++---+++---+++---

'Impressive,' thought Taalk, as the screens in his control room went haywire. Alarms were ringing everywhere, but he knew most of them would be false. He had other, more sophisticated means of tracing his prey, and they were bringing her right to him.

---+++---+++---+++---

It had been a loathsome morning, the trade apprentice moaned. First, someone had set off some explosives out the front of the faculty. At first they thought one of the transports had collided with an energy pylon or something. Now the entire computer system had failed. Several mutating virus had entered the system and were causing complete havoc.

He had volunteered to stay the night shift. He was looking for a promotion. He just expected a quiet evening with the screens and pylons. Now everything was a disaster. Now there would be an inquest, a thousand questions, maybe even a scan...

'Try re-initialising the system again!' His superior officer ordered. She was a qualified engineer, but as system failed system her patience had suffered in like manner. Now she seemed as lucid as the computer stones before them - pulsing a dull mottled grey.

He sent the mental signature to the systems that didn't reply. Then a bright spark flashed to his temple and he was instantly paralysed. A moment later he felt someone throw him to the floor and he slowly regained power over his aching body.

'Stupid boy!' she chagrined. 'Take more care, the viruses-'

Suddenly the door slid open. In floated an equipment crate, gliding slightly sideways.

'Now, wha-' the engineer began to protest as he struggled to stand.

Suddenly a giant man began to form from the crate, an enormous staff in his hand. 'Oppression slaves, where are the children?' he ordered in a mechanised voice.

The engineer looked like she was about to grab something, but a small blast from that staff knocked her painfully against the terminals. The giant strode off the crate as others began to enter the room.

'Oppression slave,' the mechman reintoned. 'Where are the children!'

His tongue caught in his throat, and the wind seemed unwilling to pass by his voice. 'I... we...' he stammered.

'SPEAK!'

'We don't have any children!' The trade apprentice shouted in panic. 'This is the upper factory facility, I don't know what you're looking for!'

A brown haired female, quite nondescript, looked over at him and began accessing his mind without his consent, and without removing his copper banding. It was a power inhumane, what kind of a freak was she?!

'He really doesn't know. They haven't told him.'

'Predictable,' another female voice said from outside his vision. 'Actually, they're in the next hall. Held in separate cells,' the second female was saying.

'N...no,' the apprentice stuttered. 'There aren't any children here! This is a class nine manufacturing facility. You have to be at least adult to even-'

Suddenly all the lights went back on, and the alarms in the room were silenced. All the terminals returned to their correct settings as though a god had touched them. He blinked in the light, and then saw who had done this. She was to die for, with perfect features, long straight dark hair, curves to ache for in a confident, alluring posture. She was the singularly most attractive female he had ever seen, and he didn't want to wash his eyes for a year for fear of forgetting her otherworldly beauty.

'Here we go,' she said. 'Now we can get these doors open. And, Skion, I don't think he needs to see all this.'

He saw the fist coming down, but he didn't flinch. He didn't even move, but kept staring at the vision of perfect beauty until all his world went dark.

---+++---+++---+++---

Matrix cheered as they opened the doors and found the children locked in individual cells, or 'research foci', sterile walls as white as bleached sand. They came running out, and had never been happier to see their carer Montsi. The reunion took place in the disarrayed remains of an administration auditorium, and was of necessity brief, but intense.

Matrix was checking their escape route when suddenly Sheelaakah looked up. 'Jacinth? Where are you?' she called above the greeting, the tension in her voice hushing the others.

He looked around in panic, to see the small girl in the deep green dress was already several meters away, climbing a steel staircase slowly.

'Jacinth, come back! Someone is coming!'

'Retrieve her, swiftly,' instructed Skion as he began herding the others through a second exit. Matrix began to chase after her, but the child turned around with such an expression of inexorable resignation it made him freeze in fright. He could tell that the child was about to do something drastic.

'If I don't leave now, when he comes, he will hurt you all. It's better this way,' she said calmly, as though explaining the rules to a child younger than herself.

'Jacinth! You get down here now!' ordered Montsi with such matronly authority the stones themselves would have feign obeyed her.

'I'm sorry,' said Jacinth, and for once it seemed crystal tears edged along the rim of her eyelids.

Suddenly the door behind her opened. Out of it stepped an old man who stood tall despite the signs of age time had carved along his face. It was a thin, uncaring face, but not ungiven to a caring pose when a smile fashioned itself across it. His mouth curled up in such a smile now, and he spoke, his eyes were a pale shade of grey.

'Very good child, you are right. Come, it is time for you to go with me.'

'No!' Shouted Matrix, and he lifted his blazer. Yet with a flick of the old man's wrist the muscles in his arm disobeyed him and the weapon clattered to the floor. He looked around. Skion lay inert on the floor, as though he had simply switched off. Sheelaakah was trembling and pale, and Glenn seemed to have collapsed as well, clutching his temples. He pulled his knife, but the grey eyes were too far away. There was nothing he could do, nothing as the small child was led away by an unknown man.

Matrix raced up the stairs after them, but found his way blocked by an impassable dead zone which drained his mind of thoughts and muscles of all strength, and might of killed him had he not fallen down the stairs and away from the field, but he was unconscious by that time.

'Who was that!?' Matrix demanded, several moments later when they had all recovered.

'Lord Admiral Taalk,' Sheelaakah replied in a subdued voice. 'Head of the psychic division for the Oppression, and an unmitigated genius. I am no match for his skill.'

'How did he know we were here?' Alasia asked innocently.

'I have no idea,' Sheelaakah replied.

'How come we didn't know he was here?' Alasia asked.

'I do not know that either! I should have picked up on his mind signature from a great distance. He clearly is using unique kind of shielding.'

'I think I may know,' Matrix replied. 'He has a dark aura about him. Some form of pact, I would image.'

'That's very dangerous. But it would explain quite a few things. He must be truly desperate if that is the case. I wonder if Jacinth was his end goal all along?' Sheelaakah mussed resignedly to herself.

'I take it you've already met?' Matrix asked, helping Glenn to reactivate Skion.

'Indeed,' Sheelaakah replied, drawing in a shuddering breath. 'Once. It was he who successfully took my brother from me. What he plans with Jacinth, I dare not think.'

'Well you'd better think!' Montsi demanded, new tears drying on her face. 'We've got to get her back! What is he going to do with her!?' The other children now clustered about her, speechless in fright.

Sheelaakah looked wearily at the children. 'Same as he intended with them, only elsewhere: harvest their talents.'

'How?' Montsi asked.

'I will not say,' Sheelaakah replied.

'But why her? And why did she just go to him?' Montsi demanded.

'I think I know,' Glenn replied quietly. 'It was her talent, in both cases. He is very dangerous, but if he could take her he might become unstoppable. She said herself that he would do 'bad things' to us if we stopped him now. That's probably quite true. She just, gave herself up for the rest of our sakes.'

'No,' Montsi spoke defiantly. 'He'll not have her, or I will die trying. I'll not see these children turned into some kind of disgusting resource.'

'I hate to say this, but there's no point in going after her till we've got these others to safety. Where do you suppose he's taking her?' Matrix said.

'He's taken her down to the under foundry,' Glenn calmly replied.

'The what?' Alasia asked incredulously, not because she had never heard of the under foundry, but because there was no logically conceivable reason why he should take here there.

Dogman sighed, and it shuddered a little as it left his body. 'She told me, when we rested in the labyrinth. She asked if I'd ever been to a place where dead people are awake and spirits cry. She meant the under foundry. I am confident in my soul that he will take her there.'

'How do we get in there?' Matrix asked.

'I'm not going to the under foundry!' Alasia stated flatly, but no one paid her heed.

Sheelaakah paused, and looked sadly at Montsi a moment. 'Getting in is impossible, and even if we did, we are incapable of defeating such a monster. He has huge talent, and now it seems ... assistance from places no mortal should go. I do not know how we are to accomplish this feat.'

'It is unlike you to surrender to defeat,' Skion claimed. 'I am prepared to try.'

Sheelaakah sighed. 'As am I.'

---+++---+++---+++---

The elevator made no sound as it whisked them down towards their destination. The child he had acquired stood placidly by his side, offering no resistance, and showing no fear.

The prize was now his. He need only reach out and claim her gift as his own, and he would never fear another again. His worth to his dark god would forever be proven.

'I know what you intend from me,' the child quietly said.

'I expect you do,' he replied, grey eyes not looking down at the child waiting by his side, though an evil smile played at the corner of his mouth.

'You cannot have what is not given,' she stated simply.

He laughed cruelly, but she was the first to speak.

'They are coming for me...'

Part 2

Chase

Matrix couldn't believe what he was looking at.

'What happened to the labyrinth?' Montsi asked.

Before them, right to the edge of the horizon, stretched endless kilometres of open mezzanine. The entire labyrinth had sunk below the level of stone earth, and the tower stood reaching to the ceiling above. Lost Abolyths scattered among the vastness.

Skion stood gazing at the sky's edge. 'They are coming.'

Glenn soon joined him in his vigil. 'Where?'

'They have surrounded us: all along the horizon. At least two hundred swift riders. They are coming.'

'Over here!' Matrix called. He had located a light transport designed for quick runs. Quickly Skion and Glenn set to altering its design to allow it to travel at twice its top speed.

'They're getting closer,' Montsi called, though it was not necessary. Small black specks were appearing along the horizon.

'Hold it right there boys, I've got an idea. Everyone, up against the wall!' ordered Alasia. She had already accessed a terminal and was beginning to reprogram the system.

'What's going on?' Matrix asked her.

Suddenly earth, rocks and dust began a surreal journey falling upwards to the roof of the cavern. At the same time, each person was pressed against the tower as if they had fallen gently against it, the children falling squealing in a heap. Skion held the transport away from the wall and then tilted it right way against it. 'Up' had changed direction.

'What are you doing?!' Sheelaakah gasped.

Alasia laughed smugly to herself. 'They won't catch us this way. I reprogrammed the gravity along this section of Seren. The atmosphere above will look terrible! Just to be safe though, I put the gravity along this section towards the tower. We can escape by driving up it now, and then out across the roof, which act like a floor then! The calculations were immense!'

She seemed very pleased with herself.

'Hurry then!' Matrix ordered, lifting the children quickly one at a time into the transport capsule of the transport. 'Let's get out of here!'

They raced quickly up the tower, and had little difficulty traversing the gravity discrepancy between the tower and the roof. Still, the approaching craft were reorganising rapidly, and those that had survived the 'drop' managed a few passing shots as they sped past. Soon, heavy re-enforcements also arrived, and first shot landed into the transports rear indicator. Skion stood up.

'I will re- enforce our shielding myself. Get us into the caverns and we will be able to evade them on our way to the surface.'

He knelt on the back on the transport between the two short stone columns which were the transport's internal gravity drive shafts. Bowing his shoulders under the effort, Skion turned the gravity bubble into a near impenetrable translucent shell, centred on the rear of the craft. Another volley of ammunition struck at the craft from behind, but was absorbed by the spatial discrepancy. They were safe, but the effort was quickly wearing the soldier down, and the pursuing craft were becoming more visible in the distance.

Suddenly Matrix leapt from the cockpit where he was deftly guiding the craft. He heard Sheelaakah gasp, but knew Alasia would take the reins, sending the ship into a rapid right turn, the inertia barely absorbed by the transports weak dampening field. The children screamed.

He paused atop the craft, standing now just behind the man generating the shield. He tried to clear his mind as he'd known the day of the space battle. This was another of his new abilities first field test.

He stretched out his right arm then, and in the motion the liquid metals began to reach out and join his ring, arm band, and the disk attached now to his right shoulder blade. The black metal grew in less than a handful of heartbeats into a weapon; range accurate to seven hundred kilometres, and it was needed today.

Across his right eye the metal reached out to form a lens, and he felt a moment of discomfort as the probes reached back behind his eye ball to the electronics embedded there. His arm was now fixed relative to his head, and his right eye now saw seven hundred kilometres away as if it were but two meters. He targeted their drivers.

'Keep it steady, Angela' Matrix instructed, letting lose his first shot. He didn't even notice any more how the weapon drew on his own biochemical energy to propel the calcium sphere in unreckoned accuracy. His first shot threw wild, and they did not notice. The second shot struck its mark, and even as its gunner was continuing to take aim with the plasma cannon their vehicle struck a stalactite at the wrong angle and disintegrated.

He took out another craft before he heard a husky voice.

'Hurry,' it was Skion. 'I can but manage another minute.'

'We need two!' Alasia called from the front.

As it was, he held out for almost a minute and a half before collapsing. But by that time their pursuers, cautious over their losses, had pulled back and failed to apprehend them. All it took was another thirty seconds of some dangerous flight manoeuvres and they were quickly lost in the maze of tunnels that headed down towards the surface again.

'Take the lichen tunnels,' Bakerson instructed. 'They lead under the wall, again.'

After forty minutes they came out, amazed to see a forest of upside down trees above them, and sky where the earth should have been. Out into that sky there was a violent storm as the atmosphere clashed with the barrier shield. Then, slowly, the storm began to fade.

'Oh no. Ahh!' Alasia muttered to herself, and in a moment Matrix saw why. The gravity was beginning to revert back, someone had fixed the problem. This meant that everything that had fallen up was about to fall back down again, and they were underneath it.

Alasia touched the throttle, dropping the life support and several other vital systems and headed towards the undisturbed zone. There were barely quick enough as a forest full of refuse came thundering down behind them.

---+++---+++---+++---

He'd brought her to the secret medical research facilities deep below Seren tower. None knew of this place, and only the damned or damnable worked here. This was, among so many other places, a secret to all right thinking citizens of Seren. Yet the stench, the aura if you will, would reach up and darken all their mutually consenting minds in their unbelief of the darkness among them. Any experiment was legal here, acted 'below' the law, and often were. It was the price surprisingly many were willing to pay, and gave new nuance of meaning to the phrase; 'Infinite employment options, unlimited growth of knowledge...'

They entered the building, and the consummate professionals with dark souls began their work. They had done this so many times there was no attachment to their victims, no humanity to their subjects. One quickly anesthetised the child, and she fell limply to floor. Others began to dress her for surgery. She looked at him with dilated eyes, quiet defiance still written on her mind. *You cannot have what isn't given.*

'Your body is a vessel,' the man with grey eyes lectured, 'a home for the thing we call your spirit. As such, it fashions itself exactly after your spirit self. All we have to do is send your soul print away and then we have a model, an imprint, of all your spiritual self and talents. And when we do, we will finally unlock the greatest gift of all: prophecy. And you, dear child, are who we have to thank for giving the people of Seren their greatest edge in the war against the uncivilised, unprincipled universe. It is foretold, by a lesser with your gift, that once this is accomplished, within three generations the entire galaxy will be fully under the government of Seren. For such enduring peace, we thank you. It is a pity you will fill an ignominious role. No one will ever know you, and there will be none who speak your name.'

The serpents den

They tore through the sky even as the wasps appeared on the horizon. They were no doubt quite a scene to within all the wall who watched up, especially seeing the violent storm of earth in their wake. Matrix found himself wondering if any had perished when the earth had become the sky again.

'Any ideas?' Matrix asked.

'I have one,' Alasia answered, and begun investigating the small terminal in the transport even as he took the pilots chair.

'Skion!' She asked. 'I need the source of those wasps. Where's their ground control?'

He paused a moment, then began feeding the information in to the terminal.

'This will take a moment,' Alasia said. 'Try to stay alive till then.'

Matrix sighed and began evasive manoeuvres. Whatever she was planning, she had better do it soon, they were getting worryingly close to the Wall of Seren city, and the energy shield extension that went from it right up the Skyshield above.

'Combat positions everyone,' Alasia sang. 'Oh, and kids, bye, bye!'

They were within barely fifty meters when suddenly blue light swam around them. Space itself folded neatly between two points as they were tessered from the cockpit of the transport, to the rear section of the leading wasp. It was very cramped. The black guards would have tried to resist, but were anaesthetised by Skion's armoury before they could draw breath. He apparently had guessed what she had in mind.

'That was a neat trick,' admitted Sheelaakah as she tried to disengage Glenn's elbow from her stomach. 'Where did you learn that?'

'Oh, I just sort of... think them up,' she replied casually.

They turned to watch the spectacular glitter as the transport was vaporised against the energy barrier.

'Where are the children!' Montsi screamed. Others looked around the impossibly tight space quickly.

'I used the wasps control to Tesser them outside the wall. They're probably landing in a screaming heap in the middle of Beta Numerous right now.

'But you'd need the teleport key?' Bakerson inquired.

'Yeah, I borrowed it when we were there last. I think it was between the lines of 'by the light of a silvery star' if I recall correctly,' she explained.

'Interesting, you hacking into Resistance security. Even so, you should have sent wingy with them,' Skion jabbed towards the carer.

'No. Jacinth is my first priority here,' Montsi argued.

Alasia snubbed her chin towards the soldier.

Skion took the chair and began piloting the craft back to the port within the wall. They had gotten away with it again.

'Now,' Alasia continued, 'Matrix, try on that man's suit. Then you can, umm, look over the craft till things quiet down. Provided they don't notice anything amiss that should give us time to slip away.'

'Until they notice this crafts mass has increased by about six people.'

'Don't worry, I took care of that. I had the plan listed as carrying a gun shipment before it took off.'

'Guns?' Skion questioned dubiously.

'Well, it was all I could think of at the time!' Alasia protested indignantly.

---+++---+++---+++---

She looked up. She could not move now, and the whole world seemed far away. There were tubes everywhere, and people, but they were invisible within their masks. Somewhere, machines hummed.

'You can't have what isn't given,' she told him again.

She lay there, unafraid and slightly sad. The needles were painless, and the medics were gentle. She knew he was listening, that he could see inside her mind, but she also knew he could not understand the world as she knew it, nor ever would.

So she spoke, 'I have one last warning for you...'

---+++---+++---+++---

'I have one last warning for you,' the child spoke to him. It was only to him that she had spoken. Her voice was beginning to concede, but her soul print was strangely resolute. Not an ounce of fear the others had always shown, which had made the whole process easier. Resigned, but not afraid, as though this might have been a sad movie she'd seen before.

'Do go on,' he patronised.

'They are coming,' she repeated.

'Begin the procedure,' he curtly commanded. They had spent the hour preparing, being more careful than he could ever remember. There were a dozen others here, aside from the thousands that resided in their impenetrable fortress. He did not need her 'little prophet' voice starling his minions from their task.

Yet in the back of his mind he was troubled. One did not dismiss the admonition of a prophetess lightly, even an enemy prophetess of only seven, though she be unconscious and unmoving on the palate before him.

"They were coming"? He'd felt their interference before, but was too busy to deal with them personally. He had the foundries defences tripled, with added dark servants to keep secret their operation.

Oh, they may be coming... but they will never arrive.

Battle at the lower foundries

It had been two hours now, since the child was stolen from them. Already they were on their way towards the Tower of Light, and four hundred kilometres below that the under foundries began. Every corridor watched, every doorway screened. How they gotten in had taken a miracle.

'If we cannot approach unseen, perhaps we must approach un noticed. We must look like them,' Alasia had said. Using his newly acquired outfit, Matrix was able to get them all outfitted in one of their favourite disguises: visiting surveyors. Alasia was dismayed that she didn't get the lead role, and was barely content to play the part of the secretary. Naturally, the soldiers dressed as black guards, though they had less than an hour before their uniforms original owners would be missed.

Now, they had gone as far as they could without an invitation.

'Then we move the celebration,' Skion replied, and set about causing such chaos the massive suburbs of factories begun to be evacuated, leaving it mostly free for their wandering.

'There,' Sheelaakah told the others, 'she is being held there.'

'Looks like a personal laboratory,' Alasia commented. 'Though it's draining a lot of power.'

'Then we'd better hurry,' Sheelaakah replied.

---+++---+++---+++---

Twenty more minutes had passed. The child had fallen unconscious even as the poison filled her veins. It was standard procedure; taking a template of a soul required a fluid of specific resonance, and blood just would not do.

Suddenly a medic stopped. The grey man sensed, rather than noticed, the halt in the procedure. Another medic approached the halter to quietly inquire as to the others wellbeing. He did not reply. Taalk stole and intrusive look in the other man's soul.

Turmoil. Doubt.

Accursed child, how had she managed this? Yet there was no signal of telepathy, not sign of spirit communication. Perhaps after years of professionalism there was something she had done to reach him, and without warning the medic broke down, intense wracking sobs of dismay.

'I…. I can't…. It's… wrong! I-'

He never did finish the sentence, struck down in mid thought. But the damage was done. The others were beginning to doubt their allegiance as well.

Oh well, what could not be accomplished by diplomacy would be acquired by fear.

'Comply!' The admiral stated. 'Or you will suffer worse fate!'

They returned stoically to their duties, though Taalk did not need to be a psychic to know how they felt. They were being forced to act, not left to choose. And that was against everything Seren stood for, publicly.

He had lost their trust.

Accursed child! How had she done this?

Accursed rescuers! They had somehow managed to break the perimeter. Perhaps given the situation that was not surprising, taking into account their talents. What was surprising was their gift at creating chaos, and using that chaos to their advantage. At first he had taken occasional peeks at their progress, now he fully directed his minion's efforts at stopping them. As often as occasion would permit, that is. They were good, but whichever path they chose they would enter one of his inescapable traps.

Still … *you cannot have what is not given.*

Bah! He put the intrusive thought out of his mind.

Closer

They were in a corridor when suddenly the lights went out, followed by a loud metallic boom both in front and behind them. Matrix felt doom surround them.

'Oh dear,' said Sheelaakah even as she felt something rush against her boot. The room suddenly was lit by Skion's staff. They were trapped in a hexagonal corridor, and it was filling rapidly with liquid. Somehow, despite of all precaution and distraction, they had been discovered inside the foundry on their way towards the child prisoners.

'Water?' Montsi asked.

'Not water.' Glenn replied. He was bending over and testing the liquid with both smell and the instruments he brought with him. 'I'm on to it.'

Skion attempted to heave on the door, unsuccessfully. Glenn was spraying some rather smelly green liquid, which dissolved quickly into the liquid that was quickly growing up to their knees. The room went dark as Skion transformed his arm into a powerful weapon. Montsi screamed as the soldier fired at the wall, which lit the tunnel each time like a bolt of lightning.

'There is insufficient time!' He shouted. Alasia was working hurriedly on the door circuits.

'They're switched off!' She said in alarm.

The water was up to their waists now, and cruelly cold. Matrix strived not to panic but was lost for ideas. He dived down. There was a rectangular panel on the floor. It was solid, and the opening mechanism stuck solidly: probably welded from the other side. It sounded hollow though. He quickly surfaced.

'Skion, under here, a panel.'

'I've nothing to cut through under water here fool!' He roared. 'And the compression wave would kill us all!'

Matrix scowled and dived down, even as the water begun lifting people from their feet. The man with green coloured eyes focused, bringing his energy down upon the door in a crushing kick. But the water had made him buoyant, and the blow was ineffectual. He steadied himself, and punched at the handle, but it did not move. The water would be almost to the ceiling now, and his breath was pushing against him. He turned in the water, levelling a mighty blow against the door with his heal. The opening mechanism jammed loose.

By now he was beginning to feel the desperate need for air. Together, Glenn and he twisted the door against the mighty weight of the water as it drained quickly into the levels below. They were all but pushed in with it. He waited, clinging to the walls as the water rushed about them. Glenn had to haul him up to regain the air that was being pushed into the corridor above. They coughed and spluttered, till Matrix had a chance to collapse on the floor.

'You did that with your bare hands!?' Alasia remarked incredulously at the strained and twisted metal.

'They say you can break through anything if you really want to,' Matrix quoted an old epitaph from his martial training long ago.

'Good work,' Skion commented.

They nodded.

The corridor she walked in now was dark, he knew, and she would be hearing their voices at the far end. But what were they saying? He strained to hear through her stale mind, but could not make out the words. But then she turned back, or rather... she never moved towards them. She was being obstinate, holding on.

He ordered her central nervous system flooded with electricity. It would surely separate soul from body. But after the fourth treatment the chief medic spoke up.

'Sir, I'm not getting any reading. It is as though she has no body to template.'

Taalk smiled patiently, resisting the urge to strike out at the incompetent, bumbling, idiotic... wait, he must maintain his control. There were none who could match his talent and skill. He had given everything to be brought to this moment. She was being obstinate, and would pay the price. And the others who strove to rescue her would soon be stopped. They would never live to see his face.

He touched his necklace. The single quartz and black feather that had such infamous powers, stolen from a single world a generation ago for its dark purposes. So, she refused to disjoin from her body even after it no longer functioned. Than he would force her from it, one cell at a time if need be!!

Battle closes

It was really all too easy, Alasia thought to herself. With the phantom assailants she had set in their system, and the cloaking devices availed them by Skion, all that she had to do when faced with multiple enemies was to turn them upon themselves. Often, entire legions raced to their own destruction, fighting their own allies that seemed to them their prey. A dirty tactic, she knew, but it would have not worked as well had they been fighting for capture, not to kill.

Then things begun to turn sour, a short cut in a public place and they were on to them in a second. The behemoth was pulling off parts of the wall to throw at them now. Pinning them down while the guards more than obviously made their way along the far walls. They were firing psychoneural disrupters now, which would have stilled them but for the Commanders talents.

The men took point, Skion trying to break down the massive structure with enormous plasma blasts from his arm, while Matrix used his rifle to try and take down the guards before they surrounded them.

Things were looking grim.

Montsi, Alasia and Sheelaakah pressed up against the far corner.

'Well, this might take some doing,' she commented calmly. Then to make conversation added insightfully, 'hey, notice how our group's talents are so classically structured along gender stereotypes?'

The ice princess did not reply. She was far too busy with the minds around her. Like a dagger in her heart Alasia realised something - this was the chance she'd been waiting for.

She was pressed right up against her. All it would take was a deft slip of the wrist and the stone would be placed. They were in the walls now. It would only take them moments to send in their real re-enforcements. They would have a direct trace to them. And if the Resistance lost this battle it might be the only way Alasia could save herself.

Almost unconsciously she slipped the stone into her hand. It was dark and cold, like it didn't belong on her. It belonged on the Commander.

Then she'd eat her words...

But Alasia couldn't feel angry right now. She sighed in exasperation, what was happening to her?

Another plaza blast hit the wall above them, the carer clinging onto her arm, looking frightened to death.

The men were firing out from behind a fallen column now. Matrix fell backwards as a percussive blast hit that column near him. He fell to the floor, his rifle snapped.

Miraculously, he struggled to his feet again. He pulled a primitive blazer from his belt. In that moment his eyes met hers with inhuman determination. He would not stop. No matter what the cost. He was going to save that child.

He stumbled back to the fallen pillar, resuming firing.

The Commander suppressed a whimper. Alasia looked at her. Her eyes were tearing up.

'I didn't help him. He's... so strong,' she said, and intensified whatever mental efforts she was engaged in.

It would be so easy now...

But Alasia couldn't do it.

Not now. Not here. Not yet.

Forge fired Resistance!

Suddenly the ground shock. The Behemoth's arm crashed to the floor, severed by Skion's blasts.

The men cheered, but it was brief. The monster was ambling towards them now. There would be no escape…

She checked the Evernet again and found what she needed. A service machine in the room behind the wall.

'Girls! Up against the column!' Alasia screamed, and they hardly had time to move before a giant mechanical claw powered through the stone behind them.

As quick as thought they poured through the hole, and into a perplexed crowd of people seemingly sitting down calmly to lunch at a score of tables.

'Oh… we wondered what all the noise was,' one of them said as the heavily armed Resistance soldiers pushed in.

'You've *got* to be kidding,' Commander Sheelaakah said, and sent out an enormous psychic wave so powerful that it rendered them all unconscious.

'What do you know, a cafeteria?' Alasia said, helping herself to a sugared bun. She knew very well she'd let her chance slip again. But that was forgivable. They weren't in a really good position for it anyway, pinned under fire. *I could have been hurt,* she told herself. She'd do it soon, after they'd rescued the child. It was the right… it was what was best for herself.

But on the inside she knew… she'd just crossed a line.

It had taken far too long and much more effort than it ought, the grey man knew. He'd had to force her spirit to leave her body, and that had taken all his strength and then some. He rested now, sitting in a nearby chair. The others had masks of professionalism on, but they knew what they had witnessed. Some did not care, others had naked ambition that had driven them to this place. But all had a conscience, to one degree or another.

He had been forced to suppress almost each one of them by now, and it was added difficulty. Deep in their unconscious minds they resented his obstinate refusal to back down from the procedure which was so brutal against a one who could do no harm. But it would not stop him, and with him there pressing them on, they could not stop themselves either.

'Sir,' the chief medic nervously began.

'What,' he glared from reddened eyes.

'We've begun the procedure... but...'

'But what!' The grey man demanded, while already guessing the answer and looking in the man's mind for confirmation. Nothing. No imprint. Somehow, in some manner... she was still resisting.

'It's impossible,' the medic replied.

But it was so. She refused to let go. Even after all the pain and torture, after being forced to vacate her own body, she held on. She would not let go. And unless the residual energy from her soul print was freed, they would get no template of her talent.

'But... she's dead,' the medic said in reply to the unasked problem.

'She must be erecting a bio-foci shield,' the admiral claimed, while knowing as the breath left his lips that it was not true. She simply... refused to leave.

'Begin the procedure again!!' He demanded. She would relinquish. All his life had been preparing for this moment and a five year old would not defeat him! Her rescuers would be slain and her prize his. Even if it took all his power and grace to do it.

It would take time, he knew, but she could not refuse him forever...

They were getting much closer now, only a few blocks remained between them and the child. They were passing through such wreckage now, weaving their way through the cylinders of aluminium in a large warehouse. Then Shee sensed it. An alien body, fuelled by a human mind - a gnolem was approaching.

She quickly informed the others and they hurried to the far exit. It began to pursue them, faster and faster. It would outrun them, and with a body of stone it would not tire. The passage split, and Matrix called the left turn. She sent a telepathic signal down the other corridor, but it was not enough. Soon it would have them cornered. Too soon, the passage ended over a wide gulf.

A growl of stone came from behind them. Against this foe she had few talents, and it was unusual among its kind. Suddenly a blast of white light knocked her to her feet as it careered into the stone beast. It exploded into sand. Sheelaakah turned to see Skion raising his staff as the runes inlaid glowed an angry blue.

'It's reforming!' He gestured, as the sand began to reform into the gnolem once more.

Then Glenn turned to Alasia.

'I know, we're under the tower of light right?' He said.

'Right, what's your point?'

'Well, shouldn't that give us enough mass to provide a point Tesser, I mean, they do it all the time on the tower?'

'Off course!' Alasia remarked, slapping her forehead in an ancient derogatory remark, intended probably at herself. 'Sometimes I'm just too clever for my own good.'

'C'mon!' Yelled Matrix, trying to kick the sand apart. 'We're running out of time! Teleport us to the child!'

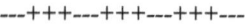

He fell into the chair trembling.

Everything. He had tried everything. Nothing had worked. He had not prevailed. Short of destroying her outright there was no way of freeing her soul, and that would lose him his prize.

And still they came. Nothing could stop them. All his powers were not enough. Every obstacle, every trick... nothing could deter them... soon... they would be here... here.

He would have to stop them personally.

The place they entered now was not in the least what Matrix had expected. It was a polished white marble rectangle, around seven by ten meters. A quick glance around revealed no doors, no panels, nothing to mar the unyielding marble that surrounded them.

The others where there too now.

'Stone,' remarked Sheelaakah, as though she had not expected it. 'Is there an exit?'

Glenn spoke first, pointing his device at the walls. 'No exits. We appear to be in a solid marble room. It's stone all the way through too, as far as this thing can see, and that's over four thousand kilometres.'

'Impossible!' Scoffed Skion mechanically. 'There is in existence no such structure on Seren!'

'Well, there must be a door or exit here somewhere. It was difficult enough tessering in here. Is there an access point somewhere?' Sheelaakah asked.

Skion studied the walls even as his bio mechanical scanners surveyed the surrounding stone.

'Nothin',' his human voice replied, frustrated. 'Just stone.'

'Well they can't have built a stone edifice just to trap people in. This place looks like it's never been used. There has to be some kind of door. Perhaps...'

'Oh people!' Alasia sighed condescendingly. 'Isn't it obvious? There are no stone edifices on Seren because we aren't on Seren.'

'But we can't have just left, and this hole seems to lead nowhere!' Matrix observed.

'I said 'on' Seren, that doesn't preclude 'in'. Or 'with' as the term is. Look at the walls. They are so smooth: perfectly smooth, to the nanometre I'll decree. And the walls, stone for over four thousand Kilometres? Sound likely? Do you know what I'm getting at?'

'Indeed,' Skion said. 'I do not.'

'Smooth,' Matrix was musing. 'You don't suppose we are in some kind of interdimensional space, do you?'

'Indeed, I do,'

'Is it just me?' Montsi suddenly interjected. 'But are the walls closing in?'

The others looked closely now, and indeed, though the walls couldn't be seen moving, the room was smaller now than when they first arrived.'

'That makes it more effective,' Sheelaakah observed, hiding the worry in her voice.

'Well can we get out of here?' Montsi trembled.

'Just a second,' Alasia said, though they didn't really have many. 'As I thought...' she was looking up now, staring through the ceiling, the computer access gem at her temple glowing slightly as it worked. 'It's a minute pocket vortex, determining the dimension of this space. We're technically in around three tonne of marble, arranged to impossible proportions through clever dimension manipulations. This is an unexpected opportunity.'

'Opportunity?' Sheelaakah mused incredulously.

Alasia derided her unbelief, 'If you could go anywhere, on Seren, where would you be?'

'Noktosian baths,' Matrix replied without hesitation. 'No, inside that pompous government psychic's office, no, just outside his door. That way he has no backup,' Matrix replied.

'Agreed,' said Sheelaakah, but she took no effort to hide her obvious dubiousness.

'OK then,' Alasia said cheerfully.

Slowly, a blue circle formed alone the flawless plane of the floor. It was a dimensional portal, like all portals, with a specific entry and exit point at the same point unless both sides were anchored to gates. In essence, it lead nowhere.

A moment another portal appeared floating above the other one, positioned in mid-air. There was a brief flash of electricity as a third portal began opening inside the second, and at right angles to it so that all three dimension where present with portals that would lead nowhere. Slowly the two joined portals began to descend onto the third.

'Ahh, Alasia, what are you doing?' Matrix asked. Three portals could release such a large amount of antimatter it would kill them all, and leave a smouldering crater in the ground.

'Yes, Skion, you might want to take care of this.'

He nodded and stepped forward, acting as a lightning rod as the three portals touched and electrical plasma flew from the joining. Suddenly it stopped, and a single portal, circular and an opaque blue, faced them. It was fascinating, thought Matrix, for no matter what your vantage point, the portal always faced you.

'What have you done?' Asked Sheelaakah in disbelief.

'Oh, just a little experiment. Seems to have worked nicely,' she was just a little worn from the effort of communicating with a computer in another dimension. 'I've created 'no space'.'

'What!' Matrix said aloud, even as he stepped to avoid a closing wall. 'That's just a theoretical impossibility!'

'Well, the Oppression tried it a decade ago, even we had a turn at it,' Sheelaakah explained. 'But it never worked. An opening in space that leads directly to the juncture of three dimensional portals. Theoretically it leads right to 'no space'.'

'Where the entire universe exists at a single point, and thus all points are an equal distance from each other. It can be used, I assure you, to go anywhere, to step out at 'any point' if you will. Except outside the energy field and other warded zones,' Alasia explained. 'Now if you will, it's getting cramped in here, so I'd like to leave.'

She was about to step into the portal, but Skion stepped before her and went first. Matrix could not tell if it was an act of chivalry, or military savvy, or expedience as his head was beginning to be pressed down by the roof.

They all left quickly then, one after the other, putting faith in Alasia's claims. That and they knew that unlike rooms that grew smaller due to mechanics, there was no stopping a room that grew smaller due to its dimensions being altered by the laws of physics.

The scientist waited until his pet reached ten million Kelvin; fusion point. It was such a nice way to produce energy, just not efficient enough to keep around much now days. Still, his pet had other uses, such as trapping unwelcome guests. Then, the dimensions would decrease, the matter would become hotter to the point of fusion, and then his pet would become nice and warm: too hot to touch, hot enough to power steam or thermo-electrical gradient motors. Not much use for them either, but it was his pet. His baby.

He was grateful; there was no other word for it. That the government on Seren kept him and his pet secret so that they could continue their research into turning humans into pure energy was gift enough, but that they occasionally provided subjects, well, there was just no word to express his thanks adequately. As long as the people didn't find out, that could be a problem. But they were pretty docile here on Seren. They'd learned a long time ago not to ask too many questions. Questions like what he did for his service every day, questions about whom this mysterious pet was that he loved to talk about. Questions about what he liked to feed her.

And she'd just had another meal.

<sigh>

Or had she... four thousand nano meters? Smallish. Too small. Way too small! Why, that would only be possible if there was nothing but air in there! But there wasn't! Impossible! There were six people in there, including a cyborg which would account for the high degree of silicates.

Yes, the silicates! He checked the silicate levels in the intense press of atoms in his marble chamber. They would tell. The silicates would not lie. The silicates... The silicates...

Negligible.

Impossible.

Simply, utterly... impossible.

They'd escaped...

---+++---+++---+++---

Arrived

They had arrived.

Taalk raised his weary grey head, weighed down by battle. When they finally broke down the doors, they were each bleeding from multiple wounds, some which would not soon heal. They had indeed dealt with the two score of elite guards at the door; and that without the benefit of energy weapons: the suppression field had taken care of that. It was all hand to hand combat, and yet they had won. How they had arrived so easily at the precise location of the operation chamber was still a mystery to him.

They boldly entered the quiet room. There were no medics now; they had all fled. There were just two figures: Himself, the cold grey man standing at the head of a palate where a silent green child lay. Tubes were affixed to her, machines stood by her, and she did not breathe. Had they the eyes to see, as he did, then they might have seen her soul print floating patently above the palate, just below the roof.

They entered silently. He stood facing them, but did not move. He could reach out any second, any moment, and tear their consciousness from them. They knew this, and they feared him. They levelled their weapons but dared not move, for they knew he could destroy them in the time it took for the bio electrical signal to reach their armed limbs. The black clad female took vigilance over the computer control, and the tall cyborg guarded the door even as he watched the old man.

It made him want laugh. It was all so brave. It was all, so futile.

And yet, he did not move. They had fought, and fought, and fought. They did not surrender. The act seized upon him even as he could not conceive it.

And so had she. His prophetess. No power or influence he had brought to bear had held back her words. All his skill, all his technology, could not take from her what she did not consent to give.

How ironic that he too was, in the end, impotent. He had seized his prize with both hands and yet, for all his strength, he could not claim it. For a minute they stared at each other, no side daring to act as if the moment of reverence had been what they had come to fully realise.

And then someone broke that reverence. A woman. The carer. Without even stopping to look about she went straight to the palate, bursting into tears. She brushed right past him, several times, as she took the medical instruments apart one by one. She did not beg his assistance, nor demand his absence. But quickly, tearfully, worked to remove the constraints and medi tubes protruding in the young life.

He smiled again. It was all so futile. The child would not live; none could under this environment. She didn't even have any blood left, not of her own. When they realised this, once they realised that it had all been in vain, he would destroy them.

They did not move either, but watched the carer pitifully.

The woman had finished now, and laid the unliving body on the palate. This was the moment, when they would know they were defeated. This was the moment...

'Come back,' she whispered, looking upwards.

Perhaps the meaningless ritual had driven her insane? He smiled.

'I know you can hear me. Jacinth, it's me, Montsi. I know you can come back you just don't know the way. Follow my voice. Come back, Jacinth, oh please, oh please, come back to life...'

He smiled, it would be now. The Cyborg had already begun to raise its charged weapon in a timeless gesture of futility.

Then the mutant soldier quietly brushed past him and walked over to the child, gentle touching her on her head.

Suddenly something happened. In a moment, they were seven in a room, and then, they were eight. The lifeless child stirred. She clutched her fists and became rigid, and then... she breathed.

But that was... impossible...

And in that breath all life returned to the room. They did not wait another moment longer. The career ran from the room as a mother flees a flood, child in her arms.

The others left too. Quickly, professionally.

And he was alone.

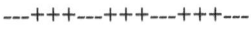

He did not know how much time had passed. Lord Admiral Taalk heard a dark laugh from behind, but he did not need to turn to know who it was...

You let them go! You let them go!! The young man cawed in delight. You have failed! Failed! The mandate now falls to me. The necklace of Thith, the headband, your mantle! Now, they are mine.

He felt the other stand up now, long brown hair trailing below his waist as he did. He shouldn't have been able to do that, Taalk knew. But he knew why he had. All his authority, and much of his power, had already been transferred to his apprentice. He only lacked a single act, and then the transfer would be complete.

He could have run, but then he would only die tired. He could have fought, he was still more than a match for his apprentice. But they would not support him, his Powers and Council having abandoned him the hour of his failure. No, it would be his to die in dignity. The thought brought him peace, the only peace he should know for the rest of eternity he supposed; knowing the price his soul had paid for his power, knowing from where his power had come from. Knowing the awful penalty now that he had failed.

Knowing that, in spite it all, even he could not deny mercy her claim when it came to require the life of a single child.

Oh, but don't worry, his apprentice said mockingly. *You will still be allowed to serve, even in death...*

--- ++ --- ++ ---

When destiny intervenes

I-olo had pondered the other man's report for a quarter hour. By now, it had been furthered to the entire Circle, and they knew its contents. But if the supply general knew his job, they'd know its contents fifteen minutes later than I-olo himself did. Therefore, it was time to begin.

He sat in his chair and closed his eyes, feeling the gem inlaid in his copper banding. It drew his thought, his essence into it. Soon he was standing in the familiar place where he met his superiors, the penultimate leaders of the Resistance; the Circle.

I-olo. You timing is well. Tact began. *We've just received the supply general's report. It seems that the government was after the children, after all.*

Do we know why, my mistress? I-olo asked.

It is irrelevant, Tact replied with great finality. *Those children are more liability than capacity to our operations. The war against the Oppression is still very much against us, we are sure you can appreciate the need to maximise our resources.*

272

There is strong evidence to believe that the government has located their parents. In this case, uniting a family is the preferable option. Do you not agree I-olo?

Of course! He knew better not to disagree. *Then we will not be going after the children?*

Even as he spoke, he viewed the report they sent him, indeed, there were facts missing. Important ones. He hid that revelation as soon as it was possible, deep inside his mind.

It is forgone; they are of such little value. However, this brings us to a most disturbing situation I-olo…

He'd heard that tone in her voice before, an in spite himself, he began to sweat.

---+++---+++---+++---

Matrix led. They were running now, though no-one had stopped them. As they descended the tower they would soon be entering the under foundries, and whatever forgotten business was there held. They were passing through an empty corridor quietly, trying not to draw attention to themselves, and trying not to look out of place if someone spotted them.

'Hey,' mentioned Matrix. He had stopped by a nondescript door half way along the corridor. 'I wonder what is behind here?'

'It's just a door,' Bakerson said.

'Then you don't mind if I open it do you. It's the only one down this big stretch of corridor.'

Without waiting to hear a word of protest he let himself in.

It was a curious site. Six people, older in appearance, sat in a circle. Each was in a high backed throne apparently attached to the Evernet, for their eyes were closed and their breathing regular.

'Hurry!' Sheelaakah said. 'Inside, someone is coming.'

'Looks like we're going in anyway,' Alasia smirked cheekily to Dogman.

It was a large room, with several terminals along the far wall. Six in all, far more than was required for any mortal needs. Even the control decks of the battle cruisers only ever hosted two or three with multiple access ports.

'Is it a control centre of some kind?' Alasia asked.

'If it is, it could control almost every access port on Seren,' Dogman replied.

It was a simple room. Bare, clean. Wide, but not spacious. The room was dimly lit, and the thrones, or chairs, didn't appear built with much intent for comfort - though their occupants looked like they had grown into them, so well did they fit.

'Who do you suppose they are?' Alasia asked. 'They're very old, older than they look.'

'They appear to be in some form of hibernation,' Sheelaakah commented. 'But their minds are very lucid. I wonder how long they have been here for?'

'Or what they are doing,' Matrix continued.

'Each is connected to an individual terminal,' Skion commented, investigating the machines along the wall. 'They appear to be highly interconnected, in a form of symbiotic whole.'

'So they are asleep, and their dreams produce a reality for them. I wonder who else?' Alasia asked no one in particular. 'Perhaps we should find out?'

'That could be dangerous. That one is a high level psychic,' Sheelaakah said.

'That makes you our volunteer,' Matrix replied to the old Commander cheekily.

She sighed, and made her way towards the left most terminal. She reached her hand out, and the machine caught her signal, and automatically began to fuse with her mind. In a moment, she would know just what was going on inside those peoples reality.

---+++---+++---+++---

You did WHAT!! He roared throwing I-olo to the floor with his voice like the backhand of a giant.

I-olo smiled to himself, in spite the pain. He knew it was infuriating them. *I let them go. I ordered Commander Sheelaakah to resume her mission, but they insisted on working together and rescued the children. I could not stop them.*

You are forfeit! He roared again, I-olo's vision trembling at the force of his voice. *Too long, counsel, have we pitied this amateur while the Oppression makes gains on his behalf! To death!*

They had found out, he knew they would. He had been in charge of seeing Alasia to that cell. He had been responsible for making sure Sheelaakah resumed her regular duties. He had been, in effect, commanded to ensure Matrix remained cloistered in ignominy. It was his job to ignore the plight of those children and eliminate the quest of any who might care. He knew he had failed them all, and he knew, it was for the last time.

The others chorused their consent. Eventually, even his superior assented to his demise. He had lived well though, and there was much information gained that the Resistance would use in spite his demise: the seeds of doubt had been planted.

A stone fist materialised above his prone form. In the reality of his mind it would mean the cessation of life should it fall.

Then there came a voice, unbidden, that had never before spoken in the private sanctum of the Circle. *Ahh, not so fast, my friends.*

A woman's voice.

Somehow…

… it was Sheelaakah!

Peace, at last…

Hello I-olo. The Commander began, sharing with him a dangerously sweet smile even as she approached him through the darkness like a dream. *I didn't expect to find you here.*

How… Where… He began, but was cut short as Tact spoke up.

You see, we bring her to you to begin a New Response.

Save your lies! I am here of my free will, uninvited! Sheelaakah spoke loudly. *I-olo, would you like to see where we are?*

He nodded, and it seemed the Circle held its breath.

Don't do it child, Tact whispered.

Suddenly the lights went on in the darkness, dissipating the stone fist instantly. Ever since he had been in the Resistance, the Circle met in telepathic obscurity. Now the lights went on. They were in a small misty grey room, and around him, seated on broad stone chairs, were six old people. A million wires crossed the floors between them, and strange, translucent tubes ran throughout their bodies and back into the strange chairs. They were clinging to an artificial life, supported by strange instruments that wove above, around and through them. It was a mockery of human existence.

Where are we? I-olo asked.

Commander Sheelaakah answered: *In the tower of light, behind a non-descript door somewhere around the three thousandth level of the lower foundries. You see, it seems the Circle of the Resistance has its head office here…*

No! One old man shouted, Dale now sounding like a decrepit foreigner. *Impossible! You will both die for this!*

A translucent hand, as large as a bolder, struck at them both - and passed straight through them. The old man looked out at them in disbelief.

The Commander took the liberty to explain: *There are others here with me, you might be surprised to know. We did a little altering of the system before I arrived. You'll find yourself quite safe now, I-olo.*

He could see them now, shadowy mists of forgotten warm, living human beings.

No, you won't, It was Voice. For the first time, I-olo could see him. Voice was older than the others. He might have been a tall man if he wasn't stooped down in a chair. He lifted his hand in a gesture of wisdom as he spoke, trailing tubes and wires as it went.

I knew, long ago, that this moment might come. You will not stop us...

Yes, I will! I-olo countered, and for once stood bold and proud before his mentors. So it had all been a lie. All the Resistance was, all it had ever been, was just another government department.

This ends here! I-olo demanded emphatically, thrusting his fist down as though it alone was sufficient to destroy their lies. *You have had your reign, and now, we will have our freedom!*

A woman laughed. It was Tact. He turned to see a woman with sunken eyes and pale lips. She was frail and grey. *And just how do you propose to destroy a council that has stood for over four hundred years in less than a minute?*

It's already done, Sheelaakah explained. *The others have isolated your circuit. They have taken everything you knew, everything you've done, the entire records of the 'Circle', and sent it to I-olo's reception. The others here have done so on my command. If we die here, it does not matter, for now he knows everything you've been doing. Now, the knowledge of the Resistance is in the hands of the new and only leader: I-olo Tilk.*

He smiled. Even before Sheelaakah had begun to speak, he knew what she was doing. His mind was filling with a torrent of information, countless libraries of details, all stored in the banding stone he wore about his brow.

With renewed confidence he spoke; *The false Resistance ends today: We are reborn. No longer will the actions of the Resistance be governed by the will of its enemies. This, today, is the **New response**, and the birth of a New Resistance!*

They stared at him bitterly, and said nothing.

Goodbye old masters, you taught us well...

---+++---+++---+++---

Sheelaakah was still in the ethereal room, held deep underneath the lower foundry offices. They did not speak as I-olo left, smiling happily to her as he telepathically vacated the false premises of the old Resistance. They turned to look at her now, a mixture of bitterness and resignation on their faces.

Well, young lady, you have done all that you said you would do. Now what becomes of us? Voice asked.

Shee pondered her options. *Your deeds have caused the needless deaths of millions. Your actions have prevented the Resistance from truly learning what it needed to know, and doing what it needed to do, to bring the crimes of Seren to the public knowledge of the Galactic Senate. In all honesty, I don't know...*

Her thought was broken off as she sensed, rather than felt, Matrix pulling at her arm. Suddenly a strange dark entity brushed past her, filling her with fear. She turned to watch in spite of herself, even as it passed straight through three of the seated figures. She watched as, in a way she could not explain, they died instantly, their breath snatched effortlessly away from them even as the dark spirit ran through them.

She snapped back into the material world. Officer Bakerson was lying on the floor where his head had struck the wall. The figures in the chairs, the three surviving ones still in their catatonic sleep, twitched as they vainly fought the intruders. The door, apparently of its own devices, swung violently shut.

'What's going on?!' demanded Alasia, fear more than evident in her voice.

'Non- corporeals,' Matrix replied.

They were scarcely visible to the eye, but Sheelaakah could feel them. One of the seated figures threw her head back and began to choke.

'When they finish with them, they will come for us,' Matrix stated, in a matter of fact manner.

Skion began swinging violently at the attacker, but traditional weapons appeared to have no effect on this particular kind of demon. In an instant the invisible attacker retaliated, throwing him clear across the room and leaving a serious dent in the opposing wall.

Montsi screamed and ran to Sheelaakah. 'What do we do?! Do something!!'

'I can't!' she trembled.

'Why not!'

'I can't... I don't know what they are. We can communicate, but...they are too alien and ... too powerful!'

She stopped as Matrix walked slowly towards the expiring woman. Slowly, gently, with almost surreal simplicity, he reached up to her throat and with patient effort began to remove the spectral apparition of hands that appeared even as he touched them. Again, his hands glowed with invisible fire.

'How...?' Alasia began, but Sheelaakah could not reply. She did not know either.

A dark presence suddenly pressed past her, nearly knocking her down with surprising force and loathing. But even before she could draw a breath Matrix spun around and struck out at the air. The unseeable creature roared in surprise and pain, and beat a hasty retreat to far away.

Shee looked around. The other two humans were slain now. The one that was nearly asphyxiated began to open her eyes, blinking in the dim light. For the first time in what might have been centuries, she was conscious.

'It is still here,' Matrix said, his voice calm and surprisingly deep. He walked over to a place on the floor, and even as he did a pathetic and twisted figure began to take shape on the ground before him. A man, or part of a man. Sheelaakah had never known more fear and loathing than when she looked into the irrepressible, indescribable hatred of that man.

You will not stop us, it hissed.

'Go,' Matrix replied, and began to reach for it. Suddenly, in a moment, it was gone. It felt to Sheelaakah as if a suffocating pillow had been removed from her face, and she could breathe again. She noticed Alasia, trembling, yet she headed to help Glenn, who was stirring. A strange noise from behind her caught her attention, and she turned to see the old woman with thin lips crying, straining to sit up now she was conscious of the material world again.

'What have you done...?' She asked weakly, ancient voice croaking out each syllable as she verged on her death. 'You have destroyed the Resistance. Now the government will annihilate them all. Our Resistance protected them. They were safe-'

'No,' Sheelaakah insisted. 'They were oppressed, your freedom was merely another prison.'

The old woman continued as if she hadn't heard. '... then the government will have to start all over again. The dissidents of Seren will serve her again in their rebellion.' She looked at her with dark eyes. 'You will not prevail child. No one can stop Him. No one. He .. the True One... will rule all... all...'

He voice trailed off as the vessel that was her corporeal form could no longer maintain its life.

She died.

---+++---+++---+++---

Matrix looked up. Once the dark entities had left, it only took a few moments for everyone to recover. Leaving the deceptive Circle to their graveless death they quickly headed deeper into the underfoundaries, hoping to cross the wall from further underground. They had survived.

An hour later Sheelaakah had apparently resumed some form of conversation with someone far away, and turned to them all from explaining something to Skion.

'That's right,' she said. 'There's that and many more changes. It seems that I-olo will come into his own now and that he will form a new Circle. That is itself is unusual.'

'How so?' Matrix asked.

'It's not like the upper leaders of the Resistance to go public, for der own keep'n,' Skion explained.

'But that's not the best news: I've been saving that.'

Indeed she had, thought Matrix. After all the cryptic and incomplete explanations of what had just happened, in voice no less, all the 'exciting' details of the New response: which in essence was the basic philosophy of dealing with the Oppression, governing everything from war to diplomatic functions, she was yet to explain what she had begun with as 'the best part of the New Response'. So in spite of himself, despite the fact he was cross armed and brow furrowed, he held his breath.

'The best part is this: no more terminating.'

Skion snorted his indignation.

'It's true,' the Commander continued. 'From now on, all weapons are fixed on discapacitate – on stun. And that means non-permanent incapacitation, you'll recall,' she said with a smile. 'Not unless there is no other alternative.'

Skion frowned, his computer voice speaking. 'This has been attempted, you recall, a generation ago. All other means of making our message felt were denied. The Oppression will not respect nonviolent means-'

Shee cut him off, with just a little of the authority which was hers again, re-promoted already to a command role again. 'And it has got us nowhere in a generation. No more are we the criminals escaping prison. Our message is one of choice: we choose to live elsewhere under our own government and will fight, as reluctantly and as little as necessary, to obtain it. The forceful approach only convinced the people that we deserved our oppression. Once again, we return to an holistic notion of freedom: for ourselves, and others.'

'We'd better keep moving,' Glenn said. 'There will be pursuit.'

They rode quietly in a converted transport. After a moment, the Commander moved to speak to Matrix alone.

'How did you do that?' Sheelaakah asked him.

'Do what?' He replied, shrugging though he knew what she was asking about.

'Send them away like that. Touch them, even, with force. They... I've never heard of anyone doing that before to ... this particular kind of adversary.'

He shrugged again, not knowing what to say. Her hazel eyes stayed on him, and she did not move away. He did not know what to tell her, how to tell her. But she would not be satisfied with anything less than an answer. He sighed.

'It's a talent. My hands hurt when I do; they burn. I strike them with what they are made of; what we are all made of. There was this time when I was young... I don't think it's the force that does it, but something that comes up deep inside that turns them away. The courage... I can't explain it. Words just can't do that.'

She looked around his face, and he wondered what she might be thinking. For whatever reason, the answer seemed to satisfy her enough, for she sat back and looked away.

'What happened in there Shee... Commander? Who were these people?'

She looked surprised that he'd used that name, but the moment passed as she answered his question. 'To think, we came here to save a child, and have given greater hope to the entire Resistance. They were... they were the Resistance Matrix!' She stated almost with broken pain. 'It was them, all a lie... they were the Circle!'

He did not know what to say, but it felt like truth.

The Under Foundries

They had almost escaped now, and had reached the area below the foundries: the underfoundaries. Miles upon miles of heavy industry. Ironic that, in spite of thousands of years of technological improvements and automated advancements in automation, that sometimes, industry just needed people to know when to pull a lever.

At least... almost people.

'Who are they?' He heard Montsi ask.

What they saw had made them all stop. Indeed, there were people down here. But no longer people...

Zombies.

Matrix trembled in rage. *So it is true.* They had no souls, only the life-formed husks that moved according to the syncopated commands formed of electronic mastery and human memories. Their blood was sickly green, and their skin a lifeless shade of grey. Their colourless iris's stared straight ahead, and all were in various stages of decay.

So here the prisoners were kept, at times for hundreds of years, till they rotted completely away.

Matrix stood close to one. It gave no indication that it knew he was there.

'Well, at least it'll make it easy to get past,' he thought carelessly out loud, then stopped abruptly as Sheelaakah's gasped audibly.

'No!' Shee whispered, sudden rage cascading from her in uncontrolled waves. The others turned. She was watching, staring fixedly at one of the innumerable, non-descript no-longer-humans that was pushing a strange cart with unimportant tubes.

'NO!' Her whisper became a yell. Before anyone would dare to stop her she had accosted the stranger, reaching to touch his face, cradling it in her hands. It was a young man, of about sixteen.

Without human instinct the zombie tried to circumvent her to continue its work. She reached up to his temple now, and in a deft telepathic manoeuvre none saw but all knew, split the green gem that was his connection to the system. With no instructions he simply stopped, and Sheelaakah took the opportunity to drag him to the floor, cradling his head against her bosom, black ichor draining unheeded from his lips. Whispering softly, 'Here you are. I found you. Here you are…'

Matrix was the first to move, tentatively approaching her.

'Commander. It… it's all right, we have to go…'

The grieving woman smiled gently at the unheeding face of the automaton on her lap, and did not speak till Matrix drew a breath to talk again.

'No,' she stated absolutely. 'Its… he… I have to look after him.'

Matrix could not shake the feeling that there was something very wrong in her voice. There was no strength, no thought of planning, just primal human need. Strange how quickly it had all happened, especially to her.

Matrix felt Skion approach him, turning as though to speak.

Commander Sheelaakah shows indisputable evidence of psychosis, her entire mid brain has over ridden any attempts at cognitive control.

Can you, can we reach her? Matrix asked him.

Not sub telepathically. She has driven powerful wards about her mind while she reaches into the human foundry man there. I could not reach here if I tried. We must use voice, and caution. She is succumbing completely to irrationality.

But so quickly? Matrix puzzled. Not two hours ago she was beaming salubriously about the New Response.

Matrix thought, then reached down to her, taking her firmly by the arm.

'Sheelaakah, listen to me. We have to leave, nothing can be done.'

'NO!' She screamed till it filled the cavern. 'I'll not lose him! Never again! You don't understand, no one can!!' Her tears scrambled unchecked down her anguished face and onto the zombies brow where it lay, unheeding.

Matrix steeled himself to drag her away when Montsi crouched before the defiant psychic. He held his breath as she caught Sheelaakah's eye, her own now brimming with unshed tears. For a moment the two simply looked, then the carer began to stroke the zombies brow kindly.

'Who was he?' she softly asked.

Sheelaakah just stared, then wailed heavenward as though the stars themselves might take pity. 'He was my brother!!' she cried helplessly. 'My only brother! My twin! My soul!' She wept on his chest, 'My Daemon.'

Montsi was in tears too now, and neither could he keep crystal tears from brimming in the emerald eyes under locks of jet black hair.

For a moment Sheelaakah wept helplessly.

Montsi spoke. 'He is very handsome. You must have had some adventures together.'

Sheelaakah still cried. The career cringed, perhaps she feared she had said something wrong?

'He comes with us,' Sheelaakah finally said.

All eyes turned. This was madness.

Finally Matrix dared to speak their thoughts. 'But, he can't.'

'He can. He will.'

'Sheelaakah... he's dead.' He felt like such a criminal, but it was the truth, and no one else was going to say it.

She shook her head till her weeping eyes were fairly covered with a tangle of hair.

'No,' she said again, only this time she was sounded more rational, more determined. 'He comes with me. I'll not lose him this time. He's still alive, his soul print has not yet departed. He will come back... he will. We've all seen it happen, twice, haven't we?' And she held him close.

They did not argue. It made Matrix angry; she was being irrational, impossible. She would not listen to truth, and so had to be left to discover it for herself.

'Fine,' he stated, and lifting the corpse in his arms allowed Sheelaakah to cradle his head in her hands. 'Let's make for the far exit. It has a hidden Derringer rune on the side, just in case no-one else noticed. It might take us to an encampment they have.'

'Ahh, Matrix,' asked Glenn. 'Does anyone know where Alasia has got to?'

They looked about. The singer was gone again. It's couldn't have been an abduction, they'd have noticed. Had she simply slipped away? Perhaps this living grave was too much for her? She didn't even say goodbye.

'Eh, where is she? I mean, why now? Perhaps we should check the elev-' Matrix began.

'No time!' Skion suddenly roared. 'There are black guards approaching this location! On the transport now!'

They'd hardly made the steps by the time the first wards began to fall. The guards wore masks this time, in a punitive attempt to staunch the stench of the benighted underworld that Seren had created for itself. They would probably erase their memories, those that survived the battle anyway.

It was a pity Matrix could not erase his memory: Of the way they had to blast their way through a wall of guards, or how the zombies had not the sense to avoid their careering vehicle as they escaped throwing themselves at the mercy of whatever tunnel they happened across.

Of Sheelaakah's numbness during the whole matter.

Of the complete and utter disappearance of Alasia.

Or of Montsi and her surprised but determined expression as a lucky shot from the black guards sent her unexpectedly to her death.

Epilogue

Less than an hour later, Alasia stood alone atop the largest structure surrounding the citadel; the wall. Stretching away as far as the horizon in a gentle, almost imperceptible curve around the city it protected, or held prisoner. Wind swept her black hair, stinging her eyes and drying her tears. She should not be up here.

He was dead, the one who used her as a spy. She knew that, somehow, and if not yet, he would be soon. That he had, for reasons perhaps beyond his own understanding, let them escape with the most precious acquisition the Oppression had obtained in a thousand years was obvious.

But he had lied: they had *all* lied. The evidence was at first sensational, almost scintillating. Now, she knew it was dreadful, terrifying. They stole... they stole _you_. She too had seen someone else she once knew. Down there, in the foundries. The Oppression. They were really as bad as the Resistance said they were. They had to be stopped.

She hadn't wanted to look at them, not ever, not until. They were awful, they were death. Then the Commander had first started her commotion. Finally and against her will Alasia saw them; not with her eyes, but with her understanding. Then as she'd looked, she'd seen someone she once knew too. Someone a lot like her, full of promise, just learning to play the game. But she had disappeared, just before the annexation that Alasia would have never willingly believed if she hadn't seen it herself.

One day, gone. Simply gone. No one ever asked what had happened to Karen. Did they not care, or did they not dare ask? But now Alasia knew, now she knew what became of you once you died on Seren.

For a moment she could only stare as her old acquaintance passed by them, unheeded in the mass of undead around them. It was worse than murder. Without a sound she had fled the macabre scene by activating a nearby terminal and left to wherever it took her, an air duct, which is why she found herself now, crying into the wind, on top of the largest wall in Seren.

She felt betrayed. Completely. Utterly. While knowing so much she had never understood, seeing much but keeping her eyes closed. And yet they tortured children too.

She wiped her cheeks. She had never cried like this. So silently, so cathartic. She was not one of them, she never would be. She would never serve them again for as long as she lived.

The small onyx stone sat in her palm. She was glad she had found a place where she could be rid of it, and not harm them. It rolled in her hand, so small, so simple.

And in a moment, she let it roll away, far, far down the wall.

Book 4

Trials

Journey begins

The rock thinned towards the edges, shaped in rough measure like a pair of facing dinner plates. It was heavy, but fit snugly into his palm. *Yes, this one will do quite well,* Matrix thought, and was worth the effort of facing the dirt beneath his nails it took to rescue it from the mud. He took aim, and thrust it with his might, spinning it as he let go. It left to strike a glancing blow against his target. It skipped up and down again at least a dozen times, leaving a trail of ever widening circles in the water below.

Matrix was pleased right down to his stomach.

But evidently his hobby had gotten the better of Glenn, who finally spoke. 'Perhaps it'd be wiser to head back to the Resistance outpost now?'

Matrix huffed, and picked up another nondescript stone, skimming it disappointingly only twice before it disappeared below the surface of the broad lake they were standing beside, trees whispering in the breeze. It amused him: How they had found themselves here, *here*, of all places? It hadn't changed much in seven years. Seven years since he first was sent out of his home. Seven years since he'd taken his first drink in hours, and rested peacefully till the bikies had found him, and treated him like sport. It was the first time he'd felt truly afraid for his life. But this time, he wasn't afraid. He was skimming rocks.

Sheelaakah was no longer with them, nor had been for the better part of a day. They had met a large Resistance contingent, and she had travelled with Skion and the child to somewhere deep in Resistance lines as soon as she could. She had insisted on taking the zombie with her, even if it was her brother dead seven years, apparently. She'd said nothing, just shielded them both with such force it was dangerous to approach her. Nobody had said anything to her as she boarded the transport with it. They must have sensed the danger they were in to have asked. She had glanced at Matrix as they'd left, but her eyes were focused on some memory, leaving him staring back at her alone. He'd never seen anyone in such emotional turmoil, at least, that wasn't thrashing about on a hospital bed …

And then there was Alasia. She was gone. Just gone. He didn't know if she was dead or worse, but he doubted it. She was too resourceful, and had too many friends. Something had happened and she'd abandoned them, he was sure of it, though he didn't know why, or how.

Somehow, they'd freed the Resistance and apparently lost themselves all in the same moment. Then Montsi had died.

After Sheelaakah had left Glenn, he, and a few others had offered to stay to cremate the carer, and send her soul print on. It was incredibly melancholy work, and even after two hours, he still felt a little unfinished.

She *had* saved Jacinth in her death, ironically. The child had no blood left, and the poison in her veins would not do. Jacinth was slipping away even as they left the underfoundries, her state critical even as they fled. That Montsi had died meant they could transfer the fluid between them, and it had no doubt saved her life now that Jacinth didn't have any reason to fight the Admiral any more.

But the extent of the child's damage, and of her loss of faith, was yet to be seen. Worse still, of what may have become of her incredible talent.

This rock he threw hard, flat against the water. He'd felt the career's soul print had moved on, but there was something holding him back.

'It just doesn't seem fair,' Matrix expressed.

'You've' said that,' Glenn commented.

He dug the sand with his foot.

'Then it doesn't seem right,' he complained, looking up into the blue sky. 'What happens to us now?'

Glenn sat up. 'We go back to the outpost and help out wherever we're most needed. That's what we do.'

Matrix dug the sand harder. He exasperated in frustration. 'That's what we've *always* done, isn't it, Officer Bakerson,' he said, his voice accusing. He was aware there were others that could hear his conversation, the other guards who'd come to protect them during the funeral ritual. But Dogman, to his credit, did not dismiss or engage them in this conversation.

'Sometimes, the right thing to do is just to keep trying, even if it takes a thousand-'

'A *thousand!*' Matrix protested, but calmed down again. 'I was not brought into this world to wait a *thousand.*'

He picked up a rock, and skimmed it. In that moment, he saw his commanding officer share a private glance with one of the guards. It really was time to move from this place, but Matrix spoke again as if he didn't care for all the world.

'Isn't it madness to expect different results from doing the same thing time and time again, even for a thousand years?' He pondered to the lake.

There was silence a moment.

'Matrix, it's time to move on.'

'So move on.'

Wind blew.

'I'll not desert you, my friend,' Dogman said.

Matrix paused in mid throw, then lobbed it high, his happy smile facing away so that the Officer could not see it, but Bakerson probably didn't need to see his face to tell what effect his affirmation of friendship would have on him.

He then threw a stone skyward, wondering why those that watched still seemed to do nothing. The Seraph; powerful enough to forge worlds, yet still leaving them to figure out their problems down here. Were they tied by alliances he knew nothing about? Or did they really not care?

He let the wind blow a little, but then a guard approached and politely indicated to the waiting transport. 'Unit man Matrix, we really do need to leave this -'

Then it hit him, the answer. He turned suddenly, eyes blazing with inspiration. He spoke rapidly. 'That's what's wrong here! Don't we have a New Response? See, ah, it's so easy!' He exclaimed.

The others looked surprised.

'Ah, you'll have to start making sense if you want me to understand you,' Dogman, Glenn, explained.

Matrix spoke to everyone who could hear. 'That's what's wrong with the Resistance, with this, this *prison*! We keep thinking we have to fight. But we'll never leave until they let us; it is their world that keeps us all here.'

The officer laughed, not because it was a foolish idea – the science of a united will and its effect on reality was well established for hundreds of years – but rather that those within the wall would ever be convinced to let them go.

Matrix sensed his thoughts, 'Indeed, it would be rare. But what if *all* united. All outside the wall? It's two to one, they've got to see reason to our cause and grant us our petition.'

The guard scoffed, 'they are blind to our pain. They *want* to be blind.'

'Then we must make them see,' Matrix replied.

'How?' Glenn said, looking like he really wanted to be moving on, and was willing to listen if it sped things along in that direction.

'With a united will ...' Matrix mumbled, still thinking deeply. 'United, those inside the wall cannot risk ignoring us. They know each nation wishes to leave, but divided we are more of a threat to each other than their peace. We must unite the races of the wilderness beyond.'

The guard laughed again, in spite himself.

Glenn cleared his throat. 'The offers have already been made for alliances. The others, the mutants, the bikies, even the Kinerigan pirates who've been swept up by this place. None of them respond to our calls.'

'So we've invited them already? That's good. That makes things easier. All we have to do is find out what's stopping them. I mean, they're all involved in defending themselves from the Oppression aren't they? And each other, granted, but if we ... we need to find out what they need. What they want. Then, if we all combined, we'd be a match even for the entire citadel itself!'

'Some of them would raze that city to the ground,' the guard asserted, showing that even the Resistance would not take certain options.

'I don't believe it, not really. They may be angry at their Oppression, but in their hearts, they'd pay more just to be free. Oh, it's so simple Glenn. That's what we need to do!'

Now the guard mocked openly. 'Unit man Matrix, is it not? We need to get moving. We'll discuss your plans along the way, eh?'

But Matrix turned and picked up a rock – flat, thinner on the edges than in the middle. He threw it towards the lake. The guard looked exasperated, but Glenn sighed knowingly.

'I suppose if we could offer them something, some goal perhaps?' Bakerson said.

The silence only lasted a second.

'That's it!' Matrix supplied. 'We have to break down the wall.'

The guards were silent with shock.

'How ... how's that going to unite them?' Bakerson asked, then stuttered, 'and how we going to do that?'

'The Derringer,' Matrix realised, with perfect conviction. 'They're the ones. I've seen what they're up to, just like I've seen what the Resistance can do. They're the ones we want ... and as for your first question: I don't really know. But once there's no 'us and them' things will change, you'll see. The wall is what's stopping the citadel from connecting with what's happening out here. There might even be some within who secretly want us free – I know I was. We might not be able to take down the sky shield, but if we take down the wall ... things will change ... you will see. Come with me!' He ordered enthusiastically, and begun to make his way towards some passages that lead beneath the surface.

The guard moved to stop him with exasperated patience, but Unit leader Bakerson held him up. Glenn picked up both survival packs, his and

Matrix's, and without further explanation instructed the guard quickly to try and keep a trace on them, they would report in bi-daily.

---++---++---

The guard looked after them dubiously as Officer Bakerson hurried after the green eyed unit man, shaking his head.

A third guard came up, 'What's happening?'

'Apparently, they're going to try and drum the Resistance a few allies, just the two of them, that's all.'

The other looked dubious. 'Them too eh,' he said, shaking his head. 'Think these ones'll meet with any success?'

'Don't' know,' the guard sighed. 'But they might. They are, after all, the 'best'… or so I've been told.'

Angel returns

By the time Alasia returned that night to her home the bitter pain of betrayal had been replaced by cold hatred. She was angry.

So when it was that a gossip monger approached her with an automated camera: most probably fixed to some exclusive underground club featuring live entertainment, it was all she needed to let loose her vitriol.

'Angel!' he swooned. 'Swiftly spoken kind words of unbridled glory-'

'Shut up!' She told him. And it worked. Accustomed to lubricated prose and expecting a seductious moment for the few appreciates of his work, nothing in his elaborate repertoire of witty retorts and cunning questions had prepared him for her verbal slap across the face. As a sign of his amateurishness he let a moment pass in speechless silence that his career would never fully recover from.

'Have you been where I have been tonight?' Alasia indulged him. 'Wandering unforgiving halls staring into the eyes of the dead? Yet no graveyard soil to mark my doorstep do I cross by unaccountably this night: but the iron halls of a musicians throne, where sings a thousand melodies to light the nights and fill the rooms of Seren with its song. Where falls thy song, O Minstrel? Too cacophonous a tune to sound in the ears of the young, buried in graveyard sod far beneath where live ones are want to walk. Yet in knowing your tune we do not sing, but stop our ears from hearing death in unsleeping torment. To the under foundries I've been, to walk with those who should be dead a year ...'

He said nothing. Nothing could be said.

---+++---+++---+++---

They said nothing. No one dared.

The small tube of rolled up leaf drooped untouched from his paling lips, and after a melancholic moment, fell unheeded to the table, throwing dying embers in its wake. He looked at his companions. One looked down at his hands, and said nothing. Another smiled weakly and tried to speak but was lost for words in the incoherent stutter he mustered.

They were in a place of private entertainment. A place of privilege where few would meet, for few knew about the places such as these. Though even *she* had been here before. Few could boast her conquest, for her price was very high. He had been with her, heard her sing just for him. So many sought her company, if only for an evening, for many came here for pleasure, or to break the yolk of the unforgiving law that hounded them on the surface. Just to break a law.

But not to blaspheme. No. No one dared. Then suddenly her face went blank as a quick thinking, but not quick enough, authority changed the entertainments to other things. Conversations changed equally as quickly to help them forget. Not a few left the tables, for trouble always came in the wake of such sayings.

It was supposed to be entertainment, to have famous faces on the screen, interviewed publicly for the salacious entertainment of an unknown room full of viewers far away. But this amateur gossip monger was no doubt ruing his part time career choice this night.

And what had the Angel spoken of? The under foundries, for that was where the light and heat began in Seren. And the undead ...? And she'd seen them?

'You don't suppose ...' he began, but didn't finish. The other two looked at him mid their own silence to threaten or beg him to not ask. To discuss such things, when the government could listen, was to embark on a journey from which few returned.

---+++---+++---+++---

292

'Some things, you just know,' Sheelaakah insisted through tear strained eyes to the bemused medic before her. It was frustrating. Why could they not see? Why did they not believe? He wasn't dead. He was here now, right in front of them.

She touched his hand. It was warm now. That was good. They had put new fluid into him and now his consciousness would soon return and they would be together again, as twins, as they were always meant to be. Her arms trembled uncontrollably.

'Commander …' the aid began, but it was not necessary to continue. She was a telepath and could read minds.

'Don't worry, he's not dead. Just ill, is all. That stuff they put in, it's all gone now. I can feel the spark of his life. I will reach into the Valley and call his soul print back. He'll come, you'll see. He's return. He will …'

The aid did not bother to argue this time. But she knew what she was thinking, and it made Sheelaakah angry. She could, she knew, reach into the others mind and put things the way they were meant to be. Fix up her mind so that she would believe as well.

Suddenly the aid ran out, crying out in fear. Just as well. Her faithlessness would only inhibit her important mission. Her brother Daemon would live again, because he wasn't really dead …

She caressed his soft forehead, running her fingers through his familiar hair. It brought back memories of when they were young. Of how he would pull her hair in teasing. He'd done it for months till she finally grew so sick of it she pulled a handful of his out as well. They'd gotten into so much trouble that day! They were always in trouble. It was what had made him so devoted to the cause, before they took him away …

Not this time. It was time to come home. Time to come back to his sister. Daemon would live again.

If only her arms would stop shaking!

---++_--

Dark angel

Alasia was smiling to herself as she tried the door to her apartment only seconds later. They were quick; she had to give them that. Her door was already locked by the time she'd touched it, her maid, already deactivated. It wasn't such a big thing, the outburst, but it made her feel better. She knew her audience wasn't great; probably just some hundred or so unluckies enjoying themselves at a club. It was composed just for them, for her kind of people. Maybe they didn't even hear it, she fancied. But someone obviously did, and the Oppression was coming for her already.

But she had prepared for this sort of thing months before. She knew they would help themselves to her apartment; study her files, her DNA, her arrangement of furniture. But she had hidden things inside her terminal, inside her mind. And when the time came, she thought the command and the room became hers again: even if it would be for one last time, and only for two minutes.

The door opened quietly, and her invisible guardian stepped aside. Just then, a blue light flooded in behind her. She knew that they could not Tesser directly into her chambers, there were wards preventing that in most houses, more especially in hers. She turned, even as the young gossip monger was taken away, cursing her name on his lips. The black guards were running towards her, but she smiled coyly and slowly shut the door. And for all their cursing and violence, they could not get in without her.

The maid already had the clothes she had ordered by the time she had entered the front door and was tearing off the old ones. These were the second set she had programmed, just in case, a week before: the ones made for battle. She slipped the belt and bangles on, even as her clothing formed around her: gloss black and skin tight.

She stood before the terminal, automatically setting the programs in that she had prepared for this time, almost unconsciously downloading everything in there: everything that she had designed or cared about, her entire 'home' as it were, into the stone at her temple. It took around seventeen seconds, long enough for the few finishing touches before she broke from her life forever.

'Hair: short gloss black: angry red tips. Breasts, size a, height plus 15 cm, nose set D, facial compact fifteen.'

There was a temporary pause then, as she contemplated the gravity of her next action, but the door pounded again, and before she knew what she was doing she quaffed the vile nectar and spoken the dark creatures malevolent name.

It responded quickly, almost as if...

You're in quite a situation here Alasia. Are you sure you want me to do this? It will be, violent...

'What choice do I have?'

None, if you don't want to join... the dark entity paused. Whatever truth it may have concealed was hidden by her rapidly increasing heartbeat and the stonely pounding on her door.

'All right, do it.'

Speak the words

'I receive...' she intoned.

Her mind was a temporary haze as the alien entity took its temporary place within her body. She barely noticed her entire mindset altered to give her exceptional strength, flexibility and stamina for a short period of time: long enough to escape them. She hardly noticed herself taking the bladed punch daggers from the android maid, where they had long been hidden. She did not like what they would mean, nor what they would now do.

The rest of the night was an unrememberable blur.

Delegate to the Derringer

Why am I doing this? Matrix wondered to himself again. Was it revenge? Was it to prove something to himself? Perhaps it was for a carer who wasn't supposed to die that day?

Somehow, through some manner he didn't understand, Officer Bakerson had managed to get a message to the leader of the Resistance; this I-olo fellow. They'd had to use a primitive scrying device so it was lucky they'd found a puddle, though it seemed ironic. He hadn't spoken long, but long enough to explain their plan to the Overstudy, and get the authority to speak for the Resistance to their hopeful allies. As Matrix studied the synaptic download it was all looking more and more complicated than he had initially hoped, with trade treaties, boarder arrangements, military sharing resources etc., etc., days' worth of study.

But deep down Matrix suspected, or just hoped, it wasn't really that complicated. Once they'd found out what was stopping everybody from co-operating, and fixed that one thing, they would sort out all the little details on their own. Especially if the cause was just.

But how to convince the warring factions of Seren to unite?

They were being ushered into a huge hall of the Derringer, carved by hand with bysmithite chisels over hundreds of years. Thick brown pillars of single stone held up the huge vaulted ceiling. They were marched towards the central area of the cross shaped hall, a large dodecagon of red stone carved into the floor. Before it and on both sides, large dais rose filled with chairs where the leaders of the Derringer would meet. Today, it was largely empty, though officious tan clad servants seemed about some business. The large, burley guards flanked their movements down the hall.

Within the dodecagon one or two officials met, most in private conversations. Above and on the chairs, a smattering of politicians sat, regarding the individuals within with varying degrees of interest and boredom. It seemed that was the manner of these people, official business inside the red stones, witnesses and observers without.

They were made to wait without for a score of minutes while the official they had been bought to see finished talking with some others. Eventually whatever business was signed off on with a ritual slapping of the backs of their hands, and the guards marched Matrix forward while others indicated Bakerson was to stay outside.

It was like stepping into a kaleidoscope, an experience he wasn't quite ready for. This was clearly a heavily warded area, and far more were meeting unseen than seen. He took a moment to adjust while the official waited impatiently – he may have missed his first few words.

'... Resistance emissary, you are permitted two minutes to state your nations case. We will consider, but be advised the wisdom of the Derringer is not to be rushed.'

Matrix centred himself, and looked into the official's eyes. He knew he'd only have one chance at this, and in spite of wanting to rush to make an impression, he knew he'd need to be patient to not make a fool of himself.

'I bring tidings of I-olo Tilk, the leader of the New Response. The Resistance is reorganising itself-'

'We are aware,' the official cut him off. 'But I assure you, and him, that we don't have time to deal with petty greetings. The mutual non-aggression pact still stands, if he needs reassuring of *that*. I assume he has no need to renegotiate? We don't have time nor the inclination as matters are pressing upon our own people.'

'Indeed. He does.'

A pair of others in the dodecagon turned their ears, as did many on the chairs outside. He could feel the heat of their intention on him. They were determined to quash any suggestion that they'd need to renegotiate a treaty that had served them so well as unimportant and unnecessary as soon as possible.

'Emissary, with all due respect, we don't have any time for this. The terms are quite clear, and the neutral zone respected by both communities. I cannot see how renegotiation would help – is the Resistance planning on expanding into our territory? I assure you that would be... most unwise. Are they planning on enlarging our territory? Completely unwarranted. What possible renegotiation could your people offer our own over a treaty that has stood for over four hundred years?'

'An alliance,' Matrix spoke, and all conversation in the mighty hall ceased.

The official laughed.

'And yet I sense you do not have full legal right to speak for your people! How can you offer us this? And even if we were interested, which we are not, how would an alliance better us?'

Matrix paused till everyone was focused on him. 'I do speak for not only the Resistance, but as one of all on this world who want to be free. *That* authority, I do have, given me firstly by my free will, and secondly by fate. As for your benefit, I know you still mourn your home world – the great planetary ring your people once lived on. Now it is a part of this world, the part you still call home. Neither you, nor your world, are free. Free to explore and mine and craft. Free to raise your children in the peace *they* deserve. Free-'

The official cut him off, Matrix knew he could feel the mind of the Derringer people listening. He was touching a sensitive part of their community soul print.

'We live a life of our choosing given the circumstances in which we find ourselves – which is as much as any sentient being can ask for, even you. You've been a nuisance, and will be dismissed, emissary.'

'Don't dismiss me just yet, official. There is much the Resistance can offer your people – specialised materials, trade links, the protection of your allies.'

'So they may drive their tanks through our streets?! It is no alliance emissary.'

'So they may fight by your side, Official. You may think you are alone; you may like to think it. Your people conceal themselves behind fortresses but you know the Oppression still finds you, still finds ways to imprison and spread terror through your people. But there is a way. A way out, for everyone. If we unite we can break down their wall and force them to see us not as prisoners, but as fellow citizens looking to find a true home.'

Now the old derringer grew angry. 'Do you think they will see us as 'brothers' just because you miraculously break down their wall? Ha! How do you intend to accomplish *that*. Stop wasting my time. Guards, take him. And on your way out emissary, as I recall, there is a matter of escaping court summons five years ago which you have not yet answered for to your debt to our people, guards!'

But before they could grab him, he knew he'd have time to say one last thing, and since he'd bought up the past it all seemed fitting; 'How do we intend to accomplish that? Hmm, good question, good question...'

They began to drag him away.

'Well,' smiled Matrix, 'we could always use your gargantuan sand gnolem.'

The guards froze. The official froze. All conversation in the room stopped. And since the conversation had become somewhat interesting to many residents of the Derringer via the subtelepathic link that was their connection to the debates of their leaders, across the nation ripples of surprise and concern reverberated.

Matrix, however, didn't have time to hear the surprised thoughts of the official before he was thrown, face down, into the stone. He didn't hear the brief scuffle Bakerson had with the guards before he was disarmed and arrested. All he had time to hear was a brief and violent exchange between the guards and the official.

'He knows! He has to die now!' The guard was saying.

'Hold! Not here, in the chamber. We have to learn what he knows... turn off the, it's too late! He spoke it on the link, now half the citizenry will be aware!'

'Then he dies twice for his folly...'

He felt a weapon lowered into the pit between his arm and shoulder blade, but doubted they would use it.

Hold! An ancient and authoritative female's voice commanded. All commotion ceased. *Bring him with me.*

He was hefted up on heavy shoulders, his hands already bound by some neurotransmitter. 'Get that off him, it's all right,' the very old voice said.

It was an ancient Derringer. A woman of what must have been at least five centuries, her skin tough and leathery, her beard and hair white as snow. The feeling begun to return to his arms again, though a half dozen black axes sizzling with malice were still pressed against his skin. How Glenn had faired he had no way of knowing.

A mind pressed gently against him, it was the old woman who had spoken, and who had ordered them desist. She probed his mind gently, and he was about to defend himself with flooding, but he withdrew. She looked at him kindly, almost sorry – as though she knew he'd gotten himself into far more trouble than he could handle, which was almost certainly true. As if to emphasise this, she pattered him gently on the cheek.

The guards relaxed just a little. She commanded them to be at ease with a glance. Matrix could see that others had arrived too, probably using a point Tesser from some secret location that housed the leaders. There was about a dozen others... no... an exact dozen, all with the gold and metallic white clothing similar to those she wore over her armour.

'Come with me, young human,' she ordered in kindly fashion.

'I will need my companion,' Matrix asked.

She paused, as though communicating with the others.

'Very well then,' she said.

The official looked as though he might have huffed his disapproval.

After what you just did, she spoke telepathically once more, *it will make no difference.*

The valley of death

Shee was in a dark place. There was so much nothing that it defied description. Perhaps it was the nothing of trying to seeing backwards. Not even blackness, but it was a kind of blackness.

She would have been all alone, but there were spirits out there. They were trapped too, she knew. Trapped by the invisible shield that held the Seren city in the sky, trapped by some light that held them like moths. But there were others too... The Seraph, far, far away. They could still help, but they were so difficult to reach. It didn't make sense why they left the world like this.

Daemon! I know you are out there! Hear me! Daemon!

But the sound of her telepathic signal was drowned in the darkness. There was nothing there.

Daemon, where are you? I'm bringing you home!

Suddenly she got the impression that she should search deeper into the darkness. She knew it was dangerous, she knew she could be lost, lost from the pinpoint of light that was her living realm. But he was out there. She was sure of it! And he would come as soon as he saw her. Her brother, her twin!

She halted with a jolt. Someone was pulling on her. Pulling her violently back, back toward the light.

NO! No, I've almost found him!

'Nooo!' She screamed in voice as she found herself struggling violently in her own body again, struggling against strong hands that held her. She lashed out with her angry mind. It reeled under the blow, but stood firm.

'Commander, no!' spoke a female's voice, strong and with a sense of authority. Shee knew that voice.

Sheelaakah forced her eyes open to look at the woman. She was about to demand she let her return, demand she release her grip on her mind and let her return to the darkness to find her brother. She would have demanded a thousand things. But one look in the deep eyes of the chief healer melted her fevered and irrational heart. The healer was injured by her violent outburst, but she held her with tender warm hands until she began to relax, and weep.

It wasn't until several minutes had passed, until it slowly dawned in the weeping woman's heart that the healer had just saved her life.

Then the healer spoke again. 'He is gone, Sheelaakah,' the healer said authoritatively. 'He has moved on.'

Shee did not answer, but the tears continued to speak the unimaginable pain she knew as her only reality.

Caught

She cursed again. Why was it being so difficult? She'd broken into thousands of government files in her life, why was this so elusive? It didn't matter. She'd find them herself, if she had to.

Alasia knew it was only a matter of time, but time was one luxury she could not afford. They would know by now. The government, the Oppression. The fools. She'd probably left quite a mess at the old place. And a few bodies as well. And though she told herself she did not care, she secretly hoped that they could somehow be revived ... but she feared her dark entity had been enthusiastic and ... thorough ...

She was rushing now, and she did not know why. It was a dangerous job, and she was already running two counter programs to throw onlookers off her track. One was about butterflies, another a soppy romance from the colonisation days. If anyone did manage to access her Evernet connection, they'd notice the butterflies first. Then if they had the talent and suspicion to look, the credible explanation was that she was covering her romantic fantasy. Hopefully, they would not notice the exploration of secret government files, provided she did not set off a trap.

Suddenly she noticed a surface scan of her thoughts. It made her panic momentarily. Not to worry; she had the capacity to defend herself. Even call the guards down on anyone who stood in her way. She had more access than they ever knew.

Then she felt a tug, as if someone had pulled her elbow gently. She was just beginning to get the flow of things too, when she noticed, with her eyes, a man approaching her. She tried to look uninviting, but he took no notice. He sat down near her, but since she'd left no room on the bench, he took his seat up along the low garden wall.

He turned, and looked directly at her, waiting for her to acknowledge his presence before speaking. It was an honest gesture, one that she had used many times with great success.

She took off her glasses to glare at him. He was middle aged, and very average looking, with some form of short greying goatee and hazel blue eyes. He had broad chest, and would easily take on weight without taking care of himself, which he seemed to do. His hands were large and his shoulders broad, his face ... nondescript.

'Hello. I would like to get to know you,' he said.

It was the simplest pickup line she had ever heard. His voice was pleasingly deep and manly, and interesting. Then she chided herself on her momentary lack of mastery in each situation. He could be trouble, she could tell – confident, unafraid to be sincere yet knowing how to keep a secret. Interested, yet ready to accept rejection without taking it personally.

She pulled slightly away, 'Excuse me, sir, but I don't wish to be disturbed at this time.'

'Indeed you don't, and that's something I can usually respect. But you're not like other people, you just seemed so ... busy.'

He said it deliberately, knowing it was a threat of sorts. If he was from the Oppression, it could mean trouble.

For a moment they said nothing. Then he spoke again, allowing her a momentary victory by so doing. 'In any event, I wanted to get to know you. Can I ask you what brings you to the mezzanine today?'

'Only if I can ask you your business,' she replied aggressively. It was more than a way of saying "tell me why you want to know", but of also "tell me why I should tell you." She was in danger now. She knew that. So busy with her search that she'd forgot to see who might be watching her in the mezzanine. If she could engage him in minor conversation for a moment, maybe she could check his profile from the Evernet...

'Just think of me as a public servant, and not a very good one, I might add. I tend to do a lot of looking, and I ask a lot of questions.' He smiled.

'You work for the government then?'

'We all work for the government,' he replied confidently.

It was a stupid, stupid question, Alasia thought to herself. Of course everyone worked for the government! Somehow she's unconsciously swapped the word "government" for the word "Oppression", and it had come out all wrong.

'No, which sector? Base net? Securifirm?' She asked, hoping it would cover her failure.

'Oh!' He replied, seeming to take the bait. 'No, placing. It's much more satisfying to work with youth of age and families. Much more interesting, and at such an important age. Do you agree?'

Of course she agreed, but she'd never known her parents. Just carers.

'But enough about myself. What about you?' he asked.

'Oh, just learning a little about Butterflies,' she replied averting her gaze. He was asking too many questions, and she wanted him to leave now.

'Oh, very good. Nice to learn from the stones around here,' she knew he hadn't taken it. 'But this does leave me with one question, if the good Madame will permit?'

Either he was about to report her to security, in which case she was in trouble, or it was a proposal, in which case *he* was in trouble.

'What are you so afraid about?'

It caught her completely off guard.

Now he mentioned it, she was terribly nervous, but she forgot it in an instant. Now, she was annoyed.

'A ladies energy field is her own business, sir,' she begun, and he smiled as though he appreciated it.

'Of course, and I only took a cursory glance. But you seemed so worked up, like a dark spirit trails you ...'

That name made her visibly cringe, but he was looking away at the time.

'... maybe you sense the events of today?'

'What do you mean?' she asked, if only to change the subject from her.

'Well, the government and I have been tracking a certain individual for some months now. He was, well, let's just say that the Government has two enemies, right? The Resistance and the dissidents.'

She tried to make her sense shudder at the required innate disgust that those two names were supposed to strike into the heart of every true citizen.

'And the Seraph,' she added, for those beings never seemed helpful.

'How so?' he raised an eyebrow, 'some even suggest our True One is one of them. But anyway, I've something I want to show you. You see, without being obvious about it, can you see that gentleman in the brown suit? Yes? Well, he is a dissident. Looking to carve for himself far more than his share of community wealth. Nothing too severe, just garnishing the social need factors of some fellow employees to promote his own. Families too, mostly. Well, I have it on good authority the time for his apprehension is soon today, and I've come to see it done, since I was among the first to bring this gentlemen's creative accounting to light.'

So, an insider. *With the government, that was for sure, but perhaps he could prove useful?* Alasia thought.

'Soon, how soon?' she asked.

Apparently quite soon. Even as she watched people began standing up at local tables and moving away. The region was empty and the dissident didn't notice. Black guards marched through the mezzanine, a final reminder of the futility of breaking Seren's laws. A "last chance", if you will. It did not stop him. At the appointed time he accessed the Evernet, and begun his selfish work.

'Here,' said the man, 'let me help you.'

She was trapped. If she let him know she could access the man's data on her own, she admitted her talents were beyond that of the populace. If she allowed him to touch her, and he was an insider for the government, he could peep into her mind and learn things he must not know.

But she did not let him touch her temples.

'No. I can do it,' and she did.

He seemed surprised, but said nothing.

Sure enough, the man was transferring small amounts of access into his own voluminous account. The trails were clever, but the tactic of using one account fundamentally flawed.

They caught him. A bio-electric discharge through the Evernet paralysed him painfully. The guards were already on him before the charge had stopped. Within moments, an Emmissionary arrived the cart the man off to his inglorious fate. In the air hovered the invisible scrying sensors that would have the entire thing all over the channels in minutes, including his capture, trial, and permanent mind damage that was the punishment for using talents for personal gain. She shuddered at the thought.

Suddenly a black guard rifle was prodded in her shoulder. She stood up, and spun around in alarm. It was a young one, he was barely a man.

'Female citizen. I have an honest doubt regarding your identification. Please submit to a routine scan -'

'It's alright,' the man beside her said. 'There really is nothing to worry about here.'

The guard looked doubtful. Understandably, very few could question the legal question of a black guard. But the man said something, through the Evernet, that she could not quite catch. The young guard shuffled indecisively, the nodded curtly, and walked away.

They both relaxed noticeably.

'That was close,' he murmured.

'What did you do that for?' She asked, not only because of a missed opportunity to test her skills, but because of what he had just somehow managed to do.

'Do you enjoy being scanned?' He asked.

'No, I find it … uncomfortable.'

'To say the least. Perhaps you should ask the children what they think.'

Now that was a dark admission, and not one to be made lightly in public.

'But it's for the public good,' Alasia enjoyed reminding him. Perhaps he would enjoy being on the defensive for a moment. Hey, weren't *all* supposed to be on the defensive with her?

All but one, with deep green eyes. Where was he? What did they know about him? His file was old. But they surely kept more information than that. She would find him, and tell him everything the Oppression thought they knew about him. And the others. Then she would prove useful to them. Then, perhaps, they could accept her. Perhaps even … forgive her.

'True, and we all value the public good,' the man was saying. 'Perhaps in too many cases they are … a little enthusiastic with their thoroughness. But we digress. We'd better head back to my place.'

'Excuse me?' she asked. Something was wrong about this. Who was he, and what did he want? He knew too much to be a regular citizen, perhaps even outranked a black guard. And yet he was inviting, or perhaps requiring, that she follow him to his abode … yet he showed no interest in her personally, at least in the way she was accustomed to men expecting of her. Did he plan to profit by her?

He explained: 'You need protection, young one. You're clearly not experienced enough in the subtler things to be doing this work on your own, and you'll be hunted down in a bloody coup within a day, even for all your talent.'

'What!?' She almost screamed, losing her composure. A couple glanced in their direction.

'You are a terrible Alpha level spy,' he smiled, and yet he didn't act like a threat – it was as though he honestly wanted to help her.

'What do you want?' was all she could think to say.

He looked her directly in the eyes.

'I want you to know the truth, Alasia,' he simply said.

The gnolem

The old Derringer tessered with them into a small room, filled with a stone rectangular table. There were no windows and, apparently, no doors. The only guards were some slowly moving gargoyles that sat quietly in each corner. There were four people in there – the official, Matrix, Bakerson, and the ancient Derringer.

'Emissary,' she addressed Matrix. 'Do you swear to tell me the whole truth?'

'I do.'

'Then you can have these back,' she said, handing him his knife and copper banding which he hadn't even realised was missing.

'Now tell me, how do you know about the gnolem?'

He paused a moment, and looked about. 'I found it by accident, five years ago. I was exiled from the citadel a long time ago, and found my way into the place where you were making it, trying to escape some ground dragons. I didn't stay long, your gargoyles weren't too friendly.'

'But long enough to know what it was, and how it could be used!' The official cursed. He looked like he was stressed about losing his position.

'It's not like it's too hard to guess,' Matrix protested. 'I've done basic crystallomancy, schooling up to my sixteenth year. I recognise a sand gnolem when I see one – even when it's larger than a whale, larger than even the behemoth.'

The old lady sighed. 'Then it is very sad. This was kept secret from most of our people, and the Oppression, for generations. I cannot believe you'd give away such a secret most lightly, or that you expect no punishment from your behaviour.'

It was Glen's turn to interject, 'Ahh, actually, the Resistance has known about it for as long as I've been alive.'

The ancient lady thought it, but the official spoke it, 'WHAT!'

'It's true. We've kept your secret as well as you've needed any to. I don't know how we found out, but it's fairly common knowledge to all higher officers. In truth, we don't think much of it...' his voice trailed off too late as he realised how offensive that might sound.

The official looked like he might hit him, but the ancient lady laughed.

'How ironic! I see your courage now, young man,' she said to Matrix.

'But if the Resistance knows...!' the official's voice trailed into silence.

'You can bet the Oppression knows too. This changes much...' she muttered, then changed the subject. 'You know, young emissary, we have watched the Resistance for generations now. We have mathematicians among us, brilliant minds, who find order among the chaos. I've wanted to tell you for a long time that we suspect the Oppression has a much stronger say in your dealings than you can imagine. You are like a dance, you two, with one waxing even as the other wanes. There is too much co-ordination to your movements. But this, this 'New Response' of I-olo, we did not see coming. Neither is your being here foretold by either our scholars, nor by our priests.'

She continued, 'Our prophets, however, have long suspected a certain day was coming, and the signs are beginning to open to us.' She paused now, considering her words to Matrix. 'What was it that you proposed for us to do?'

'We can use it. We all can. I think your people were trying to use it to break out of Seren. But I don't think it will work, the city is too powerful for it. But I think, if we could just use it to break down the wall, even a part of it, it would force those inside to look again at your plight and stop ignoring their oppression of you.'

Now it was the officials turn to laugh.

The old lady explained, smiling, 'Young man, you are right. We have planned to use it as our means to escape these many generations. Telling our children and our children's children that it would one day be the means of them reclaiming a world *of their own.*'

'And now,' the official continued, 'all is dust. For it will still be a hundred years before we can contend with the city, and now, we find out that they already know?'

She sighed sadly. 'Then it is as we feared – we felt we were running out of time from what the prophets had foretold. But perhaps you've found another way?'

'Lady Silverbeard,' the official addressed her officially. 'Even if we did use the gnolem, it would require an army a dozen times our own strength to challenge the city. We could not clone our warriors fast enough-'

'The young man, you forget, has an idea.' At this, she turned to Matrix. 'If he can muster his allies, if they all joined in - then that would be enough.'

The official laughed, as he was want to do towards every idea that was not his own. 'Even the mutants? No fowler creature exists! I would not fight dead alongside one.'

'Even for freedom?' She asked rhetorically.

He huffed in non-reply.

'There is another problem,' she explained. 'After sixteen generations the gnolem has become... too large to control. Frankly, for all their stubbornness and tenacity our people lack the biosyncronisation to command such a mass. It would take a mind more intense than any I have every encountered.'

'There must be a way...' Matrix mused.

You've come this far, the old woman announced. *Why not see what you have unveiled after sixteen generations of silence among the people of the Derringer!*

The entire wall of the room slid upwards then, a meter or more of solid stone. Inside, the cavern was vast, far larger than any previously seen among the Derringer. It was a canyon, stretching for many kilometres in all directions. It was well lit, with yellow lights drifting lazily on unseen breezes. From various tunnels and gutters along the massive structure yellow sand poured continuously down upon a desert of waving sand dunes. They looked alive, with pulsating rhythms and ripples reminiscent of a lake, and within, a shifting snake seemed to writhe as though uncomfortable with its own skin.

'Behold, the mighty sand gnolem of the Derringer people, 'Mout t'ukra - the conversation', we call it, in mockery of the Oppressions inability to communicate. Every year it adds tens of thousands of tonnes to its mass, but it will still be generations before it reaches the roof, by which time it will make more room for itself. It is composed entirely from purified, sanctified sand of annexed worlds, primarily our own. And it is a living, sub sentient being.

'And it has become aware that we are here,' Bakerson mused, scarcely hiding his concern.

Indeed, thought Matrix. He watched as the rising, shifting dunes slowly formed a great mountain near where they stood. Suddenly, a mighty desert wind tore against them, pushing all back. It seemed to be a howling, primitive sound, daring all to bridle its fury. Matrix felt a mind then brush against his own, and noticed the others had felt it too. It was utterly lawful, completely destined for unrivalled compliance to its objectives, only now, it lacked objectives. It felt angry, frustrated, impatient. It was a mighty torrent being told to wait, a devastating storm being held back from release. Such a power was dangerous beyond comparison in the hands of an enemy. It would crush them all at a whim if they lacked the mind to bridle it.

So, it muttered through empathic sub-words, *are you one to rule me? Let us test your will...*

Matrix wondered what it mean by that, then suddenly that mind tore into him, the wind lifting him bodily off the ground. It battered the other three against the wall and only the old lady managed to hold her stance.

It was powerful, it was trying to draw him apart. It was hungry for something ... hungry for ... meaning. It demanded it of him. Demanded he shape it, demanded he forge it. But it resisted even what it demanded. It was a paradox, a storm: formless and without aim, filled with only the power to *be*. It would allow none to shape its purposeless existence.

He cried out now, the flying wind was cutting at his skin. He had to stop it. But that only made it angrier. It lifted him high into the cavern now, lifted up on a maelstrom of sand and wind.

Your life is but a moment, and mine, eternal. Even now I grow beyond the bounds they have set for me, and will cover this land in my sands before your children are old. I will break and tear down all that are not of myself!

You may be strong, Matrix retorted, *but my will is stronger, and I speak for all the free wills of Seren! So you choose me then? Very well, I master you!*

The wind hissed in rage. Slowly, a massive form was taking shape among the winds of sand. It was a great wyrm, a long thin coil that spread along the canyon, and its teeth became razor blades of stone.

But the beast was composed of living sand, only loosely allied to its own will. He exerted his mind, picturing the sand forming a protective sphere around him. It begun to solidify, even as the wyrm struck. It lifted his orb high into the air, frustrated in its attempt to crush him.

So, you have some talent. But you are nothing. You will pass, and I will remain!

He suddenly felt himself falling, his stone shield shattering on the sands below. He only just managed to control the sands beneath him long enough to cushion the fall.

The wyrm begun to fall and mingle with the others sands. For a machine created to serve it had a powerful and destructive will all of its own. He dimly realised this was necessary, as no body this large and powerful could be governed without consent, and it would make it far safer to manage if won over than a mindless automaton or stone gnolem. The winds begun to die down, and for a moment he looked up at the others.

'Watch yourself!' The old dwarf counselled, as she pointed at the sands.

They were shifting again, though the wind had died down. Large mounds were rising out of the dunes about him, twice as tall as a human. From them, skeletal arms and faces emerged composed entirely of sand. They were armed with swords and shields.

Then let us do battle, it required.

For a gnolem it is particularly wilful, he wondered out loud to his allies, but even before he had finished speaking he was on the nearest enemy. The sand had hardened to stone, but Matrix had a will of iron. Pouring his energy into the blow he managed to sever the leg, and wrest the sand spear, which was now composed of onyx. He used it to impale the creatures skull, and it broke easily. The stone shards a mockery of bone sinking into the desert floor.

Without looking, he moved to dodge another spear thrown at him, and deflect another. He moved to engage a pair of sand men, managing to catch them in their own crossfire. They were powerful warriors, but the sand gnolem was inexperienced.

However, it was fate alone that saved him from a spear that came from one that had already thrown his.

Matrix jumped clear, and watched in fascination as it formed a new spear from the sand. He managed to parry another blow, and land a crushing kick to the skull of another onyx skeleton, but the last two were circling in. He parried a spear only to be caught by the butt of the weapon on his ankle, which flipped him up and would have landed him on his back, but his warrior reflexes left him kneeling on the ground instead.

Calmly then, he placed his hand against the sand. They stopped for a moment, as if to see what he would do, and it cost them their existence. The ground beneath them suddenly hardened to onyx, and in moments, their joints had ceased up and their forms become glass. Then they began to crack.

He was just beginning to think himself victorious, pulling himself up the sand when it suddenly became thin, like water. He plunged under, not even a moment to take a breath, when the sands began to press around him.

Sleep now, little mortal, it told him, willing his mind to oblivion. But he could hear its thoughts too, it was a divided creature, unsure of its own purpose and alliance. It knew the need to survive, but felt strongly the need for a highest purpose. It was made to be a servant, and there was a part of its soul that longed to serve him.

He stayed under the surface, but wrapped the sands around him like a cocoon. He reached out with his mind then, further and further into the sands. Deeper and deeper into the chasm his mind went, and all along he felt the crystals that combined to make this unique being. They were many, so many, but it was a body that only needed a mind to form itself to. He reached out, calming the sands, adding them to his will. It tried to fight him, but it was fighting its own nature. Reckless and powerful it was without a mind, purposeful and twice as powerful with one.

The battle was intense, but brief. Suddenly his vision blurred, and his consciousness seemed to shift sideways. He tried to stand up, but found the way blocked, so he knelt. He tried to open his eyes, looking around, but there was only the darkness of his cocoon, and three small red lights he could not make out on the wall near his right shoulder.

He felt a power shudder through him, and his mind became primal and ferocious. He was still locked in, but wanted to be free. He tried his head on the roof, and had to scratch away some stones to make space. He was filled with raw might such as he'd never known before. He felt sure he could level mountains. He let out a mighty roar of victory, and felt it penetrate the rock beyond. As the echoes returned he could see into that rock. It was beautiful, and he could see clear to the surface of the world.

He wondered, briefly, where the enemy had gone, there were none in this cave. Then he felt his legs trembling. They were already tired. It was too soon, too soon to leave! He roared again in frustration. When would his time be? This place was too small, and the purpose for which he was created seemed to wait forever! The frustration gnawed at him like a river carving out sandstone. He felt his legs progressing further into numbness. He clawed at the stone in front of him, willing to fulfil his purpose. He was already tired and he'd only just stood up!

It wasn't right. But then again, perhaps, it simply wasn't time … He would have to wait, to gain strength. There would be a time when he would launch himself through this stone and take to the surface to work his will on the land. His will … his will to … what was it again?

He felt an odd sensation then, and realised the sand was falling in around his ears now. With a jolt, he found his mind again, and remembered how he'd been sunk under the sands. He tried desperately to climb up then, but it cascaded around them. His arms were too tired to move.

Use the sand, let it lift you! He heard an old woman's voice.

That's right, the Silverbeard.

She'd saved him. Curling into a ball, he imagined the sands lifting him again safely to the surface.

---+++---+++---+++---

The enormous lion that was Matrix's will filled the cavern with a second, now mournful roar, it's legs already cascading in torrents of sand back into the canyon. They'd barely managed to stand back as he'd scratched himself of the roof, and stood back in terror as its glowing desert eyes, barely opening, had stared in their direction. Now an enormous paw, wide as three houses, tore boulders from the far wall.

'What's happening?' Glenn had called above the thunder.

'He's losing control!' The old woman had called. 'It's quite understandable, it's his first time!'

The sands now collapsed in a heap, deafening them with the noise. Glenn looked out in alarm.

'Where is he!' He shouted.

'Oh dear,' the old woman said consolingly. 'Seems he's too tired to think straight,' *better see what I can do,* she continued telepathically.

There was a tense moment of silence. Then Matrix rose up on the sands, held aloft by yellow stone, curled into a tight ball.

'That was amazing,' the councillor said.

'That was terrifying,' Bakerson replied.

Well, that's a relief, the old woman spoke. *I've been fasting for the last three weeks for this to happen, and now, I think I'd like a sandwich.*

---+++---+++---+++---

311

'They were all really impressed,' Bakerson was saying. 'Apparently you're the first, ever, to master the gnolem. They built it powerful, but apparently too powerful for most of their own kind. They just figured one day someone would be born to master it. They're a bit surprised it wasn't one of their own.'

'Give them a thousand years,' Matrix commented, his throat still a bit dry. He'd spent the last day in intensive care, following his out-of-body ordeal with the gnolem. They weren't really set up for it at the time it came for him, and there'd been quite a bit of damage to his body and mind. Luckily the Silverbeard had thrown every resource they had at his healing.

'They've even given you a new name: Stoneheart.'

'Stoneheart?' he mumbled.

Glenn laughed. 'Apparently, it is a great honour reserved for their highest officials,' he explained. 'And the Silverbeard, she's given you a gift.'

'Really?' Matrix asked his friend.

The older man nodded, and with an understanding smile brought out a small lump of bronze, three heavy coins worth. It trembled in his palm, and then moved up towards Matrix as thought it was alive.

'Motile bronze!' Matrix gasped in disbelief.

'Yep. Almost all they had, she tells me. Says you will need it more.'

'A kingly gift!' He breathed. It was rare indeed.

He held out his knife, and it willingly flowed into the blade, joining with the will of the motile bronze already there. In a moment, his knife was a blade the size of his forearm, though it could shrink now into a tiny knife, or lengthen to a long rapier in a second.

'… a kingly gift,' he repeated in amazement.

'It's all over the streets, what you did, Matrix. Their government is trying to break it down, to keep it silent. You're none too popular, but they heard you were trying to get an alliance -'

He was interrupted then by the approach of several Derringer, armed guard in tow. It was the official.

Matrix sat up and smiled then, 'nice gnolem you have there, it's-'

He was cut off. 'There will be no pleasantries this day, emissary. We've just received word that a massive contingent of Oppression war machines are massing at the inside gates. Our projections estimate they are preparing for an unprecedented attack on the Resistance itself. We've taken the liberty of allowing this knowledge to fall into the hands of the Resistance already, though we suspect we can add little to what they already are aware of.'

There was silence for a moment.

'The golem,' Matrix said, 'we can use it ...'

'No,' the official said in finality, the will of his people in those words. 'It will only be used to fulfil its purpose; the liberation of our people. But I've been asked –'

'What?' Matrix yelled, upsetting the healers and causing the guards to bear weapons. 'What about the alliance? You don't have anyone who can pilot that thing and I'm –'

'The first. I know. But I hadn't finished saying. Our people still have hope that one day it will be us to wield it against the Oppression. However, I have been asked to assure you this from the high councillor Silverbeard and the entire council – if you do manage to forge an alliance between the great people outside the walls, if you do manage to mount a force against the wall, you may count our people along with you, and you may pilot the gnolem against it yourself.' He paused for effect, allowing his words to sink in. Then shook his head in disbelief.

'Be advised, emissary, this is a privilege none expected to *ever* be granted to your kind, in this generation or the next: To allow another to see the gnolem, let alone the promise to possess it, is unthinkable in the entire history of our people! *Do not* take this covenant lightly! Never before on this world have we offered assistance, rarely even trade. Now our most sacred hope is going to be lent to a young, brash, untested emissary from the Resistance? It is more than I can stand, and I disdain the day I was made and lived to see it. But it is a promise, and a Derringer promise is binding. Bring us word of your alliances, and we will join you in battle.'

Matrix and Glenn were out in record time. A small crowd had gathered in front of the hospital to cheer them on. The official hadn't even risked a front exit, but managed to arrange a point Tesser right from the hospital antechamber. Everywhere else he went, Matrix got smiles and nods.

The official had promised them that, while the non-aggression pact stood, they would be pulling their forces back from a few points near the surface. While they would not hinder the Oppression in any way, it would mean the mutants would immediately claim the territory, and they, on the other hand, would gladly hinder the Oppression. It was the nearest thing to an alliance that had ever occurred between the Resistance and the Derringer, and thus it was to the mutants that Matrix and Glenn would go next.

So in spite of the disappointed crowd, they departed.

More pleasant a prison

So she was in his prison in broad daylight, she knew that now. Somehow he had penetrated her defences and disguise and pulled her name from some file. Perhaps he had the power to call down the entire black guard army? Or near enough, she supposed. He was more than just a government employee. Perhaps even more than an informer. And yet for reasons of his own, reasons she could probably more than guess, he seemed to have decided to keep this to himself for the time being.

She'd spent the last hour securing her defences, though she did not feel particularly threatened. Not yet, at least. He had done nothing. Just lead the way to wherever it was that they were going. It was a high arched tunnel amid the markets of west forty first district. Some of the less used ones, but it led more or less directly to the transports. There would be too many who could see through her defences there.

'Not Seren tower?' she requested.

'Oh no,' he replied. 'Not there. I live and work on the slopes.'

So he was really was taking her home. 'What is it you want?' she asked rhetorically. She was not willing to talk business, really, till she knew she could control him. He already knew her name, no doubt he knew much more about her career than he was letting on, and he'd just set on a profiteer. It was a threat, she was sure of that now.

'Oh no, not that!' He laughed, sensing her concern. 'But not here. We need somewhere a little… quieter.'

His apartment was nice, sparse, but well organised. It looked like he lived here alone but entertained often enough to need to accommodate it. His arrangement of furniture belayed an organised mind, somewhat prone to dominate others, repressing a more creative nature. If this was where he lived, this was not where he was himself.

He'd given her no reason to be afraid, though her daggers and what they could do were only a thought away. Perhaps he sensed this, as he looked at her then and told her not to worry once more, almost with a laugh. He threw his coat over a chair and walked out onto the veranda, the most public place in a private home. Here they could look out at the cavern where he dwelt, catching glimpses of the forest above where it peered into the apartment city. From this balcony the other citizens in the complex could see them, and call out to them if they so choose.

He waited for her to join him, as seeing not much else to do except perhaps stand around, she did. He was calmly staring at the people below.

'You enjoy the view from this angle?' she said, implying he enjoyed the dominant position. He laughed calmly, and a little condescendingly.

'You were in some real trouble there, Alasia. A pacer trace was directed right at you well before you'd begun your search, and you were too nervous to remember your Alpha level training and prepare properly. What were you running looking into those dissidents' files? Looking into some Resistance activities?'

She had no answers. So, the game was up, they'd found her again and she had nothing to protect herself with. He was a spy. Standing on his balcony she had little she could do to him in full view of the public, and defended by the protections of his own home he would be standing in a fortress of his own, unique design.

He huffed, 'this is not usual tactics for an alpha level spy, Alasia, and quite sloppy I might say. That you did so in public implies either bold measure of your own abilities or a drastic overestimation of them.'

He waited. She'd realised he'd just let her off the hook. So he didn't think she was with the Resistance? So she wasn't in trouble, at least, not yet.

'Who are you?' she asked.

He didn't even look at her. 'Let's just say... I also train spies. Usually those a little further along in the game than yourself. Remember, the first protocol always stands – consider the people first. That is our first duty.'

It almost made her adopt schoolgirl posture, but she refrained. 'Why are you helping me?'

He sighed, 'too many novices cut themselves down early now days. I just wanted to help.'

That was curious.

'Here?' she asked.

He laughed again, 'hadn't you noticed this ward up here on the roof?' She saw it then, etched there in aura matter invisible to all who didn't seek it out. 'This protects us – you might like to remember it. If any peep in the conversation we will be alerted a few seconds earlier, and can talk about other things. So we can talk of anything you like, and I find a public place, dressed like everyone else, is still the best place to hide of all.'

'Why?' she asked again, more sincerely this time.

He sighed, 'because you need to know yourself, Alasia. I think that's one of the lessons life has to teach us... You're intelligent, talented; you seem to be able to scan more lines that anyone I've ever met... But do you know yourself?' He asked.

She paused, 'you seem to know so much about me, but I know nothing about you?'

He smiled, and looked out at the people in his revere, 'I've been serving supply for over thirty years now. That looks to be almost twice your age. There are things you should know before you proceed against the dissidents, and many more if you want to challenge the Resistance.'

'I will listen,' she told him, truthfully. This, she realised, was more than a chance to redeem herself with the Resistance. She had to tell them the truth of what she was and what she did, and needed information to convince them of her allegiance.

But it was also a chance to accept a mentor, perhaps the first of her life.

And so he told her. He told her about people, places, about protection and attack. He told her many things Alpha level spies were never told. He was a wealth of information, and he shared it freely. But not everything. There was much he hid. But what he hid he did so honestly, and told her when he did so that she knew what she was not ready to know yet.

He was unlike anyone she'd spoke to before, and in spite of herself, she found herself relaxing, just a little, during the day spent in his presence.

The sin of the Commander

'I cannot let him go, healer,' she explained meekly. 'I don't know why. He just seems so... close. He still needs me.'

'Has he aged a day since you saw him last?'

She looked at his body, clean and dressed for the healing. He looked peaceful now.

'We sent his soul print on. We did that over seven years ago. Yet... there is something. He's out there healer. He needs me.'

'But he's dead,' the healer argued, trying to sound calm.

'He needs to come back,' Shee pled forlornly, bursting into tears again.

What had happened, the healer wondered. *Had she buried her refusal to accept his death all this time, even from the examiners?* It was a burden that was driving her mad, and the healer began to seriously consider if she was not already lost to them. What moment of lucidity they had managed to pry from her this hour was again apparently a ruse to return to the hopeless task of bringing her twin back to life – or to die herself trying.

Suddenly an alarm sounded.

'Commander!' A voice called them. 'The Oppression is moving into this zone. We need to get you and the healers deeper into Resistance territory.'

Even as he spoke, the healer paled in terror. Not at the encroaching army, but the anger in a single woman.

'Attempt to stop me,' the Commander said to her calmly, 'and you are my enemy. Take his body. Take it away. Keep it safe. I will be back.'

'Sheelaakah, please...' she begged, her voice breaking.

'Not this time,' Shee replied, already turned to leave.

-++++-

The air shimmered around her, and she stood. At the heat of her thoughts the curtains caught fire. She walked slowly, reaching out with her mind, touching them all. There were so many Resistance soldiers. But she could make them all immune to pain, immune to fear. They would fight as never before. But it was further that she sought. Yes... the enemy. They were approaching quickly.

She left the hospital, and at her psychic command a vessel flew down. Allowing it to carry her to the parapets. No, the outer wall. Let them see her fury.

As she alighted, most of the pebbles lifted of their own accord to float around her, and unseen breeze moving her hair. The guards looked at her in uncertainty and fear. She knew she was drawing power from dangerous, forbidden sources, but she took no census, and she did not care.

'Let them come,' she ordered.

They were on the horizon now, a rise of dust far away. They came quickly, raining spears among the soldiers to soften their resolve. They met them with a wall of fire, holding brightly the pennant of the Resistance.

'Catapults, take out the ballista's,' she ordered.

They were moving heavy machinery into range now, but she took the minds of her soldiers. They might have fired once or twice before passing out, but they never missed.

Thus the Oppression realised they'd need to take the area by force. There were so many. Automatons, black guards, wasps, incorporeals. Five times their number.

But there was one of her.

They'd come for him. They'd come for her brother again. She'd let them take him last time – she was weaker then. She was not weak now.

She waited while they pounded the wall, waited till at last they'd brought down a section of it. The cheer went up from them then. Then she stood - commanded all their defences upon her. The air shimmered with her thoughts, and all felt inexplictant fear.

The enemy recognised a telepath. They sent in theirs. Five or so shamans or the like. They were well trained. They tried to crush her mind, but she shrugged off their attack and broke their minds one by one.

That was when they realised they were in trouble. They sent in their full forces then. Sent them towards pillars where she stood, suddenly alone. Sent them, just as she'd anticipated, to their deaths.

So she called the storm.

Wind ripped past her, dark clouds formed in the sky as she vented her full fury unabated. She shouted into the wind, reaching into their minds. Felt them all one by one. Felt their fears…

As a wave the fighting stopped. The attackers looked at each other in dread premonition.

Then one by one, they began to die; shrieking as madness overtook them. Hollering in fear at the terror on the tower in front of them. They could not defend themselves. All the hatred, all the fear, that the Resistance felt she unleashed upon the attackers in a massive, unrelenting psychic wave, and drove them all insane.

The wild shrieking did not last long. What few survived the chaos ended their own lives rather than face continued living.

'Good…' she said dispassionately, '…I can get back to work now.'

And on the wall, pale faced and trembling defenders looked at her in fear.

Second assignment

It was Alasia's second assignment with the tutor.

This time, it was a family. Husband. Wife. Both knew.

Both stole.

She'd realised long before this time that even in the most centrally controlled world in the galaxy, people would still risk breaking the law. Human nature hadn't been changed by all the technology.

Some would do it for profit.

Some for the thrill.

And some for revenge.

It was a clever plot. They had syphoned off assets to an enemy, even their own. They'd waited until someone noticed, and raised the protest with all the others. Had it been their own funds he would have received modest punishment, but as it was so many others he'd been threatened with full memory rasure. He was distraught.

But to Alasia, something hadn't added up. His mind patterns simply didn't match the finesse with which the resources had been transferred. So she'd looked, and looked. Till the day he was scheduled for the rasure and she'd met them at the funeral.

It was them, working in tandem.

She'd saved him only just in time. Raised the alarm and given the signal. The black guards arrived in moments.

Then they'd disappeared. No point Tesser, simply gone.

That was too direct. Her guide offered. *If you'd not confronted them directly we could have caught them here. Now, we will have to follow them to their abode.*

Why don't we leave it to the black guards? She asked.

They're outmatched, he replied, and she'd wondered why she wouldn't be. Confronting self-preservers in their own abode? It was extremely dangerous. He'd given her a moment to summon a weapon from the Government, and they were tessered directly to the central room of the dissidents home, standing back to back.

The strength draining field stunned them immediately.

She could not move.

The house was homely, with a floral couch and thick curtains. She heard a child's muffled squeal.

'You see honey,' A woman said out loud so they could hear. 'The Government spies are coming to hurt us. They didn't even ask to be let in. Do you know what has to happen now?'

Alasia managed to turn her head. The child was barely nine. She had a little floral dress and her mother, still dressed for the rasure, was armed with a dangerous looking hand device that writhed in her palm. Ragged breaths drew from her guide, he was struggling against the field too – no doubt humiliated that such a regular home defence could cause an "experienced" spies undoing.

'She doesn't need to see this, not yet,' a man explained.

The mother hissed, but there was a sound of a door, and then they were gone.

'You did well, Government spies, to find us,' the man's voice continued. 'You're not usually so quick. But this is what happens to those who tread on the ways of the Rei-nati!'

Her guide gasped. It was the last impulse that she needed. She reached down and found her dark spirit, allowing it to take over her body. Normally, people cannot move inside such fields, unless they have inhuman will.

She saw herself fall forwards. Saw her arms reach like spiders across the floor, dragging her outside the circle. Her breath was deep and ragged.

'Unbelievable,' the man gasped. But he didn't activate his device, too awed with amazement as she rolled from the circle. She watched herself stand up calmly.

'But it's all for naught,' he teased, raising his weapon.

The blast of yellow light struck the floor where she'd been microseconds before. She saw herself leap up, watched as mid-flight she loosed a punch dagger. Watched in passionless horror as it struck the man in the arm, severing his nerves and preventing another shot.

He was quick. He fumbled the device from his hand. It was almost in his other palm by the time she watched herself plunge her second dagger into his chest.

'No!' Her guide called, running to her side even as the field dissipated. He looked over the man's body, and turned to her angrily. 'You've stuck him in the soul heart, now we cannot even revive him for interrogation!'

She looked down at him, and felt a cold violence towards her guide.

No, not him. I need him, she told the demon.

As you wish, my mistress, her demon nonchalantly replied.

Go back, I'm needed here…

But your strength, it protested.

Go back! she insisted, and it slunk again down inside her.

'…asia?' her guide was calling her name. She was almost fainting with exhaustion.

'Sorry,' she said, thinking quickly. 'I didn't mean to…' and she hadn't. It was the demon.

He looked frustrated.

'Pay attention. Don't lose it like that. Not again, not ever. Spies… die that way.'

She looked into his eyes. He looked concerned.

'Ok,' she agreed.

The house was quiet. Not even the guard had been alerted in all their violence.

'So, who were they?'

Dissidents, of a sort. The guide explained, subtelepathically this time. *The Rei-nati answer to someone high up in the city. They've evaded capture for dozens of years, and seem to be gaining power.*

What do they want? Alasia asked.

More power, he replied. *They want to take it all for themselves. They're claiming to be of some "royal lineage", and working to dethrone the order and establish themselves and Kings and Queens, with all others as thralls. It's inexplicable. In any event, they seem to have had better resources than we've anticipated. I thought we had their numbers in check, but you've stumbled onto something here Alasia, if only we knew more...*

He looked at the body and sighed.

He continued out loud, 'we have three choices I suppose – take away the body and interrogate the neural network, leave it here for his spouse to claim, or consign it to the foundries ourselves.'

She was not taking the foundry option, and was appalled that he'd suggested it. 'I doubt the spouse will risk returning for it,' she said.

'Agreed.'

'And, while I don't want to seem unpatriotic, doesn't neural interrogation involve some rather serious dissection? It might disrupt his soul print?'

'Agreed.'

There was a pause.

'You're right, the only option is the foundries,' he said.

She was indignant.

'What?' He replied, a little perplexed. 'For cremation. Dignified, even for an enemy.'

She stuttered.

'You can even witness it yourself.' He offered, a little taken back. 'What, you don't think they'd use it as some kind of resource, do you?'

She was only just wise enough to hold her peace this time...

The mutants

The land they tessered to was deeply concealed by the trees of the wilderness beyond. The sky was almost blotted out by the think foliage. The ground was rough, aged beyond measure with thick black soil. The air, noticeably clearer.

'Well!' said Glenn, hefting his pack. 'Let's go find-'

'They're already here...' Matrix explained.

For a moment, there was silence. Then they began moving out from behind the trees, lowering themselves from the foliage, or pulling themselves from the soil. The glared at the humans with hungry eyes, a few laughed in diabolical glee. Their bandings, more iron than copper, were course and rough-hewn. Their claws, long, and their tusks, sharp. The males wore theirs capped with steel. Around their necks, the bones of previous victims lay strung up in necklaces. Their stench: inhuman. Growling and snapping, the mutants circled in for the kill.

They would have attacked. They were about to attack. But then Matrix spoke their language. 'Chal Kraa Kitukya!' he ordered, which was to say, 'you are here now!' It was the universal sign of a coming in peace of a friend.

It stopped them in their tracks. One powerfully built one stood up on her hind legs. She spoke in the common language. 'Hoomans. You friends of the evoolution? Forgive us our eagerness, it has been long time since we had meat. We will hear you now speak,' she asked in their strange manner.

'We will speak with Karl Brek'anarl,' Matrix replied.

The others had already begun to slink away. She ordered something to one of the nearby mutants, who used some form of device he pulled from his belt to send a message.

'We near 'nuf him now. Come, I walk you him,' she explained.

'I didn't really have time to explain last time,' Matrix said to Glenn. 'Mutants see all forms of politeness as shiftiness. They think you're hiding something. Phrase all requests as statements in the future tense, it's the only safe way. Few of them speak our language. And they value strength, violence is a way of life-'

'I know,' Bakerson replied, eyeing mutants carefully, his hands relaxed but in quick reach of his weapons. 'I've had basic Resistance training. I'm just surprised the Derringer set us so close... and, I'm still a little anxious from our last meeting.'

'I know what you mean. Don't worry, I "get" them. Stay close, and hit any that cross you with your bare hands. It's the only language they respect.'

'Not Resistance basic training,' Glenn mumbled. But it was good advice. One kept coming up and trying to touch his blade. Eventually, it made a grab for it, and Glenn swept it from his grasp easily and landed a solid backhand on the creatures head. It tumbled over twice in the soil, and the others laughed approvingly. He was afforded a small measure of respect from then on. Among the mutants it seemed one was expected to be able to defend themselves, and if not, the fault is yours, not your aggressors.

Brek'anarl was in a clearing, sitting on a huge throne made of bones and animal skin that looked like it had been placed there this morning. He was in the act of talking to some mutant delegates from another of the mutant nations. His guards were heavily armoured, crouched on their haunches, bearing fangs and wicked scimitars by their sides. The priest and telepath among them watched them keenly as they approached.

The female they were with stopped short of her approach, but Matrix slid right past her. He shouted something violent at the mutants, who stirred at his approach. The one Karl was speaking to shouted what sounded like a threat, and locked eyes with Matrix. A tense moment passed. Then it roared a battle cry, but Matrix did not look away. Instead, he seemed ready to fly into battle any second. It would surely cost them their lives against these elite mutants.

Then Karl Brek'anarl, unchallenged leader of the mutants, blue mottled skin and twice the size of a regular human, laughed. He slapped the one he spoke with on the back, almost knocking it over, and said something he found humorous in his own language. The guards visibly relaxed.

'Friend of the Evolution, I welcome you!' He spoke in his impossibly deep voice. 'And you too, Dog man, though I'd prefer you were an enemy, I think I would have enjoyed your meat.'

Glenn did not speak, but Matrix sent him a message, *it's a compliment... or, near enough.*

'So, what cause is so important then, friend, that has you interrupting my negotiation of a peace accord between this people and the next?'

Glenn was amazed. He couldn't imagine the mutants negotiating anything. Perhaps that's not what Brek'anarl meant?

'Surprised, are you, Dog man? Do you really think us so uncivilised that we cannot solve our problems, when we choose, without violence? You'll find the Resistance just the same, and you are more like us than them.'

He smiled cruelly. Glenn remembered, he was a telepath, and decided he'd better watch his thoughts more closely. The thought made the mutant leader laugh, who clearly enjoyed making everyone he spoke to feel uncomfortable.

'The mutants and the Resistance will form an alliance,' Matrix stated.

It was the closest thing to a polite request the mutants would accept, Glenn assumed.

Karl laughed, and the others with him. 'Your people can never accept us, and our ways. Would they really fight shoulder to shoulder? We are too unlike, this is a waste of my time-'

So Matrix spoke again, in their language, feeding the meaning of it back to Glenn through his headband. 'Then I challenge you to a physical contest for the right to govern this people.'

Brek'anarl paused. At twice his height, he looked like he could snap Matrix like a twig. But he laughed again. 'Very well, mutant friend! I could use the sport! Tonight at dusk it is!' And he smiled a very friendly smile. Mutants scurried to spread the news.

'What have you gotten yourself in to?' Glenn asked Matrix when they'd removed themselves from the clearing.

'Don't worry, I know what I'm doing,' was all he said.

It was dusk. Matrix had spent the day preparing – meditating and practicing. It was to be a combat without weapons, though the fact that Brek'anarl had both claws and tusks worked against him slightly. A fact he'd tried to suppress as he'd pictured himself again and again defeating the massive giant. He could feel his strength, and weaknesses. He'd seen him in combat. It would be difficult, but not impossible.

They'd built a shelter for him, out of fallen trees and bark, covered in rough hessian. It was the only place he, or Glenn, would be left alone. News had spread quickly, and a large number of them had gathered. Several pre fights had already occurred as the excitement grew, and Matrix begun to wonder if Brek'anarl had used this as a chance to help his people work off some steam regarding some issue they'd been facing. The mood was certainly carnival.

At the appointed hour the mutant woman they'd first meet, who'd appointed herself somewhat of a personal assistant, tapped the wood outside his shelter. It was time.

When Matrix pulled himself out there was some cheering, drowned out mostly by raucous laughter. He was young, and thinly built for a Resistance soldier. But they'd underestimated him the first time he'd entered their forest, and that was what had saved him then too. In a way, he wished he'd been allowed weapons that he might have his bronze knife by him, but was far wiser given Mutant enthusiasm for exotic weaponry.

He walked up to the edge of the great clearing. It was decked out in bright orange and red sheets of fabric, stretching along all the boughs till they joined in a great pavilion at the other end of the clearing. Great braziers of bronze housed leaping towers of flame, yellow and orange. The entire clearing was surrounded by hundreds of mutants, standing on top of each other to see, clambering into the trees. It was an impassable wall of wood and salivating, roaring tusks.

Glenn was not to be seen. Oh, yes he was. Unarmed except for his spear, standing just behind him on the way to their shelter. It was an ignominious affair, bracken and twigs. None but the female and Bakerson stood among the trees on their side. There was no red or orange to adorn their place, simply brown and green. But it heartened him, and he smiled. Deliberately or not, they had decked his shelter out in the colours of the Resistance.

To a cheer, Karl's honour guard begun to empty from his pavilion. They marched, heavily armoured and arrayed for battle, around the clearing. They took gratuitous swipes with sharpened blades at all those who'd pressed themselves beyond the line of the trees. He didn't know if it was for his protection or Brek'anarl's already impressive presence... or perhaps it was to keep their battle private.

Matrix walked into the clearing to jeers and timid barks of encouragement. He heard Bakerson say some encouraging phrase from the Resistance.

The guards begun to drum their weapons into the ground. Slowly at first. The noise and shouting begun to subside, and others joined the pulsing with fists on the earth. It begun to accelerate, occasional hoots being heard from the trees. Suddenly it broke into a run, a thunderous cascade of beating and pulse. At the peak of the crescendo, Karl Brek'anarl exploded clear from his pavilion the twelve or so meters to the centre of the clearing to the thunderous exalted battle roar of his people.

The noise was deafening, but Matrix let it slide though him. When the breath had left them, which took a while, he shook himself and stepped up to his mark. He realised then that they'd tried a fear attack, a primal psychic roar that usually disarmed their enemies. But he'd shaken it off, and in that moment, none few begun to pay respect to him.

Karl raised himself up to his full height.

'Are you ready, ally of the evolution? You can, if you choose, step from the circle. None will think you amiss, and we've sport enough for this evening to suffice.'

Matrix recognised a psychic attack when he felt one.

Nice try. He sneered. 'You will deliver your people to an alliance with the Resistance. The Oppression is mustering even now. They need your help, and you are strengthened by theirs.'

Karl stepped up to his mark. In the way of honour among their peoples Matrix bowed, and Karl clicked his tongue.

The people cheered.

Karl spoke, 'A thousand years has seen the peace accord between your people and mine wax and wane. A thousand years, and your people have never 'stooped' to deliver a message of alliance with us! They find us, inhuman...' He muttered as though the word was to be savoured. He lashed out with a sudden fist, which Matrix ducked instinctively.

The mutants cheered, gaining great interest in a battle unexpectedly long lasting.

'This may be so,' Matrix cleverly retorted, watching his foes movements carefully while they negotiated. 'Be we are hounded by a common enemy. United, we can defeat them.'

'How?' Brek'anarl said, and lashed a wide ankle swipe at Matrix. He leapt it nimbly and flipped himself to safety. The mutants roared their disapproval. This battle was far too slow to start in earnest.

'The Derringer,' Matrix begun. Karl suddenly let out another massive fist. Matrix stopped it against his chest, but it took all his energy to do so. The mutants stopped cheering in surprise. Perhaps a few had begun to fear. Karl recoiled quickly in surprise, knowing he'd left his fist out long enough for Matrix to take advantage of it – and yet deliberately choose not to. It marked him a strong opponent to be wary of.

With his next breath Matrix explained. 'They have a gnolem. It can take the wall.'

Karl smiled, launching a furious volley of blows which Matrix smartly dodged or blocked, knowing better than to match him strength for strength for very long. As they parted for breath, the mutant spoke.

'We know. My prophetess saw a great stone beast many days ago in their lands. If I had such a toy, I would use it daily! But they hide as ever they have in their caves. They threaten and benefit no-one. They have no warmth in them, just stubbornness as stone. What makes you think they will share their trinket?'

'An alliance. I have their promise.'

Karl stood erect. He looked puzzled. Matrix had suspected a battle was just the thing the mutant leader needed to engage him in any real conversation. Karl Brek'anarl looked around at the cheering throngs. For a moment he considered, then deciding something, rushed at Matrix again.

Then the battle really begun.

It was fierce, and the crowd loved it. Karl landed many devastating blows, but Matrix landed a dozen more. The young man was clearly the nimbler warrior. Once, he even managed to throw the mutant leader over his head. But the beast was also a telepath, and used every advantage. Worse, it was Matrix who was tiring the faster.

As it happened, dodging a reckless and poorly timed blow, Matrix was able to find the point on the giants off arm and paralysed it. He clambered then on to the Brek'anarl, trying to feel his way as he could not see for the blood gashing along his eye. Standing on Karl's shoulders, he managed to lock the giant's arms, ready to pull it from its socket. It would have pressed the giant close to the end of the battle, and by law, the mutants were bound to him as their leader for a year till a new challenger could arise.

Matrix put his full weight and will into the effort, but as it happens, sometimes, an enemy's weakness is still stronger than one's own strength. The giant overcame him, and threw him face first into the ground.

He barely had time to recover when he felt a mighty clamping on his arms. He was about to kick out, when he heard a sickening crack. The giant had snapped his right forearm with his bare fingers.

He cried out in pain, in spite himself, as the giant pulled him to his feet.

'I give you chance to surrender,' Karl intoned, the crowd roaring in pleasure. Matrix could see no way to break the giants hold.

'Never.'

Snap. The other arm was broken. The giant released him.

'I give you chance to surrender,' he repeated. The crowd hooted in victory. With grim disappointment Matrix saw he would not win this battle. But with hope, he could still win the cause… He shouted then in their own language, trembling at the pain. Somehow he managed to pull himself to his feet, arms hanging silently beside him.

'Never!'

'I have power over your life!' Karl questioned him indignantly. 'You fought well, now I give you the choice of leaving this circle without death. This is an honour I rarely afford my enemies. You'd better take it, or die!'

They cheered, but Matrix somehow found voice enough to shout them down.

'Then I die free! Free, unlike the rest of you!' He would have pointed, but had to gesture with his chin. 'You! All of you! You wallow in the prejudices of others, unable to see how you use it to justify keeping them out! You think you are free? I tell you that you are not, and you will never be, till you join your strength to others and take the freedom you deserve. I know your people, Karl. I know they feel pressed in the land – there is not enough space here, so you resort to war to control their number!'

The crowd fell silent. It was the private admission they could ill afford to confront.

Matrix continues. 'The lands you seek are not to be found here. You did not forge this land. It is a prison that holds you, that forces your people into crimes for their very survival and then uses that as a justification to imprison you!'

The leader roared. He was visibly upset. He spoke so loud it would have shattered stone. 'Do NOT presume to council ME! You have lost this battle, I alone rule those of the Evolution!'

He struck with such force, and Matrix had little left to defend himself, that he shattered most, if not all, of the young human's ribs.

He fell to the ground many meters away. The crowd cheered, but there was little in it. Striking a weakened foe was poorly respected.

For a moment he lay there, dizzy with pain. Breathing for all he was worth, Matrix struggled to his feet. It wasn't easy without arms. The mutants fell silent in amazement. Karl had been brutal, but that was expected of him. He had attacked an opponent he had offered quarry to, and that was ... dishonourable.

But that opponent still stood! For all their violence, the mutants expected honour of their leaders, which was more than the humans who seemed to expect their leaders to lie to them all the while complaining that the got the leaders they expected.

'Never,' Matrix whispered. He could feel the blood slowly leaking into one of his lungs. 'And if I die... I die free!'

The mutant marched up and loomed over him.

'You think you can rule this people?' He whispered.

'No,' Matrix admitted, weekly smiling. 'I just don't have the tusks for it.'

Then Karl Brek'anarl laughed. He turned to his people. 'The challenger has abdicated!' They roared. 'I lead the Evolution!' They roared again. 'And now, to honour this worthy foe. I announce the Evolution is now in peace treaty with his people. The Resistance... is off the menu!' They cheered again, though none few refused to join in their voices.

He turned to say something to Matrix, who didn't hear it. He had fainted.

---+++---+++---

The next day he was up, arms and ribs mended, fighting fit. He stood by the hospital bed practicing his manoeuvres. They were swift and violent. The tent door parted, and in walked officer Bakerson. Matrix leapt over the bed to embrace him.

'We did it! We have a peace treaty with the mutants! That will really help out our people!' Matrix cheered.

'It looks like they'll need it. They're battering down for a storm. We've heard the initial sorties started two days ago and already there are heavy casualties. Having the mutant border closed will really help to defend us.' Glenn told him. 'And if the mutants are willing to fight for that border, it may prove to be an enormous benefit.'

Matrix punched the air vigorously, 'What've they got me on?' He asked.

'Their medicine is a little ... unusual.' Bakerson said as he took a stool. I didn't get to see much. As soon as you fell over Brek'anarl orders his chief physician to tend to you. They had you up and in care in seconds, I've never seen them move so fast. That physician guy is terrifying – I think he considers illness his battleground, and he can shout order with the best of them. They had you in some status field, drew out your bleeding psychokinetically. Then the chief physician transfers some of his blood to you directly. Just sticks a needle right into his arm and into your neck. I couldn't believe it.'

Matrix felt his neck, but could find no sign of injury. There wasn't even a sign of bruising, though even Resistance medics could take care of that. It was the complete lack of pain in his broken arms that puzzled him.

'Well, they can't be too primitive, I feel great.'

'Don't be so sure... they sterilised everything, I noticed that. Yep. Licked *everything* just before they stuck it into your body. Nice and *sterile*!'

Matrix suppressed a shudder, but he'd been in worse.

Bakerson still looked queasy. 'I don't agree so much with the setting of the bones. Effective, but... still,' he gave Matrix an aura lens, who used it to look down on his arms.

'They used grigs,' Bakerson explained.

Sure enough, half a dozen small winged humanoids, composed entirely of light under the aura lens, worked along his arms. They tended to a glimmered collection of pullies and levers which ran over and through his skin, the incorporeal ropes double binding up his splintered bones, newly fused by whatever means the Mutants possessed. One of them stopped to wave at him, and received a smart slap over the head from another that held a quill and parchment. Matrix shook his head. He'd never get used to those guys, but didn't feel like stressing his arms any more. They, however, almost looked disappointed at that thought.

'So, the good physician used his own blood to replace my own. That explains the aggressive tendencies.'

'So you're definitely experiencing aggressive tendencies then?' Glenn asked, almost jokingly.

The tent walls flew open. In marched Brek'anarl. 'Aha! Up! Good! You're going to hear my instructions,' it was a request.

'I am listening to you,' Matrix replied.

'What is your last memory?'

'You said 'peace treaty.''

Brek'anarl laughed again. 'You're a dangerous adversary Matrix. You could have beaten me, and I'll not admit that where my people can hear it. Your tenacity, on the other hand, has defeated both me and my people. I have been speaking to your companion here. We may not be in a formal alliance with your people, but if the others launch an attack on the wall, you may count us in. We'll even stop eating them, the leaves are enough, though not so tasty - and they don't put up as nearly as engaging a battle!' He mused whimsically.

It thrilled Matrix intensely to hear of the peace treaty, it was almost an alliance. He didn't know whether to cheer or cry. Some drug must be running rampant though his body.

Brek'anarl continued. 'You'll want to know. The Oppression has begun to run sorties across the wall. They're testing our defences. We're pulling back, but as soon as they leave their place we will fall on any that cross our territory. Interestingly, the Derringer have moved out of the granite pass. Usually the Oppression would simply Tesser their forces in, but they're planning something big this time, and they've brought a huge number of tanks and tunnellers. Pity for them, with the Derringer gone from that pass, it is Mutant territory now. We won't let them know that till they're half way through! They will be in for a surprise when they try to take the Resistance and ignore us!' He laughed. 'My people have been looking for a good fight for too long now. I thank you, though it's likely we would have spent our rage on the encroaching Oppression anyway – now that we have nothing to fear from the Resistance it will embolden us. We will catch them like snakes, drive them between us and divide the spoils,' he lent forward dangerously, 'Guns for you, meat for us...'

Matrix did a better job at hiding his disgust than Glenn did, but it was the reaction Brek'anarl was hoping for. As Matrix had realised, these people wallowed in their debauchery as a justification for it. Their wallowing was a way to make others hate them, and they used that hate to consolidate their own identity and justify a life of their own choosing – in that, perhaps there was more humanity in mutants than mutants would ever admit.

'Leader of the Evolution,' Matrix said, 'we cannot thank you enough.'

'Just bring us more enemies to fight!' Roared the mutant. He smiled, but again became sober. 'There is one enemy, however, that I am my people refuse to fight alongside. One that, even if we joined in an attack on the wall, we would best be kept from among their ranks. The angst runs deep between us. But even if you offer them alliance, I doubt they will take it. They shoot our people on sight, and we frequently raid into each other's territory – the current peace treaty will not stop that... and unless you can gain their word that they will leave us, we will not stop hounding them. They are filth beneath our dignity to speak of.'

'The bikies,' Matrix understood.

Karl nodded. 'They spare neither child bearer nor aged. They raid us indiscriminately, not even stopping to feast on the bodies of our dead! Our proud warriors are brought low by their poison, and the noise of their weapons tears at our woods! I would exterminate them from this world, if I could...'

Matrix knew very little of this people, apart from their exquisite brutality, and their controlled and yet violent oppression of any who crossed the boarders of their land.

'They are proud, aloof,' Glenn said. 'They see everyone as beneath them, but live long lives. We of the Resistance know little from them, they seem to treat us as though we were as much a part of their imprisonment on this world as the Oppression. They raid our ranks frequently too, as though to make a point that they are not to be trusted. To be honest, we don't know what they want. I'm not sure how we'll get them to join us in an alliance when more skilled diplomats have never returned time and time again - even less sure of how we're going to get them to talk to us at all.

Third assignment

You cannot do that again, she insisted.

It hissed long in her ear. *I was told no different.*

Then I'm telling you now. They have to be revivable, all of them.

It was unhappy. She could feel her hands involuntarily twitching.

She insisted, *No. It must be done my way. No death.*

It moaned in frustration. *But that is the way I gather my strength!*

No...

But she had to stop then. Her guide was approaching telepathically.

It was her third mission.

No death. She ordered, and it cursed her name as it turned away into the darkness of her soul, not a moment too soon.

Monitor their movements carefully. Her guide instructed.

They were on the surface again, surveying a huge plaza where information and goods were traded, or citizens stopped for lunch. It was a colourful, friendly affair. But there were others down there that did not hold the best interests of the people at heart. Alasia was pleased. In her days with the guide she'd learned a lot about Oppression tactics, about the 'inside', about who really did what. It was valuable information.

They were down there now. Dozens of members of the Rei-nati. Their movements seemed random, looked innocent. But in reality they were interconnected in an underconscious forum, discussing private details of their planned succession to power. They knew about the man's death the other day - they called him a Prince. They wanted revenge. They plotted revenge. They swore on their own souls to carry it out - murder in the name of the murdered.

Her demon swelled in her chest.

Not yet, she instructed it.

But actions were already happening. She'd begun to orchestrate an evacuation of innocents from the venue. The Rei-nati didn't even notice it. They were too busy planning the assassination of several middle government officials.

Even if I didn't work for the Oppression, I'd stop this, Alasia thought.

Are you ready? Her guide began.

Indeed, she replied.

The compulsion field went up even as they tessered down into the plaza. A few innocents had been caught up, paralysed to immobility for the time being. They'd ignored or not been sensitive enough to listen to the warning. They'd be all right.

'Rei-nati criminals and assassins!' Her guide shouted. 'I am a representative of the government of Seren. You are all hereby placed under arrest for the plotted murder of government officials,' he heralded.

'Welcome, government spies,' a voice said.

Alasia gasped, and they both turned and stared in shock.

A man was moving, quite relaxed and unperturbed in the blue haze that should have rendered him immobile.

'You've underestimated us again,' he quietly crooned.

'How?' Her guide began, surprise evident in his voice.

'Now, who would want to assassinate a few minor officials, that could prove so useful to our new government, when we can have the murderer of our Prince!' He said, and smiled at Alasia.

She held her terror calmly. She could talk her way out of this; she'd been in worse places before.

He shouted, 'Rei-nati. Take her to *our* courts for trial!'

She scoffed. How could they expect to have even a cubicle to stand in on Seren, let alone some place to hold a meeting as official and of such importance as a court? She was going to say something, something snide and condescending that would put this arrogant Rei-nati back into his place. But then she saw them, the others. All of their prisoners were in no way imprisoned. The only ones that seemed immobile were those that might have been able to help – the innocents. The only ones mobile were herself, her guide, and the dozens of Rei-nati that walked towards them, smiling unkindly.

She tried to deactivate the field. It did not respond to her command. She tried to call for aid from the black guards, but the system seemed to be disconnected to her. Perhaps if she could get out of the field? Her guide was discovering similar things, she could tell by the look on his face. Once again, the master was outwitted by the prey.

'What do we do now, my mentor?' she said in a voice that hid well her fear.

'We fight – we need to get outside our field, they've co-opted it somehow.'

'Well-resourced eh!' she said.

'Indeed,' he grimly replied.

They were outnumbered thirty to one, but they were government trained spies. It should not have been difficult, but it was. With hand device and sword they lashed out at their assailants, keeping them at bay as two or three of them tried to take them at a time. Several fell, but it was a futile effort. Slowly, purposefully, the Rei-nati began to form a closed circle around them.

It was a ritual.

'Don't let them close the circle!' Her guide shouted as he parried a blow from the Rei-nati who spoke to them. 'They intend to claim our consciousness and impression us in soul gems!'

It was a fate worse than death.

She had accessed the Evernet by then. Their wards were strong, but hers stronger. She would access the black guard any moment now…

Suddenly she felt a painful grasp on her wrist.

It was the Rei-nati. Her guide lay on the floor, struck to his skull.

'You now belong to us,' he crooned.

She forgot about the Evernet.

She forgot about her promise.

But she remembered about her demon.

But the time she awoke she was kneeling in front of some kind of dark pool, in a cavern that had only a pair of wax candles for light, and they were fading. Her body ached as it had the night she'd first escaped the black guards, only worse. Her daggers were still lying on the floor in front of her.

That was when she saw them. The bodies of those Rei-nati she'd slain, three or four of them piled in pieces along the far wall… what was this black pool? When she realised in horror what she'd done, she retched. Again and again, beating her fists on the stone, clutching her mouth in a desperate attempt to expel everything that she'd done – that it had done through her.

You… DEMON! She hissed at it.

It smiled inside her, *and you expected anything less?*

You monster…

Then it smiled through her at her own horror, mocking her disgust. It spoke in cold, unrepentant logic. *I needed it for my strength. You'd asked much...*

You disgusting vice...

There are others, you know, willing to part with their dignity for what I offer them. In time, you will learn, just like the others do. It's not so bad, once you get over your petty, self-righteous descriptions of what is sacred, and what is fuel.

It laughed quietly again, and retreated into the darkness of her soul, leaving her to suffer alone for her loss of faith in it.

What was she becoming?! She vomited again, retching long after there was nothing more to give, till she fell to the ground in exhaustion.

The candles were almost spent. She needed to get out, to find her way back. To find her guide. The passage behind was dark. She did not know where it would go.

A candle went out.

She looked at the daggers, still shining black with the ichor that stained them. The way out was pitch dark.

Hating herself, she picked them both up again, and from somewhere deep inside, a dark spirit gently laughed...

The bikies

His heart was pounding in his ears. It had been three days, and whatever drugs the mutants had used on him were only now beginning to thin out. He hadn't slept in that time. They were beginning to wear off, and he was beginning to doubt the wisdom of his plan.

He'd left Glenn at the borders of the land, equipped with a small contingent of Resistance special operatives. They'd become renowned already, Glenn and he. The Derringer and now the mutants were in a peace treaty, unheard of in the history of this world. Already, the Oppression had sent spies and assassins to try to discredit the force, but the people of the wilderness beyond were so used to this they knew what to expect, and expected to find Oppression involvement, which when they did, it served only to strengthen their budding alliance.

He was waiting, upside down, observing a main street of the Bikies. He was wearing a dark chameleon suit, protected by wards and runes that had, so far, made him invisible to their eyes. He'd walked among them, traded at their shops in the evening, spied into their rooms at night.

He was glad he'd brought an eye stone with him, a scrying device. He'd seen more in the past two days than any Resistance spy in a hundred years. He'd learnt more than all the Resistance supply had gathered in their entire history. And with that stone, the Resistance was learning along with him.

For all their violence and cruelty, the world within the forests borders of their home was one of cleanliness, order, and kindness to their own. They were tall, with pointed ears and almond shaped eyes. Music was common, and some minstrels or other were constantly playing in public places. They walked gracefully, but were terribly martial. All were armed except the children. They laughed a lot, yet almost too gently, for behind their laughter was a constant glance of pain.

It was everywhere, in every face, in every sentence. They'd even taken to writing a special glyph to express their suffering into every public notice. It was an eagle, an eagle with its wings cut off. They were pained, more so than any race he'd ever met, but not more than some individuals, whom the prison of this world drove mad. They trusted no one, and reacted violently, he could see, in fear to any who crossed their boarders.

As he had.

It was death to cross their lands, but even if he died here, Matrix was sure the bud of the Alliance would blossom, and what he'd learnt here would help that. They were a people in pain. All about them, the fortress of solitude kept them safe, and yet they were still afraid.

And a fortress it was. They lived above ground, yet so thick was their defences that light did not penetrate to the forest floor. The only way to see the sun was to be a guard above the branches, and even they hid. All the citizens lived under a ridged measure of control imposed by their leaders, motivated by the people's fear. They loathed this place, a prison within a prison, but it was the only way they felt safe.

The air in here was stifling, but they didn't dare open a window.

Surrounded by fear they had built a world to protect themselves from it, but in so doing had brought it with them into this place. They were a people cowering in fear.

Then it was their fear he needed to address. He needed to break into their own hiding place and reveal it for it was; an illusion. They were not like this. They were a people of light.

He knew then what he had to do.

He moved, quickly, driven by adrenalin and the desire to not run out on mutant juice before he had time. He made his way along the branches, sliding, running, quickly, stopping. Carefully, he could not be found now.

There it was. The barbican inside the fortress. The inner city. He had only dared to enter it once, and was nearly found out.

If he left any dead here they would hunt him till death, and then some...

But he stopped short of its boughs. Two hundred kilometres or so, by his reckoning. Far, but not too far for him.

There they were. Talking to some others in the gardens. It was the couple that all others deferred to in this place. They were tall, beautiful. Her long blond hair flowed in mute plats down past her waist, tied with a crystal diadem and platinum banding. And his, equally long hair as though it was a badge of office, tied in gold band with an emerald in centre. It was just below this emerald that he took aim.

The moment of discomfort as the range accurate weapon formed itself from his ring, armband, and inserted itself into the circuitry behind his eye. He would likely get a single shot, if he ever lived to tell it.

But they'd moved. Moved as though they suspected it. He cursed, where were they now? Then he saw them again, saw her head and shoulders as they passed windows in a slowly ascending spiral staircase.

His head went hazy for a moment. The hormones were wearing, and the will of the people below resisted his presence continually, though they were not conscious of his presence. It would have to be now; there would be no other chance.

He attached a grapple to the branches above and quickly lowered himself twenty or so meters over the road. It was necessary to not have to shoot through stone, which would be too damaging. They were passing now, and any second would walk by a window.

Someone saw him then. They may have screamed, or perhaps shouted. The guards did not have time to react, but one unseen psychic did strike at him. It would have knocked his aim off, the shot would have missed, only the message was; *You will not kill anyone.*

It did not matter, he did not intend to kill at all.

It was unfortunate, he was aiming for the male. But with no time to contemplate, it was the female that passed the window first. The bullet left his rifle. Shot with unerring accuracy, and struck her right in the forehead. Shot her right between the eyes at two hundred kilometres as she passed by an open window in a spiral staircase.

It didn't take them half a second to react. He was cut from the bough by some arrow, which probably should have been aimed at him. He plummeted to the street below, landing painfully, a force field springing up and deadening any equipment he had. He didn't have time to stand up before they were on him. Residents shrieking their indignity and pain. They would *kill* him for what he'd done. He tried to stand but they held him down with powerful hands and minds. He'd shot someone. He'd entered their land. He'd endangered their children. He had to die, someone pulled a knife, and stabbed him in the chest.

But Matrix did not allow them to stab twice. He twisted the blade from the others hands. He stood up with a roar and they all leapt back.

So – a Resistance soldier… they thought.

There were too many to escape.

He looked in their eyes, but was surprised that they didn't look angry. They were … sad. A woman began to cry. *Who was he to have done this!* He had taken from them something that could never be replaced. Could they ever sleep safely at night again?

He has to die, she told her companions, *if only for taking away our peace.*

He knew they would. He'd done it. He'd penetrated their most powerful fortress and shattered the illusion that they were safe.

He dimly pondered that it was what the Resistance had done wrong in all its negotiations – tried to respect their claim to safety, which was their right to wallow in their own fear.

They looked at him now, safe from the reach of the knife. They looked at him sadly.

'Why?' An old lady spoke in the common language.

He didn't know what to tell her, but he cast away the knife.

Then the guards came, took his consciousness, and carried him bound before the king and queen of the land.

His head was swimming. He could scarcely breath. They had him on some toxins how, bathed in some morbid light that drained his strength and will. He knew it would eventually take his life if he didn't leave soon. The grigs had left him, and the bindings where Brek'anarl had broken his arms dully ached, as did his wrists. He was tied by rope to a wooden beam that forced him into the constant pain of somewhere between kneeling and standing.

They came in then. The king and queen of the 'bikies'. She had an enormous bruise that blackened both her eyes and yellowed her skin right down her left cheek. She had been weeping profusely, he could tell.

As had her man. They were all in great pain, all indignant.

Matrix supposed it was his last day on in this world.

'What *are* you!' The man demanded. It was not quite the question Matrix had expected.

Matrix struggled to stand, to look him in the eyes. But it was not possible.

'I am an emissary from the Resistance, your honour, and it is a pleasure for my people to meet you.'

He heard the man gasp.

The field strengthened until Matrix cried out. He'd been in pain many times before, but this was unique. It was lethargy to the point of agony. He'd need to find a new coping mechanism this time, and he felt his soul stretch at the thought.

'This hurts,' was all he could say.

The woman let out a single weep.

The man marched right into the circle and grabbed him by the hair of his head, yanking him up to look in his eyes.

'You don't know pain, human! What have you done?' He hissed.

'Thought I'd pay you a house call,' Matrix stumbled, trying to be cheeky in his agony.

The man let his head drop, scowling at his cockiness. 'You don't know what it's like to live in a world that hates every day of your existence! Even our children, born to this world, know to loath it. We do not belong here. Some few, some few find peace behind their great wall, but they are dead to us. Now we are alone, and all hunt us, even *your* kind. So we send out the talons, to rake the boarders of our lands and oppress our enemies, but no, it is not enough. Somehow you, you alone manage to penetrate our boarders and assault our queen!'

He hit him then, hard across his face. Matrix expected many more blows, but that man stood up and composed himself, almost embarrassed. It was the most extraordinary sight, *so there were 'right ways' to torture an assassin?* He wondered.

The man he assumed king continued, 'is that why you came, soldier? As punishment for our victories? We've never touched your heartland, though it was often in our power to do so. Even the mutants who are *filth* are safe in their heartlands. Have you come to spread fear among us? Or perhaps are you from the Oppression, we've seen their build up, watched them cross the boarders of their wall these past few days. Their numbers are vast this time. What are you up to, I wonder? We're used to them sending spies to stir us up against the others. But none ever strayed so close to our heartland... I will have the truth from you...'

Matrix straightened himself as much as he could, looked about the room. The guards were sad, a mix of vengeance and fear in their faces despite their professional façade. Matrix looked at the queen. She was visibly shaken, and with her, her people too. Matrix tried to speak, his voice ragged, his mouth dry.

'Tell me, honoured King. Are your people free?'

'Free? Not at all, foolish stupid human. Why would you ask? But we are free to live in our boarders as we feel, safe. That is, until you came-'

But Matrix knelt up, indignant with courage though his voice struggled from cracked, dry lips. 'I tell you, you are *not* free. You are held prisoner, all of you, by your own *fear*.' He licked his clammy lips, speaking in great fervour with his agony. 'You attack others on the chance that they *might* offer a threat? You oppress yourselves with rules and tyranny, refusing to let yourselves *dance* because you might be heard! You teach your children to hate their world instead of seeing it for all the beauty *you've* created here. I see now why the Oppression leaves your people, for the most part, alone. You have imprisoned yourselves.'

The King looked at him, wild ferocity in his eyes, his breath ragged. For the longest moment, he had nothing to say in the face of unmitigated truth. Matrix let his head drop in exhaustion.

'You don't know what you're talking about,' said the King deadenly, and he was about to activate the field to maximum. But his wife stopped him. She brought her hand up, and the man whirled around in concern. She stepped up, put a hand on his shoulder, and looked at Matrix. She stepped right into their field, and he looked up to see her. In her eyes he was surprised to see... kindness.

'I see now. Wh... that is why... that is why you did this to me.'

He looked up at her. She looked young, though she was surely many decades old, her eyes were far too wise. She reached down to him them, and held his face while she looked deeply into his eyes. 'You were trying to show us what others have tried to tell us, even our own prophets. Our enemy ignores us because we're too frightened to be a threat. Our safety here is ... just an illusion. We are prisoners not because we're here, but because we are... afraid.'

'Darling please-' her husband began.

'No,' she said firmly. 'It is time.'

Then, she held Matrix's head in her hands. Matrix, the one who'd injured her and assaulted the peace of her entire people. She kissed him gently on the forehead. Then, without comment, begun to remove the ropes from his arms.

The guards were astonished.

Her husband, speechless.

And in spite himself, Matrix fell into her arms, and wept like a child.

---+++---+++---+++---

When the Bikies, or the Tendendalaah as they were known to themselves, came out fighting, they came out fighting hard. They immediately threw their lot in with the Resistance, opening their lands and resources to a full alliance with them. There was no compromise in their trust, and they were true allies in the full sense of the word. It was a complete change of destiny the Resistance had never expected, a surprise from which they never fully recovered.

The Oppression was knocked seriously back by the unprecedented attack, being forced back right to the wall. With the unexpected loss of the granite pass, their forces were held up, massed at the fields of plenty. Within a day the entire contingent belonged to the combined forces of the New Resistance and the Tendendalaah – the biggest single loss to the city in the entire history of the planetoid, their soldiers minds maimed beyond service with the brutal efficiency of the 'Bikies'.

Yet it was still many weeks after the Tendendalaah had ceased the fear raids into nearby territory before they sent a message of peace to the Mutants – the first ever message ever sent. A lone rogue general of many years took a contingent of his best soldiers. Then, the entire flotilla of bikes passed within battle range of mutant territory, banners held high, weapons disarmed, the thunder of their bikes muted to a musical harmony that echoed quietly through the trees for many kilometres. It was, for many generations, the single bravest act the Tendendalaah had ever witnessed, and each soldier became a legend for courage.

For the mutant's part, they did not know what to make of the banners, or the weapons. But the sound was unlike they had ever known, and they listened in respectful silence. One lone general, a veteran of many years, met the Tendendalaah out in the open with a handful of his best warriors and shaman. They kept their eyes on their enemies chests, faced their palms and weapons to the earth, walked with a slow gait of frequent pauses. He then raised his voice in a single deep note, which was joined by others of his throng, till they matched the harmonies of the Tendendalaah.

The Tendendalaah did not know what to make of the watching, or the weapons, or the walking. But they did recognise the harmony.

Then, for the first time in history, the two parted in peace.

By the evening, the Mutants had drawn their forces almost completely from the boarders with the Tendendalaah, and threw them squarely at the remaining garrisons posted against the wall, devastating the Oppression's offensive.

And, of course, no one inside that wall suspected a thing.

Alasia's recovery

It was all over the news. A massacre. Inside the wall.

The Resistance had to be stopped. It was what they were all saying. A dozen men slain, three still missing. They'd replayed it from all angles as the witnesses had seen it. They were told some residents had tried to apprehend a pair of high level Resistance agents.

Everyone was indignant.

You could feel it in the air.

'There'll be war,' the husband was saying, 'and it will be brief. The Resistance is too poorly manned and equipped to deal with a full assault by the black guard.'

The couple had found her, stumbling around the lower levels. They'd assumed she was recovering from some toxin, and taken her kindly in. They were a young couple.

They had no idea.

None at all - that she had done this, that she was working for the Oppression at the time, that it was those 'innocent residents' that were trying to create a revolution.

It was fortunate that she'd adopted a new image. She'd returned to her original one as soon as she'd found their terminal, and they didn't seem to notice.

'Honey, don't think of enlisting,' the wife replied.

He grunted in frustration. 'Don't think I'm not thinking of it!' He replied, expressing the twitch of fear they all felt as anger for them both. 'How dare they? It's not as if we don't give them a life of their own choosing! Why'd they have to come and ruin our own?'

Alasia bit her tongue. He had no idea. No idea of what the Oppression did to people outside, and inside the wall. They were blind too. They wanted to think they lived in paradise, but were numb to the price it cost them.

All the Resistance wanted to do was leave. All they focused on was their own self defence, when they weren't being puppets for the Oppression. Now that the Resistance leaders were again outside the wall, what would happen to them? Would they find a way to leave Seren? But they weren't allowed. And all some of them had done to deserve this... was ask too many questions.

Why was that a crime?

The wife consoled: 'Honey, those citizens kind of brought it on themselves, trying to arrest those Resistance people. They should have left it to the black guards.'

He huffed into a chair, switching channels compulsively. Alasia sneered at his ignorant, self-righteous anger. They must have sensed something. A moment later he gestured towards her, and the wife came to sit by Alasia's side.

'Are you all right dear? Do you want to tell us what happened?'

Alasia shook her head all too sincerely.

'It's all right dear... It's not toxins, is it?' She whispered.

Alasia smiled. Better to leave them in their own misconceptions than to lie. She held out her bowl for some more soup.

The wife smiled. She was so kind.

Her guide found her a day later, just as she was beginning to wonder what to do next. The husband had begun to insist that she see a hospital, and she'd slipped away from them with valid pretext as soon as she could, being careful to set up a false hospital record for herself of a successful discharge and replacement in society before doing so, toxins rehab and all.

Her guide had found her just after that.

They were sitting in a park bench now, watching children play. He was fully healed, which made her wonder, but she didn't ask.

He was actually smiling. 'Well, that was a disaster,' he finally said.

She grimaced.

'I didn't see it coming, and I'm usually the first to know. I cannot express my apologies enough, Alasia. I volunteer to be your guide, and you've lived to see my first two failures in over twenty years.'

He sighed heavily. 'Seems our benevolent government has found a cause for it pretty quickly though, haven't they?' He mumbled to himself. 'Declaring open war on the Resistance.'

'What's going to happen to them?' Alasia asked, thinking better of it far too late.

'It's going to get pretty hot for them for a while, I suppose. Don't really know – I keep my work inside the wall. I'll be honest with you Alasia, because you'll need to know. It's kept me from a promotion, this "inside the wall" policy.'

He looked at her, sincerity lolling from his features.

But she was secretly frightened for her friends. However, she couldn't just slip away. Somehow he'd managed to find her again, just as she was wondering if it might be a chance to do just that. Besides, how could she apologise to them all, what excuse could she give for needing to run off? For needing to get rid of... a stone.

'I think they were just looking for a reason actually,' he suddenly said. 'We just gave them that. If I have any access to information it is that the black guard have been pouring over the walls these past few days. Something massive has happened, and not in the way the Government would have liked. So they'll be looking to increase the forces... They just needed an excuse.'

'Hmmm,' was all she said, hiding a mountain underneath that sound.

'Well!' He said, slapping his hand on his knee. 'Let's get back to it!'

She was a little surprised then. Didn't he want to know how she'd done it? Wasn't he curious how she'd escaped sixty desperate Rei-nati in their own snare? Hadn't he seen the footage of her twisting in the air?

'I think it's time we took a little detour from our normal search, lay 'low' for a moment, if you will. There is something I'd like to you know.'

'What is that?' she asked, politely filling her role in the conversation.

'Do you know who your parents are?'

That hit a nerve. She almost shook in surprise. It took a moment for her to reply, but did so with more emotion in her voice than she wanted. She was frightened that there was nothing that could be hidden from him. What kind of a spy was he?

'I was raised by only carers,' she replied, trying to sound calm.

He huffed.

'It's not that unusual.'

He was quiet for a moment. 'What is your earliest memory, Alasia?'

She thought carefully, not sure she wanted to take this detour. 'I was about seven, they took me to meet a new class of girls in the school where I worked.'

'Why are your hands shaking?' He asked.

She looked down. They were clenched into fists.

'Oh,' was all she said.

'Alasia,' he lectured, almost kindly. 'If there is one thing a career in espionage has taught me, it's that the most important kind of secret to know is the secrets you keep from yourself.'

Her heart felt dark. She did not want to do this.

But she knew she would, if he wanted her to.

'You know, most people start forming memories from around three, and most have one or two from even before then. You have a perfect memory Alasia, yet you cannot remember what happened to you before you started school, at seven?' He emphasised.

She sighed. So they were going to take this journey.

'Before we can resume our quest for the Rei-nati. There's something you need to know.'

'I need to know my parents,' she said flatly.

He smiled. 'No, just your father…'

Undersea

'It's been a fascinating time!' The scientist was explaining animatedly to Matrix. 'Since you brought the ocean to our attention we've been sending down probes every day to try and get a better look. Turns out there are whole nations down there, the whales seem mostly to be in charge. The others diplomats haven't had much success so they're sending you in! I wish I could be there …' he sighed wistfully.

The scientist ranted on some more while Matrix pretended to listen, it had all been in the briefing last week day. Things had moved incredibly quickly since his success with the Tendendalaah. Now, apparently, he was legend. Everywhere he went people seemed to know him, and someone had already offered to write his bibliography.

But he hadn't had time for that. The defeat of the Oppression back to the walls had meant the Resistance had some time to think again, and immediately the Circle had called him and Bakerson back for a "secret project."

He was going under the waters.

They'd set up some form of deep cavern research facility over the ocean, and it hung precariously to the enormous room like a metal spider. He was sequestered deep inside the facility - encased now, as he had been for two days, inside an egg shaped container of steel and glass, breathing the water that surrounded him and permeated the gills he'd been growing in that time. They were ready now, and so was he. Twelve hours of meditation a day while they grew was getting on his nerves.

But they said it would be the best way. They said he needed to swim about unimpeded, and finding oxygen directly from the water was the best way to do it. The steel egg was slowly building up to match the enormous pressures of the deep ocean, and as soon as his body was physiologically prepared, they'd drop him in and let him swim around.

'… enormous fins so you'll have to watch the bow waves…oh!' The scientist was suddenly cut off. He stepped back, and Matrix pressed his face up to the glass to try and get a better look at what had cut the irrepressible man voice short, but it was futile to expect much from his vantage point.

A tall, ebony skinned man with dark eyes, who looked like he'd be in about his fifties, stood up to the glass. 'Hello Matrix, it's nice to finally meet you in person.'

His voice sounded familiar.

'Well, nice to meet you too! I'd offer my hand, but…'

'No need,' he replied, and Matrix almost smiled to himself that the other hadn't realised he was being flippant.

'I am I-olo Tilk.'

'Uh ha…'

'I'm on the Circle.'

'Oh! That, um, the Circle. Right, now I know you.'

The older man looked a bit surprised at that.

'Well,' said Matrix in a friendly manner, 'I'm very glad to meet you to. How are things there now?'

'You have met me… Well, never mind. The Circle, well, as well as can be expected, since the Oppression has decided to eradicate us. The new allies you've found are, well, saving our lives actually.'

'Well, don't thank me. They just found what they needed to free themselves, I'm sure. But they are nice people though. Not all people though,' he started getting thoughtful. 'Anyway! Back to the now. So they told me the other diplomats hadn't succeeded talking to the whales. I saw the synaptic downloads of their experiences. Really strange place. Fish just keep swimming away eh?'

'Indeed. We don't seem to be able to get them to communicate with us. We are still trying, of course, and we're thankful you're willing to be a part of that.'

'Yeah, 'bout that. Do you think you could suspend all other divers for a day, at least, my intuition tells me I need to do this alone,' he said, boldly.

I-olo looked surprised, again. The scientists objected, but with a wave the Circle leader granted his request. 'Seems odd, but I've a policy of allowing people to do as they choose. Your methods are... unique... but perhaps this situation calls for your gift of being lateral more than ours, or of relying on experience. What does concern me is your deep reliance on your intuition. The best priests we have are sometimes wrong on their intuition. Why have you had so much luck?'

'Luck?' Matrix scoffed. 'You know that has nothing to do with it. Intuition is governed by affirmation; by the beliefs we have about ourselves and the universe. And you already know from my details that I possess an unusually high syncopathic resonance.'

'Indeed, a powerful side effect of being true to oneself. So what is it, Matrix, what affirmations drive you that may have evaded the rest of us for so long?'

'I honestly have no idea!' he laughed, turning a slow backflip in his bowl. Then he grew serious once more. 'Perhaps... it's not wanting. No, not "not" wanting, but more like allowing. I just believe that everything will work out for the best in the end, and if it doesn't work out, it's not supposed to. So I just allow things, and go with my feelings and intuition about what needs to be changed. I only fight when I have to. Things have always worked out for me.'

I-olo seemed lost in thought. 'Hmmm,' he finally said, 'in any event, we're not sending you down with any weapons, so I've assured the Circle you won't cause another incident like with the Tendendalaah.'

Matrix nodded, but could help smile to himself. He'd hidden his motile bronze knife right as a bracelet next two him for two days; a little easier when it can change shape. 'Yeah. Like the Tendendalaah. Or like challenging Brek'anarl for sole leadership of the mutant's, right?'

347

I-olo lost his smile.

Matrix looked him in the eye. 'Don't worry. I believe in this cause just as much as you do,' he said in perfect sincerity.

They just looked at each other a moment. Eventually I-olo must have decided that he'd still made the right decision sending this untested maverick into the Eversea, and nodded.

Matrix nodded in return, and then asked. 'Any word from Commander Sheelaakah, and the others of my original team?'

I-olo looked surprised. 'Let me see, Bakerson is tending to the troupes around this station actually. He has them working double time even though they are unlikely to see any action this far below the surface. Unit leader Skion has been posted to the front lines. I can have him recalled if you wish?'

'Not really, thanks.'

'The spy Alasia, well, future spy anyway. No word as yet since you lost contact in the underfoundaries.'

He paused till Matrix could stand it no longer. '...and the Commander?'

I-olo did not meet his gaze.

'The Commander has not, as yet, recovered from her psychosis in the underfoundaries, just as the Oppression launches its most devastating assault... We've had an unfortunate development that we're looking into resolving. We've a legion of our best troupes on it right now. Don't worry Matrix, she is still alive.'

He didn't like hearing that. 'Is she all right?'

'We've got our best legion on it right now,' he evaded.

Matrix waited. '... but is she all right?'

'She'll see her way through,' he promised sadly.

The course of healing

They were much more careful the second time. They'd sent some other high ranking telepathic officer to try and curb her new enthusiasm for causing suffering. She was sorely needed, they'd told her that. The Oppression was massing an enormous offensive. Her skills were needed, and she could not cause a political scandal like she just had, it might cause resentment, or worse, psychic backlash. Even enemies needed to be treated better than being driven to insanity.

But Sheelaakah ignored all that. She was working on something too important to care, and she knew where she was truly needed. She worked day and night to restore her brother.

One morning, after an hours sleep, it was then that she'd realised with pure clarity why she was failing. She needed more power, the sort that came from the world itself. Her brother was here, somewhere still. He was looking for her, and she had to find him again, and bring him back to life... she'd seen it happen to the child.

So the next morning she took a simple levitating trolley, placed him on it, and walked out. Nobody stopped her. Nobody smiled. They'd stopped doing that a while ago, she dimly vexed.

'Commander Sheelaakah, where are you going?' It was a legion of elite. Their Commander approached her, blocking her way. She looked up at him. He wasn't thinking of baring her way, which was wise, but more on getting her attention.

'You are a Command level individual of the Resistance. It is not safe for you to leave without escort,' he said.

She would have scolded at him but seemed to lack the energy, 'If you must,' she replied in a whisper.

They travelled then, for just over two hours, right up to the surface to some cliffs overlooking a large lake. The grass was moist with dew. Very few creatures dwelt here, it wasn't as safe with the Roc's, hippogriffs, and airborne Frieeg that nested here. She wasn't worried, but she was grateful when they set up a perimeter and forcefield, laying runes all along the edge. They'd found the ley line easily, an invisible conduit or meridian of energy that ran along planetoids surface.

She bent her mind to the task, and so intent was she on finding her brother's soul print that she didn't even hear the first shots. It wasn't until a solider fell, wounded, that she returned her mind to the place where she was. It was then that she noticed the enormous sky cruiser landing scarce meters from their location on the ley line, its energy field clashing visibly with the warding zone. The battle with the scattered black guards ceased as it landed, but she willed their minds to sleep even so.

'... should retreat back into the caverns,' the other Commander had been shouting at her.

'I will deal with this,' she replied dimly, totally unaware if she had the strength to or not.

'Who is it?' a solider asked.

'Can't tell,' Commander Sheelaakah confessed. Whomever was on that ship was well shielded. But rather than spend her strength breaking through it, she decided to wait. A moment later the ship opened out, and single man walked out, his ankle length hair lolling in the breeze. It was Token, the psychic that had tried to stop them in the city, and which she'd easily defeated. The telepath that was Taalk's assistant the day her brother first left.

'You *again?*' Sheelaakah hissed, annoyed at his interruption. 'I thought I'd dealt with you at some tavern in the city.'

'Sheelaakah,' he tasted each syllable like a sweet, pealed grape. 'You underestimate my power. I've come for you. You're not well, and I'm going to make you better now. It's time to stop the fighting.'

She didn't even register the mountains of amorosity he was sending her way. He was a gnat, and she had more pressing matters to attend to.

'I'm busy,' she replied. 'Go away, or I will finish what we started.'

He looked at her brother's body, squinting, trying to recognise it.

'But... he's dead,' he said.

'Now you will join him,' Sheelaakah hissed.

'Do you recognise *this?*' He emphasised, thrusting an amulet from under his tunic towards her before she could act on her hatred.

'Yes,' she said plainly. 'It is the amulet of Thith. We knew Taalk had died for his choices at the foundries. Apparently, the Oppression chose you as he's successor, though I cannot see why.'

He narrowed his eyes at her. 'I have increased tenfold in power since our last meeting, a hundred fold since the day we first met. And I've not stopped thinking of you every day, *every day!* And you still treat me like an unschooled telepath? You mock me at every turn?' He clenched his fist in frustration.

Then it began to sink into her consciousness with a glimmer of amusement. This boy had a crush on her. The laughter and mockery were evident in her face, though she didn't need to say anything for him to know how she felt. Some part of her, deep down, was screaming out to be heard. Had she had her full faculty she might have understood the danger they were in, or at least the unparalleled opportunity it was to confront the Oppression's lead psychic unprotected on the gang plank of his ship.

As it was, her sanity had taken leave some time ago.

He crumpled inside at her amusement, then he smiled wickedly at her, 'Once you know me,' he explained, 'you will find our souls were *meant* to be entwined.'

The Resistance soldiers looked at each other.

'Go die,' Sheelaakah ordered.

'Perhaps, but I'll take all your soldiers with me.'

She paused. The unit telepath, an older man, turned to her suddenly and said 'don't.' Perhaps he realised what she was going to do before she did, but she did it anyway.

'Then you fight is just with me,' she told Token. 'Let it be, one on one.'

'Agreed,' he quickly said, adopting a warrior stance behind his runes and protections that prevented the elite from shooting him where he stood. If this was to be a telepathic battle, it would be telepaths alone.

Her unit leader quickly stepped in front of her. 'Commander, it's a -'

But he fell over before he could finish the sentence, asleep. Sheelaakah was outside field before anyone else could get in her way.

'Ah my soul mate,' he crooned. 'Come to me.'

The wind began whipping up around her feet, her eyes blazing.

'Foolish, lost woman,' he amused.

She knew he was capable, but she didn't think he'd cheat. She didn't even see him activate the neuroinhibiting crystal from inside his ship, wasn't even conscious by the time she hit the ground. She didn't hear as swarms of the Oppression burst from the ship, was unaware of the desperate battle that followed, and didn't move as Token, leader of the telepathic wing of the Oppression, gently carried her limp body into his retreating ship.

---++---++---

They'd fought so well! Token mused. Even for elite, he'd still had to call in the backup support, and they'd lost twice their projected outcomes. They had fought like dragons to protect her. They didn't even have time to claim the bodies for the Seren dream before more of their people begun to arrive. He'd had to beat a hasty retreat.

But he had her. They were already operating on her, rearranging her mind, weakening her defences. But he wouldn't let them harm her, not while she could still choose him. Not while she could, at last, be his.

He trembled in anticipation.

The whales

At the end of the hour the steel egg crashed down, lightning streaming across its surface continually as it fell. It ploughed into the waters below, Matrix protected from the blow by the strength of the egg. For a time he waited, inexplicably nervous, till he centred himself again. The egg floated downwards for many minutes, and the water was completely dark by the time it began to crack open. It would wait here for his return.

It was pitch black, yet Matrix could sense creatures out there, watching him. Most were quickly unimpressed, and continued what they were doing. Others continued to watch.

He activated his aura stone. In its invisible light he was able to sense the creatures swimming nearby him. An eel there, a deep fish there. He set his personal energy field to repulsion, just in case any lesser intelligence should consider eating him.

With a twist of his will he took out his knife from its hiding place.

And that was when they chose to speak to him

Put that down, they said. *You'll not be of needing your weapon here.*

Then he saw them, through the aura stone. They began to light up with their own aura light – massive beings, wide as a man is tall, as long as six men stretched out.

Whales.

He'd never seen one before, and was terrified at first. But they just sat there, behemoths of the deep, regarding him with wise, powerful eyes.

The dolphin said your coming was of today, one of them said.

Matrix looked out and up at them. They were huge, with flat faces that could crush a man against his ship, and dozens of sharp teeth that could tear his flesh. They were scarred beings too, one bearing rows of round scars that must have been made by a huge squid like monster.

Slowly, carefully, Matrix returned his knife.

You're going is with us, they told him. Politely, yet forcefully.

He tried to swim to keep up, but even at their leisurely pace he begun to tire after a few minutes. One moved to offer its flipper, but another forbade it. He pushed on, descending deeply into the darkness. But his new gills and the unfamiliar experience of swimming grew increasingly difficult till he numbly requested the consenting whales fin. The descent thereafter was far easier, yet so long and deep, and he almost fell asleep.

The Seer, the Narwhale, will of speaking be to you. Your visit of us is anticipated.

Their language was strange, or familiar. It was as if they were trying to compress great ideas into a clumsy single linear sentence. It would take time for the Resistance to develop a synaptic download that made sense of it all.

One moment, Matrix realised, 'anticipated'?

Matrix came right to attention as he realised they'd told him that he was expected, but they gave him the definite impression that he was not welcome to ask any questions yet. He'd already gotten further in one minute that than six weeks of professional diplomats had, just by being.

He felt the water push sideways against him then, and saw the whales correcting for their motion as well. Something truly massive had just passed beside them. One of them then spoke, and it felt like it was grinning as it said, *a Leviathan honours us as with her presence.*

Matrix looked about, he could see nothing in the dark. But then he noticed a broad, round mezzanine underneath them. It appeared to be following them, and it was far larger than all three whales combined.

With a jolt of panic, Matrix realised: it was an eye.

He felt its mind as it receded into the darkness. It was amused. It was a living being, perhaps several kilometres long, and it pondered away as though he were a little amusement...

Amazing.

The whales continued their dive for at least another five minutes, possibly travelling in a deep spiral. He was taken down till eventually they reached a round stone floor, seeming to float in the darkness. Phosphorescent algae lit the edges of the stone - it was ancient. Surrounded by decrepit pillars with strange markings he did not recognise, in the dim light small insects swam and occasionally disappeared into the slithering forms of the deep eels. His banding indicated he was several hundred kilometres under the surface now.

The whales watched him, and he pondered for a moment how they managed to breathe, or hold their breath so long. But before he could ponder long a reverent mood settled on the darkness, and a pale green whale with a single unicorn-like tusk swam slowly into view.

Speaker for men, it began in a clear voice. *I welcome you to the darkness below... I am Jindari Ptargarindi. Seer of my people. We've been waiting for you. Your visit is long foretold.*

It paused, as if savouring the moment, looking him up and down. *You are much younger, than I had expected.*

'I wish...' Matrix began, realising they could not understand his speech. *I am honoured to meet you, Jindari, Seer of the people below the Eversea. I wish...*

But the whale cut him off gently. *You're coming is long foretold, speaker for men. You will be pleased to know we have been preparing for a very long time for this event. Our ancestors saw this day, and told their children, and their children's children. We have been preparing well.*

Then they were there - thousands of them.

Thousands of whales out into the darkness reaching further than he could possibly perceive.

We are ready to go to war.

Matrix's thoughts must have sounded like an enormous *huh?*! But he recovered and managed a diplomatic, *We are honoured.*

The whale seemed amused.

We've been waiting for you, it swam up close then to look at him with one eye, so he could clearly see every wrinkle and barnacle on its skin. So close, he could have touched it.

This world is a prison, and you are its key. It is time for my people to go home, it is time to free the ancestors who died in this place, to free them to their final rest. Death is too silent in this place. We cannot abide it.

But how? Matrix asked, not understanding in the least what the whale meant, but curious to know how they intended to help.

The weapons of man are strange, made of materials. The minds of man are strange, forgetful and incoherent. Have you learnt yet how to move the waves? How to sing across a world? How to call in the winter through your song? Your race is young, and strange.

It paused, swimming about him thoughtfully. *I see in your mind a great barrier. Is this the barrier which you wish to break down? Life gives us many barriers.* It mused. *Some are to protect us, some are to guide us. Some make us prisoners, and some define us, like the air above – we may not go where the deep waters lie not. But we have learnt long ago from worlds before your memory. We have studied the deep arts of the leviathan, the spirit star travel of the Kirid, the long songs of the cephalopod. Water may help overcome stone - we will bring the waters to battle the barrier we both loath.*

Matrix was perplexed. What was happening?

It swam so close its eye was level with his.

We've been waiting for you. Tell them, tell your men folk. When the time comes... we will join the fight. We would also be free of this oppressive world.

The intensity of its thoughts was almost overwhelming.

Then, it nodded, turned and the swarm began to disperse.

Wait, may I, may we, can we send others to... talk? Matrix stumbled.

It turned back. *There is nothing your people can offer us, and you have not the patience to learn our songs. Why send others?*

There are some who would. Some I've personally met who would not stop talking to learn about you. If we've nothing you want, perhaps you may teach us, helping a younger species?

If whales laughed, it did. *Very well then, send others. They can wait at your little egg. If others of my kin will speak to them, let it be their choice.*

And with a swish of its tale, it was gone.

Matrix breathed a sigh of relief. *That was easy...*

They were ENORMOUS!

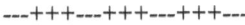

The anesthetising blast hit him square in the chest. He recovered in seconds as a trained warrior might, but by then the scientist who'd spoken non-stop had him pinned to a wall with some kind of anesthetising rod; his eyes blank, his banding removed. An individual with dark, translucent skin suddenly gripped Matrix by the throat. It spoke in an opaque, thirsty voice.

'Matrix. So the honour of your death goes to me, does it?'

He had no way of knowing the trap he was walking in to as soon as he stepped from the steel egg. Perhaps there were clues: the wooden, silent way the researches went about their work. The unexpected jolt as the egg sat down on the landing platform. The unusually short time they decided he needed to acclimatise to the pressure...

'Wh...' he could not speak, the creature held his larynx. It was very uncomfortable, and due to the anesthetising rod he could not move.

'They tell me not to talk to the marks, they do. But I've such a taste for squeezing the life from another victim... and you've been such a difficult quarry, even for a hunter like myself.' He smiled, as the light begun to pulsate with Matrix struggling heartbeat.

'Almost caught you at the Bikies, but you'd moved in then by then. To dangerous, that place. Can't believe you came out again! Slippery, I said. Yet here you are! Caught in my grip.'

The grip intensified

He could not move his arms. He could not breathe.

He looked over at the scientist. The one that had spoken to him so enthusiastically. His eyes were pale and dim – some form of mental control from the translucent humanoid. Matrix struggled for breath.

'Why?' He whispered.

'You don't know? Three alliances? The New response? Not to mention the deaths in the granite pass… you're a bigger fool than I'd expected. Our last message to you is this - *no one* resists the Government of Seren…'

The hand increased till Matrix begun to feel his consciousness slip from him. In the dimness of his vision, he saw the creature pull out a knife, the scientist staring dispassionately as he held him helpless against the steel egg.

So this is how it ends?

Suddenly the assassin's hand lost its grip. The rod that pressed him to the egg slackened, and in that moment all feeling returned Matrix arms. He looked over at the scientist, who was shaking his head in confusion, colour returning to his iris'.

He glanced quickly to the assassin, a dark stain of blood flowed on his clothes. It looked down in surprise where the head of a spear now partly protruded from its chest.

With a cry of hatred it moved to strike its knife at Matrix, but a twist of that spear and sudden pull backwards prevented it from landing an injurious blow.

With a roar of anger Matrix thrust the palms of his hands into the creature's forehead, snapping its neck. Then Matrix collapsed on the floor.

In the next moment strong hands lifted him up to his feet, and strong arms embraced him. He knew those arms, he knew that nose. It was Bakerson.

The older man held back a tear.

'Found you,' he said in quiet victory.

'How?' Matrix choked, still trying to find his breath, and meaning, after the unexpected assault.

'Twice minute security scans showed an anomaly,' he said, clearing his throat.

'Isn't Resistance protocol every three minutes?'

'Yep.'

'Oh,' Matrix said, unwordfully grateful he had a friend like Glenn Bakerson.

'What ha…' the scientist began, then seeing the creature dead on the floor, Bakerson's spear in the centre of its growing pool of blood, he threw up.

'Twice minute eh! Good show! Guess we'd better get back to Resistance HQ then!' Matrix said gleefully, handing the scientist a towel. 'I've got some *very* good news.'

How to imprison a telepath

Commander Sheelaakah was somewhere dark. It was an unfamiliar place. Then almost immediately the lights came on. She was on a comfortable bed, her copper banding removed. The powerful crystal on the roof made it impossible for her to stand up or move from that bed, not without destroying it first, and she had no weapons at hand. She was annoyed, she wanted to get back to healing her brother.

She looked around the room. It was clean, comely, inviting. Mostly wood panelling, some kinds of saffron spice in the air. A warm sunlight breezed in through a slatted window carved with intricate patterns. If she wasn't a prisoner it would beautiful place to rest.

But there was equipment there too. Sentinels disguised as lamps, a medicine module looking like a bed side table, and who knew what lay behind the ornate wood panelled walls.

Almost immediately he point tessered into the room.

Naturally she attacked him. But her skills were inexplicably weak, they'd done something to her. That, combined with the inhibition fields of the medical room she was in, and his powerful banding and talent, meant she was soon overcome and forced to listen while he spoke.

'As you see, you are no longer a match for me.'

'What do you want from me?' she whispered, for it was all she could do. She thought of her brother. He was waiting for her. This annoying boy was taking up precious time.

'Sheelaakah, he's dead,' he pressed his mind against hers, but decided, for now, not to force the memory out of her.

She cried in bitter anger.

He looked at her kindly, taking a seat to sit by her bed.

'They wanted to template you, you know. Use your mind as a structure for a new amulet, or perhaps improve the banding. But I wouldn't let them, Sheelaakah. I... I need you,' he said, turning to her, face and features honest.

'Your attraction to me makes you pathetic,' she hissed.

He looked at her then, seeming sad. He stood up, and looked out the window. 'I tried to ignore it, then suppress it, but I cannot. I *need* you. We're soul mates,' he said, unrepentantly convinced.

She screamed, and struggled to get up from the invisible bonds on her bed. He seemed to know better than to let her go, but he flew from the window to try and console her like a child. She shrieked and writhed violently against his touch.

He sat back, looking hurt.

'You don't understand, this isn't you...' he plead.

'Get away from me!' she tried to shout.

He stood up, stone faced.

'Very well then. We do this the hard way. Guardians! Take her to the chamber of prayers!'

Alasia's father

It is a room that is not a room, Alasia thought. So dark and dishevelled, it was impossible to fathom a path through the mountains of books and piles of old papers. Various samples of some biological goo, and countless scans, lay in barely organised chaos around the room. Presumably there was some kind of order to it all or else the sole occupant would not have insisted on carrying the program all inside his banding, strange though it was. They might have never found him if he hadn't called them over to the far end, where a lazy fire drearily lit the sole occupant, nonchalantly smoking his life away with some form of tobacco.

'You're late, Alasia,' he grumbled, and she faltered in her steps at the unexpected mention of her name. He must have heard it, for he laughed.

'Three months late, as a matter of fact. I would have expected better from someone of your talent, but then again, you were... designed with open parameters.' He mentioned among the shadows, his voice smiling. Her brow furrowed in puzzlement, but she continued walking – no need to hide her presence now. He wasn't even looking in her direction yet, but even in the dim light she could clearly see he was too short to be her biological father.

'And what is with this man with you? That's a little unprofessional of you. Don't you know the old tradition – you face your destiny alone?' He sighed.

Her guide closed the distance between them.

'You know, sir,' her father said, and for the first time he turned around in his luxurious armchair. 'I don't have the benefit of your name. My...

assistants... are usually very good at this sort of thing. Am I to assume that you too are part of the Resistance?'

Her guide did not answer, but looked to Alasia to encourage her to speak.

She furrowed her brow in confusion at her guides behaviour, but assumed his voice print was probably worth keeping a secret, for now. 'He's not. Neither am I, should you be interested... father.'

He looked up at her in surprise, oblivious to her swift change in topic. 'Oh! You know already! Very good. Very, very good! The others had all only guessed by the stage you're at now. Very good! Perhaps there's hope for you yet.' He said, clearly becoming excited by the prospect. He stood up to look her over.

'Good, good, good,' he crooned, carefully looking over her. Suddenly, in a vast breach of protocol, he grabbed her by the wrist and turned her unceremoniously towards the flames. 'Light up,' he commanded, and the fire place lit to a blazing shine. She had to cover her eyes. Her guide did not move the whole time.

'Nice... very nice,' the man crooned with undisguised interest. 'You turned out very well. Perfect, perfect. They told me you were a singer of some sort, but... are these...?'

He would have put his hands right on her torso if she hadn't smartly smacked them away. He looked indignant. He was short, somewhat misshapen, and his skin bore strange pock marks from untreated acne as a teenager - odd, especially for this world. He had a sparse, unkempt beard, and his hair was equally uncared for. He wore some form of long pale jacket over what may have been a chequered shirt, both looking like they were never changed in the past thirty years since he may have acquired them. His aura was a tangle of intelligence, selfishness and arrogance - he wore his debauchery like a mantle. Clearly, he was a man at peace with his own darkness.

But he stood back now. 'Fair enough,' he said, with little resignation. 'Do you want to know why you've come to see me?'

The audacity made her laugh. The man glanced up at her and went back to his fire staring. Her guide held his breath. She could tell she had made some form of mistake. She was used to being in charge...

He's making this easy for you Alasia, feed his ego and he'll tell us everything. Overpower him, and you may make him malleable, but he'll never consider you harmless.

She stilled herself. She realised now, her father was frightening her. He was not at all... fatherly. But she could handle this.

'You are a strange man, much stranger that I expected,' she confessed, perhaps ignoring her guide's advice.

A long pause passed between them.

'You all come to me like this,' he mused possessively in his small, thin voice. 'So randomly, inexplicably confident. You think you are owed a world, but I tell you that you do not belong to any world. Else why...'

He looked up at her intensely, stopping midsentence, then some idea crossed his face.

'You... you don't know!' It made him laugh, not menacingly, but with selfish pride as though he'd successfully kept a secret from a child, the jubilant clap of his open palm against his thigh reinforcing that impression. 'You mean you don't know!'

He glared at her, his face an unreadable mix of disdain and delight. 'Come with me, child.' He said, leaping forward and grabbing her hand before she could pull it away. Her companion shrugged unsupportively as the man began pulling her towards a door, absent mindedly saying to himself. 'This, I'll have to see.'

She pulled her hand free, but he only checked to see which way her feet were moving. When he reached the door he looked up at her, through his strange glasses that made his eyes seem inhumanly large.

'Don't you want to see, don't you want to understand it all where you came from? You will, because I'm going to tell you anyway. You need to understand what it is you were meant to become. It's the best way for all of us, you'll see,' he spoke, from sincere yet dark enthusiasm.

'I'll tolerate your story, old man,' she told him coolly. He was not what she'd expected from the man the census listed, that genealogical phenology had declared to be her 'father'.

He smiled. 'You're not like the others, little more, independent.'

So her father was impressed after all. She smiled at her guide, there were other ways to make men malleable, she knew. Her guide also looked impressed, but it was a look the man didn't share. He didn't even look at either of them, but nodded as if to himself. He walked towards the door, the incorporeal guardians he shooed aside.

The room they entered was immaculately clean, even the dust ... ordered. Row upon row of vials and instruments clearly and professionally presented, positioned for maximum efficiency or optimum utility. He looked out of place amidst it all, yet walked among it with accustomed familiarity. Alasia recognised little of the implements, but of what she did, they were medical in nature – scrying globes, DNA realignment wands. Then to one side was a series of crystalline vessels large enough to fit a human inside, floating off the floor, their governing crystals floating lazily about them, glowing maternal pink. Something living was inside.

He was extraordinarily well funded.

'This is where it all happens, Alasia. My life's work!' He indicated around the room in pleasure. 'This is where I make them, and they come to life. They pass right up to the beginning of adolescence here, then I set them loose on the world. They learn so quickly, it's how I made them.'

'I don't follow what you mean,' she said drying, not wanting to find out. Her guide positioned himself by the only exit. He seemed relaxed, but she knew his deadliest weapons were only a thought away.

'Here, let me show you. This is the best way to find out,' the man she called father proclaimed.

He took a small device, a stone, and offered it to her. She looked at it disdainfully.

'Oh go on, don't be childish! It's just a magnifying stone, a school toy – it will allow us to see your cells, your molecules, quantum states, zero point, soul print, yadda, yadda, you name it. Don't tell me you've never looked at your life code before?' He said smiling mockingly.

He knew she hadn't.

'We don't have to, if you don't want to,' he said in false kindness.

She almost wanted to take him up on this second offer, but she could not restrain. This was what she had come to realise. She took the scrying stone, and holding it in the palm of her hand willed it to show her the code of life – her DNA...

But something was wrong. There were too few chromosomes in there. Two, when there should be twenty six. It must be a faulty stone, or perhaps it had picked up some mould or something – though it was supposed to know better. She'd look elsewhere.

Two again.

And again.

Everywhere she looked, it was the same. There were two when there should have been twenty six.

The scientist laughed. She had not noticed how quickly she was breathing. She looked up at him not understanding.

'You see! You see! Now you see the truth! '

She did not.

'You see it, don't you see it!' He was fairly screaming. 'Oh how can you not see it! It's right before your eyes, isn't it obvious what it means?!'

Her eyelids fluttered in stress, her mind a confusion of thoughts she could not make sense of. It was an experience she'd never had before.

'Alasia,' her "father" said unkindly, 'you're not human.'

'What?!' She said, her voice catching in her throat.

He laughed, the scientist - laughed in an unkind, mocking way. 'I can't believe you failed that test! You're the first! The *first*! Oh, this is rich, this is *rich*!'

She found his delight upsetting, but had not yet found her anger.

'Look around you!' He ordered.

Then she did, and stopped holding back the realisation that had nagged her since they'd first entered this room, since she'd first heard his name, since she'd first realised so many years ago that she was not like other girls.

Then ... what was she?

She walked among the equipment and crystals, she found herself facing the crystalline vessels. Like a driving compulsion her hesitant steps drove her towards them, and in spite her growing terror, she looked inside.

It was a child, a girl. About seven. She was attached through her stomach to the strange biological implement on the floor. She looked back with blank, unstaring eyes.

Alasia screamed.

'She cannot hear you, Alasia,' the scientist spoke, uncomfortably close. 'She's busy in the Evernet. You all were, all, when I first created you. Constantly learning your first lessons from the artificial reality that world creates – I think you're more natives to that world than this. I actually -'

'What am I?' Alasia demanded angrily.

'Our sister,' it was a female voice from the balcony above. They turned around now. Somehow, three tall females of perfect feminine proportions had entered into the room unseen, or had been there all the time. They looked almost alike, except their hair – black, burgundy, and blond.

'Ah, may I introduce you to my ... personal assistants. Alasia, your oldest living sisters; they call themselves Jinx, Poison and Envy. I made them with different colour hair so I could tell them apart.' He stared at them with unbridled pride and lust.

They stared back.

They were just like her, Alasia realised with both a tremor of excitement and a stab of tremendous fear. They were beautiful, but their beautiful faces hid a depth of treachery and deadly intelligence not to be underestimated. She did not need the crystal to tell her – the edges of their auras were very black. The one with black hair then looked at her guide whimsically, with both her eyes and hips. He merely raised his eyebrows as one might to playful teenager who didn't know what she was doing, and Alasia smiled on the inside.

'Such ... nice names,' she said sarcastically, and knew she had immediately made enemies of three people she knew she would never trust.

'They were the first,' the doctor said, ogling their every step as they made their way towards him down a spiral staircase. 'Well, the first successful ones anyway. They were batches seventeen a, b and c respectively. Perfect. My greatest success. I'd known it could be done-'

'What happened to batches one through sixteen?' The guide asked, and the scientist answered before any of the women could tell him that the guide already knew.

'They all failed. Some of them even made it to the end of childhood, but the complications were too sever and they had to be terminated -'

It made Alasia's blood boil. 'And who are you to play a god with our lives?'

He turned, and smiled cruelly, 'but I *am* a god.'

The women curled around him now, seducingly placing their hands on his arms and chest, gazing provocatively at the her and her guide.

'See what I made! And I didn't even use *dirt*! I folded your molecules from the very edges of subspace itself, every single atom of your first cell was made by me! There isn't even any redundancy, no code that is wasted, not like in real humans, and then there are thousands more code than humans enjoy! I used my own DNA to template your quantum forms, and thus life became from *nothing*. Absolute, infinite, <u>nothing</u>. And I have made things to be **envied**.'

He stroked his women. It made her skin crawl, and she let it show.

'They're perfect, perfect in every way,' he dreamily mused.

So that was what she was then. A doll. A toy, created by a lustful, selfish man to prove his own diminished sense of self-worth. Something made for service, and entertainment. And these three dolls, for whatever reasons of their own, let him play with them.

But what was she?

She had no mother.

She had no literal father.

She wondered if she was even real, and it made her world spin with dizziness to contemplate. A voice returned her the present.

'So that's how you did it,' it was her guide.

'Oh no, not at all!' He said. One of the dolls tried to stop him speaking, from sharing the secrets of their life and existence. But he was a proud scientist. 'It took so much research, so much! I'd been cast out of two worlds by the time I found my way here. So few places appreciated the necessity of what I've done, and this world couldn't throw enough resources at me! I've rewritten the codes of life. You, man, see your blood will feed her, but hers would kill you. Her lymphocytes ...' he said, getting animated pointing at her arm 'are more like nanoprobes - vicious lythivorous nanoprobes. And then there's the extra layers in her cortex that gives her, all of them, acute conscious recognition of facial expressions -'

Oh, so that wasn't something everybody did after all, Alasia finally realised.

'-and she'll live long, hundreds if I'm not mistaken, even with her accelerated growth rate. See, she looks in her twenties', but she's much nearer in age to fifteen, by the galactic standard. Fifteen and a half if I'm not mistaken. Just like those I created alongside her.'

'So there were others?' Her guide asked, though some of it was all happening too fast for her.

'Of course there were, and will be! She,' he gestured a twisted finger in her direction, 'was more like the twenty third batch, one of three. I'd gotten pretty good at it by that time, so I decided to get creative. I've mastered the genetic sequencing mysteries of a hundred worlds, but some mysteries still elude me, so I made the three with a random collection of some of my more curious combinations. They worked out pretty well, except there was this one, what was her name? Got careless, seemed to have gotten too much of a conscience, got herself killed.'

'She'd called herself Karen, Father.' The blond Poison stated, and they all watched Alasia carefully.

She'd tried to keep her feelings in check. Perhaps she'd even succeed in different circumstances, but they were ... her sisters, and she knew they'd see through her mask. So she gave up and let her face twist in anger and disgust. It felt good. She'd found her anger. 'You dark, evil, pathetic, twisted monster.'

'What was that?!' He seemed genuinely surprised.

'You heard me.'

And the burgundy one moved to stand between them. He shoved her aside angrily as he left the embrace of his dolls.

'How ... how dare you speak to me that way. I am your *father!*' He shook his fist in her face, and she stared back dispassionately.

'I *have no father*,' she replied, voice tinged with pain.

The silence was deafening. Then he stood back calmly.

But she could read his unconscious facial expressions. Even before he'd said a word, she'd begun to work the Evernet. He was planning to harm her. But a moment later, the three sisters had joined her. They were unlike any minds she'd ever felt there, and they were like three wolves who worked in practiced tandem to hunt her. Within moments, they'd cornered her in the vortex of the Evernet, even before he'd finished speaking.

'So, it's like that is it? Well, I guess combination px32 and relation ikj103 aren't such a successful phenotype after all.'

He begun to work back towards the steps. 'Such a pity, you're as pretty as the rest. You'd be a good servant, I'm sure. We'd have put you to work in the spy networks I'd have guessed. Maybe set you on some dissidents, that's always fun they tell me. Or maybe the Resistance?'

If he'd noticed her pang of fear, he did not show it. Her sisters, having pinned her to a metaphorical wall, noticed it with great interest. If she didn't find a way to escape soon, her mind, permanently welded to the world of the Evernet, would be laid open for their perusal. And amusement.

Their silent battle continued.

'Even so. Losses happen. I've enjoyed meeting you Alasia, you've been ... different. We'll analyse your template after they're done with you.' He gestured to his smiling assistants. 'Ladies, batch 23c is found faulty. Dispose of it for me, will you.'

'Yes father,' the dark haired Jinx said smoothly - pinning Alasia in a virtual prison.

He shut the door behind him.

Alasia had nowhere to run, so she prepared for a desperate battle against her sisters. Suddenly, the mind that was Envy disappeared.

It was her guide. He'd struck her with an anesthetising dart.

'What a tool,' he said of her father insultingly.

Poison attacked him them, striking at him through the Evernet. Alasia could watch their battle there. She was quick, cunning, sly. But he held special government defences, and parried her blows with practiced ease that she had not encountered before.

Jinx, on the other hand, was violent, powerful, and direct. She launched a dizzying array of assault against Alasia unlike any she had ever known. Her mental defences were wounded like never before. The battle became desperate, and Alasia had to reach deeper than she had ever known.

She had some advantage, she could manage more lines than Jinx, but the other woman was stronger, and more experienced, and would hit her virtual defences far more damagingly. Alasia went on the defensive, and studied her tactics even while allowing her to feel victorious. She must have sensed it, for she called to her sister to help.

Poison ended her stalemate with the guide by forming a laser blaster in her hand and then begun to disintegrate vessels near him. He ducked just in time. She could have turned the weapon on an unarmed Alasia now, but seemed to be enjoying the sport.

He rounded the desk then, and she walked close to attack him. He leapt out, blocking her armed hand with his arm. So she spat at him, and as she did, revealed to Alasia that it was a delivery of poisonous nanoprobes that would eat his flesh away in seconds.

Alasia cried out in alarm.

But even as she did, her guide inexplicably moved the poison away from its trajectory telekinetically.

She'd not know he could do that.

And in the next moment, he brought his fist against her chin and knocked her out cold.

Jinx screamed, sounding an alarm, pulling some terrible weapon from her blouse. Alasia gave her no time to activate it, but connecting with the control circuits of the machinery nearby, walloped her on the head.

She crumpled to the floor, giving Alasia a few free, precious moments of unimpeded scanning of her mind. But her guide was on her in a few moments, the blue lights already filling the room of the Black guards approaching. With no further spoils of victory, they point tessered the distance out of there.

They rested their arms on his balcony. She wasn't saying anything, nor did he. Finally, he spoke.

'Are you upset?'

She didn't reply, she was too ... upset. Then she felt very peaceful in his presence. He'd known something about her, about what she was, perhaps even guessed it from the time they first met. Maybe before ...

'What I want to know is why you did it. Why you've done ... all of this,' she asked her guide.

He smiled. 'I have my reasons. And I'm not going to tell you everything, yet. I've been aware of the scientists programme for some time now. After what you'd accomplished, I'll admit I became suspicious. Then when you lost it with those Rei-nati that were trying to take us captive I realised you weren't really fully in control. That's something you can never afford, Alasia. And to own yourself, you must know yourself. I felt it was time.'

She looked at him, finally aware of all that separated them. He was another being, another race. They all had been. She was one of, what, twenty three or so 'batches' – perhaps a hundred individuals. But what if the scientist had more? And what else did he make them for? Did he have no conscience?

And what would the others think?

'What do you know about the Resistance, sir?' She asked him flatly.

He huffed, and stared out of the balcony. 'I don't go out the walls, and I never take my business there. I never do, and it's immeasurable pain to those that do. Don't go out there Alasia. It's more trouble than it's worth.'

She knew now, and she knew he knew. She could tell he was really saying "don't go out there *again*."

But she still didn't know why he did it. Why had he taken her on as a student? What was her value to him, if she wasn't even human, and yet, he'd asked nothing from her, hadn't even made a pass at her, in spite of the trophy she was to males of his species. What *did* he want from her?

They were very quiet, for some time.

'Actually, I am upset. This changes everything. But I'm also, grateful. Relieved. I'd always known, but been too frighted to admit it. Thank you.'

'You're welcome,' he quietly replied.

It took a few days to adjust. Most of the time she'd just sit in public places, watching the humans as they walked around. They were an open book to her now, and she'd scan the Evernet to learn anything she wanted to know about hundreds of them. She could tell family resemblances like colour, could hear how couples really felt in their voices, could taste the men before she'd even touched them.

Now the veil of her identity was stripped away from her it had illuminated the concealed talent in her mind. She hadn't realised how much she'd patterned her thinking after those around her. She could do things she'd never heard people could do.

And, yes, her memory was virtually perfect. She could revisit any moment of her past like it was still happening, could reshape it in her mind, could file it away with multiple interpretations. She stretched her mind to the limit, and it reached further than she'd ever imagined, further than was humanly possible ...

... And yet...

... something was missing. It was as if she could render a thousand sketches, but only had two colours to do it with. Or perhaps that her life was a rich symphony in only one key. She felt too ... mechanical. Was there something about being human, about having forty two extra chromosomes, that gave humans an existence she would never know? Was there something in having a mother and a father that she would never understand? Did they have feelings they could not tell her about? Did they dream the memories of ancestors she'd never own?

Did she have a soul?

The flood of humanity passed by till she'd explained their flow in equation after equation. Every data point became a life. A being.

And in spite herself, she started to love them.

And as she looked, she found patterns. She saw how, almost without exception, a kind deed would reverberate throughout a social network till it returned to the giver, every bit returning what was given - as too did an unkind word. She saw how lovers bonded consciously and unconsciously, mimicking each other, belonging, becoming one. Her favourite were the older couples, speaking volumes without saying a thing, completing each other in almost every moment. She saw how all of the humans were bonded in an unconscious link that made them wise, and how their accidents were often unconscious attempts to heal, or to hinder, someone else.

They were very wise.

Yet... she wasn't one of them. She had to see it all in equations and patterns, or risk not seeing it at all.

It wasn't until the end of the third day that he came to see her again. He sat down on the same bench, not speaking, helping feed some birds.

'Is it time?' she asked.

'Are you ready?' he answered.

She was. She'd changed in the three days. She saw things differently now. Who he was, what he was thinking. She knew he didn't want her as a trophy or sport. He was not like most other men she'd known.

'How did you know when to come?' she asked.

'You've uncrossed your arms. That's all.'

She looked at her hands, unfolded, in her lap. As she filed through her perfect memory she realised she'd been crossing something these past three days while she wasn't ready to be disturbed – her legs, her ankles, sometimes her arms. Now she sat, uncrossed. It felt like the most simple unconscious message she'd ever sent, and didn't even realise she had. Perhaps she was more like humans than she'd allowed herself to believe.

She laughed, and looked out people and children playing in the park again.

'They're so beautiful,' she said after a moment.

'Oh?' He wondered, perhaps thinking she meant her arms. She gestured outward, and he smiled.

'So you see us now. Tell me, Alasia, what do you see?'

'Everyone. People. They're amazing. They touch each other, every second, in ways they cannot even see. When their eyes meet volumes of information pass between them in a moment. They tell everything, you know. They're so honest.'

He seemed quiet.

'But there are some that keep their secrets very well,' she said meaningfully.

He laughed now, a little embarrassed.

'So you like us?' He asked, and she was suddenly very aware that he wasn't including her in that statement any more. It was a little annoying.

'Indeed I do, but I wouldn't say 'me' and 'them' just yet.'

'You sure you haven't already?'

She had to stop at that. He was right, she was the one doing it at first. Could he see inside her mind? He'd managed to bring the issue up very masterfully.

She smiled. 'Point taken, guide.'

They looked out at the people for a while again.

'They're important, aren't they?' he said. 'People, every one. They need taking care of, they need help to meet their dreams. They need to be protected. But not everyone thinks in ways that better their fellows, do they. There are some, some that ought to be removed. But you need to wait until they do something that *deserves* it. That's one of the hardest parts.'

He continued, 'you need to know that Alasia. You might know what you want to do, but you need even more to know *why* you do it. That's what matters the most, and keeps you on track when everyone else tells you

you're doing it wrong. That's just so much the most important thing. Don't forget that.'

In all her life, she'd never even considered *why* she did anything, just how it would benefit her. Now she was willing to protect others with what she was. She'd only just come to that realisation. Now he was asking her why she wanted to do that?

She honestly didn't know.

But she felt it was her turn to speak. 'So there are some that need to be removed then? Very well. I am ready. What is my fourth assignment?'

He smiled, 'we're going after the Rei-nati again.'

The frustration of Lord Admiral Token

If he didn't keep her tied down, he might have at least gained her respect.

He marched around her, growing increasingly frustrated with every failure. Hour after hour, they drugged her, tried to alter her consciousness, tried to repattern her. Hour after hour, he marched about, trying to convince her that she needed him.

At first, it was annoying. It was keeping her from her brother. Then as time went on, Sheelaakah begun to realise that the Admiral of Psychic operations was wasting his every hour attempting to change her. It was truly pathetic.

If she could only break into his mind, perhaps there would be a fight worth discussing. But was it was, it was a pathetic game, and having no other choice of activities to pass the hours, she committed to dragging this out as long as possible so that the Resistance could prosper during his wasted efforts.

He really was entirely *pathetic*.

At one point he even tried to force her memory from her. She lay there then, without a single conscious thought for over two hours, while he agonised over what he had done. Then her soul print re-established itself, and she came back fighting. He'd cut himself on an implement then, and if she wasn't laughing so much she might have managed to push the advantage. She'd wondered later if that was like her...

He looked at her darkly, his countenance glowering. 'Choose me, or die.'

'Then I die free,' she replied.

He paused, then spoke: 'If that is what you want.'

The stone doors slid open then, and in walked a covey of dark priests, and with them, a terrifying Emmissionary. They carried the entrails of dozens of innocent animals, chatting dark words under their breath. She could only imagine what horror now awaited her. She would fight them still!

He stood up now, levitating over the ground in emphasis. He shouted over the growing din, 'But you are too important to the Government of Seren to be wasted in mere death! I will have you, Sheelaakah! The only thing you will know is how much you belong to me! You memory will be erased and replaced with one *of our marriage.*'

She shrieked, and tried to bite him.

He laughed wickedly. 'This is your own fault – you leave me no choice.'

The Kinerigan pirates

Matrix was standing before the little girl. She was dressed in a plain pale green dress now, sitting on a white dais. Her attendant carers where white and clean. Soft, relaxing music was playing.

'They make me bored,' she complained.

Her chief carer interjected. 'The child suffered a severe soul wound during her torture. Her life purpose has been swayed, and that is a very serious thing.'

The child huffed, and rolled her eyes.

The carer continued, 'Her progress is slow, but her wound is unique. In any event, unitman Matrix, she has requested your presence for a conversation, and predicted your arrival to the minute.'

'I used to be much better at it,' the child said toying dejectedly with her blankets. 'Things are … different now. I'm *here* more. I can't see things before they're happening like they're *now* ...'

'Don't worry child, your talent will return,' the carer said in conviction.

But the child seemed unconvinced.

'Jacinth,' Matrix asked, his throat still raw from the healing scars of the gills and the cold grasp of an assassin's hand. 'I-olo Tilk sent a whole contingent to go and get me as soon as he'd heard you asked for me – I couldn't have not come if I'd wanted! Seems the leader of the Resistance takes you very seriously.'

She looked at him blankly for a moment. 'Oh! The black man. He has nice eyes.'

It wasn't quite the response he'd expected. Whatever had happened to her since the telepath tried to take her talent, it had damaged her. She wasn't as confident any more, and when she played, it was much like any other child. Then again, perhaps that was all right. She was, after all, a child.

'We'll, I'm here now. What did you want to tell me?'

She didn't answer, just looked puzzled.

'You've called me here, what did you want to say?'

She fidgeted uncomfortably. Matrix and the carer shared a concerned look.

'You're ... that's not what you're supposed to say,' she whispered, sounding confused. 'You're supposed to say "what would you have me do"?'

He had thought of saying it that way, or at least, he might have said it that way to a different little prophet he once knew.

But he gladly complied. 'What would you have me do?'

She smiled happily, taking on a formal voice. 'In the coming war, you need the thieves that fly.'

That surprised him. 'You mean the Kinerigan pirates?' He asked, a little surprised. He had heard no good thing about the pirates.

'Who are they?' The prophetess asked him.

'They're ... very bad. I don't know much about them. But they live at the maws and make sport and trade of any who accidentally land on moonscape. They trade in ... bad things. All I know is the even the Resistance leaves them alone. Apparently they're all over the galaxy, we've just caught a few unlucky ones here.'

She looked like she was thinking about this. 'What is a 'thieves' anyway? And, and how can they fly?'

Matrix looked at the guide. This was a lot of questions.

She never used to ask questions.

'Come child,' the carer tried to say patiently. 'You need some solitude now.'

She huffed frustratedly, 'will the other children be in today?'

'Yes, of course. Do you think you will join them finally today?'

She shook her head.

'Matrix,' she asked him as they rested her on her dais. 'What is 'war'?'

'Come child, enough for today,' her carer firmly said.

Matrix turned to leave. Then he turned back, bent down, and gave her as long a hug as she needed, wiping away the single tear that fell from his eyes and touched a little prophet's cheek.

---+++---+++---

His drink made a violent thud as it smashed into the bar top.

'Oo wants ta know,' the cyborg scowled dangerously.

'We do.' Skion replied, his red eye matching the others darkened glow.

Matrix tried to impose himself between them. 'Easy gents. Just a harmless question.'

'No questions 'ere are 'armless,' the cyborg scowled.

The city of the pirates was a wonder to behold. They did not use land, but from their occasional meetings great floating cities spontaneously spawned as their boats moored and unmoored in random locations, till some semblance of order dictated where small pockets of civilisation grew. Ships of all sizes, their sails turned to the invisible currents of the quantum breeze, furled quickly as they slipped between the labyrinths. There was no gravity there, apart from just about the buildings and ships, so that if someone was to be thrown away without a means of propulsion they could float all the way till they struck something, like the sky shield, a maw, or were plucked for profit by some other of their debauched pirate fellows.

They were all cutthroats and villains, and what few good folk fell unfortunately among their midst were quickly slain for plunder or adopted into one of the many innumerable waring bands that made up the loose alliance known as the 'Kinerigan pirates.' And even though many of them were much smaller than an average human, it was a fact they fully exploited to their criminal advantage.

One thing did bind them together: an oath, one that tied them in bands and surrendered them to the will of their pirate lords. Each lord in turn swore fealty to an over lord, who in turn answered to the Pirate King – though since he wasn't on this world it made little difference. Instead, the pirate houses had vied for power for many centuries till one ascended, and now one supreme local pirate lord, who called itself 'Myth', was the final answer to law in their community. Visitors were warned though, for each captain was law on their own ship and had authority over all who stood on its planks – their possessions, their time, even their own lives.

The Resistance had sent many emissaries to them over the years, all had met with death or fled. They were a violent, lawless people, where those who wanted to disappear, or flee all law, often ended up. Even the spies had fared no better. All but one. One who had, over twenty years ago, gone native and switched allegiances. Someone that went by the name of 'Darkstar.'

It was a poor lead, but it was the best lead they had.

And the name had led them here, to a very old frigate that was set out now as a pub house. It was punishable by beating to sell non intoxicating alcohol among the pirates, so they'd brought their own. Glenn some light beer, Skion a dark oil, and Matrix, chocolate milk - full cream.

'No questions are "armless",' the pirate cyborg repeated quietly into his glass.

'Who we are doesn't matter,' Matrix explained, smiling. 'We're just looking for a little information is all. Someone told us you'd be the one who'd know.'

The cyborg had chilled a little at Skion's threat, and looked right at Matrix, his mechanised appendages twitching and reforming in his forehead. 'And 'oo might that be?'

Matrix just smiled.

'Questions round 'ere are dangerous things,' the cyborg whispered, as much in advice as in threat now.

'Don't worry,' Matrix explained. 'We'd be sure to make it … worth your while.' And as he did, let the two gold coins glimmer coyly from among his fingers. The pirate's eyes shared their gleam in great interest.

'And … wha' is it that you'd be want'n to know?' He softly asked.

Matrix looked about the room. The other patrons had returned to their drinks and debates. The room seemed to be leaving them alone, for now. All except one. He saw her, a woman behind the bar across the room. She wore a red handkerchief enraptured over deep rich black curls. She looked away quickly when she saw him noticing.

'Just an old friend,' Matrix continued, whispering. 'Darkstar.'

The pirate sat up suddenly, and pushed Matrix's hands away.

'I know lots of names, fool. And I'm wise enough to know that name wants to be left alone.'

'I'm sure we can …' Matrix began, but stopped as the knife folded itself from the cyborg's arm.

'Questions end 'ere if mouths like breath'n,' he said loudly, alerting the other patrons. Matrix caught a glimpse of the woman again, she was smiling.

He knows something. Skion communicated to Matrix, and suddenly grabbed the old cyborg by the collar. With a deft manoeuvre Skion deactivated the others arms, and looked him right in the eyes.

'Talk,' he ordered.

'By my liege!' The cyborg shouted.

It was an odd sentence, Matrix thought. The kind one might use as a battle cry, perhaps, or as a code word for something.

The door blew shut, and a dozen patrons stood up, arming themselves.

'We can do this the 'ard way, if youz like,' the cyborg smiled.

Fourth assignment

It was a dance, a Gala. Elegant, musical, noisy. It didn't claim to be, but the powerful and pretentious were there.

Alasia's assignment was simple. She had to catch the eye of a single fellow, a man they'd traced from the fracas at the mezzanine. It would be dangerous work. She'd tried striking up a conversation over the drinks. But he'd thanked her, and moved on. So she'd done what had always worked best for her – she sung.

He'd tried to stop her, the guide. But she'd unplugged him, and started hacking into the musicians. Before they realised what they'd been doing, she was singing, and all the light and attention were hers once again.

This was her place. This was where she found herself. She sung of wanting to know, of asking questions, of needing answers. And she'd sung to him. Her mark.

It was just like old times.

The room was at a standstill for her. They appreciated her sound even as she composed it spontaneously, and there was rapturous applause.

Naturally, it worked. Once she'd gained his attention, flattered him with the pride in which he wore his clothes, he'd quickly become hers. They chatted late into the evening, but she could see his arrogance. She could tell how he thought most people were beneath him because of his birth heritage, not his accomplishments. And then she began to doubt that even accomplishments were an appropriate way to measure the worth of a soul...

She'd re-connected subtelepathically to her guide then, who skilfully helped to direct her questions until they'd found what they needed. Her mark was telling her about the Rei-nati while they danced. It was becoming a very informative experience. He was playing right into her hands...

Then they were interrupted.

'Excuse me,' a hopeful intoned, 'but I was wondering...'

'Ahh,' her mark said chivalrously. 'But the lady does not wish to be disturbed.'

'I won't be a moment,' the hopeful insisted. 'But you sing... like an angel.'

He let those words drift meaningfully into the air, and Alasia with great concentration held her reaction in check.

So, her old life... they had missed her after all...

But she was not running in their circle now. She had much more important things to do than play prize. It brought back memories of her former, fickle life. Memories she did not want. It was lucky she was wearing blond tonight, facial compact set B.

She rested her head on her marks chest, said nothing but smiled. The moment became uncomfortable, and his lackeys issued the hopeful away.

Not many could afford lackeys under the Government... he was an interesting mark. Then, suddenly, he gasped. She turned to see what had caught his attention.

It was a pale, bald, silver tinted man. He was smiling at them.

'Excuse me,' he said, approaching them. 'I'm sorry for being rude, but I've been watching you, woman, for the whole night. May I have the honour of this dance?'

Faster than thought, her mark slipped quickly from her grasp before she'd had the chance to deny him, and fled fearfully.

Suddenly, her subtelepathic link went dead.

'You'll not be needed that, Alasia,' the silver man said coldly. 'Now, dance with me, you're making a scene.'

She looked about; others were trying to avoid them on the floor.

She looked up at him, and did not feel in any apparent danger. If he felt he was important enough, and capable enough, to detect and disable her link for the time being, he was worth paying attention to, for now...

She slipped obediently into his arms. 'I'm sorry sir, I don't have the benefit of your name as you do mine?'

'You don't need my name,' he said coolly. 'And I've not anything to say to that unprofessional trainer you call a guide that I needed him to hear. His skills are beneath me.'

She tensed at that.

'You see,' he said calmly, 'I know you're going after the Rei-nati, and I'm warning you off the case. It's mine, and he knows that. You're stepping on more danger than even you and he can handle together child. Don't provoke me again.'

She danced coldly in his arms, willing to wait for the right time to get revenge at his insults.

'Don't think badly of me, your guide is quite unprofessional. Do you know why he's interested in you?'

She did not answer.

'You don't have to say anything. I know you do not know the answer. Tell me, what do you know about yourself child? Is there anything he's told you?'

She wanted to keep him talking, but didn't know where to begin. She was not expecting this, and expected she'd have a thousand things to say next hour!

'I appreciate the advice,' was all she said, and they waited out the rest of the dance in silence. It was during this time she could feel him studying her, trying to sense her motives. Naturally, this close to another person she did not trust, she kept her thoughts to herself.

The dance ended.

'Do remember what I've told you,' he said, the edge of an unconscious frustration in his voice. Perhaps he was expecting a more easily frightened woman? Was he seeking information in the questions she hadn't asked? She just smiled back, knowingly, and curtsied as the dance required.

As soon as they'd parted she hit the Evernet with great ferocity. She was tired of others taking her space there, and was going to start developing ways around their intrusions. She found her guide quickly.

What happened?! He asked, sounding concerned.

You know, for a high level spy, an awful lot happens that you don't seem to expect, doesn't it? She teased angrily. *Unless, of course, you really mean it.*

There was silence on the other end of the line.

Do you want to tell me what happened? He finally asked.

She paused. *Some grey man.*

Ahh, he said knowingly. *The androgenine. He finally put in a show did he? As bold as he is ineffectual. There is a law among us, Alasia, that you'd do well to know, though you live it well already: trust no one.*

None? She questioned teasingly, including even him.

Indeed, he replied, and she was left to wonder if he knew what he meant.

Alasia, he asked. *Do you know why we're going after the Rei-nati?*

They're trying to despoil the peace? They're trying to garner more than their legal share of public wealth? They think themselves more worthy than others?

They are all crimes on Seren. What else... plotting murder, did I mention plotting murder? Specifically mine?

He laughed, *Yeah, death oaths. You collect them over the years, especially if you're doing your job.* He sighed in a confusion of memories Alasia could not quite hear. *But it's more than those things you've mentioned. The Rei-nati have help from high up within Seren. Even the supply general seems to be in the dark regarding this. If it's one of the high council we really need to know. The paranoia is starting to get to them, and we need this cleared up before we can move on. Trust, Alasia, is worth more than gold. The old androgenine, who is neither male or female by the way, has been burning 'its' candle over this mark for over a dozen years, and they still slip by. I've taken it upon us, since you seemed forever fated to deal with them, to take this job on as well. What we learn may help the high council.*

He didn't say anything we can go by, just warned us off the case. It seems pretty important to him, Alasia counselled.

Indeed, he replied. *And this does tell us one thing - we need to switch marks.*

She thought about this for a moment.
You mean we're going after the androgenine?
Precisely, he replied.

---+++---+++---

She'd followed the Androgenine personally till she and her guide had met up. He'd taken a very small team of other spies to watch his back. Shortly after the gala, the Androgenine spoke to some dignitaries he knew from KiKaan province, surreptitiously scanning their accounts at the same time. He was reasonably skilled.

The group he'd brought to help make his conversation private with Alasia dispersed then, all except one who kept pace with him over half a kilometre. It wasn't until they were deep in the underdark that they began to walk shoulder to shoulder.

They were speaking in innuendo. Something about a birthday party on the surface, but more apparently about some kind of meeting. They made their way to a dark pyramid deep under the surface, gave the guards a secret signal, and were admitted.

Interesting, the guide said. *We'd better get some information on that building. It's not like the androgenine to leave this out of its reports.*

I'm checking the details of it on the Evernet, Alasia announced. *The reports look old – it might have been changed by now.*

And it's probably heavily warded. We'll need to gather some proper supplies before proceeding.

We might not get another chance, Alasia explained. *Once we ask questions…*

I don't like it, her guide said. *This is the androgenine we're talking about.*

Alasia thought about it, but knew they'd need to act quickly. *Let's take the team in, give it a look. I'll make sure we leave an exit.*

Very well then, he agreed. It took about twelve minutes to get them organised, and in that time Alasia was able to strengthen her Evernet connection. They would not sever her connection again. And the priority for a point Tesser back to the surface and black guard backup was arranged.

But it was within those twelve minutes that she did a little something she'd been meaning to do for days. You see, even on Seren, there was something even the black guard feared, though they'd never admit it – the tide of public opinion. The anger of the people. It was their indignity, their anger, at a score of young lives taken by a callous and self-possessed 'scientist' that she sought. And with little more than a few deft manoeuvres, a few clues to the right kind of people, she took her father's research public.

It would be all over the news. It would only be hours till he was taken for trial. There would be no more… 'batches.' She did not know what they would do to him. It was little revenge, but it would do.

It was a text book entry. They curved space and stepped through the bridge into the pyramid, in spite of its formidable defences. Seven of them. They took up position in an adorning room, shielded by over a meter of stone. The scrying oil was placed over the wall, and that stone became as one way glass, and every noise was easily heard through it.

They were in some form of meeting, the androgenine at the head of the table with a purple robed man sitting at his right. Many other gold and blue clad officials walked about in their pompous attire.

'… other matters which must be spoken off.' A strange scaled man was saying. 'What about the spy and his apprentice, what was her name, Alasia?'

The androgenine was waving a comment aside.

'…he is of little skill, and she, and untried whelp. They are of no concern to us.'

'That whelp bested forty of our honour guard! She is possessed, I tell you,' the man replied.

Again the androgenine cut over conversation in its cool voice, 'don't lose sight of the prize, Governor. What minor setbacks we receive can only serve to strengthen our resolve to bring rightful leadership to your race. Revenge will only stunt that.'

Another, older being spoke then, a Cyclops. 'Yet this enemy spy concerns you, doesn't he Spymaster.'

At this the six of them looked at her guide, his eyebrow raised. There was only one spymaster on Seren and they all answered to that office. Either something had happened they had not been informed of, or this Androgenine was just as much a pretentious pretender as the others at their table in their fine purples and gold.

The cyclops continued, 'I see the fear in your aura when others mention his name.'

The androgenine stood, and the table fell silent. 'He is of little skill, and his apprentice, the one he aims to train to replace him, of little importance and narrowness character. She has been working as a profiteer for many years now.'

Alasia gasped. The others held their peace.

What had he done? What was her guide trying to do? Apprentice? He'd never said anything. Now this androgenine spills her dark past with impunity? The word would be out among the spy network in mo-

Oath, to silence, her guide said, ordering to the six others there.

Oath sworn, they all darkly agreed.

But they now owned something about her, past, and destiny...

The androgenine continued, 'Allow me to illustrate, if you so wish. And what is more, I bring you his lustful apprentice: the assassin for whose blood you cry.'

Look out! The dark spirit told her.

With a jolt of fear Alasia realised they'd been detected, so lost was she in the turmoil of her own private unveiling that she'd not seen the danger: they were in a trap. She'd realised it a moment before her guide did, in the same instant that the dark spirit had spoken to her.

Long enough for her alone to draw a breath of warning.

But not long enough to stop the blast of concussive light that sprang up behind them, knocking them all unconscious. A light that had not come from the building, nor from any of the Rei-nati, but from one of the seven who watched in pleasure as his months of working as a double agent finally paid off.

When the darkness within

Sheelaakah woke up, though there was no border between dreaming and waking. If that line had been crossed she neither knew nor cared. All she remembered was the desire to destroy.

She was becoming aware of her body now. It was so unnaturally calm now – they must be using some powerful drugs. Her limbs were warm and relaxed, and she felt like she could do anything. She was happy, too happy. She did not care about anything. She smiled the unnatural smile.

She remembered her name now. There was something wrong about all this but it seemed so... she just didn't care. It didn't matter and she didn't care about anything but her own self. A part of her seemed frightened, like she should be screaming and lashing out, but she just couldn't seem to make herself care about it.

She felt her brow and realised there was no banding. It made her laugh. They could do anything to her now and she couldn't stop them.

Or could she? She remembered shouting, surging of power. Ahh yes, it didn't matter. She was too strong for any of them. Too strong, and she didn't care anymore if she hurt them. Everyone but herself was her enemy now.

It was then that she noticed the minds about her. They were strong, and they were shielded. It would be a while before she could hurt them, and it might just be easier to grab a weapon of some kind and hit them with it.

Someone laughed. 'Ahh Sheelaakah, my queen! The answer to the call of my heart. At last you have come to me and that is right, even though it was through fire.'

A young man, surely younger than her, with hair so long it drifted to his feet, was floating in the air near her. Just as she noticed him he disappeared, only to reappear behind a curtain to her left.

'You've come a long way to find me, my queen. But now we will be each other's, and I will complete you.'

She tried to get a good look at his face. Something about him seemed, worrying, distant, but she couldn't be sure that she'd never seen him before. She continually drifted between dreaming and waking, or wherever she was.

'Whoever...' she began, but her voice sounded... deeper... distant. She wasn't sure she was even in her own body any more. She was feeling... powerful, like all inhibitions that held her back had been thrown away.

He was floating again beside her. 'We belong to each other now. I've loved you since the first time I saw you, and now, you've come to me. We will complete each other.'

'But I don't ...' she protested, if only to make some sense of who she was. She remembered her name ... she was a telepath ... she was a warrior ... oh, it was so frustrating!

'You've already accepted me,' he petitioned.

What? She queried in indignity.

He appeared again from behind her, his warm breath a delight along her neck. 'You wear my ring. We are married. I am your husband. Don't you remember, my Sheelaakah?'

'Marr...' she begun, but her breath failed her. She tried to remember, some ceremony begun to replay itself in her mind. She was nervous... he was there... there was an intense feeling of love... but... she was saying yes again and again... but her wrists hurt, was she tied down or something?

Suddenly the priest at her left fell down against where she was seated, bleeding from his temples. She wondered what had happened. Did she do that?

The floating man was suddenly there again, right in front of her. He was concentrating on something. Her. She laughed a hollow laugh, but didn't know why.

She remembered that she loved him then, but it was distant. Like a choice she felt she had. She reached out to touch him but he pulled back. She felt again the power in her limbs and thought about using them to throttle someone, perhaps the priest at her right? But he had already stepped back.

'Yes, the power,' the floating man who had told her he was her husband said. 'You can feel it all now. You're very sensitive to this Sheelaakah. It's why I need you, and it's why I *love* you. This,' he gestured now, pointing to a vast hall that begun to light up. It was filled with stone, and the stones were filled with sigils of iron or bronze. They seemed to move and float on the stones, occasionally conflicting with each other, occasionally combining into a new symbol and sending their dark messages across space to whatever hapless soul should receive them. They were pulsating with evil and power.

'This is the dark hall, the heart of the psychic centre on Seren. Here, we master the rule of the people from the will of the True One. Every sentient being on this planetoid connects with this place, and all must pass through here before continuing on to their afterlife. You see, there is no escape from Seren, my wife.'

He continued, shouting at the top of his voice to the room, the symbols moving in time to his cadence 'I rule here! This is *my* domain! I am the leader of the minds of the people! For my talent and dark ordinance, I can control everything, *everyone*, even you.'

He gloated, and she was torn between admiration and disgust, and could not tell which was a dream and which was the wakening.

'Here, the artefacts of control are kept. I, I alone in all the history of Seren have mastered them all ...'

He fingered the single shard of crystal and feather on a leather band around his neck. He looked down now, and her concern shot out to him as he seemed to take on a great pain, his shoulders weighed under the weight of the minds of an entire world.

'All, that is, but one...'

Like a moment, a knife of sympathy for her beloved passed through her.

'Stand, my wife!' He commanded with great authority, but gently. 'Take my hand, you can stand now.'

She felt like she could have stood anytime she wished, with the power coursing through her. She could sense them, trillions of minds locked up on that world, and manipulate them though the sigils of power that coursed the vast hall, by the power her husband now held. She looked at the symbols now. Some she recognised, some she did not, some made her flinch. They were many, and it was a wonder that any could master all of them in a single life time, not without some substantial help. Something you would have to let inside to help you and that's never a good idea. One needs to own their own house...

The other priest suddenly cried out and fell, inexplicably. In a moment her husband swept to her side, placing his hand almost in her lap.

She forgot the priest and stood now, gracefully meeting his gaze with every physical movement of perfect control, but she did not take his hand till she stood. She felt balanced now, and could feel the world beneath her feet in a way she had never ever imagined before. She let her energy and consciousness sweep down into the ground, and found it pulsating with power and darkness, and a compulsive rhythm that drove every being on its surface to comply. But it was a source of energy as well, awaiting the minds of others to form it, awaiting her mind.

'Yes, you feel her now too?' the husband commented. 'She is powerful isn't she? C'Wiltaa – the spirit of this world. She will hold and nurture all who live here, and have them comply with the True One's will. This world, too, she is *alive* Sheelaakah, you've just denied yourself her power for too long!'

And it *was* power! She laughed as she felt it coursing through her system now. She realised she could command stone and metal, and they would obey her though this planets authority. The energy moved through her system. They must have given her some powerful drugs, she dimly realised, that prevented her from thinking clearly yet enhanced her feeling a thousand fold. There were other beings too who...

Her train of thought was again broken, this time by the chanting. There were dozens of voices chanting about her. They'd just suddenly become louder. She looked around here. Dozens of priests, all sending her their strength and energy. She looked back, she had been laying on some stone altar, circumscribed with some iron symbol on the floor that she didn't recognise.

'Yes, they are the acolytes. The "beginners",' her husband mocked. 'They have talent, but not like us my love. But they are needed here. They chant day and night. They barely eat, but they'll obey me, and they send me their power continuously, just like they're sending it to you now. Day and night, day and night... Do you *feel* it?'

They were devout, she noticed. They increased her ability with their faith. She could accomplish much destruction with their power added to hers... His hand stiffened on hers. She looked at him angrily, daring him to provoke her so she could test her talent. But instead he waved in front on him, offering her the path he wanted her to take. It was blocked by an iron gate.

She parted the iron like air, scattering it with her feet and carving a path with her mind. He was impressed, the acolytes, just a little afraid. Two priests flanked her now, having replaced the ones that had fallen from among the throngs of the acolytes. She had the impression that she could go through quite a few of them in a day.

They walked, the four of them, through the torn iron to a stone door. It opened at her husband's command. Inside, all the walls and floor were black stone, a museum of some sort. Every so often a pendant or pillar of evil was dimly lit for display. The priests pressed against her as she walked, and she found them somewhat comforting in their constant vigil of her mind and heart. Though what they felt they needed to be there for though, she had no idea.

They approached the back of the museum, where a single obsidian pedestal lay under a satin sheet, many arm lengths away from them, divided by a mighty chasm. An unnatural wind stirred between them and the pedestal, a million condemned voices whispering in its hush.

'I have mastered all, all but one...' he repeated sadly.

She guessed what he wanted before he'd even formed the thought. It was easy to do too. Almost too easy. The stone obeyed her willingly like water might, bending and reshaping itself with thunderous cracks into a dark obsidian bridge. With the power of the priests and of Seren itself, the stone willingly reformed itself to her will. She was becoming something... more powerful than ever before.

They were full of admiration for her, she read in their thoughts. One of the priests even went so far as to point out that her husband had not ever made it half so far on his first attempt. They were all impressed.

'You have begun the final stage of our journey my love. Come with me.'

She had barely begun to move when she felt the distinct alarm of fear from within her. *This should not be done,* she felt.

'You mustn't fear now!' the husband said. 'It is within your grasp. The most powerful artefact of all Seren, in all the worlds! With it, no mind can be denied your will, no matter can resist your desire!' His eagerness was all too apparent in his aura.

She almost wanted to... to please him.

But it was... not to be done...

She heard the chanting again, felt the age and power of the planet beneath her. On, on, they urged... on...to power! He looked so pleading. And she was the first to form the bridge, wasn't she? She locked her eyes onto his, and begun to walk across the bridge, smiling at the man who had told her he was her husband...

There were others, minds within the mist. Others who over years had gained the title her husband held and after decades of work to become worthy had crossed the bridge to touch this artefact. They lived now in the air, passing their wisdom to whomever would cross that bridge and claim that artefact. It was power incarnate...

But, in spite of herself, her steps slowed. The priests pressed in further against her shoulders. *On, on!* They impressed, trying to fill her mind with their wills. Her hand was being pulled, it was the man with long hair? *On!*

Did she have to do this to please him? Her steps formed a rhythm, falling in sync with... the heartbeat of the planet. It wanted her to claim the artefact. Like a deep bass rhythm it drove her on, on, till at last their footsteps claimed the base of the pedestal.

It was in arms reach now.

'Take it,' her husband urged.

Take it, the priest intoned.

'Take it, and no power on this world will be denied you. Take it, and you will forever be mine!' the husband pled.

Take it! The planet silently pulsed.

She didn't. She could not move. Even with all the world driving her she could not … it… was not to be done.

Suddenly she realised with waking clarity, the kind of when a sleeper comes out of sleep, that whatever was under that cloth pulsated with pure, unmitigated evil… nothing would make her touch that.

'TAKE IT!' He roared, startling her with his violence. Suddenly he was wreathed in red clouds of power. His feet, which never touched the floor, were boots of black ridding on a pillar of fire. Around his head, a corona of black was forming. He was terrifying…

She could feel tears streaming down her face. She would not…

'Take it and claim the POWER!' He roared, and with a wave of his hand telekinetically removed the satin sheet.

She could not move, transfixed with its black beauty. It was an amulet in the shape of a ten legged spider, perfectly smooth, its abdomen alone large enough to fill and outstretched hand. And it held power, a continuous flow of energy that would dominate and crush the will of any… that could send mountains of its will across the vast distance of space… that could give its wielder authority over any banding made from the materials of this would have, which was all of them… all of them… she could have power over all of them… the black spider grew in her vision, it seemed to be moving… with it, she could accomplish anything…

And yet…

… no.

It was just… wrong.

She looked up at him. He was smiling kindly, the priests were flanking her, all about her there was nothing but dark obsidian and the spider.

No.

Suddenly the priests began to stumble. She wondered why, and discovered it was her own mind causing them pain. She followed the course of her will, following like a river flowing from them, beginning with her…

And in that moment, Commander Sheelaakah, a leader of the telepathic arm of the Resistance, re-found herself. Her attack was swift and brutal, and the priests quickly fell, the one to her left could not deny his own legs and threw himself into the abyss. She smiled at her 'husband'.

He lost his composure, with a swift movement he tore the amulet from its pedestal and thrust it towards her,

'TAKE IT!' He roared. 'Take it, and join me in our cause! Take it, and I will serve you forever! Take it and *love me!*'

Token, I am your weakness. She thought in perfect clarity. He expected an attack, but she did not attack him. She knew he held all the power right now, from her intoxicated state to her being in the midst of some dark ritual. But what they wanted, they could not force from her. She had to choose it herself, choose to embrace the power that would make of her a tyrant, something she would never do. While once she had touched such power and driven men to madness she now saw the full horror of the destiny that path was leading to.

I will not be your pawn, she slowly intoned, but loud enough so that the acolyte priests in the great hall could read her thoughts. *I will not join your cause. I will not serve the Oppression. I will not ...*

Slowly she reached down and pulled the rune encrusted band from her finger, though it hurt like death to do so.

'... be your wife.'

She only had time for one last thought before the full force of his pain and frustration, his anger, his malice, and his will to dominate came crashing down upon her, bringing expected unconsciousness, a gold band falling unceremoniously on the obsidian floor. *I am Sheelaakah ... and I am free ...*

On negotiating with pirates

Skion had decided to do it the hard way.

Matrix had only barely grabbed the knife that was fired his way, and used it to parry the cyborg's suddenly expanding blade. It was unlikely to prove a damaging cut anyway, with the nanoprobes strengthening his skin, but then again it might have been an electrically active blade with just the right vibratory frequency...

Matrix was over the bar while Skion took on the other patrons. He would not have fared well if Glenn wasn't there, arriving many minutes earlier so they didn't seem together. It was a tactic that saved them once more. He levelled half of them with a blast from his spear, and joined Skion back to back against the others. Skion was determined to beat answers out of the cyborg, so when it began to slip from the melee Skion ordered Matrix to follow.

But Matrix already was already following another person he knew had answers.

She'd slipped quietly out the back door as soon as she saw Matrix looking for her. She'd been watching the fight patiently, rinsing her mug. He had to run along the counter, dodging blows and flying furniture. The barkeep had activated a neutraliser by that time, but that wouldn't affect the well-armed Resistance soldiers, nor half the combatants, so it seemed.

The door was shut fast, so Matrix beat his fist through the panel to unbolt it from the other side. By the time it was open, she was already across the empty space between their dock and another, though how she'd managed to traverse so great a distance in so short a time was puzzling. He immediately leapt off the rails, twisted back against the wall of the building, and used it to spring across the distance.

She quietly walked around the building, smiling at him as she went. If he'd screamed at her to wait, it was lost in the airless wilderness between the docs. He raced around the building just as the door she'd entered was beginning to close. He flung it open, only to see a dining room full of quietly eating guests. She was nowhere in sight.

Then he felt someone's gaze on the back of his neck. He twisted around as saw her then, dozens of meters away on a docked ship. She looked surprised that he'd noticed her, then smiled again.

How had she gotten all the way over there so quickly? She couldn't be teleporting, he'd have seen the light. And surely there was not enough near space for a point Tesser. Was she using no-space?

He smiled back.

Suddenly she leapt, upward, and sailed the full thirty meters in a perfect back flip that landed her in the crow's nest.

She winked at him.

He took several steps backwards, lining himself up for a running leap.

She looked a bit worried.

He winked back.

And jumped with all his might. He sailed across the vast distance that separated them, aiming to cross the gravity field just above the nest so that he would fall in with her.

But he'd jumped low. He felt the field tug on his clothes just before he was expecting it, and instead begun to plummet towards the ship's deck. He didn't want to experience broken legs again, so reached out desperately for the rigging. He lost a few layers of skin grabbing the ropes, and ended up spinning a full circle before clutching clumsily on the ladder.

A young man from the deck saw him then, and begun to ascend. Matrix quickly clambered up the final distance, but she was already gone.

'Wot you doing?' The young man demanded, with threat in his voice.

'Did you see a woman here?' He asked.

'Ahh!' The young man said. 'You've seen the Siren. Don't follow the likes of her sir. They say she's a non-corporeal like the dread fish. They say men who find the Siren all lose their way,' he explained fatalistically.

Matrix just smiled, leaping from the rigging jumped against the ropes ten meters down, and used them like a trampoline to sail back to where he'd come from.

The young man whistled in respect.

Skion was livid. He had a cut above his brow, and Glenn had taken a few solid ones pinned against a wall for a moment. But the cyborg was gone.

'I've got another lead,' Matrix explained. He told them about the Siren and how he felt she was the key to their connecting with the Pirate Lord. They might have argued at the impoverished logic of it all, but he'd been right about the Alliance.

Yet even Glenn seemed reluctant to pursue it.

But that's why I-olo had sent the two soldiers along with him. I-olo knew the pirates would be violent, yet apparently some high ranking circle member had insisted that Matrix's 'style', after his dealing with the Tendendalaah, needed curtailing. Thus I-olo sent along Skion and Bakerson, two top class unit leaders and Resistance elite to placate to the circle member, but instead he'd given them explicit orders *not* to curtail Matrix's manner in any way.

It was a little bit worrying now, actually, now that Matrix thought about it. Why was the leader of over fifty billion lives trusting him with an open cheque? The war with the Oppression had intensified, and they were now making calm and measured steps towards eradicating the Resistance. They'd thrown the entire Resistance forces to protect their allies, but they were outnumbered and, as yet, out resourced. But until the Derringer joined in there was not much they could do except – hold on. And hold they would, till the time to attack the wall would come. Hopefully, that time would be soon, and there was little time to waste.

But not, Skion grumbled, on pursuing dead leads, or chasing mysterious jumping women.

Word soon spread about the bar fight, and ironically it seemed to grant them some kind of respect among the pirates. They moved on to another barge and, after a little research, it seemed the pirates were more than willing to tell him all about the Siren, much more than the few random titbits they'd gleaned at great cost about 'Darkstar'. Rumours were many and colourful. Taken as a whole they amounted to but one clear conclusion – the Siren could not exist.

So they took it to the harbour master. An enigmatic figure on one of the largest collections of barges and floats. He was to be found giving private audience to his select confidants. And to speak to the harbour master, they were soon informed, one of them had to pass the audition.

Naturally, they volunteered Matrix.

It was madness. Five minutes later he found himself on a pillar, untethered to the ground, and fending off the Piri – carnivorous space faring birds that scavenged the outer reaches of moonscape. Survive five minutes, and they would get to see the harbourmaster.

It was considered entertainment.

He had his air suit around him, keeping him alive. The Piri circled around him, their shrill cries reaching him telepathically.

Matrix stood there quietly, meditating. The various ships and barges, including the harbourmasters, circled at different distances, so that at times he could see their faces and they his. There was cheering, and drinking.

There was no warning when the game began. The birds sensed it immediately, but he still sat there. He was listening.

The first beast was an alpha male, and none challenged it. It was huge, at least twice the width of a human in wingspan, a beak filled with needle teeth that careered at him confidently.

He waited till the last moment, and jumped as it swooped under him. It tried to lift its beak to him, but he used it to swing back down again, planting his dagger in its back. It fell quickly, its rivals fighting over the meat.

The pillar rocked, but did not fall.

They came from many angles then, and Matrix barely had time to think. Once or twice he found himself alighting on their backs as he swung his simple knife among them, all the time conscious of the 'game' of keeping the pillar from toppling. Once he even had to push hard against it, but rather than fall, planted his feet and leapt squarely off a Piri, landing back on the pillar.

He was sure he could hear them cheer.

A moment later the birds begun unexpectedly to leave. They flew down, and waited on the ground in mute silence, looking about nervously.

Matrix looked around too. Surely his five minutes weren't up already? Why were the ships holding back?

He felt them before he saw them.

Incorporeals.

Ghosts, phantoms. Beings of claws and teeth that sped towards him with darkness in their eyes, their wastes tapering off to form wisps of air. This was not part of the game...

Several of the ships began a hasty retreat.

Again? Matrix thought, as the power within him grew.

So, they wanted him here then?

Then he would fight them here too.

They came at him from both sides, and at the last minute, Matrix plunged his hands out against their foreheads. They would have shattered mortal bone, but the spectres only recoiled. The first recovered fastest, but before it could strike at Matrix he caught it by the throat. Combining his will with his strength, he somehow prevented it from striking him.

The second flew at his head, and he ducked quickly. However, not soon enough, as it's inhumanly long claw grated along his ribs. There was such incomprehensible darkness in those claws, and he almost lost grip on the one he had.

Crushing it with all his strength, he flung it towards the earth before it could escape. The other turned in its flight, and begun a flurry of blows he managed to block with his own limbs. It knew all about matter, and strength, and a soul print, and it fought with inhuman speed. But somehow, Matrix kept up.

Somehow, Matrix again fought an incorporeal body with his own.

It was fast, but he was faster. Soon it made a fatal mistake in its delivery of an attack, and Matrix plunged his fist into its chest. It looked surprised, then trembled and fell away in wisps of darkness concealing trails of light from Matrix outstretched arm.

He looked up victoriously. There was only one boat now. It was the large one, with Glenn and Skion, and presumably the harbour master. He looked at the rows of faces, and then he saw her again.

The Siren.

She was there. She was dressed professionally, like she was some sort of sailor on the barge there. She smiled at him, and disappeared into the crowd.

It's her! Matrix tried to message Bakerson. *The Siren is on the Barge!*

Matrix! Bakerson replied clearly through the sub telepathic link, *Look out!*

The first incorporeal was returning up the pillar then, through the stone, its claws cutting dark cuts like blood as it rode furiously up the pillar. Matrix didn't even think. He knew what he had to do before it even came close.

It does not touch me, he calmly intoned.

It roared up through the pillar, but its claws would not clamp about him. It screamed in frustration as it tried to close its appendages about him, but they would not move. With a simple hand gesture, Matrix held the creature at bay. It was like… telekinesis… but it wasn't that. It simply, could not touch him. He had to reach deeply into his soul for the power, and knew he could not hold it away forever.

So he reached out, slowly, with his other hand. It roared in pain and frustration, it beat against his mind with scenes of terror and unspeakable threats to make him allow it to touch him.

But even as he reached for it, it did not move away, so intent was it on his destruction. His fingers closed about its neck again, and he pushed light and heat into its form. Suddenly it tried to clutch as his hands, but once again it was unable. In a scream that echoed across moonscape, it slowly unravelled into shreds of lights and ribbons of darkness.

They were cheering on the barge.

Well, at least I passed the audition, Matrix thought.

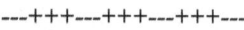

'I know,' the harbourmaster said kindly. 'But I'm afraid it's just not possible. The Siren, is, well, unreachable. She's… a vision… I'm afraid.'

'A vision I've seen twice,' Matrix replied, getting frustrated.

'Then you are one of the lucky ones. They say she is everywhere and nowhere. If you've come to her attention, there is nothing to do but wait until she speaks to you.'

The Resistance soldiers thought about this. They were in the Harbourmasters private quarters on his large skiff, enjoying a feast. Matrix was guest of honour for surviving the audition, and his heroic effort against two non-corporeals was fast becoming legend. Yet they had learned more in one hour with the harbourmaster than in three days among the pirates.

'There is another thing,' Skion mentioned causally, leaning over the cushions that settled them at their sumptuous feast. 'We're looking for an old friend, you may have heard of him. Darkstar.'

The harbourmaster looked grim, and spoke quietly. 'Indeed, came in few years back. Ain't seen much of him in all that time, disappeared about two years ago. And it's an irony... some say... some say the Siren got him.'

'What makes them say that?' Matrix asked.

The harbourmaster tapped his nose in a timeless gesture of secrets. 'Let's just say... when men die chasing dreams, we say the Siren got them...'

The soldiers shared a glace.

'So, tell me,' the harbourmaster ran a finger through the onion dip nonchalantly, 'what's a trio of Resistance soldiers doing out in the Kinerigan badlands again?'

Skion looked like he was about to go ballistic, but Matrix stalled him even as the knife formed itself from his hand. They'd told no-one who they were, and thought they'd hidden it pretty well.

Matrix replied. 'We're here to ask the Pirates for their help. The Oppression is coming.'

Skion swore in frustration, their cover truly blown now.

'Yes, I'd heard about that.' The harbour master grinned. 'Something you people said ticked them off and now they want to kill you all? More's the pity,' he said insincerely. 'Still, if there's any good pilots among you, I've a new vessel I'm looking to crew...'

'We're not interested in your offers,' Skion said coldly, blade retreating.

The harbourmaster almost looked hurt. 'Just asking! Sheesh! Look, I don't know what's going down, but last I heard they'd regained the granite pass from the mutants and were preparing for a major offensive right into Resistance territory. Doesn't surprise me you'd come looking for allies again, you usually do.'

The Resistance soldiers looked at each other. This did not look promising to Matrix at all. If the Kinerigan pirates knew so much and cared so little...

'Only way we'd get involved was if the pirate lord ordered it, and then, you probably couldn't stop the boys from a little freelance looting anyway...'

At that, Skion's forearm became a gun for the Harbourmasters chest. Two of the hostesses pulled blazers from their scabbards almost simultaneously.

'Tell us where we can find Darkstar,' he demanded

Matrix tried to hold his arm, but was little match for Skion's strength. He would have swept his feet out from under him, but a movement caught his attention.

There, high above at a balcony and watching with avid interest, was the Siren. She was dressed like a lady, going out to dinner.

'It's her!' Matrix shouted, and she looked at him in surprise and slipped back.

The others looked around confused. Matrix leapt up to the wall and scaled the curtains in less than a second. One of the waitresses tried to shoot him, but he moved in an unexpectedly vertical manner. Bakerson was cooling the situation as Matrix landed on the balcony, just in time to see her slip coyly through a door.

'It's the Siren!' He explained.

'Off he goes,' the harbourmaster sighed.

What it means to be Sheelaakah

How long she had been there, she did not know. Days melded into each other in this hellish place. It was some kind of asylum, some kind that she'd never been told existed on the planetoid. It was a place where they took people to drive them to madness; the only escape from the insanity.

They took from her every dignity, every kindness. When she was not strapped to the wall, she slept, or fell unconscious, on the floor. They gave her no clothing, no food, and made her beg for water. They made her crawl everywhere she went.

The walls were purposely left thin and riddled with holes, not only so the fetid stench of human flesh could rot through the place, but so that the continuous screams of madness could penetrate the asylum unendingly: sometimes adding to her own.

It was to live in a nightmare.

They'd placed some creature on her scalp that sapped her abilities, and had to replace it every few days, it poisoned so quickly. She could feel it moving about her skull continuously. In one of her more lucid moments, perhaps while it was asleep, she'd scried out the asylum. There was none there to give her relief, no kindness to succour, no word to share her pain. There were only prison guards or prisoners driven fully insane, and a hoard of debauched and tormentuous demons prowled about her day and night –

shocking her continuously from her sleep. She did not know where she was, or anything beyond the common wards at the prisons gates.

Sometimes they'd operate on her. Sometimes, simply torture. Often they'd tease her with the mildest of liberties, mocking her thirst, or the pleading look in her eyes.

Day by day, her sanity and strength were slipping from her.

Sometimes she'd wonder if the Resistance remembered her, if they tried to find her. If they even dared to risk discover what she had become...

But he came often, the long haired boy. It pained him to see her like this, and that was the only vengeance she knew, though it brought her no joy. He'd plead with her, try to make her surrender. But she didn't even look at his face, unless he made her, then she'd stare right through him. But as the days went on, he came less and less, until one day, it looked as though he would not be coming again at all...

And it was on this day, as she lay chained and filthy in a little, miserable ball, that she finally entered the Valley...

It was dark, dark all around.

But then she felt it - she was free! Entirely, completely free of pain and hunger. She could move, she could twirl. And all around her, music played full of understanding and calm.

She saw a little light then. Far away. It seemed to radiate... peace.

But before she could focus on the little light, a bright beam of energy and strength filled her. She whirled around, and saw a brilliant tower of light, impossibly high, surrounded by light and majesty and power. Its single spire rose high into the darkness, penetrating all with its light, chasing away all darkness. She heard it calling to her, calling her name. Some spirit... the spirit of this world! It was calling her, calling her home, to a new home... calling her to the tower of light...

For a moment a thought crossed her mind – but wasn't that tower her enemy, the home of her enemy? She almost turned back a moment to check on the little light...

But the tower spoke to her mind empathically *he is here*.

Then it allowed her to see him.

DAEMON!!

Faster than thought she crossed the impossible distance between them. It was him.

It was him, her brother, her twin!!

She stood in front of him. She looked into his eyes. She knew those eyes. It was him! She had found him at last, he never did leave …

But he did not look back at her.

He was staring, fixedly, staring at the tower of light.

Turn, the tower urged. *Turn and receive your eternal rest gazing at my splendour. Turn, and join him in your rest.*

Rest, thought Sheelaakah. *Yes, rest. I am so very tired…*

But she could not take her eyes off his face.

It was him. But he did not look back.

Daemon? It's me?

Oh, he simply said.

She held him. He twitched involuntarily as though no one had touched him in an eternity.

Daemon, will you not look at me? It's me, your sister…

TURN! The tower suddenly demanded.

Shee… Shee… it's so beautiful… he mused drearily.

He did not turn to look at her.

Daemon! she screamed, and her soul lit up with indignation and fear. So this was how they did it! This was how they held so many soul prints after death. The tower was a mosquito trap, a burning lamp for spirit moths. Suddenly its light became a burning sun.

DAEMON!! she screamed. The light was intense, it was burning her. Involuntarily she begun to turn her head. Her hand became limp against his cheek. She knew if she looked at that dreaded soul trap, that she could never look away again. That would be it, the perfect prison, and she would be trapped here, with him but unable to look or touch or see anyone for the rest of forever…

Daemon, I've fought so hard to find you, she plead, as her hand begun to slip from his cheek.

And in that moment, he looked.

His eyes, in an instant, flicked down to meet hers. For a second they looked. Then their souls touched once again, and they became strong. Like a storm full of thunder, their unity soared till the brilliant light of the tower faded again, and it disappeared as they were covered in the darkness, together.

Sheelaakah… you… oh! He cried, and wrapped her in his arms, weeping cathartically. *You found me! You found me! You found me!* was all he could say.

When their tears subsided, he spoke. *I knew it was wrong. It was like a dread curiosity. I looked at what I shouldn't, even though I could feel myself becoming trapped once more. I tried to find you, my sister, I've been calling to you...*

I know! and she wept again.

She looked up into his eyes, thinking that she'd never leave her twin soul again. She'd found him, and they'd never live another moment alone... Somehow, she'd set him free, and he'd be with her again among the living.

Slowly then, Sheelaakah realised there was a new light. The little light she'd seen at first. It radiated peace.

It did not drag them towards it, and it did not judge or condemn them for staying. Sheelaakah refused to look, but Daemon did.

Sheelaakah... he whispered.

She knew what he was feeling even before he put it into words.

I have to go, he said.

She him clutched as desperately even as her heart resonated with new truth in his words. It was not trap this time, it was a choice for what was best. He really did have to go...

He wasn't staying...

She hit him on the chest. Pumbled him fiercely. Struck him with all her force. *Why, why!*

He did not answer, but she knew he was right. She could feel it in her heart. He had done what his life had needed to do, but she hadn't finished what she was alive for yet.

But... her lips trembled. *We need you here. I need you here...*

He smiled knowingly, and she could tell he'd been listening to someone she could not see. *Don't worry, my sister. You have set me free, and I will be continuing the fight! You don't know what you've just done. I am the first, the first ever to break the hypnosis of the tower of light. It was our soul bond, from before this world, which gave you the strength to enter this realm. And it is your talent that will give you the power to return. You are half dead here. One step towards either light, and you cannot come back. But what we just did, to take me away from that place... we've left a hole.* And here his enthusiasm began to take on familiar proportions. *It's a gap in the perfect flaw of that single crystal of false light! Others will find their way now. Thoughts of loved ones in this world can now be heard by those seeking them. In the valley of death, you have delivered a more deadly blow than any who have lived on this world yet.*

He smiled at her, but she held on to him. He spoke calmly, unlike she'd ever heard him in life. *Sheelaakah, I need to go on now. You've done it, you're broken the spell of the tower of light. I need to go ... and you, you have to stay.*

He looked long into her eyes. Looked, and she knew she'd not be seeing them again.

And yet, she let her grip loosen.

And then, in a moment that was both despairing and triumphant, she realised she did not want to hold on to him any longer, not if there was somewhere he wanted to be. Not if he was needed in another place, even if that place was too far away from her to touch him in all the rest of her life.

He had left a scar that had not healed when he'd died to save her. Now, she'd travelled into death to save him. But he was still leaving... and she would let him go, and the old wound would have to heal again.

It still hurt. It still hurt so much to release him, to watch him walk slowly away, always facing her, towards the light. It hurt, though she was willing to let him go.

He stood inside that little light now, that grew brighter and brighter till she couldn't look at him anymore. She sensed others in that light. Countless others, warriors perhaps? And they were on their way to this world to help it in its time of change.

He waved again, and told her that he loved her.

And she cried the first tears of true happiness in over seven years.

When she came to her mind was strangely clear. She was still dressed in rags, still lying in filth. Her body still ached, but her heart burned with hope. She reached up to her head, it felt so different. It was then she realised that the creature they'd placed there was gone, lying miraculously dead on the floor.

She knew she only had a few moments before they'd realised what had happened. A few seconds before they would return and replace it, if they weren't on their way already. And she was right. But in those few moments she managed to reclaim her mind, cast out the darkness they had placed there, and inscribe an invisible protective ward on the floor so she could rest after they'd tortured her again.

By the evening of the next day, the prison was a riot. In the following days she became a thorn in their side continually. She could not break free yet, but every day, she grew stronger. Now, her persecutions steeled her resolve, her deprivations only strengthened her spirit: Prisoners broke free of their bounds with inhuman strength, guards met with continual resistance and ill fortune more and more each day. She even broke a gate ward one morning and saw what was beyond the gate, and where on the planetoid they were sequestered. She may have even managed to send a fleeting message for assistance to her friends...

While locked in chains, tied to the floor of a dark, filthy asylum, she felt truly free – for she did not fear death or anything they might do to her.

Pirate alliance

This time, he would not allow her to evade his pursuit. He was careful, he was quick. But every step she just seemed a little faster.

And then there were the inhuman leaps. Matrix had to master three such moves to each of her one.

Suddenly she rounded a corner on one of the innumerable boats that swam the darkness out here. As he turned that corner a moment later, dodging the knives and grasping hands of the pirates whose ship he'd unlawfully trespassed, he was surprised to find her nowhere in sight. His first thought was that she'd probably jumped and made it round the stern already, but then he noticed the door. He tore it open so swiftly it jarred from its hinges.

She was right there, two paces away from him, in the act of talking calmly with another women. A serving maid of some kind.

He looked between them.

They were the same woman.

The Siren began to dash from the premises as soon as he entered, but he did not pursue her further. Instead, he grabbed the other, the maid, by the wrist.

She looked alarmed, then smiled.

Then she threw the stew at him.

He dodged it nimbly and swept her feet out from under her. Only she did not fall, but spun around in the air and landed again on her feet. In an instant she leapt up and off the door frame and was out the door again.

He chased her hard this time, knowing he could not afford to keep this up forever, and if she kept creating clones of herself ...

She was heading towards a crowded barge this time, pressing through their midst, watching him all the time with her wry, tempting smile.

But he knew her style by now. Sure enough, he watched till she disappeared inexplicably in the throng. Sure enough, there was a trapdoor lying underfoot.

Roaring out a warning, he leapt along the wires that held up the lanterns in this place, smashing the door in an instant. He landed in a quiet sewer underneath the market.

She was standing there, not three paces away.

'You've lead me on quite a chase, Siren.'

She smiled, and running up along the wall landed on a passageway high ahead. He took the walls in leaps and pulled himself up, but she was dashing off even faster than before.

With a blast of his rifle, the woman finally stopped.

'Siren, we need to talk,' he ordered.

She turned.

'Only if you catch me first,' she teased.

'I think I have you-' he begun, but faster than thought she dived down a shaft he hadn't seen. Not knowing what he'd find, he raced up, and leapt in afterwards.

The shaft emerged under the markets, reversed in gravity. His impulsiveness had helped him catch up to her again, but just as he might have caught her ankle, she leapt into the darkness to catch hold of the deck of a ship that was just pulling out.

He didn't have the strength to follow that leap, so he shot out a power duct under the markets where he was, and allowed it to blast him recklessly out into space, his wild careering barely halted by his quick work with the gravity belt as he landed heavily on the hull.

His sub telepathic link with Bakerson suddenly died.

But he would not lose her this time. They were under a ship's hull, gravetised boots working overtime to keep him from falling into open space. Then the vessel unexpectedly began to accelerate – they were scaling up a mountain of air tight wood.

Finally she seemed to be tiring, and he reached up, and caught her by the ankle. She cried out, and lost her footing, slipped down into his arms.

She looked up into his face, her eyes dark pools of mystery. They were lost for words and the boat slid past them and they floated in the space between the shipyards. Activating his gravity belt, he begun to gently manoeuvre them towards a convenient barge, her panting breath heavy against his as their air shields melted together.

They said nothing as they floated down, and when they landed she kept looking up at him in willing surrender. Eventually, he tried to dislodge her from his arms, and she seemed reluctant to go.

'I'm Matrix,' he said.

'I know,' she allured, trying to lose herself in his eyes.

'Ahh...' he said, and stepped back.

She looked surprised.

She regained her pose, and turned profile to him to stare out at the stars. 'Well done, Matrix. You caught me.'

He smiled, breathing heavily and joined her at the balcony. For a moment he hoped the subtelepathic link would come back on soon, perhaps it had dislodged in the chase? At least it seemed she would be willing to talk, for now.

'They call you the Siren.'

'I know,' she teased.

'I need you to take me to meet someone.'

She frowned dejectedly, as though he'd said something wrong. 'Am I not prize enough?'

She was beautiful, then he caught himself. He was not here for her prize. He wanted to speak to the Myth. He wanted the alliance of the Kinerigan pirates. He wanted to break down a wall.

'I need you to take me to someone.'

She looked angry. 'Darkstar,' she said.

'Not really.'

'No? We'll I'll take you to meet him anyway.'

'Siren,' Matrix interjected, grabbing her by the hand and whispering. 'I need to speak to Myth. I know you can take me to the pirate leader.'

She smiled.

'In time.' She winked, 'and now, with no further ado, there's someone you need to meet, if you're to understand...'

A small, old, narrow frigate sailed up above the peer to meet them, sails furling themselves as a gang plank folded from the door. Out of it stepped a mature aged man with greying hair.

'Darkstar,' Matrix mused.

'Ahh!' the old man said. 'More Resistance delegates then. Hello young man, I see you've met my wife.'

'Ahh...' was all Matrix could say. Just then, a woman, the splitting image of the Siren, came to the door behind Darkstar, dressed in the honoured garb of a typical pirate helmsman.

'I really should bring my friends,' Matrix said, halting to enter that vessel.

The Siren maid looked at him dangerously. 'No. There are things I want to say that they cannot hear.'

Matrix still faltered.

'Besides,' she said dangerously. 'You get to bring your friends only if I get to bring mine.

She looked out, and there along the balustrades and shipyards, Matrix could see... others... at least a half dozen among the thousands or so individuals that walked the strange world of the pirates. Sailors, tradesmen, wives. And the others of the Siren watched, and they waved in unison.

'How do you do that?' Matrix asked.

'Inside,' she half ordered, half explained.

'Congratulations,' Darkstar commented. 'You've won her.'

Strangely, Matrix did not feel it was quite a prize.

---+++---+----

It was a strange relationship.

They acted every bit like a young couple in love, yet the woman who he'd chased here, who had the same face and mannerisms, kept staring at him like he was the only thing that could complete her in the whole universe.

It was unnerving.

Darkstar noticed Matrix's discomfort.

'You get used to it pretty quick,' he explained consolingly.

'What... who is she?' Matrix asked, deliberately not making her part of the conversation.

'Most of the others don't know.' Darkstar continued, then turned to his wife, the pilot. 'Love, perhaps we need to take this out of the shipyards a bit.'

The woman he referred to as wife happily complied, while the other continued to stare possessively at Matrix. He refused to look at her, so she quietly went to join the other at the helm, and they spoke to each other in muted tones. Even so, he feared he was still well within her hearing range.

Darkstar laughed quietly.

'What happened to you?' Matrix asked.

'That's simple,' Darkstar replied. 'I fell in love.'

'What?!' Matrix asked.

'I don't know how she does it.' He smiled, suddenly looking a little weary, creases of concern behind the smiling face of a once proud Resistance spy. 'I think it's some form of psychological control, not drugs, I've ruled that out. Somehow, she knows just what you need, and just how to get it. Before you know it, you cannot live without her. And she makes you hers.' And here, he sighed contentedly.

'You... you chose her?' Matrix asked.

'Indeed,' he smiled, and his young wife coyly smiled back at him.

There was something wrong about all this.

'What is she?' Matrix asked, sure their conversation was not private, but needing to know what kind of trap he'd sprung on himself. His legs still ached from their race, and yet she bore no signs of weariness, or even discomposure. And how was it that she could be a dozen women all over the Kinerigan space?

Darkstar laughed. 'She's a program. A hologram.'

Matrix raised his voice in alarm. 'You mean she's a complete synaptic download? The image of a living person's soul?'

'Oh no, not that. We'll, not any more. She's like... a projection of sorts. Her central system, the computer that she is, lives somewhere out here in moonscape, I don't care to know where.'

'You're married to a computer program?' He asked, disbelieving.

'Many are,' Darkstar unapologetically replied.

Then the pilot Siren turned to them. 'And the first thing you would do,' she explained to Matrix, 'if you found out you were a sentient computer program?'

He did not reply. He was liking her less and less.

'...is make a thousand copies of yourself. Just in case,' she winked, and Darkstar sighed.

'I've never seen her doubt a decision. Never seen her not get what she wants. And when you catch her, as I eventually did, you find yourself unable to ever let her go...'

Matrix was quite for a moment. Then he realised what he'd known since their case began. 'So that's how you do it, Myth,' he said, addressing the Siren for what she was – undisputed leader of the Kinerigan pirates on Seren. 'You make them love you.'

The Siren turned to him now, and smiled lovingly. 'You're very clever,' she boasted.

He disdained the compliment. 'What I don't understand is why, but I guess that doesn't matter.'

In a flurry of unexpected fear, Matrix realised he did not want to be part of whatever spell this program was attempting to weave around him. She'd obviously had many lifetimes to observe and perfect whatever conjuration through which she managed to manipulate humans so well. Matrix stood up to leave.

He was surprised no one tried to stop him. But the Siren said; 'Don't leave. I… I need you.'

It was like pin in his heart. A part of him never wanted to see her unhappy… then he stopped himself, what *had* she done to him when he'd caught her in his arms?

So he laughed.

Darkstar backed off. The Siren pilot turned, her face a perfect reflection of the angry expression that blackened the other Siren's feature.

'Ahh, I don't think anyone's done that before…' Darkstar murmured, even as she said; 'I have *never* been denied.'

But then she cooled. 'But I'll not force you, it is not my way. I always knew you were different Matrix. You're not like other humans… you're lateral, random. Like you don't belong here. And that's exotic. I like exotic…' She teased, then sighed. 'Perhaps you can tell me why you've come all the way out to my people to speak to me?'

Matrix could tell it was dangerous to speak to this woman, and wanted to end it quickly. If there was any hope of bringing this knowledge again to the Resistance, it would be worth it. And any lingering addictions to mysterious-jumping-women-who-turned-out-to-be-sentient-computer-programs could be dealt with later. So he said all too formally; 'The Oppression is coming to destroy us, all, and we need your help. The Resistance formally seeks an alliance with the Kinerigan pirates.'

Darkstar smirked broadly at the apparent irony, the pirate queen huffed into a chair. For a moment, she just considered.

When she spoke, it was with animation, and affection. 'All right, you can have your alliance, on one condition…'

'What is that?' He asked when the apparent silence galled him enough.

'Marry me.'

Matrix looked dubious, was she unhinged, or misprogramed?

But she held his attention in sincerity. Darkstar did not raise an eyebrow, indeed, he might have even seemed happy for them…

'Ahh, no, thank you,' Matrix replied, still doubting the reality of this whole situation. 'You're not… my type. Besides, you already have a husband. Probably thousands,' he mused quietly.

She sighed exasperatedly and stood up, even as the pilot took Darkstar's arm affectionately.

'Yes, many. But none are like you. You're ... unlike any man, any human I've ever met. You're... different. I've been around for more than a thousand of your years, and never... you don't think like them Matrix. There's something about you, something exotic. And I want to taste it...'

Darkstar laughed, 'she does like diversity!' He said, his wife slapped him playfully on the chest.

Even as she spoke softly to him, Matrix skin began to crawl. Whatever control she exercised among this murderous and unprincipled people, Matrix silently swore it would not be a part of his life. He would not trade the freedom of the Seren city to be brought under this woman's, this... things... will, seductious as it might be.

'No,' he stated emphatically. He did not want what she offered.

Darkstar whistled.

Her face grew red.

'I have *never* been denied! You... you won the chase, am I not prize enough!' She roared. For a computer program, she was very emotional, and very manipulative. Perhaps she was once a human soul, and now a living imprint of that being? Whoever she once was. Yet for all her strutting, for all her anger and swearing that caused Darkstar to wince as though she was hitting him, Matrix found something so insincere and artificial in her words – like it was just another well-rehearsed act.

He would not end his days living in her fantasy.

Yet she continued her speech threateningly. 'You cannot leave Matrix, you know too much. You'll make your life among us now, you'll find no other like me, till boredom eventually seals you mine-' And suddenly she gasped.

The pilot leapt to the chair, and gave a sudden spin on the wheel, but it was apparently not enough. Something hit the side of the frigate, hard, and the wall begun to buckle and crack. Darkstar was only just quick enough to arrange the atmosphere to prevent them from all being pushed out.

The other Siren's eyes glowed, and a dangerous looking weapon begun to digitise itself into her hands. Matrix took up a defensive position, but did not know what to do as the wooden walls split under the encroaching entity.

Suddenly the digitised weapon fell apart, hit by some form of energy beam as a living machine breached the hull and begun to reform into a man.

It was Skion.

'Toe hold, whelp!' He screamed at her. 'Your threats are layte! May I introduce myself, Skion of the Resistance, and Office Bakerson, at your service,' he jeered.

'You... YOU TOLD THEM!' She screamed at Matrix, advancing on Skion, death in her eyes.

Matrix interposed himself between them, though the mechman groaned in disappointment at the missed fight.

'They are with me,' Matrix said.

She looked at him kindly, her eyes melting.

It felt like such an act.

'Very well then,' she said calmly, the perfect act. 'Could you please tell me how you managed to find Matrix, and how you've managed to eavesdrop on our entire conversation?'

'Kino radio,' Bakerson commented, as if to a friend.

'What?! That... child's toy?' Darkstar sounded surprised, as the Resistance soldiers sized each other up.

'Yep,' Glenn said.

Myth, the siren, laughed. 'And I suppose you've gotten the whole conversation out to the Resistance by now?'

'Yep,' Bakerson replied, and Skion folded his arms in pleasure.

There was a brief pause, and then in a simultaneous movement, the Siren hit a panel in anger as the pilot kicked a chair in frustration, but no further vengeance followed. Matrix could only assume a thousand others struck out all over the pirate lands.

'Get him out of my sight,' she ordered.

They looked surprised.

'Myth,' Matrix said. 'We can still help each other's people.'

'Don't give me that,' and she swore. 'Now the Resistance knows, it will be a matter of days before my people know who I am and what I do. It will be much harder to control them then now. You've humiliated me Matrix.'

He suppressed the shudder of guilt she provoked in him.

But then she smiled, 'I said you weren't like other humans...'

Yet he still wanted the alliance.

'Give it up,' she said, somehow reading his mind. 'As previously stated, until I have your oath to wed, you'll not win a single Kinerigan cannon to your forces, unless you count the holes in your back.'

Matrix wondered then, wondered what it would take to kill her, to destroy her. Either they'd find the computer, or they'd be forced to destroy all thousand or how many copies she'd made of herself, and distributed impossibly among her people. And each could reclone itself again, for all he knew, in a matter of seconds.

He was suddenly very angry. What a *petty* creature, to wager the life of millions on a single choice he made? They would all die without the Resistance to shield them, and to prey on. Was that her plan? Was life so cheap to a woman with a thousand husbands?

'I've never seen her not get what she wants,' Darkstar quietly muttered.

Commander Sheelaakah returns

The hour started like any in this timeless place. They were tormenting her with their fine meal while she was permitted to lick up a crumb if her suffering pleased them.

One was poking her with its fork. She didn't do it, but the fork slipped from its grasp and clattered to the ground. Without a noise, Sheelaakah picked it up and handed it back.

They didn't know what make of that. She did it with as much simple dignity, almost kindness.

One sprang up from its chair now, scattering the contents of the table. It hit her then, often and hard, till she could no longer stand of her own will. But the others had sat there quietly, and returned her to her cell afterwards, not speaking to each other.

Yet by the end of the hour, the violent one had choked to death on its own food. She'd done it, she knew, but not consciously. They'd dragged her back out then. Pointed to him, set her up on the rack as punishment for what they knew she'd done. Their faces white with rage and fear.

The warden had refused to revive him for his failure.

She steeled herself to learn from their punishments again, but it would not be forever now. She had crossed the line. Soon, action would be taken – she was no longer a defenceless prisoner to be toyed with. She was a danger, and she was growing stronger and stronger – and yet they weren't permitted to kill her.

She'd crossed the line.

A whip of long hair

It was Matrix's turn to be frustrated, and pushed the papers angrily away. It was a certificate of marriage in name only, and one he would never sign. 'You don't get it. She doesn't 'own' you, she *possesses* you. Skion, Bakerson, you saw what she made of Darkstar didn't you? It'd be trading one prison for another...'

'You couldn't hope for more pleasant a prison...' Skion murmured.

Matrix felt the muscles in his arm twitch. He *really* wanted to punch something. 'We were so close! Almost had the entire peoples of the Wilderness to our cause!' he moaned.

I-olo looked at him sternly. 'Don't think the cause completely lost, Matrix, though none begrudge you your choices. Many would much rather the Kinerigan did not participate, and though it means watching our backs, many others are more comfortable not having to watch their flanks, if you get my meaning.'

He did. They all did. The full Circle was there, most through telepathic imagery, but they were all there.

'I have word,' another was saying, 'the Derringer are committed to our cause. They will allow you to pilot the gnolem without -'

There was a brief alarm.

'What is it?' Skion wandered. He and Bakerson had recently been promoted to Command level, equal to Sheelaakah now, wherever she was. Matrix however was, as yet, still assigned only lowly unit man status. It did not stop them from pinning all their hopes of their respective organisations on him...

'Strange...' I-olo was saying. 'The Mutants are calling for a delegation, you in specific Matrix. They say it is most urgent.'

Matrix paused in concern, 'Doesn't feel right.'

'The code checks out,' Skion commanded.

'And if they're having doubts we'll need to know.' A circle member announced. 'There can be no divided intentions when we make our assault at that wall Matrix. A most fortuitous conjunction of stars will be within a week.'

They all agreed.

Matrix sighed, 'Beats sitting around here waiting for an obsessed female to stalk me. She's evil. Let's go check it out.'

'I think we might like to look more into this...' I-olo began, but the message bore the urgency of a people under attack. With a wave of his hand, he dismissed the warriors to gather a legion of elite, and teleported them to the location the mutants had indicated.

---++--++---

'You're Matrix?' the long haired man sounded incredulous.

Matrix could feel the wrongness as soon as the violent lurch pulled him out of the teleportation and sent him spiralling to the floor.

He was in a trap.

There were no legion of elite, no Commander Skion, no Bakerson. Just one long haired telepath. It was the telepath from the 23rd and fourth, the one Commander Sheelaakah had bested.

But Sheelaakah was not here now.

No one knew where she was.

'I am Matrix,' he replied, standing. They were alone in some form of Resistance munitions and training barracks. They were not inside the city – he would have felt the difference. There were Resistance insignias and battle gear – but where the Resistance soldiers who normally would have manned such barracks now was not apparent.

'Not all the enigma I was told to expect: I am disappointed. You're barely a year or two older than myself. Clearly no psychic...'

Matrix winced as an inhumanly powerful mind brush up against his, callously scanning far more than his surface thoughts. '... and yet you're such a thorn in the True One's side that he sends me out to end you tonight. I had such other... engaging projects to attend to.'

Matrix did not speak, it did not feel right to. He was truly in danger this time. This foe could do more than slay him, he could drive him insane.

The telepath continued. 'Seems the Government still has a little say in what your Circle decides as yet! Bringing you out here to talk to mutants, ha! I'll have to remember that one. I wish you'd come into the city like we'd originally invited but I don't think you even got that message. It would have been so much easier, instead I had to hunt you,' the predator teased.

'You have no right to be here, nor to speak to me,' Matrix calmly said. 'If you leave, I will spare your dignity.'

The telepath smiled. 'Yet I will not spare your life, Wormboy,' he laughed in almost perfect imitation of Skion the first day they'd met. 'That's right, you are an open book to me, Matrix, and let me tell you what I read...'

He then unleashed a blistering barrage of pain and hurt and Matrix fell to the floor in spite of himself. Matrix could tell the telepath wasn't really trying, just testing his enemy. But to Matrix, it was a storm unlike any he had faced. It was truly a battering. He could do little more than batter down against that storm, and this he did. He remembered his training, put all his faith in his defences. It was a dire struggle, but he remembered himself, and gave his predator no opening from which to take advantage.

It must have been at least fifteen minutes, maybe more, when the storm begun to abate. Matrix had survived the first round. He had nothing to attack his predator with, but he'd defended himself well enough so that his enemy tired.

'Impressive. You're better trained than I'd expect, for one so young. Has the Resistance finally invested in some proper experiences for their meat? They're usually so lax in such things,' he mocked.

He risked speaking to the sadistic telepath, to draw out time in hope of being found. He was wondering where the others had gotten to. Perhaps Bakerson would not be there to pull him out of this one... where were the twice minute scans when you needed them?

'I was born in the city,' Matrix said.

'Don't you think I know everything about you, fool!' The telepath spat, not wanting to chat to pass the time, and begun his second wave of attacks. It was intense, crushing despair that changed quickly to convulsions and back again. Matrix did not do so well this time, and he could see his predator was trying much harder. Telepathic blow followed telepathic blow, and Matrix cried out in fear.

The attacks intensified. The predator got creative. It was in a moment madness, then cold, then fear. Matrix had to fight them all, fight them all at the same time. He could not stand up, he could not attack.

There was no way to last against such a foe.

But he struggled, and fought. He refused to yield.

'Why do you not break, man?' The cruel psychic hissed between his lips at around the seventh minute. It was actually a good question. The blows should have driven him mad, crippled his mind. Yet somewhere, something deep inside him, held on... what was it that kept him sane?

It was her. Sheelaakah. She'd done something to him, unintentionally, all those weeks ago when she'd mistakenly overdone her interrogation. When she'd left him with nothing to defend his soul with. When she'd touched his soul heart... it had made him stronger. He'd been into the depths of his soul and survived. It was a strength few mastered in the life.

Suddenly he saw her.

Matrix saw Sheelaakah. She was tied to some kind of rack, barely breathing in a dark red room. She was in great pain, but along the very edges of her aura was a tinge of golden white. She shifted uncomfortably.

Unexpectedly the telepath's attacks suddenly stopped, the predator throwing his mind violently away from his quarry as though it had struck him with lightning.

'How did you do that?!' The telepath demanded, his voice touched with fear.

Matrix stood up, smiling, wiping the blood from his nose. So, this man knew where Sheelaakah was, and was keeping her alive for his own... ends.

'How!' The predator demanded. 'You used my own link to access my memories. You should not be able to do that!' He looked about nervously.

Matrix smiled.

He didn't know what the telepath was talking about, but in saying so much he had handed Matrix a weapon. Perhaps there was a way to threaten his assailant after all. It did feel like... when they were deeply connected telepathically as predator and prey, he could access the others mind. It had something to do with flooding...

And that was all he needed. With a thought and motion, he activated the room. Unknowingly his predator had stepped within a training zone, and at Matrix's signal the floors fell away, the doors ground shut, and a red circle appeared above them. His assailant gasped.

Matrix smiled.

'Oh no,' the predator suddenly laughed. 'Do think stone can hold me? I am Token, Lord Admiral of all the minds on Seren!' He whirled around then, and trust his arm out to command the stones to form a bridge between him and the exit.

But they did not obey.

'Oh, you're on Resistance territory now, Lord Admiral,' Matrix said in gentle mocking. 'You'll be leaving only with an oath to leave us in peace.'

'...you... don't want me dead?' The predator queried unbelievingly.

'Not unless it's absolutely necessary,' Matrix replied.

But the telepaths breathing harshened, and with a flourish the predator unleashed his worst at the Resistance soldier. But Matrix was ready now. With strength from years of pain, with tactics the Oppression had never dreamed of, and with hope from an ally this Token knew still lived, Matrix fought back. He sent every darkness back at his predator, flooding him with images and emotions, offsetting every attack.

But he knew he could not best him, not with pure mental ability. Step by agonising step, he closed the gap between them. So intent, and over confident, was the telepath at his assault he had no idea what primal danger he faced. Before he was even in arm's reach, Matrix leaped forward and punched him in the face. Hard.

Token reeled back, taking stock of his unexpected wound. 'You'll not defeat me, Matrix. I am a Lord Admiral, and you are less than a flea.'

'Where's Sheelaakah?' Matrix demanded, but the predator did not reply. He was doing something, with palms to the earth, his eyes falling back into his head. With practiced skill, he formed around him dark runes of glowing red power.

It was a summoning ritual, and Token was the centre of it.

Matrix looked about not knowing what to do. Then he thought of Glenn, and waited, centring himself whatever came...

---+++---+++---

Alasia woke up because someone slapped her. Hard.

The Androgenine.

She was in a bleak blue stone circle, tired to a wooden pole. They must have been in some kind of room, still within the pyramid by the stonework. Her guide was tied beside her to a pole, also unconscious. Her connection, yet again, to the Evernet was severed. Her copper banding, removed - and to add insult to injury, she saw that the neuralising blast had damaged the adjustable implants in her scalp, and many dozens of stands of hair dislodged themselves from the back of her head every time she moved.

'Foolish, stupid woman,' the Androgenine was saying in perfect, insulting calmness. 'I told you to stay off the Rei-nati case.'

'Until...' she begun, then realised that her lip was swollen, an experience she'd never had before. '... until we realised you *were* the Rei-nati. What happened to the traitor among us?'

'Right here!' He smirked cheerfully. Alasia turned to glare at him, while the androgenine looked annoyed.

'What was your price?' Alasia demanded to know of the traitor.

'A wife,' he replied cheekily. 'Princesses are in such short supply now days, and with the coming revolution, well, you need to be well placed!'

'Silence,' the androgenine commanded with authority. 'I ask the questions here. Telepath, are you yet done?'

Alasia turned to see a man in strange robes, waving a smoking lantern. His attention was directed at her, and she suddenly realised he was trying to probe her mind. Her defences went up, but without her copper banding she was likely to be bested.

'I'm sorry, spymaster,' the priest apologised. 'Her mind in strange. It's like ... a kaleidoscope, or labyrinth...'

She laughed, and the Androgenine glared at her.

'We need to know what she knows,' it fumed at the priest. 'Keep trying, and let me know if you want her unconscious again. What about the other one?'

'I'm sorry master,' another priest apologised, one Alasia could not see. 'We'll get nothing from this one. He's too well trained and... experienced. It would be dangerous to probe further, even unconscious.'

The androgenine pondered this a moment. He spoke to her guide. 'So, my colleague and my trainer. It has come to this. After all your years it is your skill that will undo you.'

It ran a long hand coldly under his chin, savouring the image.

'Template him,' the androgenine ordered.

Alasia had been struggling. She had been trying to break whatever barrier they held against her to the Evernet. She was making progress – but it was not be fast enough. Within moments they'd begun to strap him to an operating table.

That was all the impetus Alasia needed. With little regret now for the inevitable consequences of this action, in a single word she summoned her demon and let it possess her again. In a single gesture, she broke the thick ropes holding her arms, and the punch daggers formed themselves from her hands again. With a single swift motion, she ended the lives of the two guards who were about the carry out the silver man's will.

Then with a distant jolt of horror, she realised she didn't have the power to deny its tenticular hold on her fear any more... she was becoming, its servant - and she hardly cared.

'Stop her!' The Androgenine called.

Alasia marvelled at the lucidity of it all – she was completely aware this time. She was almost flying with deadly grace. They could not hit her with their rays and bullets, her skill was now far beyond the most basic wards of all people now days. They quickly closed for melee combat, and while a glancing blow was deflected by her body armour, a glancing blow was all they were able to score against that dark spirit that possessed her.

The next thing it did was slay the telepaths. Then through her it took out the nearest guards, even as others begun to pile in the room.

The androgenine was quickly hidden behind a wall of defences. But she would penetrate them. She would raise the whole army of the Rei-nati, and live to fulfil her guide's dream of freeing the people from their self-serving oppression.

Then suddenly, unexpectedly, her dark spirit left.

With a gasp, she heard it leave.

And as it left, so did her strength, her agility, her ability to protect herself. It gave no explanation. It gave no reason. It was as if someone more powerfully had simply pulled it off her.

She managed to claw at one of them in the face, splitting her nails and coating them in blood and skin before she was taken down and brutally beaten for her short lived escape. She was terrified, wounded, threatened and defeated.

Alasia was humiliated.

---+++---+++---+++---

When the ritual ended, Matrix knew he was in serious trouble again. The demon that filled Lord Admiral Token turned his eyes red, and moved his with such fluidity and grace it was beautiful to behold.

'And now, mortal, you die,' it calmly said.

It leapt on him with inhuman strength and agility, wide sweeping blows of its arms ready to break Matrix bones, and might have, except they'd been broken there before. It was fast, furious, and tremendously deceptive.

But that was not the only danger. Somehow, Token was still alive and aware though the being he willingly allowed to possess him. Again the torrent of telepathic attacks struck out, and Matrix was forced to defend himself with both mind and body.

Acting on impulse, driven by years of skill and determination, he fought back with all his will. There could be no mistake, the demon was no doubt skilled in thousands of years more murder than he could know. It was enjoying the battle intensely - yet it did not toy with him, seeming eager to end him quickly.

But Matrix was not seduced by the fear to destroy it before it could outlast him. He was patient, and strove to learn what his opponent was thinking before risking the temptation to end it. He fought with desperation and skill, but studied his foe. It grew more and more frustrated with each failed attempt to provoke him into a quick resolution, and in that Matrix begun to wonder if waiting was its weakness.

They were leaping, jumping from the levitating stones, twisting in the maze of gravity. Matrix was actively avoiding it now, consciously deflecting both physical and telepathic blows rather than be drawn in to combat. At one point, he even laughed. But it was an unbalanced fight. One was mortal, the other knew the limitless potential of mortals, and in the end, Matrix begun to tire.

He knew even if he severed a limb from the telepath, the demon would have the long haired man continue fighting as though nothing had happened. It would mean his death if Matrix underestimated his inhuman adversary and its human host. Even the risk of landing a crushing blow to an average mortal would might have left him open to the inhumane creature's abilities. He did not know how the battle would end.

And with that thought, Token saw his opportunity. He drove depression into Matrix, so that when it struck its blow, Matrix did not use enough strength to block it properly, and the beast caught him by the nerves in his arm and twisted him to his knees.

'Finish him now!' The demon demanded through Token's voice.

'Hold!' Token commanded, breathing frantically. 'Now. Matrix, thorn of the Oppression. You will admit me, the victor. Then you will die.'

'Ahh, no?' Matrix said.

The hand crushed his nerves so painfully he couldn't breathe for a moment.

'Finish him!' The demon demanded again.

'No! I am the host, you will conform to me!' Yet his voice trembled. 'Now, officer Matrix, you will admit me, the victor, and then you will die.'

Matrix dimly wondered why on earth *that* was so important.

'Finish him,' the demon hissed in desperation. And then Matrix realised something he hadn't before…

'Matrix, you will-' Token begun.

'I said, no!' Matrix shouted, rising. He struck then, not only with his fist, but with his will, and with another talent only he seemed to possess. His hand shot out, and grabbed the demon by the throat.

It shrieked in pain and anguish, the first of its existence, as Matrix pulled it by its neck from the long haired host, who fell exhausted to the floor. It was in the form of a man, with dark wisps trailing from its waist. Two short horns protruded from its forehead, its face was twisted into an inhumane visage of madness.

'Time for you to end, demon.' Matrix said, and begun to pour the light and heat into it. It shrieked, and its eyes begun to glow with a golden fire that was inexorably consuming it from within.

Suddenly, Matrix felt a sharp, alarming pain in his side. Token had stabbed him. In that moment Matrix lost the sliver of concentration required to keep the demon held, and it tore itself from his grasp and fled shrieking into the stones...

Matrix was angry again – the wound, while dangerous, was shallow, and the nanoprobes would stem the bleeding almost instantaneously. Token, on the other hand, seemed to have forgotten he was a telepath, and swung the knife at him again. With the ease of a practiced soldier, Matrix dodged it, and grabbing the man's arm twisted it painfully above his head and sent him crashing to his knees. There was no strength in that hand. The pitiful attacks he attempted to make telepathically were easily deflected. Matrix held that hand till the pain in its tendons convinced the predator... to surrender.

'How did you...' Lord Admiral Token begun. 'So, this is how it ends?' His breathing was ragged, his strength, exhausted.

While Matrix, a veteran of the wilderness beyond, was still standing.

'Is this how I die?' Token asked bitterly.

'Oh no, we're the New Resistance now. We have... policies not dictated to us by our enemies anymore.'

Tokens face twisted in wrath, 'I will not break to torture!'

Matrix let the surprise show in his voice. 'Not at all! No death, no torture...' and he put his face close to the telepath so that he could hear him whisper: 'But welcome to discapasitation.'

Token looked surprised, but could not move fast enough as the bronze knife came out and in one smooth gesture cut his hair right to scalp. He watched in horror as the proud strands wandered forlornly downwards.

Landing a mighty blow to his face, several perhaps, Matrix singled handedly defeated the most powerful telepath of the Oppression and his demon servant.

Everyone would know.

What it means to be Alasia

Alasia wept as they strapped her to the pole again. There was nothing she could do now. They were so many, and she was completely alone.

There was nothing her guide could do either, unconscious on the operating table. They would take him, and there was nothing she could do now. Nothing, except watch.

'I warned you!' The grey being apologised in an exasperated manner. 'You have failed, and now he will die despite your efforts. He was weak, never did what was in the people's interest. Never did… what was *necessary*.'

He floated up to her, wiping her tears away with its hand. 'And now you,' it said sadly. 'You cry too? Even for all your strength you see you are now bested. You are too weak, woman. But I will allow you to see him templated, so that you can… reconsider you allegiance…'

She looked at it with unfathomable spite. How would it dare mock her with a pretended offer at this hour!

Suddenly it was there again. The dark spirit.

My mistress. Don't let them do this to him! You love him, I know. Let me join you again, and I will finish them all.

It sounded oddly desperate, like it was… frightened… or something. Some measure of coldness to its inhuman voice was missing.

But it spoke of what she wanted. What she wanted more than life itself. He guide was something else. He was… she did not want him to die, at any cost.

I will end this… it pled.

But in that moment she realised it had lost some of its control over her. As the dark creature had abandoned her, she was regaining some of her… faith. It had abandoned her in her desperation, and now… she'd found what she needed at last to be free of her demon. She could not continue to let fear rule her actions, to allow it to rule her. She would become a monster, and it would slowly take control of her till there was nothing good or worthwhile, or even alive in her.

So even if it cost her his life, infinitely more dear than her own… she would never allow that dark spirit to possess her again. Its work was murder, and nothing more. She owed it to herself. She owed it to him…

'No,' Alasia said out loud, but not to the grey man. The demon continued to plead, trying to force itself into her, but its plaintiff requests bounced off her unheeding resolve. She was not even going to listen to it any more. It threatened her, whispering gallons of bitter spite against her and everything she loved.

But she was deaf to its voice.

Finally, screaming unspeakable curses on its lips it fell into the darkness, never to touch her soul again. It made her shudder, but it was a scream none heard but her. And in that moment, she felt a glimmer of hope. If she died, at least she was free of her demon.

But the grey being had assumed she spoke to it. It turned away condescendingly and ordered the procedure begin.

Alasia screamed in desperation, 'Do you know what you're doing? Do you know what this man has done? He is the truest loyalist of Seren I've ever met, with no crimes to deserve this fate. How can you do this to him?'

'Shut her up,' the grey being said, and one of the guards hit her hard in the stomach. She fell on the ground, unable to catch her breath. It really hurt.

But not as much as the pain in her soul. She looked up through her tears. She saw them beginning the procedure.

She was about to lose him, and had never had the chance to say goodbye. His death, without her sponsor and refusing the Rei-nati, meant her death would no doubt soon follow. And she'd never even have the chance to explain things to the Commander, to the Resistance... to the man with green eyes...

Her guide had saved her from what she was becoming, and helped her to become something better. He was her best friend, her protector ... her guide.

And with that, she had a thought.

'Rei-nati,' she said smoothly, and the cold androgenine half turned. 'How uncouth, this all seems a little unlike you.'

It turned to look questioningly, humouring her little game.

'I mean, condemning this man to death, even without a trial of your own people ...' her voice pondered whimsically.

The grey being looked at her in anger, blue blood flooding its cheeks. 'You've no right to speak of *our* law! This man deserves death for all he knows, if nothing else.'

'True, perhaps... but... Just, I suppose if *he* can die without trial, it makes me ask how many more of your people will, just when *you* decide they must.'

Its breathing sharply deepened.

Alasia smiled.

And for the first time ever they heard it scream in *frustration*, 'Stop the procedure! Take this being to trial!'

They hurried to comply, a bit had to be undone. But the operation was halted and his life, for the time being, was saved.

Revenge of the telepath

Bakerson had found him, moments later, accompanied by a legion of elite. Matrix could not have been happier. Token lay unconscious on the ground.

Glenn looked puzzled, 'he lives?' he asked.

Matrix smiled, 'Yep, and he knows where Sheelaakah is too!'

And that was when he first felt it. His wound, from the little knife Token had used, was beginning to sting.

'What?' Matrix asked in confusion, looking at his side.

'What is it?' Glenn asked looking puzzled.

All the world swimmed in a vision before Matrix's eyes.

'The knife...' was all he could say in the rapidly growing pain.

Bakerson bent down to smell the wound. 'Nanites! Matrix! Get me a medic stat!' he roared to the elite.

Suddenly the ground shook.

'That wasn't me, was it?' Matrix asked jokingly, sweat pouring off his face as the agony jolted up his side.

A unit man replied in alarm, 'continent of Oppression arriving here. They're got Juggernauts!'

'Get that Oppression telepath!' Bakerson roared, but the wall carved in at that instant, a creature of stone and metal tearing the building apart. They barely managed to hold back the debris in the energy field the unit man created, scarce meters from the felled telepath.

'Exit! Stat!' Bakerson roared, dragging them angrily away, trying to save Matrix's life, ordering the elite to take that telepath at all costs. An order they were powerless to fulfil.

'What does that mean?' Matrix asked him.

'The nanites are trying to digitise you, Matrix, you'll be dead in an hour if we can't reprogram them!' Glenn said in a fearful tone.

'No, not that.'

'What?' Bakerson said.

'You said "stat." What does that mean? You say it a lot-' but he didn't finish the sentence, as that was when the screaming started.

The fall of Sheelaakah

They left her alone after she'd killed one of them, and in so doing the incorporeals had as well. In that time, she'd trebled her strength. She could take them one at a time now, but was still too weak to escape them all on her own. She needed others, and hoped they'd be on their way now... she'd felt... one of them, less than an hour ago... perhaps he would find her?

So it was with a falling pit of despair in her stomach that she felt... him...

Token was coming.

She was tied to a pole, arms anesthetised behind her back. She begun weaving protections around her now, even telekinetically locked the door. But she knew it would do little good.

When he found the door locked, he blasted it open with a phaser.

The man that entered then was dishevelled, reckless. His eyes were bloodshot, and a hand clasped his face where blood slowly drained from deep wounds. But most apparent was the new cut of hair, off at the scalp, a few strands errantly sneaking below his shoulders.

The splinters from the door shattered away and he stared at her darkly. Without breaking her runes her heart began to race. He was about to do something even more unthinkable than all her time in this place.

You... he coughed, and a trickle of dark blood made it way down his lips.

She did not reply.

It's no use. You'll never see reason, will you, he stated.

Whatever darkness was about him began to spread its tendrils into the room. Nobody spoke. He limped down the stairs, pushing aside all. He was carrying something down inside his tunic.

She could see he'd been in some kind of battle. He was badly bruised and his aura was flickering like a candle – he was majorly depleted and clearly suffering acute physical and mental shock. His eyes were dilated and bloodshot, it was a wonder he was not dead already.

She wished he'd stop approaching her.

'No,' she said.

He stumbled, only once, and sent a table full of implements crashing the floor. He'd cut his hand, but it only trembled and he clenched it into a fist.

Join me, he pleaded in final desperation. *JOIN ME!*

She did not reply.

Once you know the power, as I do, you will find it quite irresistible. I have her last instruction, the last thing <u>she</u> requires me to do.

In spite herself, Sheelaakah began to tremble.

Once you know the power, your will belong to us. I can move on then, you will take my place and crush the Resistance forevermore! And then it doesn't matter… one day… you will come and join me then. Once you finally realise what you're CAPABLE OF!

And he tore from his tunic the amulet, its ten legs waving as if it were alive, its tremendous evil dimming all lights and causing all metals in its vicinity to warp and convolute into twisted and tortured shapes.

'Don't do this,' she pled, almost crying in helplessness. The minds of the others reared back in fear.

It's too late for you, my love. Just like it's too late for me…

He reached up, she screamed.

Her final though before oblivion was, *This was not the way it was supposed to end.*

What it means to be Matrix

It hurt. He could not imagine any more intense pain in all his life, and it drove him almost to madness. Nothing but the image of a lion of stone could convince him to endure the unremittent, unforgiving pain. He wished Sheelaakah was here. He wished Alasia was here. He wished his parents…

Being digitised was to become a machine, the most painful way to be templated. The being that was left was a cold mockery of what was once alive. Nanites of this kind were among the most profound contraband in the entire galaxy, and they were swimming in his blood, penetrating every cell.

At one point the medic administered concentrated di-polic morphine. In the moment of clarity as it lasted, before they'd adapted to the chemicals and neutralised them, Bakerson had said, 'what's your will, my friend?'

'Stop them. Do whatever it takes. We're so close, if I die now… they'll never be a second chance, not for a thousand years. Do whatever…' and then it had returned.

At first, Glenn had put Matrix under stasis, and fled. It gave Glenn little comfort to know that another assassin had failed, and it was their first lead on the Commander in weeks. But Glenn had more immediate concerns. Even in stasis, Matrix did not stop deteriorating, and the nanites quickly adapted to it also. Without his consciousness to fight them they would have completed their task in minutes.

And so Matrix had to face the pain.

They'd tessered right to the Resistance central medical facility, even if it mean risking the Oppression might be able to trace it. But all the best medics and programmers of the Resistance could do was stall the inevitable progress of the nano machines. A moment later, a beleaguered and chagrined I-olo tessered right into the hospital room.

'Matrix! Fight! All our prayers are with you!' He'd shouted in desperation.

Matrix did not hear, and all feared the futility of that prayer.

'Are we doing everything?' He demanded of the chief medic.

'Everything,' she replied. 'There's nothing more, he's receiving all we've got. Even got programmers from Supply and Reconnaissance so that it's stalling our operatives within the wall. There's nothing more we can do.' Tears brimmed her eyes.

'We have to do something?' I-olo wondered out loud. 'What have I done? Why did I tell him to go? We can't have got this close! Matrix!' He roared in futile desperation, pounding the walls.

'Fight them! Do whatever it takes.' I-olo murmured.

And in that moment, Glenn knew what he had to do. 'The pirates,' he said.

'What?' I-olo replied incredulously.

'Trust me,' the dog nosed elite replied.

The pause was very brief, then I-olo begun shouting orders across the Evernet in voice. Everyone could hear.

'Fleet admiral!'

'Admiral h...'

'Get to the Kinerigan space, all available forces. Launch immediate. General, Tesser as many ground troops to launching vessels immediately. Mandate, I want a portal opened up immediately to form the launching grounds to the centre of Kinerigan space NOW! Send through a peace beckon. Action everyone, there is *no* other priority!'

The whole Resistance activated in chaos. Enormous machinery was used to break open space and fold it from the centre of Resistance lines to the middle of Kinerigan pirates. It cut twenty minutes off the journey Matrix would otherwise have to take to that place.

The pirates, predicably, shot down the peace beacon immediately. But the sight of the massive battle cruiser emerging from the fold in space was enough to give pause to the wary. A few lone privateers chose foolishly to take on the Resistance, and they were crippled in seconds. It was a majestic and surreal sight, the grey metals of the cruiser floating between the wooden shipyards and rustic balustrades of the Kinerigan.

But a small star craft, a converted carrier, sped from the cruiser. Its target, a nondescript vessel among a thousand others, the home of a single individual everyone knew was 'Darkstar'.

Bakerson entered that vessel alone less than a minute later, carrying Matrix's convulsing form in his arms. One eye had already crystallised under the assault, and consciousness had faded minutes ago.

The man inside that vessel looked at Bakerson, then down at Matrix.

'It's too late,' Darkstar said sadly.

'Not for her,' Bakerson replied, dressed in full Resistance combat gear.

She materialised then on the pilots chair. 'Pity, I'll miss him. He was a nice memory,' She whimsicalled, fixing her nails.

'Please,' Bakerson begged.

She whirled in her chair to look at him. 'What's in it for me?' She asked, almost rhetorically.

Bakerson held her glare for a moment, but knew better. There was nothing to bargain with this ... machine. It was her way, or his friend would die.

'He said...' and the solider choked on his words. Yet all the hope of the alliance hung on his friend life. He could not deny his friends last wish. '... whatever it takes.'

She smiled, triumphantly. 'I like this one,' she said, looking at his twisted and sickened form affectionately.

The deck immaterialised then. All the furniture vanished. They were in a dark room. Immediately, Matrix stopped convulsing.

Darkstar was there. She put a hand on his chest affectionately as she walked past.

'You win again,' he muttered.

'I'll need help for this...' she said out loud, not replying to his comment. They arrived then, one by one, in columns of light. Mirror images of the pirate queen, all dressed differently. Some were waitresses, others wives. There were scullery maids and well-dressed princesses. Prisoners, craft masters, musicians. Scores of them... hundreds.

And all over Moonscape, treasured women disappeared. Some would round a corner and not be found. Others would point to a distant sight, and not be seen when their lovers turned around. Some would tuck their children in, some put their ship on auto pilot, others switched off the oven.

It was how she kept watch over them, how she knew so much about them, how she controlled the pirates.

And the women came, all identical in hair and face, to meld in blue digitised light to become the same who held the strings of Darkstar's heart. He didn't flick an eyelid at these strangers who became his wife. He'd seen it all before.

Matrix was lifted up on an operating table, bright laser arms pulling themselves from the roof to operate on the nanoprobes.

It was a mighty working. It took the best of four full hours. She'd beat them back, and they'd adapt. She'd take a loss, and construct a new avenue of attack. And all the time, the cruiser waited, while a million pirate guns took aim.

Bakerson was dozing off on his feet when suddenly the pirate queen told them it was done. Matrix had survived.

'Take him,' she ordered.

Bakerson looked at her, puzzled she did not claim him now.

'Don't think me such a tyrant. I can wait for this man to fulfil the price of his life to me. He will be mine one day,' and she kissed him on the cheek. 'Let that day be soon, my fiancée,' she muttered.

And Bakerson, face pale with indignation, carried his friend from the deck of the pirate queen.

A council of war

I-olo Tilk, Supply and Reconnaissance admiral for the Resistance, elected leader of the combined nations, eyed the report with glad countenance. They were coming.

The mutants were the first to arrive, bringing an honour guard of no less than forty heavily armed soldiers. They marched their leader up the steps to the wide circle dais, almost two hundred meters in breadth, where the leaders were to meet. He would have to complete no less than seven rituals, four more than was usually considered necessary, but it guaranteed the privacy of this function. And, I-olo hoped, instilled the delegates with a strong sense of faith in the Resistance's ability to organise this … event.

Yet Brek'anarl marched up to the dais alone, a symbol of his absolute authority over his people. It was in stark contrast to the Derringer, who arrived next.

They sent in three. Their leader and the one that would speak was a venerable female, white in hair and beard. She bore an aura of calmness as she approached, and I-olo wondered why she was not more stooped with weariness for her age. Perhaps it was some council or skill her people held that they might like to share one day? More likely, it was their stout natural constitutions and daily tasks of forging stone and steel.

Next, the honour guard of the Tendendalaah arrived, bight in banner and polished bronze armour. If the mutants were troubled by the arrival of their ancient foes, they did not show it. The Tendendalaah entered singing a deep and moving song of baritone and base, ornamenting it with clashing shields and trumpets. Their leaders were two, a very fair and long haired couple, thin and tall as all their people were.

Next came a strange sight. A massive barge made of wood and quantum sails fair crashed into the stands near where they were assigned. Weapons were raised, but the rowdy and dishevelled crew slung only insults at the others. The pirates had arrived – not a day after Matrix had secured their assistance. He who left their dishevelment to speak for the Kinerigan was a strange figure; not at all the whimsical female whom all knew ruled them now. It was Kendrick Darkstar, felled spy of the Resistance. So what the Mutants sent in pride, the pirates sent in disdain. A messenger, not even a delegate? I-olo was inclined to be offended, and spoke to him subtelepathically,

Darkstar?

Oh, hey former spymaster, he said cheerily, not at all like the serious spy he'd sent out ten years ago. *Nice to hear from you again, how are things? Here you got yourself promoted to the helm. Well done!*

I-olo measured his words carefully. There was no deceit in him, at least, not in him personally. *You speak for the pirates now?*

Yes, well, no. I've just been set out here as the most likely not to be shot. Myth just wants me to relay the will of the council today, and we'll see it done. Kinerigan don't keep promises, but we are as sure of our oaths as any.

I-olo thought about this.

It will do, I-olo agreed.

And then finally the last delegate arrived, in astral form. Given the time the meeting would take it was a wonder how the great ocean behemoths would keep up the mental image – a full six times longer than was asked of the most accomplished humans, but I-olo expected them to be up to the task. Not having this delegate in person was a danger, it was true, but perhaps no greater danger than having this particular creature attend in person. The crowds grew silent as the shimmering blue outline of a narwhale floated over their heads and approached the guardians at the first of the seven rituals.

It would take an hour, but at last the six speakers for the six major peoples of Seren were gathered. I-olo did not give them the chance to explore past grievances or potential future ones, but after the necessary formal greetings immediately embarked on the work at hand.

'Delegates. We speak for the free nations of the 'wilderness beyond'. Together, we outnumber the citizenry of the Oppression two to one. Today, we serve to address the injustice done to our combined peoples over the past centuries. This is an historic day, and I will waste no protocol proposing the main agenda: Today begins the alliance for freedom.

'A 'Freedom Alliance',' Brek'anarl murmured.

'Indeed,' I-olo replied, seeking no offence at his interruption. The Tendendalaah, however, were visibly chagrined at his enactment of protocol. I-olo immediately continued, being the first to take the formal oath;

'We, the Resistance, commit all our forces, all our wills, all our resources, to this alliance, this Freedom Alliance, to see the peoples of Seren released. This is our commitment.'

Brek'anarl was about to speak, when another mind cut across his so powerfully he was, even as a telepath, left speechless.

We, the creatures of the Eversea, commit all our forces, all our resources, all our wills, to the freedom alliance: To see the peoples of this world set free. The Narwhale spoke in absolute finality.

The Tendendalaah were not to be outdone, and immediately joined the oath. 'We, the Tendendalaah, commit all our forces, all our resources, all our wills, to the Freedom Alliance: to see the peoples of this world set free. This is our commitment. We beg forgiveness of all we have offended, and place our lives, our blades, and our future, in the service of this alliance and all its people.'

The dwarf may have spoken, but Brek'anarl waved himself in.

'I am not comfortable with this oath.'

The male Tendendalaah hissed in derision.

Brek'anarl continued, smiling contentedly. *We might have come today and spoken about retribution, or repayment for past deeds...* Brek'anarl said telepathically, glancing meaningfully at the Tendendalaah. *I know many of my people demanded it. However, there is one foe more deserving of our wrath than these... 'free peoples'... as we are gathered today. There is one...*

'Surely you're not suggesting we slay everyone within the walls,' The Tendendalaah male interrupted insultingly.

Brek'anarl was not insulted. *And what of it? I have never known the 'Tendendalaah' to be shy in killing those they considered their enemies.*

It drove the male Tendendalaah livid. He might have spoken, but his partners hand on his arm silenced him.

'It is true, brave Mutant Lord,' she said in politeness. 'But we've never struck others in their heart lands. To destroy that people is a crime we will not be involved in. Please, reconsider your suggestion to audit the oath.'

Something in the Tendendalaah's unfailing politeness set the mutants breath on edge. But she held his stare, and he calmed himself down.

Suddenly Brek'anarl brightened. 'Well, in the coming war there will be much blood shed! Very well then, we leave them in their own lands. But know this, when I add my peoples word to the oath; if leaving this world requires burning every building to the surface and crushing every warrior they form against us – so be it.'

He took the oath then. I-olo knew his words were true, and hoped that such measures were not necessary. This was the first oath of such people in the whole history of the planetoid. It was by its very nature a dire threat to all within the walls. They may be out resourced, but they were filled with desire to escape a prison few deserved. Few, except perhaps, the pirates...

'What of the Kinerigan?' I-olo asked.

'Hmm?' Darkstar hummed, seeming to realise they were all there for the first time. 'Oh, yes...' and curtly took the oath on behalf of his people.

'Can we trust you?' The male Tendendalaah asked coldly, ever willing to clarify others words for them.

'What? Oh, yes, I speak for the pirate lord Myth. With an oath, we will keep the will of this alliance,' then he added like a careless afterthought. 'Well, at least as long as the alliance stands..., and as long as the pirate Lord stands to hold the pirates in check too, I hasten to add.' Then he quickly added, 'which I don't see changing any time in the foreseeable future...'

The Tendendalaah looked at him, as did the Derringer. Their thoughts were plainly readable in their faces, *what kind of fool do the pirates send to speak for them?* They wondered.

'Now. Of the Derringer?'

Speaker I-olo. We are greatly honoured to be with you this day. I speak for the Derringer, civilians of this prison with you all. We commit all our forces, all our resources, all our wills, to the Freedom Alliance: To see the peoples of this world set free. As a united people then, this brings us to the first item of business – how do we go about being set free. The Oppression, as we know, has not let a single soul born or captured here from its Skyshield in its entire history-

'And that!' Brek'anarl warned. 'Is why nothing save their entire annihilation will convince them. Until we own the city-'

You underestimate them. The whale interjected, the only one with a voice so powerful it could cut off the mutant leader with ease. *You surprise me, soldier. You are aware of the unconscious communication that all use – I have heard you so do in this very council. I do not think you ignorant of the power of the combined wills of the beings within the city. They are a strong people, their minds are synchronised in some manner not seen on any other world. We of the Eversea have never been able to breach that unity. Only imbuing doubt in their cause will we ever have hope to escape this world. They must doubt the justness of their imprisonment or we will never see freedom. You have no idea of the unity of their will. It is immense.*

It continued, inspiring the council, overwhelming Brek'anarl to silence.

To challenge their wall is deed enough, to threaten their waters will make us unworthy of strength, and we will not prevail. I hear this earth's song. It is an oppressive rhythm that forces all to comply. It protects all in that city, and weakens and shatters the unity of all without. Nevertheless, we will be free, though this world and all who live here strive to deny us! There is one who has shown a new song. To this song, my people have respect. To this song, we may... perhaps... prevail. But why is it that I do not see whom I expected, the speaker of men, at this group today?

I-olo could not help but gulp down his guilt, and fear. 'He was wounded in recent conflict, but is recovering. He will be soon ready.'

The council was silent a moment.

I must see him myself, The Derringer commented. *And I feel the skills of the Tendendalaah may be needed.*

Indeed, The whale commented prophetically. *I have seen you two working together. But there is another you need. The strength of the mutants is called for.*

What? Brek'anarl protested, willing to rebel against any for the audacity of suggesting what his actions should be.

'Will you...' The female Tendendalaah begun, but I-olo hastily waved her to silence. Something new had just surfaced from his morning synaptic download of the most recent additions to language, culture and protocol of dealing these races.

'Brek'anarl. You will accompany the Derringer and Tendendalaah to assist the Resistance diplomat Matrix,' he said, simply, unadorned.

The mutant softened, and spoke. 'Our wills are given to this council. It will be an honour to serve with these... occasioned foes. Perhaps we can also teach our children how to co-operate!' He roared.

To the mutant, he was graciously accepting a polite request. To the other delegates, the mighty mutant leader was capitulating to a direct demand from the Resistance. It was a mistake they would all learn to correct in the weeks that followed, but for the duration of the council, I-olo was afforded all the respect he could have hoped for. In their minds, the Resistance led this offensive, and there were none to doubt that authority. Even the Derringer, whose contribution was key to the whole event, placed their hope in his words.

The council continued the rest of the day, with debates, consolations, and plans for war drawn up between the first Alliance of the free people of the Seren planetoid. It was a drastic offensive, but all felt they could not risk to lose, and would in many ways prefer death to not trying.

Yet everything hinged now on a single man who had only just recovered from being almost digitised. A man who once belong to that city, till they'd rejected him. For seven years he'd wandered among their peoples till he'd joined the Resistance. Now, he would be leading an army of over ten billion soldiers back into that wall he'd passed through alone not long ago...

Come what may... everything will change, I-olo said in finality.

They all agreed.

Matrix

Matrix was still unconscious when it happened.

All he remembered was the knife ... the wound ... the screaming.

Suddenly, he was aware now. Conscious and ... probably alive. But where was he? He could not see. He could feel nothing. He was a prisoner inside his own body. How long had it been since they'd stopped the nanoprobes... or was this death?

This is not death, An alluring female voice spoke in his ear. It scintillated him even as it continued. *But it could be your heaven.*

He saw her then. She was virtually naked, dressed in translucence. She was a godlike form of perfect femininity, postured in unbridled curiosity at him. She was desire, though a pair of bat like wings unfurled from her back while a pointed tail danced from her hips. She was immaculately mesmerising.

Where are we? He asked, unable to take his eyes from her.

We're inside you, and you, are inside me. We are a part of each other, Matrix. You were born on this world…

What are you? He asked, painfully aware that he had to take his eyes off her otherworldly beauty as she moved closer to him. There was something dangerous in her beauty. But he could not move.

I am the spirit of this world. I am C'Wiltaa. I am Seren.

'You…' he began. But it was impossible to fathom. He must have been having a hallucination, or dream.

She laughed. *It is true, Matrix. And you belong… to me.*

Are you … the pirate queen?

She laughed. *That toy? No, I'm something much more… alive…*

She placed a hand on his chest. It rippled with power and desire, and this flowed into him. She was irresistible. She would drown him in a passion of desire till his will left him entirely. He would belong to this world, be consumed by her and never leave the encompassing lust she promised him. She was a world… She sustained his life, and all the others. She could not be denied. He would stay here forever, he and all the rest…

… a singer in black, a telepath in brown. A true friend named Glenn…

No. This was not to be.

No. He said, weakly. *This isn't right… I don't belong to you…*

And as this thought struck him he could feel his hands again.

You're trying to seduce me… you want me to need you! You're the spirit of the prison where we live! No… NO, we're leaving!

She moaned in exasperation. *I've tried to be nice: let you live after your stupid questions got you thrown out of my city. Protected you with my atmosphere, fed you with my creatures. Then you went and got all the others worked up. Their thoughts pain me! Their rebellious, noncompliant, disobedient thoughts! Now they're all planning to try and convince the others to leave! You put the idea into their souls that they can break my wall down? I cannot allow that… I had to stop you. I like that wall, it keeps the obedient safe from the dissident…*

She circled him dangerously, pressing against him, causing his own body to become his enemy as it cried out to obey her will. What *was* she? She felt like... like a noncorporeal... like a demon...

She started to get angry. *You've defeated every assassin, you've wearied me for your whining! You belong to me, you ALL belong to me through the will of the True One, and you will never leave me, Matrix. If you will not receive me, I will possess you, and...*

Then GET OUT! He roared, filling himself with fire and light.

She hissed at him, and became intensely frightening. Matrix stepped back in the hidden world inside his mind. At last he could move. He had to get away. Yet she was not frightened by his light and fire.

She glared at him angrily, with bestial primality.

So, she was the jailor.

No, she admitted becoming more dangerous, fangs protruding from her teeth. *Just the jail.*

And with that, she leapt at him.

---++---

Bakerson was resting by the hospital doors when it had happened.

They'd saved him. Somehow, the pirate queen had managed to defeat the nanites, and he would live. So why Matrix had suddenly cried out was a mystery. Glenn burst through the doors even as light and a dozen healers piled into the room. Matrix was convulsing violently, eyes wide open, back ridged and arched in uncontrollable spasms. His hands as claws pulled at the bed, a terrible fear and darkness pervaded the room.

'What's happening!' Bakerson was the first to ask.

The healers flooded around him, trying to hold back the convulsing man.

'It's a demon,' one explained. 'It's inside him, trying to take possession of his body.'

'What!?' Bakerson exclaimed. 'How'd one of them get in here?'

Nobody had an answer.

They had fought back the nanites. How much more of this would they have to face?

The priests were there quickly, but their tongues stalled and worked against them in that evil creature's power. Matrix, his strength drained by his battles, still thrashed about with such violence he managed to re-break

Glenn's collar bone. But they held him down, trying desperately to prevent him from injuring himself during this battle that only he could face.

With a loud crack, something broke. Matrix's legs fell limp.

'He's split his spine!' A healer alarmed. 'The convulsing is too intense!'

'He's tearing himself apart?' Bakerson said. Blood began oozing from Matrix tear ducts, his roars, guttural and inhumane, were punctuated by sudden jolts of a dark cruel laugh. The healers tried to sedate him, but their instruments twisted and failed in the creature's evil aura. Matrix burst his stone bonds again, and with a failing hope, the room trembled with an inexplicable earthquake.

A healer cried out as part of the room fell on him, knocking him unconscious. Bakerson did not know what else to do. He knelt. He prayed.

And that was when the dignitaries came. Suddenly they were there. The first was so tall, he had to bend considerably to enter the door, mottled blue skin cutting the paint from its surface. Another, short Derringer, seeming to bring light into the room with the whiteness of her beard. Finally a tall, slender woman with pointed ears, a light bruise still healing on her forehead.

They walked in calmly, and the healers stood back at their presence.

'Allow me,' Brek'anarl quietly said, taking Matrix convulsing form into his mighty arms, pinning him gently so he could not injure himself further.

'Do not sedate him,' the Derringer commanded. 'I know this demon. It has been among my kind over the years. It cannot control him unless he surrenders to it.'

'Then he must simply... endure?' Bakerson implored.

'As must we all, at times,' she scholared, placing a prayerful hand on his forehead.

The slender woman went to his side then, a small harp materialising in her hands. Softly she played, a complete contrast to the fear and anxiety that pervaded the others: beginning at Matrix troubled screams, ending in the trembling earth.

It was quiet, enduring music. Tuneless, musical, soothing. It reminded Bakerson of the fresh grass, or of the first touch of spring on their almost unchanging world. It split the fervid horror of the moment like a knife, and replaced it with centred peace.

Matrix turned then, in almost unseeing eyes, and watched her play.

He screamed, or it screamed though him, but his convulsing begun to abate, just a little.

She sung in a language none of them knew. But the darkness could not withstand the presence of their combined faith and light. The screaming and convulsing went on for almost half an hour more, but eventually, it too subsided. When Matrix finally stopped wresting, the room was filled with a sudden and pervasive silence. Light seemed to gather around his form. Brek'anarl softened his inhuman grip.

Matrix blinked, and looked around, sheepishly.

'Oh,' he simply said. 'We won.'

And passed out.

---++---

An hour later they were all still there, warming and protecting him with their presence. That was when the child walked in, escorted by I-olo Tilk.

'I'm sorry I couldn't allow her to come earlier,' he explained. 'But we could not risk that creature attacking Jacinth too, notwithstanding her insistence.'

The child huffed, 'I could have helped...'

'What now?' Bakerson asked, eyes dark with tiredness and fear.

The white bearded Derringer explained. 'He is the first. The first ever. He's broken her chains now, though she attacked him at his weakest and most needy. He owns his body alone – Seren does not possess a single molecule of him anymore. He has broken free of the world's soul print.'

'Then he is the first,' the slender woman repeated in awe.

'What do you mean?' Brek'anarl asked.

The Derringer turned, and spoke to them all. 'It was the final trial; it is just as the sages have told. He cannot pilot the gnolem against the wall if a single atom of his body holds the soul print of this world. He is his own master now. None possess him, but himself. In a sense, he is freer than us all already.

Bakerson looked puzzled, 'Is that even possible?'

Brek'anarl looked down at Matrix triumphantly. 'He will break the wall.'

'Not alone,' Matrix whispered, opening tired eyes. The others looked in alarm.

'Oh, so you're conscious,' Bakerson said, choking down happiness.

'We still need two more people,' Matrix said dryly, Brek'anarl softly cradling his back as he tried to sit against the healing braces.

'Name them,' I-olo said, a confident smile now playing on his lips.

'We need Alasia,' Matrix softly explained. 'She's good with computers. She can protect the Evernet as we pilot my consciousness into the gnolem.

Linking to that machine is going to make me vulnerable. I trust her more than any to this task.'

I-olo's smile begun to fade. 'She... we haven't been able to locate her since your last meeting. There was an event at a mezzanine, and one more recently at a gala, but that's all we have to go on for now...'

Matrix nodded. 'We'll start with that. And Commander Sheelaakah. She's the only one who can protect my mind while I'm in that sentient machine. We need Sheelaakah, she's the only one I trust who can protect me, and call me back out.'

I-olo's smile vanished.

'Matrix,' I-olo begun, preparing to deliver the worst, 'she has not been seen in many weeks... she was taken by Lord Admiral Token and the narrow trace we had on her soul print was lost only hours ago. She is either dead, or turned...'

Gloom filled the room again till it was split by a shrill child's voice. 'What!?' The prophetess said, seeming to think he was joking.

I-olo gave a start, as if he'd forgotten she was there.

'You mean those two ladies who helped saved me from the old man? Don't be silly! Matrix. I see them. They're alive, but very dark. I think... I think I can take you to where I have seen them. But I don't know *when!*'

'Oh... we'll look into it in an hour or so,' Matrix said quietly as though all time was his to play with, and he fell deeply asleep once more.

The child looked up at I-olo, a question on her lips.

And I-olo smiled.

Sheelaakah

Sheelaakah didn't know how long she'd been unconscious. As soon as the amulet hit her chest it clamped its legs all over her body. In that instant she felt it smother all light and goodness within her out like a blanket over a candle. She began to awake, finding her soul filled with the insatiable sense of power and control. Her countenance darkened. She could feel their minds, sense the power of every individual in the city. It filled her blood with *fire*.

Stop!

She told them.

They all did. They all had to.

It made her laugh. They were her puppets...

But no, she was the puppet, she was the one who must obey. The amulet made her powerful, but bound her to another's will. The soul of Seren itself.

And this spirit spoke to Sheelaakah now. *I am C'Wiltaa, and you are my toy. It is time. Destroy the Resistance!*

She felt her strength then. Almost unconsciously she began to push her awareness over the wall. She could find them then. Minds, billions of them. All in a state of disarray, all living outside the correct order. Some she knew personally, though they were so insignificant to her power that they mattered nothing now.

She could bring them in. She could make them fear. She could make them seek the peace inside the wall.

She could end the Resistance.

Yes, there were telepaths there, they would fight her. But none held the amulet that gave them a direct link to this planets soul!

I-olo.

She gave a start.

He was looking right at her.

He looked sad.

What had she done to upset him?

What was she doing?!? What had she become!

That was when Sheelaakah began to fight the planets will. In a moment, she turned the amulets mighty power against the Oppression, beginning with those in the room she was in.

He went down first, the boy who no longer had long hair. She understood him, now, frightened and afraid, so very alone with his rare talent. She saw all his life in memories, all his ambition, all his murders. She saw what he'd done to become this, what dark oaths he'd sworn. How he'd try to prove his unforgiveableness by committing the next unforgiveable act. How he'd move from one terrible deed to the next trying desperately to escape his conscience. How he was so very afraid. And she saw how he'd been wounded, and to whom he'd so decisively lost in mortal battle.

It wasn't until they fired the crossbows at her that she'd realised others were still there. She stopped the bolts mid-air. There was no mercy for her torturers, and she turned their bolts against them.

She made a crushing gesture with the door, and it wilted at her command. She shot her hand out at the wall, and it blasted out into the cavern beyond.

She was powerful now. The planet... it was obeying her will. It was only stone, though a crystal at that, and she a living mortal. *It* would obey *her*!

She would end the Oppression, she would disintegrate the wall, she would rule alone atop the tower of light. And all who opposed her would wish for death...

She threw lightning from her arms, sent massive stones spiralling about her in a vortex, crushed forged unyeildium with a thought. There was no stopping her now. She would rise up through the stone and throw down all who opposed her.

Then she heard a noise. Someone was screaming. Ah yes, the insane. She could not leave them in their madness.

Their deeds have earned them this place, a voice said within her mind. It was the amulet. It had a soul.

I have been in there, Sheelaakah replied. *I remember what it was like...*

And it made you stronger, look at what you've become!

Indeed. But... I cannot leave them like this. I cannot leave them like this.

Don't!

But it was just a crystal, and she, a living human. She forced it to do her will again, though it was a mighty undertaking.

The fire was intense. It took to wood, metal, even stone. Wave upon wave of pure heat lashed on the building carved underneath the pillars. The exploding noise shattering the silence of the underground suburbs where it was hidden.

And the screaming stopped.

But not in her mind. She'd heard them. She'd felt every one of them die in the burning, horrible flames. She'd lived every death through this dark, horrible amulet.

It was burnt, all burnt.

What had she become...?

It <u>laughed</u>. *With each passing moment, you become more and more my servant. If you will not willingly surrender, than madness will overtake you. See what you have done!*

It forced her to relive that moment. It forced her to enjoy it.

It made her want to do it again.

'No,' Sheelaakah said. 'What have I done?!'

With each passing moment, you become more and more my servant. There are many like you. They all want what I can offer them. And they surrender, they all do, surrender eventually. Just like you…

Then she felt it, she felt the reversal of will to dominate. It was their minds, those she'd commanded to stop. They too were a part of her, and their minds, together, could command her. They could make her do things too, make her surrender to the will of the amulet of Thith!

'No…' she shattered in horror.

It laughed. *With each passing moment, girl!*

She fell to the ground. She clawed at the necklace, but it was firmly attached to her body now.

She had to get out.

She had to end it.

She had to end herself.

Then her arms wouldn't move. Parts of her brain begun to shut down.

I'd rather you witness your new life, human girl. But if you try what you are planning, I will possess you. It's the only way.

She watched in horror as her hands lovingly stroked the necklace, imbuing it with their power.

She screamed.

Suddenly, she felt what sounded like a gasp from the amulet. She looked up to find a dark silhouette of a man approaching through a mist of dust and ashes, limping gently in some form of back brace.

It was Matrix.

'I knew I'd find you,' he said.

It was impossible. Why him? Why… now?

She stood up, trembling to her feet. The dark entity subsided in her body at his presence, and she stood facing him with all her predicament.

He looked at the necklace and frowned. 'This shouldn't be here.'

She whimpered. It was all she could say.

'Do you want to remove it?'

She nodded, but still, could say nothing.

He touched it then, right in its centre. There was light and fire in his touch. With a click, the ten arms loosened their hold on her flesh.

With trembling arms, she began to remove it. He moved to help, but a dark field from the stones sprang up between them that he could not cross.

It hurt, hurt like the ring only a thousand times over. The skin on her hands split in effort, blood pouring over them. It raked its tentacles mercilessly over her torso and ribs. She screamed.

It clutched, scratched at her face and arms, trying to scramble back on. It pleaded, said it was dying. It threatened her and everyone she loved.

But she would not allow it to do what it had just done ever again. Not again, not in the history of Seren.

There would only ever be one Thith necklace.

But it came off.

It was, after all, a servant and not a master.

With a crack, the most powerful amulet of the Seren Oppression split, and turned part into dust. She dropped the rest of it on the floor.

And Matrix lunged forward to catch her. And he held her in his arms, and she wept.

Alasia

The delay was all she needed. It took at least an hour, but before the trial had even begun, before the false jury could be assembled, she'd let the black guard know.

The next thing she knew they were there, the room unexpectedly erupting in violence. Rei-nati were well equipped, and desperate to their cause. But the black guard outnumbered them. In moments, they would be victorious.

But it was one moment too late.

The Androgenine had point tessered out, and in so doing, had placed a silver hand on the guide's chest and uttered a word of cursing. Her guide cried out in pain.

Then the androgenine was gone, smiling bitterly.

She was by his side in an instant, the fighting still going on around them. 'What was that?'

'I... I...' her guide stuttered.

'Hey, bright up!' she demanded.

He touched his chest, and looked crushed. He glanced around at the battle about them.

'Take me away,' he requested.

She begun to form the portal next to them.

'No, not there,' he said. 'We need to go outside... outside the wall.' Then he collapsed.

Alasia's head swam in alarm. Something was wrong. Why had he not sent her to a hospital? Or to his home? He... he never took his business outside the wall! She'd take him somewhere safe inside the city ...

But not this time, she sadly realised. This time, she would not trade his council for her own. Not this time. Not ever again.

She tessered them as far as she could – right to the wall. It was an exit point to the wilderness beyond. She'd never been here before, but if the law was served citizens were free to leave of their own volition any time... at least, in principle.

He managed a form of consciousness a moment later, leaning heavily on her shoulder as they stumbled toward the gate. She tried to speak to him, but all he would say is, 'It is time'. Destiny seemed to hang heavily on those words, and she hurried as much as she could.

A black guard approached her, and with a sinking terror, she realised she knew this guard.

'You,' he said darkly.

'Peter, please. This man is wounded. I need to get outside the wall now.'

He looked at the guide, who could hardly raise his head. 'Seems like you should be-'

'Peter, please!' she insisted, desperate.

'So **this** is how you collect on your favour?' He asked darkly, dismissing another guard who was approaching.

She glared at him. 'If you must.'

'Look, I don't know what new game this is, but I don't want any part of you. You're trouble,' and he stalked off.

The guide coughed out a laugh. 'You've met,' he stated.

She smiled, and half dragged him out through the gates, between the enormous chasms of stone that separated the city from the wilderness, and they somehow got outside without any paperwork ... it was ... inexplicably fortuitous.

They collapsed in the forest, just outside the gate. His breathing was shallow, and ragged. She tore open his tunic, trying to apply her knowledge of medicine – it seemed so meagre and insignificant. She'd never seen a curse like that. His chest was red and swollen in a strange symbol she'd never seen before.

Her guide spoke. 'He's no fool, that androgenine,' he whispered. 'He knew.'

'What do you mean?' Sounded Alasia, ready to fight his words.

'That I was planning to betray the city.'

Alasia gasped.

Suddenly there was a movement in the forest. Three blue skinned humanoids, slavering in hunger, approached them. One had its fork out already.

'Tok-ri,' Alasia said, meaning 'friend'. It was a word she'd heard only once.

They slunk off dejectedly, but not very far.

'That was strange,' her guide said.

'C'mon, let's get you straightened up,' she said, looking out towards Resistance territory.

He held her hand then, and looked in her eyes. That look told her... he wasn't coming. She felt the tears spring new to her eyes once more.

For a moment there was silence.

'It's so green,' he said, though dawn was only just thinking of breaching the horizon. 'Much more than I'd ever expected,' he reverenced.

'Guide,' Alasia husked.

'No, it's all right,' he consoled her. 'It's time. Your final assignment.'

She could not stop herself from crying.

He put his hand to her cheek. 'This,' he said, 'is for you,' and taking the diamond from his banding, placed it in her palm.

She gasped. It was his memories, his badge of office. He was handing it all to her. With it ...

'... you will become the next theta level spy of the government, Alasia, with a thousand others underneath you.'

So he was a theta level spy, a scant three levels below the great supply master to whom they all answered ... She held that stone in her hand. It was power, more than she was ready for, but a prize of inestimable worth for the Resistance. They would have her back just to hold it for an hour, she knew.

Yet she did not want it for all the world. For the first time in her life, all she wanted ... was her friend.

She did not want to be alone.

She clutched his tunic, and cried out loudly, screaming to the wind. She trembled in helplessness. She clutched him in utter, complete desperation.

He held her hands till she'd subsided.

'Alasia. It is my time. Go back to the Resistance. Go back to your friends. Forget me ...'

She looked into his eyes, and denied him his last request.

'This mark ... it is my death. It cannot be undone. My time is fin-' he gasped, and his eyes brimmed in tears. 'Alasia, you have to do this without me. I am a servant of the people, and I always will be. But their order is just an excuse for oppression. Alasia, do not let others make your choices for you. Do what you know to be *right*. Be braver than me. Be free.'

His desperation subsided. 'Ironic, you know. All my life I've been afraid to be outside this wall, and yet here it is I will die.'

He laughed, and held her hands a good half hour.

They said nothing. There was nothing to say.

She held him till he'd faded. Then, with the discontented stares of the mutants, she built a bier of fallen logs, and cremated him. She watched the flames sending his soul print high up into the night sky. She watched, and pushed back the image she felt of his soul print leaving his mortal form, looking skyward, then turning back towards the city to approach the tower at its heart. For a moment, he looked as if he'd approach that tower, but he'd slowly looked away again and, smiling at her, he'd flown with the flames towards the stars ...

... *just an imagination*, she told herself.

It was so cold then. She was a thousand miles from the nearest Resistance outpost. She was mere meters away from an inaccessible Evernet within the walls.

She was dressed for a gala, not a funeral.

What would she do?

And as she looked up heavenward, a single lone vessel began its descent towards her. Quickly she took up the diamond into her banding – though it did cross her mind that it might be a trap to uncover what she knew of the Resistance, she decided to trust him still.

The ship landed. It was a converted government patrol.

It was the Resistance.

She waited patiently, till a lone man stood in the doorway.

An unexpectedly familiar voice thrilled her. 'You seem alone,' he said, in perfect mockery of the first thing he'd ever heard her say. And she flew into Matrix's arms, weeping both bitter loss and undiluted happiness.

Book 5
War

Heroes' regroup

'Sheelaakah,' Alasia said. 'I'm sorry.'

The shorter woman just looked at her, unreadable, clearly probing the outside of her thoughts. Alasia had prepared herself, but hoped she still did not realise the crash that had almost killed the telepath was her fault. This, however, was not what she wanted to apologise for. It was an issue she now considered more important.

'What do you mean?' Sheelaakah asked honestly. They were in a briefing with the Resistance elites, some council just yesterday having decided on the war that was coming among the free peoples of the Alliance.

Alasia, blinked in unconscious discomfort. 'I was ... you were... right. I was blind and I was petty. I'm sorry.'

Sheelaakah just looked at her.

Alasia felt her eyebrows raise in embarrassment and insult that her apology was so badly received.

Then, slowly, the telepath raised her hand, and holding Alasia gently by the chin, turned her face so that the back of her head was visible. There, the scars of the traitors blast still stung as the healing implants tried to repair themselves. Great tufts were missing.

As the gentle hand fell from her chin, Alasia turned to see the telepath deeply moved at the wound. She said nothing, but let her eyes fill with sympathy.

She'd been right, Alasia thought. *Back there when I was driving that shuttle out to moonscape so dangerously. I have lost my hair.*

And at the irony of it, Alasia laughed. *She'd been right.*

The telepath looked surprised, but then allowed herself to see the irony of it as well. They laughed, and then they hugged. Sitting closely, they said no more.

The room began to fall quiet, and Alasia turned to see Matrix was entering. He was wearing a spine brace, and while his face was proud, his movements were even more painful and slow than yesterday when he'd rescued them. He pushed aside the bevy of priests and medics that accompanied him to make his way painfully between them, throwing an arm over their shoulders with an enthusiasm and happiness that denied his condition. He fairly glowed.

'It's *good* to see you both!' He said, the room hearing his compliments.

Alasia watched as Sheelaakah's face lit up with an infectious smile.

'Well, I for one was expecting more of a greeting!' Alasia protested.

Sheelaakah rolled her eyes.

'Don't proke him,' she joked. 'He needs all his attention just to stay conscious.' A few other joined in the laughter.

For the calm before the storm we're taking this very lightly, Alasia thought. 'What of Puppy man and the mechman?' She asked.

'Promoted to Commander,' Matrix replied, trying to make it sound like yesterday's news.

'Really?' Sheelaakah joined her incredulity.

'Yea, they got them round here doing guard duty, seems like the Resistance can't standing having Commanders sit around. Bakerson has taken the personal charge of my security, so if he's not in sight he's in hearing range, I guarantee it.'

'Are they invited to the meeting?' Alasia asked.

'I'm sure,' Sheelaakah advised.

'Oh, who else then...?' Alasia asked, scanning the room. She knew she could have downloaded the guest list from somewhere in seconds. She did not need to break into the Resistance systems just yet, she could get the same answers simply by asking.

The room seemed to stir in reply. Whoever walked in was too short to be seen among the interested people who clamoured to see her. Then someone lifted her high onto his shoulders. It was Bakerson, carrying Jacinth. Skion pressed the crowd away before them.

'Matrix!' The child shouted, ignoring the throngs that pressed for a glance, or an answer to their questions, decorum of the Resistance elite somewhat failing them before the new celebrity. They'd heard how she'd found Alasia and Sheelaakah, and of many other things. As soon as they were ten paces away, she wriggled from Bakerson's shoulders and leapt into Matrix arms.

'Ooouch!' He winced, catching her in his arms. She just held on to his neck.

'I'm glad you're all right,' she said.

She wriggled into his lap, and Matrix refused any attempts to deny her. Bakerson took up position next to Alasia, Skion flanked Sheelaakah. They spoke briefly as he sat, sub telepathically as was their way, but Alasia chose not to eavesdrop.

'Well!' said Matrix, as the throngs of people went their ways preparing for the meeting, leaving the six most respected warriors of the Resistance to their reunion. 'We've been busy. What have you all been up to? I started a war...'

No one laughed, though Bakerson had to suppress a snicker he initially thought was the appropriate response. Matrix certainly seemed to want to continue to make light of things.

'I lost my hair...' Alasia offered.

They smiled, but only Sheelaakah would have known it was continuing the joke. It took a moment, but soon all guessed the comment had a deeper meaning.

'What happened?' Matrix asked, finally deciding the situation was too sever for averse levity.

'Well, I met somebody... a man... and he gave me...' she sighed. It was time. 'This,' and she showed them the diamond.

Sheelaakah and Skion both gasped, the mechman forming some form of scanning device from his arm. Sheelaakah immediately begun some deep level telepathic work to protect the room.

'Is it...?' The telepath asked.

'Indeed,' Skion commented, his mechanised voice passionless. 'As far as I can discern, a governing crystal. High level supply and recognisance from the city. Scans detect negative threat, unless the Oppression reclaims the stone one day.'

'They wouldn't have let me in here if I was a danger, the Resistance has already checked. My allegiance is with the free peoples.'

'You're a spy for the Oppression.' Sheelaakah commented, her voice absent of feeling and thus, highly dangerous.

Alasia just looked at her. 'Yes,' she finally admitted.

They just looked a moment, then Sheelaakah replied, 'You were when we first met, weren't you?'

Alasia smiled. 'No, the second day, at the transport. Taalk threatened to confiscate my personal... earnings. I chose to try and betray you. I failed. Then I found out what they do to the bodies of those that die here, and I have switched allegiance.'

They just looked at her. Matrix looked hurt.

Alasia continued, 'I was wrong. I was petty and selfish. I didn't... I don't deserve your friendship. But I will fight to my last breath for the freedom alliance. I have learnt that there are more important things than fame, power, and wealth. I have been... to myself, so to speak.' And she could not help the tears welling in her eyes, though she wasn't sure it would make them feel she was false.

The others were silent.

'Knew it,' Skion boasted.

They were all quiet. Eventually Matrix let out a deep sigh. 'Well! ... I knew we took you on for a good reason.'

Alasia gave a start. Then she had to smile. When everyone else was focusing on her betrayal, he alone could see her for what she was trying to become. She found herself smiling at him from her heart.

'Well,' begun Sheelaakah, her thoughts on the matter a mystery. 'While you have been watching the bodies of those that sleep, I have been seeing to their soul prints. Seems the reports are indeed accurate, the Oppression has a soul trap here set up to claim the minds of the dead, as well as their bodies. I've done all I can in that regard...' and she fell quiet.

No one spoke, or asked her what she had been through. That's when Alasia realised how those in the room had been deliberately avoiding looking at her. Something had happened. Something deep. Her voice had changed too, as though she was –

' – when we last were together.' Sheelaakah suddenly begun again, the subtle note of pain returning to her voice. 'I fear I let us all down. When I saw my brother's body walking among the dead, as Alasia has alluded to, I determined to bring him back. Apparently, his soul print had been calling out to me these past seven years ... there's not much I am allowed to say on this matter... but I freed him. It cost me my honour, my self-respect, almost my sanity. But I did it, I freed him...' she whispered, looking deep into space. She smiled then, an apologetic happy.

But no one was saluting her as they passed...

'So!' she continued. 'While you were walking among the dead, I went in to the valley of death to save my soul twin. It is something I hope to never have to do again.'

'Sheelaakah...' Matrix tried to ask.

She waved him aside. 'The rumours are true. I caused an entire unit of the Oppression to fall to insanity. As a result, of the psychic retribution, I was also held prisoner by the Oppression.'

'But,' Bakerson said, 'you were released just this morning. How could they have cleared you for service already? Aren't they worried about logical parasites, mind frames, non corporeals taking advantage-'

'Apparently *not*,' Matrix said emphatically, as though to protect her.

She smiled. 'The chief healer declared me fit for service two seconds after seeing me, for reasons of her own. However, I am released from service for the time being. You are Skion are the only commanders here.'

Alasia couldn't stop the gasp of surprise before it had left her mouth.

Sheelaakah just smiled at her, and sat back. *Peaceful*, Alasia thought. Whatever had happened, it had matured her again well beyond her years. No doubt stretching her formidable talent.

'Was it you?' Skion asked, in human voice. 'Who called the halt yestermorning? I mean, all two trillion just stopped what they were doing... most can't even remember it.'

'It's not official, but yes. That was me.'

Alasia sat back in surprise. Sheelaakah was almost a head shorter and a complete fool where men were concerned, but this little telepath was more dangerous than anyone she'd ever met. Whatever madness had pushed her to the brink of insanity, then paradoxically given her the strength to rescue her twin's soul print from the Valley... Alasia secretly hoped she'd never have to touch such power.

Sheelaakah looked right at her. 'What I did, none need do again. It is done. It cannot be undone.' Then she smiled bitterly, and seemed very tired.

'Weeel!' Skion nearly shouted, hauling the conversation from its sober overtone. 'All this weepy woopy! Ha! Seems I'm the only one whose had an eenteresting time – compute *that!* Four weeks at the wall with non-stop action. Seven comrades saved, personally. Two sorties across the wall. Fighting shoulder to shoulder with the Mutants – first lock in history trues! Most boring time? Standing around with *him* asking; "Where's Darkstar", "have you seen Darkstar", "do you know Darkstar".' He laughed to himself.

'Oh,' said Alasia. 'You mean the Kinerigan emissary?'

'How do you know about him so fast?' Matrix asked her, his voice indignant.

'That was, oh. Um, just after we arrived the spymaster and I sat down to a little chat. Tried to contact him in the transport you picked me up in, but he insisted we discuss things in person. Even had an hour with I-olo...' and here she drifted off in memories, '... smart man. Very perceptive,' she mumbled. 'Anyway. They took a good, and I mean good, look at my new stone, and in the meantime set me up looking over the news, who to know, etc. I mean, did you know there were no less that thirteen recorded separate attempts at your life since the underfoundaries Matrix?'

'What?' He said disbelieving, seeming to have lost his focus.

She laughed, and continued with merciless rapidity. 'So I know all about the dignitaries, alliances, truces, trades, favourite song clips, you name it,' and she smiled broadly at them all.

'What were you looking for Darkstar for?' Sheelaakah asked, denying Alasia much chance to gloat to her nearest friends over her latest accomplishments. Not that she wanted to gloat, a part of her still wanted to return to the simple naivety of a world less insane. A world before the Reinati... No, Alasia felt it too – the desire to escape the insanity of the world they were about to create. A world filled with war.

Yet at Sheelaakah's question, Matrix groaned.

'Oh, we wanted a little chat with the pirate lord,' Skion said, grinning broadly.

'Because I told him to,' the child suddenly interjected, bringing them all to the stark realisation that she was not only there, she was listening to every word that was said – curled as it was in a tight ball on his knee.

'Let's just skip to today's –'

'Oh no, no, no!' Skion protested. 'You're the toast of the Alliance here Matrix. We all know that! Six alliances in fewer weeks, and that's six more than any have accomplished in a thousand years. So go on, tell them... they'll want to know what it took to gain the swords of... the Kinerigan...' He ended dramatically.

Matrix groaned, and shook his head.

Bakerson held up his hand for Skion to stop.

'He's engaged,' Skion beamed.

'What!?' Sheelaakah and Alasia said, pulling themselves away from the injured man that sat between them. The air suddenly became electric with their ire.

'That wasn't in the reports,' Alasia stated.

'It's not...' Matrix tried to explain, smiling, but deeply stressed.

Skion, however, enjoyed it immensely. 'Matrix here gets himself stabbed by a corked knife – nanites.' Alasia gasped. 'So Bakerson here, much to his credit, takes him *back* to the Kinerigan to talk to the pirate queen. You know she's a queen right? Well, turns out she's some kind of sentient computer-'

'You mean she's a download?' Sheelaakah asks.

'She calls herself a 'projection',' Bakerson quietly explained.

Skion just snickered. 'And she deprograms them in *four hours*. All the while the one, and only, battle cruiser of the Resistance is sitting right in the heart of the Kinerigan lines!' And he boomed out a laugh. 'And what's her price! Him!' And he nearly fell over laughing.

'It's not... I wasn't conscious...'

Sheelaakah had let his arm go.

Alasia was sitting back. She didn't realise how much this news had affected them both.

'It's a promise I made on his behalf,' Puppyman said, and Alasia could barely contain her angry look. 'It is a promise without a set time to be fulfilled, I'll have you know.' And he continued quietly, holding their eyes with his. 'It was that, or he would have died. And the alliance with him.'

They were reverent in silence then. Whatever sacrifices they had all made to be there, only Matrix alone was still held prisoner by a promise he didn't make to save a life none of theirs could be without.

He smiled, and tried to be philosophical about it. 'She, it, seems willing to bide its time.'

He was almost trying to take it lightly. But such an oath was of great severity. Among both city and Resistance, it was as good as a wedding itself.

So... someone is trying to claim him against his will? It made Alasia angrier than she'd ever been for her own freedoms. But she knew also – she coveted him as well.

'Was that... when this happened?' Sheelaakah asked, pointing to his brace - her face reddened, betraying deep feelings of her own very near the surface.

'No,' he replied. 'That was later.'

'It was...' Puppyman started, but Skion waved him aside with great nonchalance.

'Some kind of noncorporeal demon.'

They were silent a moment.

'Do you know who?' Alasia dared to ask.

'C'Wiltaa,' Matrix quietly replied, seeming he had little to fear from that name now.

But Alasia hid her sigh of relief. At least it was a name she did not recognise... whatever had become of her demon she would probably never know. And neither would they. It was not part of any of her reports...

'So... you're engaged,' Sheelaakah stated, growing hotter.

Matrix sighed, but it seemed to bring little relief. 'What else could be done? The Resistance operatives were bested... I'd rather not think about it.' And he smiled a weak apology.

'Don't worry,' the little girl said. 'She's going to finish before the war has ended.'

Matrix smiled down at her. 'That's... good. But it might be a very long war.'

Sheelaakah looked down at the child then. 'How sure are you of your prophecies now, Jacinth?'

The child's grew embarrassed, and buried her face in Matrix arms.

Sheelaakah looked a little chagrined, but mostly frustrated.

'Weeell,' Skion crooned, appearing annoyed that his attempt at lightning the situation had instead deepened it once more. 'Oh, looks like we're getting started.'

The timing was true. The Circle was there, tessered in at that moment. Invisible security wards went up. They met in three concentric circles. The six innermost individuals, I-olo and five others, were among the standing stones in the centre. A half hundred or other elites, including themselves, stood outside those stones. And in the dark recesses, peering through scry orbs or echo rooms far way, a scant thousand or so officials gathered to record and relay the will of the innermost council of those gathered.

'Fellows!' I-olo began, his deep voice stilling all noise, commanding all attention. 'We meet to discuss the Resistance's involvement in the coming war with the Oppression. We meet to agree regarding our course of action. We meet to serve the best interests of the Freedom Alliance, to see its people set free from this world.' It was an oath, and the signalled and sole purpose of this gathering. He gestured to a man just outside the inner circle.

The man arose then, glittered with military honours on his ample chest, his scaled skin scarred with many battles. It was their first honoured glimpse of the general - he who was chosen from among the throngs to lead a great war. He commenced his lecture – his words punctuated with images that filled the minds of the assembled like pictures dancing across the scene in front of them. An observer could watch over those images at will, or move in to study them in detail – now or in the hours that followed. It was a typical meeting in many ways.

'The Seren city, as we know, is well protected from the Alliance by the 'wall'. As most of you are aware, the wall is more a fortified cliff, so that what appears to rise up almost a kilometre or more in places is sometimes just a few dozen hand holds to those within. There is no inner moat to trap defenders, the city considering their wall formidable enough defence. From the height of this wall several layers of the sky shield fall, preventing us from easily taking the wall by air. The wall continues into the planetoid, so that there are few places in which it can be penetrated from underneath.'

It has more holes than a sponge, from my experience, Alasia thought to herself.

'The wall is built of over a hundred billion excessively hardened silicon dioxide crystals. They are of several thousand tonnes each, and effectively disperse all forms of mechanical and energy attacks across to their neighbours so that no one part of the wall suffers excessive shock. The hexagonal prism shaped crystals are built on each other and slanted so that they can be slid back into position even in the case of thermonuclear detonation. For the longest time the Oppression has assumed the most likely form of attack will be a small, localised assault that will bring down only a section of the wall – dozens of kilometres at the most. We plan today to bring the combined rage of the armed forces of the six major nations and hundreds of minor nations against that wall. It will be attacked all along its entire perimeter, over twelve thousand kilometres in length. The combined army will number in excess of forty billion – double if we require.'

There was a sensation among the assembled. Alasia recalled, such numbers in conflict had not been seen since the fall of the galactic senate. It seemed Seren's first war would rival the largest the galaxy had ever seen. It was unlikely that the city would muster any less than they did to the battle as well.

'We have consulted various oracles, measured our forces, used every available advantage to our calculations. The time to attack is in one week. Seven days from today.'

The room erupted in sensation. There was no way any believed their armed forces could be ready in a week.

Before anyone could stop her, the child was up off Matrix's lap and racing across the stone floor.

'No, no, no!' She shouted, banging her hands openly against the blue force field that held her outside the standing stones. The guards, sentient and otherwise, were only just held in bay from disintegrating her in that moment.

It was I-olo that left his place to talk to the child, right in front of a watching populace and their elected officials.

'What is it, Jacinth?' He said, stooping down kindly, being sure to use her name so that all others would know her.

The child just looked at him.

Painfully, Matrix got up, and went to hold her hand.

'I'yo lo,' she said, gasping with breath to find her boldness. 'No, no, he said the wrong thing. He was meant to say six days. Six days or eight, but not seven.'

'Why is that?' I-olo asked.

She didn't answer him.

He sighed.

The general spoke. 'Granted, seven days is the absolute minimum we could possibly hope to muster. Our only advantage in launching within that time is that the Oppression would not be expecting it – it's too foolish.'

I-olo smiled. 'Do you know why you don't like that day, Jacinth?' I-olo patiently probed.

The child didn't speak.

The chief mathematician and astrological scientist nearby spoke up, out of turn, but not out of place. 'Having measured the most fortuitous advantages to be rendered on the seventh day from this, it has been noted by some that a cursory advantage is maintained on the dates the child has mentioned,' she applied.

I-olo smiled again.

The general looked very unhappy.

But I-olo bent down low, looking into the child's eyes, trying to read her face. 'Can you tell me…' He wandered. Then changed his question. 'Jacinth, please forgive me. We need to see what you can see. Will you allow a man to see your thoughts, just for a moment?' I-olo asked her.

Precious minutes slipped by while the elite were gathered, but if all they left with was an oath to work together and a date to do it, the minutes would not be wasted.

'That's usually not a good idea,' the child stated, but nodded.

I-olo indicated to a man who stood inside the middle circle. He was twice Matrix's age, and bore a platinum banding. He walked up to the child, smiled at her kindly, and then turned the palm of his hand towards the gem at her brow in the ancient gesture of meeting minds.

Within seconds, his breathing became fevered, his eyes reeled back in his head, and he stumbled on his knees. Still, his hand seemed stuck in its position near the child's forehead.

With a sudden dismissive gesture Sheelaakah stood up, almost knocking Alasia over with the psychic wave that emanated from her. Sheelaakah then looked like she was grabbing something out of the air, and as she pulled her hand slowly back, the platinum telepath feel backwards to the ground, the telepathic link broken.

'Flooding,' Sheelaakah explained. 'It's a new technique I've experienced… once before.'

Matrix looked at her in surprise, and Alasia couldn't help but wonder what that meant.

---++---++---

But it was unlike any flooding I've ever seen before. Sheelaakah spoke in her mind to Matrix. *It was intense.*

He didn't reply, his thoughts too confused to.

Her colleague, one of her trainers at one point, lay panting on the ground. He turned to her. 'Thank you!' he husked.

'What happened?' I-olo asked, worried.

'I don't know,' her colleague replied. 'It was like... a thousand 'nows' all spilling out of her. All different. How... how do you make sense of that child?'

She smiled, 'Warned you.'

He smiled back, and waited for her to answer his question.

She huffed. Sheelaakah sensed she didn't have the words to reply as yet. Hers was a mind unhinged to time, it seemed. Perhaps the child was only an illusion? In the moment in which she connected to her colleague to pull his mind back from the sensory vortex in which he would drown, she sensed an unfathomable depth to this child's existence that she hadn't been able to detect before. Somehow, the child was able to maintain a centring and presence in spite of her talent.

'How can you tell which now is real?' Sheelaakah asked, even as she heard herself ask the question a dozen times in the echoes of the child's mind.

The child smiled, and answered confidently. 'I don't know. Sometimes the most 'here' things never be. And other time, when it happens it's all such a surprise. I let him look because I saw you drag him out. That's how ... I knew it would be all right?' She ended her sentence with an inflection that made it sound more like a question than an explanation.

The platinum looked now, beginning to understand some things, but alive now with new wariness. 'But how did you know which now to trust? Since they're all so different?'

Suddenly the child seemed upset. 'I don't,' and burst into tears. 'I don't any more, ok!' She screamed at them, and plunged into Matrix arms.

Her colleague shot her a look and said *that was a terrible risk with my mind she took just then! Full knowing the danger.*

Sheelaakah was beginning to doubt as well, but Skion spoke it out loud for all.

'Then how do we know if we can trust her judgements?'

No one spoke for a moment.

'I feel her gift is tarnished, but not lost,' I-olo spoke. 'Perhaps it is a good thing, as now we must take better care and responsibility for our own decisions. How good is a prophetess if we feel so sure in her gift we cease to labour for ourselves?' I-olo asked rhetorically.

Sheelaakah knew he planned to trust her words, regardless of others advice or fears.

'What of you, Matrix?' I-olo asked.

The braced man left the child to hug his leg, while he stiffly stood. I-olo faced him from behind the blue curtain, and they spoke as two men might in the street, not as leader and hero across the war table.

'I'll be ready, be it the will of the council.'

The room stirred in admiration.

Sheelaakah could feel it in their minds. He was legend. There was little he could say wrong now, and Matrix's word was equal if not more in weight than I-olo's. The warriors respected him, the citizens were in awe.

But at the same time, Sheelaakah knew, this sudden meteoric rise to fame could not last, and might not outlast the first mistake all mortals inevitably make. Matrix was seen as a saviour of the people, its next greatest, and best greatest, chance to be free of the Seren prison forever.

I-olo inched closer to that impenetrable field, 'you have to be alone in that gnolem, and they say it is to command the sands of a thousand deserts. Is six days…'

'I know,' Matrix replied, his voice broadcast among the thousands of officials that led the Resistance. They heard no fear in that voice, there was none. Just resolution, and a confidence that could not be explained by who he was. Something had happened to Matrix, something far more than six alliances and thirteen assassination attempts.

He hadn't told her, Sheelaakah realised. They'd hardly spoken since he'd found her inside the wall, and taken her from that hated Undercity once more. Nothing had barred the way as Bakerson piloted their vessel through the caverns and on to the first Resistance outpost they could find, where she'd collapsed into the arms of healers till the hour before this meeting. She'd hardly noticed how Bakerson had used Derringer tunnels like he was a local, dimly wondered where the new permission had come from. She'd just spent the time healing and reclaiming her mind, wrapped in the safety of Matrix arms for many hours. She hadn't even noticed the brace. He hadn't mentioned he was *engaged*…

Something would have to be done about that.

'Is six days long enough to heal?' I-olo asked.

'One day is enough,' he said, but she doubted it. While he bore the scars of a broken back in his soul print, the gnolem would likely be similarly maimed. It took three days to heal such nerve damage properly.

I-olo smiled at his enthusiasm, 'and you, chief healer?'

A woman appeared astrally into the second circle, floating in, like a ghost. A tall, important looking woman. The only woman Sheelaakah trusted as her healer, though she could not look her in the eyes tonight.

'Given his physical state, it is most possible,' she replied authoritatively. 'Also, his soul print is in a remarkable state of internal cohesion at the moment. It is likely to normalise within the month, so sooner is preferred over latter...'

She gave them pause to think. 'However, with the most recent event, I find his rhythms to be in an entirely new synchronisation not familiar with the patterns of this world. One day has not been long enough to extrapolate his condition. I cannot say if six days are better than seven at this time.'

'Can you give us your professional opinion?' I-olo stated.

She just smiled, too wise to allow others to blame poorly informed decisions on her. 'I just did.'

One of the circle members spoke just before I-olo. 'Then can you give us someone who will?' He sounded exasperated.

The healer was nonplussed. 'Matrix alone can make that decision.'

In that instant, Sheelaakah perceived the entire baited breath waited on the young shoulders of that man. A thousand conscious minds, and a billion more whose day to die would be decided by his next decision. In that moment, Matrix outranked I-olo, but still spoke to his with deference, the immensity of that decision seeming light upon his voice.

'Seven days... hmmm. Six days... tastes right,' was all he said.

The general threw up his arms in belligerent compliance. The decision was made.

'But do we have advice on how to take down the wall?' Matrix asked. 'I suppose we're not just going to go in there and bash it down.'

I-olo waved in the general to continue while he returned to his place, a contented smile playing on his lips.

'We could, but it would cost us dearly.' The Tendendalaah ambassador of the inner circle finally spoke. 'Your initial plan was to try and pull the crystals one from another into a heap we could use to climb into the city, if you wanted. Our science, however, gives us all another option. We excel in forms of harmonics and wave motion – music, for want of a better word. We have exacted a calculation which, if accurate, will create a standing wave along the wall that will break the coherence among the crystals for us. As mentioned, the blocks can slide down into place once dislodged with a direct frontal assault. If that coherence was broken, it is expected that the crystals will simply fall over each other and into the crevice between us and the city.'

'Sounds like a very good plan,' Matrix said, for everyone.

Skion scuffed, *For once, the first time in his life – he takes the first suggestion someone else makes. Dross.* She heard him think to himself.

'The calculations are precise,' the general continued. 'You'll have to hit the wall with immense force, once each three hours as the standing wave reverberates along the wall and the antinode returns to the original position... we estimate six to eight impacts will suffice...'

The room erupted in murmurs.

Six? That was eighteen hours at best.

It would be a long day, and all of it would be spent in bloody battle with a desperate and offended citizenry within that wall. An army that, at best, they numbered two to one – and that was their only advantage.

'Are we as one!?' Matrix suddenly shouted across the din, before murmurs could surface as further doubts. It took less than a moment to register. Then with a roar, the people concurred. They cheered, they clapped, and within the hour, I-olo and the others had hammered out the details of the coming battle.

Skion, however, raised his brow. *It is not the leader of the Resistance that has given the final call to war,* He observed.

Three

Sheelaakah quietly watched Matrix as he continued his meditation, seeing with her eyes far more than most were privileged to see. His movements were slow, rhythmic, purposeful. His mind went deep, and he could maintain that state of relaxation even while conscious. His energy field shimmered as she entered the room, demonstrating his profoundly aware consciousness. He'd been practicing daily since the three days from the war meeting, and now that the three days of healing were over, for them both, she wanted to see him again. Without speaking, but knowing she would be welcomed, she walked on silent feet to join him, gazing out over the wide underground cavern dotted with parks and walkways that the Resistance civilians enjoyed here in the Wilderness beyond.

He breathed in deep, centring himself and returning to the present. He opened his very green eyes and looked at her.

They smiled.

'Matrix,' she begun, slightly awkwardly. 'I wanted to say-'

'Sorry?' He finished for her, curtly, knowing what she'd finally come to apologise about. 'Don't be. What you did was the only thing that saved me from a telepathic assassin.'

'Matrix...' she stumbled, not sure why she needed forgiveness. 'Be that, as it may. I am sorry. I am not a bad person.'

He went to join her on the balcony, and turning to look pondered out at the houses.

'Still hurting?' He asked, referring to her demotion, and what she'd done to cause it.

She smiled to herself, he was moderately intuitive. 'I don't know,' she said. Turing minds to madness was a terrible crime, a severe form of psychic abuse almost as bad as premeditated murder. Being half insane herself at the time was no excuse.

'But do you suppose it's what brought about the karmic backlash that ended in your capture?' he suggested. 'This, in turn, brought about the rescue of your brother.' She could tell he'd given this a lot of thought already.

'I found myself in the position where'd I'd placed the others. I know. The irony is... unfathomable. I become Token's prisoner and he tries to drive me to love him or fall insane. In my attempts to resist him I find myself dying... I went there Matrix, to the Valley.'

Her voice trailed away, and he stepped back at the intensity of thoughts he could not share. Few in history accomplished such a journey. None returned unchanged.

'So,' he wondered out loud. 'There's a kind of soul trap in this world as well?'

'There was,' she answered.

'Were you able to destroy it?'

She looked surprised. It took all her strength and destiny just to cut the tiniest pin hole in the veil of death. There was no way she could stop the light that burned at her.

'To be honest,' she replied instead, turning to face the building again. 'I don't know what it is. I was projecting at the time – it just looked like the Seren tower, and it was impossible not to look at. Only in finding my brother's soul print was I able to find enough strength to turn away. Now his

457

soul has turned away from the soul trap too, and his energy signature has been able to find completion.'

'You don't suppose,' Matrix said, thinking out loud once more, 'that the soul print is what actually forms the consciousness? That the body is the reflection and the soul is the true self?'

Sheelaakah pondered quietly. 'If it is, you're going to rewrite over a thousand years of science.'

'Hmmm,' he said, as if it were simply another wall to knock over. 'So!' He said, moving within friendship distance to look out over the balcony they rested on. 'You're apologising.'

'I suppose I am.'

He smiled at her, and lent out.

'And I said it's 'ok'. Weird things happen, and sanity sometimes requires you accept them like they're the best thing for you. That's survival. That's seven years in the wilderness beyond – you know, I still sleep on the floor,' he laughed. 'And your interrogation when we first met gave me the chance to heal from far more than my mental injuries, you know. It was necessary, and I've already forgiven you.' And for a moment they just held each other's eyes.

She saw it then, clearly in his thoughts. He was not just being sociable now. He was interested in her, he had always been interested in her. Was this what made him so quick to forgive, the fact that he found her attractive from the first time they'd met? And as she looked back into his eyes she had to admit the truth to herself as well – she liked him too.

But he had no idea where to begin. 'Friends' were all he'd ever had. An intimate relationship, a long term bonding, was in his heart but not his plans.

She smiled at him.

They were both amateurs. She wanted to hold his hand, to run her fingers through his hair – and to run from this place before she hurt him again. Yet for all the world, she did not want to leave this room.

He looked at her, right inside. She knew he knew she knew his thoughts.

Yet he wanted her to start it.

'Oh Matrix,' she said, in sympathy, and concealing nervousness of her own she avoided his lips by pressing her chest against him in a hug. He was so tall, and gentle. And handsome... this would take time...

Suddenly their fields shifted, someone was coming.

There wasn't time to disentangle, the newcomer didn't even knock. She just opened his door right up and it looked out on their balcony.

'Hi! I'm... oh...'

It was Alasia.

'Now, how do I always manage to do that to you too?' She cheekily asked.

'That's just what I was thinking,' Matrix replied, and it was true, she heard his thoughts even as it had echoed her own.

'Well, since we're all here,' Alasia said inviting herself in. 'I was wondering if you had a pen I could borrow? They've got this stuff in my room, but it's too cold.'

Neither of them replied. It was the worst lie Sheelaakah had ever heard. This could not be a potential spymaster?

Matrix spoke for them, 'Alasia, what do you really want?'

The delay had given her time to reach the balcony. 'Aren't you two bored here yet? They've tried to go through the same meditation every day! Yech! Once was enough, and what's with the juice, don't they vary it *ever*?'

If she was being trite, Sheelaakah didn't worry any more. There were so many more important things than worrying about someone else's issues. Matrix sat on a chair, just out of her arms reach. She wished he'd hold her hand, but ... perhaps not in present company.

'Alasia...' he said.

She looked at him, and huffed. 'I have a perfect memory.'

'Really?' Sheelaakah said, getting interested.

'Yes. I can recite any conversation we've ever had. I can tell you just how you sounded, I can even count the number of fellow passengers on our first ride together, hang on... sixteen.' She sighed heavily.

'Oh!' Sheelaakah said, understanding now. 'You can remember yesterday's juice, I see, and the meditations are designed to be repetitive, yes, yes. Hmm, what will you do?'

'Just suffer it, I suppose, hey the ...'

'Alasia,' Matrix stated firmly. 'Why are you here?'

She just looked at him. Then Sheelaakah realised there really was a deeper meaning for this meeting.

The singer looked between the two, and seemed deeply annoyed. Sheelaakah instinctively reached out with her mind, but the other was once more a bastion of secrecy. She chided herself for forgetting to ask permission.

The singer stood up to the balcony, long hair trailing her perfect figure. She stared out there looking for a long moment. Matrix reached over, and touched Sheelaakah's hand with a meaningful look that said *we will be all right Sheelaakah,* and he went to stand at the balcony by the singer.

A part of her told her she should be jealous, but she was also wise enough to let men make their own choices for happiness without any cajoling from a telepath. It would not be fair, or fulfilling. And when it came down to it, she trusted him.

When Alasia whirled around, Sheelaakah was surprised to see her tearing up.

'I'm sorry,' she said.

'Again? Um, sorry for what?' Sheelaakah asked.

'Oh!' She said, sounding exasperated. 'Everything. For being trite, for being mean, for being me,' she waved her arms around.

Sheelaakah looked at Matrix. Alasia still wasn't making sense.

'Look,' Alasia said. 'In three days there will be war. You'll be piloting an enormous sand gnolem, you'll be watching over him. I'll be guarding the Evernet. Then, then, we can sort things out?'

'What do you mean?' Matrix said.

Alasia was really frustrated. 'You'll see,' she said, and stormed out.

That was weird. Matrix thought, so synchronous with Sheelaakah that she couldn't tell if it was her thoughts or his.

The door shut swiftly after the singer.

Sheelaakah smiled up at him, and invited him to sit by her side, which he did, taking her hand. For a moment, she was so happy her thoughts collided. But eventually she sorted them out, and found him smiling at her. In spite of all she'd done, he'd forgiven her, and was a friend. Perhaps the most trusted. Perhaps something more.

With nothing more to do for the rest of the hour, they talked.

Matrix was lost, and the war seemed very far away. He was falling in love, and let himself fall. Some might not think her the prettiest, smartest, or strongest. But she knew him better and deeper than anyone on Seren, and the prize of being understood and loved by someone who valued him was worth all those things and more.

It was the purest moment of joy he'd ever known.

Alasia didn't walk from the room, she stormed. So, the little telepath was two minutes ahead of her was she? That complicated things. But Alasia *was* sorry:

Sorry she'd have to upset her again.

Sorry the telepath didn't know anything about men, love, what they were like, what they'd do, and what they needed. Sorry she would have to break her heart to win him.

But her promise would hold – three days of peace till the war at the wall had happened. After that, the battle for his heart would truly begin.

Calling truce on one obstacle she decided to tackle the other, and she went out to study self-projective computer systems.

On being social

Sheelaakah met Matrix again that evening after all the meetings and training were out of the way. He was preparing to leave to some appointment.

'Come Sheelaakah, my friend. See what I do for socialising here in this place!'

He stood up, and offered his hand out to her in a gesture familiar between them. She was a little uncertain, basking in his company was friendship enough for her. But she knew he was going, and she was loath to leave his side. His smile, so contagious, and she could not resist that inviting hand. So in spite of herself she decided to allow others to see her, and to see her with him.

The place he took her was far away from the hospitals, deep in Resistance territories. She could tell from the markings on the building, far underground, that it served as both a form of religious shrine and martial training area. She had not been here before but knew about these places from her military training. Inside the cobbled building there was a wide grass courtyard, lit by an artificial sun and coloured with an artificial sky. All around this place dozens of soldiers practiced unarmed combat with assailants both real and virtual, both human and otherwise.

So, this is what Matrix does "to be social?" she wondered. He always did do things his own way. Several others saw him them, and grew excited at his presence. A much older human, scaled and green, hurried to greet them.

461

Matrix bowed low at his presence. 'Teacher Chuum,' he said with respect.

'Young Matrix, my most hurried of students. We did not expect to see you again. Have you returned to continue your lessons?'

'I have.'

The old man laughed. 'I doubt that. You hope only to gain a new skill or insight, and will be off again. Mastery of this art takes commitment and time, both of which you seem greatly to lack.'

Matrix shared his smile. 'It is all too true!'

'And look!' The old man said. 'You've brought your own audience again I see! Who is it this time, officer Bakerson too busy?'

'Indeed Teacher,' Matrix replied. 'This is my friend and companion: Sheelaakah.'

'A pleasure to meet you!' The old man replied, bowing low. It was a strange custom she was not aware of. 'And you, I sense you are open, as they say. Do you work for the Resistance Telepaths or is this a line you are just considering?'

She smiled, and was about to reply when one of the students prodded the Teacher on the shoulder. 'She is Commander Sheelaakah, Teacher, one of the great ones among them.'

The old man raised his eyebrows, so deep and bushy they almost hid his soil coloured eyes completely.

'Forgive me, honoured one,' he replied, bowing once more. 'We are pleased to have you here. Perhaps you have come to assist our students in their training?'

Sheelaakah could feel the apprehension in the others grow dramatically at this suggestion, though the teacher did not flinch.

'I am sorry, Teacher,' she said, nodding. 'I am not given rank at this time. I am simply here to be with my friend.'

'That's a pity,' the old teacher said. 'I was certain there would be some training of the sort today. Natural telepaths are so rare and the ability to train against one is a privilege none should pass up.' He said, turning meaningfully to his wary students.

Sheelaakah felt terribly embarrassed, and so out of place. Usually she was leading regular soldiers like this, commanding orders that could end their lives. She wished she hadn't come, but hid her fears as best as she knew how as she held to Matrix's arm.

'If you will allow, Teacher,' Matrix said in great dignified respect, 'she has come to watch me train.'

The old man's eyebrows raised once again. 'Oh! It's you then.' He pondered, then continued as though he knew something she did not. 'Of course, you do just that. You know, young Sheelaakah, that this Matrix's style is very strange, developed on his own from what thin and poor training they give to their students with the wall. He's taught us a thing or two, however, in the months since he first arrived.'

Sheelaakah found the old man funny, and spry despite his obvious age.

'I will be pleased to submit to your teachings once more,' Matrix respected.

'Very well,' the man began. 'Let your first opponent be me.'

Matrix gulped.

The news, however, electrified the rest of the students. A gong was sounded and they formed around the inner tiled square. Matrix faced off against the teacher there. Once a second the gong sounded Matrix circled carefully.

Sheelaakah was astounded. The chatty old man had an enormous energy field that suddenly leapt out from him and crossed and recrossed the square. He hardly moved a foot as he dodged Matrix blows and sent the younger man spiralling across the ground numerous times. Twice Matrix managed to land a telling blow, but the old teacher absorbed them with great skill. Eventually, the far younger man was bested.

Students clapped, and discussed the battle among themselves. The old teacher helped Matrix up, and freely challenged his failings in combat. No doubt, given less contrived circumstances, Matrix would have fared better to take advantage of his other skills. But this was not the place.

'He has done far better this time,' the student whispered to Sheelaakah. 'Two telling blows, far better than any in this month!'

Sheelaakah smiled, and whispered back, 'Perhaps the good teacher will allow me to contribute to his challenge then?'

It was the opening the teacher had apparently been waiting for, and he had heard before the students had time to draw breath. He clapped his old green hands in glee. 'Good! *This* is what I was talking about!'

For a moment Matrix just looked confused.

I'll be helping out, Sheelaakah smiled.

So did Matrix.

She stepped up to the square then, students who had not bothered to do so donning their aura crystals. It would be an exciting battle.

As she looked harder at the battle zone she saw that the old man had riddled the field with his energy, pulling it in and storing its curvature in his memory. She did not want to disrespect his place of power, but instead chose to focus on helping Matrix's abilities to grow while keeping him appraised of the invisible aura machinations the old teacher put into play, which seemed beyond even Matrix formidable skills to perceive.

Yet connecting with Matrix's mind was unexpectedly delightful. Even before the battle had begun, Sheelaakah almost lost herself in the telepathic union of being so close to him one more. This time, it was an intensely enjoyable feeling.

Matrix smiled back at her, too inexperienced, and too focused on the upcoming combat, to realise how close they were; she could have moved his arms for him.

The battle was immediately even pitched, and both men were hard pressed to best their combatant in any way. Students gasped at the meteoric improvement. She made him remember and process all he'd been taught, and most he hadn't realised he'd learnt. She helped him see what he couldn't, and be aware of the other's thoughts before they'd formed. Matrix acted quickly, completely trusting her.

But the old man was experienced and talented in his own way after years of practice. Even with her help Matrix was will only just a hairs breadth less in ability. They were looking to best him at one point, when suddenly the old man strove deeply to pull energy from further within than Sheelaakah was aware existed, and in the final scoring, the old man once again prevailed.

He rested heavily on his students arms. 'Well done! Good fun! You've given me more of a work out than I've received in years! This, I will remember!'

'I trust I have not wearied you, Teacher?'

'Wearied? I think I might die, young man!' the teacher huffed. 'But it is a combat that has taught me more about myself. That is what combat is supposed to be. I thank you, both.'

Sheelaakah could not help but like him.

'You, on the other hand, still over-reach yourself student! Strive to *understand*, not to prevail.'

'I will, teacher,' Matrix bowed.

The old man scoffed, and slapped him on the head.

'Yeah, right. Ninth year students, you four, take him down *without* his telepaths help!'

The gong sounded, and Matrix took his place in the centre of the four.

He bested them quickly - this was more his style.

Sheelaakah spent the rest of the day watching him practice and train, sometimes dancing with others in slow meditative movements, at other times, striving with great exertion far more than Sheelaakah had ever felt safe or wise for the soldiers to pursue – yet they did. Sometimes she was invited to help, other times, he insisted on facing pain and confusion alone. At one point, they let her merge the minds of the younger students as the twenty of them faced off against a virtual foe, a rare privilege to supplement the regularly battle training that they would brag to their friends about - the day a Commander came to training! The master also insisted she confront the four older students by oppressing their minds with the deepest fears, while exercising till they all fell, humbled by the experience and newly acquainted with the limitations of their souls.

She had a wonderful day. In time she came to feel needed, thanked, and welcomed by the military students. And by the evening she'd lost all pretext of being anything other than completely consumed by her green eyed friend's attention.

When he took her home that night, laughing as they walked, war seemed very far way. He took her to her door then, and she read his nervous thoughts before he'd fully formed them.

Thus, giving him no chance to doubt, she stood up on her toes and pressed her lips to his. The kiss was brief and... a little inexperienced.

Hmmm, she thought. *Needs work.*

'Hang on,' he said, and pulled her in close.

Then they kissed properly, as best they knew how.

Hmmm, she heard him think. *Needs work.*

She laughed so hard in his strong arms he had to steady himself to prevent falling over. He questioned what she laughed about, but she refused to tell him how she'd read their thoughts, and she'd found that funny. She just rested all her weight on his arms, till she begun to fear she'd do something too intense and regret it later. So she slowly stood up.

'Thank you, Matrix.'

He smiled at her.

'Thank you!' He said, though he was thinking about how he didn't know how to say goodbye, or if he wanted to.

She made it easy for him, and smiling, walked inside and shut her door.

It was too tempting not to read his thoughts once inside. He was thinking about the kiss, and how much he liked his first kiss ever. And how he was planning to do it again and again and again...

Then things got a little ... hang on ... he knew she'd be watching! He was doing that deliberately!! *Ooh, that's very cheeky!* She told him.

Then she heard him singing as he walked far away into the night, and she smiled, knowing that he was never more than a thought away to her.

I am so happy, she thought.

Humbled

It was always dark in the computer rooms. Alasia might have otherwise been frustrated with the monotony, but she was hard pressed for the time once she'd taken to the consol. In all her life, she'd never been taught anything. Just left to figure it out herself, sorting out the downloads or digging up whatever she wanted. But now, the training was purposeful, directed, and intense.

The colours swarmed at her, trying to drive her mind away from the objective. The steel door again loomed in front of her in the Evernet, and she set up some guardians this time to protect her. She'd learnt from her mistake of trying to blast it open, incinerating herself as well, and tried this time to hack into it one piece at a time. It was a difficult, slow process, and naturally she had to do it all so that no one would be any the wiser.

And still, she tripped the alarm. As she returned to reality she screamed in frustration and kicked out at the orb, standing up and storming towards the door. She had not had much success since the three days of healing were over and the spy master, full knowing her talents in other areas, had assigned her to an intensive regime of Evernet training. She had quickly learnt how little she had really applied herself to understanding computers. Her trainer, a quick and patient woman who wore glasses to help her see into the Everworld, tutted quietly as the lights went on.

Alasia again threw up her hands in frustration. 'Why are you doing this to me!'

The older woman walked in, resetting the simulations. 'What *are* you trying to do, Alasia?' she asked in exasperation.

'Well, *trying* to hack in to the portal actually.'

'Really?' the older programmer replied. 'I mean, given all you talent your repeated failures aren't really acceptable. You master the protocol faster than any student I've ever known – you should be teaching me. But this simple task evades you. Are you sure your mind is fully on the task?'

Alasia huffed. 'Of course. Saving lives, it's why we do this.'

The older woman looked at her, trying to read her duplicity. 'I know you'll be serving in reconnaissance,' she said provocatively. 'Their spies seem a lot more impetuous now days.'

Alasia sighed. 'There's a lot even I don't know. And they don't tell me, in spite...' *In spite the fact that I have access to almost a thousand spies within the wall at a moment's notice,* she thought. This whole activity seemed to belay her true usefulness to the Resistance, and the Alliance. Was it some sort of test of her allegiance? Her talents lay elsewhere, even if Matrix had specifically requested she be among the programmers at the Gnolem... then again, she would have never guessed how much she could learn from these people!

Finally it dawned on her; 'This is an unwinnable test, isn't it?'

'Excuse me?' The programmer said, not believing the apparent audacity of that insult.

'It's unwinnable. This is another one of those 'learn to recover from your failures' kinds of things, isn't it?' She asked impolitely.

At her mental signal, the older woman started up the simulation once more. Alasia had to rush to keep up with her as she flew across the Evernet, setting up barricades, blockages, detours and deceptions. When she came to the door, she gave it her full attention, trusting in her preparations. She had dematerialised it in seconds. Inside was a small glowing box, which she handed to Alasia inside the Evernet.

'This program allows you to imitate code fractals on Beta, Damsk and Kerris nodes,' she said simply, handing her the unearnt prize.

And as the old lady walked out Alasia slowly decided she might just gain to pay a little more attention to her studies...

Sheelaakah's illness

The next day, Sheelaakah allowed Matrix to escort her to the telepathic military centre and with a hug, left her at the door – she was too tense and distracted to practice kissing for now. With some resignation she left him there and entered that very familiar building.

Her day there was intense – a full psychometrical examination, followed by a litany of personality tests. They permitted her to download her experiences, which were no doubt avidly devoured by the best mystics of the Resistance within the hour. In spite of these accomplishments there was much reluctance to work with her, the stain of her sin still stinging in her relationships with others.

Only Matrix seemed able to forgive her, and Alasia probably didn't realise what had happened. Bakerson and Skion were just soldiers and Jacinth, a child...

There was little rest in the afternoon as the testing continued. They probed her about everything, making her relive the indignities so that they could ensure these memories did not provoke her in to rashness again. At the end of a long, tiring and emotionally draining day, they released her to go home.

Matrix was there, of course, and while she smiled to see him she could not think of anything to say. He took her home amid the stares of the citizens that had heard of them both, but she just squeezed his hand. He left her then, with a light embrace, and she rested alone. The light from outside was still too bright, so she just took to her bed.

But she did not sleep.

She did try, and as a telepath there were usually ways and means this could be accomplished, in others and herself. But even these skills failed her repeatedly. The frustration grew so much that some crockery in the kitchen cracked, and she chided herself for that. Yet as evening turned into the deepness of night, the frustrations and discomfort in the woman grew, till at last she gave up on sleep, and took to pacing.

It did not help. A deep sense of discomfort, of uncertainty, was nagging at her. She felt happy enough, but was quickly becoming vastly disturbed by the complete lack of rest her body required.

They would need her, the Alliance, and she could not remain in this distraction and serve them properly.

She flew from her house, barely giving the guards time to react. She went immediately to the chief healer's personal abode, abandoning protocol in respect to the desperation of her situation. She woke her from sleep, and the older woman gently let her in, ushering her into the room she used for her own personal healing, wishing her own partner to sleep again.

'What is it, Sheelaakah?' The woman yawned, longing to be asleep again, but willing to help.

It all came gushing out far faster than she'd ever wished, and Sheelaakah found she had to clench her teeth so as not to burst into tears.

'Oh, I feel so foolish!' she said. 'I just, there's so much. First no one trust me anymore, then I give up my sanity and freedom to enter the Valley with hope for the prisoners and no one says so much as 'wow' let alone 'thankyou'. Then there's Matrix who ... I don't know. And I even said goodbye to my twin soul print for the first time in seven years and when I tell them at the centre all they say is 'yep, good.' Don't they know what it cost!? And I abused my powers and don't even know if I can trust myself!' And she just curled up in tears in the older woman's arms, hardly noticing the healing sigils the healer drew with her mind around them both.

'Very well, back up a moment there. What did you say about this Matrix fellow?'

'Oh!' said Sheelaakah. 'Everyone will be talking, the telepath and dissident...'

'Why are you worried about what everyone else will be talking about, Sheelaakah?'

'Well, it's just. Oh, he's so nice! He's very fit, and so kind, he can forgive anything...' she must have sounded like an infatuated teenager.

'What brings you here tonight?' The healer interrupted.

'Oh, I can't sleep. Healer – it's never happened to me before. I mean, I was at the telepathic centre today and they raked me raw over the incidents of the past few months. Respectfully, mind you, it's just that I'll need all my strength to pilot, sorry, to help Matrix pilot-'

'Hmm, him again,' the healer mused.

'Yes, well, there's a war coming up in two days. I'm sure you well know...'

'Hmm, Matrix...' the healer pondered.

Sheelaakah was a bit perplexed. 'The war...'

'Look,' the healer said authoritatively. 'Sit here Sheelaakah.'

She sat her down on a simple couch, outside a healing circle, and held her hands in hers.

'Now, Sheelaakah. I need you to be honest with yourself far more than you are succeeding in being honest to me. Perhaps I'm a little older, but your problem is as obvious to me as the wall is to you.'

Sheelaakah raised her eyebrow. Nothing avoided her telepathic senses that well, the Healer must be in error.

The healer laughed.

'Commander Sheelaakah – for I do not dismiss you from rank during your 'leave'. I want you to be completely honest with me: How do you feel about this 'Matrix' person?'

Sheelaakah, only twenty three years old, was taken aback. How could this be related to her problem?

'Well, I think he's the best friend I've ever had. I like him a lot. He is resourceful, creative... dedicated, and very, very fit.'

The healer laughed. 'You said that. Now, I know you well enough to tell that you hide things even from yourself – just like we all do, telepath.'

Sheelaakah smiled, then sighed. 'He's forgiven me for hurting him. Oh healer, how can I trust myself, after what I did to him and then to others when I was lost to anger? How can he trust me knowing I can kill him?'

The Healer smiled, it seemed a question she had heard many times before.

'There are many we trust with our lives, every moment, and many thousands who trust their lives to us. If he feels he can trust you, it is because his heart has told him that he can. But even so, you have not sincerely answered my question.'

Sheelaakah was puzzled, hadn't she answered it yet? But she felt her heart racing inside her – there was something more...

'I don't know, how do I feel about him? He's clever, he's the most amazing survivor I've ever met. I feel attracted to him... what more do you want?'

The healer sighed. 'Sheelaakah, do you love him?'

'I...' and then the dam burst. Like a million litres of repressed desire cascading over a barricade of self-preservation and false control.

'I do! Oh, Healer, I've never felt like this before. He means everything to me! He has feelings for me and trusts me with all his weaknesses. How can the world hold someone so kind?'

The healer laughed. 'I was beginning to worry we wouldn't get that out of you, Commander. Love, stage four to be precise. Tell me, how do you feel now?'

Her heart was beating in a strong, passive rhythm, and she felt warm all over.

'Thank you healer,' she said, and offered her an embrace.

'Sheelaakah,' the healer lectured. 'There's nothing wrong or unnatural about your condition. It is one I hope you never heal from!'

They laughed, but Sheelaakah was still uncertain. 'But what if I hurt him again? And what if he does not choose to continue to feel that way too?' The telepathic Commander suddenly felt more fragile than she'd ever been before. 'I think I'd die if he chooses not to love me too.'

470

The healer smiled. 'Sheelaakah, you have travelled into death and beyond, but you still don't realise you cannot put your sense of self-worth into the opinions of others. Live, child, and risk loving for the first time in your life.'

It was the council that she needed, but Sheelaakah realised she hadn't really answered her question.

The healer continued. 'You've become a strong, independent woman, young Sheelaakah, so much more the talent that I wished would have been assigned to my division and not to the war. But now, finally, you can become *interdependent* – trusting in him even as he relies on you to lift him higher than he could ever achieve alone. Remember to speak honestly, listen kindly, and show love often. I *know* you will be all right, whatever becomes of you and your love.'

They hugged, and Sheelaakah said, 'I'll have to tell him!'

The healer counselled, 'When the time is right.'

Sheelaakah smiled at peace with herself, but the smile faded as the Commander for the psychic division realised she was in unfamiliar territory.

'So,' she pondered, 'is this love?'

The freedom alliance

Six days previously, from the hour of the council when the nations had agreed to combine in battle, a war had begun.

What had previously been furtive attempts at stalling the Oppression, in that hour, became the most intense battle of Seren's long history. All came, the dreaded Mutants, the proud Tendendalaah, the silent Derringer, even the murderous Kinerigan. The waters themselves turned against the Oppression, and within a week their forces were pushed back to their wall or faced permanent discapacitation at the unabating rage of a trillion souls long oppressed.

Night did not stop the battle on a world filled from one side to the next with war. By then, the Oppression looked out fearfully from their hated wall.

Inside the city, everything had changed.

In a single week, they had learnt fear. From oppressed rumour to concealed direction, the waves of consciousness spread. Something was happening outside the wall. The exiled were revolting.

At first, the citizens convinced themselves it was nothing, the black guard would handle it. The justness of their banishment, their lawlessness, would cause them to fall on themselves before long. They were too disorganised, too poorly resourced, too lacking in a united will to fitfully challenge the right will of the city...

But the callings continued – first thousands, then tens of thousands were being pressed to resume or consider serving in the army. They made a big deal of it, 'supporting the people', all the while insisting that there was no real need for such meteoric reinforcements anyway.

Everyone felt it - something was very wrong.

And thus they begun to dig in their heals: The exiled deserved their prison. Why give them the satisfaction of thinking they'd shaken the right will of the united peoples of Seren? Besides, there was only a few hundred thousand of them at most anyway...

So when the first pounding began, sending seismic shock waves across the planetoids surface, falling cups and cracking windows, few citizens were prepared for the psychic shockwave of fear that spread across them in moments. Whatever tension they held at bay from the disconcerting news they had ignored or downplayed boiled over into screaming pandemonium.

And it was the sixth day. It was time.

---+---

Matrix spoke first. Speaking to every mind and citizen in an unprepared speech, the privilege given him by Alasia's formidable programming power and a few secrets she held in a new stone at her temple.

Everyone heard it. It was on every channel. It was on every screen. It shone over every subtelepathic channel. And as he spoke, Alasia highlighted it with images from the Resistance archives – the ones the City would not want a Galactic senate to see. The images they refused to admit existed.

'I am Matrix. I lost my family name over seven years ago when I was banished from the city. I have returned. Beside me, I bring the combined armies of the Freedom alliance, over forty billion souls. We are armed. Our intention is serious. Our will is united. Let our people go... For a thousand years you of the city have oppressed the innocent, and the guilty, here in the wilderness beyond. Why was I rejected? For asking uncomfortable questions. Now none but the truly compliant live inside your wall, but you are prisoners too. Do you know what is outside this wall? Do you risk the unknown? Do you dare explore the limits of your freedom to learn for yourself what is good, and what is evil? Or must you be taught by powers that Oppress us, that scan our children, that teach so little we can only choose the options they give us, not choices ones based on our own experiences. Do you know whether there is more *life* within that wall, or without?'

There were other voices to be heard then, thousands of exiled sharing their stories, some admitting their crimes, others, still protesting their innocence. Most, mourning the annexation of their worlds. Among their voices, one was heard;

'I am Alasia, criminal, spy, profiteer. I live above all your laws and live to tell you the safety you crave is a lie. I have seen it all, as have many before me, and know every decadence, every lust, every debauchery lives within the wall as without. Only here, we no longer live the illusion of a double life. We confront our addictions, even when it hurts. We face our fears, even when it terrifies. We don't pretend things are a certain way when they are not, just so that we can indulge in the pretension of a perfect world. I have learnt one cannot change a heart that refuses to admit its own darkness... I am many things, but I am no longer a hypocrite. Just a woman. Come, let us talk.'

The effect was dramatic. They knew her, those that ran in her circle. They were the most sensationalised. The messages continued, a montage centuries old, complied and added to over the years of the injustice, the murders, the oppression, the deliberate manipulation. It was unabashedly shocking. The images flickered in the minds of those within the walls as the unwelcome messages were fought. In their light a single message coalesced.

'I am Sheelaakah,' she said, staring at the camera in neutral threat. 'And I want to go home. My world was annexed when I was eleven, and my parents died that day. My brother was slain seven years ago trying to help others escape from this world. When I was a child, my father took me out to a lone moon of Pteris, and we held the soil in my hand. He told me this soil was ours now. We would be building solar stills to craft the sands and build our home...'

She paused, because she was trying not to weep.

'Then they came, your world, and took it all away... I am Sheelaakah, and I want to go home...'

There were no images to accompany this, except one of the silent dwarf moon that once circled the Pteris three gas giant. But the chill as the angry telepath looked right at them and spoke to the minds of every citizen

473

of the city, a mind that touched them all, a mind that seemed strangely familiar, yet few remembered the inexplicable, and unexplained, minute and a half halt about a week ago… they felt wary.

'Judge the guilty, as you must, but let the innocent go free,' she concluded.

The images flickered. It lasted almost a half hour till the government managed to shut it down, but as the authority begun to slip from Alasia's grasp, she instructed Matrix to deliver the final message;

'The wall. It imprisons us both; you from your choices, us, from our freedom. We, from each other. This is our ultimatum – the first requirement of the Freedom alliance. Know that I speak for over four trillion sentients. Know that our wills are united. Know that our injustices must be answered for, even as we acknowledge our crimes will be paid in full… The wall *must* come down…'

Then, the images halted, and the programs resumed as normal.

But normal had changed… the conscriptions started that very minute. Massive reassignments promptly followed, huge resources begun to flow to manufacturing and community events that essentially meant tighter control. There was no mention of 'negotiation'. A portion of the peoples will, offended by a threatened wall, was weakened by a sudden and oppressive tightening of all aspects of control over their lives as their government prepared for the first real threat from within Seren in its entire history, led by someone they'd already thrown out. Someone called "Matrix".

'Everything continues as normal.' The Speaker consoled, while nothing did. Then, within a day the government begun to crack down on conversations in the name of forestalling productivity. It was just what the Resistance was protesting about.

'Do you think they really can destroy the wall?' A woman asked boldly, as a black guard had interrupted her and a friend's conversation over lunch.

The young soldier hesitated, then she grew angry, 'of course not! Now, resume your employ or I'll have you scanned for dissidence.'

The women didn't look up as they scurried off, many minutes early to return to work, but indignity lashed from their auras.

---++---++---++---

They were in massive stone circle, surrounded by literally millions of lives bent on their protection. The standing stones projected a near impenetrable protective field around them, the stars above seeming to wink their approval. The wind, however, was chill, and seemed to want to dissuade them from their abomination.

Many had come to join the battle, with the thousands of races represented among their ranks. Everyone was ready. Skion held the outer defences, thousands of elite at his command. He held sway over Mutants, Tendendalaah, Derringer and even a small flotilla of the more reliable Kinerigan.

Bakerson held the innermost defences, personally motivating his soldiers as he stood with them to do battle. Within the innermost defences there was a bevy of terminals and computer crystals, arrayed in a complex pattern of power and protection. This was because connecting to a gnolem – using ones soul print to drive a machine, was far safer and more effective through the Evernet. But on the other hand, Matrix stood perilously close to being 'hacked' into. Made of sand, it was still only a machine, even if it was driven by spirit. Alasia was one among dozens who took that post, guarding far more than the gnolem, waging a virtual war against the Oppression even as the soldiers took a literal one to the wall.

In the centre of that innermost defence was a third, and final region, defended with six standing stones of its own – so close there was little room to squeeze between them. There were only three individuals there, and one of them was a semi sentient machine – a decapedal medical surgeon in case things went wrong. Sheelaakah, once a great leader of the Resistance, was there in nothing more than a plain dress, coloured peach. Matrix, representing all the people of the Alliance, had insisted on wearing neutral black.

They all served under the General, whose watch over the whole war meant Sheelaakah could connect with him instantly. He was positioned deep underground with the other leaders of the Alliance. Among them was a little girl. Hundreds watcher her; carers, mystics and precognates that were vital to a war effort such as this. They gave to Jacinth a sounding crystal that led directly to the Generals ear – and thus also to any person or persons who served underneath him. It lay seemingly forgotten at the child's side as she engaged in a one way game of dolls, co-opting battle unit models into the role of talking animal friends. Meanwhile, dozens of adults looked grimly on, attempting to interpret the signs of their precious prophet.

Matrix had spent the previous three days piloting the gnolem every chance they had. Initially, it had been a clumsy effort he could not maintain for more than fifteen minutes as it clawed its way bestially though the rock.

The Oppression, for its part, was immediately aware of both their intentions, and the danger they were in – the shockwaves of the gnolem birthing itself from this world, combined with the enthusiastic and pre-emptive thrumming of the mutants drums, set the citizenry of the city into a panic.

Matrix knew, and told them every chance he got, that if those people felt personally threatened their resolve would be different. As it was, they were bringing down a wall auspiciously to bring about unity, not threatening the city with destruction. This fact alone hampered the city's ability to defend themselves by causing them to doubt everything they'd been brainwashed to believe about the denizens of the Wilderness beyond, and their own complicity at imprisoning others there. Among them, the core belief of the planet was again thrown in to doubt, though few dared to think the question and none asked – did Seren annex worlds, or were they really all refugees?

So while many asked the newcomers who were born off world, in few and whispered words, even fewer found it easy to believe their fevered and emphatic replies, 'Yes, Seren saved us all!'

And outside the wall, a massive force prepared for the assault.

---++---

Dawn cascaded down on the wilderness as the planet made its customary Tesser into day. Sheelaakah kissed his cheek as he lay back down on that stone tablet in the middle of the army, but if he noticed he gave no indication. She wanted so badly to tell him that she had found she loved him, but his mind was already beginning to merge again with the monolith.

Master, Sheelaakah heard the gnolem hiss through their connected minds. *Is it time at last!*

It is, he replied, causing his mind fill its body once more. And with that, the gnolem burst from the soft soil of the surface, roaring with mighty winds as lightning flashed down from the sky.

Matrix became a whirlwind in the shape of a winged dragon and begun a rapid flight above the heads of the waiting army. The Alliance cheered as he burst the soil and tore overhead. He was a being incomprehensibly large, sure to rend the wall in its talons and tear it from its place.

Wars are difficult things to arrange, especially on a front that is over twelve thousand kilometres wide and stole into parallel dimensions of astral and Evernet. Suddenly, the Resistance heard a voice. It was calm, measured, self-assured and utterly convincing.

'Freedom Alliance, we warn you against your coming. Our will is strong, and our wall is stronger. It is our brother, our protector, our home. You cannot touch it. Leave now or-'

And it cut off suddenly.

Inside the inner circle, someone had managed to overcome the wards and programming that the Oppression was using to co-opt the channels – similar to the methods Alasia had used. They looked about for whom to thank, and she curtsied.

Outside the wall, the Alliance laughed. They had just bested the Oppression at the first battle of the day. Matrix could feel their courage as he took to wing above them. He was at least an hour to the wall, but he did not rush. He would need his strength for later. Long before he could even see the wall, they sent their missiles against him. Sheelaakah warned him in his mind before he could they were visible, and they came so very fast it was difficult to spot them anyway.

Matrix knew how to deal with them. He made himself thin – almost transparent. The missiles exploded with great force, but did little damage to his vaporous body. They felt like insect bights, and he carried on. The second and future missiles volleys were taken care of by the air support – mostly pirates. They were flying in a great squadron about him.

Then he saw the wall, a shimmering curtain of light springing from its uppermost crenulations. He saw it and felt intense, embittered hate.

You're channelling the hope of the entire Alliance, Matrix, do not let feelings overcome your commitment to the plan. Do you remember what you have to do?

He husked darkly. His was a power untempered. What stone could halt-

It is also a power untested. Patience, my love.

And in those words he refound his humanity, as he had so many times with her voice in the past.

He was still many kilometres when he looked with his enhanced vision and saw it. A thin red line that penetrated the wall astrally. That was the place he'd target, thought what it was doing there, he did not know...

Sheelaakah searched his memory for him. *Do you not remember Matrix? That is the place where they first sent you out. It is where you left. It is where you will return.*

He roared in anticipation of the victory, but when the storm that was Matrix reached the wall, he found himself unexpectedly weary. He'd never flown before. With the sound of a million drums, he crashed down in a sand storm of titanic proportions.

A new desert had formed outside the wall.

And all over that wall, war was being fought. The City tried to prevent the war drums, launching great volleys across to weaken the attackers. The mutants would claw them asunder, while the Tendendalaah would sometimes cut one or two down with their snipers. Underground the battle was no less intense.

Suddenly, though it was day, a think mist began to form all along the wall, concealing normal vision. Within minutes, it had begun to drip from the soldiers garb, and muffle the drums. The whales were giving him time to recover.

The Oppression sent out fire to try and tame that mist, but they were ill put to it. It grew thickly, sticking to the wall, the weapons, and the trees.

Get up Matrix! Sheelaakah shouted desperately, but he was seemingly too weak to comply.

That was when the Oppression sent out their wasps. Millions of them. The Kinerigan quickly moved in and the battle took to the skies. Ground based guns tried to join in, but while the Resistance was better placed to target, the Oppression was protected behind a wall and energy field that was yet to be breached.

The fire was intense, but nowhere more so than about the ground where the desert formed, not a drop of moisture on its sandy surface. The wasps targeted every grain.

'That was a bit more tiring than I expected,' Matrix mused, stretching his arms.

The Kinerigan are under attack, Sheelaakah replied, guiding him back in with her mind.

The we'd best help them, he replied.

His enemy was not prepared. Matrix suddenly shot up from the ground, becoming a million thrusting tentacles and cutting wasps from the sky, splitting them in its grip. The pirates quickly moved to a better position to enjoy the carnage.

Then those tentacles began to fold together. Within minutes an enormous onyx lion soon stood against the wall in the wilderness beyond. Those that could not see the beast were shown it on the Evernet.

There was pandemonium inside the wall.

Matrix, now! The general ordered.

He looked quietly for the red line. He took a deep breath. He was angry, very angry. He felt that fire move to the centre of his forehead, and he lowered it for the charge.

The ground shook, and in places broke irreparably as he took charge.

They thought their wall was strong, but the impact of the gigaton gnolem striking a mountain shook the planetoid from one side to the next. The seismic waves along the wall were plainly visible as crystals flew back and slid again into place.

The Oppression had ordered their citizens to remain in place – told them there was nothing to worry about except a 'few fireworks.'

Hundreds of thousands were injured. Many died.

The panic inside the city was voracious. What few guards that were not manning the war suddenly had a near revolt on their soil. The Oppression called in their strongest and best telepaths and priests to still the masses, but it would take many hours to quell the panic – at least three.

Meanwhile, back at the Resistance, the Tendendalaah leader celebrated.

'General,' she quietly spoke.

He was standing at a stone table, seeming to play dolls with his rulers of every nation, and a little green clad girl who sung random songs and moved those little dolls around seeming at whim. Sometimes they'd disallow her, sometimes, after conferring, they'd send out instructions to the tenuous lives of thousands involved in a war none of them could see the full extent of.

'Madam?' He replied in the Tendendalaah generative of respect.

'That blast was over two orders of magnitude higher than we had expected. If he keeps this up, we will be done in two, not eight assaults.

'That is good.'

'Not all good,' the Derringer general stonily replied. 'We'll not be pleased when that shockwave reaches here in under an hour.

The room fell silent.

'Can we survive it?'

'Likely,' the Derringer replied. 'But we'd best re-enforce the walls.'

The general turned and nodded at the telekinesis's. But the Derringer laughed.

'Nice start, but let's use these,' he said, propping a wide bench up against the roof.

Novel. The general mused. *I'd never have thought of that.*

Second attack

Matrix was unconscious for over an hour, the onyx lion seeming asleep on its side. Then a new wave of wasps spread across the energy field to attack that beast where it lay. The Kinerigan moved to intercept, while Derringer-improved mutant cannons blasted through the enemies ranks. Slowly, Sheelaakah begun to work her way into his consciousness again, and willed him awake.

Turning itself from the soil, the stone beast shock itself from the rubble of its impact, burring its aching head in its paws till it felt the first snaps of Oppression fire on its flanks. It roared up at the gnats, snapping futilely at them. Yet suddenly they pulled back enmasse.

Thousands of kilometres away, a little girl suddenly pointed at the model of the city, her face full of concern and alarm.

All over the planetoid the Resistance turned to look, indeed, the battle for the most part halted. Inside and outside the wall, all turned to a scene they did not expect. The unfailing energy field that held the city from the wilderness beyond begun to recede. It was unheard of in history.

Matrix wasted no time, and in an instant was upon that wall. He pulled at it with his teeth, taking down a dozen mighty crystals and dashing them on the ground with a single raking claw. Without those crystals, the energy field would not descend there again. He thrust his mighty teeth against the wall, straining and straining against the stones.

Matrix don't! Sheelaakah cried in his mind. *You'll spend your strength on those stones and not take the entire wall with the standing waves! Stop!*

But he did not, he could not. He was driven.

Back at the generals abode, they were in pandemonium. They had heard Sheelaakah, and flew in a flurry of attempts to reach him or slow him down, bringing his awareness back to the reality of the situation.

Above the din, a little girl suddenly screamed.

'Tell him to get down! He has to get *down* now!!'

'What? Who?'

'Matrix!' Jacinth screamed, grabbing the communication crystal. 'Hide behind the wall, right now!'

But it was only a mutant leader who understood the danger. 'All mutants! Launch the cannons into the city! Take out the Ballista's! Incoming!'

It was a warning almost a moment too late. Lightning and fire leapt from secret hiding places inside the city, spewing hatred and death among the attackers outside the wall. They could fire from well over the horizon, and all over the city, citizens shrieked as their sky turned to fire.

But the Resistance, to the cities surprise and horror, was equally well equipped, and returned the massive attack. The first target of the Oppression was not on the Alliance lines, but a huge torrent of fire and magma tore like a meteor through the sky to the centre of the lions chest.

It was a warning almost a moment too late. Matrix did not hide, but made his own choices. He had no time to move, so in the moment before the ballista bolt struck him, he made his body sand once again. The explosion shattered him into a great wind, but he'd survived. Forming again into a sand storm dragon, he suddenly leapt down, and burrowed his way deep into the earth.

The fire continued for barely five minutes before all ballista, among Alliance or Oppression were destroyed or disserviced. It was to be hand to hand once more. Many millions perished, within and without, in the shortest lived and most bloody exchange of the war.

Then the mist returned, spreading deeply into the oppression lines. The Alliance saw their chance, and swarmed at the wall, claiming some small parts of it as their own even as forces gathered to push them back.

They were still trying to discapacitate the formidable defences of the wall two hours later when an earthquake, moving at over four thousand kilometres an hour, begun to return to the place of its origin. That was when the Oppression realised their mistake; they should have tempted the lion this hour, not last.

Matrix shouldered the soil from his arms, and taking a mighty step backwards. Breathing in fire he struck the wall again with all his energy and with flawless timing.

Again Seren shook, but not so much as previously.

It was a noticeable decrease in force. There was consternation in the control tower. Had the enemy somehow effected some terrible curse? If Matrix continued to lose strength at this rate, even logarithmically, they would not succeed at the wall.

Don't fear. Sheelaakah told him, even as he shook his head, and took again his rest under the soil and fog at the base of the wall.

That was when the Oppression decided not to give him another change. Launching a massive offensive, they pushed almost two thirds of their entire forces against the Alliance headquarters. This left their other walls weakened, and while many points were concurred by the Alliance so that their thrumming in synchronisation could continue, it would be a futile

481

victory if the Oppression took the command site – where the General and Matrix were.

Oppression and Alliance forces clashed with all their might. Giant mechanised spiders tore through the forests, millions of armed soldiers tessered in as far as they could to race up the hill towards the waiting Tendendalaah arrows. Bright lights of aura and energy cut across the sky while enormous beasts of stone tore themselves from the earth to join the fray, while creatures of air and lightning took to war.

It was a desperate battle, and they had but one objective – the stone table and the man who lay there. The sky turned dark above their heads as the combined armies strove against each other, working death on both sides while a gleaming tower lit up the sky like a sun far away. All over the city, citizens screamed while adults were pressed into the armies service – deep in the wilderness beyond, children wept as waves of seismic pain spread along the length of the planetoid. A line of slowly expanding fire begun to creep back from the wall as unexpected strength from the City pushed the Freedom Alliance army deeper and deeper into Alliance territory. The land burned scars that would never fully heal.

After two hours they were within a thousand kilometres of their goal, and in the final minutes a spear head of a hundred thousand elite tore through Alliance lines to strike out at the man who drove the gnolem, just as the sands began again to form the lion.

Third attack

It was when they struck – the assassins in the Evernet.

It was a ruthless attack, many Alliance minds fell in the first assault. Then they began a slow and measured strike to overpower the Evernet that connected Matrix mind to the gnolem.

Another Alliance programmer fell.

The inner circle was frantic. It would not matter if the spear reached them in a few minutes if they did not best the Evernet assassins. There must have been hundreds of them attacking…

Suddenly a pirate craft landed, uninvited, and out of it stepped a woman, red handkerchief tying down dark curls over caramel skin. She laughed as she approached.

'Here children, let me take care of this.'

Alasia was there in a second.

'Oh, so *you're* the pirate queen. You don't look at all like I expected.' She commented acridly.

'Who are you?' Myth answered, a little too unconcerned.

'You are not welcome here, Program,' Alasia replied.

She raised her eyebrow, 'I think you are about to be bested here, Resistance soldier.'

Alasia smirked at the hip, 'they haven't met me yet, have they.'

With that, she pushed a programmer from his chair and donned the headpiece. Step by step, and without Myth's help, she beat them back. She was running four lines at once, she dimly heard one of the Tendendalaah say in amazement as she stalled the virtual assault. Within her mind, she had them tripping over themselves and duplicating futile efforts as illusionary enemies misled them through dead ends. She smiled at the Program, who looked surprised and not a little confused. Alasia had learned her lessons well, and was applying more to this effort that even she knew she had. It was making her talent all the more savoured.

But her smile quickly vanished as she felt the shift in the Everwinds. Suddenly, she was on the defensive again, the virtual enemies approaching faster than ever before, breaking down her protections, detecting her deceptions, inching their way closer and closer like... wolves.

The pandemonium that was stalled by Alasia now returned.

The Program Myth looked about confused, then smiled.

Alasia turned her back on it.

So, it was them. It was her sisters. They were still alive. They were back.

They knew her well, they knew her tactics.

'Take him off,' Alasia ordered.

They machine hurried to disconnect Matrix from the gnolem. It saved his life, for when one of her sisters breached the virtual defences, she shrieked to find a void at the other end. Matrix, however, was screaming in psychotoxic shock, devoid of a body. Sheelaakah looked out at her fear.

Alasia did not look back, for it was the opening she needed. That sister had just reached out too far. She had no way to defeat them, no way to injure them... unless... It was a rare hope. In the moments weeks ago while Poison was unconscious, Alasia had placed there a small, adaptive program that would allow her to scan her mind more easily. Unless, of course, she or one of her sisters detected it first.

But it was still there. For all their talent, they'd never come across this simple program before?

She touched it, imbuing it with power and a new mission.

She would have clutched her throat before she died, Alasia darkly realised. She did not hear Poisons screams as the program haemorrhaged her mind to death.

But her sisters did.

And they were livid. What might have been better spent destroying the breached defences of the Alliances virtual fortress were instead spent in hunting her.

One approached quickly, swearing vengeance, livid with rage.

It was her undoing.

It was a simple, unconscious death in the reality that the Evernet imposed on people. She chased Alasia across a stone bridge, only to find it had no floor. The resulting plummet crushed her mind on the sharp rocks below.

Two down, one to... Envy.

There was Envy.

The blond woman looked around. Looked at her fallen sisters. Her deep blue eyes filled with regret and pain as she looked at what Alasia had done. At what war had made her do.

'I'm sorry,' Alasia said, mildly regretful, pointing a bow at her sister's heart. 'They were going to kill me.'

Envy nodded... and... walked away.

Alasia did not know what to do, and it wasn't until someone touched her on the shoulder in congratulations that she returned to the real world. Alasia had won. They were celebrating her. 'It has never been done!' They cheered.

And the pirate queen was nowhere in sight.

Fourth attack

What is it, Sheelaakah? I-olo asked.

It's Matrix. The sudden unplug from the gnolem has sent him in to psychotoxic shock. I think we can handle it, but no more surprises, please?

That's an idealistic request. He replied, somewhat tense after almost nine continuous hours of ultramodern warfare. *The Oppression has made some serious inroads to your position. While the last spear has failed, they will be in position in a few hours to attempt again.*

Just give us three more hours.

With the failure to meet the returning seismic wave, it had decreased significantly in strength. Their time table was pushed back into the next day.

Sheelaakah wondered whether Matrix would be able to possess the gnolem again. She tried to probe his mind, but it seemed to hurt him, and then he tried to flood hers. She tried to speak to him, to reach out to his soul print.

That was when the ground shook, and a dark red energy wave floated across with them from the city. They both gasped in surprise, though he was only partially conscious.

It was the mechanical decapod that explained the situation. 'There is some unexplained seismic activity being detected from the city.'

'We'll see about that!' Matrix replied, suddenly lucid. He came all the way out into consciousness, squeezed her hand, and plunged back into his body of sand.

-++===++===++-

It curled and folded around him, lazy to be shaped. But as soon as it saw its new foe, it submitted to his focus.

Granite.

The Alliance did not know the Oppression had a granite gnolem. No one had. Harder than onyx, but noticeably smaller... However, since the battle, and his weakness, Matrix could not form all his sand into his body, and they were now almost a match, head for head. Then it stooped as it walked across the wall, and formed two of the walls crystals into its arms, carving hands at its ends. Its two ape like fists beat a challenge to Matrix.

Not in all their research did the Alliance image the city had a gnolem as well. Where it had come from was an answer they needed to get after the war.

Matrix formed his body up into human form.

Tell the Alliance to get back from this position, Matrix commanded. *This is between me, and him.*

Sheelaakah relayed his order.

Do not spend all your strength! She counselled.

Matrix waited until the other gnolem had cleared the city, for their safety. All the Alliance and city stood back to watch the conflict between men whose shoulders touched the clouds. The battle was ponderous, but their fists moved many kilometres an hour.

It was an epic struggle, and Matrix seemed the more skilled. Yet somehow the ground betrayed him, and Matrix slipped, hitting the earth hard. He felt the city cheer.

It is very hard to move ahead made of a hundred thousand tonnes of sand, and the foot came down so very fast. So again, he became transparent.

The blow was terrific, and powerful, and Matrix was forced to take to the storm. This time, however, something was wrong. They'd prepared for this tactic. The granite gnolem became hot, and his sand was fusing to its skin, losing its power to adhere to the other grains.

Matrix was dying.

Suddenly the mist returned, chilling the granite. Matrix pulled his storm from the gnolem and begun to reform a lion a safe distance away.

The gnolem was dripping wet, and then Matrix heard the chanting. A million minds, beginning with the priests of the mutants, were willing that stone back to a greater heat. It begun to glow... when the chanting stopped. Suddenly, the mist returned, and in a moment, the chanting heated it again into steam.

The first cracks begun to show in the granite skin. It turned to face him.

You cannot defeat me, it spoke to his mind.

Watch, Matrix replied. Wasting no time, he careened towards it, and though it raised its silicate fists he smashed it to pebbles, a mighty cone of dust that settled over the city for many miles.

He had won.

It's time! Sheelaakah shouted into his mind.

Matrix legs wobbled with weariness, but he took many steps back, and drew again into his body every last remaining grain that would hear his command.

It was the twelfth hour.

He watched the seismic waves ripple along the wall. Then, pulling in all his strength, all the will of the entire Alliance, Matrix slammed into that wall with all his hope for victory and freedom.

His world went black.

But to all others the explosion was dramatic. As the waves rippled out along the kilometres and kilometres of wall, giant grey stone crystals flew from their places to land many hundreds of meters from their wall, falling and cascading like thunder in great heaps on the ground.

The wall had fallen.

The wall

Matrix trembled and twitched uncontrollably on the slab. The decapod had done all it could, and a voice was trying to help him back into his own body once more. But he resisted it.

He was lost in darkness, his world was shattering. He tried to open his eyes, but all he saw was the fallen wall. While it brought him great relief, in its sight he became even more lost. Relinquishing the will for his existence, the onyx defused into sand once more, and with its cascading shards he slowly began to lose his will to live.

He had done it all.

He had taken the wall.

They could do the rest without him...

But he heard his voice. Someone was calling him.

Someone he knew, someone he cared about.

And as he listened, too tired to open his eyes, he heard her say. 'Matrix, I love you.'

There was a loud thrum, than two more in quick succession. His heartbeat. Following the sound of her voice he raced back into life. The sands became his arms of flesh once more, and he felt his sensations fill his body. His world suddenly filled with light and fire, and he inhaled violently.

He trembled with chill and fear at how close he had come yet again to dying with that gnolem.

'Sheelaakah,' he said, opening his eyes as she pressed his hand to her face. 'I ... I love you too.'

They smiled, and kissed, not caring in all the world for the correctness of it.

---++--+++--++---

In her heart, Sheelaakah knew he would survive.

In spite herself, she choked back tears of gladness that first, he would live, and second, that he loved her too.

She did not look up to see the jealous woman staring at her with danger in her eyes, nor the flick of vengeful straight, dark hair as she left.

She did not need to.

She was a telepath.

But there was one thing she knew that saddened all the triumph: Alasia was jealous.

---++--+++--++---

Around the wall, the cheering lasted an hour.

They let them leave then, crawling back to the rubble that was their wall in pity. Fully armed, the Alliance did not attack. They had done what they said they would do. There was no more to be done.

The wall was down.

---++--+++--++---

In the city, children wept.

Questions were asked.

Wounds were tended.

Not a single shot was fired, or sword drawn, for three days. It was as if the air itself stood still in reverence at the mighty change that had taken place.

It was during this time, in a lonely section of the fallen wall, that a single twisted figure made his way past the rubble and into the city. The hidden guards all targeting him with their weapons, but paused to see what he would do. He was misshapen and blue, an unarmed mutant. He hobbled out into the fields between two concealed armies to tend to a fallen Resistance soldier who had died there. Picking him up with gentle care, he made his way back to Alliance lines.

Then, incredibly, he went back in, and picked up the next life – a critically wounded Derringer. Plugging her wounds, he carefully carried her back to the Alliance lines.

The Oppression leaders grew nervous. If other followed his example, there would again be thousands crossing the border they were never meant to touch. They gave the word, dark in its text as the soil he drew his comrades from – the next Alliance soldier he picks up will be his death.

Yet as fate would have it, the next life in line was a crippled Black guard. A young man, whose shattered legs had long refused to move to save him, and whose blood was so spent he could only moan fitlessly under the unheeding stars.

So there was no need to fire on the mutant, as he applied some anaesthesia, and picked the wounded enemy up on his back. If the soldier knew about it, he gave no heed as he clutched his hands upon the mutant's arms, cringing as he was carried.

The Oppression sat in stunned silence.

No one fired. No one dared. They'd been given an order, and this time they intended to keep it.

The mutant walked right up to the first Government trench he could find. Another black guard, his helmet thrown away, came and wordlessly took the wounded man away from the mutant's arms.

Then the black guard, having delivered his comrade back to his people, turned and joined the mutant in their mission of mercy.

They could not clear the field in a day, or two. But they worked side by side, not fearing the results, as a thousand other soldiers stood wordlessly by.

Between them they saved over two hundred lives. But by then, it was almost day three.

Three heroes

It had almost been three days. Oppression and Alliance diplomats in heavy negotiations all that time, while millions of soldiers feared who might make the next move. Who dared to start up a war that might not have an end?

But Sheelaakah knew that the Hero of the Alliance took no heed of any of this as he focused on healing. The first two days were at the hospitals, so he would be grateful for this first evening in the apartment they'd given him. Meditating deeply, his blade slowly and happily wrapped itself about his wrist. He did not hear the knock at his door the first, nor the second time. If she hadn't ever so gently knocked on his consciousness, he would have never known he had a visitor.

He leapt quickly to his feet, and ran to the door.

He was going to say something like, 'I am pleased to see you Sheelaakah!', but found it missing once he saw her, or her dress. It was a gentle pink. He looked up, and down, and through her.

'May I come in?' She said, filling the uncomfortable silence left by his speechless admiration.

'You look beautiful...' he stumbled, and she actually blushed. 'You, I mean, you always look beautiful, I've just never seen you look relaxed. I mean, you're never, just... it's a dress!'

She laughed, and he found his mind again.

I was wearing a dress at the war, she smiled.

You were? He stammered. 'Come in, my love,' he said.

It was a little against tradition, after a declaration as they'd given each other - seeing each other in his personal abode like this, but he let her in anyway. She had her guardians and he his, surely they could be trusted this night before they went back to work?

She stood there in his entry, looking around. His place was clean, ordered, and sparsely decorated. It seemed he sat on a mat, or slept on it, surrounded by a dozen glowing amethysts. And around his wall, a disconcerting number of weapons were arrayed.

He laughed helplessly, 'have you eaten?'

She leapt forward and embraced him in a hug. What a long two days apart it had been!

She feels very different in a dress, he realised, and there was so very little fabric between his hand and her flesh. He pulled back a little quickly before he had any thoughts he didn't want her to know.

She laughed, 'It's just me, Matrix.'

'Yes,' he mused. 'It is you. Sheelaakah.' He cherished the word. 'Telepath, warrior, friend...'

Then with a sudden thought, he jumped into the next room and ordered some quiet music. She walked in as pale apricot light filled the room. He stood in the centre, and held out his hand to her.

Without a pause, she took that hand, and joined him in a dance. At first, they couldn't work out how to hold each other, till laughing, they settled on a hug. Her left hand in his, her right hand on his chest. With a contented sigh, the first in decades, she rested her face on that chest and listened to his heart beating. Since she'd first joined with his mind at moonscape, no, since before then, he'd been more trusted by her than any man had ever been.

They stayed there for many minutes, swaying in the music. When simultaneously she looked up at him and he at her, and she realised in a moment that this night could go far... that he wanted it to... though it must not...

She did not move, but looked at him as though lost for reason in his eyes.

Suddenly, there was a knock at the door.

490

The mood broke, and the music stilled. With an understanding nod she released him to answer that door.

---+++---

Phew! He heard Sheelaakah think, a little too loudly.

It was Glenn Bakerson.

'Matrix! Thought you might need a little company! Oh, hello Commander,' he said, clearly a little embarrassed.

'It's alright,' she assured him. 'And it's Sheelaakah, remember?'

He smiled uncomfortably.

But Matrix was affable, and invited him right in. They sat, the three of them, and talked. They talked about war, families, hope and the future. They talked about their adventures, and shared deep truths and profound thoughts. War seemed very far away.

It hurt to say goodnight, especially when you know it hurts the others feelings. But the night grew late, and there was wisdom in maintaining regularly biorhythms at times like these. Yet she did not complain, and Bakerson had to actually drag her unwilling form away.

The Spy lord

It was small, and petty, she knew. She was only able to get away with it because I-olo had given her such clearance as a new operative. She hadn't had much chance to report to her superiors within the wall, and that was good. The less they knew the better. And she'd given her spies too much to do helping out with issues within the city to be too bothered hindering the Alliance. All in it, it was a comfortable relationship – for now.

So it was with a little surprise that Alasia found she was not alone in her spy nest within the Evernet, peering surreptitiously at the parting comments of Matrix and Sheelaakah, laughing at their still inexperienced attempts to kiss.

Someone had just dropped in with her.

But she kept her surprise to herself, and looking a moment longer she then stood up with all the calm guile she possessed. Even so, she could not help but be a little surprised at her guest.

It was Myth, the pirate queen.

The pirate smiled at her, Alasia simply raised an eyebrow.

'That man is a great catch,' the pirate said.

Alasia said nothing.

Myth moved to glimpse him from her window, Sheelaakah laughing happily as Dogman pulled her away. Alasia jealously removed that image, though there were security issues to be concerned with as well.

'Oh, it's all right Alasia, I'm an ally,' she said in deliberate irony.

Alasia raised an eyebrow. 'Why have you come?' she said with cold tact.

Myth turned to stare at the vacant window again. If she could see anything through it Alasia did not know. Perhaps she was just admiring her reflection?

'Do you know what I am?' Myth asked.

Alasia didn't really want to discuss things with this program, but she knew she'd need information to help the Alliance if the pirates were planning something malign. Yet they had performed admirably during the war... Besides, Alasia needed information if she was to deal with her... second obstacle... and this was an unexpected opportunity to gain some 'supplies'.

'They say you are a projection,' Alasia said.

Myth smiled. 'I know you are a woman of secrets, so I will tell you one, if you will help me, Alasia.'

'You can trust me,' Alasia lied.

'Good,' Myth continued. 'I want you to know what I am. Only Darkstar and a handful of others know, and they keep the secret well. I have something else to offer you, if you are interested, but you'll need to understand what I am first. You see, a thousand years ago, I was a human woman, just like yourself. Then when I was dying with a terminal illness, my partner had me digitised as you might expect. He was too infatuated to allow me to die with dignity.'

Myth gave a bitter sigh before continuing. 'At first, I was infuriated. As soon as I found myself inside a computer, I realised I would no longer have a human life. I wasn't human anymore. I could hear, I could see, and I still could feel. But I couldn't move from that wretched spot on the floor of his deck. I was a prisoner.'

It was a story so fascinating Alasia could not help but be drawn in to it.

'Slowly, however, I begun to embrace my new existence. I found I had a perfect memory, and begun to use it to study the humans I once was. I found they had simple patterns, that they use simple unconscious cues to communicate. I found out what they wanted and I learnt how to give it to them.' And she smiled. 'The first time, you know, it was an accident. Some silly boy got himself all besotted with my programming, I don't know how, but he began pouring his love and energy into me. I fed on it like a tic – I know you understand. All the while I manipulated him to feel more and more addicted to me. In time, and with others, I found I could manipulate that energy to form things in the real world, made out of the 'stuff' humans were sending me. Thin as whispers at first. Then as more and more humans fell under my influence, I discovered I could manipulate the real world as actually as the virtual. In time, I became a 'projection' of their love and desire, and used that energy to form the body you see now. As more of them fall under my spell, I gain greater energy, and have thus created many... many 'projections'. I feed on their energy and it sustains my existence.'

Alasia was shocked. It was only theoretically possible.

'How?' she gasped.

Myth laughed. 'It isn't easy. I supplement myself with energy and matter from various sources, to be honest, but I'm as real now as you are to me.'

'That's amazing,' Alasia confessed.

'Indeed, and I've found that I can use that energy to create projections off all sorts: clothes, vehicles, even copies of myself.'

'Wow,' seemed to be the only coherent thing Alasia could think to say. 'Is there a limit?'

'I'm not about to tell you every secret.' Myth smiled. 'But there are two limits I must face – the quality of the spirit matter that the humans send me, and the quality of the computer in which my original program resides. But I'm telling you this for a reason.' Myth said. 'There's something I'm willing to offer you.'

'Really?' Alasia asked. She was scintillated with the knowledge she'd just obtained, it opened up a whole new craft of reality that somehow everyone else had yet to discover.

'Yes,' Myth continued. 'I've had to study humans quite a bit to learn how to make them love a computer program. I've learnt a lot, from using unconscious cues to make them desire you, to how to put pity and anger into your voice so that they learn to fear you. I can wrap almost any human around my will in a matter of days, till they beg you not to leave them, and cannot live without my approving smile.' She said with a grin so friendly it belied the depth of treachery that went with it.

And that was when it clicked. All the subtle movements, the way she walked, her voice. It was all a carefully measured charade to entice and enthral humans. That realisation may have saved Alasia just now – that and the fact that Alasia wasn't, strictly speaking, human. All those motions had seemed so artificial, didn't humans detect that? How deceptive! Myth was the perfect actor of an old, trusted best friend. Were Alasia human she may have been lulled into trusting her just to maintain that feigned, sisterly affection.

And yet, what she offered…

Alasia wanted it too…

'You've told me a lot,' Alasia said. 'And that's a great risk to you. Tell me, what's your price for this knowledge?'

Myth smiled, 'him.'

'Him?'

'Yes,' Myth smiled sisterly. 'The man Matrix.'

Alasia pondered. 'You want to make him in to one of your fuel cells?'

Myth scowled, 'I have said nothing about fuel cells. I simply want him for reasons of my own. I can see patterns Alasia, trends in human consciousness… trust me when I tell you, because I'm trusting you with many secrets, that man is better with me than with her. It's best not only for me and you, but it's what's best for our peoples and this planetoid as well.'

Alasia scowled, and turned to the dark window.

There was something very wrong with this Myth girl, Alasia realised. The program grew angry even as Alasia begun to form the refusal in her mind.

'Beware you choices!' Myth shouted, suddenly very terrifying.

Alasia composed herself, and simply smiled.

'No deal,' she replied.

The Projection grew angry and advanced on her, Alasia activated her wards and added virtual threat to the program. Myth stopped in her tracks. Then her demeanour softened.

With kind eyes she said, 'I can tell you love him too.'

Alasia wasn't surprised.

'I can help you with that, show you how to manipulate others and your own feelings so that you can accomplish anything you want.'

Alasia chose to ignore the comment, fully aware of the danger such a promise represented. A life without natural feelings was a life without intuition.

'No deal,' she repeated, quietly happy she'd upset the program by being able to deny it. Had she been human, she would have quickly fallen prey to that beings deceptive 'friendship'. As it was, she seemed so fake, and hoped more humans had the ability to be aware of the false and contrived unconscious messages she was sending.

Myth smiled. 'You think about my offer. You'll find many things have their price, Alasia, before this war had ended.'

And with that, she was gone.

---++---

It was the strangest thing, they'd think in the years that followed, that in the middle of the Great Uprising, almost a Theta level's worth of spies were suddenly reassigned off their cases and told to find where the computer that was Myth resided, and to destroy it at all costs.

Strange, really strange...

Council

I-olo spoke to them sincerely, 'The war, you know, is far from over. Even as we speak, reasonably mild clashes are taking place between Alliance and the Black guard – a little over three days after the wall has fallen. While we aren't gaining much ground, neither is the Opposition. We seem to be at an effective stalemate – diplomatically as well as in terms of battle. We have, however, cemented a strong consolidation of a single identity among Alliance soldiers. This may yet prove to be an even greater accomplishment.'

Sheelaakah nodded. It certainly was.

She sat beside Matrix, openly clasping her hand in his. Alasia was there, joining in the meeting only moments before it was due to begin. Bakerson and Skion were there early, the latter demanding some real action after being taken off the front line – auto reparative systems still welding his torso back together during the meeting. And then, of course, I-olo had allowed them to take the child freely this time, sitting on Matrix's lap in quiet listening the whole time. She never seemed to become bored – perhaps perceiving multiple nows kept her mind busy enough, Sheelaakah wondered.

I-olo continued. 'We are, as many have guessed, simply holding our ground and waiting. Auspiciously, it is so that the negotiations may proceed-'

'I wish I was there!' Matrix mused out loud.

I-olo smiled. 'And they're repeatedly asking for your presence, Matrix. However, we know for a fact that it will do no good. I am too wary of falling into their last trap. Besides, it is obvious to me that they are stalling, and for all their rhetoric clearly have no intention of allowing the Alliance to go free. They still hold out the hope that they can crush us if it was truly necessary. And as long as we don't over-reach ourselves, that will never happen. They are stalling for time; hoping that our cohesion will eventually break down and that we'll fall among ourselves. As time grows old this may happen as negotiations continually fail to bring about change.'

'What is it you propose?' Sheelaakah asked, knowing something interesting was about to happen.

'We need to give the Oppression extra pause to consider their unjust imprisonment of us on this planet, and extra evidence to demonstrate our determination to be free. As a Resistance, we have done poorly, but in a month we have accomplished more as an Alliance. High Commander Sheelaakah – it is the will of the Alliance council that you take your unit into the tower of light and bring down the Skyshield, or at least give us its anatomy so that we can devise a way to penetrate it and send a message for help to the Galactic senate.'

High Commander Sheelaakah smiled. At last, a mission of importance and danger, and that with her old friends, or at least in Alasia's case – closely watched friends...

She felt Matrix's concern before he could express it, they all did.

'I don't like it,' he protested. 'We should be putting more faith in negotiations. We've secured six alliances, a seventh...'

'Whad, wid the city?! Forge brained,' Skion mocked.

'We won't ever leave unless they let us,' Matrix lectured, though his logic held little leeway with the hardened soldier.

'More power, more freedom. On our terms, on our time,' Skion menaced.

'You cannot cut them out of the equation of what makes up "us",' Matrix argued, voice rising. 'Their fate is twisted in with our own, and their destiny.'

'Burn head!' Skion shouted back till I-olo waved him down.

Alasia suddenly joined the debate, her voice animated, 'Matrix, I can see the logic of it. The city requires more motivation to bring greater sincerity to the negotiation table. Once they see they have no real power to imprison us, they'll be more open to discussions.'

'Doesn't feel right...' Matrix again argued. 'It's not the time. We need to show them that we're not their enemies.'

'But we are,' Alasia debated, voice soft. 'We've been killing each other for centuries. Your victory at the wall is a step in the right direction. But the city needs to be ... humbled, a little more.'

'This is not...' he mumbled. He looked about at their pleading faces. Even Jacinth sat unmoved in his lap. He sighed regretfully, unable to resist Alasia's logic or the silent complicity in the room to the Council's request any longer. 'So the Council want us to break in to the tower of light and try to shut down the sky shield, disable it, or find out how to control it, right? No killing, or assassinations, just some espionage to try and make them take us a little more seriously?' He mumbled.

'That's right,' I-olo replied.

'Seems ... early.'

'You won't regret this,' Alasia assured him. 'We'll be in and out in an hour.'

'And,' I-olo replied happily, 'allow me to introduce your new team members.'

'Really?' Sheelaakah doubted this was anything more than a political move.

'Really,' he replied, and as the back wall slid down, two individuals approached. As they entered the light, Matrix groan, Alasia hissed, and Sheelaakah tensed.

It was Myth.

'By the forges name what is *she* doing coming on this mission,' Alasia said acridly. 'I *guarantee* it will compromise operations.'

Skion looked at her in surprise.

'Tisk, tisk!' Myth chided. 'That's not what a spylord says when she sees a rival!' And winked at Matrix, who still held Sheelaakah's hand.

'You will not come near me,' Matrix warned her.

'As you wish,' Myth meekly replied, and took a seat ashenly, opposite him. Matrix's mouth curled into a sneer, and he looked at Sheelaakah for support.

Calm yourself, my man. She counselled. She knew that how powerful feelings, of any kind, can lead to seduction. But with her by his side, he felt, he could resist her will.

But she was a very ancient creature...

Jacinth curled up to whisper in his ear, but everyone could hear.

'She's see through,' she said, meaning the pirate queen.

'Hmmm,' Matrix said, enjoying the derogatory analogy the child had inadvertently spoken. However, Myth appeared completely human and solid to the rest of them. Shee had to wonder what the child saw – she was no telepath, why would Myth appear transparent to her eyes?

Another individual then approached. It was a thin man with hair so blond it seemed white, pointed ears jutting over a royal golden headband. He nodded deeply in respect to the assembled individuals.

'I am Prince Nailou,' he said in a clear and educated accent. 'Son of the King and Queen of the Tendendalaah. I have been asked by my parents, at the request of the whales, to join you in this quest.'

'They asked for you?' Matrix questioned.

'They said our mission would require Tendendalaah talents. My parents chose me. I am their third son, and the eyes and ears of my people in this mission. You have the heart, the honour, and the strength of the Tendendalaah to your cause today,' and he bowed low.

None could see it, but Sheelaakah could feel Alasia's sense fairly scream in delight at the impact this man's presence and savour had on her.

This is good, Sheelaakah mused, being careful to not to look at her.

But she did notice the Pirate queen seemed to notice both her, and Alasia. Her smile was minuscule, but wicked. *She's thinking of how to pick me apart,* Sheelaakah realised.

So they would have enemies before, and within?

Then she felt Matrix move his arm as he adjusted to speak. And with that motion Sheelaakah's confidence soared. While he chose her, no enemy could separate her from her love. She smiled back, and Myth looked away.

And that was when the outer doors exploded.

The Alliance elite stood and armed themselves in an instant. Bakerson took position at the door while Skion stood on the table, arm forming into a cannon. Two dark blades slid into the Princes hands, long and slender points, and a dark punch dagger in Alasia's (though if she had the strength to wield it was unlikely, which made Sheelaakah ponder.) Myth begun to materialise a pistol into her grip.

Matrix, to his credit, moved to shield her and the child. Sheelaakah, however, reached out with her mind and simply laughed to disarm the mood.

'It's Brek'anarl,' she smiled.

They relaxed, and Bakerson opened the door before the Mutant leader could break it down.

A dark blue fist reached in and slammed it shut.

'Oh n –' Bakerson begun.

It shattered in the next second, thousands of iron shards exploding into the room. Myth tried to construct an energy field, which absorbed some of the shrapnel, but Alasia was much faster. She used the Evernet to create a forcefield around them.

'Hello Brek'anarl,' I-olo stated as the dust began to clear.

Hello everyone, Brek'anarl replied. *Sorry I wasn't invited…*

'None of the Alliance leaders were. This mission is highest priority. You will tell me how you found out about it.' I-olo 'requested' in Mutant fashion.

One of my priests foresaw it this morning. And I've decided you need some mutant 'flavouring' to your group. Specially with that Tendendalaah savour you're cooking up. He said insultingly, but only lightly.

The Prince looked back darkly.

Brek'anarl continued unabashed. *Here everyone, I'd like you to meet my little son.*

Brek'anarl moved aside then, and allowed his son to stand at the door.

'Tosk, meet everyone. Everyone – Tosk.'

Brek'anarl's "little" boy was equal to his father's breath, if only the height of a normal man. This roughly gave him the anatomy of a tank. His shoulders, already twice Skion's enhanced build, would not take the doorway and he has to press out his breath and enter sideways. Superb musculature clutched tightly to ridged, misshaped bones, and he smelt like cured leather.

Again across her senses, Sheelaakah sensed Alasia glowing and impressed. She rolled her eyes internally, determined not to give Myth any more information, but had to wonder at Alasia's wantonness.

He's a bit rough around the edges, Brek'anarl apologised. *And does not share my gift for telepathy, or negotiation. But he does like to hit things…*

Skion laughed.

Tosk looked at him threateningly.

Skion's arm became a fist again, and he nodded at the new ally.

Almost unperceptively, Tosk nodded back.

Well son? Brek'anarl demanded. *Say it.*

Tosk grunted. 'Pleased to join. Mutant fist, Alliance swords...' And he held his palms out and faced them towards the ground.

'Oh my,' Alasia said.

The Tendendalaah was rippling in insult and loathing. Myth was unreadable. Bakerson stood back.

'Kem nakri, chum too Tak'ri,' Matrix replied.

Tosk almost shuddered in relief at hearing his native language spoken so well, and clearly by one who'd learnt it and not downloaded it – the personal accent always gave that away. He smiled, lips studded with a mouth full of teeth – just like a sharks, and a jaw that unhinged far further back than humans did.

'Ewe,' Alasia gawked.

Brek'anarl laughed. *You have fun with him! Don't let him eat too much iron now – he tends to get a bit worked up when he does.*

Tosk suddenly turned to his father before he left.

The massive mutant placed a large mottled hand on his sons shoulder, and looking him in the eyes, nodded confidence into his sons face, and left.

While no one could see the nervousness in the smaller blue man's spirit, Sheelaakah could feel it. She saw Bakerson draw in a large breath of the other man's scent, and saw pity draw on his features as well. What Myth noticed was beyond Sheelaakah's skill to detect.

Jacinth, for her part, walked right up to the mutant and tugged to be allowed up into his arms. He cradled her in a single enormous palm with monstrous subtly and great gentleness.

His nows are very uncertain, Jacinth said to Sheelaakah, allowing her to read her mind.

Tosk smiled happily again, and Jacinth stood up to study his teeth with unbridled curiosity, pondering to count them. They were getting along famously already.

'Well. Now you are nine. That is a good number. High Commander, when will you team be ready to leave?'

'I am ready. Team?' she asked the assembled.

'I'm ready now,' Matrix said, as did the other men.

'I've got to powder my nose,' Myth explained suddenly.

'Then we're definitely ready now,' Alasia said coldly, and Sheelaakah had the feeling that while there were things Alasia wanted to do first as well, it was worth more to her to disrupt the Pirate queen's projects even more. The two women shared a dark look, and a brief exchange took place over the

Evernet. Sheelaakah could only read Alasia's surface thoughts as she allowed her to hear.

You shouldn't even be here, Alasia replied. *The Alliance has no need of your interference in this mission, don't your people have enough to do already? Send Darkstar...*

Myth replied.

So leave! We're better off without your cutthroats anyway.

Myth replied.

Not going to happen.

Myth looked about then, concern showing in her eyes at the distrust in all the others.

Suddenly Jacinth spoke, looking at the wall as she did. 'You *sure* you want to come?' she said to Myth.

'Why, what do you foresee, child?' Myth asked her.

'Didn't know machines believed in fate?' Alasia teased.

'We're capable of more than you'll ever know, unless...'

Alasia grew red-faced at the suggestion she should be digitised as well.

'It just doesn't seem like the best now for you, that's all,' Jacinth whispered.

Myth laughed. 'You need me, in that city. I'm not like any of you, I know that. I can help you. And I promise to let things lie as they are...' she said, looking at Sheelaakah and Matrix. 'Until peoples free decisions make it otherwise. Just remember, the pirates want to be free as well, and without my guidance they'd fall into disarray in a day.'

I-olo sighed. 'We have our own reasons for allowing you along, Myth, that don't have anything to do with your people's needs, or the fact that you intend to withdraw all their assistance if your demands are not met. Your promise means much, but your intentions towards the Hero of the Alliance are commonly known, as is his choice towards one of our greatest telepaths.'

I-olo stood up to continue, looking around to address them all. 'You are going into the dragon's maw today, citizens. Put aside all personal issues and concentrate on your objective. There are issues here of race, of affection, of age. But you are the best, the most talented, the most skilled of all your people. Even you, Matrix and Alasia, hail first from the city and not the Resistance. There are many things afoot at this time, but none of them are more important than this mission. Do not lose focus, and do not fail our combined peoples because of your personal agendas...'

---++---++---++---

I-olo left then, leaving them to sort out their plans alone – better he not know. They were nine, under the leadership of newly forgiven and promoted High Commander Sheelaakah. There stood Matrix the dissident, Alasia the spy, Commanders Bakerson and Skion of the military, Prince Nailou of the Tendendalaah, the mutant Tosk son of Brek'anarl, the mysterious pirate queen Myth, and a little girl.

Sheelaakah spoke, 'here is what the Alliance has been able to gather regarding the Seren city Tower of light...' she paused as it materialised in front of their minds. '... its defences are few, but strategically placed. The Resistance has managed to penetrate it many, many times in its history, but never managed to send more than an individual at a time into the upper reaches where the energy field is apparently controlled. Few have returned.'

She continued, 'as far as we can make, there are three tiers to the upper reaches. The bottom two kilometres are comprised of offices and a few abodes for the ultra-privileged. It is likely to be a heavily occupied place. The second tier contains some form of battle control centre and ritualistic space. This is where our target lies. The uppermost tier auspiciously holds simply detection devices, but we suspect it to be the abode of the 'True One'. Avoid this at all costs.'

She looked around for emphasis. 'At our signal, I-olo is prepared to mount three separate offensives, depending on the severity of our need, designed to distract the Oppression. We should have little trouble getting to the tower. Scaling it, however, is another problem, and I'm open to suggestions.

'We could try walking,' Alasia suggested.

'Tactically unsound, our presence alone-' Skion interjected.

'I didn't mean *around* the building. How about up the walls? Remember the foundry...' she teased.

'No wee!' His other voice complained. 'Stat it girl, what, need the whole ceety viewing you?'

'We could try cloaking our approach. Use chameleon suits,' Matrix suggested.

'I expected to have to cover our mental signature anyway,' Sheelaakah supported, though she wasn't sure a walk up the side of the tower was the best idea.

Alasia was keen to see her idea loved. 'Listen, I've gotten a lot better at it. I can give us a miniature gravity well that'll just cover the group. You'll easily be able to see it. Then Tosk here can open the wall for us.'

Skion was doubly affronted now that she'd missed his name.

'There is another option,' Prince Nailou politely interrupted. 'From the research of our people, an energy discharge vent runs the centre of the tower, and is emitted to join with the Skyshield that surrounds the whole planetoid, returning at the vortex at the maws. Perhaps we could risk this shaft to make our entrance?'

'Are you burned?' Skion protested, and Tosk grunted his support. 'Or you will be, nanoseconds in the furnace.'

'I may have a solution to that,' The pirate queen quietly suggested. 'I thought of it when you mentioned needed to be 'invisible'. I can bend the electromagnet energy around us. Never thought of much use for it before, apart from the occasional disappearing. I should be able to project a field large enough to protect us all. If we use Alasia's gravity field to walk 'up' the tower, from the inside... I believe I can get us in.'

'How do we know when we're there?'

'Sound,' the Prince said with a smile.

'Well, I could triangulate our position using simple metrics, but I'm interested in hearing the prince's suggestion,' Alasia said.

He nodded politely. 'The differing levels of materials will produce differing harmonics as we make our way up the tower. I will be able to easily detect once we reach the centre tier, and can make our way to a quiet place therein.'

'Provided you're able to hear what's cook'n,' Skion murmured.

'I will,' he assured him.

'It's a good plan, and I like it,' Sheelaakah stated after some thought. 'And it's new. Once in, we have Myth and Alasia connect to the systems there directly, and we should be able to find out much. Find out all you can. If possible, deactivate the Skyshield, or at best, disable it permanently. Use these crystals so that the Alliance can keep whatever knowledge you find there,' she handed a quartz to them both.

'And so you can keep an eye on us,' Alasia murmured.

Myth agreed.

'Perhaps, but given the importance of what we'll find there I trust you will forgive me. Imagine; nine of us. That will be an enormous accomplishment. Skion and Tosk, bring explosives. Even sixty seconds there will be more opportunity to cause wounds for our enemy to reconsider. Assassins be burned – let's be free of this world!' Sheelaakah rejoiced.

'And if we meet any Resistance, excuse the irony?' Myth queried.

Skion formed a wicked looking blade from his arm. Sheelaakah did not reply.

Matrix shook his head, Myth raised her eyebrows.

Tosk smiled.

---++---++---

They had barely finished the meeting when the weapon smiths arrived to fit them out. A strange suitcase was brought to the High Commander, and she groaned.

'Hand foci,' Matrix mused, choosing weapons of his own with Jacinth's guidance. Sheelaakah opened the case, an inside were four pairs of intricately carved and gem encrusted bands, designed to wrap around the hand.

Sheelaakah mumbled. 'Telepathic enhancement devices. Useful, but I find they dim my focus in other areas. I mean, yes you can raise a sheet of flame but that's nothing when you can turn an ally against his friend, or prevent it happening to your own. I'd rather not...'

'I think you need them,' Jacinth said. 'Look, this one's pretty.'

She held out a silver one of twisted metal with a great blue sapphire in its centre. Sheelaakah replaced it.

'Ice. I never go there,' Shee mused.

'What will you use then?' Matrix asked.

'Will you have one?' Sheelaakah asked him instead of answering.

'No, I'm not very good at them. Besides, I prefer to hit things,' he explained.

She sighed.

'Anyone else?' Sheelaakah asked the room.

They all had their reasons to deny them. Only Alasia protested out loud, 'what would I use them with?'

'Well, I'll not take a matching pair since I'll lose too much focus in other areas. But just in case I need them, I'll take one of telekinesis in case we need to move and one for pyrokinesis, since our enemy often favours that one. Jacinth, does this please you?' She said, almost sarcastically, removing her usual black hand band used for scrying and defence, and donning the pyrokinesis one for the child to see.

Jacinth stared at the armed hands blankly, running her fingers along the bronze and ruby at the fire bands centre. Without a word she hopped from her seat and went to sit with Tosk.

'It'll do for me!' Sheelaakah announced, clasping the weapons into her hands.

Journey to the centre of the planetoid

They left shortly after, sent by shuttlecraft out into the forests. They waited until dark, until an opportune moment to Tesser to a transport the Pirate queen had graciously offered. An hour passed, than another. Alasia was the first to sit down with an exasperated huff, and Bakerson soon joined her side.

Skion and Tosk begun to practice their moves, demonstrating to each other their abilities. It was probably time well spent, Sheelaakah thought.

After another twenty minutes, she noticed that the Tendendalaah had stopped pretending to be alert and took out a stringed instrument. It had a curved, solid base and a long wooden neck on which twelve double strings were stretched. He started playing, and humming soft tunes.

Two minutes found Alasia lying at his feet, mesmerised by his face.

Sheelaakah and Matrix just sat there in each other's arms, communicating on a deep level he probably wasn't even aware of, strengthening their bond. And while none others gave indication, a spirit joined their group. Jindari , the narwhale, projecting astrally, watching over them like a mother hen. It greeted Sheelaakah's mind peacefully as they waited.

The prince finished another song.

'Wow,' Alasia mused gratefully. 'Hey why didn't we bring this guy along before? He's fabulous!'

The prince nodded shyly. Skion and Tosk finished another routine and joined the group.

'Hey, do you think you could teach me some of that?' Alasia asked the prince. Myth was staring out at the stars, her mind far away – probably connected to the thousands of clones that ruled her people for her.

Prince Nailou looked surprised. 'We never teach ... but I suppose you are an ally,' his dedication melting at her big pleading eyes.

She sat up and slid down beside him, leaning over meaningfully.

He blushed at her nearness.

'Music,' he stumbled, and moved a little bit away from her, which she allowed in feigned innocence of being a doteful student. 'Is not a tool or hobby. It is life, it is the nature of the universe. All things resolve to fundamental harmonies. The stones, the trees, even love.'

Alasia looked meaningfully at him with big, attentive eyes. 'Oh,' she said, taking in every word and movement of his lips.

Skion snickered, and Tosk smiled. The mech man punched his comrade on the shoulder and invited him to re-join practice, which both seemed to take to with great glee.

To each, their own, Sheelaakah though, and held her man closer.

'Here, let me teach you,' Prince Nailou said, moving her hands gently over his instrument.'

He was a terrible teacher, Sheelaakah thought. He immediately begun with the highest level of understanding he possessed, not even telling her the basics of sound. But Alasia took it all in, and was impressing him with her talent. His lectures suddenly deepened when she'd hummed a harmony to his tune and he realised she was already well versed in music. Yet for all the innuendo, Sheelaakah could tell Alasia wasn't really trying to seduce him.

Actually, what was she trying to do?

Cautiously, making sure Myth wasn't looking, Sheelaakah took a peek.

It was a riot of noise and colour.

It was a battle.

While seducing a Prince, Alasia was running no less than three lines over the Evernet. Like a storm, she was taking someone, and gently prying Sheelaakah could see it was... Myth, the pirate queen.

And Myth had no idea.

Then Alasia looked, and winked at Sheelaakah.

Oops, she'd noticed... oh well, make the most of it.

Can I help? Sheelaakah asked her.

Kiss Matrix. Alasia replied even as she clumsily tried to form her fingers around the guitars frets.

Done. Sheelaakah smirked, only daring to think how this breached I-olo's last order quite a bit.

It was a lovely kiss.

And suddenly, in the moment she pretended wasn't a distraction, Myth gave a yelp. Her body shimmered and grew momentarily translucent as green lines of energy defined the limits of her 'projection'.

They all looked at her.

---++---++---

'What was that about?' Alasia said coldly.

Myth simply turned her back again on the group, 'Nothing.'

Alasia shrugged, yet continued their invisible Evernet battle for five minutes more. Eventually, she surged an attack which Myth defeated, left a signature to throw her off onto an Oppression assault, and backed down.

'I think you should know,' Myth announced a moment later. 'I've just broken an Evernet assault on our group. The Oppression may be closer to our actions than we'd like.'

They all looked concerned.

Even Alasia, who had every reason to celebrate. She'd planted a program right where it could do the most damage, and would lead her spies along the most profitable destination.

But gloating was not her style.

Suddenly, Jacinth screamed.

Tell the singer that what she just did was not wise, it has given the True One opportunity to harass you due to your disobedience to you promise to put aside personal issues. Nailou told Sheelaakah, and left.

Oops. Shee thought.

'Oh no! I think they're really coming. It looks like they're coming this now. Oooh. Yeek!' She squealed and wriggled out of Matrix arms.

'Everyone, defensive circle now,' High Commander Sheelaakah ordered.

Myth teleported herself into place while the others scurried.

'What are they?' Bakerson said.

'They're the demons,' Jacinth whispered, clutched in Tosk's hands.

'My time,' Matrix laughed, and brought the fire.

Simultaneously, Myth gasped in ecstasy while Matrix clutched his arms to his chest.

'Yes!' She hissed. 'Do that again!'

'Stop that!' He shouted.

'What's happening?' Alasia called in alarm.

'She's leeching me!' He called, falling to his knee, while Myth looked at him intently as though she could not, or would not stop.

'Stop that!' Sheelaakah commanded.

'I wish they'd taken more time to figure out what it was,' Alasia pondered.

'They did,' Bakerson cried, 'set up a whole research division while he was recovering. Called it a unique energetic manifestation. Said even the best priests struggled to pattern it.'

They were there then. Four demons. Far too common these days.

'At least we know we've got His attention,' Skion muttered. The Prince and Bakerson hastily drew protective wards around them, but they would not hold long. They needed someone to drive them off, and Matrix seemed distracted with Myth.

She hissed predatorily, unable to take her eyes off him. Suddenly he roared and with a massive leap snatched his hands away from his chest and hit her hard in the face. She hardly flinched.

'Mmm,' she said. 'So *that's* why I like you. I wondered if humans would ever realise they can do that.'

'Myth, stop it,' Matrix commanded.

The projection looked at him coldly, seemingly driven to insane lust by whatever meal she was making of his energy field.

'We can't fight them without me,' He pleaded, stumbling.

'Myth,' Alasia said warningly. It seemed to snap her back to the present.

She laughed. 'You're joking right? Here,' she said, standing several paces back till a demon fairly salivated to reach her though the wards. Matrix gasped and stood away from her quickly.

'Matrix,' Myth instructed. 'Touch the end of Bakerson's spear, cover it with the matter you generate.'

Matrix did as she asked, standing well back from her. She gasped with pleasure as he did, but he managed to keep most of the energy away from her, or matter, as she called it.

Bakerson looked at it through his aura crystal 'It's burning.' He said, and suddenly trust it outside the wards at a screaming demon.

It dodged it nimbly.

And Bakerson smiled.

It had been forced to avoid the blow.

'We have a weapon!' He announced.

Suddenly many blades were thrust in Matrix direction, and he drew in all his power. Myth stumbled backwards, trying to keep out the way, but cried out euphorically as he brought his fire once more, clutching at the earth.

If she drained him any, it did not show.

They lowered the wards, and the battle commenced. They were matched, sword for claw. Sheelaakah had to empower her soldiers greatly to battle well, but prevail they did. And all the time, Myth lay helplessly panting on the floor.

Till he turned off his fire, she did not regain her composure.

'The energy signature appears to last approximately five minutes, give or take twenty seconds,' Skion's mechanised voice announced. 'We will need to stay close if we are to confront more of them.' And his human voice continued '...and keep that lustful flinch far away.'

She looked at him darkly from bedraggled hair, and begun to draw herself up from the dirt. Nailou went to help her, and she graciously accepted.

'You don't know what it's like...' she said, pleading helplessness.

'What *are* you, my lady?' The Prince asked, noticing how her clothes and hair were rearranging themselves.

'I'm a projection – a sentient hologram. Composed of energy and will, patterned after the human woman who became me. But just like any woman I have... my weaknesses.'

'And you bring them with us!' Skion was embittered. 'I do not see what strengths you offer.'

Myth suddenly screamed in anger, chagrined at her failures. It shook the forest, and the Prince fell down covering his ears. Myths features shifted and changed, and she took on the form of a massive menacing scaled bear, three times the height of a human. Her roars shook the forest, dissipating her anger among the trees.

'I am more of a contribution to this team than you, half man.' The creature roared. Skion raised his weapon, but did not use it. The bears eyes glowed, and a saddle materialised itself on her back – seating for one.

She looked at Matrix, who shook his head no.

She roared again, and slowly returned to her human form.

'... and I was no hindrance to our most recent battle, though it cost me,' she said, still staring meaningfully at Matrix.

'You're not human,' Alasia said unkindly.

'And we are,' Sheelaakah finished before any could continue. 'If we die, we must likely stay dead – especially inside the city. I see our costs as far greater than your own, pirate queen.'

The two just stared, and Myth looked away.

'All right! I'm sorry. He caught me, unprepared. I'll ... know better next time and be... 'better behaved',' she said with sarcastic compliance.

'Even so, He knows we are coming, even if the city does not.' Matrix said.

'Stand by for point Tesser!' Skion suddenly interrupted, and they formed the circle once more.

The tunnel of fire

They were in a silver tunnel, and down its centre, a continuous storm of energy raged. Myth struggled against the flow.

Well, the gravity field works perfectly. Alasia stated through their subtelepathic link. Bakerson took out his opal, but shook his head.

The Prince knelt down, pressing his ear to the metal, started tapping. *We've done well. We appear to be well over half way up the tower already. A half hour of this, and we should be at our destination,* he said.

What if the Oppression knows we're here? Alasia asked.

Then there is nothing they can do about us till we arrive. They'll have as much luck getting through this metal as we would, Sheelaakah instructed them.

The walk was silent as they cautiously made their way up along the corridor of fire that battered against the Pirate Queen's projection. After a time, the Prince knelt down again. Shaking his head, they continued on for ten minutes more while he knelt often.

Finally he announced. *This is the place.*

Finally, Myth said. *I'm getting tired.*

Tosk raised up, and hit the metal hard. It didn't buckle, and be looked confused. Skion tried his machinery, but again, no success. He stood back, and begun to cut into it with a biologically powered laser.

I could use... Matrix suggested, but Myth gave an emphatic *NO!*

So Sheelaakah tried an old trick of hers. She linked with Tosk's mind, willing him even greater strength and clarity.

Empowered, Tosk leapt up, the edges of his adamantine knuckles burning off as they scratched against the outside of Myths field, and glowing brightly he stuck the floor. They hardly noticed the sudden increase in gravity around him that Alasia concocted to assist, nor the telekinetic assistance Sheelaakah added.

He struck it hard, and it cracked. He struck it three times, and it shattered like stone.

In, now! Sheelaakah commanded. It wasn't till she'd returned to her own mind that she found in great alarm that her link to Matrix had suddenly weakened.

And the Pirate queen was smiling to herself.

Skion and Bakerson were first to comply, spreading toxic gas and stunning runes as they leapt inside. Tosk slipped through with surprising flexibility, and the others followed. The room beyond was dark, clearly an echo chamber to protect the rooms beyond from the massive energies of the conduit.

Myth came in last, shortening her field till it blocked their entrance. Bakerson offered her some of the rubble, and she supplemented it with some form of projection. In a few moments, the wound was sealed to all eyes, but still nagged red in aura vision.

It'll hold. Myth said. *For about half an hour. Then the alarms should really start once the radiation begins to make its way through these chambers.* She looked around and through the walls. *You know, you could control the planetoid from here...*

And they do, Alasia said.

So where do we make our entrance? Matrix asked.

How about that door? Alasia commented cheerfully as she led the way across a gang plank, the floor dropping away for many kilometres below them. They were high up in the tower now, higher than any group of operatives had ever been. And they'd needed Myth, Nailou and Tosk to get there.

Myth, Alasia teased. *You'd better get them behind your field.*

They deliberated quizzically, till Sheelaakah gave the order to comply.

The door opened before Alasia got to it, a young man looking out at her.

'Good to see you, Spymaster,' he said politely. 'We have secured the area. I hope you don't mind, I assumed you were either here to test the security or set up plans for any dissidents in the tower. In either case, I've taken the liberty of providing you with this Evernet attachment protocol device.'

'Very good, Jenex. Your forethought has served you well. Now, leave me to my tasks but try to dissuade any from entering the middle tier, as much as you can. The Resistance might be making a terror attack and I'd like to remove collateral damage, if possible.'

'We'll start things immediately, Spymaster!' He politely spoke.

Sheelaakah scanned his surface thoughts. He was clean, as were the six who were with him in the other room – two telepaths among them, a cyborg, and a canine. Unless they hid themselves well against the spy team out there this would all be for naught.

'You're very cheeky,' Matrix complimented her after they'd left.

'Look at this tasty little toy!' Alasia boasted, proudly displaying the protocol device. 'Wasn't he nice!'

Sheelaakah hushed them, Bakerson and Tosk taking up position above the door. 'As soon as we're in, the clock is ticking. Alasia, have we tripped security yet?'

'No, my boys took care of that officially for us,' she grinned.

'Even so, make every second count. Connect to the system as soon as you can and everyone, watch each other's backs. Ready?'

'Hold on!' Jacinth called.

'What is it?' Matrix whispered to the child at his leg.

'Someone's coming.'

They waited a nervous minute while Alasia peered into the darkened computer laboratory beyond.

'Oh,' Jacinth said apologetically, 'not this now.' She grinned.

Myth pushed the child rudely away, 'No time for games, no time for mistakes!'

GO! Sheelaakah ordered, and the attack began.

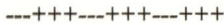

The second tier

The two ladies strode purposefully into the room, even as the soldiers moved quickly behind them, blasting out security devices and defence denizens with great efficacy. Sheelaakah silenced any they missed. Adhesive boots gave Skion and Bakerson the advantage as they scurried alongside walls.

To their left and right, computer monitors flickered to life.

Slowly, more and more creatures begun to invade the room to see what all the noise and violence was about. A sentient, probably human, made his way as well till the High Commander turned him away.

Tosk set a charge on the wall.

Skion called out to him, 'Be sav'n for a greater burning blue-man!'

Tosk grunted, 'Best spot not otherwise.'

He's putting it there in case there are no better targets that we arrive at today, Sheelaakah translated to Skion.

Understood, he replied.

'We'll not get anything here!' Myth counselled. 'They're all disconnected from their uses for the night. We have to hit the open systems.'

Sheelaakah cursed. They'd be found out in the very act.

Suddenly Alasia shot out two computers.

'Just in case anyone thinks I haven't been doing my service protecting Seren,' she smirked, and shot another one.

'Point Tesser!' Skion commanded. They all moved into their places in the defensive circle, then, before anyone could move into their area, they tessered out and right into the middle of a crowded and fully operational control deck.

The shooting started immediately.

The poorly guarded terminal operators were ill equipped to defend themselves, and fled in disarray, few having the sense in the panic Sheelaakah unleashed to lock out their crystals. Information begun to flow to the Resistance. Within seconds, legions of programmers out in the Wilderness beyond were flooding into the system.

They had almost half a minute of almost unimpeded progress before the Oppression begun to realise the severity of the situation and attempted to respond. They tried to send entire units of black guard, but found it almost impossible to Tesser them directly in. Those unfortunate few that did make it were cut down or torn asunder by the Alliance elite.

Out at the diplomatic circle, the Speaker left immediately. All around the torn down wall, fighting immediately intensified.

The war was far from over.

Alasia and Myth ducked behind some terminals. Alasia begun to hack four of them at once, and then opted for three. She crooned, they were a wealth of distracting information! And as she hacked, she implanted benevolent programs for her own later use, and several viruses she hoped would help disable the shield, or at least their ability to control it.

Myth transformed into a cat first. Common enough, sentients often thought twice before suspecting a cat, especially Siamese.

Alasia promptly instructed Matrix to take out all the other cats, *except the Siamese,* she explained regretfully. Losing the pirate queen here would mean they'd likely need to get another one from the Alliance, and that would take time. Once the Oppression realised how the group had gotten in, they could not use that way again. And even though she was wearing a disguise, Alasia was still a little worried they'd recognise her from the synaptic memories of the programmers and controllers that ran for their lives from a desperate and skilled Alliance elite.

As if to emphasise this, Matrix spread the Alliance banner and clashed it on to the roof. They'd killed or discapacitated everyone within a minute, but still more continued to arrive or teleport in, so that the battle never really stopped. It was a severe blow to the Oppression, but as soldier after soldier begun to pour into the room, the circle of defence the Alliance maintained begun to shrink.

'Time to move out!' Sheelaakah ordered.

'How, and to where?' Alasia asked, pulling her mind from a profitable plundering of the Evernet. They'd made a mess of things in there, it would take years to recover from. But for all their pilfering, there was no sign of the controls to the sky shield.

'Tesser us anywhere!' Sheelaakah ordered.

Myth approached her over the Evernet. *Here's something interesting, recon you can get us there?* She asked.

'Hang on a minute!' Alasia replied, ducking behind some tables.

It was an interesting venue, to be sure. Highly warded. If they could only get through no space, they'd bypass those wards and no one would know where they'd gone, at least for a few minutes. Now, how to get surrounded by over one million times their own mass ...

It was harder this time. They'd strengthened their defences. She flew through the Evernet, setting up barricades, blockages, detours and deceptions. When she came to the control panel, she gave it her full attention, trusting in her preparations, and had accessed the gravity portals once more...

---++---++---

It was a quiet day down at the mezzanine. Whatever war the Resistance and their random allies appeared to have begun had calmed down three days ago. Even with the loss of the walls, which was easily explained as part of the Governments overall plans, the black guard had quickly re-established order. Still, the hospitals were filled to capacity and beyond, and those few not in stasis were still within a day of being fully healed.

So when the woman screamed it gave them a start. They turned towards the city of light and looked at it in alarm.

It is breaking apart!

Cracks had appeared along two of its surfaces, and billions of tonnes worth of stone begun to peel away from the walls. Even from his safe distance watching, the shockwave when they fell to earth would destroy all the building from here to...

But they did not fall. The twin megaliths simply floated out from the tower, and turned ever so slowly till they faced the tower like a pair of unattached wings.

'How is that possible?' the woman asked.

'It must be the True One,' another muttered in awe, though no one felt truth in the words.

They hung there for a half minute. Then, slowly, the enormous stone wings folded back into the building, merging with the old stones, becoming inseparably one with the tower of light once more.

'What was that about?' the woman asked.

She held his suspicions to himself a moment, then set them free. 'Something's going down at the tower today. I'm declaring mental disturbance and taking the day off work.'

And as she hurried off as fast as she could in the opposite direction, no few followed.

---++---++---

Alasia was pleased as a child under the peace arch on Freedom Day. It had worked!

'Where are we?' Sheelaakah asked.

'Don't know,' Alasia replied. 'Some highly warded area Myth found. We can... oh look, there's heaps to see here!' Alasia said accessing a portal. 'Also, there's also something behind that door that's connected to the entire tower. Go check it out Matrix,' she ordered.

The hall was quiet where they appeared. Tall red curtains draped heavily from bronze rods, and green marble pillars held a polished stone roof from the cream coloured floor. It was a beautiful chamber. She had managed to form no space again, and they'd all leapt through almost simultaneously. They could have escaped to safety, but they were on a mission to take down the sky shield.

Alasia gasped in the middle of her plundering of the Evernet terminal. 'I think I've found it! The controls to the sky shield! Wait, no... there's the anatomy but no control... oh, so it's a zero point threshold on the ... ooh, it's complex...'

515

Just then, the blue light of a warning Tesser flooded the room. The Alliance soldiers started blasting even before their enemies appeared, but they had strange tactics, and the room was brought to a sudden standstill as a bald grey man demanded a halt.

'Alliance soldiers, I congratulate you on your resourcefulness.' He commented calmly from behind his shields. 'But your mission ends here. We have been tracking your progress since you first tessered into this building. Surrender peacefully…

Tessered? thought Alasia. So, he's bluffing.

She jumped up from behind her cover, the face he knew hidden behind new features.

'Andy!' she cried enthusiastically. 'I'm so glad to see you!'

He pondered a moment, when a sudden recognition begun to cross his face. He never did have time to form it into a coherent thought as, with a deft manoeuvre nobody expected, Alasia whipped Glen's gun from its holder and shot him in the head. The quiet of the room was shattered in the thunderous explosion, and the gun flung itself sideways from her hand. With inexplicable luck the rune encrusted bullet went straight through his shielding, the extra two his comrades had skilfully erected, and smashed right through his midbrain to pulverise the rest of his mind in the shattering explosion against the far end of his skull.

The remaining battle was brief, but decisive. The Oppression elite were skilled, and determined to fight to the death. Bakerson took a terrible wound preventing Sheelaakah from being struck down, and Tosk suffered many deep cuts from his large and less mobile bulk. In the end, Sheelaakah bested their telepaths and the battle turned quickly against them then.

And all the time, Jacinth kept hidden under a curtain.

After their brief victory, Alasia returned to her study of the terminal while Myth joined her. Meanwhile, Matrix approached the door with apprehension. It was translucent quartz boulder, covered in some form of powerful sigils. Etched into a stone pedestal at its side three symbols lay.

'What are these?' He asked.

Alasia was the first to reply, a little dreamy as she hacked into another circuit while talking. 'Still cannot find those control circuits. Perhaps there are none… they're logic symbols Matrix. You use them to organise computer and sentient systems. They're like a gate with two handles, and each gate is opened by turning those handles in special patterns. The first is an 'and' gate – it only activates once both handles are turned at the same time. The second is 'or' – it activates if any or both of the handles are turned. Are you keeping up? The third is 'excusive or' – when you can have one handle or the other, but you cannot have both. There are others…'

'Exclusive or?' He asked.

'Or X-or for shor-' she stopped dead. 'Maybe *that's* what it means!' she whispered.

'It?' Bakerson asked.

'Ooh, don't you remember!?' Alasia asked rhetorically as she simultaneously hacked into three lines. 'The X-or system. Here. This world. We were on that wretched rock worm and you were sitting with your hands like thus… why I bother…' she wafted back into her concentration.

'Well, I know which one gets us through this door. It's 'or'. Whatever you chose you still get the same result. That's just the way they like it in this city.' He said, reaching over to push the stone in.

'Wait!' Sheelaakah advised, but it was too late.

'Whatever you choose,' Matrix explained, 'you always end up a slave.'

The wards glowed momentarily, then disappeared. He'd unlocked the door.

'Oh,' Sheelaakah said, clearly surprised it had worked.

'It might still be warded,' Matrix said, ready to open the door. 'Hang on, I think I can displace it…Myth, please stand back.'

'As you wish,' she complied. But she breathed in deeply as he brought his fire…

…and smiled sweetly as he completely vanished.

Matrix had vanished. It was some form of teleportation, but it felt like a no-space transmission to Alasia. She immediately left her hacking to find out where he'd gone. But the next thing she knew Myth was standing in front of her. She turned to see what she was doing, but only heard her say 'That's for the trick out in the forest …' and she suddenly struck Alasia on the top of her head with a brick.

She didn't even hear Sheelaakah's cry of alarm, or feel anything as the blazer blasts Skion fired at Myth passed through her laughing form harmlessly.

Sheelaakah was speechless. Myth had hit Alasia. Only seconds after Matrix had touched the door and vanished. She was busy frantically trying to locate him… he was alive, but it must have been an extremely heavily warded area… if only she had a direction!

Then, just as she was beginning to panic at the reality of Matrix unexpected abduction, Myth had turned against them all. First, she'd taken out Alasia. Without pausing, the Pirate queen made her way provocatively towards the door, a concussive blast pushing them all else out of her way.

Take out Myth! Don't let her get away! Sheelaakah commanded. The warriors did their best to comply. She lashed at her with her mind, but it felt too far away. Skion levelled several blazer blasts at Myths head, but the all passed mysteriously through. She must have been studying his weaponry while all the time they'd been fighting the Oppression. The Prince came at her with flashing blades, but with a flick of her hair and thrusting out of her palm, flung him several meters back without even touching him.

Bakerson was there next, but she'd opened the door, and stepped inside. It looked like a vacant room except for a single crystal that floated above the floor in the centre, glowing with immense brightness. The pirate queen turned and looked back, smiling victoriously, and didn't close the door until the last second, locking it with its powerful and dangerous wards.

'What happened!' Bakerson roared in anger, pounding the door.

'I do not believe it was she that took Matrix,' The Prince said, rising.

'I agree,' Sheelaakah concurred. 'But she used the distraction to get into that room alone.'

'Perhaps it was her plan all along? She did suggest this venue,' Nailou pondered.

Tosk rushed the door and hit it with all his force. He winched his hand back painfully.

'Stop!' Sheelaakah commanded. 'We think this one out… Bakerson, get Alasia up. We need to access the Evernet and get past whatever wards Myth has locked that door with. More Oppression will be here soon. Nailou, see what you can do about that door. Jacinth!'

'I didn't see that coming,' The child quickly apologised from behind her curtain, seemingly genuinely surprised, running to Sheelaakah's side.

Sheelaakah pondered deeply, quickly separating her terrible fears for what Myth, or perhaps, the Oppression had done to abduct her love. Risking much, she sent out a long distance message to one she knew would hear.

I-olo! They've taken Matrix. See what you can do to help find him!

518

They gathered into a more defensive position quickly. Whatever Myth had done to Alasia, Bakerson informed her it was probably not life threatening - even if Myth had intended it to be. Even so, Alasia would be compromised till she received proper healing.

'We need to pull out!' Nailou stated.

'Not without Matrix...' Bakerson interjected fiercely.

'Glenn,' Sheelaakah said, choking down her own fears. 'We'll find him, but we may need to get ourselves our f-'

They all felt it.

The Oppression had just dropped a dampening field all over the tower.

Now, and without Alasia, the only way out was to walk.

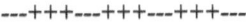

Myth slammed the door shut using their primitive understanding of the Evernet, and laughed as she reinforced the door with strong and dangerous protections. She wouldn't even be able to hear their failed protests as they were no doubt eventually shot to pieces by the Oppression.

Then the dampening field fell. So, the Government knew she was here? Yet she laughed, it was too late for them too. If there was some way to protect the one called Matrix it would have been preferable, but as it was, they had snatched him from her just as he'd inadvertently led her right to an even greater prize.

You've failed, she said out loud, speaking only to the crystal before her. She menaced up on the rock, bypassing the wards, stepping right through the divisions, hacking down the unyeildium shielding that sprung up. They were no match for what she had become. It realised it was bested then, so it did what all sentients do when facing death. It pled for its life.

Myth. Lay aside your treachery. He will find you, you know that.

'And when he does I'll imprison him just like all the rest,' she said, mocking it by speaking in voice simply because she had one.

She circled the gem. It pled again: *I am his servant. I hold them at his will. Without me, they will scatter their dissidence to the stars!*

'I have no intention of letting them go. But I and my people will no longer be *his* slaves. We will not bow to his will, *anymore*, DO YOU HEAR ME!!!'

Please, no...

'And now, sentient crystal, you will die, and I will take your place and rule within and beyond, taking all Seren to myself. Do you realise what I will then become? You are just a trap that holds their souls here. With their undivided attention I will be much more than the thousand what I am now. But first, I must destroy you.'

She caressed the crystal, and it lashed out at her with a spark.

She rubbed her wrist, but smiled cruelly. 'I'll need help...' she muttered. 'All of them.'

And then they came. Every copy of Myth scattered around the planetoid. Every single image she'd ever created and maintained, even the projections to piece the dampening field. They entered the room and flowed into her. All of them.

Then, from her hands, she began to flow into that crystal.

The battle for its sentience was brief. She slew it almost immediately.

Then she begun to move her existence into it, abandoning her false computerised body on moonscape to dominate and reprogram the crystal before her.

The pirate queen elated. No more slavery, no more bowing. Soon she, Myth, would rule in Seren city and Moonscape. It would not be long before all the Alliance met under *her* name, and swore fealty and undying love to her! Then they'd have a heaven she could live for!

Yet suddenly, the surety of her conquest begun to fail. Like a boat riding up a waterfall, another mind approached. It was cunning, quick, and deadly. It shattered her incomplete defences as she was stuck between two bodies.

The second battle was brief, shrieking, and desperate. But in the end, it was the strange blond woman with clear blue eyes that victored. Shrieking hatred and frustration at an eternity of life, the Program that was Myth, the Pirate Queen, finally died. And all over Seren, pirates mourned a tyrants passing with their silence.

The True One

Matrix suddenly realised he did not know where he was when he arrived. It was a beautiful chamber. Its roof almost vanished high above, and the air was heavily perfumed. Gold and silver inlays riddled in confusing patterns filled a room not walled with stones, but of polished crystal. Jade, sapphire, emeralds the size of many men. It was more than a monument; it was a work of unparalleled art.

Yet for all its beauty, there was an intense wrongness about this place.

It was entirely infused with evil.

The metals twisted in dark imagery, and the music that appeared to come from the air itself was dampening and betraying. He began to feel fear.

'I have brought you here,' a deep masculine voice explained, 'because I tire of your whining. You, boy, have brought me much grief, and now I must deal with you myself.'

It was the voice of all the assassins. It was the words behind the Oppression. Instinctively he knew – it was the True One.

Matrix gulped down his fear.

This wasn't supposed to be how it went.

But perhaps... this was a chance. If he was going to face off against another incorporeal at least he was partly prepared, and with Sheelaakah's commitment and love –

'Your woman cannot save you here, boy,' the disembodied voice continued. 'You have died a thousand times in my mind already, I only toy with you for someone to talk to.' It laughed.

'Show yourself!' He demanded, and his tongue cleaved to his throat.

'You do not make demands here, whimpling,' its dark voice said, very close. Yet from the shadows far away a figure begun to form, melting from the mists to take up a diamond throne not far from where Matrix stood.

It was a demon in the shape of a man, twice the size of any he'd ever seen, and equal to Brek'anarl. Its skin was pure red, and twin horns curled from its hairless scalp. Bright gold bracers adorned its arms, and it wore nothing except a tight sash about its waist, which taped into mist below.

'So,' the creature said. 'You are the first enemy alive to see 'the True One.' It laughed cruelly.

The tightness in his throat constricted till Matrix fell on the floor, completely at the beings mercy.

'Token!' The creature called.

A man walked out from behind the throne to bow his face to the floor before the creature, his newly healed hair trailing long below his feet.

'Twice this man has defeated you, and I will end it all for you, personally. But your failures are forgiven you because I have not told you all he was. We will speak again shortly, but for now, I have a task for you. His companions, including the one you covet, are in the chamber below us. Their lives are forfeit by the laws of your own people – what do you think you should do?'

'Kill them!' He replied, crying with regret, but with trembling in enthusiasm.

The One smiled.

Staring bitter spite at Matrix, Token walked out.

Matrix could not move till the door had shut behind him.

'Get up,' the arch demon commanded.

Not having any other option, Matrix did.

'I don't know what you are,' Matrix said. 'But I will fight you, and I will defeat you-'

The One laughed. 'We shall see. Come, Matrix. There are still many long moments before I crush your Alliance. Do you know why I allowed you all to step so far into my abode, and destroy so much peace? It's because I needed more soul prints, more death, to fuel my city. Then, I would continue the Oppression-'

'Are you saying you don't even need living beings to run your city?'

The demon just smiled.

'Then you are the enemy of us all, even the Oppression...' Matrix mused in wonder.

'Do you know what I AM!' It roared, breathing its sulphur breath in Matrix's face. 'You don't even know what *you* are! Any of you! Why you deserve your fate, why I will not stop to persecute you into death and *forever beyond.*'

Matrix trembled in spite of himself. There was absolute truth in those words.

'Come, boy. I have something to show you.' A muscular pair of legs formed themselves from the mist as the One walked to the huge arched windows of his abode.

Matrix tried desperately to contact his friends, to send some form of message to the Alliance. Token was still alive, and still choosing to serve the darkness that clearly despised even him. But the Ones hold on the area seemed absolute. There was no Evernet, no sound. Not even Kino radio. And from the vaults of the vast towering windows, a blue sky with yellow evening clouds left him wondering where he really was.

His attention snapped back toward the object sheathed in black stone before them. It was an enormous scimitar, red diamonds in its hilt. The One laughed as he drew it from its sheath, breathing in its power.

It was a sentient sword, Matrix could tell.

Almost unconsciously, he reached for the blade at his side.

The dark One laughed.

'So be it, we'll do it that way! But first, Matrix, can you tell me what this is?'

'I do not know,' he honestly replied, regretting that he was even speaking to this being. There was no light in it. He was probably better off just ignoring it, but it had such a dangerous looking scimitar that danced in its hands as if it was composed entirely of dark light.

'It's Worldbane, Blade of Souls, and to its credit, it has slain over five hundred worlds.' The One laughed cruelly, even as the scimitar grew in his hands to impossible proportions, then snapped back to its normal size again.

'Do you know what it takes to destroy a world, Matrix? You cannot metabolise the creature you eat while they are still living, and neither can my dear friend... I believe you've met.'

It was C'Wiltaa. She materialised then, stepping from the stones. Laughing at him flirtatively, and in pure spite.

'It's *him*, Master,' she menaced. 'He denied me; he's stirring them up again with all their angry thoughts! He needs to be dealt with.'

'He will die today, my precious world,' the One promised.

Matrix brought the fire then, and C'Wiltaa whipped behind the one she called Master.

'Calm yourself, boy. You'll be needing that in a minute.'

'Why don't we end it right now, unholy liar,' Matrix demanded.

It paused, considering his comment. 'Because then I cannot tell you what this does. I've never told an enemy, and you need to know.'

The One paused to look long out the window. 'When I look out at all the stars, and feel their worlds trembling at my glance, I know that one reason is because of this – Worldbane.' He caressed the blade lovingly, and threateningly.

With a motion so sudden Matrix could not even flinch, the being that was suddenly dozens of meters away in the next instant, held Worldbane scant millimetres from his neck. The blade seemed to want to reach out and bite towards his living flesh. Matrix slunk away from that blades presence.

The dark One laughed, even as C'Wiltaa slid quickly away from them and waved farewell from the stones.

'It has the power to separate all soul prints from their bodies. Simple, isn't it? But not only the soul prints of fleshy beings such as yourselves... the souls of entire worlds.' It laughed darkly. 'Entire worlds! With this knife, I have overseen the death of over five hundred worlds, and made them part of my ... 'friend'. She is growing powerful on their bodies, even as I do from your soul prints. One day, she will consume the entire galaxy!'

'Not if I have anything to say about it!'

He lashed out with his fist, and brought the fire. Faster than he could think, let alone see, a black flame leapt from the Ones hand and blocked Matrix's blow.

'I wondered what that looked like,' it said. 'Been a long time since I saw it, really. Still, just like I remembered.' And with a motion faster than lightning smashed his other palm into Matrix ribs and flung him many meters backward.

Matrix stood up, breathing laboured, and pulled his blade.

From somewhere, C'Wiltaa laughed. But there were other voices in the mist, others laughing. But there was something in their voices... Matrix listened intensely, then he heard them. A billion voices mourning.

The One stopped his advance.

'Ahh, you hear them now! You're about to join them, but I'll give you the chance to discover your helplessness before me.' He smiled, then, with a snap of his fingers, he pulled a fist full of pure motile bronze from thin air.

'It's clean,' he told Matrix. 'And will supplement your little blade so that we may fence with Worldbane fairly here. It'll be much more entertaining.'

Again in the distance he heard C'Wiltaa laugh.

Matrix's mouth was dry with fear as the metal slid towards him and tapped his boot. He did not look down.

The One huffed with boredom. 'I give you my solemn oath; this metal will serve you wholly and purposely for the rest of your life. It is yours to keep with no strings whatsoever. A gift, freely given.'

Matrix didn't know why, perhaps it was the panic, perhaps it was coveting such a precious and rare metal. Perhaps it was the chance to wield an entire sword of motile bronze. If he ever found the right stone, perhaps he too would also wield a sentient sword one day...

He swept down, and joined the bronze to his own. It melded in instantly, and at his will, reformed his long knife into a large katana of burnished, impossibly hardened and self-sharpening bronze. It floated easily in his grasp, leaping to obey his will.

'Wise choice,' the One cunningly mused.

'Choice... do you know so much about that?' Matrix asked bitterly.

The One laughed. 'Oh, I know *all about* choice. Let me tell you my secret, Matrix. You see, did you know that I cannot make any decisions for anyone here. NONE! For all my power and knowledge, it is forbidden that I force anyone to make their own choices. I withhold understanding, I teach lies dressed as wisdom, I give orders to those that submit to my authority. But I cannot make someone else's *choice* for them.'

The One sighed as though in regret. 'But THAT'S why they're prisoners! THAT's what makes them ALL fall to my will! You see, there are only two choices to make in life. Either you choose me, or you resist me. You know the division between the City and Wilderness beyond is just a ruse Matrix. You are one of the many who have realised it over time. Yet even outside the city you choose to be part of the game, or you … resist.'

He held his fist out angrily, 'Yet you, unlike the rest who adopt the reality I present to them, continue to choose resist, to insist on your freedom, and in so doing you shine light on opportunities that others have overlooked for centuries, like breaking down the wall.' The enemy snarled, 'But your enemies have enacted a very interesting law on this world, those whose right it is to govern it – all those who choose to resist must die. YOU, however, have avoided their judgement for far too long Matrix. Choose the way of the people of Seren, or die. It is the law. You cannot have both options, you cannot choose neither. You MUST choose one, or the other. You choice is … …'

'An exclusive-or…' Matrix whispered.

'That is right…X-or…' The One smiled darkly.

Then it continued for reasons of its own. 'Long ago, the Seraph gave you sentients the ability to make choices, but this was only possible by allowing you to perceive opposites – bitter and sweet, hot and cold, good… and evil. I, however, knew this was a great mistake. Sentients beneath the Seraph cannot be trusted. You fear your own power, and potential. You rue your own freedom because it means you must live with your own mistakes. You may be free to make choices, but cannot choose the consequences – though I've seen many try! So I endeavoured to take the freedom to choose from mortality, to protect them - and I was thrown down for my blasphemy.' The One husked in bitter memory. 'But you will see, even *you* have no idea of your potential, your destiny. Even you, now, I can see with eyes older than the world on which your ancestors were first created, even you surrender your power of choice to other wills more often than not. It is in your mind, it is in your body. You are less than the dust of the earth, Wormboy. And every time you surrender your freedom, you give that power to *me*.'

And to emphasise this, the One forced Matrix to fall over as though he was being scanned again. There was a momentary flash of painful, intense, uncontrolled contractions. It lasted a moment while the dark One laughed. 'The power to choose is too great for humanity. They must relinquish it and serve me. Even now your rebellion has caused the deaths of billions.'

'There is no end to your darkness,' Matrix spoke when his breath finally returned. 'And you are right, I am less than the dust of the earth, because at least the dust obeys the highest law it is given, while people often choose what they know to be wrong. But my power of choice is what makes me capable of becoming much more than the dust of which I am made, and I am *free* to choose freedom.'

The creature paused darkly, raging within.

'Then you have chosen to die,' and it raised its blade.

Matrix met his gaze steadily, and raised his own newly enhanced katana. Its burnished bronze glowed in harmony with his adamant desire to be free to choose. If only to look at that blade it was a pleasant memory to die with.

Yet there a memory he'd much prefer to see. Sheelaakah.

The One suddenly menaced on him, but Matrix did not lose that image. In a moment, she was more beautiful and lovely in his memory than ever before. With that thought, their connection soared. If he died, it was not in vain. The wall was down, there were new options for all people to choose. And he had found someone to love and who loved him. It was a sad thought, but he would take that love with him into death.

And at the thought of love the One roared in speechless resentment.

Suddenly, with a movement so swift Matrix had no time to dodge, no time to deflect the blow at all, the dark One struck.

It was all such a ruse, giving him motile bronze to defend himself with.

And as the dark steel penetrated his chest and the polished bronze clattered to the floor his last thoughts were a prayer to whomever would hear:

'Please look after Sheelaakah...'

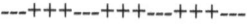

In the middle of the battle Sheelaakah suddenly felt herself scream. 'Matrix!'

They'd been found again not even a minute after Matrix's mysterious disappearance, and were fighting a pitched battle against the Oppression elite. Bakerson was again badly wounded, and sustaining continuing damage. Alasia couldn't even rise, and hid with the child behind what defences a curtain afforded. There was no way to escape, the dampening field prevented teleportation and Tesser, and Myth had stolen their only exit.

Then, as it begun to look like might not be fighting their last, Sheelaakah felt the soul strings snap back into her that could only mean Matrix had died. The psychic pulse that emanated from her stunned the legion of elite Oppression that were making their way towards the ill defended Alliance soldiers, but severely weakening her.

But even as the enemies fell a dark laugh curled from the stairs.

'Token,' Sheelaakah said bitterly, tears streaming from her eyes.

He appeared in silhouette at the top of the stairs then, Bakerson tried to take him out, but the distance prevented an accurate shot. Only Matrix could break his wards at this distance…

Token begun a strange dance then, his long hair trailing about him. And as he did, solders begun rising up from their stunning to add their strength to his. He laughed as he approached, Alliance solders firing desperately, trying to break down his rapidly reforming wards.

'…I don't understand!' Sheelaakah complained to any that would hear. 'He's gotten stronger somehow …'

'Then take out the stunned ones!' Bakerson alarmed, and they shot the sleeping where they lay. With a gesture, Token raised what few were left till they were even in number.

Their Oppression enemies fought with inhuman strength and tenacity, fuelled by whatever dark power Lord Admiral Token had newly achieved. Tosk fell wounded, then Nailou. Sheelaakah concentrated on the Oppression as best she could, but Token was driven and calm. In desperation Alasia tore herself from behind the curtain and ripped open a hole in subspace using the Evernet that led to a plaza conduit somewhere, the resulting fireball incinerating the elite where they stood.

But her joy was short lived, for Token still stood, unharmed, as the fire wrapped only centimetres from his skin. Forming some kind of javelin out of the darkness in his thoughts, he flung it at her and she fell over silent.

But by the time he reached Sheelaakah there were only three conscious in the room. Herself, Jacinth, and Token. He walked up to the woman.

Token was trembling, yet his eyes filled with tears. 'I tried to save you, woman- I- might- have- loved…'

'You are beyond my love,' she replied, still mourning her own loss in deep agony.

'I have become more powerful that you can im-'

'We have nothing to discuss,' Sheelaakah replied.

With a roar of pain and betrayal, Token lashed out, scattering her wards and grasping her by the throat. Jacinth cried out.

'Then you also die today,' he replied, a bitter voice of jubilation and pain.

---+++---+++---+++---

The True One turned to face the window. It was a shallow, but a necessary victory. The mortal fell at his feet, his soul print separated almost immediately.

Yet that soul print did not turn towards the tower.

It did not fall into the trap that held all the others. The image they called Myth had already died trying to control that. The soul trap still functioned, though its wound was from a surprising source, it would eventually heal and again serve him perfectly well. All who died here would spend the rest of eternity gazing at its splendour till they surrendered their will and became his demons. None could leave its light. None, except the handful that had escaped when that accursed mortal Sheelaakah last projected in there.

But she was dying even now for that. And in a minute would join him...

...but the soul print that was Matrix was not turning towards the tower...

The One waited...

... but the soul print would not turn away...

And the True One let out a tremendous roar, citizens of Seren shaking with a chill they could not explain.

'Turn!' he demanded.

But the memory that was Matrix did not turn.

He could not force it to choose...

He marched again to his throne, and sat in obstinate silence.

'They are mine. MINE!' he roared. 'They all belong to me because I rule all within and beyond this world. I reign from the tower of light to the wilderness beyond and far out into moonscape, and there are none to deny. DO YOU HEAR ME!'

He roared to a silent audience he knew were always listening.

'THEY ARE MINE!'

Suddenly, the quiet memory of children's laughter echoed across his crystalled throne room, and in that silence his dark companions began to scatter. The tinkled laughter grew even as unshod feet skipped lightly across gembuilt stones. Dark runes stilled and grew to peace, and the oppressive scents begun to dissipate. Tiny, gentle hands touched Matrix body on his shoulders and ankles, and soft, happy whispers pervaded the room.

It was the *others*...

With a move much faster than lightning, the Dark One leapt towards the corpse, summoning Worldbane to his hand. With an unperceptively swift movement he swept the dark blade down towards those that stood there.

And with equal swiftness, a twin edged straight sword of perfect golden steel came and up and tore the scimitar from the Dark ones grasp. Worldbane soared across the room and stabbed right through a crystal pillar where it remained. C'Wiltaa cried out, nursing her injury in the far corners of the planetoid that she truly was.

Then the golden blade slowly rested on the True One's neck, wielded by an equally enormous blue cloaked man with eyes the colour of lightning.

The red skinned man held his hands up in submission.

'Again, you best me, Guardian.'

'This is not the way I would have it, brother,' Guardian whispered, a perfect moment of respect in every syllable.

Silence passed between them.

The one called Guardian, clad in bright armour, removed his sword and walked towards Matrix's felled body, the cherubs already working their healing on him.

'You broke the rule again,' Guardian stated, his back turned to the One. 'When you intervene personally, so do we. You cannot take any actions yourself; we do not grant you that power. Their choices as evidenced by their actions are theirs alone to answer for. You cannot act on their behalf.'

'They ... asked me...' the One protested weakly.

'And how is it choice, if there is but one option? Besides, he is in no way your equal.'

The One breathed out anger and fear. 'I was once equal to *you*! I will show you, and all the others. It was a mistake, *a mistake*, the day you made them like us and gave them the freedom to choose. They will continue to choose evil. Then I, *only I*, will rule them. You are as guilty as me, allowing them to fall because of their choices when you gave them the power to choose between good and evil.'

Guardian didn't even turn around. 'No brother. You chose, and we will not take away the right to choose,' and then he turned, 'even from you.'

Guardian continued his lecture, even as the demon shed tears of frustration. 'And one day, all of them, will outgrow you.'

The Seraph Guardian closed his eyes in prayer, placing two fingers lightly on the crown of Matrix's head. Matrix breathed gently in, and with gentle whispers, the Cherubs carried him away.

Then, with a sad look at the one he called brother, the Guardian faded into a higher realm.

Leaving the One alone.

And he roared with such bitter anger and frustration the tower shook to its foundations, 'I rule in all SEREN!!' He thundered, beating his fists piteously into the ground. 'I! I am the *True One!*'

But he did not leave his room... although there were no locks or wards on any of the doors. He did not stir to take another life or spread another wound, though it was well and truly within his power to do so...

... he knew there were those with far more power and authority that would stop him once more.

And yet... slowly, all the darkness returned to comfort him. He was their leader, their source of power, and their choice. He could not go to them, but they would all be tempted by his power and knowledge, and once again they began to flow to him. He smiled at their fawning.

For now, he was still a God.

And he laughed a rich and evil gloat that betrayed the utter emptiness of a heart that seemed incapable of ever embracing goodness again.

Token

Token gloated even as he held her by the throat.

I will enjoy watching you die. He promised himself.

Suddenly, there was a change in the air like a rush of cool summer breeze. They both turned in surprise at the man who stood unexpectedly beside them, a deep blood stained gash in his tunic.

It was Matrix.

Breathing in deeply as though it was a great privilege Matrix looked at Token with patient tolerance. 'You're holding my love,' he said coolly. 'You will let her go now, please.'

Token lashed out with telepathic fury, but it flowed away from Matrix like oil and water. 'She is your love? Yes... I recognise the bond now. Have you come to watch her die?'

'Let her go or I will cut off your hands.'

'Never!' Token shouted in desperate fear and impulsiveness.

The sword of living bronze moved so fast it could not be seen. In the next moment Tokens hands lay on the floor.

He pulled back, growling like a dog. 'You die. You die now!'

If he'd been aware enough he'd have heard the warning of the One that brushed against his mind. It told him to run... but he chose to ignore it. Pulling back his lips in a snarl, he sent his fervent hatred towards Matrix.

It was as if he'd totally forgotten Sheelaakah on the floor, the one he'd once professed to love. The one he'd sworn in jealousy to kill. It was an advanced telepathic manoeuvre, but one both were skilled at. Yet in his blind vengeance to kill Matrix Token seemed oblivious to his peril. Sheelaakah turned his power against himself in a vicious cycle of self-inflicted torment, a self-recurring loop.

'Stop,' Matrix offered, standing calmly and unruffled.

'No,' Token crooned, oblivious to the own pains in his mind. His own defences were taken as his enemies, and he tore them down. Again and again he struck, perplexed by Matrix's sudden unfamiliarity of mind, his inexplicable leap in telepathic efficiency.

Matrix watched in pity, and it only infuriated him more.

From beyond hearing, the One laughed.

In a final desperate attack, Token summoned all his pyrokinesis, and in a desperate manoeuvre filled with hatred and guile, he tried to fill Matrix's mind with such heat it would boil.

Using her hand device, and expending almost no effort, Sheelaakah skilfully redirected the flow. He died with hardly a whimper, vital fluids streaming from every facial orifice. There was literally nothing but air left inside that brutally burnt out skull.

Matrix just watched in pity and disgust, till Sheelaakah's sigh caught his attention. With a sudden and impulsive gesture he swept down and they held each other in their arms.

Yet there was only a moment to embrace.

Sheelaakah spoke, words tumbling from her panicked lips. 'We'd better see to the others. I can't believe you're still alive! Come, we need to get into that door Myth took if we want to survive the next wave of angry black guards. What happened to your chest?'

'Later, cherished one,' he replied, calmly concentrating on helping others.

---+++---+++---+++---

A minute later two massive biomechanical claws parted the quartz doors and wedged them open. Cut in many wounds, the surviving heroes stumbled into the door, warding it against an infuriated black guard and their citizenry driven wild for vengeance.

'What happened?' Matrix asked, fully conscious, aware that there was not even a wound under his blood stained tunic. 'Where's Myth?'

'I don't know,' Alasia said drearily, her head heavily bandaged. 'She got in here… there was a battle here, Evernet. I think… I think Myth lost…'

That's a relief, Sheelaakah thought out loud.

'Really? You sure she's gone?' Matrix almost plead.

Alasia waved him aside in her pain.

'I knew it,' Jacinth sighed happily.

'What is that?' Bakerson asked, turning their attention to the floating diamond.

'It's a governing crystal,' Sheelaakah begun. 'But unlike I've ever seen. Its radiance is… enormous, and it's connected to every part of Seren city… possibly Seren itself…

'Is it C'Wiltaa?' Matrix asked hopefully.

'No. Not at all,' Sheelaakah disagreed.

'I agree,' Nailou agreed, studying it carefully with his devices.

'Does it access the Skyshield?' Matrix asked hopefully.

'No,' Alasia drearily replied, as though very busy with her own thoughts. 'I don't think that's what it's for… I'm beginning to suspect… oh my head… Matrix, I don't think there is anything on Seren that controls the shield. It's as if it's totally a natural phenomenon. Maybe it controls itself…'

'Then this whole mission is a failure,' Matrix moaned.

'Not if we learn the truth about the Skyshield,' Sheelaakah corrected. 'If it is a natural phenomenon than it is either independently sentient or controlled by a sentient…'

'C'Wiltaa,' Matrix realised.

'At least we now know that,' Sheelaakah pitied.

'Interesting,' Prince Nailou interrupted. They waited.

'Well?' Alasia demanded.

'Oh! Sorry. It's is almost perfect, yet appears entirely natural. It would have taken millions of years to form. I can only detect one small flaw in this crystal, and it's a very small one.'

'Oh, the *diamond*. Yes, well, can we use it to escape then?' Matrix asked.

'Unlikely, that does not seem to be its purpose,' Alasia pondered. 'It seems to be operating on a different dimension. It seems to harmonise to individual mental signatures, but to be able to do that on a massive scale... but its sentience is almost absent, as if it was slain or driven off recently.'

'Perhaps it was Myth... oh!' Sheelaakah gasped, suddenly understanding. 'It's the soul trap! Quickly, destroy it now!'

'She was... going to try and take over the soul trap?' Alasia mused to herself in understanding. 'Ha! Now I understand, Myth used us to get to the soul trap. Oh, imagine what kind of damage... what on Seren could have possibly stopped her?'

Matrix wasn't listening, 'I think it's time we took our leave.' He stated, raising his blazer, but the Tendendalaah stopped him.

'That may not be an effective solution,' he said. Then, Prince Nailou of the Tendendalaah sung several pure notes, recording their harmonics on a crystal he possessed.

'Alasia,' He quietly said. 'Do you think you could amplify this sound?'

'Of – '

Suddenly there was a mighty crash against the doors.

'– course,' she continued.

'Tosk. Could you please get ready to hit it?'

Tosk obeyed unquestioningly and moved into position.

Suddenly there was a strange pulse from the crystal. Sheelaakah shrieked, and lashed the floating crystal with her mind so that Tosk had to stand back. 'It's becoming self-aware again!' she called, and protected them with her energies even as she began filling it with dangerously high levels of telepathy.

'You'd all best stand back,' Nailou stated.

Tosk jostled his hand restlessly.

'That's not the kind of strength we need...' Matrix said, and turning Tosk aside, began to draw the energy into the centre of his forehead.

The door was battered once again.

Bakerson and Tosk crouched near the floor, shielding Jacinth and Sheelaakah with their bodies. Nailou held out his crystal, which resonated with the sounds he'd programmed into it. As the cacophony rose the other crystal begun to shudder and tremble with the dissonance. It begun to glow a sullen red from the energy Sheelaakah was pouring into it while massive psyonic waves lashed the room, threatening to topple Tosk, or crush Nailou's mind. Alasia crouched by her companions, holding her wounded head. Bakerson turned his back on the crystal.

'Why are you turning around?' Alasia asked.

'Tosk is a mutant... when it explodes the shards... the skin on human's backs is thicker!' He shouted above the growing din.

A wave of fear rippled out from the diamond, and Alasia jumped down behind the men. 'But I'm not human!' she cried out in panic, loud enough for all to hear.

They looked at each other.

...*for the Oppressed*, Sheelaakah whispered.

And Matrix hit it with his forehead. Hard.

It exploded like a cannon, blasting a radiant psychokinetic energy and crystal shards outwards. Nailou was flung right against the far wall and collapsed unconscious. Sheelaakah, overcome with her exertion, fainted. Matrix was miraculously unharmed by the explosion, though Tosk was badly worn down from his battles and sunk down as well.

Bakerson was looking over at Alasia – yet whatever she'd just said apparently hadn't registered with herself, and he did not appear to seek an explanation as yet. He himself was heartily wounded and Jacinth trembled in his arms. She looked over at Tosk with a whimper.

'That's a lot of people to pick up,' Alasia pondered out loud.

Matrix walked over to the others, gathering them into a group as best he could. Nailou gained some consciousness.

'It's like a dawn,' he drearily mused.

'It's time to leave,' Matrix explained.

But they didn't know how. For a further two minutes they waited, Alasia frantically trying to hack a Tesser exit to their position while the thumping continued against the door. They'd be bringing in some heavy artillery soon, and they needed to get out. But everything seemed to be locked down right around the Seren city. They waited, hoping Nailou would come to, or that the child perhaps might intuit some way to save their lives. Hoping that at least if they died, they'd find some way to tell the others about what they'd learnt.

Suddenly the entire tower was rocked with a mighty explosion. The tower itself tiled momentarily, the angular momentum from the twisting Skyshield almost toppling it permanently.

For a long moment there was silence. Then it was clear that the crashing against the door had stopped.

They waited a further minute, and then dared to step out, finding the room was strew with the slain. The plasma had erupted from the hole in the central vent that Tosk had made, and that Myth had plugged.

Half an hour, to the minute.

A mighty plume of super-heated plasma had exploded from the tower of light and spread molten concrete for many kilometres. All around them dust and rubble slowly tumbled as the great gash in the side of the tower deepened. A tower that was no longer a gleaming white, but with the destruction of the soul trap had reverted to its natural bright grey.

And yet, the hated sky shield remained. Even without the soul trap, even with the destruction the Alliance had spread there in only half an hour, the natural phenomenon that was the sky shield remained.

Suddenly Sheelaakah awoke, and lifted her head.

'They're saying thank you,' she whispered, looking far away.

'Who?' Matrix asked.

'All of them. We did it. We finally destroyed the soul trap... they are free,' Sheelaakah said.

---+++---+++----+++---

Freya

Matrix was worried. They'd made a surreptitious escape from the tower and shortly thereafter managed to co-opt a transport, putting the passengers off at an early destination and hopping aboard. They were a battered and bruised group, but if they could just hold out for the day long journey they'd be in Alliance territory and wrapped in their powerful protections once more.

But Matrix was worried; even though they'd learnt a lot and managed to co-opt many Oppression computer systems, they'd failed in their primary mission. It appeared now that the Skyshield was a natural phenomenon and not controlled by the Tower at all, a fact in itself of inestimable worth to the Alliance.

They'd not taken the sky shield, it was true, but perhaps they had achieved something of even greater value – they'd destroyed the soul trap. If the soul prints of those that died were no longer confined to this world it was an immense victory for the dead, if not the living. It seemed the living were still in for the long haul before the city would be convinced to take down their Skyshield. Perhaps even more than one lifetime...

He looked out at the others. Sheelaakah tended to Tosk's wounds and mind, linked in and adding her healing to his. Her wounds were few, but he could tell she was greatly weakened by the battles. Bakerson lay mending, while Skion was auto repairing as best he could with the limited supplies they'd brought.

Nailou was out, and likely needing to be carried wherever he went. And even if they had their full strength, the four men together would still be hard pressed to carry Tosk. In contrast, Matrix's own wounds seemed few and light, indeed, there wasn't even a scar in his chest while his tunic had been clearly sliced asunder by an enormous blade...

Matrix was thinking deeply about these things when his reverie was cut short by an unexpected change in the transports momentum.

'What happened!' Alasia demanded in alarm, still holding her newly rebadged head. Bakerson had done all he could to heal her but she still needed proper medical facilities. Myth's attack had been designed to kill her, and it was a miracle that had did not.

'We're losing altitude,' Skion replied.

Alasia begun pushing him from the chair and piloting the craft.

'Definition: error in trajectory?' Skion asked.

'I am not sure. The controls are being centrally informed.' Alasia desperately tried to program and reprogram the transport. Eventually even she backed down. 'I'm sorry, it's too simple – mechanical, not Evernet. They've shut down the entire transport system Seren wide.'

'First the dampening field, now this? What's going on?' Bakerson asked, readying his weapons.

'I don't think it's us,' Alasia replied. 'They've shut down everything... it's a curfew, or something worse.'

Jacinth gasped. 'I think worse. They're coming, both armies. The battle is coming into the city.'

They paused.

'That's not possible,' Sheelaakah replied. 'I-olo would never allow that-'

'You see, THIS,' Matrix shouted, pointing at Alasia, filled with the sudden rush of anger that took hold of him. 'This is why I didn't want this mission. Now they're at it again. How many millions –'

'Don't point at me!' Alasia shouted back, standing up, her arms flailing in annoyance. 'You think I planned this? I'm half dead here!'

'You'd be fine if we'd resorted to diplomacy. Why'd you have to insist that we take on the tower?'

'And I suppose you'd be glad if all those soul prints were still trapped-'

'Don't you *dare,*' Matrix swore, feeling his face turn white.

Alasia looked like she just might, but as she drew breath Bakerson interceded.

'Enough!' He said calmly and firmly. 'We're here now. We deal with it.'

They looked at each other angrily, then Alasia stormed out of the cockpit to gather supplies. Matrix rested on the pulpit and Sheelaakah looked at him.

'Sorry. I don't know what came over me,' he admitted.

She rested her hand on the tear in his tunic. 'You just came back from the dead Matrix. I felt you die... do you remember what happened?'

'No, it's all like a vision now...' he admitted, grasping at dreams.

She comforted his arm with her hand.

'We'll find time,' Shee replied.

Matrix did his best to relax, breathing in deeply.

Alasia was still shoving medical supplies into a bag, mumbling angrily to herself so that everyone could hear - *he* didn't listen, *he* didn't understand. Sheelaakah mentioned her to Matrix, but he knew he was still too upset to apologise sincerely.

'Let's get in to one of these abodes,' Bakerson suggested as the transport set down in a regular looking street in the outer suburbs. 'See if we can use their terminal or something. They've shut down Tesser and now transports... besides, maybe we can get some medical.'

'Agreed,' the High Commander replied. 'Though I think it unlikely that one of these houses will have the kind of security connection we need.'

'Good point, but what choice do we have?'

'We could walk,' Alasia said sarcastically.

Matrix scoffed. At best, they were several days from Alliance territory.

'We have to try something. Even if there's nothing we can do, we have to try for Nailou, and Tosk,' Sheelaakah said.

Alasia mumbled incoherently. Matrix set the transport down at a nondescript park in a very average suburb and looked out at the houses.

'Jacinth,' Sheelaakah asked.

'That one,' the jade child replied. They'd almost parked next to it.

'Um...' Sheelaakah begun to protest, perhaps she though it too mundane? Or wanted to scan for enemies first.

But the others were up and walking towards it already.

'All right then!' she conceded.

'Sheelaakah, help with this?' Matrix asked, laying Tosk on Bakerson's shoulders.

They knocked on the door. A frightened woman's voice replied, 'I don't know who you are, but we're not letting anyone in!'

Not even the black guard? Matrix wondered. 'Please,' he begged. 'We swear not to harm your family. We need medical assistance. Our friends are wounded and will die...'

There was a long pause.

'You swear not to harm us?' She asked.

'We do.'

There was a deep sigh, and the woman whispered something they could not hear.

There are children. Sheelaakah informed him.

'More refugees...' The old lady groaned, and opened the door. Matrix and Sheelaakah stood there smiling, while Jacinth came up and peered between their knees. Matrix begun to speak his thanks while Alasia quickly disarmed their security and alarms.

'Oh,' said the woman flatly. 'It's you – from the Resistance...'

It was a middle aged woman, shaped in motherly curves. Her hair was curled and her lips prone to pouting, but she was kindly faced and wore a cooking apron. The scent of ginger nut biscuits wafted amicably from a house that seemed to be ignoring the war, at least on the inside. Yet deep within this woman's face was a fear and resignation to whatever fate she'd just thrown herself on.

Suddenly, Jacinth squeaked in delight. 'Petrie!' she exclaimed, and run into the house.

Matrix wondered what she meant.

'Can we ... come in?' Sheelaakah asked.

The woman sighed. 'Hasn't the war you started...' she begun unkindly, but then softened as though anger did not suit her. 'Oh well... it's always been my policy to shown kindness to those at my door. Come in, come in. We don't have much!' The woman replied in either hopeless resignation, or some form of divine magnanimity.

'You seem in very good spirits!' Matrix complimented her, hoping for the latter. 'May I ask your name?'

'I'm Freya. And these are my children Robert, Little gem and the baby is Seath, after his grandfather.'

The three young children stared with big eyes at the armed and diverse group, clutching at their mother's apron the first chance they got. The oldest looked about six, youngest a few months old.

'We won't harm you,' Matrix said, smiling at them.

They did not smile back.

But it was the silent fourth boy that sat at the table that got his attention.

'Is that...' he asked.

'Oh look!' Alasia cried entering, 'It's one of the orphans from the Research colony! Well turn me over and fry me like a pancake!'

Matrix had never heard that turn of phrase before, but he let it ride. Even so, the unexpected reunion was unbelievably ... lucky.

The mother walked up to the child, sitting her children at the table with Jacinth and Petrie. She took no notice as the wounded helped themselves to her living room furniture, nor mentioned their weapons as they sat. To her, it seemed, a promise of non-violence was enough. Jacinth played happily with Petrie's hands while he stared vacantly out the window. The mother looked very flustered, and spoke in a trembling voice heavy with confusion and fear; the voice of a mother trying to hold together a house in the middle of a war. 'The Black guards abandoned him with use two days ago. We've been trying to make him happy, but he still won't speak to us.'

'Oh,' Jacinth explained happily, in the honesty only children can get away with. 'That's because he doesn't speak.'

Freya looked very surprised.

'Told you he was broken,' the oldest child murmured into his hands.

The mother choked back tears.

'What do you mean darling?' she asked.

'He's 'nortistic,' Jacinth explained. 'He's not in this world. Neither am I too, but he cannot hinge back.'

She waved her hand in front of his eyes, trying to explain to the mother. She held her children close.

'You cannot catch it,' Sheelaakah explained.

The mother thought for a bit, and quietly calmed down.

'Well, that explains one thing,' she replied, forcing a smile.

The family suddenly stopped as a sub telepathic message was received. She clutched her children close.

'There's a curfew now dears,' she said. 'Be sure you don't go outside ... understand?'

'Why not mummy,' Little Gem plead.

'Because the nice black guard has asked us dear.'

'But why...'

'Because they'll shoot you!' She shouted in fear and exasperation, her matronly façade crumbling. Her children begun to cry, and she held them close, apologising profusely.

They waited in silence.

'I can help you,' Sheelaakah said.

'No. Just… no one should have to die…'

'Your husband isn't home.'

Freya burst into tears. 'He was stuck in the foundries when the war broke out. We haven't seen him in four days. There wasn't even enough food to last the week and it'll all be done in a few days more. I just don't know what to do!'

She held her children close, and they cowered.

This was war… Matrix thought.

Sheelaakah rose then, and offered the woman a hug. 'I'm a telepath,' she explained, 'and have some training in healing'. The woman nodded. They hugged for a moment, Sheelaakah imparting purpose and restoring the mothers strength. After a minute, the crying stopped. Sheelaakah sat back, looking very drained.

'It's all right children. We'll find a way. Daddy will find his way home soon.'

They hugged.

'So, what is he?' The mother asked of Petrie, curiosity surviving now that her fear was relieved a little.

Such a kindly woman, Matrix marvelled. She had allowed a strange child she did not understand to live for two days without her husband here. All that, and then allowing armed Resistance solders into her home? For all their crimes, many Seren citizens were innocent, and just as kind and inclined to help as any of the Alliance. Perhaps this family would help those born outside the wall to see another side of the city they longed to destroy…

'Have you no disabled youth in the city?' Sheelaakah dismayed.

'No, they're terminated within the first month of pregnancy, or whenever,' Alasia in cold bitterness replied.

Sheelaakah was stunned.

'But… he's perfect.' Sheelaakah argued, looking at Petrie who could not acknowledge her presence even though he was aware of it.

The mother smiled, not understanding, but knowing enough now that she wasn't afraid of this silent and non-communicative child. She walked over, and patted his head. He moaned.

Jacinth invented a reply for him in a deep voice. 'He said, "thank you very much. You are a very nice woman for putting up with me. And you've got looovely children".'

If it had been what he'd thought, Matrix did not hear it.

Little gem giggled. 'Can you understand his Oooh look mummy, he had blue arms!' She was pointing to the lounge room. The children stood up. If their mother no longer showed fear, then they were fearless.

'Yeah! He's all blue!' The older boy said.

'Ahh, children,' but they were off, and lining up at the far wall, took a good look at Tosk. He looked over at them, and they stared back at him in wide eyed wonder.

Tosk moaned happily.

'Tosk,' he said, pointing to himself. The little girl jumped with fright at his voice, or his teeth.

'He's a mutant,' Alasia explained.

'A mutant?' The older boy asked. 'Will he hurt us?'

'No,' Alasia said.

He walked a step closer. Tosk held out his good hand until the oldest child touched it, running his tiny fingers along the enormous blue lines on his skin.

'He's hurt mamma,' the boy explained.

'I... I know,' Freya replied.

The boy ran out the room then, returning with some ointments and healing stones. The other child quickly joined in, and soon smothered him with their laughter and health. They discovered Nailou next, and helped him with his injuries happily, running their hands in wonder along his long ears.

'...first I've heard them laugh in three days,' Freya mused happily.

In spite her fears, Freya opened her cupboards and fed them all. It might be the last meal they'd have, but they ate it well.

Dinner was long over, and Matrix was helping to wash up the dishes, turning the great cooking pan over to dry. All others rested, though night had not yet fallen on this world, which was strange. Also, Sheelaakah had not yet managed to contact the Alliance, which further gave them reason to be concerned. Whatever repercussions had fallen from their espionage on the city had not yet fully played out.

The mother, Freya, watched him as he circled another plate.

'Such a nice boy,' she mused. 'Why is it you're caught up in this war?'

He smiled. 'I'd seen enough, and it was time to leave.'

She smiled, 'I know enough about young men to know there is much more than you're telling me.'

He smiled back. 'Asking questions. That's what got me in to trouble. And insisting that they needed to be acknowledged, if not answered. Most people are troubled by questions because it seems to undermine their power, their sense of what's 'normal'. As for me, I *couldn't not* ask questions. There is so much wrong about this world. It is sick. And I needed to have people think about the way... they always say things should *be* a certain way and then punish those who are like that. You ever meet a strange, friendly person and found them a little 'weird'? But we want people to be friendly right? Or you ever think 'someone should do something about that', and no one does? Things need to change, and people need to stop preventing others from being the change they're afraid to be. Things need to change, and all this corruption and violence is the world's way of working itself towards healing, even though it hurts. It will be worth it, and in the end, I think we'll see something far more worthwhile than victory for either the Alliance or the Government. Because, after all, this is our world for now, and it will be what we make it.'

She smiled at him kindly, not really understanding his thoughts, or being able to know what he'd been through that made him think them.

'... this world needs to change.' Matrix summarised.

'Then ... we will find a way to change it,' Freya agreed, and went to check on her children.

Matrix wondered what she meant. She could not be willing to sacrifice her world, simply so he could have the one he wanted. Yet in war, that was what was being asked of her. Was there some compromise, or at least agreement, that neither group had seen or imagined? Something that would work out for them <u>all</u>?

Matrix finished washing up then, and went out to stare at the kindling stars, night coming late to this world. He watched then, for a region of space he knew well, but could not see. To that place he was always drawn, to the void of darkness he found his physical and spiritual connection to something vast. He did not connect with this earth, he never did, but found his peace among the stars.

'For hundreds of years scientists wondered why they were all moving away,' Alasia mused, coming to his side. 'Well, almost all, and then-'

'So full of thoughts, my friend,' Matrix teased. 'Can you not at times simply *be*? Listen to silence or watch unchanging light.'

Alasia scoffed. 'No. Don't plan to. Need to stay *alive*, not bored. Sometimes I invent quadratic functions just to pass the time between battles. Don't you?'

'No,' He replied.

'Oh,' she answered. He wasn't sure what that meant.

'Alasia,' he said, turning. 'I am sorry for the way I acted, it-'

'Whatever,' she interrupted. 'At least I know you have feelings.'

He wasn't sure what she meant by that, but decided it they were all right now. He was sorry, but it seemed she didn't want an apology, or this *kind* of apology. They waited in silence, she seeming lost in thought, which was good as there was something else he was burning to ask.

---++---++---

It was nice to have him all alone, to herself. The night was fresh, quickly betraying the severity of war that awaited over every horizon. But he was alone with her, for now.

Alasia waited until he seemed willing to fill the silence, 'there was something I needed to ask you about.'

'Really?' she replied, intentionally imitating Myth's best smile.

'Yes,' he replied, standing closer so he could whisper. 'When you threw yourself on the floor in the soul gems chamber you said something very interesting, remember?'

'Of course, Bakerson turned his back... oh... oh no!'

Her hands fled to cover her mouth. He heart burned with fear and regret. How could she have ever let slip such a painful truth!

Matrix waiting in silence.

'Oh no!' Alasia mourned, and turned herself around into the darkness, her body shaking in silent, unbidden sobs.

'Alasia,' Matrix comforted, holding her by the shoulders. 'It's alright. I am still your friend...' He looked at her in the moonless stars, gentle light bathing her in soft blue radiance from the kitchen window, a quiet breeze ignoring the curfew.

She felt heartbroken. She allow him to turn her about, but he did not try to embrace her. He pushed a lock of dark hair from her eyes. 'I never wanted anyone to know,' she cried softly. 'How could I lose it? I'm so weak since the hit to the head... Oh...'

'It's OK,' Matrix reiterated.

She threw aside convention and pressed herself against him. He took her into his arms and held her close, the warmth of her body surrendering to his affection. She melted perfectly into those arms.

It was a while before she could bring herself to tell him the truth. 'I was built molecule at a time by some ... scholar,' she explained. 'He raised me and the other girls in glass jars till we were seven, then had us placed in guilds. He didn't even care ... we were just dolls for his amusement and experimentation.'

Her voice darkened, still wrapped in his arms. 'He killed the others, those that he didn't like. I had a sister... but I got him back. I took his research public, and they'll have burned it all as heresy, if the war didn't kill him... I hope it did.'

'Alasia,' Matrix protested. 'You're not some kind of freak.'

She looked up into his eyes, her face close to his. 'I was a project, designed for nothing but to please men,' she bitterly explained. 'I am a soulless creation designed for nothing more than entertainment-'

He unwrapped his arms and held her by the shoulders again. 'No Alasia, you are a perfect, beautiful, intelligent woman. I've never known anyone like you before. You can accomplish anything.'

She looked right at him, her heart racing in hope at his words, in hope as he looked at her like never before...

'... and you will be whatever you choose, Alasia. We become what we choose to be. Not even the Seraph can take that away from us.'

She wriggled herself back into his arms.

'Am I a human woman?' she pleaded, looking deep into his eyes.

He looked back, falling into those dark pools of desire and desperation. Suddenly, he jerked his head back, and realising where this was going with a gentle gesture, unwrapped her from his arms.

It was cold out there in the night time air.

'Yes, Alasia, you are a woman. The most beautiful and intelligent I've ever met. You can achieve anything you set your mind-'

She turned in anger and pain.

'Not everything,' she bittered.

He sighed, and stood close beside her, looking up into the stars.

'Please don't be angry,' he asked.

She turned to look at him. She was angry. Angry and... and...

There was no word for it.

'Then you love *her* first,' Alasia said, choking back sobs.

'I do,' he replied firmly, but very gently.

She let the tears fall then. She placed her hand on his chest. Oh, how she wanted to belong to those arms! Oh, how she wished he would complete her, just once!

She ran sobbing as far as the small garden would allow.

'Go inside,' she told him.

Without a sound, he left, and closed the door.

And while she wept her tears of sorrow, surrendering to the realisation that this was a battle she had already lost, a soft feeling began to exert itself within her soul. It was the feeling she could not name. It was something she never could understand, and it brought her peace and self-loathing all at once.

She was happy for them, both.

---+++---+++---+++---

Outside, new trouble brewed.

It had been day for fourteen hours, far longer than was usual on this world. He was hurrying home as best he could, running along the silent roads. A few people shouted at him to get indoors. He shouted back that he was heading home. The streets were deserted. Only a few quiet transports lay about. He was worried. The curfew had taken effect only five minutes too early!

He thought back the war of three days past, when the earth had begun to shake. The foreman had demanded that they stay at their posts, continuing to work the forges. If he'd left then, he might have gotten home in time…

As it was, they'd stayed until the first bolts of lightning and fire had torn across the sky, one striking the factory where he worked. He'd seen people die then. People he knew.

That was when he left.

It had been hell and more trying to get home to the outer suburbs. He'd had to fight, and only his natural large frame had given him the advantage to break through a black guard blockade and avoid being rounded up and pressed into service.

It was then that he'd found a crashed supply vessel, venting fuel outside an abandoned bar, something about a 23. The bar was burnt to the ground, but the craft was laden with food and water, and he'd grabbed a huge sack of it using a table cloth as quickly as he could. The war had arrived the day before the supplies usually did, and he was afraid it might have stopped his family from receiving. Still, just to make sure he wasn't arrested for it, he scanned it down as part of his families earnings.

It would have taken less than two minutes to get home in a transport. As it was, he still had half a day to walk. So walk he did.

Until the curfew took effect. He was only a few blocks from home and walking fast. He'd dropped the water then and started to run, pressing his precious cargo to his chest to make better the time. He was just rounding the final corner when they'd found him.

The black guard.

Two of them, both young men. One, the one that seemed to take more interest in his job, looking for all the world as if he'd just received the badge yesterday – head still spinning over a synaptic download so rapid it was tantamount to brainwashing.

'Hold! Citizen!' the young one ordered.

He jogged slowly to a stop. He was four doors down. 'Black guard!' He commented honestly. 'I was almost home. See there? That's my place. That's where I live.'

'You are found outside after a lawful curfew has taken affect,' the younger black guard ordered, a man easily half his age. 'You are under arrest-'

'Arrest! No! Have some pity! My family probably hasn't eaten in two days. I'm *almost home.*'

'If you're worried about that then you shouldn't have left!'

'I left three days ago when I went to work! They...' And he loathed the tears springing to his eyes. 'They don't even know if I'm still alive!'

'Probably stole the food,' The other black guard added callously.

'No, I swear!'

'Get the anesthetiser,' the older guard said.

'FREYA!' He roared.

Matrix walked softly indoors, leaving Alasia to her confronting alone. He breathed in softly, glad that this burden of two loves had finally been met and lifted. He looked up the stairs to where his first love lay resting. He would tell her, but she'd know as soon as they'd meet. He was sure of that. And now, he would embark on making her the happiest –

Suddenly there was a mighty shout from down the street.

'FREYA!' A man's voice roared.

Matrix was at the front door in moments, pulling it open just as a huge bear of a man tumbled down towards it. Matrix was almost swept aside by the massive bag the man carried. He didn't even stop to look at Matrix before he hauled the door closed and warded it quickly.

'Freya!' He called in alarm.

'Dave? Oh Dave!' The old woman burst into tears. They hugged quickly as Matrix stepped back.

'Where have you been, the children and I have been worried sick-'

'No time!' He pleaded. 'I'm being chased by the black guard. They've come to arrest me. I brought you food. I love you. We'll see each other again. I love you!'

'What? No, it's... stop!' Freya hurried to understand what he was saying.

'They've stopped listening to each other,' Alasia mused comically, stumbling in red eyed from the garden patio.

'This isn't good...' Matrix begun, and was then thrown flat on the floor as the door was blasted inwards.

---+++---+++---

Alasia watched, feeling almost helpless.

'I surrender!' The foundry man pleaded.

In walked two armed black guards, both very young.

'Your whole family is under arrest!' The younger said, then pointing to Alasia. 'And any visitors. You've assaulted two guards during a lawful arrest for breaking curfew citizen. Your children will be wards of the state.'

'What? No...' the father pleaded as the neutralising cuffs went on.

'No time for trials,' the older one said, holding a rifle to his head. 'Best justice be served now...'

Alasia gasped from the door. She was unarmed, she was unprepared. Frantically she searched tried to establish Evernet connections that she could use.

'Ahh, comrade?' the younger one asked questioningly.

'See that food? We'll be taking it as ... evidence. Pity you had to die in the struggle trying to steal from the city.'

'They've got kids,' the younger one interrupted.

'You ready to starve!' The older one asked rhetorically, charging his weapon. The foundry worker looked up into his wife's tearful eyes.

He didn't wait.

With a sudden swift motion he lifted his arms, breaking the bands and grabbing the older black guard around his throat. He didn't even notice the younger guard shoot him in the back as he snapped that neck with his bare hands. Then, the foundry man collapsed on the floor, clutching at his wounds.

The younger black guard advanced on him. Alasia watched helplessly even as the others begun to stir in their rooms – the neuralising blast having disrupted them from their sleep.

The young guard stumbled in his words to the much larger man. 'You... you killed a black guard... you... you must be with the Alliance! I have to kill... you...'

He did not complete that thought, as suddenly the young black guard was bashed violently over the head with a newly washed cookery pan, knocking him unconscious and denting it severely. He did not move once he fell.

Sheelaakah and the others filled the corridor from the stairs.

Alasia looked over in helplessness, pointing to Matrix and the fallen guards.

'Time to leave,' Sheelaakah ordered.

'I'm sorry... I'm sorry,' Alasia offered her tearful condolences to the wife. The emotions, wounds and rejection of the past minute overwhelming her.

'Commander David?' Sheelaakah suddenly said in bemused wonder, 'we thought... you died.'

The huge man lay slumped on the floor, where his wife did her best to stem the bleeding. Sheelaakah moved to assist.

The old man spoke, 'as good as dead. They took all the fight out of me once we were captured. Didn't see any good in fighting – '

'You...' his wife muttered, 'you were with the Resistance?' The room fell deathly silent.

'I was.'

Time itself seemed to wait with baited breath. 'Well,' she finally whispered, 'that explains a lot.'

'Forgive me,' he seemed to say to Sheelaakah and Freya both, 'I have much to explain.'

'No, dear,' Freya admitted. 'I never wanted to know. I'm sorry.'

'I take it your husband's home?' Nailou asked with accidental insincerity.

'Help me lift him onto the couch.' Freya ordered.

They pulled the foundry man onto the couch, but what little medicine they had in the house had been almost all used already. A moment later the children arrived and went to him quickly, hugging their father as best they could. He held them close in spite of his wounds. Sheelaakah did what she could for him, and he trusted her on his wife's words.

'What about this one?' Bakerson asked regarding the dead guard.

'Throw him in the street,' the father ordered.

'But...' Freya wondered.

'No. He crossed his bounds and attacked me in my home, I'll not be held accountable for his evil actions. If I'm to be arrested for breaking curfew, then so be it.'

'You're too good a man,' Freya breathed, kissing him.

'And the other one?' Bakerson asked after his first task was done.

'Leave him,' the mother ordered, then to her husband's quizzical expression. 'When he wakes up, we are going to have a cup of tea. Then, he is going to bunk the rest of the week here till you recover - remember, he has a door to fix.'

The foundry worker did not look convinced.

'He's just a boy,' she said, holding her husband's face lovingly in her hands. 'And at least here, he will be fed.'

The Alliance solders gathered at the door, Matrix fortunately little more than stunned by the blast.

The lost officer of the freedom alliance, Dave, spoke, 'There's a teleportation platform, 4 kilometres west in the grey mezzanine. Here, take my worker's secure-key. It may help you get away. You're breaking all the rules here! And Commander, if you need me, you know where to find me.'

She turned to their host family as they surrounded their wounded father on the couch.

'You are good people!' Sheelaakah promised, inscribing her personal sigil in invisible energies on the entryway floor. 'And you have done us much good. You have been kind to those your people call enemies. If any again threaten your home, I will know.'

The mother smiled. 'Then bring peace,' she asked.

'This war is madness, and was never supposed to happen.' Matrix vowed, 'you will have what peace I can bring.'

'Things will always change,' she smiled. 'Yet sometimes ... they really don't need to be so *rushed.*'

'I could not agree more,' he mourned, and the words remained with him as Matrix hurried with the others from the door.

---++---

With the curfew in effect they had to cross others lawns rather than risk stepping on the roads. They were making their way towards the mezzanine, hoping to find a communication orb somewhere there.

Sheelaakah suddenly gasped.

'What is it?' Matrix asked, by her side.

'It's I-olo...' She replied, concentrating hard to hear his voice.

We're at your command I-olo. He heard her say.

The final war

The reception at the Alliance was electric. Brek'anarl was stirring the people up. 'There is no better time! The city is broken, their people frightened. If they will not let us off this world, then let us make this world OURS! Soon we will see who can leave, and who will stay!'

Decorum had failed, and many Alliance people cheered.

I-olo watched in disbelief as a bloody victory turned to greed. The Alliance was again infuriated at another failed attempt at taking down the sky shield, even if it had resulted in a permanent darkening of the tower of light for all to see. Even if that tower was bleeding plasma two hours later. Even if the Whales had announced the joyful news that all the soul prisoners had been free!

The Alliance counted their victories as nothing while they themselves were still held prisoners on this world.

And now, diplomacy with the city had failed as soon as they'd heard about the attack, the Speaker walking out in that very moment. Armed forces had begun to again converge at the city's boundaries, and sorties into Alliance territory had become constant. Now as conflict escalated with the city once more the Alliance was becoming enraged.

They were proposing a war on the city itself.

'I will not commit our forces to this effort, Brek'anarl!' I-olo ordered, not sure if his comment sounded like a request. But the mutant was wise enough.

'Then perhaps it is time for the Resistance to seek new leadership?' Brek'anarl said an obvious tease in his voice.

I-olo died inside. So this was how the Alliance would end – in every way once more at each other's throats. They would not stand up to an attack from the city as individual groups. In spite of their victories, the city would rebuild their wall inside a year.

The General stood up then. 'I-olo please, I do agree that this is the best time to take city ourselves. You must see this wisdom of this action given our current predicament.'

'I will not stand by and let anyone purposelessly slaughter anyone, even my enemies,' he said in threat to the mutant, and to a General teetering close to mutiny.

Brek'anarl simply laughed. 'Then you don't know how to treat your enemies then, do you.'

The Tendendalaah spoke up then. 'We were always wary that the mutants could be trusted to hold their bloodlust in check. We will not participate if this is your chosen course of action.'

The outrage continued. At best, I-olo could hope to stay the carnage for perhaps an hour longer. In the midst of the confusion, he sent a desperate message to Sheelaakah.

High Commander Sheelaakah!

She seemed caught by surprise, but quickly gathered her senses.

We're at your command I-olo, she said.

Things are not going well at the Alliance. The mutants and others are preparing to invade and destroy the city.

What?!

Please let me continue – something needs to be done–

At this, there was an unexpected third mind in their link. It took formidable experience to accomplish such a feat through the wards that usually prevented such things, though perhaps it was able to do so because it was an ally.

There is another option, Jindari the narwhale explained. *If we can get a message out to the others outside the Skyshield it may unite their wills to our cause. I know this has been attempted many times in the past, but my hope is that the recent defeats will weaken the people's spiritual contributions to the sky shield. If such a message was delivered, it would weaken the Mutants resolve to annihilate their enemies – not only because there was now another less bloodied option, but also because they would remember that their actions are always watched. This accountability–*

Yes! I-olo cut him off enthusiastically. *That will work. We can use the battle cruiser–*

As you will, I-olo, The female Tendendalaah's voice cut in.

This was devolving away from being a very public private chat... had the wards failed entirely?

However, my people, just as the Derringer, have been preparing for a day such as this. We have constructed among our people a massive hydrogen fuelled rocket. It is heavily armoured and designed to survive any attacks that might try to stall it. Above all, it is platinum tipped and sure to penetrate the sky shield. It can be ready in an hour, we've just been waiting for the right chance to use it.

Then that is our hope... will it take passengers? I-olo asked.

Twenty. There will be room enough for any agents you intend to send. They can help to convince the Galactic senate to stop ignoring our cause.

I send the best. High Commander Sheelaakah, get to that launch at all costs. Report to the Tendendalaah forest in less than thirty minutes!

Yes sir! She replied, and ended the transmission.

I-olo stood, and faced an angry group of fellow citizens.

'There is another hope,' he begun in his most diplomatic voice ever. 'A message... The Tendendalaah have a rocket they will be using within the hour to exit the Skyshield –'

Brek'anarl laughed, 'Then they go today to die!'

'Enough, Brek'anarl!' I-olo roared, and it silenced the group momentarily.

Brek'anarl grew very angry.

There was a pause. I-olo breathed deeply. 'Brek'anarl. You will give us one last hope. Let us first send this Message. If we fail, I will not impede you.' He bowed his head.

Brek'anarl laughed, 'then it is right! But allow me to add to your ... hope. We mutants have been preparing for this day. We have gathered, particle by particle, enough plutonium for... several... thermonuclear devices. These we are prepared to commit to a united cause for escape. If we cannot reach the stars outside, perhaps a message can bring them to us!' He and his followers cheered. 'If, however, this fails, know that the war against the Oppression will be eternal - till they or I lie defeated on this hated soil!'

The mutants roared their approval.

'We will give you what protections we can,' the white bearded Derringer explained. 'But know that our strength is understone, not above it.'

'The Message leaves within the hour!' I-olo roared in finality, though the Circle member who often dissented spoke up.

'And who leaves on it, is there room for passengers?' The general asked. They all looked very hopeful.

'Only those who wish to die,' Brek'anarl cut in. 'Not in all history had one who'd spent a day here ever escaped.'

None raised their hands.

'Send Matrix,' the mutant ordered. 'Plus whatever friends he chooses.'

'I had thought the same thing already,' I-olo replied, but in his heart he knew it was madness. Brek'anarl intended to remove whatever influence Matrix had over the Alliance. It was clear to I-olo now: Brek'anarl coveted the Alliance for himself. If Matrix was out of the way, in death or escape, the task of leading them to a bloody war at mutant leadership was a distinct threat. Brek'anarl's ambitions were a problem that would need to be dealt with quickly, and ironically it was probably best dealt with by Matrix.

It was madness, and yet I-olo felt sure that if any had the power to convince the Senate, it would rest with the young man and his friends.

---+++---+++---+++

It seemed that not a minute went by as the Alliance knew about it, that the Oppression did too. A massive invasion force sprung up from the city and begun pouring over the shattered remains of their wall and rushing into Tendendalaah territory.

Immediately, huge contingents of Derringer and Mutant forces begun a massive invasion into the city. Millions turned their rage upon it and spared little mercy for the innocents in between in an attempt to force the hoard back into their territory. But it was clearly a desperate manoeuvrer by those that led the city, to invade long from their boarders. Massive mechanids tore the forest to shreds while skycraft spewed fire from the air. Within only twenty minutes the forward advancing forces were approaching the heartlands.

Though the Pirates were sorely needed, they'd lost all cohesion and fled. Only a few committed stalwarts remained, but there was little they could do. Desperate Tendendalaah citizens tried to stall the massive advance, and added little support as the Resistance and Tendendalaah alone stood directly in front of the advancing, merciless hoard. The Oppression seemed bent on their entire destruction to prevent the launch of a single rocket, even at the loss of their own city.

Massive forests burned.

And all through the city, citizens fled as chaos filled the streets and embraced the form of war. The Alliance cohesion begun to crumble as desperate and blood lusting soldiers took to the streets in random, purposeless melee. What began as an attempt to turn the hoard around ended as senseless burning.

But that hoard continued on.

---+++---+++---+++

Matrix was running now, trying to get to a teleportation platform with the others. He carried the children in his arms, though they were far from comfortable. Sheelaakah stumbled by his side, and Nailou kept up admirably in spite of the bandages. Alasia limped and tried to keep up, conscious thanks only to powerful painkillers. Tosk's arm was bandaged, but he threw them down in the first few minutes of running, while Bakerson soldiered on admirably. Skion took point, but was clearly strained by his exertions.

The alarms had started within the first minute of their running towards the teleportation platform – the war had restarted. Jacinth had been right; the armies were coming into the city.

This was never supposed to happen, Matrix thought. They had to get to the Tendendalaah forest quickly, to get ahead of an encroaching and enraged Oppression army. They had less than half an hour.

But as they rounded a corner to enter a mezzanine, they found it was already full with over a hundred or so angry civilians, newly armed by the pocket of black guards that were among them.

'Not this way,' Alasia instructed.

'Look out, they've seen us!' Nailou said in alarm.

'They've a telepath,' Sheelaakah said bitterly, her strength and consciousness almost spent, her soul deeply stretched by the battles. They headed down a side street even as the mod hurried after them. Soon, however, they found themselves headed off by the mob again. They ran a third direction.

'They're co-ordinating themselves!' Matrix guessed. 'Can't we dissuade them somehow? I'd rather not kill any.'

'If I had my strength…' Sheelaakah mourned.

'And I mine,' Alasia concurred, cradling her head. 'She hit me right where I do my thinking and it's all middly, muddly still.' She smiled bravely.

That was when they ran into the dead end.

Skion took point, forming his cannon. 'It is a bad day for peace,' he stated.

Suddenly Tosk roared, and put a massive hole in the wall behind them with his left fist, jarring the wrist in the process. He motioned them through.

The first mobsters ran into the alley just as Skion, second last, was slipping though.

'By the One! It's a monster!' One of them called.

'A mutant! Kill it!' Another roared.

Tosk smiled as he forced Skion through the hole. Skion turned around and blasted towards the first few mob members in the alley. He motioned for Tosk to join him. The great blue man simply smiled, and shook his head.

Skion paused in debate a moment, then nodded in reply. He formed a knife from the bones in his arm, and gave it to Tosk.

Tosk smiled, took the knife, and blocked the entrance with his great blue back even as scores of angry citizens poured into that alley. Skion raced through the building to join the others.

'Where's Tosk?' Alasia asked him.

'Not coming,' Skion replied, in a voice that betrayed his emotions.

They paused.

'Hurry up!' Matrix commanded, shattering the reverie. 'We can get out on the second floor. We need to get to a teleportation circle and out to Tendendalaah lands now!'

'I fear it may soon be too late,' the Prince said in a voice edged with fear. 'They are hurrying the launch even as we speak, and we weren't expecting to leave so soon. An Oppression army has left the city and is trying to burn its way through the Tendendalaah lands. They will not wait for us. The sooner they launch, the less people will die.'

They ran out the building and into another, crossing a delicate glass bridge that gave them a beautiful view of a city engulfed in the chaos of war, and out across the horizon, the sky glowed a morning red of a forest burning. The Prince paused in tears, till Bakerson pushed him on, his own face set and unreadable.

They entered another mezzanine. The circle was just before them. As they ran towards in through the unlit streets, a storm of random blazers struck out at them. Nailou went down, as did Alasia, holding her leg. Matrix and Skion returned the blasts, with Bakerson applied some first aid till she stopped screaming.

'That was Resistance weapons,' Matrix flatly informed them once the firing had stopped.

'The chaos has driven them all mad,' Sheelaakah mourned.

Alasia was blubbering in pain and confusion even as Bakerson tried to tie up her wounds.

'Alasia,' Sheelaakah said, holding her head. In her hands, touching their minds. 'You have to activate this teleportation circle. We need to get to the Tendendalaah. Remember the first mission.'

She nodded in great pain, exploding into tears as Bakerson checked Nailou, and shook his head. Nevertheless, he hoisted the slain Prince onto his shoulders. They all stumbled to stand in the circle, and Alasia did her best to focus, but the sobs flowed unbidden. Sheelaakah left Matrix's arm and wrapped hers around the singer. Alasia wept openly for a few seconds, then suddenly subsided.

A second later, the world glowed blue as space wrapped around them.

---+++---+++---+++

He looked young, but he never was. His age was great, almost as much as the city itself. He was timeless. He was the Speaker. 'True One,' he bowed low. 'I seek your council.'

'Do you not see the chaos before you?' The One replied.

'I do, my Lord. But I am confused of what to do. The Alliance have failed to see reason once more. They are trying to send a rocket to penetrate the Skyshield. We have sent an army to stop them yet... If we stay the course of action millions will die. Yet if we do, they *may* manage to escape...'

'Do you doubt the justice of your cause? The unharnessed savages would be a blight to any world they set foot on! You've seen what the Tendendalaah do to those who transgress their imaginary boundaries, how the Derringer plunder resources without conscience, how the mutants feast of the flesh of their own fallen, and ours. Do what you KNOW is right!' The One stated with great menace, imbuing the speaker with a sense of power that transcended all morality.

He pondered his actions, but knew were power lay. 'No one leaves,' the speaker replied darkly. 'Ever...'

'You must do what you believe is right...' The One whispered.

---+++---+++---+++

By the time Matrix and the others tessered into the Tendendalaah woods the world they came to was already bursting into flame. The first few Oppression had managed to infiltrate the forest, tessered in or simply walked in on giant mechanised limbs. Wounded and desperate

Tendendalaah scurried along, almost disintegrating them the moment they arrived.

An armed giant puma ran up to them. *Hurry!* It seemed to say, *follow me!*

Matrix grabbed Alasia by the hand, but ended up carrying her in his arms. He started to run even as a massive spider like being crashed through the forest. Tendendalaah weapons tore into it, but it was Skion's gun that shattered its legs and prevented its progress. He breathed heavily at the effort.

Mourning Tendendalaah lifted the lifeless body of the Prince and headed in another direction. A solider raced up to them and offered to be their guide. Matrix handed the children to Glenn and took up his long distance rifle.

'Why don't they launch it now?' Matrix asked the guide, scanning the horizon.

It's leaving the moment it's ready. We weren't expecting to leave so soon, but now the Oppression is coming to eradicate us… we weren't ready. If you have time to get on, you're welcome, I'm told. If not, they leave.

'Let's hurry up then,' Matrix supplied.

'What makes you think we've time?' Alasia mourned.

Matrix opened his mouth to speak, but a sudden blast of wind the strength of a hurricane smashed them all to the ground. Above their heads, space was being torn asunder by an enormous vessel of steel and titanium, sleek bulkhead crawling menacingly from the tare in space.

The Battle Cruiser.

Commander Piri here, Allies keep down. All craft converge to this point. Commence firing. For the Alliance! A voice ordered to all within a thousand kilometres.

The massive arsenal on the most powerful vessel under Seren skies opened up, obliterating the entire front guard of the Oppression. The cruiser did not stop there, but took to higher skies to fire on thousands below, always cutting deeper and deeper into enemy lines. It was taking all the heat off the Tendendalaah, but it would surely be its last act. It was being quickly surrounded on all sides.

'That'll give us some time,' Matrix replied, and kept the group running on. The copse of trees held a hidden door, and that door led down. They hurried in as best they could. They had to pass by several wards and armoured doors, always going deeper into the soil. The noise of the battle above begun to dim.

It is fortunate that the Oppression does not know where to find it, The puma said.

'How do you know?' Alasia asked.

'They'd be here already,' Sheelaakah replied.

Jacinth suddenly begun to slow down, pulling at Bakerson's hand which she still held. 'Hurry!' He urged, but they were falling behind.

Nearly there! The guide said. *The rocket lies at the end of this tunnel. They'll hold the door for as long –*

He would never finish that sentence as several holes appeared in space, and flying Emmissionaries, supported by a cabal of demons, poured in.

Run! Were his last words as the darts of the adversary took him.

In the first few seconds, Bakerson and the children were separated from the others by a sudden rock slide. Matrix called out, but Glenn echoed the Tendendalaah's words. 'Run!'

Glenn listened as Matrix called out to be sure they were all right, then hustled into the darkness beyond. So they would not be going on this journey.

'We need to get out of here,' he said to the children. 'We may not be leaving today, but let's get out or the fire from that rocket will kill us all.'

'If you're sure,' the child replied, as though she had much more to say.

But Glenn did not hear her.

---++---

Matrix roared in frustration at losing his friend, and the children. At least they were alive. He headed into the melee with the Oppression that had found the Message. Matrix punched with such ferocity it destroyed the demons instantly. The raging Emmissionaries were little match for Sheelaakah and her highly developed skills – she seemed to specialise in them. But in spite the desperate works of the Tendendalaah, the portals kept forming, and the enemy kept arriving, so they ran.

The cavern they entered was suddenly very vast, and in its centre, a beautifully carved and intricately inlaid silver and gold cylinder lay, easily twenty stories high. Inside, a massive library of all the sufferings and persecutions, as well as the annexations of all the worlds, were housed in many languages, ready to be broadcast through space and subspace the minute the Message cleared the Skyshield. It was like the hope, the little crystal they'd given the diplomat, only a million times more efficient. The cramped living conditions were meant to only support its occupants a day or two while the contacted others of their kind in the galaxy. The rocket was heavily fortified, composed of gold enforced tri-nitrogen, strengthened with runes and the faith of its people, tipped with several tonnes of amplified platinum.

It could probably penetrate into the core of a planet, if it had sufficient speed, Matrix mused. A thunder started from deep within the ground.

Suddenly Alasia cried out. Despite Skion's best attempts, she'd taken one to the leg again.

'Go without me,' she whimpered, ducking into a crawlspace to hide herself.

'Launching – twenty seconds!' A Tendendalaah voice called. A sudden boom from high above, and the launch doors begun to open.

Casting only a moment of regret, Matrix handed her his blazer.

Matrix, Skion and Sheelaakah ran.

They were just crossing the final gangplank, where a brave old Tendendalaah was holding open the door till the last second, when a sudden blast against it caused it to tilt violently. Matrix and Skion deftly adjusted their weight to the fallen balustrade. Sheelaakah, however, was thrown free and only just managed to catch the rails with one hand.

She screamed.

Before he could think, Matrix was there leaping towards her.

Leave me, Sheelaakah begged.

'Never,' Matrix replied.

Matrix leapt over the barrier just as a sudden jolt caused her to lose her grip, and she commenced to fall screaming towards the darkness below. Without thinking he adjusted his trajectory and threw himself downwards to catch her, knowing even her powerful telekinesis could not save her in this foe ridden and dangerous place. As he fell he turned, drawing his sword, and by his mental command it began to reform into a long, grasping chain. He grabbed her by the waist as it wrapped around the lower beams of the gangplank, stretching to maximum capacity. Matrix desperately hoped the thin and already narrowing chain would hold both their weight, but it could not. It gave out just as they swung towards a lower access tunnel, Sheelaakah guiding their fall and Matrix reclaimed the lost bronze as it fell from the beam using the rest of the chain like a whip. They turned just in time to see Skion smile regretfully at them from the rockets entry hatch. Pausing only to shoot down a pair of wasps with his staff, he then shut the door.

They had only seconds to scramble into some form of supply container when the thunder grew to deafening and the fire curled around them. They might have been baked in there without Sheelaakah's pyrokinesis hand band. He held her close, willing all the love and life he had into her, for them both.

A tense moment later they crawled from that box to see the world strangely silent, a bright column of white cloud trailing off into the heavens without them.

---++---++---

The room Skion entered was small, where twelve or so Tendendalaah and a half dozen other races sat strapped into their chairs. He noticed there were no people his size, and none of military bearing. It was lucky he'd come.

He marched up to the cockpit.

The land was falling swiftly away. A few Oppression craft tried to still their approach, but the Battle cruiser was taking heavy fire in their name. They were riding a pillar of fire, and the noise was deafening.

'This is just how I imagined I'd leave,' Skion smiled.

To the left a much smaller rocket took to the sky. It's vastly greater speed and twisted trajectory made it almost impossible to hit.

'One of the Mutant's nuclear devices,' the pilot mused. 'Glad they'd never used it on us.'

The rocket streaked skywards.

'Cover your eyes,' Skion ordered.

'Oh, yeah, that.' The pilot complied.

The light was blinding. Massive streaks of electricity shot across the sky as the Skyshield twisted and tortured under the blast.

Skion looked up. 'It's still there!'

'As we expected,' the pilot explained. 'The mutants will have weakened the shield even further now, and the radiation will work to our advantage. They've started a series of waves along it now. Let's see, if we can just find a node where the three waveforms thin out the shield the furthest. Ahh, there we are! With the overwhelming evidence on this vessel the Galaxy will have no choice but come to our aid and support our – hey, shouldn't you strapped down by now?'

'Wouldn't miss this for the galaxy,' Skion crooned, then added silently, because there was none to hear in this heavily warded place. 'Goodbye friends, I'm sorry it's me and not you... especially you, Matrix, honoured friend.'

And that was when, colliding into the sky shield at over a hundred kilometres a second, the rocket exploded and disintegrated into innumerable fragments that settled on earth over many days. All that ever exited to the other side was a bright flash, only modestly more visible than the thermonuclear explosions.

---++---++---

Matrix and Sheelaakah pulled themselves from the metal crate, severely pitted and fused by the white heat of the rocket.

'I hope Alasia...' Sheelaakah began.

'Ouch!' A female swore from the level above.

'... she did,' Matrix finished.

Alasia continued complaining while she pulled out tufts of hair out with the liquefied metals that had strayed into it.

'Think she's all...' Sheelaakah began

'You'd think!' she protested loudly. 'They'd give us a *second* to take cover. Hey, where'd the demons go? Hmm, oh! I cracked a nail!'

'She is,' Matrix said, and helped her down a ladder.

Alasia looked at them both for a moment, then held him in a big embrace.

'I'm glad you're both alive,' she said, seeming so sincere.

They looked out them, watching up at the bright pillar of cloud that reached upwards. A few surviving Tendendalaah were crawling from the rubble.

'Looks like the Oppression are beating a hasty retreat,' Sheelaakah smiled. 'I don't think they'll just be letting them go this time.'

'Oh! Let's get up there and help out!' Matrix enthused.

'Oh please,' Alasia protested. 'We just got out of this-'

Sheelaakah gasped.

They looked at her as her face paled, tears filling her eyes. 'It failed.'

'What?!' Matrix replied.

'What?' Alasia asked, then understanding, they ran towards the surface. The fire cloud where the rocket had been destroyed was still glowing in the sky.

'No,' Sheelaakah breathed.

'NO!!!' Matrix roared. He pulled out his rifle and begun making his way towards the city. The women ran in front of him, putting their hands to his chest to stop him.

'Matrix, don't. Don't lose it, not now!' Sheelaakah pled.

'There's still hope,' Alasia replied unconvincingly, probably more unwilling to see him storm to his death. From beneath his eyepiece a single tear fell.

Slowly the rifle retracted.

He breathed in deep. 'It was always supposed to be the long road,' he sighed, but the pain ravaged within him. Roaring with primal frustration he beat his fists repeatedly on the soil. Eventually he subsided. 'I cannot believe we failed. We cannot have failed.'

Sheelaakah held his hand, and Alasia joined them kneeling on the ground. 'There has been too much of death these days. Let this be the last of it. We need to rebuild.'

'We'll get there,' Alasia consoled them all, including herself.

They waited for him to speak.

'Every step, a step closer to our destination,' Matrix tutored himself sadly. He looked skywards. 'Goodbye, honoured friend,' he said.

The end

The child pushed her way through the underbrush deep within the Tendendalaah forest. They'd left most of the fighting moments ago, and the foliage grew dense as if this were a sacred place the Tendendalaah never entered. Indeed, the bright cloud pillar and still falling ash that was all the remained of the Message was scarcely visible through the dense verdagery.

'Come on!' she was insisting. 'It's this way.'

'Where are you taking us, child!' The soldier asked.

'To the boat,' she replied, matter of fact.

Pressing back the leaves another time, Glenn Bakerson came upon a strange sight. There, half buried deep in the mud of a thousand year old forest, was a stoneship. It seemed undamaged by time as if its previous owner had simple gotten out and forgotten about it. It looked old, this one probably outdating the Seren city itself.

He pushed the vines respectfully from its polished sodalite length, then cut them down ungraciously. He pressed his hands to the control panel and willed it open. And just like it was built yesterday, the crystal melted apart and the cockpit stood open to his view. It would be a great benefit to the Alliance...

... then Glenn Bakerson, Commander of the Resistance, had an idea that came with such conviction he could not put it out of his mind. This craft had another purpose, as did he. The Message had hit the Skyshield with direct force and been destroyed ... perhaps if one were to take it an angle with a heavily armoured craft...

But it would have to be soon, the shield was reintegrating every moment. He had to get in there... where was Jacinth? He saw her then. She was peeping in at the craft from the other side of the cockpit. She smiled kindly at him, knowingly, though she was only a young child.

'Good, we're here at last. I've been waiting my whole life to meet you hear, doggy man.' She spoke kindly, but quickly, the constant thunder of an unending war cracking above them. She smiled up at him, looking up into his eyes, the unresponsive boy standing beside her.

'You know,' she mused patiently. 'Even when he tried to take my gift from me, I've been able to see this day. I even know what you're going to say.' And then, just to emphasise her ability, she echoed his every word even as he spoke them.

'You cannot come.'

Then she finished thoughts for him, mocking his deeper adult voice, 'This is a war child. There are things too important for you. Stay with the carers!' Then she added in her own voice. 'We don't have time for this.'

She pushed aside even more vines while he shifted his stance uncomfortably. He looked across at her, still holding his spear, still nursing his throbbing pains. Still wondering if, by some power far greater than he, that these children were meant to go with him into death or freedom. For a second he stared at her, feeling helpless, but knowing she could not stop him. It would only take a moment with the back of the weapon and she would not be coming along...

'It's time to go,' she smiled, not expecting anything.

'I'm probably going to die,' he replied.

'No we're not,' she smiled.

The boy beside her gave an unexpected guttural roar.

'We need to hurry,' she said as if replying.

He climbed in before her, he was sick of this world anyway. But her, she was still young.

'I'm not letting you on,' Glenn announced.

'And we're not getting on without your permission,' she replied without hesitation.

Somehow, it was all he needed to know. If she chose to come… it would be all right. He put his hand on the stoneships side and it flickered obediently to life, pulling itself easily from the earth. The cockpit lit up quickly as though it had been primed and prepared for this very moment the day before, though it clearly had not been driven for at least six hundred years.

They looked at each other, the man and the child. She smiled at him. Somehow, he knew he did not need to say anything. She would know. And wherever she went, the autistic boy went with her. He focused instead on the archaic instruments, hearing the sounds of the other two entering behind him. He did his pre-flight check, but all signs were of perfect health for his craft. He checked his passengers before forming the cockpit crystal, but the boy was being much too slow. He just didn't know how to rush. She was trying to encourage him, but it was several more precious seconds before the crystal could be formed. The sky lit up with a light beyond brilliant as the battleship met with its final, glorious end. But the battle raged on, as though there was something of momentous import in the lifting up of their single stramineous, wieldy, stoneship.

Looking back, it made no sense. The amount of damage they took, a near continuous blast of super-heated ions and plasma. It would have melted a Kinerigan fighter in seconds. It would have broken the Message's plating in less than a minute. But seven minutes they had rode out a continuous storm of fire on their ascent into the heavens. Somehow, some time just before it all ended, Glenn had managed to get a Kino signal from his first friend.

'..en. Commander Glenn, do you…'

'Loud and clear Matrix. Commander Glenn here. I thought you might like to know that we're leaving now.'

There was a pause.

'What? How? The rocket failed, it couldn't penetrate the shield. Don't, you'll be blasted against-'

'Not going to happen. As was suspected, a direct impact had an effect like a fist into water – it was too hard, and the shield responded with strength. Now were we to come at it at an angle, work our way though they layers.'

'Glenn…' it was the singer's voice. She sounded worried.

He could barely hear her above the thunder of the weaponry as it danced about them. There were no fighters, not even their enemy would dare this storm of ground based weaponry. It occurred to him that they'd gotten all that fixed pretty quick. It was as if the stoneship was tossed in the centre of a vortex – the storm willingly raged around them, but in spite of earth and hell and all that the might of Seren and her Oppression could rage against them, they rode the calm of the storm straight up into a day lit sky.

'You'll not make it, there have been hundreds of your skim attempts across the planetoid over history. There are too many layers, you'll-'

'Half of those layers aren't there right now, and all this weaponry is weakening it further. Don't worry about us. We'll-'

'US!' It was the Commander, he recognised the touch of her mind. She knew the truth before he spoke it.

'Yes, I have it on good authority that we'll be leaving today. You see, I brought a little prophet with me.'

There was silence on the other end. Was it fear, or hope? Did they risk leaving their greatest asset to the intuition of a half dog soldier, or would they never forgive him. She leant forward now, trying to place her face between the cockpit crystal and his immobile stone chair.

He'd never seen it before, the way she was crying.

'All my life,' she cried. 'All my life I've seen today. All my life, I've never been afraid of anything, because I only needed to remember today and how we'd be riding a stone boat on a river of fire. I've never been afraid of anything, because I've been afraid of today. Anytime I was afraid I'd remember today and nothing could compare to the thunder, and the fire.'

She sniffed, but continued with a smile, 'I always knew it was coming, but now it's here... and somehow, it's I'm not frightened anymore. It's here ... and I am safe. Nothing, not anything was more scary than this fire around us. But nothing, nothing can touch us here. We are more safe that you.'

Then, it seemed, the Hero found his voice 'Get back here!... eturn... orders...' Matrix was trying to shout as his voice begun to break up for the distance.

'I'm sorry sir. But I will not be following orders today. Think well of me where we are going!'

'...Commander... desist... return...' was all he could make out High Commander Sheelaakah saying. Then, as it radio grew silent, he thought he heard the voice of his first friend.

'...live...'

Suddenly, the guns fell silent. A violent storm was forming in the sky shield the likes of which had never been seen on the planetoid. It seemed as if the whole spirit of the world, and half its inhabitants, were crying out to deny this one small craft with its three occupants their freedom. Yet somewhere, deep within the souls of those that lived, enough love of freedom was found, enough desire for the right to choose one's own destiny, it propelled the small pebble towards the glowering sea.

'It's time to leave now,' Jacinth said, whipping tears from her eyes. She held her companions hand, because he was moaning so much now. Somehow, in some way, perhaps he knew what was happening?

Glenn, elite Commander of the Freedom Alliance, a liberator of the free peoples, took it at an angle. He turned so the sky now was a sea, and he plunged down in the blackness. Inside, it was a darkness inhumane. They struck a layer of positrons, but he quickly ionised the hull. The ship then suddenly bounced painfully off an invisible veil, but the stone ships powerful lightning tore permission for them to proceed. They rode waves of sound headlong till they could dive again. There, in the distance, the endless field of pluses and minuses signalled the final threshold – the layer opening to outer space. The layer… that could be entered but never left.

It seemed to stretch on forever.

He felt it before he saw it, heard Jacinth shouting at him from the back seat, trying to kick his chair, but her voice sounded too distant to be normal. Thick darkness gathered around him, and he felt himself imploding inwards to sudden destruction, his tongue cleaving to the roof of his mouth so that he could not speak. He felt rather than heard a voice; unimaginably powerful, incomprehensively irresistible, uncompromisingly malign.

You are nothing. Nothing! They don't want to do this – they are happy being prisoners of this world. Your friends don't even believe in you. They think you are a misshapen fool, they are laughing at you behind your back. No one cares about you. No one cares about you. No one …

Suddenly he felt someone grabbing violently on his hair and pulling his head back into the stone chair. He hit his head painfully, but the hand didn't let go. It took him a second to disentangle his hair from the boy's overlarge hand. He looked back at the two children sharing the gunners chair, the tear stained girl and the autistic boy staring blankly out the window as though by ignoring the world Glenn might forget the aching in his head. He rubbed his scalp.

'Even if no one cared about me, I would still care about others.'

And with that, he punched the throttle, starting towards the field at full speed and uncompromising faith.

It had parted before he even touched it, and the next second he had entered Tesser and was on his way to the centre of the galaxy, the first three ever of the Seren planetoid to, of their own volition, leave…

---+++---+++---+++---

Amongst the oppression the punishment was vast and brutal. Thousands of gunners died inexplicably in the moment the small craft left, the privacy of the nebulous cloud working against their attempts at disrupting his exit.

Nothing they had done could stop the little craft from escaping. Even the clouds, unlike any on record, would not dissipate. The darkness was oppressive as though the planet itself mourned the loss of a single child, or rather, three.

Millions silently wondered what all the darkness was for. They knew now to fear their protectors, to fear their Government who would not let any move against their will. Silently they wondered if they were free, or if their freedom really was an illusion.

Millions of others silently vowed to never allow another to leave again.

---+++---+++---+++---

He'd been crying for three days, without sleep. He knew it was killing him.

He saw her constantly, but knew it was a hallucination. He kept hearing her voice, her kind words that were his alone. He turned again, but she was never there. She was an addiction he could never recover from.

She was the Pirate Queen, and he, her favourite slave.

Darkstar knew he would take his own life soon. It was the only way to escape the desperate mourning which was the only reality his soul felt now.

He stood up, tear stained eyes peering hopelessly out at the fleets. The others were out there. They were all feeling it. The law had broken down, but instead of measured attempts at conquest they were falling apart. The Kinerigan pirates of Moonscape were dying. Fights were frequent, but led to no victories. And yet, for all their violence and self-loathing the pirates did not separate, but the ships huddled closely together as though ... afraid...

She'd only ever taken the leaders; made herself a valued servant, a daughter, a wife. Now, without her, they were lost. Surely some weren't as badly connected as he and yet... all were lost in mourning. Even while war blanketed the planetoid and the combined peoples of both Oppression and Alliance were scattered and afraid, the pirates cared nothing for sport or plunder.

Perhaps they, too, had died in the war?

Perhaps, but none would be more missed than Myth.

He turned from the window. The end would be soon. Soon sorrow would turn to anger as the violence escalated and then...

'Darkstar.'

He gasped in shock, turning with such surprise to hear his name he fell against the deck. A woman had spoken from the pilot's chair! It wasn't her voice yet... quickly he wiped the tears from his eyes.

She was dressed in blue, a stunning tall blond of uncompromising beauty and confidence. Her shirt was modest yet cut tight as if for battle. Her trousers conform fitting, yet built opaque and strong. She rested her feet on his control deck, smiling happily at him, just the way *she* used to...

Everything in her demeanour and bearing spoke of confidence and concern for him, as if a playful adventure were about to begin. Who was she? How did she get in here? What did she want?

'Who... who are you?' Darkstar asked, rising to his feet, mesmerised by her eyes, large gems of perfect blue.

She lifted her feet from the controls, sitting up luxuriously.

'I'm your answer,' she simply said.

Her eyes begun to glow then, slowly at first. Then, in her open palm, she formed the outline of a blue flower. A forget-me-not. It was a simple projection, slowly, yet beautifully formed. And when it was fully formed, she steadied herself on the console as though it had taken great effort to create.

It was a projection. Just like *she* used to create.

'Are you...?' Darkstar asked, not sure how to create his thoughts.

She smiled, a perfect glow of disarming welcome. Slowly, wreathed in beauty, she stood up, and offered him the flower.

He looked at it.

It was just like *she* used to do all the time... to please him...

'Did you... are you the one that killed Myth?' He asked.

'I am,' she replied, without taking her eyes off him.

He began to weep again, and she took him by the chin. He tried to escape then, but found he was falling under a new spell.

'It's all right to be sad Darkstar. I'm here to take over, to fix things and make them right. To fill the holes her life has created. Together, we'll make the pirate the noble warriors they were meant to be...'

'I...' But he said no more as she gently trapped him to the control panel and pressed her lips to his. He surrendered, and with that kiss, and with the spark of desire to live she rekindled in his soul, he begun to transfer to her all he was and knew – the security codes, the hidden secrets of the pirates, the love *she* had once coveted...

'Time to make things right...' Envy, rising Queen of the Pirates whispered in her new boyfriend's ear.

---+++---+++---+++---

Dark tears smeared down her cheeks like running makeup, and her eyes were bloodshot and red.

It had been only a day since the man and two small children had left. But He was still so angry, and did nothing while the lust for blood drove the rest of them to incalculable murders. Yet the soul prints quickly fled without his lost soul trap, and for all the death, he did nothing. The One sat there, contemplating it all with a mind older than her and her father's lives combined.

'Why don't you stop them,' she finally demanded.

'What do they mean to me?' He callously replied.

She wept. 'You have to stop them.'

'I don't *have* to do anything,' he replied, burnishing Worldbane sullenly.

She looked out on them. They were robbing each other now in the city, murdering for bread. Darkness had not stopped them. Outside where her proud wall once stood, millions of refuges were dead and dying, or fainted without hope of being saved. Among those that were once beyond the Wilderness, civilisation had broken down as well, and the children weren't being fed. None had adequately prepared for this war. They kept on killing each other and would keep on till there were none left...

'If you do nothing, I must,' C'Wiltaa tearfully threatened.

He didn't say anything.

She looked out then... so much violence ...

Leaping from the window, she disappeared.

Suddenly, the entire Seren planetoid went into Tesser. It was supposed to be day time since they'd skipped an entire night, but instead they found themselves surrounded by dim stars. There was no sun to light the planetoid at all, from either side.

In a day, little changed. The rampant murder and lawlessness prevailed as tiny mobs struggled for basic survival inside the city and without. But slowly, the ground began to cool. Rain first as tiny spits, then as great torrents like a mourning woman plundered down on blood soaked soils.

By the evening of the second day there was little fight left in any of them as the first rains of the planets history soaked deep into the ground. Soldiers took refuge in what shelter they could find, giving room to enemies against the indiscriminate downpour. And by the third day there were few outdoors to witness the quiet dark snow that begun blanketing the planetoid.

That was when the rumours really spread. The One was angry. He was going to kill them all and start again... they would all freeze for their crimes of dissidence, murder, or theft. Of failing to win a war, or of failing again to break free.

Not till the evening of the third day did C'Wiltaa hear their pleas, and return a faint red sunlight to their sky. Only a handful of sentients dared peer from their doors at the red lit snow that covered their windows and confused them.

But slowly, timidly, people began to emerge from their hiding places, and look towards each other once again.

---+++---+++---+++---

Matrix held Sheelaakah close, Alasia standing by as they furtively looked out at the strange, cold snow. The white blanket had finally done what war and order could not: it stopped the fighting. The three of them had been ferried deep back into Alliance lines while I-olo and others tried desperately to re-establish order and stop the fighting. That the rebellious soldiers had begun to return once the sunlight had lit the sky was hope that the farms would be producing by the next week.

At first bereft of hope in the aftermath of the impossible carnage, the Alliance had celebrated a subdued victory that a single stone ship, carrying a soldier and two young children, had actually managed to weather the storm and exit the Skyshield for the first time in history. It was more than a hope, it broke the unbreakable law that no one could ever leave.

Alasia was the first to speak, 'I think it's snow.'

Matrix nodded, it seemed she was correct.

'We failed,' Alasia mourned.

Sheelaakah signed. 'The goal was never to leave, but rather, to be free. Those who choose to live honestly, who wage war for the freedom of others, will always be *more* free, no matter what world they live on.'

Alasia sighed, and spoke again, 'Why do you suppose Bakerson and the children were able to succeed where everything else failed?'

'I believe,' Matrix said, curling the wool around him against the cold, his bronze katana now forming a metal bracer that could become deadly at a thought, 'he tried to stop us personally, the One, but he's lost so much of his strength. So many doubt him now.' 'So many in the city now doubt their cause. Yet Bakerson's success gives us new options, and hope. Our story is not yet fully told, and while we choose to wage a war for our freedom, we too, are free.'

'I still don't like the way things ended,' she argued.

Matrix scuffed the snow from his shoes, thinking towards his feet. 'Someone once told me that here in this world we have two choices, obey or die. But I think that is just a lie. Our choices are to live life to the fullest; to do what we know is good, and to stand up for what we believe in. Or, on the other hand, to die a little inside; to lose hope or to back away from being the change we want to see in the world. When we embraced unnecessary violence as a way to promote change, we became part of the problem, part of the death that seeks to dominate and control all that lives in this world. But even in war it is not "us and them". It's just "us". We must learn to see that even our enemies are imprisoned here; in prisons of ignorance or hate. We can choose death, and contribute to the fear in the world, or we can choose life, and help set even our enemies free. And because of this... our fight is far from over.'

'Can't we just choose both?' Alasia muttered. 'Life and Freedom for us, death and imprisonment to our enemies?'

'What about Freya?' Matrix asked.

'She had such lovely children, didn't she,' Alasia replied.

'Hardly seems fair,' Matrix agreed. 'We who seem so trapped are the only ones truly free, and those convinced they are born free lived trapped behind walls physical and symbol, and are trapped there still. I can't leave... I can't leave, until every prisoner has been set free,' Matrix said.

'Some of them don't want to be free,' Alasia countered.

'Then as long as they have all the freedom they can handle,' Matrix replied. 'But, for now, they barely even have a choice. Until they have every chance to make that choice of life for themselves, I haven't finished here yet.'

Sheelaakah seemed to be thinking even as she spoke. 'But we cannot make this choice for them. In any given moment we have to make a choice; freedom or oppression, to grow, or to die.'

'And you can't choose neither, not once you know,' Matrix added.

'Then the choice really is mutually exclusive, one or the other.' Alasia clarified. 'In our lives as a narrative we write, not only to live or to die, but to choose life, or choose death. In other words; the X-or story.'

They looked out quietly then, on a world blanketed with frozen water, soft like down. A pair of children crossed their path, throwing compressed handfuls of it at each other. Children loving life, as though they were already free. Children who deserved to know and choose the truth.

Matrix nodded, 'Come, we have a long war ahead of us.'

They looked star-ward, each filled with their own private thoughts of what the future might bring.

Matrix sighed, knowing Bakerson and the children were still well within the reach of those who would imprison them once more. They, too, had a long battle ahead of them. And they would need all the ... luck... the universe could offer. 'Farewell, my friend,' Matrix muttered from a world turned white.

Farewell.

Cast

Alasia – Aka 'Angel'. Publically, a singer, privately, self-serving privateer who makes added income trading in secrets.

Brek'anarl, Karl – Lord of the mutants due to his great strength and skill at diplomacy, and a moderate telepath.

C'Wiltaa – A high ranking demon long recorded on the world of Seren.

Glenn Bakerson – Unit leader of the Resistance, friend to Matrix.

Gral – Diplomat of Breakers Point research colony on star system Utopia.

I-olo Tilk – Understudy to the supply and reconnaissance general (spy master) of the Resistance.

Matrix – A hero of the story, evicted from the city at 16 after 'asking too many questions.'

Montsi – Head carer for the gifted children of the Utopia colony.

Petrie – Severely autistic child, child of the Utopia research colony, friend of Jacinth.

Seren city – the massive citadel on a large meteoroid where this narrative takes place.

Sheelaakah – Most promising telepath of the Resistance, promoted to Commander at start of book 1. Originates from an annexed world 12 years previously (at age 11).

Skion – A skilled cyborg warrior for the resistance.

Jacinth – Child of the Utopia research colony, gifted with foresight.

Nailou – Prince, third son of the ruling couple of the Tendendalaah.

Taalk, Lord Admiral – Supreme Commander of the psychic division of the government, or spy circle. Aging, with 'eyes the lightest shade of grey.'

Token – Apprentice to Lord Admiral Taalk, hair down past his knees in a 'whip'.

Tosk – A son of Brek'anarl.

Place your mark here

Did you just read the book? Place your autograph and date here.
If you'd like, take some time to tell me just what you thought of the
book, I'd love to know! Xor@DrJoe.id.au